I0761937

ROSEWOOD HIGH

#5-7

TRACY LORRAINE

HUNTER

ROSEWOOD HIGH #5

PROLOGUE

Poppy

Three years ago...

"Zayn, your turn," Ethan says, his eyes moving around the circle until he finds Zayn's excited dark eyes.

It's his birthday, he should be excited. Unlike me, who's been forced to attend a fifteen-year-old boy's party while ignoring the fact he doesn't want me, Ruby, or his sister here.

We stand out like a sore thumb among his football friends, but for some crazy reason Jada, Zayn and Harley's mom, seemed to think it was a good idea.

I roll my eyes at her naïve plans. At least Scarlett, their older sister, had the sense to argue and has hidden herself in her room.

The tension in the room ticks up a notch as everyone stares at the empty bottle that Zayn spins in the middle of the circle we're all sitting in.

All the girls around me, bar Harley, seem to hold their breath in the hope of getting a chance at seven seconds in heaven with Zayn.

I try to keep my breathing steady in the hope of covering up that I'd also be more than willing to lock myself in the closet with Zayn.

He's hot, and I can't deny that I haven't had a crush on him since they first arrived in Rosewood last year.

It's just a shame he's one of Jake's football buddies. They might all only be sophomores, but I only have to take one look at the varsity team to see what they're going to be like in two years. Their egos and wannabe god-like personas are already growing larger than life.

I have no interest in getting tangled up with that. I'm not a popular girl, I'm not destined for the cheer squad or one of the sport teams. I'll just hide in the shadows while doing my thing and counting down the days until I can leave for college and finally take charge of my own life.

I let out a sigh, lost in thoughts of a future without the weight of my family weighing down on me. Being fourteen shouldn't be like this. I shouldn't be worrying about everyone else more than myself, but sadly it's my reality.

The bottle slows to a stop and my heart jumps into my throat as realization dawns that it could be about to land on me. I glance to Harley at my side and smile, imagining everyone's irritation—mostly Zayn's—should it land on his sister.

It misses her though, and when the bottle comes to a stop, it's pointed directly at me.

My eyes fly up in shock as I look up at Zayn.

"No. No fucking way," Jake, my cousin barks, his eyes narrowing on Zayn.

"Calm down, man. It's just some fun. Poppy, you're up for it, right?" Ethan looks at me expectantly.

"I… um…" I hesitate as all the sophomore girls' eyes drill into me.

"Just let him spin it again," Shelly pipes up, one of the cheer wannabes. "Zayn doesn't want to kiss a freshman anyway. She probably doesn't have the first clue about what she's doing."

I part my lips to argue, but really, she has a point. My experience with kissing is limited to an awkward lip press with Christopher back in junior high during a game of kiss chase.

"No second spins," Ethan spits, reiterating the rules that he laid out at the beginning of this stupid game. "You get in the closet or you forfeit, and I'm pretty sure none of you want to do the dares that I've got running around in my head." He smiles wickedly and Shelly pales slightly. I've heard all about Ethan Savage's dares, and so has everyone else in the room looking at their faces. "So…" He waves his hand between the two of us and the closet being used for this game.

My nerves quadruple to the point I worry if I'm going to be able to actually walk over there.

I push to stand, feeling the stares of everyone around me but no more so than Harley's shock and my cousin's death stare.

I manage to take two steps to where Ethan is now holding the door open before a hand wraps around my wrist.

"If he tries anything with you, tell me and I'll lay him out."

"It's fine, Jake. It's just for fun," I tell him, but I don't meet his eyes. The last thing I need him to see are my nerves and, dare I say it, excitement about this.

"It better be. You're worth more than any of this group has to offer." I don't miss the sounds of the rest of the team ribbing Zayn for having to kiss his little sister's friend, but I zone them out and focus on Jake.

"They're your friends, Jake."

"Yeah, and you're my family. The only decent one I got. I want the best for you, Popsicle."

I roll my eyes at his overprotectiveness, although I can't help but feel loved. It's something I don't feel all that often where my family is concerned. I think Jake is the only person who actually understands, who gets me. And for that, I'll forever be grateful.

"It's all good. You've got nothing to worry about."

He releases me, allowing me to slip into the closet.

I wait in the shadows for Zayn to join me while the hoots and hollers from his friends continue.

"Make sure she gives you one hell of a present, Hunter," someone calls, making me swallow down the lump of anxiety that's climbed up my throat.

It's only a kiss. I can do that. It's no biggie.

Right?

There's no doubt in my mind that he's only doing this because it's a game. There's no way in hell he'd ever willingly kiss me. I might have imagined what it would be like a time or two, but I suspect it never so much as crossed his mind, let alone in this capacity.

The door widens, allowing a sliver of light to illuminate me before it clicks shut, bathing us both in darkness.

My heart beats so wildly I swear he must be able to hear it. My hands tremble and my temperature spikes.

Every noise he makes sounds incredibly loud despite the fact I have blood rushing in my ears faster than I'm sure is natural as he closes the space between us.

"Poppy?" he asks, his voice sounding calm, like this is just an everyday occurrence for him.

I remind myself that it probably is. Jake, Zayn, and the others have girls hanging off them wherever they go. He's probably well-practiced in this sort of thing.

"Y-yeah," I whisper, hating that my voice cracks, showing my nerves.

The heat of his body hits mine. "Do you have any idea how long I've wanted to do this?"

His words throw me off for a second and it takes me longer than it should to register them.

"Y-you want to k-kiss me?" I sound pathetic and I kick myself for not sounding more confident.

"Yeah. There was no one else I wanted that bottle to land on. This is the only birthday present I wanted."

"Oh God," I practically whimper when his fingers find mine.

He steps into my body, pressing me back into the wall. I gasp at the feeling of his hard body against mine as his fingers tickle up my bare arm before he grasps the back of my neck.

"Ready?" he asks, his voice deeper than it was only moments ago.

My head spins as I fight to remember to breathe.

"Y-yeah, I—" I don't get to finish my thought because his soft, full lips brush mine.

At just that small contact, my knees go weak. He must sense it because his other hand lands on my waist. It feels huge as his touch burns my skin, causing sensations to swell within me that I've never felt before.

His lips stay on mine, unmoving for what feels like forever but in reality, it's probably not more than a second before his tongue teases at the seam of my lips.

I have no idea what I'm doing, but it doesn't seem to matter because my body seems to know what's expected of me and my lips part, allowing him entry.

If I didn't already know he'd had experience, then I did in that moment as he took control of the kiss. His tongue sweeping against mine.

My arms stay rigid at my sides as his fingers twitch at my waist, obviously wanting to move, but he never moves.

He kisses me like I've seen on TV, but it feels nothing like I imagined. I'm not nervous. Not self-conscious. I just let myself go and allow him to sweep me away.

All too soon, he places a chaste kiss on my lips and backs away from me. I miss him almost instantly, to the point I actually reach out for him, but despite my eyes having adjusted to the darkness, I don't manage to make contact with him.

"Poppy?" he asks again, his voice husky and rough, it does things to my insides I can't explain.

"Yeah?" I ask eagerly, desperate to hear it again.

"Don't repeat a word I said to you."

Lead fills my veins at his warning. I should have known he was lying.

I'm too devastated to respond, desperately trying to fight the tears that are already burning the backs of my eyes.

I thought he really meant it. That he's been thinking about kissing me like I have him.

Stupid, stupid girl.

He pushes the door open, the sudden light makes me close my eyes as a chorus of cheers erupts from the other side.

My heart sinks into my feet as I wonder how the hell I'm supposed to walk out of here with my head held high.

You're not, a little voice in my head says. *You just totally screwed up.*

The ruckus only gets louder as a victorious Zayn steps from the closet after his few seconds in heaven.

"So..." someone prompts. "Did she give you the gift you've been dreaming of?"

Before he answers, he looks back at me. I might be back in the shadows but he sees me and our eyes connect for the briefest moment.

"Nah, she's a frigid bitch." He walks away as his friends erupt in laughter and a couple of the girls descend on him, probably offering to do everything I apparently couldn't. All the while, I pray for the ground to swallow me up while continuing to hide in the shadows.

How long can I stay in here? Will anyone even notice?

1

POPPY

I rush out of the Hunter's kitchen with a drink in hand, ready to find Harley and Ruby to celebrate the New Year together.

Butterflies erupt in my stomach, despite all the crap in my life, this is an exciting moment. One year closer to finishing school. One year closer to taking control of my life. One year closer to leaving this place and everything I despise about it behind. This year we're going to become seniors, we get to start seriously thinking about our futures and what we want from life. I might not have it all figured out yet, but I know one thing. My future isn't here. There are too many memories and demons lurking in the shadows for me to ever want to stay.

But while I'm stuck here, I figure I'd better make the most of it.

I see a flash of Harley's bright red hair and I can't help but smile. At least I have a couple of good things in my life, my two best friends are definitely that. I have no idea how I'd survive this place without them.

The sound of the party around me begins to lessen as kids head outside, ready to watch the fireworks that are about to illuminate the sky.

I shouldn't have come tonight but despite my parents' obvious irritation that I was going to spend the night enjoying myself and they weren't, I packed a bag and walked straight out the front door. Most days I allow them to blackmail me into doing as they wish, tonight wasn't one of those nights.

I knew it was safe being here. It's mostly the seniors who are partying at the Hunter's, the majority of our junior class are elsewhere, thank God. It means that for once, I'm able to let my hair down and attempt to enjoy being a seventeen-year-old girl if just for a couple of hours, forget about the weight that presses down on my shoulders every other day of the year.

I'm almost at the door when a warm hand wraps around my wrist. The grip is hard, meaningful, and my heart jumps into my throat. A shiver of fear runs down my spine.

He's not here, I remind myself. *You're safe right now. He is not here.* It doesn't matter how many times I repeat those words in the millisecond I have before whoever has touched me makes themselves known, the fear threatens to swallow me whole regardless.

I kick myself for letting my guard down tonight, for allowing myself to think that I could have just one normal night. For once, just enjoy a party like everyone around me does without constantly looking over my shoulder, waiting for the devil to strike.

"You're looking hot tonight, Pops."

His deep, rough voice flows over me, and instantly my shiver returns, only this time it's not with fear.

Steeling myself, I lift my chin, ready to fight.

"Get your hands off me, Zayn."

I try to pull myself from his grip but he's holding too tightly. Before I've even had a chance to plan my next move, he's taken control and pulled me back until the cool of the wall bites into my skin.

He stares into my eyes and as always, I hate that he can see so deep.

"Why aren't you enjoying yourself like everyone else?"

"I... um... I am. See?" I lift my drink and tip it toward my mouth, only it doesn't meet my lips. Instead, it's taken from my fingers and pressed against his full lips in a heartbeat.

"That's soda," he states, his brows drawn.

"So?"

"Don't you want to let go, have a little fun? You're always so uptight."

I flinch at his words. I spend most of my life trying to cover up how I really feel, what's really going on with me. I really don't need him digging and finding the ugly things that I try to keep away from everyone else.

"Don't you want to have fun?"

"Who says I'm not?"

"Aside from the soda, your face."

My lips part to respond but I fear I have no argument.

"The others don't see it, do they?" His fingers lift and he tucks a lock of hair behind my ear, his touch burning all the way down to my toes.

"Don't see what, Zayn?" I snap. I shouldn't ask. I'm terrified to hear the answer, to know what he really thinks of me but that's the thing about my best friend's older brother. He affects me in a way that no one else ever has. It annoys the crap out of me.

"I don't know," he muses, staring deep into my eyes. "But I want to find out."

"Fuck you, Zayn," I spit.

"Now there's an idea. You think that'll help loosen you up a little?" His eyebrows wiggle in excitement as I will all of my muscles below my waist not to clench at the thought.

I told myself years ago that I wasn't ever allowed to lose myself in Zayn's smooth lines. He shattered my young heart all those years ago in that closet. I may never have forgiven him for that, but hell if I don't still dream about it. I tell myself that should the situation arise ever again that I'd tell him to go to hell, but I'm pretty sure I'm only lying to myself because even now, I can feel that kiss.

"Let me go," I damn near beg.

"Why, so you can go and pretend to be happy? Tell me how to make it better, Poppy. Tell me how to put a genuine smile on your face."

"Why do you care?" I ask, my eyes narrowing on his sparkling ones.

"I've always cared. I watch you, you know, when you're not looking."

"No," I argue, knowing that it can't be true. The thought of it being true and him discovering what I keep hidden is scarier than him admitting that he might actually care.

"These frown lines," he says, his finger gently running between my brows, smoothing them out. "I want to know what puts them there." His finger continues down over my nose until it connects with my lips.

I suck in a ragged breath as I watch his eyes follow its journey. It lingers on my bottom lip for a beat before pulling it out. His eyes darken as he sucks on his own bottom lip like he's imagining all kinds of dirty things.

I've seen the look on him before. Usually right before he makes a play for a cheer slut. But despite the fact I know that, it doesn't make me move. In fact, right now, with his scent filling my nose and the heat of his body seeping into mine, all it does is make me want to find out where he's going with this.

I don't need to look up to know we're alone right now, someone has turned the music down and all the voices that can be heard are coming from the garden.

I should push him away. Harley, or worse, Jake could see us and jump to conclusions. What I really don't need in my life right now is more drama. But as I remain locked in his stare, I'm powerless to move.

His hand wraps around the back of my neck, his fingers squeezing in the most incredible way.

"What keeps these muscles so tense, Pops? What are you hiding?"

My lips part to respond as he rests his forearm against the wall beside my head. He steps closer, completely surrounds me with his size and I feel like a little girl once again. I feel like I'm fourteen once more and about to experience everything I'd been dreaming about.

"Zayn," I warn as he slowly closes the space between us, the crowd from outside beginning their countdown to the New Year.

"Celebrate the New Year with me, Pops. Let's bring it in style."

He steps closer still. His hard, powerful body pressing mine back into the wall. His muscles meld with my softness and my knees threaten to give out.

Right as the first firework explodes, his lips connect with mine. His grip on my neck gets tighter and my lips part without any instruction from my brain.

You shouldn't be doing this, the little voice in my head screams. But I already know I don't have the strength in me to stop it. Not now that I can taste him, feel his tongue dancing with mine, feel his hardness pressing against my stomach.

Fuck, he actually wants me.

His tongue delves past my lips once more, searching mine out. This kiss is different to the previous one we shared. There's no hesitation whatsoever. He knows what he's doing this time.

As he should, he's been with half of the senior girls according to the gossip.

"Oh God," I mumble against his lips, the realization of what I'm doing slamming into me full force.

Pressing my palms against his solid chest, I push in the hope of making him back up.

"Zayn, stop," I beg the second his lips part from mine.

Keeping my eyes on the fabric of my shirt, I fight down my need to pull him straight back to me.

I miss him already. It's crazy.

"You shouldn't have done that," I whisper, needing to at least attempt to tell him how wrong it was.

"Why?" His voice hits me exactly where I don't need it to. That combined with how ferociously his chest is heaving doesn't help my resolve at all.

"Because nothing good happens when we..."

"When we?"

I roll my eyes at myself, at the fact he needs me to say the words out loud. "When we kiss." I lift my eyes to him, needing him to know how serious I am.

"I don't have a black eye yet, do I?" he says, referring to what happened after that horrendous experience of our last kiss.

I might have wanted to hide in that closet for the rest of eternity but the second I heard Jake's angry growl and the girls start screaming, I didn't have a choice but to step into the light and watch as Jake rained hell down on Zayn's face for what he said about me.

"Give it time."

Our eyes hold, mine hold a warning whereas I swear his hold a promise, although I'm not entirely sure what he's trying to promise me. All I do know is that the tingles continue to race through me and my temperature doesn't decrease at all with his stare burning into me.

When the fireworks are over, the crowd starts to disperse and their chatter and laughter filter down to me. I know I need to move. I can't be standing here in this stare-off with Zayn when Jake or Harley emerges.

Thankfully, loud footsteps approaching us sound as I drag my eyes away from his dark and hungry stare.

I look up in time to see Justin clap his hand down on Zayn's shoulder. His eyes are wild and he sways a little on his feet. The guy's wasted.

I'm about to roll my eyes at the state of him when he says the words that rips the rug from beneath me once again.

"Sweet, man. I didn't think you were going to pull off your tag tonight. Right at the stroke of midnight, too."

My eyes widen as understanding washes through me. The team's little games aren't a secret around the girls of Rosewood High.

"What?" I ask, forcing the word out through the lump in my throat.

"Pop, it's not—"

"Don't lie to me, Zayn," I hiss back. "Tell me I wasn't a dare," I demand.

He swallows nervously but his lips remain sealed.

"Tell me," I damn near plead, not knowing how I'm going to deal with this again. The first rejection hurt like hell. But this time, it's so different.

That kiss, those few seconds of escape from reality, there's no way he can have any idea how much it meant to me, how much I needed it.

He gave me something that took me away, even if for a few seconds and now it's all crumbling around my feet once again.

"Pops, I—"

"No," I bark, shoving at his chest. "Don't *Pops* me. You're a fucking joke.

You know that, right? The group of you are a fucking joke," I scream, briefly meeting Justin's eyes who doesn't so much as flinch at my volume.

Assholes.

Zayn takes a step back, his eyes still trained on me. Something akin to regret filling them but I refuse to acknowledge it.

Stepping past him, my arm collides with his, sending a pain right down to my fingers but despite my gasp, he doesn't react.

"I told you, nothing good comes from us kissing. It's time you realized that," I hiss at him before I storm past.

"And what if I don't?"

Shaking my head, I march from the kitchen and head toward the stairs.

What I really want to do is walk straight out of the Hunter's front door and leave this party and his games behind me. But where would I go?

Home?

I almost laugh to myself at the thought. I think I'd rather be Zayn's plaything, the pawn in his games, than being at home tonight.

I fly up the stairs, my legs burning as I take two at a time in my need to get away. I ignore all the doors until I get to the penultimate one and I swing it open.

The safety of Harley's room makes me sigh with relief. I slam it behind me, feeling the vibrations of the force I used before I throw myself at the bed.

I tell myself not to cry. Not to waste any more tears on that asshole, but it's not a fight I can win because the harder I try to keep them in, the more they insist on being released until I'm sobbing into Harley's pillow.

2

ZAYN

"What the fuck, man?" I bark at Justin who stands staring at me like he didn't just fuck everything up.

"What? You won. You kissed your tag. What's the big fucking deal, that she didn't like it?"

I stare at him, my lips parted but unable to find any words.

He's right, this shouldn't be a big deal. I shouldn't care that she knows that it was a dare. I shouldn't have cared about the lie I told about her three years ago either. But I did, and I took the beating I deserved for it.

Things between Jake and I have never been the same since that night. I'd been in Rosewood less than a year and still trying to find my place within the team. Doing what I did was probably the biggest risk I've ever taken. If Jake didn't believe in my skills, he could have dropped me there and then. We might have only been sophomores, but he had the power, even back then.

I didn't lie to her that night. I had been thinking about kissing her. What fifteen-year-old boy in their right mind wouldn't. She was gorgeous. But not in the same way as the girls I hung around with. She was effortlessly beautiful. She hardly wore any makeup, she didn't need it. Her light brown hair had a natural curl and her gray eyes captivated me. There was so much innocence within them, but at the same time wisdom, the kind of wisdom that only came with experience, but I had no idea what that was. As far as I could tell, she had a good life. She lived with her parents and younger siblings and she'd formed a fast friendship with my sister. But there was more to Poppy than she let on and I was desperate to unearth whatever it was.

I've wanted a repeat of that night ever since. Not that she'd ever let me anywhere near her. She became distant to the point it pissed me off and instead of being concerned like I should have been, my automatic response was to be a dick.

I have no idea why she just kissed me like she did. I don't deserve it.

"Get out of my fucking way," I snap, pushing past Justin with such force that his drunken ass hits the floor. He cries out behind me, but I don't give a shit. The only thing I can think of right now is getting a drink. The new year has only just started but I'm already wishing for a do-over.

This is it. The best year of my life. Senior year. We've won both the division and the state championships. We're the fucking best team this town, our school, has seen in a really long fucking time. We're living the life. We have parties every weekend and more girls than we know what to do with. Mom ensures that I have everything I could ever want. So why do I feel like something is missing?

"Zayn!" My name being screamed from somewhere in the house drags me from my sleep. "Zayn."

"Oh fuck," I grunt, rolling onto my back, keeping my eyes firmly shut. Afraid that if I open them the light will burn them from my sockets.

My head pounds a steady beat as my stomach crashes about.

How much did I drink last night?

I think back to swiping a bottle of whiskey from Mom's drink cupboard while everyone else was forced to drink the beer she'd allowed us for the night, and I took myself to the only place I knew no one other than my sister would be able to find me. The treehouse.

We were too old to really make use of it by the time Mom moved us here, but it still comes in pretty handy. Mostly for me when I've had enough of all the female hormones running around my house being forced to live with three women.

New Year's Eve—or New Year's Day—I guess, and I was hiding like a pussy in a treehouse. It wasn't exactly the start of the year I'd imagined.

"Zayn Alexander Hunter, get your ass out here right—" The sound of my door flying open and then a loud gasp sounds out. "Oh my God." There's movement before she speaks again. "Get yourself decent, see your guest out, and then meet me in the kitchen. You have some work and a hell of a lot of groveling to do, my boy."

"Ooooh, someone's in trouble," a sickly-sweet voice comes from beside me, finally forcing me to open my eyes.

I take in the blonde who's half-asleep in my bed in only her underwear.

"Shut the fuck up, Laurie. What the hell are you even doing here?" I ask, having zero memory of even talking to her last night, let alone inviting her into my bed. Granted, it's not her first visit, but still.

"You brought me, said you needed to see the New Year in with a bang." She winks. "If you get my drift."

"You need to leave."

"But—" she starts, her hand skimming over my stomach until she's cupping my junk. She might think my morning wood is because of her, but she'd be bitterly disappointed. I have no idea if anything actually happened with her last night, but if it did, it certainly wasn't memorable. Not like a certain kiss.

"No, Laurie. It's time for you to go home."

I throw her hand off me and push from the bed. My head spins, forcing me to reach out for the wall until it clears.

"When I get out of the bathroom, you'll no longer be here." Reaching down, I swipe her dress and shoes from the floor and throw them at her.

"You're an asshole, you know that?"

"I've been called worse. You know where the door is."

She huffs in frustration, but I ignore it as I swing the door shut behind me and turn the shower on. The good thing about being the only male in the house is that I managed to snag one of only two rooms in this house with an en suite.

I grab the mouthwash and freshen up before resting my hands on the cool basin and hanging my head.

That was a dick move I pulled last night. I poured salt into an already pretty painful wound where Poppy is concerned.

I tell myself that receiving anything other than her hate would be weird anyway, and without looking at myself, I drop my boxers and step into the shower.

When I finally get down to the kitchen, desperate for the biggest mug of coffee I can find and maybe a blunt if I can unearth any, I discover Mom sitting at the island surrounded by empty bottles, crushed Solo cups and discarded cigarettes.

I wince at the sight but with last night's whiskey still flowing happily through my veins, it doesn't affect me as much as I'm sure it should.

"When I told you that you could have a party, I trusted you to keep it under control." Her voice is calm, cold even and it sends a shiver running down my spine.

"Sorry. People turned up with more alcohol and things went a little crazy."

"Crazy. The house stinks of weed, Zayn. The one thing I forbid in this house."

"I know. I'm sorry."

"You will be. I hope you don't have any plans today because all of this," she says, gesturing to the devastation. "Is all yours to fix. By the time I get back this afternoon, I expect it to be back to normal."

"Where are you going?" I ask, walking to the coffee machine.

"I'm taking your sisters for a spa day."

"Brilliant," I mutter. Scarlett may have been elsewhere last night, but Harley was here and enjoying the party, surely she should help me clean up.

"Oh no, don't even think about it," Mom warns as if she can read my thoughts. "We'll be out of your way in half an hour. Poppy is just packing her stuff up so I can take her home."

"Great." Thoughts of how Poppy and I left things last night leave a bitter taste in my mouth—worse than the lingering taste of the whiskey I can't shake.

"I suggest you start in your den. There are bodies everywhere."

She shudders as she says the words, hands me her mug and glides from the room.

Rolling my eyes, I rinse her mug out and place it into the dishwasher.

So much for a New Year's Day workout with the guys later today then.

I do as was suggested and head toward my den. I don't need to open the door to know what I'm going to find inside. The smell of weed and teenage boys lingers in the hallway.

"Rise and shine, motherfuckers," I shout, turning the spotlights on and hitting the button to open the blinds. Grunts and groans sound as bodies begin to stir to life. "Unless you planned on spending your day cleaning this house from top to bottom, I suggest you get your shit together and fuck off."

At the threat of cleaning up, everyone jumps into action.

Twenty minutes later and Justin is the last to leave as I begin sweeping the room with a trash bag in hand.

So much for being a fucking team. They were all more than happy to fuck shit up last night, but they have no interest in the consequences.

It wouldn't have been like this at the beginning of the school year. Jake, Mason, and Ethan would have stayed to help. Even a few weeks ago, Shane would have been here tidying up the mess they helped make the night before. But now they've all got their girls, they've got more important things to worry about than sorting this place out.

I'm in the kitchen getting a new bag when footsteps thunder down the stairs. Female voices fill the room and when I turn around, I find a smug Harley and a sheepish-looking Poppy standing in the doorway.

"Regretting it, yet?" Harley asks, her eyes flicking around the bottles and cups still littering the counters and floors.

"Fuck off," I grunt, ripping my eyes away from the two of them. Poppy might not have looked up at me but that doesn't mean she won't and I don't have it in me to see the hatred in her eyes, not yet at least.

"Jeez, you clearly didn't get a kiss at midnight," she mutters absently.

I fight not to react, but my spine goes ramrod straight.

Spinning back to them, I find Poppy staring daggers into me, begging me not to say anything. And I won't, not about that at least.

"That's where you're mistaken. Laurie only left a few minutes ago. Mom caught us in bed together."

I watch as all the color drains from Poppy's face and her lips purse in anger. I want to say there's some jealousy there but mostly, I think she just wants to cause me pain.

"I'm not sure that should be something to be proud of," Harley announces to the sound of Mom coming to join us.

"Ready to go?" she asks Harley before the three of them turn and disappear from my sight. Although I don't miss the "have fun" that Mom calls out to me.

3

POPPY

My stomach twists to the point I think I might puke on the Hunter's tiled floor as Zayn proudly states that he had a bedmate last night.

It's not news to me. I watched them both stumble inside as I made a trip to the bathroom before I finally fell asleep last night.

The jealousy, the anger that swelled within me like an angry beast was almost enough to force me to follow them and pull that hussy away from him.

But I couldn't. It wasn't my place. And as much as I sometimes want to pretend that there might be something between us, just to allow myself a few seconds where life might not be quite so shit, I know there's not. It's all fantasy, a game, where Zayn is concerned.

He's already proved to be a compulsive liar and last night was just another example of the shit that falls out of his mouth. It makes me wonder how much of it the cheer sluts fall for.

"Are you okay, honey?" Jada asks when both she and Harley take a step to leave, but my feet root me to the spot.

"Oh um... yeah. Just tired."

"Let's get you home so you can sleep it off." I hear the warning in her voice loud and clear. She hates that her baby is now a part of Zayn's senior year parties. But with Harley being a cheerleader now, she can hardly stop it.

Especially when all she's done is encourage her youngest child to join the squad.

"What happened to Ruby?" Jada asks once we're backing out of the driveway.

"Um..." Harley hesitates. "I think she might have gone home with a friend."

Jada's eyes find her daughter's in the rearview mirror and then narrow in accusation.

The last thing I saw of Ruby last night was her dancing with one of the guys after I ran away from Zayn. After that, the only thing I know is that she didn't spend the night in Harley's room like we'd planned.

I cast a glance at Harley who just shrugs at me, clearly not knowing where she disappeared to either.

The little bit of concern I'd been feeling about our best friend grows even more. I really don't need anyone else to worry about in my life but she's changed recently and I fear she's on a one-way street to self-destruction if she's not careful.

The conversation in the car falls silent and I rest my head back, watching the passing scenery. I don't want to go home. But where else am I supposed to go?

"Here you go, honey," Jada says as she pulls up outside my house a few minutes later.

"Thank you," I say sadly. "Call you later?" I mutter to Harley before pushing the door open.

"Sure."

"Have a great day." I put as much excitement into my words as possible but they still fall very flat. I may have turned down the invitation to join them, but really, I'd love to. A day of forgetting about everything and just enjoying the relaxation and pampering, I can't even imagine what that must be like at this point.

"It's not too late to join us," Harley asks hopefully.

"I can't. I've got stuff..." I trail off, not wanting to go into details.

"I know. Have a good one."

I wave them both off and watch as their car disappears down the street before sucking in a breath and turning toward the house.

My stomach drops the second I push inside the front door. It's in silence with only the sound of Cooper's crying ringing through the house. My stomach drops, I knew I shouldn't have gone last night.

I drop my bags and make my way through the rooms to find where everyone is. We're lucky, I guess, we've got a decent house on the boundary between the rich and poor side of town. On the outside, it might look like we're a normal, happy family. But inside tells a very different story.

"What the hell?" I bark as I swing the living room door open to the sound of Cooper's cries getting louder.

His face is beetroot red, his little fists clenched in anger as he tries the only way he can to get attention.

Running over, I scoop him up from his bassinet and cradle him to my chest. His cries lessen but they don't stop. I discover why when the smell hits me.

Mom and Dad are passed out on the couch. Neither seems to be aware that he was crying or that I've even entered.

Reaching down for one of the cushions that are falling from the couch, I launch it at the two of them.

Mom mumbles something, but she doesn't wake.

"You two are a fucking joke," I spit. "They shouldn't have allowed you to be parents."

I take Cooper to the kitchen to make him a bottle before carrying him up to his room so I can change him.

With him cradled in my arm, I give him his bottle that his chubby little hands eagerly reach for while I check on the other two.

Austin and Sofia are in Austin's bedroom playing some shooting game that is way too old for them. I want to tell them that it's not appropriate, they're only eight and six, but what else would they do? Life in this house is hell, they're just trying to make the best out of a bad situation.

They glance up at me when I enter, but they're not surprised to find their older sister and not their parents checking up on them.

"Have you two eaten?"

"I made toast," Austin says, ripping his eyes away from the screen once again.

"Are you sure playing that with Sofia is a good idea?"

He looks back at the screen with a sigh.

"We're not babies," Sofia snaps before going back to killing someone who jumps out on the screen.

"Can you play car racing or something?"

"We'll change it up in a bit," Austin agrees, looking at his little sister who's busy maiming some guy. "Did you have a good night?"

"It was great," I lie. They're not stupid, they know that our lives, our parents, aren't normal but they don't need me making it any worse. I want to show them that better exists. That they don't need to settle for the bullshit hand we've been given.

"I'm going to finish feeding Cooper, then shower. If you need anything, just shout."

They both nod, once again lost in the violent game playing in front of them.

"Where are they?" Austin asks, making the ball that's already formed in my stomach grow larger. I wish there was something more I could do for them.

"In the living room." *Just stay up here,* are the silent words spoken between us.

"Okay."

"I'll make you some lunch in a little bit. Please, change the game."

They agree and I leave them to it. Maybe I should be more insistent but the last thing any of us need is for the three of us to fall out.

I sit myself and Cooper in the chair that faces out over the balcony in my room that overlooks our unkempt yard and then the rich part of town beyond.

Jake's old trailer is tucked at the bottom of the yard. I've spent hours sitting here wishing that I could move into the old, damp thing now that he's gone.

I used to feel sorry for him, stuck down there on his own. But as the years have gone on, I've found myself craving that musty trailer more than I should. If it weren't for my brothers and sister, then I think I'd have moved in already, but I can't do that to them. Who the hell knows when Mom and Dad would have got their shit together and fed them if I didn't show up when I did.

He guzzles down the bottle in record time before almost instantly drifting off to sleep.

I rest my head back, wishing that I could now curl up in bed and catch up on the sleep I missed out on last night like any other normal teenager. But I can't. I have people relying on me.

Once he's fast asleep, I carefully place him in the travel crib I have in my room and begin stripping out of my clothes.

Probably the only good thing about this house and my fucked-up parents is that I snagged the master bedroom, seeing as I'm basically the parent under this roof.

I used to feel bad for them. Dad hurt his back years ago and has, apparently, been unable to work since. I'm not entirely sure that is true seeing as he and Mom seem to be able to make more babies than they can look after and he's able to get about and play with his beloved beat-up cars all day long. As far as I can see, he's just a lazy fuck who doesn't want to get a job.

Mom works, sometimes. But it's about as sporadic as her moods. In the past, I've begged her to go to a doctor and get checked out. I swear she's got something that could be stabilized with the right medication, but she point-blank refuses, telling me that she's fine and that it's nothing a little weed won't fix. I beg to differ.

Overall, I fucking hate my life. And after being forced to spend every day here over the holidays, I'm more than ready to get back to school where I can at least get a little reprieve from my responsibilities. Although, life at Rosewood High isn't any more pleasant at times.

Not being at school means I don't have to face the devil who roams the halls and tries to make my life a living hell.

I always thought he'd get bored when I didn't react to his abuse when it started, but he never did.

It just gets worse.

And after all these years, I have a feeling that it's not going to stop until I break.

Or he kills me.

Right now, I honestly have no idea what's going to come first.

"You ready for this?" Ruby asks two days later from the driver's seat while Harley spins around so she can study me as I drop into the back of Ruby's car.

"One step closer to senior year, right?" I mutter sadly. They both know that I hate school or more so life in general, but neither know the whole truth, the dark secrets that I keep hidden.

They know my home life is shit and that my parents mostly check out on their duties, and they know that he—Preston Hellburn—likes to try to make my life as hard as possible but they have no idea just how much effort he puts in when they're all busy enjoying themselves.

"You look tired, P."

"Cooper cried almost all night."

"Jeez, your parents really need to figure out how to look after a kid."

I agree. It's not like I can argue with that point. Only while I'm sure they're thinking that it was his crying from their bedroom that kept me awake, the reality was that I was the one up soothing him, trying to calm him down so that Austin and Sofia also didn't have a ruined night sleep.

Thankfully, Harley and Ruby get lost in cheer talk and the upcoming season and championships.

I smile as they chatter excitedly, and pride swells within me for what they've both achieved. I might have no interest in any extracurricular activities, especially those that involve sports, but even I know how hard they've worked to be chosen for the varsity squad already.

As we approach Rosewood High a shiver runs down my spine.

I've got a year and a half, then I can get out of here. I can hopefully manage to secure a place at college and disappear to the other side of the country. Guilt nags at me that while I do that, my siblings will be left behind to fend for themselves. I hate it, but this is my life, I shouldn't be stuck here because of my parents' irresponsible decisions.

There are kids everywhere when we pull into the parking lot.

Harley and Ruby jump out, more than ready to get started on the new semester, whereas I move with a little less enthusiasm.

Eyes move over to the three of us. It's normal. Ruby and Harley have been appointed into Rosewood royalty with their squad places. That uniform means that everyone now wants to be their friend in order to improve their own social status or they just want to fuck them so they can brag.

I'm used to that kind of behavior. I've dealt with it for years.

I'm related to the king of Rosewood after all. Jake Thorn *is* Rosewood High. The girls all want him, the guys all want to stand beside him, and everyone bows at his feet seeing as he led the team all the way to the top last year.

And no one wants to be Jake's little bitch more so than Preston.

He might have things that Jake never did. The money, the mansion, the daddy who gives him whatever his black little heart desires, but he's missing one big thing that he's desperate for.

Respect.

He might think he's a little version of Jake hanging out with his JV teammates and playing the part of being important, but the reality is that no one likes him. And if someone were to take away his skill on the field, they'd drop him faster than he thinks is even possible.

He spends his time forcing people to grant him the position as the leader of the junior class but really his rule is all about fear.

Everyone is scared of him. He's a loose cannon. One minute he can be completely normal, just your average school kid, and the next he's like the devil incarnate.

My skin prickles as we walk inside the building and toward our lockers.

He's here, I know he is. But then, I expected it. Since Jake and the Bears won the championship, his reign of terror has stepped up a notch.

He wants to be captain next year and for some fucked-up reason, he thinks I can convince Jake to give it to him.

What he doesn't seem to realize is that Jake would never listen to football advice from me, or anyone for that fact. He has his own opinions and ideas for his team and his word goes. He's not going to care what his little football-hating cousin thinks.

I roll my eyes at myself and the whole situation. If it weren't so insane, I might care more but at this point, I figure I just need to put up with him. One day I'll walk away from this place and never have to look him in his dead eyes again.

"Ew, what the fuck is that smell?" Harley complains when I open my locker.

My own stomach turns as it hits me, and I almost puke on my feet.

"I have no idea," I admit, my watery eyes landing on a lunch bag on top of the books I left here over the holidays.

They both lean in closer to get a look at what's causing the stench.

"Maybe I left my lunch here," I say with a shrug, knowing that it's not true but I may as well try.

"What the hell were you going to eat, a dead bird?" Ruby deadpans.

Her suggestion of a dead animal makes me heave as I remember walking out to feed Smidge, Austin and Sofia's rabbit, a few days before we finished school for the holidays to find the cage open.

I shouted at them for not closing it properly the last time they played with her, which only made them cry harder and for me to feel like the worst sister in the world.

But it wasn't them.

My stomach turns over.

Motherfucker.

My hands tremble with the realization that he's been at the house. In the past, everything he's done, any interaction between us has been at or around school. He's never once sought me out at home before.

The sweet faces of my siblings run through my mind. I can't let him anywhere near them.

"Well, whatever it is, you need to get rid of it. It's stinking up the entire hallway."

I look over my shoulder to see people starting to look this way with their lips curled in disgust.

"Great." Reaching inside my locker, I hold my breath as I pick up the bag and bring it closer.

"Oh my God, that's vile," Ruby mutters, covering her face with her hand.

I can't argue. It's repulsive.

Right as I turn to hotfoot it outside to the nearest trash can, I spot him.

He's standing right in the doorway—of course he is—totally blocking my exit with a smug smirk playing on his lips.

Kids around us seem to stop talking as they look between the two of us. It's no secret that there's no love lost between me and Preston. Unlike most of the kids around me, I'm one of the only ones who doesn't go running when he so much as looks at me.

When I said that I've refused to back down over the years, I mean it.

Preston Hellburn is no better than me. So what, his daddy has money and he lives in one of Rosewood's biggest houses? I don't care that he can throw a football better than most. To me, he is just a person. A rotten one at that, and there's no way I'm cowering to him just because he thinks he deserves it.

Holding my head up high and with the possible remains of our beloved pet rabbit in the bag I'm holding, I walk toward him.

Predictably, he doesn't move.

"Excuse me." There is no politeness to my tone. It's cold, harsh, exactly the way he deserves to be spoken to.

"Make me." His voice is low, ensuring no one else would be able to hear.

My teeth grind as he stands before me unmoving, totally unfazed by my presence.

The air crackles between us, pure hatred firing off.

There's movement behind me, but I don't look to see what's going on. I soon discover who's joined us though because Preston smiles down at me. There's no happiness in it, I don't think this guy has ever been happy, it's full of malice and abhorrence. But only a second later, he steps aside and allows me to pass.

"Everything okay?" a familiar voice booms down the hallway. I want to feel relief, but I don't. The last thing I need is Jake getting involved in this. Preston is trying to use me to get to him. I refuse to allow it to happen.

"Of course. Poppy was just taking out the trash."

He nods to his little pathetic group of followers and they all take off in the opposite direction, allowing me to run outside and dump the bag.

As I run for the bathroom, the vile scent lingers in my nose. Slamming the door back against the stall, I drop to my knees and heave.

No one bothers to check that I'm okay. I'm not sure if that's because the smell is clinging to my clothes and skin or just because they don't care. Either way, it's nothing new. I like living my life mostly in the shadows.

The only people I really expect to follow are Harley and Ruby, but they've got their own lives now, they hang out with the team and squad. And I'm more than happy for them to go off and do that. I have no intention of joining that crowd.

I know the three of us are unlikely friends with them craving the cheer spotlight and me hiding, but our friendship runs deeper than our hobbies. I don't know what it is but it's there and it means everything to me. It's why I'm not worried about their rise to fame within the Rosewood hierarchy. They won't forget me.

I wipe my mouth with some tissue and flush the toilet. I might have lost my breakfast thanks to that prick but I don't feel any better.

Tears burn my eyes as I think about what he did, but I refuse to cry. He doesn't deserve any kind of reaction from me, let alone my tears.

I wash my hands and wipe at the smudged makeup under my eyes before squaring my shoulders and preparing to walk back out there. No one else will have a clue as to what happened back there.

But I know.

And he knows that I know, and that thought is terrifying. If he's willing to sneak into my house and murder our rabbit, what else is he capable of?

I always knew he was unhinged. Well, he wasn't as a child. He was just like the rest of us then the accident happened and it totally changed him. He might have lost his mother that day but it was like he gained a personality transplant.

He turned cold, evil, selfish. He suddenly wasn't happy with his life and he needed to be the best, be the one everyone else was jealous of.

I couldn't understand it then and I still can't to this day. I'm fairly sure I never will. I just need to focus on school coming to an end and getting away from it all.

Am I running away? Maybe.

Thoughts of my future drag me down as I pull the door open and step out with the intention of heading straight to first period.

I don't look up, I don't want to see if I'm the subject of everyone's attention. Sadly that means I also don't see the person whose chest I walk straight into.

4

ZAYN

"Is Hellburn still giving Poppy grief?" I ask Jake as we turn the corner and stumble across them having a stare-off at the other end of the hallway.

"That guy's a fucking asshole," Jake mutters, his eyes drilling into the wannabe football captain.

His intentions aren't a secret, and if they're meant to be then he needs to remember that Jake and the rest of us hear everything that happens in this place. We have ears everywhere.

Although, we don't need those ears to know that he has some kind of issue with Poppy.

When I first started here, I thought that he just wanted her. But as time has gone by, things have changed.

"Should we..." I trail off, not really wanting to look like I care. Jake's still not heard about New Year's Eve but I know my time is limited. I'm surprised no one's snitched me out yet.

"Why do you care?" Jake snaps, although his stare doesn't leave the guy stopping his cousin from leaving.

"Because like you said, he's an asshole. What is that smell?" I mutter as we walk farther down the hallway.

The second Jake speaks, the entire hallway falls silent. I'm sure that more than a few of the spectators right now would pay good money for Jake—anyone really—to take out Preston fucking Hellburn.

He stalks off with his little gang of pussies before Poppy takes off running. Everyone else is too distracted to notice the speed she leaves at, but I see it.

"Hey, girl. What was that about?" I ask, sliding up to Ruby and resting my forearm on her locker.

Her cheeks are red long before she even looks up at me. "Poppy had something in her locker. Can't you smell it?"

"In her locker?"

"Yeah. Good holiday?" she asks, changing the subject from her friend.

"Uh, yeah. You?"

"I missed you," she admits, running her hand up my chest.

"That right? Because rumor has it that you spent time with Rich on New Year's instead of me. That hurts, baby."

She shrugs. "It wasn't anything like that. He's not you." Her lips curl in a salacious smile but it doesn't affect me like it usually does.

We're distracted when Chelsea makes an appearance and demands that both Harley and Ruby get their asses to the gym.

"Look out, Queen Bee is back," I call after her, earning me the finger over her shoulder.

"You got a death wish, man?" Shane asks, coming to stand next to me.

"Nah, if we get her angry, you're the only one she's taking it out on."

He thinks for a second.

"You're welcome."

He laughs and I can't help but let it affect me. It's good seeing him so happy, even if he shocked the hell out of the entire school by deciding that not only was Chelsea his girl but that he'd already gotten her pregnant.

"How're things?" I ask, wrapping my arm around his shoulder and walking us toward our own lockers.

"Oh yeah, you know. Standard shit with a pregnant girlfriend while in senior year."

"I still can't get my head around that."

"You and me both, man. I'm going to be a fucking dad. Like, I'm going to be responsible for someone else's life."

A shudder runs down my spine at the thought. Most of us can barely look after ourselves right now, let alone a kid.

"Any news from your old man?"

"Nah, he's still holed up in New York. He can fucking stay there for all I care. My kid doesn't need him as a grandad."

"Damn right, not when he'll have us as uncles."

"You think it's a boy?"

"Hell yeah, you're so having a little football player."

The others descend on us and our conversation comes to an end.

The guys start reliving their breaks, but as they talk about what they got for Christmas and the drama their families had, I can't get one girl out of my head.

"I'll see you later, man," I say, slapping Shane on the shoulder and walking away from them as the bell rings for first period.

I don't head for class, instead I go for the place I suspect Poppy might have run to.

I hover outside the girl's bathroom wondering if I should just barge in and find out if I'm right. But I don't need to because it seems luck is on my side.

The door opens and a defeated-looking Poppy emerges. Her eyes remain locked on the floor as if she's too afraid to even look up.

Moving closer, I expect her to see me, but she doesn't and instead crashes straight into my chest.

"Shit," she mutters, going to take a step back to go around me. Still her eyes remain on the ground.

Reaching out, I grip on to her upper arms, holding her in place.

"Poppy?"

Painfully fucking slowly, she lifts her head to look at me.

"Fuck." My heart constricts as I see the tears filling her eyes. "What did he do?"

"It's nothing," she whispers, averting her gaze.

"Bullshit," I spit, a little too harshly seeing as she flinches in my arms.

"Just let me go, Zayn." She fights in my hold, but I only tighten my grip to stop her.

"Talk to me."

An unamused laugh falls from her lips as her haunted gray eyes once again find mine. "Talk to you? That's a joke right?"

"No, if he hurt—"

"He didn't hurt me, Zayn. He doesn't have the power to hurt me. He's no one."

I open my mouth to respond but discover I don't have any words.

"Can I go now? I really don't want detention on the first day."

Without thinking, I release her and she immediately slips past me.

"If he does anything, you tell me. I'll fucking end him."

She turns to me, walking backward for a few seconds. "Why? You clearly hate me as much as he does."

Before I can respond to tell her that her words are bullshit, she's gone.

"Fuck," I bark.

"Mr. Hunter, you should be in class," Miss French, our guidance counselor says when she spots me in the empty hallway. I nod at her and head in the direction of my math class.

I don't see Poppy for the rest of the day, although that's not unusual. At times, I wonder if she's a ghost because despite being friends with my sister, who I can't seem to get rid of now that she's been added to the varsity squad, her best friend seems to vanish into thin air.

I don't have the same luck with Preston the prick because he's the first player I see the second I step into the locker room after school for our conditioning session.

He looks up when he realizes he has company and our eyes hold.

"What's up, Hunter?" he asks with a fake ass smile on his face. He really is a fucking snake.

"I don't know. It all depends on whatever that was with Poppy this morning."

"That, pfft," he says with a wave of his arm. "She wants me. Won't get the message that I'm not interested. I mean, she's not exactly my type. She's not even ho—"

I have him pinned up against the lockers before he manages to get that final word out.

"What the hell, man? I was trying to let her down gently. Ain't no one touching Thorn's cousin, I got that memo."

My forearm presses against his throat until his eyes widen in surprise.

People around here seem to forget that I'm not one of them, not originally. I didn't grow up with money, huge houses, and privilege like some of the kids walking these hallways.

I grew up in Harrow Creek. And that place is about as opposite as you can get from everything that Preston has experienced in his pathetic little life.

He might think I'm no threat but he needs to reconsider because while I might look like the fun, gives zero fucks about life, member of the team, he needs to remember that I was trained to fight at a very young age and with one mistake I will take him down.

"You stay the fuck away from her."

He splutters like he's fighting for breath but it's all for show, I'm not pressing that hard. Not yet.

Just as the door swings open, I release him and watch as he sags back against the lockers.

"I'm fucking watching you, Hellburn."

I don't stick around to hear his response, instead I step up beside Jake.

"Everything okay?"

"Yeah, just having a little chat with our boy."

Jake glances back over his shoulder and a smile curls at his lips at what he finds.

"That motherfucker isn't getting my team."

"I get that, I do. But who else is gonna have it? He's the best QB we've got by far once we fuck off."

"I dunno, I'm just hoping someone appears from out of nowhere."

"Amalie is turning you into a dreamer, man," I say with a laugh.

It's a well-known fact that his girl has softened his jagged edges just a little but hoping for a miracle seems a little far-fetched, but I guess crazier things have happened. And just to prove a point, both Ethan and Shane join us talking about something to do with their girls. Who'd have thought it.

5

POPPY

"This is pointless. I don't fucking get it," Harley whines, pushing the textbook across the counter until it crashes to the floor.

"You're looking at the big picture. You need to break it down," I say, hopping from the stool and going to collect the offending textbook.

"I just don't get it. I fucking hate math."

"Stop putting so much pressure on yourself." I bend down and my fingers brush the cover right as his words stop me dead.

"Well, this looks like a fun study session." I can practically hear the smugness in his voice.

I stand, smooth my skirt down and walk back to my seat.

"What do you want, Zayn?" Harley snaps. "Just because Mom has made you her bitch for the week, it doesn't mean you get to harass me instead of being out with your little team."

"My little team? You mean our championship-winning team?"

"By the end of the year, the squad will hold the same title."

"The squad with a pregnant captain. Right." Zayn rolls his eyes as Harley tenses beside me.

"Just because she's pregnant, it doesn't mean she can't lead us," she argues.

I'm used to their bickering and as usual tune them out and reopen the textbook to the section we were working through.

I might not hear the words they're saying but I'm very much aware of the deep rumble of his voice, and even more so when he walks over and stops beside me. His body heat burns into my arm as he leans over to look at what we're doing.

"I'm sorry, can I help you?" I snap, my eyes widening at his intrusion of my personal space.

"I don't know, can you?"

"Zayn, stop being a prick. We're trying to work."

"From what I heard, Poppy is working, you're having a bitch fit about it. You want a study buddy who knows his way around numbers, Pops?"

"No, I'm good."

"See, you're not wanted. Now fuck off. Doesn't Mom want you to clean the toilets or something?"

His eyes drill into his sister but while she's distracted, his fingers tickle up my bare arm.

Goose bumps erupt at his touch and I have to fight not to visibly shudder.

"Harley?" Jada's voice filters down to us from where she's working in her office. "Did you forget my coffee?"

"Shit," she mutters. "Yeah, hang on." She hops down and goes over to the coffee machine.

"While you're there, I'd love one, thanks," Zayn says, walking around behind me and planting his ass on the edge of the stool Harley just vacated.

"I'm not your slave. You're the one doing the time, you should be the one doing it."

"Quit bitching and make Mom's coffee. You know she gets cranky when she hasn't had enough."

"I heard that," Jada calls.

"You were supposed to."

"That gardening isn't going to do itself, boy," she reminds him.

"Yeah, yeah, I'm going. Slave driver," he mutters, but it's with a smirk on his annoyingly handsome face.

"She that pissed about the party?" I ask, although instantly regret it when he turns his eyes on me.

"The party, no. She gave me permission for that. The mess, the damages, and the illegal substances, she's not so thrilled about."

"I can't believe you thought it would be okay," Harley adds.

Zayn shrugs, his eyes still holding mine captive while she finishes up and leaves the room to deliver the coffee.

"You ready to talk yet?"

"Nothing to talk about," I whisper, looking down at the textbook once more, not able to look at the serious expression on his face. I'm worried he'll see just how much I'm lying because the truth couldn't be any farther from the words I just muttered.

"Riiight." He reaches out again, his knuckles brushing down my upper arm.

My eyes close as the sensation washes through me but I refuse to react. I know what he's trying to do. He's trying to manipulate me just like he did New Year's Eve so that he can get what he wants.

"I've spoken to him." His admission makes me forget all about my reaction to his touch and my eyes fly to his once more.

"You what?"

"I spoke to—"

"Yeah," I interrupt. "I'm not fucking deaf. Why would you do that? This has nothing to do with you."

"He hurt you, Poppy." His brows pull together in concern.

"He didn't. I told you, he doesn't have the power."

"Which is why you ran to the bathroom crying?"

"I wasn't... that wasn't..." I straighten my back, hating how vulnerable I sound right now. "This has nothing to do with you. I need you to back off."

"No."

"No?" I ask, my brows almost hitting my hairline.

"No," he enunciates slowly. "I'm going to find out what you're hiding," he warns, making my stomach turn over with dread.

"Just stop, Zayn." Stupidly, I reach out and rest my hand on his forearm. Electric bolts shoot up my arm at the contact and I quickly pull it away again. I shouldn't react like this to the guy who continually hurts me. "You have no business diving into my life. You're worried about him hurting me, then maybe you'd be better off looking in a mirror and thinking about how you've done the exact thing."

I drop to my feet, pushing the stool out behind me but unfortunately, he does the exact same thing and we end up almost chest to chest. The heat of his skin burns mine as his scent only gets stronger, although I can't deny it's a relief from the dead animal smell that's still coating my senses.

"I'm sorry, Pops."

"No," I say, holding my hands up in defeat. "I'm not even going there. It's done, it's in the past. You mean nothing to me, Zayn. Nothing."

I take a step back, clumsily tripping over the stool in my need to get away from him.

"You don't mean that," he warns, the edge of hurt in his voice making my steps falter.

"Don't I?"

"Not that there was anything there in the first place, but we're done, Zayn. Stay out of my life and my business." I storm from the room and almost collide with Harley, who's leaving Jada's office.

"Whoa, is there a fire in the kitchen?"

"No, just your brother. Grab your stuff, we're continuing in your room."

"What did he do?"

"Nothing worth talking about."

I spin on my heels and race up the stairs while Harley grabs her things.

"I'm done with homework," she announces, dropping the pile of books on her desk, flopping back onto her bed beside me and grabbing the TV remote. She turns it on and starts channel surfing.

"That's due tomorrow."

She sighs. "Why can't I be smart like you, Zayn, and Letty?"

"You are smart, Har. You just keep running straight into a brick wall and shutting down. You need to look at it from a different angle."

"I am, I'm not doing it." I glare at her. "Don't give me that look. I can't do it."

I hate that she's struggling with this. "Why don't you speak to Mrs. Harrington tomorrow before class, see if she can help before you miss this deadline?" I suggest, hoping our teacher will be able to show her a different trick that might make it all align in her head.

"Maybe I just... I want to be like you, you just get all this stuff."

"Trust me, Har, you really don't," I mutter sadly.

"How are things with your parents?"

At her reminder, I pull my cell from my pocket and check the time. Austin and Sofia will be back from their after-school club soon, I really should get going.

"They're... their usual disaster."

"You know the offer still stands if you need it. There's always a place for you here."

"Thank you, I really appreciate it. But I need to be there."

"They're not your responsibility, Pop."

The weight I'm all too familiar with presses down on my shoulders as she talks. She knows I do more than I should for my family, but she doesn't know the depth of it. Since Mom took a nosedive a few months ago, I haven't even invited anyone back to the house for fear of what they might witness.

"I know, but they need me. At least until Mom sorts herself out." I know I'm only lying to myself. If she was going to do anything, she'd have done it by now. "I should go."

"I'm sorry, I just—"

"Trying to help, I know. I really appreciate it," I repeat. "But Austin and Sofia will be back soon. I'd like to be home."

She nods sadly. "Can I drive you?"

"Nah, it's okay. I need the walk."

Before I climb from the bed, both mine and Harley's cell phone beeps simultaneously. It can only be one person.

"It's Ruby," I say when Harley doesn't instantly reach for hers, probably thinking the same as me. "Wants to know if we're up for a trip to the mall this weekend?"

"Ugh, I wish. We're at Dad's this weekend."

"Can't you cancel?"

"Nope. We did that the last two times and we barely saw him over the holidays."

"Fair enough. I'll tell her we can't." I start typing, but Harley stops me.

"You should go."

I let out a sigh. I want to, but while Ruby might have Christmas money to blow, as usual, I have nothing.

"Yeah, maybe."

I tap out a response that I'll let her know, leaving Harley to reply with her own excuse later.

Pushing from the bed, I grab my bag that I dropped on the end and swing it over my shoulder.

"See you in the morning?"

"You got it. We've got double practice after school though, so you might need to find another way home."

"Okay, will do." I open the door but look back before stepping through. "Har?"

"Yeah," she asks, dragging her eyes from the TV.

"Have another go at that homework, yeah. Maybe ask Zayn for help?" I suggest, much to her annoyance.

"We'll see."

It's not until I shut the door behind me that I discover that we have an audience.

"Ask Zayn what?"

I don't bother looking at where his deep voice comes from, instead I take a step toward the stairs.

"Poppy, don't do this."

"She needs help with her math homework, okay?" I snap, needing him to get off my case.

"She won't accept my help. I've tried."

"So, try harder. She's beating herself up about it. Thinks she's not smart."

"But she is." His confidence in his sister makes my footsteps falter at the top of the stairs and I do something really, really stupid. I look back.

My eyes almost bug out of my head when I find him topless with his skin covered in droplets of water.

My lips part as I take him in, I'm powerless but to let my eyes roam. I know I shouldn't, that I'm opening myself up to all sorts, but I can't stop it.

"It started raining," is all he says.

"Okay great. That's great," I say in a rush before dropping down to the first step in my need to get away from his half-naked body.

It's not the first time I've seen it, but I'm pretty sure it's the first time we've been alone while it's happened.

"Where are you going?"

"Home?"

"H taking you?"

"No, I'm walking."

"Give me five and I'll take you."

"Um... no, it's okay."

"Poppy, it's pouring, you'll get soaked."

"It's just rain, Zayn. It's hardly going to kill me."

He raises a brow, waiting for me to comply. I really, really don't want to but then I glance out of the window and see the monsoon style rain pounding at the glass and my resolve starts to crack.

Before I know what's going on, he has my arm in his grip and he's pulling me toward his bedroom.

"No, Zayn. I can't—" He looks back at me, his dark eyes cutting off any argument that's on the tip of my tongue about why this is a bad idea.

He continues forward until we're through the door. He kicks it shut behind us before I find myself backed up against it.

"Zayn, stop. Please," I beg, looking anywhere but at him.

He doesn't say anything, he just stands there staring at me. His chest heaves as his breath tickles down my neck.

"What do you want?"

His breath catches slightly at my comment, but it still takes him longer than necessary to respond.

"I don't think you really want my answer."

"Okay, great. So don't tell me, just let me go."

"I can't."

My eyes find his and I gasp at the hunger I see staring back at me.

"C-can we j-just go, please?"

His teeth sink into his bottom lip and all I can think about is how good they feel against my own. But nothing good ever comes of that happening.

"Take me home now or I'm walking," I threaten.

After a beat, he backs up but his eyes don't leave me. Instead they run the length of my body causing my temperature to spike and an ache I'm not all that familiar with to erupt in my lower stomach.

"That's a shame. You look good in here."

His words bring reality back and I rip my eyes from his to look around his room.

It's painted black with silver features and where I thought it might look dark and depressing, I find I actually quite like it. It suits him.

His hands drop to his waistband and my heart begins to pound harder in my chest.

He pops the button and pushes the wet denim down his legs.

"W-what are you doing?"

"Getting changed. I'm soaked," he says innocently, still keeping his eyes on mine as he kicks off his pants.

He stands before me in just a small pair of very tight boxer briefs and a smirk. Smug fuck knows exactly what he's doing.

As do I.

"Whoa, Jake keeps you on the team looking like that. I thought he only wanted players who were in prime condition."

His lips purse and his already ripped muscles tighten. It's in that moment I realize my mistake.

He takes a step toward me and I press my back harder into the door.

I shouldn't be here right now, and he really needs to put some more clothes on.

"I can assure you, Poppy. They don't come more... *prime* than me."

"Get dressed, Zayn." The quiver in my voice betrays me, and damn it if he doesn't miss it.

"You sure?" His eyes take another leisurely trip around my body and I can't help feeling like I might as well be wearing as little as he is from the heat in his eyes.

"Y-yes."

His eyes narrow but he doesn't come any closer. Instead he spins and opens his closet, dragging fresh clothes out and thankfully tugging them on.

"Is that why you turned Preston down? His physical appearance."

I tense at the mention of his name but I refuse to let him ruin any more of this day.

"Oh yeah, because it has nothing to do with his stellar personality."

Zayn snorts a laugh as he drags a shirt over his head. "You got that right, the guy's a class A prick."

"You had no right to talk to him today."

He looks back at me over his shoulder, his eyes saying so much more than his lips are.

"I can't not care, Poppy. He doesn't get to walk around tormenting you."

"Just leave it. If I need your help, I'll ask for it."

"No you won't."

"You're right, I won't. Shall we?" I ask, wrapping my hand around his door handle and pulling it open.

It's still raining when we get outside, although it's lighter than it was when he first pointed it out.

I hesitate at the passenger side of his truck, not really wanting to be in an enclosed space with him but knowing that he's going to leave me very little choice.

"You need a hand?" he asks, glancing at me from over the hood.

"N-no. I'm good."

Every single muscle in my body tenses the second I settle in his passenger seat, the entire car smells like him.

He turns the engine over and the car rumbles to life, the vibrations do very little to relax me as he pulls out of his driveway and heads toward my side of town.

The silence between us grows heavy as it stretches out.

"Harley said you're at your dad's this weekend," I blurt in the end, needing to break the tension.

"Apparently so."

"You like going there?"

He glances over at me. "You ever been there?"

"Uh... no."

"Then you really couldn't understand how much I really dislike going there."

"Oh. You want to see your dad though?"

"Sure, I just don't need the bullshit that goes along with it."

"Bullshit?"

"It's nothing." His words piss me off. If it were nothing, then he wouldn't have said it.

"Nothing?"

"Yeah. Just like what's going on with you is nothing. Like how we are *nothing*."

I look over at him and for a second he looks back at me, his eyes narrowed.

"Why do you look so shocked? You said it, not me."

"I know... I just..."

"Just..." he prompts, trying to get me to talk.

Thankfully, my house comes into view in the distance.

"Just nothing. Thanks for the lift."

I push the door open and slip down until my feet hit the ground.

"You know where I am if you need me."

I nod at him and slam his door shut.

As I walk to the house, his stare burns into my back but I refuse to turn around.

He should have no effect on me, and I need to work harder at stopping it from happening.

6

ZAYN

My fingers grip the wheel, turning my knuckles white as I watch her walk into her house.

My need to follow her is all-consuming, but I know I can't. I might not know all that much about her but I know that there's a reason Harley hasn't visited her house in a few months. Harley tried to pass it off with it being because Poppy's mom had a baby, but I fear it's more than that. The shadows within Poppy's eyes point toward more than that.

There's movement in one of the rooms before she appears with a baby in her arms.

My body tenses for a beat at the sight and my lips twitch into a smile as she runs her hand over the baby's head.

As if she can feel me staring, she looks up and right at me.

Her eyes harden instantly. Our contact holds for a few beats before I throw the car into reverse and head out before she starts thinking things she shouldn't about me.

I'm not interested. I don't want her, I'm just... intrigued... concerned. *Captivated*, I push that final thought from my head as I speed back toward home and Mom's punishment of gardening jobs now the rain has stopped once again.

By the time Mom calls me to say dinner is ready, I'm more than ready to give in. Coach is working us hard knowing that he's going to be sending us all off to play college football soon and then spending hours on my hands and knees tending to Mom's beloved flowerbeds means I'm exhausted.

"Feel like maybe taking a shower first?" Harley complains when I join the two of them in the kitchen.

My stomach growls as the smell of Mom's lasagna and garlic bread hits my nose. The rest of the team headed to Aces after our session for burgers. I'd have more than happily gone with them, but I knew Mom would make my life not worth living if I bailed on my 'time'.

Walking over, I rub my muddy fingers over her cheek while she squeals and slaps me.

"Where's Letty? She left us again already?" I ask, noticing the absence of my older sister once again.

"Yep, she's gone to a friend's for a few days before the semester starts."

"Anyone would think she doesn't want to be here."

"I wish you weren't here," Harley mutters, walking over to the sink so she can wash her face.

"What am I going to do with myself when all three of you are at college?" Mom muses.

"Guess you should have thought about that before popping us out one after the other."

"Zayn," she says on a sigh.

"What? The lack of time between the three of us is all the evidence we need to know that you and Dad did get along at one point."

"Can we not talk about your father please and just enjoy a meal together?"

"Sure." I pull out a chair and go to sit.

"Your sister has a point. Go clean up."

Rolling my eyes at her, I walk back out of the room to do as she suggests.

Mom changed when we moved here. Hell, she changed before that but it seems even more intense here.

After living a life with nothing and having to fight through every day back in Harrow Creek, she suddenly wants to appear perfect all of a sudden. Although I have no idea who she's trying to impress with all this.

Back in the day she wouldn't have batted an eyelid if Dad or I turned up covered in dirt and oil for dinner, she was just glad she was able to put food on the table.

But now, it's all about appearances.

She got herself some qualifications, a flashy well-paid job and everything changed in what felt like the blink of an eye.

Suddenly, we weren't trailer park kids with two parents who argued just as much as everyone else in that place, but we were packing up our stuff and moving to a fancy town and leaving one of our units behind.

When I return with clean hands, the atmosphere in the room is heavy, my fault for bringing up Dad and our past. Mom seems to think we left all that behind, but while we might no longer live there, that place will always be a part of our past, our story. She needs to embrace it instead of just running away from it.

"So how was school?" Mom asks tensely as we eat.

Harley chats away about bullshit girl stuff and the cheer squad while I stuff my face.

"I hear you're struggling with your math homework," I blurt.

"Is that true, Harley? I told you that if you're finding it challenging that I'll get you a tutor."

"No, no. Everything is fine," she seethes, while giving me a death stare.

"Zayn is in charge of washing and cleaning up. Harley, I expect you to go and work on that math homework." Mom stares between the two of us as she places her utensils on her plate and carries it over to the sink. "I'll be in my office."

Harley waits for her to leave before she starts.

"Was that necessary?"

I shrug. "Just deflecting her wrath away from me."

"You deserve it."

"I beg to differ."

"How'd you know about my math homework anyway?" she asks, crossing her arms over her chest.

"Poppy told me."

"Poppy? When the hell did you see Poppy? She left a while ago to go—"

"Home. I know, I took her. Nice of you to let her walk in the rain, by the way. Finished?" I ask, taking her plate and getting started on the cleaning.

"She was adamant."

"Well she let me take her."

"That had better be all you did."

"What are you suggesting?"

"You need to stay away from her."

"I think that's for me to decide, don't you?"

"She hates you after what you did to her."

"Pfft, that was years ago, Har. Anyway, she didn't seem all that bothered on New Year's Eve."

"Wait… what?"

"Huh?" Keeping my head down, I smile to myself. There's not much I love more than winding up my little sister.

"You just said something about New Year's and Poppy. What did you mean?"

"Don't know what you're talking about."

The dish towel that was on the counter whips across my back. It stings but I'm not going to let her know that.

"You're such a pain in the ass," she mutters, walking to the door.

"But you love me anyway," I call to her as she runs up the stairs.

Her returning growl makes me laugh.

I know I shouldn't have said anything. I'd put everything I have on the fact she's gone straight up to her room and called Poppy for the details. I have a feeling that might not be the last time I see Harley tonight.

And I'm right because not an hour later does my bedroom door fly open and she marches in with her hands on her hips.

"You kissed her. Again?"

"Ah, come in, why don't you. You know, it was a good thing I wasn't mid-wank."

"Ew." Her face screws up unattractively. "Why would you even… so gross."

I stare at her, waiting for her to get to the point.

"You kissed Poppy on New Year's Eve?" she screeches.

"Keep your voice down, Har. I don't need the whole street knowing."

"That had better not be because you're ashamed of it."

"Keep your panties on, Har. It was a game, we kissed, end of."

Her chin drops. "Are you really saying this to me?"

"It's the truth. Would you rather I lie?"

"I know the truth. Poppy told me the truth."

"Did she?" I smirk.

"Did she tell you how she was like putty in my hands?"

"You're a fucking dog. Stay away from my friends, Zayn. I mean it."

"Too late, lil' sis. I've had a taste of both."

"You fucking…" She flies at me, her arms flailing around as she tries to hit me but she's no match for me and in seconds I have her wrists in my grasp and her pinned to the bed.

"You really want to do this?" I ask, thinking of all the fights she's lost against me over the years.

"Fuck you, Zayn. Stay away from my friends."

"I try, Har. I really do," I lie.

"Pig," she shouts, fighting to get away from me.

After a few seconds, I release her and push her from the bed. She lands on the floor with a thump.

"I fucking hate you," she seethes, picking herself up and smoothing her hoodie down.

"Aw, I love you too, Har-Har," I say softly, using the name I used to call her as a kid.

Her lips purse and her tiny fists clench. I just about refrain from laughing at her. If she's trying to look menacing then she needs to try harder.

"You need to learn to fight. Maybe that's what we could do this weekend. Hell knows there are enough kids in that hellhole that could use a punch or two."

"You want to teach me to fight?"

"Sure, why not? You should be able to look after yourself. Impressing an attacker with your cheer moves isn't going to get you out of trouble."

She raises a brow.

"Did you want anything else?"

"No. Just..."

"Stay away from your friends. I'll see what I can do."

I wink and she groans as she storms out of my room as fast as she entered. Just to be a bitch, she leaves the door open.

7

POPPY

"So..." Ruby says, her gaze trained on me as we place our trays down on the table we've just taken over in the window of our favorite diner in the mall. "A little birdie told me something interesting yesterday."

I don't need her to say anything else, I already know the words that are about to fall from her lips and I'm already groaning internally. I guess my hopes for Harley to keep the gossip to herself was a big ask.

"You kissed Zayn!" she all but squeals, earning us a few unimpressed stares from the others around us.

"Yes," I mutter. "I'd been tagged, so he was just seeing it through."

"And you kissed him knowing you were a tag?"

"No, I had no idea. I kissed him because... I'm an idiot."

She rolls her eyes at me. "No, you kissed him because you'd heard how good he is."

"Trust me, knowing that every other girl in school knows just how good he is, is not the reason I did it."

"So why did you?" she asks, focusing her attention on her lunch.

"Because... I don't know. It was a serious lapse in judgment, that's all I know."

"Really? You're sticking with that lie?"

"It's not a lie, it shouldn't have happened."

"Oh, so you haven't been craving a repeat ever since his fifteenth birthday?" She raises a brow.

"No, I haven't."

"That's just bullshit and you know it."

"Why are you so keen for me to kiss him? I thought you wanted him for yourself."

"Meh," she mumbles around a mouthful of food. "I'll have him to play with if you don't want him."

"You have already *played* with him," I remind her.

"Not really. It was mostly Laurie, I was just… in the room."

"But—" I start to argue, remembering a little too well how she described that night to us after the event.

"I may have exaggerated a little."

"A little?"

"Yeah, I mean, I kissed him. Touched a bit. But nothing really happened."

"But you want it to?"

"Not if you want him."

"I don't want him," I argue.

"So he's not the one you fall asleep at night thinking about then?"

I damn near spray her with the soda I've just taken a sip of. "No, no, I do not." *Big fat lie.*

"Sure. And I'm guessing you're going to try to tell me that you haven't thought about that kiss after the event, what could have happened had it not come out that you were a tag, what might have happened if he took your hand and led you up to his bedroom."

My cheeks burn with the truth but despite the fact I know she can see it, I still insist on trying to plead my innocence.

"No. It was just a kiss. I wasn't going to… you know."

"Fuck him?"

"Shush, Ruby. People can hear you."

"And? It's okay to talk about sex, you know."

"Oh yeah, and when exactly did you decide that?"

She pales at my question and I mentally kick myself for going there.

Ruby was probably the most innocent out of the three of us, and that was saying a lot seeing as Harley and I are pretty innocent. But then *he* barreled into her life and in just a few short days, he changed her. Gone was the sweet and innocent Ruby, and in her place was a girl who wanted to do anything to help rid her of his memory.

It took us weeks to get her to talk, for her to tell us about her stepbrother's visit and the things that went down between them. I can't really blame her for wanting to erase it, but I'm not sure suddenly working her way around the football team like the other cheer sluts is the best way to go about it.

"Shit, I'm sorry."

"It's fine," she argues, but the quiver in her voice says otherwise. After she told us about what happened, she made us promise never to talk about it again. She wanted to forget he ever existed. I got it, although I'm not sure that locking it all up in a little box is the healthiest way to deal with it but she was adamant that it was over and that he was gone for good, so we had no choice but to do as she asked.

"So?" she asks, turning this back on me.

"So what?"

"You want him, right?"

I sink down in my chair and blow out a breath. "No."

"But—"

"No, there are no buts. I don't want him. The kiss was a mistake. Nothing further will happen. Got it?"

"Hmmm," she mumbles, irritating the hell out of me.

I want to continue arguing my point but something, or more like someone outside the diner window catches my eye and a shiver runs down my spine.

I didn't see a face, but I don't need to. I know when he's close. I feel it. I fear it.

"Are you okay? All the color just drained from your face."

"Oh... uh..." I keep my eyes out of the window, desperate to prove to myself that I'm just being paranoid. "N-nothing." I cringe at my use of that word. It seems to be one I'm using all too much recently.

"O-okay," she says. When I glance over, I find her looking the way I was but she clearly doesn't see anyone she recognizes either. "I'm thinking we finish up here and head back to where we first started. I want to try that dress on."

"Sure, whatever you want."

"Are you sure you don't want to get anything while we're here? I feel bad just shopping for me."

"No, I'm good. I got a ton of new stuff for Christmas." Another lie.

"Okay, well if you see something you like, make sure to stop."

"Of course." I cringe as I say the words. It wouldn't matter how much I might like something, it's not like I have the money to buy anything.

I need a job, but how do I get one of those around school, trying to ensure I get my grades high enough for a scholarship, and being the only reliable person my siblings have.

I'm distracted from my thoughts as Ruby pushes her empty tray away and lets out a very unladylike burp.

"Whoa, no wonder the team can't keep their hands off you," I say with a laugh.

"You done? I need to get my shop on."

"Yeah, let's do it."

We clear away our trays and rejoin the crowds in the mall. The January sales are in full swing and it seems that it's not just Ruby who decided that today would be the perfect day to grab some bargains.

As we walk, I can't ignore the feeling that I'm being watched. My skin prickles as my heart picks up pace a little.

I look around as inconspicuous as possible but once again, I see no one.

I've been on edge since the first day back at school and the unexpected 'gift' that was in my locker. Preston might not have approached me since, he chose to torment with his silence instead of his presence, but I know that doesn't mean he's forgotten me. He's just planning his next move. I can only hope that his need for blood has been sated with Smidge.

My stomach turns once more as I wonder what evil things he might have done to our beloved pet. I still pray that whatever was in that bag wasn't him, but I know I'm only lying to myself.

I follow Ruby into the store she wanted to return to and glance around in the hope I don't see something I fall in love with because that would suck even harder than just not being able to afford anything.

I glance over my shoulder every now and then, but every time the coast is clear.

Chastising myself for allowing him to get in my head when he's probably nowhere near me, I rush to catch up with Ruby where she's heading toward the dressing room with an armful of dresses she's collected as she's made her way through the store.

"You trying anything on?" she asks, looking back to find me right behind her.

"Nah, nothing is catching my eye." For once that's not really a lie, I've spent too much time worrying about whether I'm being watched or not to really look at anything that was in front of me. "I'll wait here."

Resting back against the wall, I watch as she closes the door behind her.

I pull my cell from my pocket and find a message from Harley asking if we're having fun and explaining that she's not because Zayn has insisted on teaching her to throw a decent punch all weekend.

I'm so lost in our conversation that I don't feel someone walk up to me until the very last minute.

Thinking I'm in the way, I move to stand straighter so they can pass but instead of doing that, two large hands land on my arms and I'm practically thrown into the dressing room next to Ruby's.

Picking me up, Preston pins me against the wall with his hand around my throat.

"Poppy? Was that you? Are you okay?" Ruby shouts, although it's muffled by the small space she's enclosed in.

Preston's dead eyes bore down into mine, warning me not to say a thing. As if I would. The last thing I want is for anyone to know about this.

"Yeah, it wasn't me. One of the shop assistants dropped something."

Thankfully, the dressing rooms in this store are little rooms with solid doors. Should we have been in ones with curtains, I'm sure Ruby would have just stuck her head out to see what's going on.

"What the hell—"

My words are cut off when his other sweaty hand clamps down over my mouth.

I suck in ragged breaths through my nose but it's not enough as my chest heaves and my heart races in panic.

"Don't talk."

He leans in close before a low, evil laugh falls from his lips.

"You really think you're something, don't you?"

I try to shake my head but his hold stops me from moving.

"When are you going to realize that you're nothing?"

Nothing, there's that word again.

"Your friends only put up with you because you make them look even more attractive than they already are."

I moan against his hands, my body thrashing about in the hope of fighting him off. It's wishful thinking but I refuse to do nothing.

"Just because you're Thorn's cousin, you seem to think you've got it all. Well, let me tell you, little girl." He leans right in, the stench of weed and stale sweat fills my nose and my stomach turns over. "You're nothing. And I'm going to prove just how pointless you and your pathetic little life is."

His hand releases my throat and I gasp, dragging in as much air as I possibly can.

My relief only lasts a few seconds though because his fingertips begin to trail up the inside of my thigh.

"No, no," I try to cry against his hand as I attempt to curl in on myself.

"Fight, go on. It'll only make it more fun for me."

I want to scream, cry, hurt him but in those few moments as his fingers get closer to their final destination I just freeze in fear.

I don't want his dirty, murderous hands on me. Tears burn my eyes and I blink wildly in an attempt to keep them in. I don't want this motherfucker to see me cry.

"Do you know what pointless girls are good for?" He pauses as if he actually expects an answer from me. "Being ruined. Used and abused until they're no good for anyone else."

Noooooo, I scream in my head as he lifts my skirt up and his fingers slip under the edge of my panties.

Please God no, don't let my first experience of this be with him.

Please, please, please.

"Pops?" Ruby shouts.

My eyes go wide as his hand stills.

"Do not fucking scream, or I will hurt you."

"Y-yeah?" My voice is rough, panic-stricken, and I have no doubt that if she could hear me clearly she would instantly know that something was wrong.

"Could you go and get me that red dress in a bigger size. I think they made this with a nine-year-old in mind or something."

"Y-yeah sure. H-hang on."

My eyes remain locked on his as I wait to see what he's going to do.

"This isn't over," he warns, causing a shiver to run through me knowing that this is going to happen again, only worse next time.

I got lucky that he cornered me somewhere where really, he couldn't do much to me. But next time, he could plan something a little more private where no one would find us, or interrupt.

My stomach turns, bile burning my throat as he steps away from me and removes his touch.

He opens the door for me and without so much as a look back, I bolt from the small room. It's not until I'm in the main part of the store that I actually breathe again.

After what feels like a long time, I locate the red dress in question and grab what she needs before hesitantly heading back for the dressing rooms.

"Rubes," I call while wiping at my eyes. I didn't cry but I have no doubt my fear is written all over my face.

I glance to the dressing room, the door is still open and I have no idea if he's still inside, waiting for me to come back.

My entire body shakes violently as I think about him pulling me back in to finish what he started.

"Thank you," she says, poking her head and an arm out to take the hanger from me. "What's wrong?"

She doesn't even have to look at me and she knows something is up.

"I... uh... don't feel well. I think I'm going to need to go home."

"Oh shit, okay. Let me get dressed and we'll go."

"It's okay, I can call an Uber or something," I argue, not wanting to ruin her day.

"Don't be stupid. I'll just get this and try it on at home. Let me get dressed and we'll go."

"Okay," I whisper, not really having the energy to fight with her. Plus, if I'm honest, I don't really want to go anywhere alone right now, even getting in an Uber seems like a risk I don't need to take.

The moment she shuts the door, I step forward and poke my head into the dressing room he dragged me into, needing to know if he's still there.

I breathe a sigh of relief when I find it empty. There's no evidence that anything happened and it's so unbelievable that I almost start to wonder if I imagined it. Although I know it's only wishful thinking because the fear, the disgust I felt as he touched me still feels very, very real.

Faster than I thought possible, Ruby is dressed and ready to go. She quickly buys what she wants and we head out to the parking lot.

"How are you feeling?" she asks once we're on the road and heading back toward my house.

"Sick."

"Do you think it was something you ate?"

"I don't know. I just... I just want to curl up in bed." *Where I'm safe.*

8

ZAYN

"Oh God, is she okay?"

The rest of my sister's conversation has mostly passed me by, it's been full of cheer bullshit and high school gossip but that one question piques my interest and I lower my own cell so I can attempt to eavesdrop.

"Why would she lie?"

Sadly, no matter how hard I try, I can't hear who's on the other end. From the cheer chatter, I assume it's Ruby.

I shift on our dad's rock-hard couch, the one I actually used to think was comfortable as a kid and try to get closer.

"Shit, yeah. I'll call her in a bit and check in on her."

The subject changes and I'm forced to wait until she finally hangs up to find out what I want to know.

"You should have just asked me to put it on speakerphone if you wanted to listen so bad," she sasses the second she lowers the phone from her ear.

"What's wrong?"

"Why do you care?"

"You sounded worried."

Her eyes narrow at me but she must decide to put me out of my misery.

"You're a pain in the ass. Something happened with Ruby and Poppy when they were at the mall."

Dread fills my stomach but I fight to keep the reaction off my face.

"What happened?" My voice is hard and clipped, and Harley doesn't miss it.

"Poppy got sick at the mall. Ruby had to take her home." She shrugs like it's not a big deal but that's not how it sounded on the phone.

"But you said she was lying."

"Ruby doesn't know that. She just felt like something was off. Poppy was fine one minute then not the next. She just said it was weird."

"And you're not worried?"

"Of course I am, and I'll call her when you stop with the twenty questions. Jeez." She rolls her eyes at me before lifting her cell and tapping at the screen.

Not wanting to look more interested than I should be, I push from the couch and go and check on the dinner that Dad's left cooking while he's disappeared off somewhere.

I wanted to go home from the second we got here Friday night, but now I have even more reason to leave.

Poppy being ill, or whatever, shouldn't be my issue but for some reason, I can't help thinking that it is.

Preston's smug as fuck face appears in my mind. I'm probably jumping to conclusions but after what happened the other day, I can't help but think that he's involved in this somehow.

I don't trust him at all and he's clearly after her for some reason. It makes me wonder if this has always been as bad as it seems to be and that she's somehow managed to keep it quiet all this time.

I stir the bolognese Dad's made. It's Harley's favorite and he makes it every single time we've come as if it makes up for the shithole we have to stay in with him. It does very little to mask that this place is crumbling around us, but I guess it does make it smell better.

By the time I get back, Harley has ended her short call.

"So?"

"Are you going to really pretend that you weren't listening?"

"Hearing your side isn't all that helpful." I don't even bother trying to deny it, we both know that I'm guilty.

"She's got the stomach flu. Hit her all of a sudden in the store. She's fine. Just sleeping it off."

Harley believes every word she just said, I can see it in her eyes. Unfortunately, Poppy's excuse for her weird behavior isn't sitting right with me.

The rest of our time with Dad drags, all I want to do is pack our stuff into my truck and drive us both back to Rosewood. Once we're finally able to leave, I gun the engine out of the trailer park, kicking up the gravel behind us and head for home.

"What the hell is up with you?" Harley mutters next to me. "Got a cheer slut on a promise or something?"

"Shut the fuck up, Har." I don't need to look at her to know that she's rolling her eyes at me. "Would you even want to know if I did?"

"Absolutely not. Just want to know how loud I need to turn my music up when I get home."

"Well, as far as I know, one isn't waiting for me naked on my bed."

"Good to know. I'd appreciate it if it stays that way too."

"Mom will be home. I'd hardly arrange that knowing she's there."

"Wouldn't put it past you."

"Wow, really have low expectations of me, huh?"

"What do you expect? I hear all the things you all get up to."

"Right, and I know all the things the squad gets up to but do you hear me accusing you of all that shit?"

"Have I kissed both of your best friends?" she asks, her voice hitching a few decibels. "No, exactly. I've gone nowhere near any member of the team."

"Yeah, because you all think they're pricks."

"Well, there is that. But even if they weren't. They're your friends, Zayn. There's like some unwritten rule about that shit."

"I must have missed that one when I did the test."

"You're a cock. Why either Ruby or Poppy went anywhere near you is beyond me."

"You love me really."

"Only because I have to. Most of the time I don't like you very much."

"If it makes you feel better, I'll give you a free pass to kiss one of the guys."

"If it makes me feel better? Fucking hell, Zayn."

"The offer is there if you want it."

"Wow, I really appreciate your permission. Now which loser should I choose to exchange saliva with?"

I shudder at the thought of her kissing any member of the team, but I have kinda asked for this.

"I can't promise I won't lay him out after, be warned."

"You can take the boy out of the trailer park," she mutters as we leave the place behind us in the darkness it belongs in.

Ignoring her, I turn the music up and try to keep my thoughts of what might have happened in the mall earlier out of my head. The last thing I need is to jump to conclusions.

It's dark by the time we get back. As usual, Mom is in her office working but as ever, I don't hold it against her. She's worked damn hard to get where she is. She studied and got her degree behind Dad's back because it was something she always wanted but never had the chance, and then she landed herself a kickass job here which has allowed her to have the life she's always dreamed of. I'm proud of her for pursuing her dream. Most people's dreams in Harrow Creek just shrivel up and die. There aren't many who manage to do what she's done.

"Have you both done all your homework?" she asks after begrudgingly asking about our weekend.

"Uh..." Harley hesitates.

"Get upstairs and get it done, young lady."

"I'm going, I'm going."

"And you?" Mom asks, turning her hard stare on me.

"All done, although I want to read over a report I've written."

"That's my boy." She squeezes my shoulder in support before I follow Harley up the stairs to unpack and get ready for a new week to start, or at least, that's what I allow them both to believe.

I sort my stuff out before changing and sneaking back out. It's not a hard task seeing as both Harley and Mom have locked themselves away.

I close the front door as quietly as I can and jog to my car.

By the time I pull up at Poppy's house, I've almost convinced myself that I'm crazy and turn back around. But even still, something has me climbing from my car and heading to her front door.

Before I can talk myself out of it, I lift my hand and knock.

There's movement inside, a baby crying and other kids shouting so when a harassed-looking woman pulls the door open, I can't say I'm surprised.

"What?" she barks, looking me up and down.

"Uh... is Poppy here?"

"She's in her room." She's gone before I even get a chance to ask where that might be.

Hesitantly, I step inside and close the door behind me. I glance around. The house is a mess, there is stuff everywhere, and the shouting and screaming continues.

Locating the stairs, I head up, leaving the chaos behind me with a wince.

The first two rooms are clearly the kids' rooms followed by a bathroom all of which are as messy as the last.

The next door is closed and something tells me that it's the one. Rapping my knuckles against the chipped paintwork, I wait to see if there's going to be a response.

"Come in," a quiet yet familiar voice calls.

Sucking in a breath, I twist the handle and push the door open.

She's in bed facing away from the door as I first walk inside and close the door behind me. But when I don't say anything, she twists around.

"What's—Zayn?" Her eyes go as wide as saucers as she stares at me. She sits bolt upright in bed as she blinks a few times. "What the hell are you doing here?"

I close the space between us as she shifts up the bed, keeping the sheets to her chest.

"Are you okay?"

"Uh... confused, mostly. Why are you here?"

I run my eyes over the small amount of her I can see, looking for evidence that she might not be okay.

"Zayn?" she prompts when I don't respond.

"What happened at the mall?"

The limited amount of color that was on her face drains away, leaving her ghostly pale. My stomach drops, that's all the confession I need to know my instincts were correct.

"I-I wasn't feeling well."

"Bullshit, Poppy." I drop down onto her bed and slide a little closer to her. "Tell me what really happened."

Her eyes bounce between mine before they drop to the sheets.

"Poppy?" I reach out, my hand landing on her upper arm and she flinches away. "Pops?"

"He was there, okay? He cornered me. Said some things, did some things. I just needed to leave, so I said I was sick. Happy now?"

"Happy?" I ask incredulously. "How could that possibly make me happy?"

She shrugs, pulling the sheets up higher in an attempt to hide from me.

"Damn it, Poppy," I snap, wrapping my fingers around her sheets and tugging them away from her. "Stop hiding from this."

Fuck.

My eyes drop from her eyes to her body that I've revealed. She's wearing a thin white tank and a pair of panties, leaving inches upon inches of smooth skin on display.

Her breath catches as she notices what's got my attention and she reaches out to take her covers back.

"No," I bark. "No more hiding. Not from me."

"I don't have the energy for this. You need to leave before my parents catch you."

"Your mom let me in. She sent me up here. I don't think she cares."

My words don't seem to be news to her. "Of course she doesn't."

My brows pull together as I study her. There's so much more to Poppy than meets the eye and the more I learn, the more it's confirmed that most people see straight past it.

Kicking my shoes off, I move closer, sitting on the sheets so she can't use them to hide behind. I'm not leaving this room until I get some truths out of her.

"What did he do to you, Poppy?"

"It's nothing." Her words infuriate me and by the widening of her eyes when she looks at me, I think she can tell. "Just forget it, Zayn. You shouldn't be here."

"And yet, here I am. Let me help you." Reaching out, I run my knuckles down her bare upper arm. She shudders, her skin pricks with goose bumps and her eyes shutter slightly.

"Zayn." I think it's meant to be a warning but it falls a long way from the mark.

"Did he hurt you?"

I hold her eye contact and shift a little closer still, her floral scent getting stronger and making my mouth water.

"N-no."

"Did he threaten you?"

A bitter laugh falls from her lips. "That's all he does. You don't need to get involved in this."

"And yet I am, and I won't be leaving until you tell me what happened."

"Fine," she huffs. "He followed me into the dressing room and… yeah." Once again she looks down at the bed, unable to hold my stare.

"Poppy," I say softly. "Did he… did he touch you?"

"Please don't do this, Zayn," she begs. The brokenness in her voice guts me.

"I'll fucking kill him if he so much as laid a finger on you."

"Can you leave, please?"

"No," I bark and she startles at my tone.

Reaching out, I take her chin between my finger and thumb and force her to look at me.

"You need to tell me what he did."

"I don't need to tell you anything."

"Fucking hell, Poppy. Stop covering for that motherfucker. I just want to help."

"You can help by staying out of it."

"But—"

Her eyes drop to my lips briefly before she cuts me off. "No buts. Please, just leave it. He's full of threats, I'm not scared of him."

"Which is why you ran away claiming to be ill?"

"I just needed to get away. Everything was just too much."

"What else is going on? What are you keeping from everyone?"

"It's just life, Zayn. Sometimes it's shit, but you've just got to carry on."

"That's bullshit, Poppy."

She shrugs, sadness oozing from her. Sadness that I wish I could take away.

Without thinking, I lean toward her.

"Zayn, what are you doing?" she whispers, but she doesn't stop me or pull away as I slip my hand around to the nape of her neck and press my forehead against hers.

"Making your life a little less shit."

"No, we... we can't..."

"Says who?" My lips brush hers as I wait for her to stop arguing and accept that this is about to happen.

"Nothing good happens after this... happens."

"Well, maybe it's time to change that."

My fingers grip her tighter as I brush my lips against hers once again, only with more insistence this time.

She remains as still as a statue for two seconds but the moment she feels my tongue run along her bottom lip, she caves, just like I knew she would.

She needs this right now, she just doesn't know that she does.

Her lips part and I greedily push my tongue past them in search of hers. A quiet moan rumbles up her throat as I deepen the kiss.

Just like the previous two times, everything around me vanishes and the only thing I'm aware of is her. It's a heady feeling and one I haven't been able to find with anyone else. It's addictive and I can only imagine how good it might be if we were to ever take it farther than just a kiss.

"Zayn," she moans when I kiss across her jaw. Her head falls back, allowing me the access I want to her neck. I brush my lips across the smooth, taut skin, feeling the thundering of her pulse just beneath the surface.

My tongue sneaks out, licking a line back up before I suck on her skin.

"So sweet," I murmur against her.

"Oh God."

Shifting on my knees, I lower her back to the bed, never moving my lips from her.

"You need more?" I ask, half expecting her to tell me to go to hell, so I couldn't be more surprised when she agrees.

"Make me forget, I don't care how."

I pause with my lips against her pulse point, waiting for her to start laughing and push me off, but she doesn't. Instead her chest continues to heave beneath me.

Sitting up, I stare down at her. Her tank is not far off being see-through, her pert nipples obvious beneath the fabric. It's pushed up around her waist, showing off the smooth skin of her stomach and her hips are covered in a lace edged pair of pink panties.

"Z-Zayn?" I hate the hesitation in her voice, she thinks that I've stopped because I don't want to give her what she needs, but she couldn't be farther from the truth.

"Shit, sorry. You're just so... beautiful."

A self-deprecating laugh falls from her lips. "I appreciate that, but I look a hot mess."

My eyes find hers. Yes, they're red from crying and she's got makeup smudged down her face from the tears she's shed. But I don't see any of that. I see the hunger, the need in her gray depths. I see her cute freckles that I know she hates and tries to hide with makeup. I see her full, pink lips and her shy little smile. I see her sinful curves that I crave to touch, to feel against me.

"Want me to prove you wrong?"

"Sure, if you think it's possible."

There are a million things I could say to her, to try to convince her of, but she wouldn't believe a word of it, so instead, I stick with actions.

9

POPPY

His lips crash down on mine once more and I forget about everything, all the reasons why this shouldn't be happening, and I just lose myself in his kiss. He makes it too easy to push real life aside and just focus on him.

It's dangerous. Too dangerous. But after the day I've had, it's more than welcome.

If Preston is serious about what he started today in that dressing room, then I may as well make the most of what Zayn's got to offer before Preston takes whatever it is he thinks I owe him.

His lips leave mine once more in favor of kissing down my neck. Butterflies go wild in my belly. I've never had a boy in my room, let alone one on top of me while I'm half-naked but hell knows there's no way I'm stopping this now.

Something coils tightly inside, telling me that things are only going to get better and I'm more than happy to find out just how good it's going to be.

His lips brush over my collarbone and the swell of my breasts.

His heated eyes find mine. Something crackles as our connection holds.

"You want me to stop, just say the words." His hot breath races across my sensitive skin and makes me shiver.

"Okay," I breathe, unable to find my voice while he's looking at me like I'm something precious. It's as incredible as it is unnerving.

He nods once before crawling down my body a little but he stops when his mouth is right above my breast. His eyes remain on mine as he closes the space between us and flicks my nipple with his bottom lip.

A bolt of lust shoots straight to my core and my thighs clench as heat spreads throughout my body.

"More?"

"More," I confirm, my fingers twitching to reach out and touch him.

He does the same again, only this time he doesn't stop at just a gentle touch, instead he lets his teeth graze me. My reaction is the same as before, only stronger.

"Oh God."

He smiles as I moan, my hips grinding against his inner thighs where he has me pinned to the bed.

"Fucking hell, Poppy."

"What?" I ask in a rush, thinking I've done something wrong.

"I want you so fucking bad right now."

"Really?"

"You underestimate yourself too much. You're beautiful..." He places a kiss along the neckline of my tank before tucking his finger in the fabric and pulling it down a little. "Sexy..." Kiss. "So fucking sexy." He pulls the fabric lower exposing my nipple but I can't find it in me to care as his eyes hold mine, showing me just how much he means the words that are falling from his lips. "And I can't get enough."

"Oh shit," I cry before covering my mouth with my hand when I realize just how loud I was. There is a houseful of people below us. Any of them could walk in at any moment and here I am laid out with Zayn's lips wrapped around my nipple. "Fuck." I have no idea if I'm cussing because of reality or the sensation of his tongue lapping at me.

He moans as he continues licking and kissing across my breast until he exposes the other one and gives it the same treatment.

"More, Zayn. More." I have no idea what I'm begging for, all I know is that I need whatever more is more than I need my next breath.

"You got it, baby."

He slides down the bed, pushing the fabric around my stomach up so he can kiss me until he hits the edge of my panties.

"Zayn?" I ask, pushing myself up onto my elbows to watch his descent. "Are you..." I trail off, not really wanting to ask in case I'm wrong and he's not about to do what I think he is. My cheeks flame red. He glances up at me with a wicked smile playing on his lips and a naughty glint in his eye.

"If you want me to."

"Um..." I murmur, biting down on my bottom lip. "No one's ever..." I fall back into the bed, flinging my arm over my eyes as I die of mortification.

Zayn's well... Zayn. Hotshot member of Rosewood's champion football team, all-around sex god and one of the boys all the girls dream about, and he's here, looking up at me like I'm the only girl in the world and offering me something that I never thought I'd experience with him, despite the number of times I've fantasized about it.

"Hey," he says, peeling my arm away from my face. "What did I tell you about hiding from me?"

I keep my eyes averted, but he moves so I have no choice but to look into his.

"You have no idea how glad I am that no one ever has." His voice is rough and my breath catches.

"You really want to..."

"Stop talking, Poppy." His fingers brush my lips. "You know full well that I never do something I don't want to."

"I know but—"

"Ah ah," he says, tapping my lips once again. "Just lie back."

He kisses down my body once more and just like last time, I watch his journey, fascinated by how he looks with his lips pressed up against my pale skin. Once he's past my hips, his fingers tuck inside my panties and he waits for me to lift a little to help him out.

I suck in a breath and close my eyes as he lowers them. I don't need to see him to know he's staring down at me, I feel it burn my skin.

"Look at me," he demands, and I'm powerless but to do as I'm told.

I rip my eyes open at the same time he wraps his fingers around my ankles and parts my legs.

His eyes hold mine as he settles himself between them before he drops to his stomach, his eyes zeroing in on my center.

I fight to keep my eyes on him, my embarrassment over his closeness to my most intimate part almost too much to bear.

"So beautiful. I bet you taste so damn sweet too."

I'm suddenly so glad the first thing I did when I got home was to shower.

His fingers brush me, parting me before he leans forward.

"Oh holy... fuck," I groan as his tongue gently licks at me. It's so gentle, so sensitive, just so... everything.

I want to demand he stops yet beg he continues. My head spins as my fingers twist in the sheet beneath me.

My back arches as he does it again, my hips lifting from the bed.

He chuckles, and it sends vibrations up my spine that only adds to the sensations.

Draping his arm over my stomach, he pins me to the bed to stop me from getting away before continuing.

"Zayn," I cry when it all gets too much. My hand reaches for him and my nails scratch at his scalp as I try to get more.

I need more. I need to discover what it is I'm chasing.

I just need… "Shit," I gasp as one of his fingers begins circling my entrance.

All of my muscles tense as something intense builds inside me.

"Please, please," I beg, needing to shatter. I've got myself off before when my curiosity got the better of me, but it was nothing like this, nothing quite so consuming and so… intense.

The world around me vanishes, we could be anywhere on the planet right now and I wouldn't know it, even less care about it. The only thing that matters is the sensations racing through my body and the ache in my core that's going to explode.

His fingers slide inside me, stretching me open but the small bite of pain only adds to what he's doing.

"Oh my God," I scream a second before I crash.

Something within me shatters into a million pieces as my body convulses on the bed beneath him.

But he never stops. His tongue, his fingers, they both keep moving, drawing every last drop of pleasure from me.

"Shit, Zayn that was—"

"Poppy?" a little voice calls from the other side of the door a beat before the handle rattles.

"Fuck," Zayn barks before practically dropping to the floor at the other side of the bed.

I wrestle with the sheets and just about manage to cover up my almost naked body by the time Austin's little head pokes inside my room.

"Hey, bud, is everything okay?" My voice is high-pitched yet rough at the same time and I cringe at hearing it.

"Uh… are you feeling better? It's just Mom and Dad have gone out and…"

"They've gone out? Where's Cooper?"

"With us. He's okay, he's sleeping."

"Jesus," I mutter under my breath. "Did they say how long they were going for?"

He shakes his head. "We haven't eaten."

Of course they fucking haven't. "I'll be down in a bit and I'll see what I can find for you."

"Thank you." He ducks back out of the room and I fall back to the bed, blowing out a long breath of frustration.

It seems Zayn managed to rid the tension from my body for all of five seconds.

Zayn, shit.

I twist to the side of the bed where he vanished to see him rising to his feet.

There's concern written across his face and I fight the need to hide, knowing what he just heard, but there's more than just that. There's hunger and it makes everything inside me clench.

"You need to go," I say in a rush before he gets a chance to make this situation any worse.

He studies me for a beat before dropping down so his nose is only a breath from mine.

"This time, I'll do as you ask. Next time might be a very different story."

My heart jumps in my chest. Next time? He thinks there could be a next time.

"This isn't going to happen again."

"You going to try to tell me you didn't enjoy it?"

I close my eyes, not needing to see the smirk that I know will be playing on his face.

"This shouldn't have happened, Zayn. You shouldn't have..."

"Kissed you, touched you, *ate you.*" His voice is so low, so dirty and suggestive that I can't help but squirm.

I flinch when his hand wraps around the back of my neck and my eyes pop open in surprise.

"This is happening again, Poppy. I need more, and I know you do too. Now go look after your family before I'm forced to start asking more questions, like why your parents just fucked off leaving you in charge of three hungry kids with no warning." I panic, assuming that he heard Austin, which of course he did..

"T-things are complicated."

"Aren't they always." He drops his lips to mine, his tongue pushing inside until it tangles with mine. My breath catches when I realize that I can taste myself on him but he doesn't stop, hell, nor do I.

By the time he pulls back, I'm a panting mess again.

"I'll see myself out."

"Make sure they don't see you."

"You underestimate me, Poppy."

With one last kiss, he stalks toward my door but stops and turns back before walking through it.

"You need me, you know where I am. I won't let that motherfucker hurt you, Poppy. All you've got to do is say the word."

"T-thank you. But it's okay. Everything is okay."

His eyes narrow, he doesn't believe a word of it, and rightly so, but thankfully, he pulls the door open and silently steps into the hallway.

What I really want to do is curl up into a ball and try not to cry myself to sleep as I obsess over every second of today, but I can't.

I've got people relying on me to feed them and keep them alive.

I give myself thirty seconds before I stuff everything about today in a box, close the lid and fling the covers off me. The sight of my almost naked body threatens to bring it all back, but I push it down. I'll do what I've got to do, then I'll let myself drown.

Thankfully, I find a frozen pizza at the back of the freezer, so I throw that in the oven and make both their packed lunches for tomorrow while it cooks.

As Austin said, Cooper is fast asleep in his bouncy chair while the two of them watch some awful-looking kid's show that has them both in hysterics every few minutes. The sound of their joy and laughter makes my heart ache. At least they're not as affected by all this as I am.

I rest my ass back against the counter and wonder where all this is going. The life we're living under this roof isn't sustainable.

I'd hoped that when my aunt returned a few months ago that it might help fix things. But her appearance did nothing for Mom, her inevitable departure however sent her on a downward spiral.

She used to have good days, good weeks. I could be normal some of the time. I'd have friends over, sleepovers even, knowing that Mom was going to just be... well, a mom. But she got pregnant again and, I shake my head, everything just went to shit.

She's up and down so fast it gives me whiplash. She and Dad are either at each other's throats or giving us all a show that we never need to see. It's... exhausting, and unless they seek out the help they so desperately need, I can't see them getting better anytime soon.

The movement of a shadow out in the garden catches my eye and has my heart in my throat, but when I look, it's just a tree blowing in the wind, the leaves catching the brightness of our outside light.

I tip my head back and blow out a slow stream of breath. Things can only get better, right?

"Is it ready, we're starving," Sofia says, racing into the kitchen and almost colliding with a bar stool.

"Yes, go and get your brother and I'll dish up."

"Yess," she squeals. "Austin, dinner!"

"Shush, you'll wake Cooper." Although as the words leave my lips, I wonder if that would probably be for the best, he should be awake right now if I have any chance of having a decent night's sleep.

Once they've eaten, I tidy up and let them carry on watching TV with strict instructions that they're to turn it off and come to bed the second the program finishes. They agree and thankfully, I know I don't have to worry about them doing as they're told. The one good thing in all of this is that they're incredibly good kids. Although, I fear that's because they see too much, understand too much and know that I'm not the one they should be giving grief to. That would be our absent parents.

I walk back upstairs with the sound of their laughter filling my ears. It makes a part of me feel lighter, but it's not enough.

The fear I felt in that dressing room earlier is still clinging to me along with the confusion over Zayn's visit.

Closing my bedroom door behind me, I pull my clothes off as I make my way to my bathroom and turn the shower on.

I'd already had one when I first got home. The only thing I could smell was him and it turned my stomach knowing that he was that close. That he touched me, that he almost...

I gag, the thought too much to take.

He almost took exactly what he wanted and I have no doubt that next time he'll be more successful. He wants to break me, hurt me, and doing that might just be the way to do it.

I don't want him breathing the same air as me, let alone touching me.

It's why I let Zayn do what he did. On any other day, I probably wouldn't have allowed it to happen.

Wouldn't you? Like you stopped him kissing you?

But the thought of it being him who touched me first, who gave me that before Preston can taint me with his own evil touch, well... it spurred me on. More than it probably should.

The water is barely warm when I step under it, but I don't notice, I'm too lost in my own head.

I think back to the evil intentions in Preston's eyes in that dressing room and a shudder runs through me. He was serious, I have no doubts about that, if Ruby hadn't had called, I have no reason to believe that he wouldn't have taken exactly what he wanted. Sick fuck.

He has girls falling at his feet on a daily basis. What's wrong with one of them? Why can't he take it out of one of the sluts who think they can use him to take a step up the Rosewood ladder?

My thoughts flick back to Zayn. Why was he even here? It doesn't take a genius to figure out that it's come from Harley, but why does he care?

I told him we were nothing, yet he turned up here anyway and helped me forget, despite the fact I barely told him anything like he demanded.

Confusion swells within me and tears burn my eyes. I don't want to cry over that entitled prick. He doesn't deserve a reaction from me but as the tears spill over, I accept that I can't stop them, can't stop myself from feeling when he constantly pushes me.

My hands tremble as I realize that I'm probably going to have to see him tomorrow... both of them. How am I supposed to look either of them in the eye and pretend like my entire world isn't currently crumbling around my feet?

My back hits the wall and I slide down until my ass hits the floor.

The barely warm water continues to rain down on me until it turns icy cold, but still I remain curled up in a ball wishing the water would wash me away with it.

10

ZAYN

"Where have you been?" comes from the kitchen the second I close the front door behind me.

My heart jumps into my throat and I feel like a naughty little boy again. I may have snuck out earlier but it wasn't because I'm not allowed, more that I didn't want to invite any questions about where I was going.

Turning left, I step through to join Mom where she's sitting at the island with a glass of wine.

"I just went for a drive to clear my head."

She nods in understanding.

Pulling open the refrigerator, I grab a can of soda and join her.

"I'm sorry, Zayn."

"What for?"

She lets out of a long sigh. "For dragging you all into this thing between your dad and me."

"It's okay, you don't—"

She cuts me off before I get to tell her that I understand. "It was never meant to end this way. I wanted a better life for all of us, I had no idea that he was going to act the way he did."

"Mom," I say, reaching out for her hand. "You don't need to do this. His reactions aren't your responsibility."

"I know, but I see the look on your face every time you come back from that place and I hate it. I never wanted to build a life there, I certainly didn't want to bring my kids up there. I had a plan, a plan for a better life but..."

"I know, Mom." She's told me this story before, and although I appreciate the truth, it doesn't change anything. Our family is still broken, we're here, he's there and the three of us are in between the two of them like punching bags waiting for the next hit.

Mom was supposed to go to college, the first in her family, she was all ready to go and then she met Dad. They fell in love, she got pregnant with Letty and that was it. She ended up with the trailer park life that she's always despised. Soon she had three young kids and no way out.

I remember the look that was always on her face when I was a kid. She was miserable. It didn't take an expert to see that she was depressed but she was stuck in hell.

She was a good mom, she did everything she could for us, but it wasn't enough for her.

We had no idea she'd somehow managed to start studying but when I found out, I was so proud of her. I still am now. She had a dream, a dream of a better life and she found a way to make it happen, something many people are never brave enough to do. She had no idea that Dad was going to kick off like he did and refuse to be a part of her future.

His decision still shreds her, I can see it in her eyes. As much as she likes to curse him out, I know she still loves him. Sadly, I think the two of them have just changed too much over the years, they want totally different things and I think it would take a miracle to ever fix it between them.

"Did you have a good time with your dad?" she asks after a few moments of silence.

"Uh... it was... fine." She gives me a sad, knowing smile.

"I'll never regret what I did. Seeing the three of you here, knowing that you have the world at your feet, it means everything to me."

"I hate going back there," I admit. "It's so... depressing."

"You don't need to tell me that."

"You're amazing, Mom."

A smile curls at her lips at my words. "Anything for my babies. Now, are you all ready for school tomorrow?"

"You know it." I wink at her.

"Any college will be lucky to have you next year." She squeezes my hand before I stand from the stool.

Now that I've turned my applications in, I'm trying not to think about it. I know my first choice, I want it so fucking badly, but I know that there's nothing I can do now. I just have to sit and wait for that letter to drop through the door that's going to decide my fate.

"Thanks, Mom."

I leave her to it and head up the stairs. Music comes from Harley's room and my hand twitches to knock, to find out if she's still struggling with that math homework, but the memory of what I did tonight stops me.

She'll never forgive me for going after Poppy after warning me to stay away. That's just the problem though. I can't. And knowing that she's being tormented by that motherfucker makes me want to protect her even more.

My fists curl as I picture him standing before me looking like the fucking weak ass pussy that he is.

Harley was right, you can take the boy out of the trailer park, but the trailer park is always in the boy.

People around here might not see me as that, most of them don't even know what my past consists of. All they care about is that I can play ball. They have no idea about the dark side of me I keep hidden. We might have left that place four years ago, but I'm not sure it'll ever leave me. Especially when we keep getting dragged back. Just one more thing to look forward to once college starts, although the thought of Harley going alone into the pit of vultures scares the shit out of me.

My room feels cold and empty as I step inside and close the door behind me. I want to be back in her room, feel the heat of her skin, hear the soft moans she made as I worked her toward orgasm. But I know she was right to kick me out. I shouldn't have even been there in the first place.

I pull my shirt over my head, her scent filling my nose as it moves, and I groan. I was so fucking hard for her as I gave her what she needed to escape. But that was just it, it was about her, not me, and I've walked away with the bluest balls known to man.

Dropping my pants, I crawl into bed, but her scent lingers and before I can stop myself, my fingers wrap around my length and I work myself to my own release with images of her laid out before me filling my mind.

I'm already worked up and on high alert before I even take a step into the school building the next morning.

My need to teach that fucker a lesson for whatever it was he did to her at the mall is almost all I can think about.

I scan the faces as I make my way down the hallway toward where her locker is. A few people try to stop me and a couple of the cheerleaders join me, clinging to my arms like they belong there. I don't shake them off like I probably should. I figure that if my entire attention isn't on that prick when my eyes land on him then it's probably a good thing.

I don't have to take too many more steps before he emerges in front of me with his little posse surrounding him.

He oozes entitlement and it makes my muscles pull tight in disgust. So what, daddy has a lot of money, it doesn't stop him from being a total fucking asshole. He seems to think he's untouchable, that daddy can cover up or buy off whatever shit he gets himself into, and to be fair, it might have worked up until now. But he's not encountered me before and there is no way he can drop a few hundred bills to make me forget what he's doing.

He scans the hallway, staring down his nose at the students around him until his eyes lock on mine. He startles slightly before his jaw clenches.

My lips curl into a smile, but it's anything but friendly. The stupid motherfucker doesn't even have the sense to look a little afraid. He's clearly already forgotten about our little chat in the locker room last week. Probably all the fucking pills he pops frying his brain cells.

Our eyes hold for a couple of seconds but someone more interesting at the other end of the corridor catches his attention.

I don't need to look to know who it is. I can see it in his eyes. He looks like a lion who's just spotted his prey.

I take a step toward him, glancing at the girl who's holding his attention. The sight of her makes my breath catch.

Her light brown hair is pulled back from her face accentuating her cheekbones and full lips. Something stirs within me as I remember just how her lips taste but the dark circles around her eyes are a stark reminder of the reality of why I did what I did last night.

I still have no idea what Preston did or how bad it was, but the ball of dread in my stomach tells me that my worst suspicions might just be correct.

Poppy was different last night. Her kiss was different, the way she reacted to me was different. She was desperate for me to make her forget, and that was because of what he did.

Her eyes catch mine and her steps falter, that is until she looks away from me and finds Preston. Then all the color drains from her face before she looks to the floor and makes quick work of getting to her locker.

Not wanting to give her the attention she clearly doesn't want, I walk toward him instead, despite the fact my body screams to go to her.

I don't stop until my shoulder slams into his.

"What the fuck, man?" he barks as all his crew stop and stare at me as if I'm about to lay him out right here in the middle of the school. It's tempting, I'll give them that but I'd hate to give him the satisfaction of watching me getting carted off by Hartmann when we're caught.

"Watch your fucking back," I warn, my voice low so none of our audience will hear.

A deep growl rumbles up his throat. "Fuck you. I do what I like."

My fists clench with my need to hurt him, it takes all my self-restraint to keep my arms at my sides and walk away from him.

His evil laugh hits my ears and I almost change my mind. Glancing over my shoulder, I find him staring right at Poppy who's still as white as a sheet at the other end of the hallway.

It's all I need to tell me that he's not going to give this up easily and that if I want to help her, free her from his twisted game, then I need to up the ante.

By lunch my muscles are still pulled tight and I'm still on high alert waiting to see or hear that the douchebag has done something else.

I don't usually listen to the senior class gossip, let alone the junior gossip but today I hear everything, and when Harley and Ruby come to join the cheerleaders at lunch, I listen to every word while the JV football team occupies the table beside ours in their need to be us.

Preston is noticeably absent from his group almost all of lunch. The rational side of me says he's probably just with a teacher or in the gym or something, but the other part of me says that he's with her.

My blood turns to lava as I think about him touching her, about him forcing her to do something.

My fist slams down on the table before me, making the lunch trays rattle and everyone to stop talking and stare at me.

"You all right, man?" Justin asks, his eyes boring into me.

"Yeah, I just… fuck. I'm outta here."

Without waiting to hear what any of them have to say, I push from my stool, all but throw the tray and its remaining contents into the trash and storm out of the gym.

If Poppy isn't with my sister and Ruby, then there's only one place she'll be. I march toward the music department.

The looks on the music geeks' faces are a picture as I pass them on my mission to find her. If I weren't so agitated about his suspicious absence, then I might be entertained by it.

I might not make a habit of coming to this corner of the school but I know where to look. Sadly, I don't make it to the practice rooms before I stumble across the one person I really didn't want to see right now.

"Zayn." Preston nods, his pretentious, asshole smirk plastered across his face.

"What are you doing here?" I seethe.

"Visiting a friend. What about you, I didn't have you down as a music fan."

"Fuck you."

"Now, now, I was only being friendly."

I don't bother responding, I push past him, my legs moving even faster than before, my need to find her even stronger.

He watches me go, I feel his stare burning into my back but I refuse to turn around and give him the satisfaction of knowing that he affects me in any way.

Looking through the window of all the practice rooms, I search for her but I come up empty. It's not until I look through the final small window that I find her defeated form slumped over a piano.

My chest constricts that he was down here doing God knows what with her while I was sitting in the cafeteria with the team.

I don't bother knocking, I just push the handle down and shove the door open.

Her entire body flinches with the sound but she doesn't turn around, she doesn't do anything.

It's almost like she's given up, lost her fight.

It fucking kills me.

"Poppy?" My voice is soft, quiet, in the hope of making her relax.

"What do you want, Zayn?"

"Are you… are you okay? Did he…"

"He did nothing. You should leave."

I hesitate, not knowing whether I should do as she asks or what I want to do.

"Why do you keep insisting on pushing me away?"

"Because it's the right thing to do. You don't owe me anything, Zayn. You have no reason to keep poking your nose into my life." Her words cut but I refuse to allow her to know it.

"What if I want to?"

A sad laugh falls from her. "Why would you want to?"

"Why wouldn't I?"

Walking over, I come to a stop beside the piano and look down at her. She rushes to wipe the tears from her eyes before she looks to the other side of the room in an attempt to hide from me.

"Poppy, what did he do?"

"He did nothing," she cries, standing from the stool and once again turning her back on me. "He did nothing, he means nothing. All of this has nothing to do with you. Just go back to your team and gaggle of cheer sluts and leave me alone."

Closing the space between us, I place my hand on her waist. She tenses but she doesn't immediately push me away.

"Zayn," she sighs. It's so quiet, so broken that it makes something inside my chest physically hurt for her.

I spin her to face me and gently push her up against the wall so she can't escape too easily.

"Talk to me, Poppy. Please. Let me help."

"There's nothing you can do."

"That's shit and you know it."

She still refuses to meet my eyes and I hate that she's hiding from me. Lifting my hand, I tuck my finger under her chin and force her to look up.

I swallow down the curse that wants to explode from me when I see the tears filling her eyes.

"He was here?"

She nods.

"Did he hurt you?"

"Not physically."

"Hurting you in any way isn't going to work with me, Poppy. How long has it been this bad?"

She shrugs and it pisses me off that she can try to brush this under the carpet like it's nothing.

"He's just a stupid boy, playing stupid games."

"You really believe that?"

"What did he do at the mall?" I try again, still desperate to know the truth.

"Enough," she barks, her eyes narrowing at me, a little of her normal fire returning. "This isn't your fight."

"It shouldn't be yours either. Why haven't you told anyone about this?"

"Why bother? What are they going to do about it?"

"What about your parents?"

"Pfft." She rolls her eyes and it's like she's thrown fuel over the fire that's crackling away in my belly.

"This is bullshit. He's not going to get away with this."

"No, Zayn. You need to stay out of it. This is my battle, not yours."

Her small fists grip on to my shirt and pull me closer.

"Please, Zayn. Don't do this. Don't get involved."

Our noses are only a breath apart, her scent fills my senses and her heat burns my skin.

"Poppy," I groan. "I can't help it." I have no idea what exactly I'm admitting to, but it doesn't really matter because the second my lips brush hers, all thoughts fall from my head.

Her muscles lock up for a beat and I start to think that she's going to push me away, but instead of doing that she releases my shirt, and she slides her palms around my back and drags me closer until the length of my body is crushing hers against the wall.

My fingers tangle in her hair, allowing me to tilt her head to the side to deepen the kiss.

Her tongue meets mine, her kiss as desperate as mine.

With my hand gripping her waist, I pour everything I'm feeling into the kiss. The anger that she's being treated this way, my frustration that she won't just tell me the truth, my need to do something about it, to make it go away, to make her life easier.

"Zayn," she mumbles against my lips as her hands flatten against my stomach to create some space between us.

"Stop fighting it, Pops."

"I'm not fighting anything. We can't do this."

"You're the only one who thinks that way."

I press myself harder against her ensuring that she feels exactly what she does to me with just her kiss.

My lips trail down her jaw.

"I'm not sure your sister or my cousin would see it that way."

"Fuck them. This isn't about them."

She shudders as I suck on the sensitive skin beneath her ear.

"No, Zayn. Stop."

Her words are like an ice-cold bucket of water poured over me, and I immediately step back.

Her brows draw together as if she's confused by me doing as she said but she soon recovers.

"You need to go."

"Why is it so hard for you to let me help you?"

"Because I don't need it."

"Okay, so… tell me what he was doing here. What did he say to you?"

"The usual shit."

"Fucking hell, Poppy." I lift my hands to my head in frustration and tilt my face to the ceiling. "Do you really need to make it so hard?"

She doesn't respond.

"If you don't start talking, I'll just assume the worst. I'll be forced to think that when he accosted you yesterday that it was so he could put his hands on you. Is that what he did?" A thought hits me and my stomach turns over. "Did he? Did he touch you? Is that why you let me last night?"

The small amount of color that was in her face drains away.

"I'm going to fucking kill him."

"Zayn, no. It's nothing like that."

"You're fucking lying. Just tell me the truth."

"Keep your nose out of it."

"No," I seethe, closing the space between us once more. My eyes boring into hers and begging for her to confess while hers pleads with me to stop.

"I don't need you or anyone else fighting my battles for me. Preston is a douchebag, we all know that, but I can handle him."

"But—"

"No, Zayn. There are no buts here. Leave it the hell alone."

"I can't promise you that."

"You don't have a choice."

My brows rise as I stare at her.

"Fuck this, Poppy. I'm not going to stand by while that prick treats you like you're worth nothing."

Stepping away from her, I storm toward the door before ripping it open.

"But what if I am?" Her voice is so broken that I almost step back inside and close the door, but I know I can't. She doesn't want me here.

"If you think that, then you've already let him win."

The door clicks closed behind me as I walk away from her. Regret sits heavy in my stomach but it's not as insistent as my need to go and find Preston and show him what I really think of him.

Anger surrounds me like a dark cloud as I make my way through the school. Kids litter the hallways, but one look at me and they pale slightly.

"What the fuck is wrong with you?" Jake asks when I pass him where he's got Amalie backed up against her locker. It's not unlike the move I just played on his cousin.

Something stirs within me, but I push it down.

"Nothing," I bark, successfully proving that there is something wrong.

I crack my knuckles, my need to hurt someone starting to get the better of me.

"Coach has fucked off somewhere. The gym is empty if you need to..." He trails off, his eyes dropping to my hands.

Without saying another word, I blow down the hallway and toward the locker room.

There are a few kids getting dressed, ready for next period but none of them are brave enough to stop me as I make a beeline for the gym, or more specifically, the punching bag that's waiting for me.

The second I see the red leather, I launch myself at it as if it's Preston himself.

My roar of anger fills the empty space around me as I plow my fists into the leather, wishing that it was his face.

11

POPPY

I might be almost at the end of my last class of the day, but my head is still back in that practice room at lunch. The last person I expected to stumble across when I walked inside with the intention of hiding for an hour was Preston.

And it wasn't just Preston, because he had Annie, a JV cheerleader, pressed up against the wall and was grinding into her like it was what she needed to keep her alive.

I went to leave, not wanting to ever see that, but the second he saw me, a sinister smile curled at his lips and he demanded that I stay and watch.

I should have walked straight back out, but his increasingly scary behavior meant that I couldn't help believing that his threats are more than just words these days.

When he tells me that I'll be next and that I will enjoy it, I have no doubt that at least the first part of that statement is true.

A shudder runs up my spine as I remember.

The things he said as he touched her, the way he compared how she was enjoying what he was doing to how I reacted the day before.

The way he spat at me that I was broken, useless. Nothing but a tease. Frigid. The way she giggled as if his words were a hilarious joke she couldn't get enough of.

All of it turned my stomach, and the final one brought back memories of a certain birthday party that needed to stay locked in the box I've shoved them in.

Even now I can hear his words like he's whispering them in my ear.

It shouldn't have affected me, but I couldn't help succumbing to the tears when he finally dragged her out. Thankfully, it was before he actually fucked her with me in the room.

I'd felt ridiculous allowing his vile words to hurt me but I couldn't help it. I only have so much tolerance for his shit.

When the door opened once more, I was convinced it was him coming back to take more from me, to attempt to make me bend to his will like that slutty cheerleader who moaned like a whore every time he so much as glanced her way.

It was pathetic. Both of them were pathetic.

I was expecting him to be in my last class of the day, so when our teacher kicked things off and his desk was still sitting empty, I was more than relieved not to have to spend the hour feeling his hateful stares burning into my skin.

Everything is normal, well as normal as Rosewood High ever is, until the boy himself bursts through the door only a few minutes before the end of the day. Only he doesn't look like he did earlier because he's covered in blood. Not that it seems to bother him.

A collective gasp sounds out around the room and he stands proudly, displaying his injuries to his loving crowd.

"Jesus, what happened to him?" Amalie mutters beside me.

"Christ knows, he had it coming though." As I say the words, realization hits me.

He did have it coming, and from someone I warned not to do anything.

He wouldn't. Would he?

As the chaos continues, I slip out of the room after muttering to Amalie that I'm going to use the bathroom. Our teacher doesn't even notice I leave, he's too busy attempting to deal with Preston who is lapping up the attention of all the girls who are offering to be his personal nurse. I try not to gag at the thought.

Just before I turn the corner, I feel his hate-filled stare trained on me.

Glancing back over my shoulder, I hold his eyes for a beat. They're cold, it's not unusual, but I can't shift the fear that snakes around my entire body.

This is not going to end well for me. Preston doesn't take well to being threatened, and I can imagine even worse to being attacked.

Leaving him behind, I turn right down the hall instead of left toward the bathroom.

I might be wildly off the mark here, but I follow my gut all the way down toward the boy's locker room. The trail of blood that I follow sure makes me think I'm on the right track.

Hesitating outside the door, I wonder if I'm about to make a massive mistake but then I think back to my warning about leaving this be, and my anger that he's ignored me forces me to swing the door back and go marching in.

My lips curl as the smell of sweaty boy fills my nose but I don't let it put me off as I march through, past the lockers and benches in the hope of finding the person I'm looking for.

The water that was running cuts off and my heart jumps into my throat as realization of what I'm doing hits me.

Walking inside here is probably the most spontaneous thing I've ever done. Preston isn't wrong when he tells me that I'm boring. I can't help wondering how much of that is actually his fault. I spend most of my life trying to stay away from him, which means avoiding most parties and all other social events that most kids at Rosewood High live for.

I continue forward until I find one person with his back to me. Water droplets cover his wide shoulders and run down his back, soaking into the towel that's wrapped around his waist.

I see no evidence that he was the one who made such a mess of Preston, but I don't need to see any, I know.

He turns and I suck in a deep breath as I prepare for him to see me.

"Jesus, Poppy," he barks, his eyes going wide and his chest swelling as he sucks in a sharp breath. "What the fuck?"

Squaring my shoulders, I take a step toward him. "Funny, because I was going to say the exact same thing to you."

"I don't know what you're talking about. Shouldn't you be in class?"

"Shouldn't you?" I quip.

"I was... eh... working out."

"Were you?" Closing the space between us, I lift my finger, running it none too gently over the emerging bruise around his eye. "Treadmill fight back, did it?"

"Poppy," he warns.

"Don't *Poppy* me." Dropping my hand to his, I grip his fingers and lift his hand so I can look at his knuckles. "I told you to fucking leave it," I shout, throwing his hand back down with as much force as I can muster.

"Yeah, and I told you I couldn't."

"So that makes it right?" I seethe.

"Trust me, Pops. Nothing about this is right."

"How many times do I have to say it, Zayn? This is not your fight. It's not your place to get involved."

"Really? So how else are you planning on making him stop?"

"I… uh…"

"Exactly. And what's going to be next, huh? You might refuse to tell me what he's doing but I know it's bad. I can see it in your eyes, Poppy. I can see the fear, the sheer terror whenever he's close, whenever someone so much as says his name. You don't have to deal with this. You don't deserve this."

"Don't," I warn as he takes a step toward me, crowding me with his large frame.

It's bad enough that he's standing there in just a towel with nothing but water trailing over his bronzed, taut skin. I watch one droplet as it runs down from his collarbone, over his chest and drops down to his abs.

Fuck.

My eyes lock on where the towel is tucked around his waist, knowing that he's naked beneath.

My teeth sink into my bottom lip as I try to imagine how it might look and wonder how easy it would be to pull it from his body.

"Go on, if you want to."

My eyes fly up to his, shocked that he's responding to my thoughts.

"W- what?"

"You're staring at the towel as if you want it to disappear, so make it."

"N- no, that's n- not…"

"No?"

He steps forward and I'm forced to take one back to stop his body from brushing up against mine.

"What are you doing in here, Poppy?"

"I… um… I had a feeling that you'd be here and I… uh… wanted to…"

He takes another two steps and I find myself once again caged between him and the wall.

"You wanted to… continue what we started earlier?"

"What? N- no. I wanted to shout at you, tell you that you're totally out of order for doing what you—"

He swallows my words as his lips cover mine and his tongue plunges inside my mouth.

"Zayn," I mumble, wanting to fight but finding my body getting sucked into his and losing myself once again to his kiss.

This has got to stop, I think to myself as my hands land on his shoulder blades before running down his back until they hit the fabric of the towel.

His thigh pushes between mine until I find myself grinding down against it. Pleasure explodes from my core as his hand cups my breast over my shirt and squeezes.

"Oh God," I cry, my head falling back against the tiles behind me.

"Let go, Poppy."

His lips trail down my neck before his tongue licks all the way back up.

"I'm so mad at you," I tell him, unwilling, even now, to let this go.

"Good, let me make it up to you." His voice is deep and gravelly, and it does funny things to my insides.

Every muscle in my body locks up tight as he pushes his thigh harder against me, the first tingles of my release begin when there's a loud crash at the other side of the room.

"Hunter, you still in here?" a familiar voice barks.

"Y-yeah, man." Zayn pulls back from me, his eyes wide in panic as realization hits me.

I need to get out of here right freaking now.

"You seen Hellburn? Some lucky son of a bitch got the chance to rearrange his face."

Jake's voice gets closer as I look around, trying to figure out how to get out of this.

Zayn looks toward where he's going to appear from, allowing me to slip from between him and the wall. Before he's even noticed, I run. Fast.

12

ZAYN

I take a huge step away from Poppy and run my hands over my head as I try to figure a way out of this. If I thought I'd done a number on Preston, then it'll be nothing compared to the beating Jake will give me for touching Poppy.

It's not until he appears around the side of the lockers, his brows pulling together as he looks at me that I glance to the side.

Where she was just a few seconds ago, writhing against the wall, is empty.

"What the—" I mutter to myself under my breath.

"Is everything all right?" he asks suspiciously. His eyes running the length of me. "Oh fuck, were you jacking off? Fucking hell, man."

"What? No, no. I was not—" Glancing down at myself, I find my still semi-erect cock tenting the towel. *Fucking hell.*

Jake's brow rises in suspicion.

"I had a girl in here," I admit.

That interests him more than the thought of me getting myself off because he starts to look around as if she's going to appear. I really fucking hope she doesn't. I have no idea where she's gone but I can only hope it was out of the other door.

"Oh yeah?" he asks suspiciously as Mason, Ethan, and Shane appear behind him.

"What's going on?" Ethan asks, looking between the two of us.

"Hunter says he had a girl in here," Jake joyfully informs them as the rest of the team make their way inside. "Well it's either that or he was beating off to the smell of your sweaty boxers," he says to Ethan.

"Fuck off," I grunt.

"I see no girl here, Hunter. I could, however, do with my underwear back though."

Flipping them all off, I march over to where I abandoned my clean clothes and drag them on ready for Jake's conditioning session.

"So you're not gonna tell us who you convinced to spend last period in here with you instead of in class?"

"Nope," I say, earning a round of moans from the four idiots who are still grinning at me. "Why do you all look so excited about this? Jealous or something?"

"Fuck yeah, locker room hook-ups with our girls is the best. This one time Rae snuck in and—"

"No time, Savage. Fantasize later about your girl."

"No need. While yours might have vanished into thin air, almost like she doesn't exist, I live with mine." He winks before dragging his shirt over his head and pulling another from his locker. "My days to fantasize are long over, man. You should try it."

"Who'd have thought it, Ethan Savage whipped by one five-foot-nothing pocket rocket."

"Believe it, bro. Hell has indeed frozen over."

The four of them fall into easy conversations about their girls as we change and I can't help feeling a little jealous. Now, I'm not saying I want Poppy as my one and only, but shit, the four of them sound so fucking happy it's almost enough to make me reconsider my ways.

Our session is... fine. Preston eventually arrives having cleaned himself up a bit and mostly pulls his weight while everyone else looks at him like he's lost his mind. I'm beginning to think he probably has. Out of all the girls at school, why mess with Poppy. He should know that it'll only end one way—with Jake Thorn breathing down his neck—so why bother? What's he getting out of this?

Jake's session is hardcore and I can't help but wonder if it's for Preston's benefit. Jake might not yet know what's going on, but he already dislikes the prick as much as the rest of us, so putting him through his paces while he's clearly in pain is an afternoon's entertainment to both of us.

Once he's finished, he sends us back to the locker rooms to get showered and dressed. The second I step inside, all I see is her backed up against the tiled wall, her head tipped back in pleasure, her lips swollen from my kiss and her soft mewls for more.

My cock swells once again, my need to finish what we started getting the better of me.

I'm in no rush to go anywhere. The guys all talk about heading to Aces, but the only place I want to go is wherever she is. I wonder if she's going to be at my house again with Harley, but then I think of the events of the day and I suspect she'd have made every excuse not to. Harley would have been in cheer practice, does that mean Poppy is hanging around somewhere on her own waiting?

My eyes flick to Preston where he's drying off after showering and a little of the fury I felt earlier swirls in my stomach.

Feeling my stare, he looks over. His lips thin in frustration. I know he hates that I got the better of him earlier. But I think he's beginning to understand that he's underestimated me.

He shakes his head as if what I did earlier and my reasons for it mean nothing. I take a step toward him, more than happy to teach him another lesson, but a hand lands on my shoulder.

I look to my right to find Shane standing there with his brows drawn together.

"What the fuck has gotten into you?"

"Nothing," I mutter.

"Tell that to your knuckles. Don't even think about lying to me about this."

"Fine, but not here," I say, knowing that Jake is only a few feet away.

I trust Shane, he's been a good friend over the past couple of months and hell knows I need to talk to someone about this.

He nods once and continues getting dressed.

The second we're both ready, we blow out of the locker room and toward the parking lot.

Music blasts down the hallway from the gym where the squad are practicing and it brings back earlier thoughts as to whether she's here somewhere waiting for a lift from Ruby.

Pulling my cell from my pocket, I find her contact and shoot her a message. It's a long shot, but I can't help myself.

Zayn: Are you still in school?

It's read instantly, but no reply comes.

Lifting my hand to my head, I rub my palm over my short hair.

I want to fix this. I want to make Preston leave her the fuck alone and I want to do things to her that I really fucking shouldn't, but I can't help thinking that both of those things have disaster written all over them.

In just one afternoon, I had beaten the shit out of Hellburn and I've almost gotten Poppy off in the locker room. Where the hell is this going next?

The fact I haven't already been dragged into Hartmann's office surprises me. I touched him on school grounds. If I were smart about this—and clearly, I'm not—then I would have waited until after our session this afternoon. Organized to meet him somewhere neutral, not have a fake note sent to him pretending that Coach wanted to meet him before the last class of the day. It was stupid and I need to be smarter where he's concerned if I'm going to do anything about getting him off Poppy's back.

"So?" Shane asks as he follows me to my truck and falls into the passenger seat.

"Ugh," I complain, dropping my head to the headrest behind me.

"Hellburn had it coming to him."

"Agreed. But why today, what's happened?"

"You gotta keep this to yourself, man."

He nods. I don't even need to ask, I know it goes without saying.

"He's bullying Poppy."

Shane's eyes go wide. "Poppy? Poppy as in Jake's Poppy?"

"The one and only," I say, something I'm not sure I like swelling in my chest at the thought of her.

"Fuuuck. Has that prick got a death wish?"

"I'm starting to wonder if he has, yeah."

"Jake doesn't know—"

"Obviously," Shane adds.

"I don't think anyone really knows. She's kept it well hidden but I fear this might have been going on for a while."

"Right. Okay," he says as he digests what I'm saying. "So what are we going to do about it?"

I glance over at him, my lips curling at his need to help with this.

Shifting in my seat a little, I think for a second.

"I have no fucking clue. He needs to be taught a good fucking lesson, though."

"More so than you did today?"

"You saw the smirk on his face all afternoon. He was fucking loving it."

"He just wants the attention. Probably his reason for going after Poppy in the first place. That guy craves the spotlight and he's desperate to fill Jake's shoes next year."

"Not gonna happen."

"We know that. Jake and Coach know that. But apparently he never got the memo."

"Fucking hell," I sigh.

"You gonna tell me the rest of it, or just leave me guessing."

"The rest of it?"

I glance over to find his eyebrow raised as he stares at me.

"Chelsea and I saw you New Year's Eve, man. You might not have claimed victory on that tag, but I know you won." His eyes sparkle with delight.

"Fuck." I run my hand down my face, scratching at my jaw.

"This is more than fighting for Poppy's honor because of Jake, isn't it?"

"I... I just... fuck."

"Oh, bro. You are so fucked." He chuckles.

"That's it, laugh it up."

"I'm sorry, it's just nice to focus on someone else's drama for a little bit."

"How's Chelsea doing?" I ask, desperate for the conversation change.

"She's good, man. She's got a little bump going on, it's pretty awesome." His eyes go all soft and sappy, and as much as I want to rib him for it. I just can't.

"I'm happy for you, man. Maybe a little freaked out for you, but happy nonetheless."

He laughs at me before his face turns serious once more and he looks over at me.

"Nice try, by the way. What about Ruby?"

"What about Ruby?"

"I thought you wanted her?"

"Nah, she's hot, but it's just casual fun between us."

"Does she see it that way, she seems pretty keen, man."

"Yeah, yeah she does." I think back to the last party where Ruby and I fooled around, I remember the sadness in her eyes every time she looked at me. It was like she was disappointed that I wasn't someone else. I know Harley is worried, she said that something had happened with a guy last year but I don't know the details, but she was never interested before whatever that was. Now, it's like she just needs an escape. I was always happy to provide that service. I figured it was better me than some of the other guys who might take things too far.

Ruby might act like she's playing it easy, but I see the barriers she's built up around herself. She doesn't really want to be one of the cheer sluts, she's just lost and trying to find where she fits in life now.

Shane raises a brow but he doesn't push any further.

"So the girl in the locker room earlier was Poppy then, I assume."

"Yep, she stormed in to rip me a new one for getting involved with Preston."

"She told you to leave it alone?"

"Sure did. I rearranged that fucker's face anyway."

We both let out a sigh, probably both thinking of the mistakes I've made already.

"You should listen to her."

"That's just the thing, she won't tell me anything. I think… I think it's bad, but she won't admit it. Just keeps trying to brush it under the rug."

"Then maybe stop trying to force her, just—"

"But what if something happens?"

He shrugs. "You want to help her, support her, then you just need to be there. Do as she asks and stop trying to be the hero that she doesn't want."

"Fuck me, Shane. Where'd all this sensible advice come from?"

"I'm about to be a dad, I need to start figuring shit out."

Silence fills the car for a beat as I think about what he just said.

"Thanks, man. I needed that."

"Anytime, and if shit gets really desperate, I know a couple of girls who can help with all the advice you might need."

"Please, don't…"

"Tell anyone about this?" He guesses when I trail off. "No worries there. I've been on the end of Thorn's fists, not a place I want to be again, I can tell you that much."

"Great."

"You need to tell him."

"Doesn't that kinda go against your previous advice to just be what she needs?"

"Uh… fuck. Yeah, I guess it does. Okay then, well. How about just watch your back. When he finds out you're banging his cousin he's going to be after your balls."

"I'm not banging her."

"But you want to, and you always get what you want, so…"

The squad emerges from the building in front of us and the pair of us watch as Chelsea starts looking around for Shane.

"Go get your girl, man."

"You don't have to tell me twice. Call me if you need me."

"Sure thing."

He climbs from the car and I watch as he pulls Chelsea into his arms and drops his lips to hers.

Maybe that kind of life isn't so bad, having a girl who looks at you like you're the most incredible human on the planet.

Taking his advice, I throw the car into reverse and back out of the parking lot, only I don't head home. I go in a different direction.

I park my truck out on the street and walk around the huge bushes that hide her house from the main road.

There are cars parked in the driveway but the house seems to be in silence, that is until I hear voices and kids' laughter from the back yard.

Walking around the side of the house, I come to a stop on the corner when I find her running around playing soccer with her two younger siblings.

"Goal," she squeals, running around with her arms above her head and high fiving her little sister in celebration. Her little brother sticks his tongue out at the two of them while stealing the ball and hurtling toward a makeshift goal that consists of two rocks at either side of the grass.

Poppy is just about to take off after him when she stops and looks over her shoulder. Her eyes find me almost immediately and her lips part in shock.

13

POPPY

The familiar shiver that I'm being watched runs down my spine and fear wraps around my chest.

With my breath stuck in my throat, I turn around, praying that he's not here. That he's not watching me while I play with Austin and Sofia. Life here is already hard enough without him forcing his way in and ruining that as well as my school life.

But when I look over my shoulder, he isn't the one I find watching me. Instead I find the one person I haven't been able to get out of my head since I ran from the locker room a few hours ago.

Our eyes lock and another shiver runs down my spine, but it's not the same one as only a few seconds ago. There is no fear, just anticipation, hunger.

My lips part to say something but the reason I went into the guy's locker room in the first place slams into me.

He ignored me about Preston and took matters into his own hands. The exact opposite of what I asked him to do.

Schooling my features, I square my shoulders and walk over to him while Austin and Sofia play behind me.

I pass Cooper who's fast asleep in his bouncer, pacifier firmly in place, and don't stop until I'm right in front of him.

"What are you doing here?"

He swallows almost nervously before his tongue licks across his bottom lip. The move isn't intentional, I don't think, but hell if it doesn't affect me. I know what those lips are capable of and it causes heat to pool between my legs at the thought alone.

"I... uh... came to apologize."

"To apologize?" I ask, my brows almost hitting my hairline.

"Why do you look so surprised?"

"I just didn't think you had it in you."

"What, to admit when I'm wrong?"

"Yeah, something like that."

"Poppy, I—"

A bloodcurdling scream from behind me stops his words.

I spin around and run before I've even realized what the issue is.

"Shit," I spit when I find Sofia curled up in a ball on the asphalt that runs down to the trailer at the bottom of the garden. "Are you okay?" I ask, dropping to my knees beside her and attempting to check her over.

Her sobs break my heart. "M-my k-knee."

I look down and find it grazed with grit and fluff sticking to it. Blood trickles down her shin and starts to soak into her white sock.

"Let's get you inside and cleaned up."

I'm just about to reach for her to carry her inside when she moves from the ground. I look up to find Zayn with her in his arms.

"It's okay, I've got her. Lead the way."

I glance down to Sofia to make sure she's okay, only to find her staring up at him as if he's some kind of superhero or something.

I roll my eyes and mumble to myself. Great, he's got another girl after him and this one's only six.

"It's a magical power. I can't help it," he says with a smirk.

He takes off for the house before I even have time to consider what the state of the inside might be like.

The second we step into the kitchen, I cringe. The air is permeated with the weed my parents have been smoking all day while we were at school and the room looks like a tornado has run through it. It's a million miles away from what Zayn's house ever looks like. Well aside from the weed, that's one rule he tries to break as often as possible.

He coughs not long after stepping inside before turning to look at me. "Should these three be in here?" he asks with genuine concern on his face.

"Probably not, but there's not a lot I can do about it," I say sadly. I want to pretend that I don't know what he's talking about and kick him out so he doesn't have to witness the disaster that is my life but it's a little too late now.

"Fair enough." He places Sofia down on the edge of the island before looking down at her knee. "You're being so brave," he says to her in the softest voice that does things to my insides. "You got a first aid kit, Pops, or are you just going to stand there staring?"

"Oh uh... yeah, sure."

I run back outside so that I can collect Cooper before rushing toward the bathroom.

"Out of the way then," I demand once I'm back with the box in hand.

"I can do it."

"It's okay, you really don't—" My words falter when my eyes meet his.

"Just get her some chocolate or something. We decided that she deserves it, right, Sofia?"

"Yes," she says with the widest smile. My heart drops because I don't think I've seen that much excitement on her face in months.

He must sense my dejection because as I turn, he grabs my forearm. "You're a good sister, Poppy." His lips curl into a smile but I can't find it in me to return it. Instead, I pull the cupboard open and pray that there's some chocolate in there somewhere.

By the time I've finished rummaging around and thankfully managing to find something, Sofia is giggling behind me, her injury long forgotten.

I have no idea what Zayn is doing but to be honest, I don't really care. The noise is like music to my ears.

"So do you think you've got another match in you?" he asks.

"Yes!" she squeals. "Boys against girls." Before either of us can say anything, she's off the counter and running back outside where Austin still is, practicing his dribble.

"She's sweet," Zayn says softly as we both watch her run back outside.

"Yeah, they're good kids."

"What's going on here, Poppy?"

I sigh, desperately wanting to keep my secrets close, but Zayn has witnessed just a small part of our lives now, I can hardly lie or try to keep it hidden. "Not a lot, to be honest. Our parents are..."

He turns to me, his brow raises as he waits for my answer.

"Well, they've pretty much checked out."

"Shit, Poppy."

"Please, don't. It's fine. I've got it all covered."

"Maybe so but—"

"Please," I beg. "Just leave it."

"Come on you two," Austin shouts.

"Go on, I'll grab Cooper."

Zayn stares at me for a few seconds too long, making me wonder what he really sees when he looks at me before taking off for my little brother. He may be a football player but in a second he has the ball away from Austin and is showing off his skills.

"I hope you're not trying to impress me, Hunter."

"Me? Never." He winks, and I can't help but laugh as Austin sets about explaining the rules of our backyard soccer game.

We run around like we have no cares in the world as we battle it out to be able to call ourselves the winners. Austin and Sofia laugh more than... well, I can't even remember when they last enjoyed themselves this much. And I can't deny that I'm actually having fun too, especially every time Zayn gets a little too close or decides to go in for a dirty tackle.

"Whoever scores next are the winners then it's bath time," I say despite the fact we're all loving life right now, reality is only so far away and it's a school night.

Sounds of Austin and Sofia's complaints fill the air.

"Can Zayn stay for dinner?" Austin asks, already becoming attached to his new teammate.

"I'm not sure—"

"I'd love to, lil' man," he says, totally interrupting me.

"Are you sure?" I ask quietly when he walks past me to get the ball.

"Yes, now come on. You've got a game to win."

"Oh please. It's so ours."

His lips curl into a smirk. "Here lil' man, get ready." He kicks the ball to Austin before reaching behind his head and pulling his shirt off.

My eyes drop to the skin he reveals. It ripples as his muscles flex beneath.

I'm still lost in my daze as Austin kicks him the ball and he skillfully dribbles it past me, kicks it back to Austin who scores the winning goal. Sofia comes to a stop where she was chasing him in an attempt to stop him and stares at me.

"Poppy," she sighs with a roll of her eyes.

"S-sorry," I mutter, irritated with myself for allowing the sight of Zayn's naked chest to render me useless.

"Looks like we win, lil' man," Zayn says, high-fiving Austin who looks up at him like he's God's gift to soccer.

"Bath time, you two. Go and get sorted and I'll be up in a little bit."

They both complain but as always, they do as they're told.

Zayn's eyes are trained on me the entire time making my already increased temperature spike.

"Those were dirty tactics."

"Oh baby, if you want dirty, I can give you dirty."

I want to laugh but his stare is so intense as he closes the space between us that I can't.

My stomach somersaults as his scent fills my nose and the heat of his body seeps into mine.

Reaching out, he tucks a lock of my hair behind my ear.

"You could have done the same thing," he whispers.

"Take my shirt off in front of the kids, oh yeah, why didn't I do that?" I sass.

"I have no idea because it was all I could think about."

He leans forward to claim my lips but I manage to get my fingers between us so when he touches me, it's not my lips he finds.

He growls in frustration but doesn't force the situation. "Why not?"

"Look up."

After a second, he does as he's told.

"Little shits." He chuckles quietly, confirming what I already knew. Both of them have run upstairs and pressed their noses against the window to watch us.

"Okay, well, I guess I'll just have to wait until they go to bed. What time does that happen exactly?"

"It doesn't matter. I'm still mad at you."

"I know. I was hoping to show you that there's really no need." He moves his lips to my ear. "You already know that I can make you feel so good. And I think we've got unfinished business from earlier."

I manage to catch the groan that threatens to rumble up my throat but I'm powerless to stop my thighs squeezing together.

"I need to go and make sure those two don't drown. You really don't need to stay for dinner."

"What if I want to?"

"Why would you?" I ask, but I don't mean for the words to come out loud.

"Many reasons."

"Put your shirt back on, no one needs to look at that," I say as I back away from him.

"Are you sure about that? Something tells me that you need to do more than look."

Fucking hell.

"You can walk away as much as you like, Pops. You know that I'll just keep hunting you down."

"Keep an eye on Cooper," I call over my shoulder.

I shake my head as I make my way into the house and up the stairs.

The TV booms from the living room where my parents are but I don't even bother looking. Experience tells me that they're not coming out for a while.

By the time I get upstairs, Austin is already out of the bath and Sofia is on her way into it. I hurry her up knowing that Zayn could be downstairs and seeing all kinds of things I really don't want anyone seeing, but without insisting he leaves—which I already know he won't do—or ignoring what everyone else in this house needs, there's not a lot else I can do right now.

I leave them both to play around in their bedrooms before stopping off in my room to change my shirt after running around the yard for the past few hours. After pulling a tank over my head, I go back to see what trouble Zayn might have got himself into.

I'm not even at the bottom of the stairs when I hear his voice followed by giggles and coos.

What Is he doing? I smile to myself as I get closer and am able to make out the words.

"Where's the bunny?" Giggle. "There he is." More giggles.

My heart swells at hearing that little laugh.

I come to a stop in the doorway, cross my arms over my chest and lean my hip against the frame as I watch the two of them.

Cooper is still in his bouncer, but Zayn has lifted him onto the table in front of him so they can play.

"Where's the bunny?" Zayn drops the stuffed toy out of sight while Cooper's face lightens up with amusement before Zayn magically makes him reappear again. Cooper laughs like it might be the most incredible thing he's ever seen and I start to wonder if I actually agree with him.

He must be able to feel my stare because after passing the bunny back to Cooper, Zayn turns his dark eyes on me.

Something crackles between us the second our eyes lock and it makes my breath catch.

"H-having fun?" I stutter, needing to fill the silence between us.

"Yeah, he's pretty cool, this one."

Zayn's eyes drop from mine to where I have my arms folded under my breasts. They darken and his lips part as he takes in my cleavage.

Dropping my arms, I walk over to them.

"Yeah, you're pretty cool, eh, Coop?" His eyes brighten as he looks at me, the way I'm sure they should when he looks at our mother.

There's a loud crash from the living room and I startle, Zayn's eyes immediately zeroing in on the door.

"It's our parents," I mutter, needing to wipe the concern off his face, not that the truth is likely to do that.

"What are they doing in there?"

I shrug. "Getting high? Wasted? Both? I don't know, I've stopped worrying about it."

"Poppy, I—"

"Please, Zayn. Don't. I know how it sounds... how it looks, trust me. But please. No one knows about this. Even Harley doesn't know how bad it is."

Conflict passes across his face.

"You can't live like this, Pops."

I jump when his fingers brush mine, but instead of pulling away like I should, I allow him to pull me into his side.

"What other choice do I have?" I ask when I finally find my voice.

His lips part like he might have an answer but he soon closes them again.

"If I tell anyone about the reality here, we'll all end up in the system. At least if I can wait until I'm eighteen then—"

"Then you should be getting ready to go to college. You shouldn't be doing this."

"Someone has to."

Our eyes hold, his full of concern and worry as the sound of footsteps pound down the stairs behind me.

"What's for dinner? I'm starving."

"Who wants pizza?" Zayn announces, pulling his cell from his pocket and proceeding to order delivery.

"No, you don't have to..."

"Please, Poppy. Just let me help."

I open my mouth to argue but my stomach beats me to it and growls loudly.

Zayn raises a brow at me, and I forget any fight I might have had.

We have a quick debate about toppings and after discovering that all of us agree that pineapple does not belong on a pizza, Zayn places the order and I set about getting us drinks.

"You've got the choice between water or... water," I say, looking in the cupboard in the hope of finding some juice but coming up empty.

"Do you know what? I was just thinking that I really fancy some water."

His smile knocks me for six and I have to fight my need to walk over and plonk myself on his lap so I can show him just how much what he's doing right now means to me.

I clear my throat after a second or two. "W-well that's a relief."

I grab four bottles of water and some plates and place them all on the table before going to make Cooper's bottle.

"How'd you learn to do all that?" Zayn asks, nodding at me as I place it in a bowl of cold water in the hope it cools faster.

"Just picked it up, I guess. I watched with those two, and when you don't have many choices, you just figure it out." I drop the bowl in front of me, and lower myself to the chair beside him.

His fingers almost immediately find mine under the cover of the table. Unable to look away, I stare into his eyes as he shakes his head at me.

"What?" I ask, a shy smile twitching at my lips.

"You're a little bit incredible, do you know that?" he whispers while Austin and Sofia bicker about something on the other side of the table.

"I'm just doing what needs to be done."

Our connection holds and for a minute or two, I swear it could just be the two of us in the room. Everything else fades as so many things pass between us, despite the fact no words leave either of our lips.

My thighs clench as he runs his eyes down my body, once again hovering on my cleavage.

"I like this top. You really should have worn it while we were playing earlier."

"Oh yeah?"

"You might have had a better chance at winning."

"I'll remember that for next time," I whisper but my breath catches when I realize my mistake.

Why would there be a next time? Zayn is hardly going to want to come and hang out with my kid brother and sister again.

He could be at Aces right now with the team, with any member of the squad grinding down on his lap and whispering slutty promises in his ear. Why would he want to be here?

Cooper growls in his seat, telling me that his patience for the bottle is waning.

"What's that look for?" Zayn asks, his hand resting on my waist, and I reach over him to take Cooper out of his seat.

I still as the heat from his hand burns through the fabric of my tank.

"N-nothing. Do you… want to feed him?"

"Me? You think I can?"

"Of course, he seems to love you."

Zayn's stare on me is intense, I feel the tingles it creates right down to my toes.

"Okay then. Sure. I've never fed a baby before."

"It's easy," Sofia pipes up. "I do it all the time." While she might be proud of her skills, a familiar sadness passes over Zayn's face to what I feel.

"You're a great big sister, Sof." She beams at my praise as I lift Cooper and place him in Zayn's arms.

My fingers brush his abs and chest as I release Cooper and his eyes fly to mine. Surely he didn't feel the same spark I just did when I touched him.

Our eyes hold for a beat before Cooper complains that we're taking too long.

Ripping my stare from Zayn, I collect his bottle, check the temperature and pass it over.

I give Zayn a couple of quick tips but Cooper is so hungry that he doesn't allow Zayn to hang around.

Sitting beside him, I look at the two of them. He looks so natural sitting there holding a baby.

"Maybe you should let Shane and Chelsea come around to babysit one time, they sure could do with some practice," he says with a laugh.

My stomach twists uncomfortably at the thought of inviting others here. He must see my panic because when he turns to look at me, he winces.

"I didn't actually mean..."

"I know," I say, reaching out and placing my hand on his forearm.

Sparks shoot from the innocent touch and our eyes lock once more.

"Do you ever get to go out? Get to be... normal?"

"I came to your party at New Year's."

He nods, probably casting his mind back to all the other parties I haven't been at.

"And I went to one of Ethan's a few months ago."

"Pops," he sighs.

"They're not really my thing, it's not a big deal."

"It's not just parties though, is it? It's hanging out with friends, it's going to Aces, the beach, the arcade. Anything."

"Please... don't." He doesn't need to tell me all of the things that I miss out on, although I don't think he really appreciates right now that it's not just because of these three monsters that I don't do all those kinds of things. Even if I didn't have kids to look after, I wouldn't be there because I don't want to see *him.*

Thoughts of Preston are like having a cold bucket of water thrown over me.

"What's wrong?"

"N-nothing." Thankfully, as I push my chair out to escape from his assessing stare, the doorbell rings.

I race to the door, desperate for a little air, but equally hoping that my parents stay put in the living room. I might not be all that happy about Zayn pushing his way into my life—my home—but it's somewhat bearable while they're hiding.

Austin and Sofia's faces light up as I carry the pizza boxes into the kitchen. The scent of the tomato sauce and melted cheese making my stomach growl even louder.

"When was the last time you ate?" Zayn asks with a laugh when he hears it over the kids' excited chatter.

"Er..."

"Shit, don't answer that."

I nod, lowering my head so I don't have to meet his eyes. He's already learning too much without being able to read my thoughts like I know he's able to.

I sit back and allow the kids to take their fill before I even reach for a slice. It's the way it always is—the way it has to be.

"Come on, I ordered plenty," Zayn encourages as he continues to bounce Cooper gently now he's back in his seat with a full belly.

"I know, I just..."

"Eat, Poppy. You need to look after yourself as well as these three for once."

I do as I'm told, mainly because I don't want to start an argument in front of Austin and Sofia, but also because I can hardly deny that he's right.

I just about manage to keep my growl of appreciation down as I take my first bite, although from the heated stare I feel from beside me, I get the idea he's aware of my reaction.

"Good, right?"

"So good," I mumble around my mouthful.

Zayn keeps Austin and Sofia entertained throughout dinner like a pro. It makes me wonder what experience he has with kids, it's hardly from Harley seeing as there's barely a year between them.

"Okay, you two need to get upstairs and get ready for bed."

"Ohhh, but it's still early."

I smile at the two of them. "You have an hour to watch TV or play. But I expect you to both be in bed and ready for sleep in an hour."

They roll their eyes at my bossiness but after rinsing off their plates they both do as they're told.

"They're good kids," Zayn says as their footsteps get quieter.

"They really are. I'm going to take him to my parents," I say, nodding at a sleeping Cooper before lifting him in his chair and walking from the room.

"You shouldn't have to do all this," he says again as I walk back into the kitchen with empty hands. Both Mom and Dad were awake, they watched me place their child in front of them although it doesn't fill me with much hope.

I walk past where he's still sitting at the table and come to a stop at the sink, blowing out a frustrated breath. I shouldn't feel guilty about leaving Cooper with his parents, but I do. He should be their responsibility, not mine. But that's not how things are in this house.

Pushing his chair out, he comes to join me at the sink to do the cleaning up.

"I know, but it is what it is."

"What's the real issue with your parents?"

My muscles tighten and he doesn't miss it.

Putting his dishtowel down, he moves to stand behind me. His fingers brush against my shoulders and he pushes down into my bunched muscles.

"Oh God," I moan, my arms falling limp at my sides as I immediately start to relax.

"Talk to me, Poppy," he breathes in my ear, sending goose bumps racing across my skin.

"Dad hurt his back at work years ago, says it's too bad to do anything other than drink himself into a coma, apparently. Mom... I don't really know. She had postnatal depression with both Austin and Sofia but managed to beat it. Although she's always been very up and down. Then she had Cooper and it's like she's just checked out. She knows there's something wrong but she refuses to seek help, says we can't afford it."

"Fuck."

I shrug. It's my life, not much I can do about it.

"All this shouldn't be on your shoulders."

"What am I supposed to do about it? Go to social services and watch as we're all taken away?"

"I..." He hesitates. "I don't know." His voice is sad and I hate that it's because of me. I shouldn't be dragging him, or anyone else, into this. It's why I've kept everyone at arm's length since Cooper was born, hell, I was doing it long before that, I just don't think I'd realized it. "I could talk to my mom. See if we can get yours some help."

"She won't accept it," I say, full of confidence.

She refused when both Austin and Sofia were born and I have no reason to believe that she'll be any different now. She's fallen even deeper into her blackhole this time. I doubt she can even see the light.

"I'm so sorry, Poppy."

His hands drop to my waist and he spins me around before stepping into my body.

"It's not your fault." The words are so quiet, I doubt he even hears them.

"No, but it still sucks."

His eyes hold mine captive, rendering me useless.

"Tell me how to make it better."

"You can't, I—"

His fingers press against my lips. "I don't mean everything. I'm not a miracle worker. I just mean right now. What do you need right now?"

My lips part. One single word dancing on the tip of my tongue, desperate to fall out but as scared as I am to admit it, I'm equally terrified of what will happen next.

Zayn's already shown me just how good he is at making me forget. If any more were to happen, I'm not sure I'd be able to give it up again willingly.

"Say it," he encourages. "I need to hear you say it."

I bite down on the inside of my lips, fighting my need to jump into his with both feet and fuck the consequences.

"Y—"

He nods, a small smile twitching at his lips.

"You."

I barely finish the word before his lips are on mine in a bruising kiss.

His hands drop to my thighs, gripping them, he lifts me into his body before lowering my ass to the counter. He pulls me right to the edge and wraps my legs around his waist as his tongue dances with mine.

His fingers twist in my hair, tilting my head to the side so he can explore more of my mouth as his hands drop down over my shoulders, brush over my breasts and come to a stop on my hips, pulling our bodies tighter together.

He grinds into me and I gasp, ripping our lips apart, as an intense sensation washes through me.

"You feel that?" he mumbles against the corner of my jaw.

"Y-yes," I whisper when he does it again. The hard length of him is impossible to miss as it continues to drive me crazy.

"You do that to me, Poppy. Every fucking time I look at you."

"Oh God," I moan when he does it again, his fingers digging into my ass.

"You always have."

"Zayn." I want to tell him to stop, to stop using these lines to get what he wants, but his name falls from my lips as a plea instead.

"Forget it all, Poppy. Right now, none of that matters. This, this is all that matters." He runs his tongue up the length of my neck and my entire body shudders in pleasure.

"U-upstairs."

"You sure?" he asks, suddenly sounding like the sensible one out of the two of us. He pulls back to look into my eyes. "I need you to know that this isn't why I came. Well, not really."

I shake my head at the boyish smirk on his face.

"Sure it wasn't."

14

ZAYN

Just as she's about to laugh at me, I slide her from the edge of the counter and carry her toward the stairs.

"Do you think they even know you have company?" I ask, although when she tenses in my arms, I immediately regret it.

"I don't really care. Pretty sure they don't either." Her lips land on my neck, the soft brush of them cut off what I was going to say. "You can do all kinds of things and they'll be totally none the wiser," she whispers in my ear.

"You're playing a very dangerous game here, Poppy," I warn, my voice low and rough, showing just how much I need her.

"Oh yeah, why's that?"

"It's like you're challenging me to ensure you make enough noise to alert them to the fact I'm dirtying up their daughter."

"Hmmm... what did you have in mind, Hunter?" she practically growls in my ear.

"Well," I say, my hands gripping harder onto her ass. "It seems that I've already captured my prey, all that's left to do is feast on her."

"Oh God," she whimpers as I walk us through into her bedroom.

We both glance over at the closed bedroom doors when the sound of kids squealing sounds out.

"They're fine. Plus, I put a lock on my door."

I pull back and look at her with a smile on my face.

"Hoping I was going to come back, were you?"

"A girl can dream. Or, I'm sure I could have found another willing friend."

"Absolutely not," I snap. "Just me. Only me," I growl, making her shudder.

"O-okay," she agrees as I kneel on the edge of her bed and lower her down. "Don't you have to be home or anything?" she asks as I hover over her, our noses almost brushing.

"You trying to get rid of me now I've got you here?"

"No, no," she says in a rush. "I was just..." She trails off as I sit up and pull my cell from my pocket.

"I've got nowhere else to be." I let her watch as I turn it off and throw it down on her bedroom floor. "No one else exists apart from you and me, baby." I wink before reaching behind me and pulling my shirt off.

I look down at her after the fabric has passed my face and find her biting down on her bottom lip as her eyes roam across my body, much like they did earlier.

"Thought you might want a closer inspection."

"Zayn, I—" She looks up at me with wide eyes like she's just been caught with her hand in the cookie jar.

Reaching forward, I take her hand and in mine and lift her fingertips to my stomach, gently brushing them over my muscles.

My cock swells from her simple touch and I bite back a groan at having her hands on my naked skin.

"Take your fill."

I stop moving when her fingers hit my waistband and her eyes once again meet mine.

She's a virgin, I know that from my previous visit, and while I don't care if we do no more than kiss, I can see in her eyes that she's freaking out about this.

I drop forward once again, sliding my hands up her thighs and to her waist.

"We don't have to do anything you're not happy with. I didn't come here to steal your innocence, Pops," I whisper in her ear before running my tongue around the shell and biting down on her lobe.

"No?" she moans. "Why'd you come then? Surely it wasn't to play dad to my siblings."

"I came to apologize. To tell you that you were right."

"I was?"

"Yeah." I don't stop kissing her. My lips trail down her neck until I brush them over her collarbone and down to the swell of her breasts. This bit of skin has been driving me crazy since she returned wearing this shirt before dinner. "I should have listened to you instead of going after..." I trail off, not wanting to say his name and ruin the moment. "I need you to take the lead, in more ways than one," I say, looking up at her.

Her lips are parted as she drags in rapid breaths and her usually light gray eyes are dark and full of hunger.

"Tell me what you want, what you need."

Her leg curls around my back before she flips us over.

"Oh-oh." I chuckle. "Like that, is it?"

"What? You think you can always be the one in charge?" she asks with a smirk.

Stretching my arms out, I rest my hands behind my head and lie out beneath her.

"I already told you, take your fill, baby. I'm all yours."

She blushes harder as her eyes drop from mine, down my body to where my cock is quite clearly tenting my pants. It's so fucking cute and totally not what I'm used to with the cheer sluts.

"I-I haven't..."

"I know," I say, reaching forward and lacing her fingers with mine so I can tug her down on me.

Her chest presses against mine and a growl rumbles up my throat as her lips find mine once more.

As we kiss, she gets braver, her hand starting to explore across my chest and stomach.

"Fuck, Pops. You're driving me crazy," I groan when she kisses across my jaw and starts down my neck.

"Yeah?" She looks up at me, her eyes wide in amazement.

"Yeah. Your touch is addictive."

I can see that she wants to argue, but she doesn't, instead, she sucks in some courage and continues kissing down over my chest.

Her kisses are so light, so teasing that my entire body locks up with need.

Reaching down, I thread my fingers into her hair, not to control her movements but because I can't stand not to be touching her.

"Jesus, do you have any idea how hot you look right now?" I ask as I watch her lick across the indentation of my abs.

My cock strains against the fabric of my pants, desperate for some action but I meant what I said a few minutes ago. We only take this as far as she's happy with.

I mean, I shouldn't even be here in the first place, so I may as well try to do something right.

She moves down until she kisses along the edge of my waistband.

"Poppy," I moan, damn near desperate for what could come next.

She pauses and sits up a little.

"Zayn, I—"

Sitting, I cut off her words with my lips. My hands run up her thighs and slip under the fabric of her tank.

"Oh God," she moans when I take her breasts in my hands and squeeze gently. Her lips leave mine as her head falls back.

"So beautiful," I whisper against her neck.

I push the fabric of her shirt up, waiting to see if she'll lift her arms for me. After a beat she does and I throw it across the room.

"Zayn," she moans as my lips trail over her breast and my teeth graze her nipple over the lace. "Off."

Sliding my hand around her back, I flick the clasp of her bra, not needing to be asked twice to remove it.

The second it clears her body, I drop my lips to her exposed skin.

"Shit," she gasps when I suck her rosy pink nipple into my mouth. "Shit, shit, shit," she chants, making me smile.

"You taste so good."

"Umm... you too," she moans as I continue.

"You want me to make you come?"

"Oh God," she cries, her fingers gripping on to my shoulders as I pull her hips down so I can grind into her.

"You feel how hard you make me?"

"Yeah."

"My cock is desperate for you."

"Zayn, shit."

I don't say it because I'm trying to convince her to go further, but because every time I say something dirty, the blush that already covers her cheeks and neck spreads lower and her grip on my shoulders gets tighter. She's so close already and I've barely touched her.

"You gonna come like this? Or do you want more?"

"More, please. More."

Flipping us, I immediately reach for the button on her pants and pop it open. She lifts her hips as I tug, helping me pull them from her body.

The moment they're off her feet, I run my eyes up her almost naked body. The only thing covering her is a white scrap of cotton.

Her chest heaves, catching my attention, her breasts are covered in my bite marks causing something possessive to wash through me.

Poppy is mine. No matter what fucking happens after tonight, no other fucker is getting their hands on her.

She. Is. Mine.

Fuck what Harley thinks. Fuck what Jake will do to me. She's it for me.

"Zayn?" Her voice is quiet and hesitant, and I realize that I've been standing here too long without doing anything while she's practically naked.

"Shit, sorry. I'm not… fuck," I bark when panic washes across her face. "No, no. It's all good," I say in a rush, opening the fly of my pants and pushing them down my legs to prove to her that I'm not going fucking anywhere.

"Oh," she breathes, her lips forming an O as she runs her eyes down the length of me. "So you're not… regretting this then?"

"Fuck no. I was just thinking…" She looks at me expectantly, but I can hardly tell her what I was just thinking, she'll run a fucking mile, I'm sure. "Shit, it doesn't matter."

Kicking off my shoes and pants, I drop to my knees at the end of the bed, and after wrapping my hands around her thighs, I tug her so her ass hangs over the edge.

In seconds, her panties are on the floor and my face is between her thighs.

When I glance up at her, she's staring down at me with total fascination in her heavy-lidded eyes.

"So fucking sweet," I mutter before dropping lower and pushing my tongue inside her.

She cries out as I press the pad of my thumb to her clit and circle until she's scratching at my head and crying out my name as her release consumes her.

"Jesus, shit," she pants, lying back on the bed trying to catch her breath. "I think that was better than last time."

"Yeah?" I ask, crawling up the bed and smiling down at her happy face.

"Yeah. I think I could do that all day," she admits.

"I'm sure we could skip a day and do just that." A darkness passes through her eyes at my mention of school. "Next time Mom is out of town, I'm going to lock you in my room and make you come over and over and over." I trail my fingers up her stomach before circling her nipples and making her squirm.

"Sounds like the best day ever. But what about you?"

"What about me?"

Her eyes flash down to my very tented boxers. "You need..." She hesitates and I can't help but smile at her shyness.

"Yeah, but when you're ready."

"But what if I want to?"

I run my nose along the length of hers. "Like I said, all yours whenever you want."

She bites down on her bottom lip, in deep thought.

"I... I need to have a shower."

"Oh." I laugh. "That's it, is it? You get yours and kick me out?"

She swings her legs off the side of the bed and nervously walks toward a door at the other side of the room.

It makes me smile that she wraps her arms around herself in an attempt to cover up yet only minutes ago I was up close and personal with her most intimate place.

"No, I was wondering if you wanted to..." She trails off, looking over her shoulder as she kicks the door open to her en suite.

"You want to know if I want to watch as water runs over your naked body?" I ask, my brows almost in my hairline, wondering if she thought there was any way I'd ever refuse an offer like that.

"Um... yeah."

"In a fucking heartbeat, Pops."

I'm off the bed and in front of her before she's had time to blink. Wrapping an arm around her waist, I pull her flush to my body, loving the feel of her hot, naked skin against mine.

"Maybe we'll add showering to our list of things to do on our day off."

"I'm not sure. You haven't shown me how good it can be yet."

"Oh, Poppy. What are you doing to me?"

I walk her backward into the room before releasing her so she can turn the water on.

When she turns back around, her breath catches at finding me bare before her.

Her eyes latch on to my solid length and she sucks her bottom lip into her mouth, making it twitch in anticipation.

"Something you can work with?"

Her eyes fly to mine, realizing that she's been caught staring.

"I literally have no idea," she whispers, backing into the walk-in shower.

"I'm sure you'll be just fine."

I stalk toward her, a smirk playing on my lips as she bumps against the tiled wall.

Water rains down on both of us as we stare at each other.

"How did we end up here?" she asks, although I'm not sure if she's talking more to herself than she is me. Her arms are still locked around her torso and I hate that she's trying to hide.

"I think it started with me fucking up and needing to apologize." Reaching out, I pull her arms from her body.

"Ah, that's right. Your stubborn ass never listens."

"I'll do anything you want me to right now," I admit, caging her in with my forearms and pressing our bodies together.

"So I just need to get naked and tell you not to fight my battles for me?"

"I'll never stop fighting your battles, Poppy. If someone hurts you then—"

"Stop," she says, placing two fingers to my lips. "Not now. Right now, let's forget everything but—"

"Fuck," I bark as her fingers slip between us and wrap around my cock.

"Okay?"

"Oh, baby. You have no idea."

My eyes shutter as she grips me a little harder. She hesitates, and not wanting her to stop, I drop my arm, wrapping my hand around hers and slowly guide her up and down my shaft.

"Fuck, Pops."

Our eyes remain locked and I watch as hers darken before me.

"You like that?"

Her lips part. "M-me? Shouldn't I be the one asking you that?" She tilts her head to the side.

"Your eyes are so dark right now." I drop my gaze down her body. "Your nipples are begging for my touch. You're wet for me, aren't you, Poppy?"

"Zayn," she whimpers.

"You want to feel me again, don't you?"

She shakes her head. I know she's lying but what I really don't expect is what comes from her next.

"There's something else I want to try more." She bites down on her bottom lip and seductively looks at me through her lashes.

"Oh yeah? What's that then?" I ask, leaning toward her until our noses are touching and my lips are just a whisper from hers.

She hesitates, before lowering herself down the wall.

"Fuck, Pops," I groan at the sight of her.

"I-I don't know," she whispers when she's at eye level with my cock.

"Trust me, as long as you don't use your teeth, you can't do anything wrong."

Releasing my hand, I rest the other against the wall to keep me upright as I wait to see what she's going to do.

She continues moving her hand, that alone is enough to have me racing toward release faster than I should, but the sight of her, the way she unknowingly licks her lips, teasing me for what might come next, drives me fucking insane.

Her eyes flash up to mine, indecision fills them.

"It's okay," I whisper, my hand threading into her hair ready to gently pull her up.

She's not ready for this, I've already pushed farther than I should. Hell, I probably shouldn't have even come here in the first place, let alone touched her again.

Just as I'm about to get her to stand, she leans forward.

"Fuck," I bark as the softness of her tongue hits me. She licks the tip, our eyes remaining locked. My fingers fist her hair as the sensation washes through me.

With her hand still moving slowly, she leans forward and does it again, and again before she gets brave and wraps her lips around the head and slowly sucks me into her mouth.

"Holy fuck, shit," I groan, my head falling back and my eyes closing so I can focus on what she's doing.

She can only suck me in her mouth twice before my balls start to draw up, telling me that this is going to be over sooner than I want it to be. Hell, it could go on forever and it wouldn't be long enough.

15

POPPY

I close my lips around him, and his taste explodes in my mouth.

He groans above me, and when I run my eyes up his torso, I find his head tipped back in pleasure.

Lust shoots straight to my core knowing that I'm the cause.

What he's done to me the last two times has been nothing short of mind-blowing and knowing that I can give him a similar experience has me craving more.

It's wrong. He shouldn't be here, and he really shouldn't be in the shower with me, but I could hardly send him away when he had that wicked glint in his eyes.

My life is beyond shit, as he's quickly learning, and he's fast becoming my secret guilty pleasure. Hell knows I deserve to enjoy myself every now and then.

He said it himself earlier that I deserve to have some fun, act my age, well look at me now doing what all the others are.

I push away thoughts of the others who've already been on their knees before him and focus on the now. The past, the future, anything outside of the room doesn't matter.

"Poppy, shit. I'm gonna come," he warns, his voice deep and gravelly.

His cock twitches and I panic. Pulling back from him, I watch as his hand covers mine once more and together, we finish him off. Hot spurts of his cum land on my chest as he growls out his release.

The second he's finished, he reaches down and pulls me up from the floor.

The water immediately begins to wash the evidence of what just happened from my body, but that doesn't stop him from reaching out and running his fingertip where he marked me.

"I think that means you're mine now," he muses, his eyes locked on the spot.

"Oh yeah? I'm sure all your cheer sluts might have something to say about that."

His eyes fly to mine, his brows pulling together. "I don't give a shit about them, Pops. Being with them…" He hesitates before wrapping his hand around the back of my neck. "Being with them is nothing like this."

The length of his body presses against mine, his already semi-hard cock presses against my stomach once more.

His nose grazes mine before his lips capture mine and his tongue plunges into my mouth.

"I'm fucking addicted, Pops," he whispers into our kiss.

After another orgasm each, we finally clean up and wrap ourselves in towels. Well, I wrap myself in a towel, the small ones we have barely cover any of Zayn. Not that I'm complaining because his body, shit… it's captivating.

I watch his muscles ripple as he dries off, my mouth watering for another taste of his skin.

"Pops," he warns when he turns and finds me staring. "Keep looking at me like that and we're never leaving your bedroom ever again."

"I'm pretty sure people would miss you if you did that."

He doesn't miss what my words imply and sadness washes over his face.

"People would miss you too," he says, stepping up to me and cupping my cheek.

Emotion clogs my throat and burns the back of my eyes.

"Not as many as you."

"Stop, please. You make it sound like you're worthless."

I shrug, hating that it's Preston's words that come to mind when he says that.

"Sorry," I whisper, looking away from him, ashamed that I allowed my insecurities about this out.

"Don't hide from me, Pops. And believe me when I tell you that you are not worthless. You're incredible. What you do here, it's amazing. Don't ever allow anyone to make you believe you are anything less than you are."

Tears pool in my eyes at his words.

"Aw, shit. I didn't mean to make you cry."

"I'm okay. Thank you, Zayn. For... everything."

"Oh, Pops. You are more than welcome."

Chemistry crackles between us like it always does and the temptation to let it consume us once again is almost stronger than I am, but I know it's time to let reality back in.

"You should go," I whisper as he leans in to kiss me.

"What if I don't want to?"

"Zayn, your mom will wonder where you are."

"I'll tell her I'm staying at a friend's. She won't care." He drops his forehead to mine, his dark eyes holding mine captive, begging me to agree, but I know I can't.

Shaking my head slowly, I force the words out that I really don't want to say. "We can't. You need to go."

"It was worth a try, huh?"

"Yeah, and I wish things were different."

"Me too, Pops. Me too."

He pulls me to him for a sweet kiss before he releases me, bends down to pick up his discarded boxers before walking back to my room as naked as the day he was born. It is one fine sight.

"Are you staring at my ass?" he asks with a laugh.

"Damn right I am."

He chuckles and the sound makes me feel a little lighter once again.

"Zayn, what are we going to do about Harley and Jake?"

I stand leaning against the bathroom doorframe while he gets dressed.

"Right now, we do nothing."

"So, I'm now your dirty little secret?"

A smile plays at his lips. "Hell yeah." He winks, making me laugh.

"Don't worry about everyone else, Poppy. Just enjoy it for what it is."

"Okay," I agree, although the word tastes bitter on my tongue. There are so many questions I want to ask him about this, about what we now are—or aren't—but I can't. I don't want to be one of those girls.

"I'll see you tomorrow, yeah?"

I nod, desperately trying to keep my sadness from my features that he's about to leave.

"Remember, if you need me, if that prick tries anything, just call me. I've got your back, Pops. Whatever you need."

"Thank you," I breathe.

"Anytime."

He gives me another knee-weakening kiss before pulling open my door and slipping through it.

A long sigh falls from my lips and I sag back against the wall as images from our time together tonight flash through my mind.

My cheeks heat and my temperature spikes as I think about the things we did. So much for telling myself I wasn't going to kiss him again. I think I've well and truly shattered that promise to myself.

As I push from the wall and drop the towel that was covering me, I realize that I don't even care. This evening has been the exact escape I needed and for the next few hours I'm going to enjoy the high Zayn left me with. Tomorrow, however, is a different story and I have a feeling I'm going to feel very different about it.

After pulling on some pajamas, I go and check on Austin and Sofia, who as predicted, are both fast asleep in their beds.

The living room door is still closed when I get to the bottom of the stairs and there's no crying coming from inside, so I decide against dropping myself back into real life already. After I get myself a bottle of water, I head back up to my room in the hope of having a full night's sleep without Cooper keeping me awake.

My cell dings as I close my door behind me and I rush over.

My heart leaps when I see Zayn's name staring back at me.

Zayn: I can still taste you.

My cheeks burn at his dirty words.

Poppy: Who says I can't say the same thing?

A smile pulls at my lips as I hit send. I feel all kinds of naughty right now. Crawling into bed, I wait for his response.

Zayn: Fuuuuuck. I'm coming back.

Something explodes in my belly at the thought. I want to say it's panic that he's going to do so, but really, I think it's just excitement that he might ignore my need for him to leave.

Sadly, he never reappears but that doesn't mean we don't spend the whole night sending suggestive messages back and forth.

By the time I turn my light out and close my eyes, my head is full of all kinds of ideas for what I want to do to him the next time I see him, and I soon find myself dreaming of some of those very things.

The next time I wake, my skin is covered in a sheen of sweat and I have a very vivid image in my head of what Zayn was doing to me in my slumber.

Knowing I need to put all of that behind me, I throw the covers back and plod to my bathroom.

Everywhere I look, I see him. Standing with his hand resting on the wall in the shower, with my tiny towel barely covering his body. His presence is ever-present and by the time I'm ready for school, I'm damn near desperate to get a look at the real him instead of just the image in my head.

"Where's Harley?" I ask, dropping down into the passenger seat of Ruby's car when she pulls up out the front to get me.

"Ugh, running late. Bad hair day or some crap. She's going to drive herself."

"You have a good night?" I ask, although I instantly regret it because I might open up the conversation about my own. I don't want to hide things from Harley and Ruby, but I can hardly tell Harley about what happened, and I don't want to put Ruby in a position where she has to lie to Harley.

"Yeah. We went to Aces and hung out for a bit after practice and then I had a ton of homework to do. That math assignment is killer, right?"

"Right," I agree. "What about you?" She glances over at me briefly when she pulls to a stop at an intersection. "Wait, hold that thought. Is that a hickey on your neck?"

Lifting my hand, I immediately cover the spot she's staring at.

"Um..."

"Poppy," she warns, her eyes narrowing at me because she's forced to focus on the road once more.

"It's nothing."

"Bullshit it is. Who gave it to you?"

"I'm not talking about this."

"Oh, hell yes you are."

"Oh my God, was it Zayn?"

"What? No," I protest a little too harshly.

"Fuck. It was. OMG. OMG. Give me all the details right now."

"Ruby," I groan. "It's nothing. Really."

"Anything between you and Zayn is not nothing."

"Look," I say, turning to her. "You know as well as I do the drama from anything happening between us could cause."

"Didn't seem to bother either of you last night," she mutters, her voice full of amusement.

"Ruby, please. This is serious."

"As serious as a hickey." She giggles. "Did you give him your V-card?"

"No," I mutter.

"Girl, why not? I have it on good authority that you couldn't give it up to anyone more... skilled."

I groan at her words. "Maybe because of that."

"Don't do that, Poppy. You're better than all of them and you know it."

"Do I?"

She pulls into her usual space in the school parking lot and turns to look at me.

"Enough, okay. I don't need a lecture. Last night was..." I trail off, trying to come up with a word to describe what it was that doesn't make Ruby think I'm as desperate for a repeat as I am. Her brows rise as she waits. "A mistake." Her lips part to argue and I rush to beat her to it. "A mistake that doesn't need to be discussed or repeated."

"But—"

"No buts. The conversation ends here and we don't speak of it again, and you certainly do not repeat it to Harley." I pin her with a look that I hope communicates how serious I am about this.

"Okay fine. But we need to do something about that hickey if you don't want Harley asking about it herself. Come on."

I follow her to the bathroom where she does a much better job than I did at covering the red mark with concealer. It probably has something to do with the fact she can afford to buy decent makeup, whereas mine is the cheapest stuff I can find at the store.

"There, as good as new," she says, checking out her handiwork.

"Thanks, Rubes."

"Anytime."

Harley still hasn't arrived when we get to our lockers and switch out books, although I do however get that familiar shiver running down my spine.

Looking over my shoulder as discreetly as I can, my eyes immediately lock on to a cold pair that turns the blood in my veins to ice.

His lips curl into an evil smirk as he watches me.

"You are mine," he mouths, making fear claw itself around my chest.

Ripping my eyes from his, I stare into the darkness of my locker as I fight to not react.

My cell dings, dragging my thoughts from his warning. Hope fills me that it might be Zayn wishing me good morning but when I wake my cell up and see an unknown number, that fear begins to grip me once more.

As far as I know, he doesn't have my number. But somehow, I know that this is him. I have no idea how, but I do.

Hesitantly, I swipe the screen and open up his message.

Unknown: Someone's being a naughty girl...

My heart thunders in my chest as I wait to see what's going to come next.

But it doesn't. Not immediately anyway.

I start to relax, thinking he's just trying to wind me up but then it dings again, and dread fills me.

Opening it once again, I gasp as I find a photo of Zayn and me in my yard last night. It's from after our game of soccer when he almost kissed me.

Fuck.

Pocketing my cell before Ruby looks over, not that she's likely to see as some of the squad have descended on her, I turn back around to where he was only moments ago, only this time, he's not there.

I look around the hallway, but he's nowhere to be seen.

My heart thunders in my chest as I think about him knowing what we've been up to. Up until now, he's never had anything to bargain with. I've never had secrets, well, aside from my home life, so he's never been able to use anything against me.

Until now.

If he goes to Harley, or worse, Jake, then shit is going to hit the fan.

Fuck, fuck, fuck.

I look around in the hope I spot Zayn. I need to warn him, but him or any of the team are nowhere to be seen.

"Ready for chemistry?" Ruby asks, dragging herself away from the squad.

"Uh... yeah, can't wait."

"Are you okay? You look really pale."

"Yeah, I'm good. Let's do this."

Ruby threads her arm through mine and together we make our way toward our first class of the day.

My skin prickles as we move, telling me that although I couldn't see him, he's still watching me.

Well, this day certainly went to shit faster than I was hoping for.

16

ZAYN

"Zayn," Mom bellows the second I close the front door behind me. All the good feelings I had running around my body instantly vanish with the tone of her voice. "Get your ass in here right now."

I already know I'm in the shit before I look at her, I can tell by her tone. I'm sure there could be a number of things that could have pissed her off, but I've got a suspicion this afternoon might have just caught up with me.

I round the corner and her murderous eyes land on me instantly.

"You've been suspended," she spits.

"Fuck," I mutter, running my hand over my head.

"Yeah. *Fuck*. Principal Hartmann said you beat a junior up for no reason."

"It wasn't for no reason, Mom. I'm not a monster."

Her brows rise. I know I'm not totally innocent and that life before our move to Rosewood was a little different from what it is now. Fighting in Harrow Creek was a daily occurrence but since moving here, I've mostly managed to keep my nose out of trouble.

"Hartmann said you tricked him out of class and attacked him in the locker room. Is that right?"

"Yes," I sigh, walking toward her and jumping up on the opposite stool. "He's not a good person, Mom. He more than deserved it."

"Well..." She blows out a breath. Mom knows that I've always been honest with her. If I've fucked up, I've confessed. I've never hidden anything from her, so I know that she wants to believe what I'm saying, but at the same time she wants to rip me a new one for my actions. "That may very well be true. But this isn't how you go about it."

"He's hurting someone I care about. I couldn't sit back and ignore it."

Her eyes narrow at my admission. I've never, ever mentioned anything about caring for someone before. I've never even had a girlfriend that she's met. Never wanted one. So I understand why she's shocked.

"Anything you need to talk about?"

I think of Poppy and everything she's forced to endure because of her shitty parents, let alone Preston.

I know that I should probably tell Mom. She could help, she would help. But I've already gone behind Poppy's back once today. I refuse to betray her twice.

"No, I'm good. I know I shouldn't have done it, Mom. But something needed to happen. I refuse to sit back and allow him to hurt someone."

"Someone you care about," she reminds me, as if I need it. I can still taste her, feel the heat of her body against mine. "Anyone I know? The girl from your bed the other morning by any chance? I didn't recognize her, but then most of your friends are normally clothed when I see them."

"Mom," I groan, rolling my eyes. "No, it's not her. It's... no one, it doesn't matter."

She narrows her eyes at me, instead of saying anything, she reaches out and squeezes my hand.

I'm about to get up and walk away when her voice stops me.

"I trust you, Zayn. You've got a good head on your shoulders. If you say it was necessary, then I believe you, but you can't go around doing this. It's senior year and you've got too much to lose."

I nod, standing from the stool.

"We've got a meeting with Hartmann first thing, and you've got to pick up work from your teachers."

"Great."

"You'd better work your ass off here this week, boy."

"All week?" I ask.

"Yep. All week."

I groan as I walk away, stopping at the refrigerator to pull out a soda before going to my room.

Well, this day really has gone to shit.

Sure, I was kinda expecting it. But it doesn't mean it sucks any less.

My need to tell Poppy has me reaching into my pocket for my cell as I climb the stairs.

My thumb hovers over the keys, but I realize that I can't tell her this yet. I'm suspended because I was trying to protect her from Preston. If I'm not there, then… *shit.* Mom's right. I really didn't think this through.

Ignoring my need to tell her, I go down a different route with my message. Hopefully one that will make her smile, remind her just how incredible tonight was before she finds out the truth tomorrow.

Morning rolls around all too quickly.

"Why aren't you ready for school?" Harley snaps at me when I join her in the kitchen.

"Didn't Mom tell you? I'm suspended."

Her eyes open amusingly wide. "No. Why?"

"I beat the shit out of Preston."

"That was you? How didn't I know this?"

"I'm sorry that the first thing I did after wasn't to go running to my little sister to tell her," I mutter, going for the coffee machine. Although, I already know that caffeine isn't going to be enough right now.

"Fuck off. Why'd you hit him?"

"Why not? That guy is a class A prick."

"Agreed but it's not like you to go around swinging your fist because you feel like it, well, not here anyway."

"It just did, okay? I'm going back to bed."

"Don't forget our meeting," Mom says, breezing into the kitchen. "I've had to move my entire day around for this, so make sure you're ready."

"I'll be ready," I call down to her.

We're almost at school when the first class of the day is about to start. I haven't heard anything from Poppy, so I can only assume that she's not heard the gossip yet. That's not overly surprising seeing as she keeps her head down and tries to avoid almost everything that happens in that place.

Just before Mom parks, I drag out my cell and send her a simple message. I probably should say more, but I have no idea how to explain what I want to say to her.

Zayn: I'm so sorry.

I stare at the screen for a minute, but it never shows as read before I'm forced to get out of the car and walk beside Mom to listen to Hartmann rip me a new one.

To be fair, the meeting isn't as bad as I thought it might be. And I can't help but wonder if that was because Hartmann also wanted his chance to punch Hellburn in the face. I wouldn't put it past him. It's no secret that Preston's father donates a hefty check to the school once a year, allowing Preston to act like a douchebag because he thinks his father owns this place.

Entitled prick.

I allow Hartmann to give me his speech about how he expects his students to behave, let alone members of our successful team. Blah, blah, blah.

My fist clench and my teeth grind with my need to tell both Hartmann and Mom just what a prick Preston really is, but without breaking my promise to Poppy again, I can't. All I can hope is that he fucks up soon before anyone gets hurt, and shows himself for what he really is.

Thankfully, my teachers have already delivered me a stack of work, and by the time we leave his office, I've got enough to keep me occupied for a month, let alone four days off school.

"Well, that wasn't so bad," I mutter as Mom and I head out to the parking lot.

"Zayn," she breathes. "You're suspended. How is that going to look to UCLA?"

"They won't care, Mom. Kids get suspended all the time. I've got a solid GPA, plus football. This is nothing."

"I hope you're right," she mumbles, unlocking the car and ripping the door open.

"They've probably already made their decision anyway."

"How are you so calm about it? Don't you want it anymore?"

I shake my head. "Of course I want it." UCLA has been my dream for as long as I can remember but I try to keep levelheaded about it. I've worked my ass off, written what I hope is a stellar application. All I can do now is wait. If it's meant to be then it will be, if not, there are plenty of other incredible colleges out there.

"Well, could you at least look a little bit anxious about it. I think I'm feeling it for the both of us."

"Everything will be fine, Mom." Reaching over, I squeeze her hand.

She nods before backing out of the space ready to kick my ass out at home so she can head to work.

A week of sitting at home on my own. Not exactly my idea of fun but then I guess this is meant to be a punishment. Even if that motherfucker did deserve it.

17

POPPY

Zayn: I'm so sorry.

My brows pinch as I stare at those three little words. Dread starts to fill me as I try to think about what he's sorry about.

Sorry about last night? About what we did?

It was all a joke, wasn't it?

My temperature spikes as anger swells within me. My stomach turns over and I have no choice but to push my chair out behind me as I run to the bathroom to save me from puking all over my desk.

By the time I push into the stall, the feeling has subsided, although the anger is still burning strong.

Tears sting my eyes as I think about everything he gave me yesterday. How light he made me feel as he took me away from the stress of my life.

"You motherfucker," I scream into the silence of the bathroom as I finally give in to the tears.

When Ruby bursts into the room she finds me curled up in a ball on the floor, still crying.

"Jesus, Poppy, are you okay?" she asks, dropping to her knees beside me.

"Y-yeah. I'm sorry. I don't know what came over me." I risk looking up and all I find in front of me are a pair of knowing eyes.

"Something to do with this maybe." She passes my cell over. The screen is now blank but from the look on her face I'm assuming she saw what made me run.

"What's he done?"

"I… I don't know," I admit.

"So why are you in here crying if you don't know what he's done?"

"He regrets it, doesn't he? Do you think it was just a dare like New Year, a game like his birthday?"

"Uh…" Ruby comes to sit beside me, our shoulders touching as she reaches for my hand. "I'm sure it wasn't."

"I need to find him," I say with renewed enthusiasm as the idea of going and ripping him a new one for treating me like this hits me.

"Y-you can't," Ruby says, her grip on me tightening.

"Why can't I?"

"Haven't you heard the gossip?"

I look at her with raised brows. "When do I ever listen to the gossip?"

She rolls her eyes at me. "He's been suspended for punching Preston's lights out. Any idea why he did that, by the way?"

"What? Why didn't you tell me this sooner?" I bark at her.

"I thought you knew. You clearly spent most of last night with him. I assumed he told you."

"Jesus, Ruby." I push from the floor and grab a paper towel to clean up my face with.

"What?" she asks innocently. "So that makes everything better now that you know he's been suspended for fighting."

"Well, no." But it sure gives me a better idea as to why he's sorry. I don't need to remember the smirk on Preston's face earlier to understand why he looked so fucking happy.

Jesus. This is a fucking mess.

"You need to talk to Harley about this, Jake too."

"Yeah," I agree.

"Come on, you ready to get back to class?"

"Yeah," I say sadly, already regretting running out like that. I've just made myself an even bigger target by acting like a complete nutcase. My MO is to keep my head down at every opportunity and try to blend as much as possible in an attempt not to give him any more ammunition to come at me with.

The second we both step back into class, all eyes turn on us—well, me—including the teacher.

"Everything okay?" she asks me, her brows pulling together in concern.

"Yeah, I'm sorry, I just felt a little..." I trail off. "I'm good now, thank you."

She nods at me, although the concern doesn't leave her face.

Ruby retakes her seat but the second I turn away from Mrs. Pritchard, *his* eyes pin me to the spot. An evil smile curls at his lips before he blows me a kiss and raises a brow.

Fear snakes around me and for a second I wonder if I'm about to run back out of the room. But I swallow it down, rip my eyes from his and march back to my seat to continue with the lesson.

I unlock my cell when Mrs. Pritchard is distracted once more and find another message waiting for me.

Zayn: If he tries anything tell me and I'll be there in a flash.

My fingers squeeze my cell.

If he tries anything, does Zayn not know Preston at all? Of course he's going to try something.

My cell vibrates in my hand once more. Expecting it to be him, I quickly wake it back up but the unknown number I find staring back at me turns my body to ice.

Unknown: While the bodyguard is away, Preston gets to play...

My muscles tense and I hate myself for reacting. His stare burns into my back, I don't need to turn around to know that he's smiling in the knowledge that he's getting to me.

Locking my cell, I shove it into my pocket deciding against replying to Zayn or being forced to read anything else from Preston.

His attention never leaves me and the second the bell to the end of first period rings, I stuff my books into my bag and practically run from the room.

I almost collide with Amalie as I make my escape down the hallway.

"Whoa, something on fire?" she asks, looking me over.

"Sorry, just excited to get to gym," I lie.

"Are you okay, you look a little terrified?"

"Yeah, I'm good. Honestly."

The rest of the school thankfully descend in the hallways and any chance we had of having a conversation comes to an end.

"I'll see you later, yeah?"

"Sure," she says, but I hear the concern in her voice.

When did I stop becoming so good at hiding how I was really feeling? *Probably about the same time you let Zayn put his hands on you, again.*

Locking down the little voice in my head, I march toward the girl's locker room, thankful that Preston isn't going to be anywhere near me.

"Ah, you decided to show your face then?"

"Ugh, yeah. I had such a hair nightmare this morning," Harley complains, running her hand over her bangs.

"Looks perfect to me."

"It should after the amount of time I spent on it. I could really do without volleyball right now, it's going to ruin it."

"I'm sure you'll still look stunning, Har."

"Whoa, you look a little too lively today. You knocked back a few Red Bulls or something this morning?" she asks when I instantly start getting changed as if I'm actually looking forward to what's to come.

"No, just feeling a little pumped."

I still when her hand lands on my forearm. "Are you okay?"

"Yes," I snap. "I'm fine. Your mom pissed then, or what?" I ask, hoping to get the heat off me.

"Pissed doesn't really cover it. I didn't know why she was in such a mood when I got in last night though. I only found out this morning. I thought she was going to blow a fuse though, and I don't think it helped that he spent most of the night out avoiding her."

My cheeks heat and I keep my back turned to her and I continue changing into my gym clothes. "Have you spoken to him about it?"

"Nah, not really."

"So you don't know why he did it?"

"No, but does anyone really need a specific reason to hit Preston? I would, given half the chance, he's a dick, and he treats you like shit."

You don't even know the half of it.

"Come on, girls. You can spread the gossip at lunchtime," Miss White shouts, clapping her hands together in the hope we speed up a little.

Volleyball helped to release a little bit of the tension that was pulling at my muscles, but it didn't last because the second I walked into every other class I had for the rest of the morning, his cold evil eyes followed.

When the bell rang for lunch, I ignored my empty stomach and instead took myself to the library. The music rooms are usually my sanctuary, but after yesterday, I don't feel safe going there. I need to do something out of character to throw him off, so the final aisle of the library away from everyone else is it.

I drop my bag to the floor before lowering my ass to the ground and tipping my head back against the books and closing my eyes for a beat.

The sound of others filter through the air, but no one is anywhere near me, thank God. I just need a few minutes of not looking over my shoulder, of wondering when he's going to strike. There's no if, it's just when and I want to be prepared for when it happens.

Each minute ticks by as if it's an hour.

I wish I had a car, so I could get away from it all then. I could go to the beach. Walk along the sand and feel the waves against my feet. I can't even remember the last time I did that. Or I could drive up to the cliffs where we used to go for picnics when things were relatively okay and just watch the clouds.

Anything other than being here like a sitting duck waiting for the inevitable.

My cell dings and I reluctantly pull it from my pocket. I pray that it's Zayn. He's sent a couple more since I ignored his messages this morning. But I haven't even opened them. I have no idea what I'm even supposed to say.

It was easy last night, he left me on a high and our banter was easy. Today with the weight of the world pressing down on me, I have no idea what to say to him.

Only when I look at the screen, I find it's not him and my stomach sinks into the pit of my stomach.

Unknown: Come out, come out, wherever you are...

My cell trembles in my hand as I stare down at his words.

I fucking knew he'd be looking for me.

The temptation to get up and run out of the school is strong, but I refuse to let him win. He will not break me.

I don't unlock my cell for fear it might open the message and show him I've seen it, instead I shove it to the bottom of my bag. My hand hits a packet as I do so and I find a smashed up cereal bar that I spend the rest of lunch nervously nibbling on.

He's not in my final classes of the day, and I almost begin to breathe normally again knowing that I'm going to be able to lock myself at home soon and try to put this day behind me.

Not having Zayn here shouldn't make any difference. I'd managed all this time without him having my back, but only a few days after he figures out there's something going on and I'm already relying on him.

It's pathetic and I chastise myself over and over before the final bell of the day rings out.

I'm stronger than having to rely on a boy to protect me.

The second the bell rings, I sweep my books from the desk and run for my locker. If I didn't have books in there I needed for tonight's homework then I'd run straight out the doors and not look back, well, not until tomorrow.

Both Ruby and Harley have practice, so unless I want to risk hanging around for a bus, my only option is to walk.

Shifting my bag up higher on my shoulder, I set off.

Every car that passes has me on edge, but almost an hour after I set off, I drag my tired legs up our street.

"Hey, good day at school?" Mom asks as I push through the front door.

I do a double take when I find that she's actually showered and dressed today.

"Uh... yeah... it was... fine." A lump crawls its way up my throat at my lie.

As I stand before her, all I want is for her to be a normal mom and for her to pull me in for a hug and tell me that everything's going to be okay.

But that's not my reality.

"You been somewhere nice?" I ask, dropping my bag to the bottom step and heading for the kitchen to find some food.

"We went to the store for some supplies."

Thankfully, I've got my back to her so she doesn't see me roll my eyes at her need for supplies. They sure aren't the same kind as other parents make an effort to go out for.

"Does that mean we have food in the house?"

"Don't be so cheeky, young lady."

"Cheeky?" I ask, astonished. I spin to her and take in her irritated expression. "Oh my God, you're serious, aren't you? Unbelievable," I mutter to myself. "Well seeing as you believe your words, how about you parent your own children when they turn up from their after-school club tonight."

"Why? What are you doing?"

"I don't know. Maybe I'll go out and get drunk like every other kid at school gets to do while I'm babysitting your offspring."

Grabbing a bag of chips and a couple of cans of soda that are sitting on the counter, I storm past her and up the stairs.

I don't usually say anything to her about the disaster that our family is but I've just about had my fill today.

I slam my bedroom door so hard that it makes the entire house shake before flipping the lock I installed after Zayn's first visit.

I didn't do it in the hope he'd come back, but as Austin interrupted us that day, I realized just how little privacy I get in this place and I stopped off at the hardware store and picked it up.

I throw the doors open to my balcony and kick my shoes off before launching myself on my bed and shoving my head into my pillow.

Today can go suck it.

18

ZAYN

I stare at the unread messages with dread sitting heavy in my stomach.

He wouldn't have done anything, would he?

I tap my finger on the side, trying to decide if I'm just making a bigger deal out of this than necessary.

Poppy has clearly handled this to a point for a while now. This hasn't suddenly just started. But that doesn't do anything to settle the trepidation swirling around within me like a tornado.

I could send her another message, but if she refuses to read that one too, I'm in no better position, other than starting to look a little desperate. That's not really a look I crave, like, ever.

"Fuck it," I mutter to myself, shoving my feet in my sneakers and slipping from my room.

It's late, the sun has already long set and the winter wind whips around me when I step from the house.

I've spent all day working in the hope I could get everything done and emailed in so I can spend the rest of my impromptu days off doing something a little more fun. Although that's unlikely with all my friends and teammates spending their days in class.

I push my key into the ignition and turn the engine, my truck rumbles to life and I set off.

Mom's not here, she's out at some dinner with some colleagues and

Harley has locked herself in her bedroom, probably fighting with some more math homework that she refuses to let me help with.

I'm at Poppy's house before I know it. The lights are on and unlike last time, I see her family all sitting around the table in the dining room like they're… normal.

It's an odd sight after everything I discovered here last night. Only, when I walk around the side of the house, I find that Poppy isn't with them.

Not wanting to interrupt, especially if she's not home, I walk around to the backyard and look up at her bedroom.

The lights are out but the curtains blow in the wind where the doors are open.

Spotting a ladder that's resting against the wall, I move it a little closer to her balcony and without a second thought, I climb.

My heart's in my chest as I throw my leg over the railing and step onto the balcony. This probably wasn't my wisest move, but I guess it's a little late now.

The room is cold and silent as I step inside. The light from the moon allows me to see the lump in the bed and as I get closer, I find that she's sleeping.

The sight of her in one piece settles something inside me.

As gently as possible, I sit down beside her. Unable to keep my hands to myself, I reach out and run my knuckles down her cheek.

Her eyelids flutter at my touch. She blinks a couple of times before she realizes she has company. She gasps, and fearing a scream is about to rip from her throat, I gently press my hand over her mouth, not wanting to alert her parents.

"It's okay. It's just me."

Her eyes focus after a beat and she relaxes, although she looks anything but pleased to see me.

"How did you get in here?" she whispers, looking to her locked door.

"I climbed. You should probably move that ladder in the yard, anyone could let themselves in here while you sleep." I drop my lips to her ear. "It might not end as pleasurably as my visit."

"You shouldn't be here." Her voice is all deep and rough from sleep and it makes my cock swell.

"But I am," I say, leaning forward and brushing my lips against hers.

"You need to leave," she breathes, although there's no strength behind it.

"What would be the fun in that when I could stay here and get you off instead?"

"I'm mad at you," she breathes, her eyes boring into mine.

"When aren't you?" Running my hand over her shoulder, I wrap my fingers around the back of her neck, my thumb stroking over the soft skin over her pulse point. It thunders beneath my touch, giving away how she really feels about my visit. "Stop fighting what you want, Pops."

"I told you not to get involved," she whispers. "Now you've been suspended because of it."

"It doesn't matter. It was worth it."

"Risking your future?"

"Jeez, you sound like my mom."

"Yeah, because I ca—" She abruptly cuts herself off.

"What was that?" I ask, my tone lighter than a few moments ago.

"Nothing."

"No, no. You were going to say something." My grip on her tightens a little.

"I wasn't going to say anything."

"I'm pretty sure you were about to admit that you care about me."

She huffs, making me laugh. "You're my best friend's brother. Of course I want you to do well."

"Oh, is that why. Not because of this." Closing the small amount of space between us, I crush my lips to hers in a bruising kiss.

Flicking the covers off her, I run my hand down her body.

"Zayn," she moans, arching into my hand. "You need to go."

"Your words might be saying that, but your body is telling me something else, Pops." I cup her breast, pinching her nipple through the thin fabric of her tank.

"No, Zayn." At her refusal, I pull back, my brows pinching together.

"What's wrong?"

"We shouldn't be doing this and you know it."

"But—"

"No, no buts. I'm doing what I should have done days ago. This can't happen between us. You need to leave."

My eyes bounce between hers, waiting for her to tell me that she's joking.

"You're serious right now, aren't you?"

"Yeah. I am."

I study her for a few more seconds before backing away. Her walls have come up, I can practically see them and I know I've got no chance of scaling them right now.

"What happened today?"

"Nothing, Zayn. You need to stop trying to protect me. Just go back to not even realizing that I exist."

"Pops. I've always known you exist."

"Well you had a funny way of showing it while you were whoring yourself around the cheer squad. Now get out."

"Fine." I push from the bed and back up toward the door. "I guess I still get to tell the guys that I got between your legs."

She gasps at my words and I immediately hate myself for making what was between us sound any less serious.

"Get the hell out, asshole." Her voice cracks at the end and my fingers twitch to reach out for her, my apology is right on the tip of my tongue but when she turns her back on me, cutting off our connection, I know I've got no choice but to do as she said.

I climb down and then take the ladder that made my entrance so easy to the very bottom of their property. The thought of someone else making use of it and letting themselves in while she's sleeping does not sit right with me.

With a glance back at her bedroom, I make my way to my truck.

I slam my palms down on the wheel in frustration. That wasn't how that was supposed to go.

I don't remember the drive home but the second I get home I run into someone I really don't have the energy for.

"Shouldn't you be grounded or something?" Harley asks, popping her hip and resting her hand on it.

"What the fuck does it have to do with you?"

"Wow, you're in a delightful mood this evening. Miss out on your daily cheer slut attention or something?"

"Fuck off, Har." I push past her and storm through to the kitchen and toward Mom's drinks cabinet.

"Mom will flip her shit if she finds you stealing from that."

I roll my eyes at the fact she followed me. Of course she fucking did, goody two shoes.

"Yeah, well, what if I don't give a shit. Go run along and tell her, see if I care."

Swiping a bottle of vodka, I slam my shoulder into hers and march from the room.

"Ow, that fucking hurt, asshole."

I don't respond. I've already said too much. Instead, I march toward my bedroom, slam the door and flip the lock to ensure she stays the fuck out of my business.

19

POPPY

My chest heaves and tears burn the backs of my eyes as I listen to Zayn climb back down the ladder.

Did I want to send him away? No, not really. But I also knew that I couldn't keep doing this.

Last night, he made me feel so incredible. With barely more than a touch, he made me forget everything.

It made today hit me harder than ever. I don't need that. I don't need to get lost in a boy.

I just need to survive.

I need to go back into the shadows, pretend that I don't really exist and get through the next eighteen months.

Once I know he's at the bottom, I climb from the bed and peer out of the curtain.

My chest aches as I watch him move the ladder. He's so damn thoughtful. It makes me wonder if I just made a massive mistake.

But I didn't.

We can't happen.

There are so, so many reasons why anything further happening between us would be a bad idea.

I blow out a breath as he disappears from my sight and my shoulders slump in defeat. I've given up asking why I was dealt this life when I could have had an easy one that allowed me to hang out with friends whenever I wanted, to have any boy I wanted and to walk through school with my head held high. But I still can't help wondering why I got stuck with this shit.

Dragging my eyes away from the darkness outside, I push through my bathroom door. I've only taken two steps inside when I sense a person already in here with me. But I don't get a chance to scream because a sweaty hand covers my mouth and my back and head collides with the wall.

Pain spears down my neck from the force of the collision and my eyes immediately begin to water.

Cold devil eyes stare down at me.

"I didn't think you were ever going to join me, Pops." He uses the name that Zayn calls me, and my stomach turns over.

He heard all of that, saw all of that.

I swallow down the bile that threatens as I hold his stare.

My heart beats wildly in my chest as my body trembles in fear. I hate that he can probably feel it, that he knows I'm scared right now.

His eyes are wide, his pupils blown and he stinks of weed.

"It's a shame your bodyguard had to leave so quickly, I thought the two of you were going to give me a private show. I would say it's a shame, but I'm not sure I'd want his sloppy seconds." He leans in, his rotten breath filling my nose and turning my stomach once more. "I much prefer to be the first. He can pick you up after I've finished with you, if there's anything left."

I try to shout, scream, anything, but my voice is muffled against his disgusting hand and my body is frozen in fear.

"You know, I thought you'd at least try to fight. Has your boyfriend taught you nothing?"

"Fuck you." I spit into his hand, not that he can probably make it out.

"And here I was thinking you were waiting for me." He lifts his spare hand and cups my breast.

I try to flinch away from him but I've got nowhere to go, and I've got no hope of overpowering him.

The tears I desperately don't want to shed fill my eyes as his hand roams, moving to the other side and pinching my nipples until they react to his touch.

"No, no, no," I chant. "Please, no," I cry as he pulls at my tank with such force it rips, exposing my bare breasts to him.

"Oh, Pops. What have we got here?" His wild eyes drop to my breasts.

Slamming my eyes close, I turn my head away, not able to watch him looking at me with that hunger in his eyes.

"Look at me, Poore," he spits, using my last name.

My eyes fly open and I'm forced to watch as he rubs himself through his pants as he stares at my breasts.

"I wonder if you taste as bitter as I've always imagined."

I shake my head wildly as he licks his lips, sucking his bottom one into his mouth.

His fingertip circles my nipple and as much as I hate his touch, my traitorous body reacts to it, heat pools between my thighs.

I don't think I've ever hated myself and my life more in that moment.

Moving from my breast, he trails his fingers down my stomach until he finds the waistband of my shorts.

My eyes are wide as he teases the skin. He's really going to do it this time.

Finding my fight, my arms fly at him, my nails scratching at any bit of skin I can connect with.

"Fucking bitch," he groans when I manage to gouge a chunk of skin from his upper arm that's holding my mouth hostage.

His hand drops and he manages to take hold of both of my wrists and lifts them above my head.

His eyes run the length of me again before he brushes his cheek against mine. "Be a good girl and don't scream. Well, not until you're coming on my fingers anyway."

His words repulse me. "What the fuck is your problem? What do you think this is going to achieve?"

"Who says I want to achieve anything?"

"You want Jake to make you captain. I can assure you that this isn't the way to make it happen. When he finds out—"

"Which he won't," he warns.

"You won't be alive long enough to play a game as a senior, let alone captain it."

An evil smile curls at his lips.

"That's where you're wrong, little girl."

"I'm fucking older than you, asshole," I spit. "The only fucking baby here is you. You're fucking pathetic." I spit at him and he backs away a little in shock.

"Bitch," he roars, backhanding me across the face. "Know you're fucking place."

"My place is not being terrorized in my own home by a fucking psychopath." The last thing I want to do right now is have a conversation with him, but I figure that the longer I put off the inevitable, the more chance I have of either figuring a way out of this or someone interrupting him.

If I had normal parents, they might be likely to come and check on me, especially after how I spoke to Mom earlier but as it is, I'm sure she's already forgotten.

His growl makes my body tremble harder.

"I'm going to fucking ruin you. Jake won't have a choice but to do exactly what I want if he wants you alive."

"No one gives a shit about me. Haven't you noticed that during all your stalking?"

"Shut the fuck up. I didn't come here to have a conversation with you."

"Fine," I say, glancing around the room, my eyes locking on something that might get me out of this sooner rather than later. "Do your worst."

"I fucking knew you wanted me." His hand loosens on my wrists allowing me to slip one way while the other plunges into my panties. "Oh, baby. So wet for me."

I fight not to retch as his fingers graze my clit. While he's distracted, I reach out, grabbing the cup I keep my toothbrush in and with as much force as I can manage, I swing it toward his head.

"Motherfucker," he barks, stumbling away from me and thankfully removing his touch.

I sag back against the wall, but I can't allow myself to relax yet.

He looks back at me, blood trickling down the side of his face.

"Now get the fuck out of my house," I demand. "Before I scream for my parents and have your ass thrown into jail."

"Oh, baby. We both know your drugged-up parents don't give a shit."

I gasp. He knows.

To my amazement, he stumbles toward the door. "This isn't over, Poore," he spits before thankfully disappearing from the small room.

Stumbling back, I crash against the wall and slide down until my ass hits the floor.

My adrenaline runs out and I drop my head into my arms and sob. My entire body trembles with the fear I still feel with the disgust.

He was in here watching and listening to me with Zayn. He was waiting for me. Waiting to… I can't even allow myself to think about what his intentions might have been.

He knows about my parents, which means he probably knows that he could get away with almost anything without alerting them.

Suddenly, I think of the ladder that Zayn moved away from the house to stop people coming up and I jump to my feet. If that's gone then how did he get out?

I stand in the doorway to my en suite, my body exposed and stare at my open bedroom door.

He just walked straight through my house after that. What if someone saw him?

Without allowing myself to think about the answer, I race over, close my door and flip the lock again.

Pulling my ruined tank around me, I suck in deep lungfuls of air, trying to calm myself down.

Okay, so he touched me, he hurt me, but I'm okay. I'll be okay.

After closing and locking the balcony doors, I tell myself never to open them again and strip out of my clothes, dropping it all in the trash. I'll never be able to wear any of it again without seeing his evil eyes and feel his bruising touch.

I turn the shower on hot and step under, allowing it to burn my skin. To singe his touch from me, to banish his scent that's clinging to my skin.

Sinking down to the floor once more, I wrap my arms around my legs as silent tears drop.

I want to call Zayn. I want to feel his arms around me and have his scent in my nose, reminding me that I'm safe, but as I walk from my bathroom, my body still trembling, I don't reach for my phone.

I sent him away for a reason. I need to be stronger than breaking my resolve only an hour later because Preston decided to pounce.

I'm in a daze as I pull on a fresh set of pajamas and crawl into bed. I curl into a ball and torture myself by reliving the events of tonight over and over.

Alarm bells should have gone off when Zayn mentioned the ladder, but that thing has been tucked alongside the fence for years, I just assumed he'd made use of it. I had no reason to believe that he was the second one to let himself in while I slept.

Thanks to my afternoon nap, it meant that I laid there tossing and turning for hours while being tormented by the memory of Preston's cold eyes and evil touch.

When my alarm went off this morning, I swear I'd only just fallen asleep. My eyes are still heavy and my muscles ache as I drag my ass toward my next class.

I haven't seen or heard from Preston, thank God. I know he's in school though. I've heard others talking about the fight he had last night and how the guy he fought is apparently fighting for his life in the hospital. I refrain from informing the gossips that it's all a load of bullshit. No one would believe me if I even tried.

He's still weirdly absent by the time lunch rolls around, but I know he's just in the shadows waiting somewhere, so just like yesterday, I take myself to the back of the library.

It's busier than the day before but I find an empty aisle and dump my stuff on the floor, ready to wait out the lunch break until I can go to class and then hide at home, with my doors locked tonight.

Pulling out my cell, I find a message from Harley asking if I'm coming to the cafeteria for lunch. I quickly tap out a lie that I'm still in class working on an assignment, before reluctantly opening the stream of messages I have from Zayn that I've been ignoring.

He starts off with an apology for last night, promising me that he'll back off, but also that he misses me. He tells me what work he's got to do today and explains how bored he is alone.

I debate replying. I might have sent him away last night but that doesn't mean I couldn't do with someone to talk to right now. But I don't get a chance to make a final decision because another message comes through, one from a number that fills the blood in my veins with ice.

Unknown: You can run but you can't hide...

A picture message follows, I stare down at a picture of me looking at my cell, much like I am now.

My head flies up in the direction he must have been in to take that picture, but there's no one to be seen.

"Fuck," I hiss to myself.

I make a snap decision.

Poppy: Are you still in the cafeteria? I'm done now.

Harley replies immediately to say they are, and I throw my bag over my shoulder and head out.

Safety in numbers and all that. Maybe hiding was the stupidest thing to do.

I spend the rest of the day looking over my shoulder, waiting for him to jump out of the shadows. But he never does.

Part of me is relieved. But the other part knows that he's just waiting for the right time and I wonder if it would be better to just get it over with.

But it seems he's not in any rush to continue what he started like he warned because the rest of the afternoon and the next day passes with nothing. Even his irritating messages stop.

As the hours pass, I become more and more jumpy, to the point I piss myself off.

When a note arrives for me not long before the end of my last lesson of the day from Miss French to remind me that I should be in a guidance counselor meeting, I don't think anything of it.

I can't deny that I've been avoiding having to sit down with her, and I've missed more than one appointment with my need to put off having to even consider any serious decisions about my future. I was hoping with application season in full swing that she'd have her hands full with the seniors and leave me alone for a little while to shove my head farther in the sand.

Sadly, it seems that's not the case.

I pack up my stuff and my teacher barely even looks up when I show him the note. With a sigh, I walk out of his classroom. No one else even spares me a second glance, they're either too busy with what they should be doing or lost in their own conversations with the people surrounding them while our teacher pretends to ignore them. Idiots.

Miss French's office is only a short walk and everyone else is in class, so I don't think to look over my shoulder as I make my way down the hallway. That is until a door opens behind me and a very familiar hand clamps over my mouth and an arm wraps around my waist.

I'm too shocked to scream, not that it would do any good. But seconds before I'm dragged backward into the storage closet, I manage to make use of my legs and start kicking in the hope of making contact and forcing him to let go of me before it's too late.

"Fucking bitch," he grunts as my heel connects with his shin. But it's not enough because the walls close in on me before the door closes and I find myself thrown up against the metal shelves that line the walls.

Pain shoots down my spine from where it connects with one of the edges before I fall to the floor.

A loud click sounds out in the silent space and my body begins to tremble.

There's only a single light bulb hanging from the ceiling that lets out a dim light, but it's enough to make a shadow fall over me when he stands above me.

"What do you want?" I snap, digging deep and finding some strength to fight him when all I really want to do is curl up in a ball and cry that I allowed him to get to me so easily.

"What do I want? I think we both know the answer to that question, don't we, Poore."

"It's not going to work. Whatever you do to me isn't going to make Jake give you his team."

"Maybe not, but I may as well have some fun trying."

"Fun? You think this is fun?"

"Oh, Poppy. You're the most fun I've had in a long, long time."

He crouches down before me, his cold eyes drilling into mine.

"Y-you don't look like you're enjoying yourself right now."

He smiles at me. It's so sinister and terrifying that it makes my stomach drop into the tips of my toes.

He's going to fucking kill me in here if I give him half a chance.

"What are you going to do to me?" I ask, my voice weaker than I'd like.

"We're going to play. Do you like to play games, Pops?"

"With you? No."

"Well," he says, reaching out and wrapping his hot fingers around my throat, lifting me from the floor as if I weigh nothing more than a feather. My back once again collides with the shelving and my head bounces off one, causing me to shut my eyes for a beat. "That's a real shame, because I really want to play with you. And do you know what? You're going to really enjoy it."

"No," I spit.

"Ah, but you forget. I remember how wet you were for me last time. How much you wanted me to get you off, how you craved my touch."

"Never," I hiss.

My arm flies up to hit him, but he's quicker, and I find myself trapped in his hold.

"We can do this the easy way, or the hard way. It's really your choice."

"I'm not playing your fucking games."

"Hard way it is then." My front is slammed against the wall, my cheekbone smarting from where it connects as he binds my hands with tape behind my back.

"Better. I'm not really into scratchers. I prefer to be the one dishing out the pain."

I tug at the restraints testing how tight they are but without a hell of a lot more force, I'm not getting out of them anytime soon. "You can't hurt me, Preston. You're nothing to me."

"You sure about that?" Before he's even finished the words, the back of his hand forces my head to snap to the side. My eyes fill with tears as my already painful cheek burns with his slap.

"Fuck you. Do what you want to me. I'll make sure you never get your way. Jake will never let you have his team."

I'm spun around, my back once again against the wall as his hand squeezes my throat so hard it becomes harder and harder to suck in air to breathe, white spots start swimming in my eyes.

"I'm going to ruin you until he has no choice but to give me what I want if he wants you breathing," he snarls in my face, his teeth bared and spittle flying from his mouth with his anger.

I tilt my chin up in defiance, not willing to show him the fear that is wrecking my insides.

Everyone is in class right now. I could scream but really no one will hear me, it would be pointless to even waste the energy trying.

"Go on then. Break me," I hiss at him.

His eyes darken with his desire before his fingers reach for the waistband on my pants.

My stomach turns knowing that there's a very good chance he could succeed this time.

I look around for something to help, for a weapon but with my arms bound behind me, I have no chance of grabbing anything.

The fabric parts and he's just about to push his fingers inside the fabric when the door rattles and the handle moves.

My heart jumps into my throat as Preston's eyes meet mine.

I should scream, alert the person who's outside as to what's going on in here but no matter how hard I try to make the noise rip from my throat, his haunted stare and his ever-tightening grip on my throat ensures my lips stay firmly closed.

"Scream and I'll fucking kill you right now," he whispers, his voice low and menacing.

He removes his touch from my body and reaches behind him. I half expect him to pull a gun on me, but the sight of the smooth metal of a blade turns my blood to ice.

Thankfully, the person outside just mutters a curse before they must disappear.

"They're going to come back with a key," I state, my voice much calmer than the riot that's happening inside me.

"I'd better be quick then. How should I let them find you? Still coming down from the high you're craving or bleeding out from when you deny me?"

"You're a fucking psycho," I spit at him.

"And you need to be taught a fucking lesson." He closes the space between us, his scent filling my nose and making me want to retch.

He places his knife on the shelf and I have a split second to act or he's going to go through with one, or both, of his threats.

While he's distracted, I lift my leg with as much force as I can manage and slam my knee into his crotch.

"Fuck," he barks, releasing his hold on me in favor of clutching his junk.

As fast as I can, I run around him pulling at my restraints with all my might. The tape digs into my wrists, slicing the skin open I'm sure, but I don't stop until it's stretched enough that I can finally pull a hand free. Snatching my bag from the floor where it fell, I run for the door as he hunches over in pain.

"You fucking bitch. You're going to pay for that." I look over my shoulder just in time to see him drop to his knees.

If I were as sick as him, I might take some pleasure in his pain but all I feel is relief.

I flick the lock and run as fast as I can without looking back.

I ignore all the classroom doors and run to the exit.

My lungs burn as I make my way between the buildings until I'm in a dark alcove.

My chest heaves as silent tears stream down my cheeks.

Lifting my arms, I push my sleeves up to look at my wrists. I pull the tape that's still wrapped around one and drop it to the ground. My skin is red with blood starting to dry around the one I pulled free.

"Fuck," I bark, angrily wiping at my cheeks. I'm furious with myself for not even suspecting that attack.

The bell rings out in the buildings before the noise of kids starting to emerge from classrooms begins to get louder.

I take off without putting much thought into it. All I know is that I don't want to be seen and that I don't want him to catch up with me.

With the thought of him trying to follow me home, I turn in the opposite direction. The kids are still at school and Cooper is with a sitter this afternoon, so if he turns up there, he's only got my parents to deal with.

My legs carry me as fast as they'll go, my need to get away from school never stronger.

My muscles burn and my skin is flushed by the time I turn up a familiar street.

I shouldn't be here but I don't know where else to go, where else I'm going to be safe and to forget all about the last hour of my life?

I don't bother knocking, I never do, so it would be weird to start now. Plus, the lack of cars in the driveway point toward only one person being here.

I let myself in and after finding the kitchen empty, I head up the stairs.

Music hits my ears about halfway up, telling me that I'm heading in the right direction.

It's not until I wrap my fingers around the door handle that I begin to question why I'm here, but then the image of Preston staring down at me in that storage closet fills my mind and I know that I don't want to be anywhere else.

20

ZAYN

I hear the front door close before footsteps race up the stairs, but despite the fact that Harley should be at cheer practice and Mom told me that she was in meetings all day, I don't really think much of it.

That is until my door swings open and I find a distraught looking Poppy standing there staring at me.

Her hair is a mess, her eyes are red-rimmed and there are tear tracks down her cheeks.

My heart jumps into my throat at the sight of her.

"Fuck, Poppy." I'm off the bed and in front of her before I've even realized that I've moved.

I take her face in my hands and wipe her tears away with my thumbs.

"What's happened? What has he done?"

Dread settles in the pit of my stomach. All of this is my fault. I lost control and now I haven't been there to keep an eye on her.

She lifts up on her toes and brushes her lips against mine.

"Please, Zayn," she begs. Her hands slip under the fabric of my shirt, her fingertips brushing over my abs. The heat of her touch makes my cock swell. "I need this. I need you."

Her tongue licks across my bottom lip and my restraint snaps.

My fingers thread into her hair as I give in to her kiss.

Desperation pours from her as she clings to me, and as much as I know this probably isn't what we should be doing right now, I'm powerless but to give her what she says she needs.

My tongue sweeps against hers as she loses herself in my kiss. Her hands frantically explore my body before she wraps her fingers around the hem of my shirt and begins pulling it up.

"Off," she mumbles into my mouth.

Reaching behind my head, I grab the fabric and pull, ripping my lips away from hers for the shortest amount of time possible.

I forget about everything I should probably remember in these few moments. I forget about how she sent me away the other night, I forget about what she might have been through today if the look on her face is anything to go by and I just follow her lead.

Her fingers slip inside my sweats and before I know it, they're pooled around my ankles, her hand already beneath the fabric of my boxers, palming my ass.

"Fuck, Poppy," I groan, dropping my lips to her neck and nibbling on the soft, sweet skin. "Up," I encourage, pulling her hoodie up her body then throwing it behind me the second it leaves her body.

"More, Zayn. Everything."

I still at her words.

"Poppy, what's—"

My words are cut off when she presses her fingers to my lips. "Please. I need this. You."

"Fuck, what are you doing to me?"

I stand before her, both our chests heaving, our breaths mingling as our eyes remain locked on each other. She practically begs me not to stop, not to allow her time to think, while I desperately try to do the right thing. But my brain isn't winning in the thinking department right now.

"Please. Make me feel good."

My lips take hers once more in a dirty, wet kiss. Her nails rake down my back as I press her against the wall. Hitching her up, I wrap her legs around my waist, allowing me to grind into her.

I hiss in pleasure as the burning heat from her pussy surrounds my cock. "So good," I groan into her kiss.

"More."

Pulling her from the wall, I find the clasp of her bra and flick it open, ripping the fabric from her body.

My lips drop from hers and down to her neck.

"Oh God. Oh God," she chants as I kiss each of her breasts but ignore her peaked nipples.

Her back arches in pleasure, trying to give me more but still I resist.

"You wet for me, Poppy?"

"You should find out," she breathes, her voice deep and raspy.

Flicking the button on her pants, I push my hand inside.

Her eyes hold mine as my fingers part her and find her swollen clit.

"Zayn," she gasps when I press against it. "Yes."

I push lower, finding her soaked entrance.

"Oh God." I push two fingers inside her tight channel, my cock aching to feel just how hot it might be. "Oh God."

"That good?"

"Yeah," she pants, her eyes locked on where my hand disappears into her pants. Her head falls back against the wall as I circle her clit. "Bed, now." She says it so quietly, I'm not sure I've actually heard the words but as her hand wraps around my forearm and she tugs, I start to think it wasn't my imagination.

Lifting her into my arms, her lips find mine as I carry her over to my bed. The sheets are a mess from this morning, seeing as I had nowhere to go. I quickly sweep them aside before laying her down in the center.

I hesitate with my fingers wrapped around the waistband of her pants but with one nod of her head in agreement, I pull them down her legs, kissing down her torso as I do and finally sucking her nipples into my mouth. She thrashes beneath me, her nails scraping across my head and shoulders as I tease her.

"Zayn, please. I need to feel you."

"You don't need to ask me twice, Pops."

I kiss down her belly, dipping my tongue into her navel before pushing her legs wide and sucking her clit into my mouth. I lick at her, nip her and push two fingers deep inside her, bending them exactly how she likes it.

"Oh God, yes, yes," she chants as her muscles begin to clamp down on me and her body starts to tremble as her release surges forward.

Sucking harder, I push my fingers a little deeper and it sends her over the edge.

"Zayn," she cries as her body convulses.

I pull back once she's come down and stare at her on my bed. Her light brown hair is fanned out over my pillow, her cheeks are flushed, the desperation I saw in her eyes when she first arrived is long gone, completely replaced by heat. Her flush continues down onto her chest and I continue running my eyes down her curves.

"Zayn?" she asks, hesitation creeping into her voice.

I don't say anything, I can't. She's so fucking beautiful, and even better laid out on my bed.

Pushing my boxers from my hips, I crawl onto the bed with her, groaning when the heat of her skin hits mine.

"You're so beautiful," I whisper before sliding my fingers into her hair and crashing my lips to hers once again.

I settle between her legs, the head of my cock teasing her core, causing my desperation for her to skyrocket.

"I want you," she breathes into our kiss.

"Pops," I groan. "It shouldn't be me," I admit, kissing down her neck.

"Says who?"

"Fuck."

"You'll never get to take this back. This is kinda a one-time thing."

"I know," she says, her hungry gray eyes locked on mine. "I need it, Zayn. I need you."

Pushing up from her, I wrap her legs around my waist and take myself in hand, rubbing the head through her heat.

"Oh God," she moans as I tease her already sensitive clit.

"Are you on birth control?"

She shakes her head. "No."

Reaching for my nightstand, I rummage inside until I find a condom.

Her eyes burn my skin as she intently watches me rip it open and roll it down my length.

When I glance up at her, I find her teeth attacking her bottom lip, a small smile playing on them.

"Last chance to change your mind."

"Nope, not happening." Her eyes hold mine as I bend over her, I can see her determination in the gray depths. I probably should question it but right now with my cock lined up at her entrance, I'm not exactly thinking clearly.

"Please," she breathes. "Fuck me, Zayn."

"Jesus." I drop my lips to hers as I grip her ass in one hand and slowly push inside of her with the other. A moan rumbles up my throat as her heat engulfs me, and I'm forced to break our kiss so I can focus on the sensation and attempt to find my restraint. "So tight. So good," I groan, needing her to know how fucking incredible she feels.

A smile curls at her lips.

"More. Don't hold back."

"Pops, I—"

"You're not going to break me, Zayn."

"Fucking hell." I drop down once more, plunging my tongue into her mouth as my hips surge forward.

She cries out into my kiss as I push past her barrier before stilling.

"You okay?" She's gone as hard as stone beneath me and has tears pooling in her eyes. "I'm sorry, I'm so sorry," I whisper, wiping one that drops with the pad of my thumb.

"It's okay. Keep going, please. Make it feel good. Take me away."

She's said so many things since walking through my door that should make me question this, but I'm too lost in her to think straight.

Pulling out of her slowly, I slide back in, keeping our kiss at a similar pace.

It takes a few minutes but before long, her arms emerge from under my pillow in favor of running down my back.

"Okay?"

She nods, her hands dropping to my ass and pulling me tighter into her body.

I drop my lips to her neck as I up my speed, giving her exactly what she craves.

All too soon, the familiar tingles of my impending release start to race down my spine.

"Poppy," I groan. "You feel so good."

"Zayn," she cries, her already tight pussy starting to clamp around me.

"Are you going to come over my cock, Pops?" Just like I suspected, at my dirty words her muscles tighten even more. "You like it when I talk dirty to you, don't you?"

"Zayn," she moans, her back arching.

Sitting up, I change the angle, locking her ankles behind me in one hand and continue to thrust into her.

"Oh fuck," she cries when I press my thumb against her clit.

"You look so fucking hot right now with my cock inside you, baby." She thrashes about on my bed.

"Please, Zayn. I need… I need…"

"I know what you need, Pops."

I grind into her, hitting her deeper than before and after only three more thrusts, her entire body stills for a beat before she falls over the edge.

"Fuuuuck," I groan as she forces me over with her.

I keep moving until we've both come down before pulling out of her, tugging the condom off and dropping it over the side of the bed. I fall down beside her, wrap my arm around her waist and pull her into my side.

"Kiss me," I demand and without missing a beat, she turns her flushed face to me and offers up her lips.

We kiss for ages, just enjoying the feeling of each other's bodies pressed up against the other. My cock aches for another round, but that's not what this is about right now. I want to show her that I can take my time and treat her how she deserves, unlike how rushed we were when she first stormed in.

"I shouldn't have done that," I admit to her when we break apart in favor of dragging some air into our lungs. Our legs are still tangled together and my arm locked around her body.

"Done what?"

"Took your virginity. Not like that. I'm sorry."

"You're sorry?" she asks with a laugh. "I'm pretty sure I asked you for it."

"I know but..." I push up on my elbow and look down at her, my hand lifting to the red mark on her cheek that has anger stirring in my belly. "Why did you come here, Poppy?"

Her body tenses, telling me that I'm right. Not that I needed any kind of confirmation, I knew it the moment she pushed the door open and I took advantage.

"I needed you."

"Yeah, I know." I can't help a smile tugging at my lips. "But why? You've ignored me since you sent me away and then this."

She breaks our eye contact. I hate that she still thinks she can hide from me.

"Poppy?" I ask, cupping her cheek and turning her face back to me.

She lifts her arm as if she's going to pull my hand away, but she doesn't get the chance because I find something that I've missed this far.

"What the fuck is this?" I lift her arm up in front of me, inspecting the welts and cuts around it.

She tries tugging it away but I'm stronger by far. "It's... it's nothing."

"Bullshit. What happened this afternoon, Poppy?"

"It's nothing."

"Stop lying to me." My anger explodes within me, my muscles twitch to get up and start pacing, do anything to try to expel my need to do something but I fight it and keep her in my arms.

"What good will it do? The last time you knew something happened, you got yourself suspended. I refuse to allow this to ruin your future."

"My future. What about your present, Poppy?"

"It doesn't matter," she whispers.

"Like fuck it doesn't. You don't deserve any of this. Fuck." I throw myself back on the bed, my irritation at her being able to just brush it off like it all means nothing pisses me off beyond belief.

"Zayn, please. You've already done too much. Just trust me to handle it."

"Handle it?" I sit up, grabbing both of her hands and staring down at her red wrists. "He fucking bound you. What else did he do, Poppy?" Lifting my hand, I brush my thumb over the red mark on her cheek.

She shakes her head, still refusing to give me the answers I need.

"You need to stop protecting him," I snap.

"So what am I supposed to do? Tell the teachers? Hartmann? We both know that his daddy will make sure everything is swept under the rug. Or should I tell Jake and watch as he ruins his own future by going in all guns blazing like you did?"

I blow out a breath. "I don't know, Poppy. But you can't continue like this."

"He'll get bored eventually."

"No, he won't. We both know you're just lying to yourself. He won't stop until he gets what he wants."

"Not happening."

"Fuck." I drop my head into my hands. "He should not win. It's fucking wrong."

She climbs from the bed. "You think I don't know that? This has been my life for years, Zayn." She lifts her arms from her body in exasperation.

"Years?"

"Yeah, well… not quite like this. The past week or so, it's been worse. He's suddenly turned into an even bigger psycho."

"What's changed?"

She bends down, swiping her discarded clothes from the floor and begins dragging them on.

"You. You are what's changed."

I gasp, not expecting to hear her say that. I thought it was just that it's senior year and his time to shine was almost in touching distance.

"Because I beat the shit out of him?"

"No, Zayn," she breathes as if I'm an idiot. "He knows about this." She gestures between us.

"H-how?" I scoot to the end of the bed, not happy with the distance she's put between us.

"It doesn't matter. He just does."

"How, Poppy?" I ask, standing and stalking toward her until she has no choice but to back up.

"Just leave it. Coming here was a mistake. I shouldn't have—" Her words are cut off when she hits the wall.

Lifting my arms, I cage her in.

"How does he know, Poppy?"

"Fuck." She looks over my shoulder, unable to keep eye contact but I don't fight her on it, I know I've already won. "Where was the ladder when you climbed up it the other night?"

"Against the wall a few feet from your.... No, no, Poppy do not tell me that he—"

"He was already there. I just assumed you found the ladder where it's always been. I never in a million years thought you meant it was already up against my balcony."

"Where was he?"

"In the bathroom."

"Fuck," I roar, my knuckles connecting with the wall beside her as she cowers away from me. "Shit, I'm sorry. I'm so fucking sorry."

I wrap my arms around her trembling body but she fights me.

"No, I need to go. I shouldn't have even come here in the first place."

"Poppy, please." My voice is bordering on begging but I don't give a shit. I can't have her leaving and putting herself in danger. "I'm not letting you walk out of here alone."

"Well, then I guess it's a good thing that you have no control over me, isn't it? I refuse to cower down to that prick."

"No, no," I shout. "He can't touch you again. He just fucking can't."

"Why, Zayn?"

"Because you're mine," I roar, my chest heaving as our eyes lock.

Her breath catches for a beat before she recovers from my admission.

"That's just it though, isn't it? I'm not yours, and I never have been. You haven't treated me much better than him over the years."

"I'd never hurt you, Poppy."

"Physically, no. But do you have any idea how many nights I've fallen asleep crying because of you?"

My lips part in shock.

"No, exactly. You have no fucking clue."

While I'm standing frozen in shock, she pushes her feet into her sneakers, rips the door open and disappears from my sight.

I made her cry herself to sleep?

"Shit, Poppy, wait," I cry, fumbling around for my boxers.

They're only halfway up my legs when I follow her out of the room and toward the stairs.

"Poppy, please, stop. Just…" I race down the stairs and find her with her back to me and her hand ready to open the front door and leave.

"You don't want me, Zayn. You never have. I'm just a plaything, a toy that you had some fun with when your friends weren't around. Let's not pretend there's any more here than there really is."

"No, that's not true."

"Well you just scored the ultimate win. All the way with your sister's best friend, that must get you some points with the team, right?"

"You think I… fucking hell, Poppy. It's never been like that for me." When I finally reach her and place my hand on her waist, she startles. But not allowing her to hide from me, I spin her to face me.

My breathing catches at the sight of her tear-filled eyes and the river of ones that have already spilled over running down her cheeks.

"Poppy. Fuck."

The second I pull her into my arms, her first sob erupts.

I drop my lips to the top of her head and hold her to me as she crumbles, hoping that I can at least help in a small way.

After a few long minutes, her breathing starts to even out but she still doesn't pull her face from my chest.

"Do you remember what I said to you in the closet that day?" I ask softly.

She nods but no words leave her lips.

"I meant them. There wasn't anyone else in the room that day I wanted to kiss more than you. I thought all my birthdays had come all at once when the bottle landed on you."

"But what you said after," she whispers.

"It was bullshit, Poppy. I shouldn't have said it. I regretted it the second the words fell from my lips, but as the entire team turned their stare on me, I just couldn't help it. I didn't know how to admit that I liked my little sister's best friend."

"You liked me?" She lifts her head from my chest and the vulnerable look in her eyes guts me.

"I've always liked you, Poppy." I brush my thumb over her cheek. "But I don't deserve you."

"You can't say—"

"I can say that," I cut her off. "Because it's true. You're so beautiful, kind, thoughtful. Innocent—"

"Was," she adds with a laugh.

"You still are, Poppy." I drop my lips to her head. "It's why I can't have you going out there and taking this on by yourself."

"I've done okay this far."

"You have, but you shouldn't have to. You should have told someone."

She shrugs. "So what do you suggest? You already agreed with what I said earlier."

I think for a minute. "You own a gun?"

"Zayn," she gasps, her eyes impossibly wide.

"It was a joke. I'm joking." *Kind of.*

"Okay, good. He might be a prick, but I don't want to kill him, Jesus."

"We'll think of something. Come on, let's go back upstairs before Harley catches us."

"You ashamed of me?"

"No, not even a little bit, Pops. I just thought that maybe you might want to tell her about this instead of letting her walk right into the evidence."

She nods. "Yeah, good thought."

Taking her hand in mine, I lead her back up to my bedroom.

21

POPPY

Zayn locked his bedroom door the second we walked back inside and after pulling on his sweats, we crawled onto his bed and he pulled me into his arms.

He found something to watch on the TV but even now, over two hours later, I'm not really sure what we're watching.

My head is still back in that closet with Preston breathing down on me.

Feeling Zayn's eyes on me, I turn to look up at him.

Harley still hasn't come home, nor has his mom, so it's easy to hide out in here like the real world doesn't exist right now.

"Stay the night with me."

My chin drops in shock as his dark eyes continue to hold mine.

"Oh my God, you're serious, aren't you?"

"Deadly. I want you safe, Poppy. He's already got himself into your bedroom while you were sleeping. What's next?"

A shiver runs down my spine because I really have no idea. He keeps telling me that he's going to ruin my life, but what exactly does that mean? My life is already pretty shit as it is. There's not really all that much he can destroy.

A thought hits me, making the ball of dread which seems to have taken up permanent residence in my belly grow larger.

"He's going to come for you."

Zayn's smile drops. "He's not that stupid," Zayn says with confidence.

"Well, I beg to differ. Everyone thinks going after Jake's cousin would be a stupid move, but it seems nothing stopped him going there."

"No offense, but he probably thinks he can overpower a girl. But if he's got any sense, he won't try anything with me."

"You make out like we should all be scared of you," I say with a laugh. "I hate to tell you this, but you're hardly scary."

"I know a few people who probably have a different opinion."

I narrow my eyes at him, begging him to explain.

"How much has Harley told you about where we came from?"

"That it was a trailer park." I think for a minute. "That's probably about it, other than she hated it."

"Yeah, well, she had a very good reason to hate it. Harrow Creek is not a good place. It's full of drugs, guns, and violence. You either accepted that kind of life or you got out. It's lawless, run by the guys who have the most money and power."

"Sounds like something from the movies," I mutter.

"Yeah, it pretty much is. I wasn't brought up like the kids in Rosewood were. I was taught to fight, to protect what's mine and defend until the end."

"So what are you telling me exactly?"

"You need Preston to go away, I can make it happen."

"Whoa, I thought we were joking about killing him?"

"With my own hands, yeah. But for the right price, I could find plenty of people who'd be more than willing."

"Fucking hell, Zayn," I breathe, pushing away from him and sitting up as his words settle into my head.

I look back at him, and it's almost like I'm seeing a different person for a moment.

"You ever kill someone?"

"Poppy." He laughs, sitting up with me and taking my hand in his. "We left when I was fourteen. Mom worked her ass off to ensure we all got out before it was too late. So no, I've never killed anyone, thankfully, I never had the opportunity. But if we stayed much longer, I'm sure it would have been inevitable."

"Jesus."

"When you don't have money readily available, people will go to all kinds of extremes to look after those they love."

"I get that."

"I know you do. More than most."

I blow out a long breath. "He's not going to go away, is he?" I drop my head, allowing myself to accept those words for the first time.

"No. Not unless he gets what he wants, and even then, he's such a prick that I wouldn't put money on it being over."

"I don't want to kill him, Zayn."

"I know you don't, baby." Goose bumps race over my skin at his name for me. It makes me feel much more secure and happy than I probably should. "Those are extreme measures."

"Jake won't give him the team," I state.

"I know. We need another way, because you're right about his dad's money and influence, he'll make sure nothing sticks."

"This is a mess."

"We'll sort it out." Wrapping his arm around my shoulder, he pulls me back down to the bed with him. "I meant it, Pops. Stay with me tonight."

"I can't. I have the kids to look after."

He brushes the hair from my face and stares into my eyes. "Then let me stay with you."

"Your mom will freak. You've already been suspended."

"Then let me hide you in here with me." He rolls on top of me, dropping his lips to my neck. "Just think of the fun we could have."

I giggle like an idiot as he tickles up the sensitive skin of my neck with his tongue.

"Okay, okay. But I need to go home, see what state my parents are in. If they can look after the kids, then yeah, I'll stay."

"Come on then," he says, jumping from the bed.

"Excited much?"

"I just want you to myself."

"You mean you want me naked again?" I raise a brow in his direction where he's busy pulling on a clean shirt and hiding his toned olive skin from me.

"Something like that." He winks, making me shake my head at him.

"Come on then but be prepared to be disappointed. My parents aren't known for being reliable."

"I've got a good feeling."

Zayn holds my hand the entire drive to my house and to my surprise, I find Mom in the kitchen being normal again.

"What's all this?" I ask, very aware that Zayn insisted on following me into the house. I'm not sure if it was to protect me or because he was worried I might lie to get out of spending the night with him. Truth is, just the thought of falling asleep with his arms around me fills my entire body with tingles.

"Just cooking dinner, is that so weird?" Mom asks, her face actually looks shocked that I've commented. I guess that just proves how far gone she is.

"Yeah, it is. I'm going to stay the night at Harley's, is that okay?"

She looks over my shoulder, her eyes narrowing on Zayn.

"That's not Harley," she states.

No shit. "Zayn's just giving me a lift because Harley is still at cheer."

She nods, accepting the lie that fell flawlessly from my tongue. I guess when you have absolutely no respect for the adults that are supposed to care for you, lying comes easily.

"Okay, great. Go for it," she agrees before turning her back on both of us as if we've already left the room.

"Great, thanks," I mutter, rolling my eyes at Zayn the second I turn to him and find his concerned stare on me.

He follows me up to my room and stands with his back pressed against the door while watching me collect a few things I'm going to need.

"Mom's working late," he says after a long stretch of silence. "Says to get our own dinner."

I look over my shoulder at him staring down at his cell. Walking over to where I dropped my purse when we first walked in, I dig mine out, praying there isn't a message from *unknown* waiting for me.

Thankfully, the only people who've sent me messages are Harley and Ruby. Guilt swamps me that I'm doing all this behind Harley's back. I tell myself it's to protect her. It was at first, the fewer people involved in this shit with Preston the better, but now... I glance up at Zayn who must feel my stare because he looks up and flashes me his megawatt smile. My tummy clenches with desire and my, although tender, core aches to feel him again.

Somehow, I manage to rip my eyes from his and look back down to my cell.

There's a message from Ruby telling me that Harley is going back to hers to work on an assignment we were all given earlier and asking if I want to join them.

"Harley is at Ruby's. They want to know if I want to join them."

I look up just in time to see a sexy smirk pull at one side of Zayn's lips, "Perfect," he says, pushing from the door and stalking toward me. "An empty house means I can make you scream."

A whimper falls from my lips as his hand wraps around the back of my neck and heat heads south of my waist.

"What if I want to go hang out with my friends? Tell them all about what I've done today."

"Oh? And what's that exactly?" he teases.

"That I lost my V-card to an insanely sexy senior."

"Insanely sexy, huh?"

"Some would say so."

"Some?"

"Ruby for one."

"There's nothing between me and Ruby, Pops."

"I know. She told me."

"So did you want to go and tell your friends all about my cock, or would you prefer to feel it again?"

"Zayn!" I squeal, swatting his shoulder playfully. "Your sister definitely doesn't want to know about your cock."

"Hmmm... I guess that decision's made then," he says, nuzzling my neck and breathing me in.

"I can't get enough of you, Pops. I'm pretty sure I've been addicted since my fifteenth birthday."

"Don't," I beg.

"Don't what? Tell you the truth?"

"If I find out you're lying, Zayn, I'll never forgive you."

"Trust me, Pops. I never wanted to walk out of that closet that day. I was so fucking hard for you."

My cheeks heat and I tear my eyes away from his.

"Don't pretend you're embarrassed. I know for a fact that you like my dirty words."

My lips part to argue but then I remember just how hot they made me feel while he was inside me and I realize that I can't.

"Hurry up and I'll be able to prove my point sooner rather than later."

"You don't need to prove anything. I remember," I admit.

"Hmmm, me too."

Zayn bites down on his bottom lip as his eyes track down my body, turning my temperature up a notch instantly.

"You're going to ruin me, aren't you?" I shove down the feelings that that word threatens to drag up. This has nothing to do with that asshole, and the only ruining Zayn is going to do is going to be very different from his threats.

"Nah, baby. I'm going to fucking consume you."

"Oh God."

"Hurry up." He swats my ass before dropping down onto the end of my bed and resting back on his elbows, his eyes locked on me.

"Okay, I'm good. Let's go."

"Finally." I watch as he reaches down and rearranges himself in his sweats before standing, although his rearrangement didn't do much to cover his hard-on.

"Issue?" I ask, quirking a brow at him.

"Yeah, I'm in a room alone with you," he says it like it should be obvious. "Don't tell me that if I were to push my hand into your panties right now that you wouldn't be wet."

I shrug, fighting the smile threatening to spread across my lips.

"I thought we were going?" I walk toward the door but am abruptly stopped when his palm slams down on the wood from behind me before I get the chance to open it.

His lips brush my ear, his breath tickling down my neck as his palm skims down my spine before his fingers disappear under the waistband of my pants.

"Zayn," I gasp.

"I need the answer, Pops." His fingers part me before one digit pushes inside me. He groans as if he's in pain.

"Glad you know now? Did it help your little issue?" I ask, looking over my shoulder at his pained expression.

"I should bend you over right here and fuck that smart mouth right out of you."

Fuck, how is it he's even hotter when he talks to me like that?

"You could. Or you could wait until we're locked back in your room with no chance of interruptions."

"Let's go." He takes my bag from my hand before lacing his fingers through mine and all but drags me from the room.

I shout a bye to my mom, but I don't hear her say anything in return. I hate that I feel guilty about leaving my brothers and sister with them, but I can't help it. I should feel confident that their mother is going to look after them like she should, but I don't.

Zayn throws my bag in his trunk before holding the passenger door open for me.

"Ah, he can be a gentleman."

"What's that saying? Gentleman in the street, freak between the sheets."

"Oh my God, you're insufferable."

"You love it." He leans in and steals a quick kiss before closing the door on me and jogging around to the driver's side.

"What do you want for dinner?"

"Uh..." I hesitate, thrown off by his sudden subject change. I really thought he was going to race home and feast on me.

He glances over after backing out of my driveway and I can only assume he can read my thoughts because he says, "Oh, don't worry, that will happen after."

"Oookay. So... Chinese?"

"Chinese it is."

We swing by a takeout place and pick up dinner before Zayn continues driving in the opposite direction to his house.

"Head Point?" I ask when he pulls up into the deserted cliff edge parking lot. "Isn't this where kids come to hook up?"

"You haven't been here before?" he asks, pulling a box of noodles from the bag and passing them over to me.

"Do I need to remind you that I live a very different life than the football god and the cheer sluts he usually spends time with?"

"I love that you're not them. It's refreshing."

"So how many of them have you spent time with up here?"

"The team? I don't swing that way, baby." He winks, flashing me a wicked smile.

"Nice try. You know that's not what I meant."

"A couple," he mutters before stuffing a load of noodles into his mouth.

"Well, I guess that's better than the entire squad."

"Hey," he mumbles around his dinner. "I'm not that bad."

"Oh really?"

"Hell yeah," he says after swallowing. "Savage used to be way worse than me."

"And look at him now," I say with a laugh.

"Yep, pussy whipped motherfucker."

"Is it so bad?" I ask, finally starting to dig in.

"Nah, they all make it look pretty fucking awesome, if I'm honest. I've never seen any of them happier."

"That's nice. Jake deserves it after everything."

"They all do. None of them have had it easy."

"Being a kid is tough, huh?"

"You can say that again."

"Says the boy in the huge house with all the money and one of the kings of Rosewood High?" I tease, knowing that he has his own issues beneath how his life might look.

"Or the boy who's been in love with his sister's best friend for like, forever, and not able to do anything about it?"

I damn near choke on my noodles as his words register.

"I mean, you know what I mean. I wanted a repeat of that kiss for a long time," he says in a rush, trying to cover up his previous words.

"Right. And here I was thinking you hated me."

"Never, Pops. I just hated how much of a fucking tease you were. Always at the house wearing short skirts, flashing about everything I couldn't have."

"Now I know you're lying. You never looked at me twice."

"That's what you thought."

Zayn relaxes back, clearly happy that I don't say anything about his accidental admission, not that I think he really meant it. He turns on the radio and the soft sound of some singer I've never heard of fills the small space around us.

"This is nice," I say, looking out over the horizon where the sun is starting to descend, turning the ocean a gorgeous orange color.

"It's not just for making out up here, you know."

"Oh really. I'm disappointed. I was hoping to tick off make-out session with a Rosewood Bear at Head Point off my bucket list."

"Oh? Well, now when you put it like that, I'm sure something could be arranged."

22

ZAYN

"I like seeing you like this," I say, watching Poppy where she's resting back in the passenger seat with her feet up on the dash and a small smile playing on her face.

"What's *this* exactly?" she asks, turning to me, a line forming between her brows.

"Relaxed."

She sighs, looking back out to the ocean. "It doesn't happen all that often and I already feel guilty about it."

"Stop," I say, reaching over the center console and lacing her fingers with mine. "It's okay to forget it all for a few minutes."

"But what if Mom doesn't feed them? What if they stay up too late?"

Reaching over, I lift her from her seat and settle her so she's straddling my lap.

"I love how much you care, but they'll be okay. Your mom has cooked, they have food. And if they go to bed too late, does it really matter? They'll be a bit tired tomorrow and probably have an early night to make up for it.

"They're good kids, Pops. You're an amazing sister. It's okay to have a night off."

"But—"

I press my lips to hers to cut off her words.

She smiles at me but lifts her hand and tugs my arm down.

"Harley is going to hate me when she finds out I've been going behind her back."

"So tell her."

"And Jake?"

"Yeah, we can tell him too."

"You're serious enough about this to tell Jake and risk the consequences?"

"What's he really going to do? Try to give me a black eye and a couple of broken ribs? I've handled worse, I'm sure I'll cope."

Her lips twist as she thinks.

"Talk to me, Pops. Tell me what's going on in that head of yours."

"Can we… can we deal with Preston first?" She wants to say more but slams her lips shut, stopping her from saying it.

"Of course, if that's what you want. What else?"

"I'm just worried…"

"Worried about…"

"That once all this is over and he's no longer a threat, that you won't want me. That this is all just a game."

"You need to stop thinking like that. None of this is a game, Poppy. I want this," I say, cupping her face in my hands and rubbing her cheeks with my thumbs.

"I want you. I've wanted you for a long time. You're not just my little sister's best friend. To me, you're so much more than that."

"Zayn," she breathes, tilting her head to the side.

"Whatever you want to do, just tell me. I'll follow your lead. If you want me to be your dirty little secret, then I'm happy to be. If you want to stand on the school roof and shout it for everyone to hear, then I'll stand right beside you."

Her eyes flood with tears at my words.

"And here I was thinking you're an asshole."

"Oh, baby. I'm still that. You just bring out my softer side."

Bringing her face closer to mine, I brush my lips against hers.

"Now, tell me. Are you ready for your first make-out session with a Rosewood Bear at Head Point?"

"So ready."

"Good, me too."

Dropping my hands, I wrap them around her hips and pull her closer until the heat of her core is right over my cock and her breasts brush against my chest, making my hold on her tighten as her tongue pushes past my lips to find mine.

We make-out for hours as the sun descends around us.

By some miracle, no other cars join us but that doesn't mean they won't.

"Zayn," she moans, kissing across my rough jaw and down onto my neck as her hips grind down on me.

"You gonna come, baby?"

"Hmmm," she groans.

"Sit back," I instruct and she does so without questioning me.

With a little space between us, I can just about push my hand inside her pants.

I find her wet and ready for me, and in record time, she's coming on my fingers.

"Better?" I ask when she sags against me, an exhausted mess.

"You could say that."

"We should head back before the others do."

I lift her back into her seat and start the engine.

"But..." She glances down at my crotch where my cock is trying to punch through the fabric of my sweats. "Don't you want..." Her face drops as if I'm refusing her advances.

"More than I could explain. But we're on borrowed time here. Someone else will pull up and I don't want anyone seeing anything of you they shouldn't."

"O-okay."

"You can make it up to me once we're home."

Her smile knocks me for six when I look over at her. How the fuck did she agree to this? I don't deserve her, that's for fucking sure.

Thankfully, the driveway is still empty when we pull up so we're able to grab some drinks and lock ourselves in my bedroom without being caught.

We might have been lucky tonight, but I know that time's not on our side. There's no way we're going to be able to sneak around with Harley's room right down the hallway. Tonight is going to have to be a one-off. Somehow, I'm going to have to trust that Poppy is going to be safe without me and allow her to go home.

My fingers twitch to reach out to some of my old friends from Harrow Creek to come and deal with Preston once and for all, but something tells me that she'd never forgive me if I were to do something like that. I have to follow through on my promise to allow her to do it her way. As much as it pains me. Putting a bullet through the motherfucker's head is too tempting.

"Here, wear this," I say after rummaging through the closet.

"What is… oh, really?" she asks nervously, and when I look up, I find her staring at the red fabric in disbelief.

"Yes, really." I walk up to her and grip on to the bottom of her hoodie, pulling it up and over her head. Her bra goes too, revealing her pert, rosy pink nipples to me.

"Zayn?" she asks, as I stare down at her body.

"I changed my mind." I pull my jersey away and drop my lips to her breasts.

"I'm not here to be your plaything," she snaps but I know she's teasing. Something tells me that she'd be more than happy to comply. "Give me that." She reaches forward to where I pulled my jersey behind me and tugs it from my hand and over her head.

I take a step back and look at her. I can't even complain that she's covered up her tits because she's standing before me wearing my fucking number. I shake my head, as if I can't believe I'm actually seeing it.

My cock swells at the sight.

Mine. All fucking mine.

"Do you have any idea how hot you look right now?"

"Me?" she asks, pointing at herself in disbelief, but she's got a naughty glint in her eye that makes my temperature increase a few more degrees.

"Yeah, you."

She takes a few steps back. "You want me to stay like this?"

"Yup. You're mine now." As I attempt to close the distance between us, she steps back once more. The tension crackles between us as she teases me.

"So you wouldn't want me to remove these?" she asks, her hands going to her waistband.

"Hell yeah." I watch with a smirk as she kicks her pants from her legs.

"And what about these?" she asks, hooking her thumb in her black lace panties. "Would you want me in *just* your number, Hunter?"

My mouth goes dry at that thought alone. The sight of her long legs sticking out the bottom is fucking incredible but knowing her perfect little pussy is beneath, bare for the taking. Fuck.

"Every fucking day, Pops. Take them off."

"While you're fully dressed? I don't think so," she sasses, dropping her eyes down my still fully clothed body.

In record time, I'm standing in just my boxer briefs, her eyes feasting on my skin.

"Better?" I ask, attempting to get close to her again.

"For now." She laughs and it makes my heart constrict.

"Fuck, I can't get enough of you." I press her body up against mine and slip my tongue past her lips, desperate to feel her against me once more. My hand slips under my jersey to palm her ass and she moans into our kiss.

Without warning, she drops to the bed, her face in line with my cock.

"I think I owe you one." She winks.

"I'm not counting, Pops."

"That's a shame, because I am." Her fingers wrap around the waistband of my boxers and tug. My cock springs free, making her tongue run along her bottom lip, her eyes locked on mine.

"I'm pretty sure you couldn't look any hotter than you do right now."

"You sure about that?"

She leans forward and sucks my length into her mouth, her heat surrounds me and almost makes me lose my damn mind.

"Fuck. Yeah. Okay." I thread my hand into her hair but allow her to take control as she sucks me deeper and deeper.

I just let out my release, my heart thundering in my chest when the front door slams and feet run up the stairs.

Poppy looks up at me with wide, panicked eyes.

"It's okay, I locked the door."

Dropping my hands to her waist, I throw her up the bed. Her hand slams over her mouth as she lets out a shriek of surprise. That is until her entire body tenses as a knock on the door sounds out.

"Zayn?" Harley calls.

"Yeah."

"I've got work from your teachers."

"Leave it out there," I grunt, desperate for her to just go away.

"What are—fucking hell, are you jacking off again?" she asks, her voice higher pitched than normal.

Poppy rolls into my side, shoving her face into my chest.

"Yeah, could you knock again and pretend to be the maid coming in to polish my—"

"You're fucking sick," she screams before she runs to her room and the slam of her door makes the walls shake.

The second we know it's safe, Poppy barks out a laugh.

"Pretend to be the maid?" she manages to get out through her laughter. "Please, for the love of God, tell me that you don't have a maid, let alone one that polishes anything of yours."

"We have a cleaner, but I wouldn't let her anywhere near me with her feather duster, don't worry."

"You're a nightmare," she says, falling back down into my side and snuggling close. Her bare leg drapes over my waist and I can't help but to trail my fingertips over the smooth skin.

"What?" I ask innocently. "It got rid of her, didn't it?"

"Yeah, and probably scarred her for life."

"She'll cope. She can consider it karma for the fact she now crashes all my football parties in her slutty little dresses."

"Oh, because you haven't been torturing her for years? Did you ever think she does those things out of karma to get back at you?"

"Huh..." I think back over our childhoods and all the things I've done to torture her over the years. Poppy probably has a point. "Nah, that can't possibly be the case. I've been the most awesome big brother ever."

"Sure," she says with a laugh, tapping my chest gently.

"Maybe you just need a reminder of how awesome I am."

I roll her onto her back, settling myself between her legs and capturing her lips to cut off any argument that might have been about to fall from her lips.

We hibernate in my room all night. Harley doesn't bother knocking again but I do slip out to see Mom to reassure her that I've done all my work and got the extra Harley collected for me once she came home.

She looks at me weirdly the entire time, as if she suspects something and it makes me nervous that she's about to race up to my room. But she doesn't say anything and after a few minutes, she allows me to go back up to my girl.

"Poppy?" I whisper when I return and flick the lock once more before finding my room empty. My stomach bottoms out for a second that she's run the second I've left her alone.

I only have to wait a second before she emerges from my bathroom with a plume of steam billowing out behind her.

"You've got a bath," she states, running her eyes down the length of me.

"I do. I never use it though, so eat your heart out."

"Oh, I was thinking you could use it tonight."

A smile curls up at my lips as my brain catches up with her plan.

"You know, I was thinking that tonight was the perfect night to christen the thing." I walk toward her and gather her up in my arms.

"Shit," she gasps, running her fingertip gently down my neck. "I didn't realize I left a mark."

A smile plays on my lips.

"What?"

"That explains why Mom looked at me suspiciously."

"She knows?"

"I doubt that. She probably just thinks I snuck someone in this afternoon."

"Which you did," she helpfully points out.

"Hmm... so I did. She's not going anywhere either."

23

POPPY

I wake with a happy smile on my face as I open my eyes and find I'm laid on Zayn's naked chest and with his arm protectively wrapped around my waist.

I have no idea if he's awake or not but I can't help running my fingertip around the lines of his stomach that the sheets reveal.

Each time I make contact, his muscles bunch and I smile.

"Hmm... I could get used to this," he says into my hair before dropping a kiss to the top of my head.

The move takes me back to relaxing in the bath with him last night. There was no point where he didn't have some kind of contact with me and as time went on, I craved it more and more.

He rubbed the tension from my shoulders, gently cleaned around my sore wrists and peppered kisses up my neck while he played my body to perfection. I'm not sure I've ever felt so relaxed as I did in his arms last night.

I blow out a slow breath, this might feel incredible right now, but we both know it's not going to turn into a regular thing.

"Skip today. Stay here with me," he says, his fingers wrapping around my hair and tugging gently until I have no choice but to look up at him.

"I can't, Zayn. It won't do any good. I've just got to hold my head high and carry on."

"Are you going to tell me what he did yet?"

I shake my head. If I tell him any of the details about Preston accosting me, it'll just make him angrier than he already is, and I'd hate for him to end up hurt because he was fighting for me.

This is my fight. My problem. I refuse to allow anyone else to get in the middle. It's exactly why no one else knows just how bad things are.

"Just tell me one thing. Did he… has he touched you?"

"No." It's a half-lie, and it tastes bitter as it passes my lips, but I know I can't tell him the truth. He's barely holding it together as it is where Preston is concerned. I can't do that to him. "I should get ready for school."

I push from him and swing my legs over the bed.

"Wait," he says, his hand wrapping around my wrist, preventing me from standing. "I'm not letting you out of this bed until I feel you coming around my cock."

His lips trail down my spine, sending goose bumps racing across my skin.

"Well, if I have to," I concede and fall back onto the mattress when he encourages me to do so.

After a short argument that I ultimately lost, Zayn drives me to school once I've sent a message to Harley and Ruby to let them know that I'd make my own way.

That hardly ever happens, so I know for a fact that they're going to have questions for me the second I step foot on Rosewood High soil.

We waited until everyone else had left the house. I thought it was just so we wouldn't get caught but Zayn pointed out the moment that we were in the car that it was mostly because he didn't want me in school and anywhere near Preston for a second longer than necessary.

I swooned, hard. But no matter how protective he is about me, I think we both know that it's not going to stop him. If Preston wants to get to me, then he will.

The parking lot is almost empty of students by the time we arrive seeing as the bell for first period has already rung.

"If I get detention then it's all your fault."

"You're hardly late. Come here." He leans over the console and crashes his lips to mine.

"I will be if you continue doing this," I mumble against his lips.

"I'll miss you."

I can't help but laugh at him.

"What?"

"Nothing, just wondering where bad-boy Hunter has gone, is all." I wink at him and reach down for my bag.

"Oh don't worry, baby. He's still here. I might even unleash him on you later." That promise has more desire than probably necessary coiling around my lower stomach. "Last chance to skip with me. Empty house..."

"I can't, but I really appreciate the offer."

"I'll pick you up later, yeah?"

I nod, thinking of the place he told me to meet him after school to give us less of a chance of being spotted.

"Okay, now go. Your cleaning lady might be waiting."

He laughs as I climb from the car, close the door behind me and make my way to the building.

The closer I get, the harder my heart beats. I look around, praying that no one is watching us and I'm almost at the doors when movement behind a tree off to my right catches my eye.

My footsteps falter as I keep my eyes on whoever is clearly hiding.

I take one step up to the building when he emerges. My entire body turns to ice at the look in his eyes. His warning is even more stark than normal.

"You're done," he mouths. Fear explodes within me, and I rush to get into the building to be surrounded by other students.

"Where the hell have you been?" Ruby asks the second I drop into my seat beside her.

"Sorry, family shit," I mutter, refusing to look at her, knowing that she'll be able to read my lie.

She studies me as I pull my books out and flip my textbook to the page the teacher has written on the board, ready to go.

"Family shit, huh?" Before I can respond, her finger tucks into the neck of my hoodie and she pulls it away from my skin. "Feel like telling me the truth this time?"

"Fuck, Rubes."

"Little morning hook up, I like it." She winks and I groan.

"Can we not, please?"

"Not what? Talk about how a certain player is rocking your world in the back of his truck?"

"Yeah that," I mutter as the classroom door opens and Preston strolls in like he's not almost ten minutes late. Our teacher doesn't so much as look up at him. But then I guess that's the kind of thing you expect when your father pretty much owns his ass. It's a harsh reminder as to why I'm not sitting in Hartmann's office right now explaining everything that Preston has done.

Lowering my eyes before he spots me looking at him, I stare at the desk in front of me, praying that all of this will just come to an end without anyone getting hurt sometime soon. Sadly, I can't see how that's going to happen. He's not just going to give up now. Senior year, and what he thinks is rightfully his team, is almost in touching distance.

Thankfully, that's the last time I'm forced to be in the same room as him. He was supposed to be in my class before lunch, but his chair was tauntingly vacant. It has me on high alert, expecting something to happen that would drag me from the room and right into his hands.

The interruption I'm expecting happens almost twenty minutes before the end of my final class. I was beginning to think that I was going to escape and be able to run to Zayn's car and to safety very soon. But the second the classroom door opens and Principal Hartmann steps into the room, my heart falls into the pit of my stomach.

I don't know how I know that it's got something to do with me, or that it's my name that's about to fall from his lips, but I do.

"I'm so sorry to interrupt," he says to our teacher. "Miss Poore, could you please come with me?"

Harley shoots me a concerned look from the other side of the room. I force a smile onto my face and try to play down the panic that's beginning to rise within me.

As predicted, she threw question after question at me about my absence this morning, along with my refusal to hang out last night. I used Mom as an excuse, but I think, despite her being a disaster parent, that my excuse is starting to run out of steam. The time to come clean is coming, before they dig and find everything out themselves.

I collect up my stuff and follow Hartmann out of the room and all the way to his office. He doesn't say a word, which in itself is concerning. He always has something to say.

When I step into his office, I'm greeted by two police officers and a woman in a suit.

"Poppy, please take a seat."

I do as I'm told, but mainly because I'm so confused, my brain too busy trying to figure out what's happening to consider defying him.

"Poppy," he breathes, as if he's using the time to find his next words.

A million and one thoughts run through my mind about why I could have been dragged in here. I've seen all the films, usually it's when the girl gets told her entire family was killed in a car crash and her life is about to change forever.

My breathing starts to increase as I stare at Hartmann, wishing he'd just spit it out.

"I'm sorry to have to tell you but your home was raided this morning and your parents have been arrested for possession of illegal substances."

"Oh my God," I sigh, falling back into the chair, my hand coming up to cover my racing heart. "Everyone is alive? The kids?"

"Y-yeah. Everyone is alive," he confirms, looking from me and to the woman behind me.

"Good. That's g-good," I stutter, trying to process what he did actually tell me now that I know I'm not about to attend five funerals as an orphan.

"Hey, sweetie. I'm Bea, I'm a social worker, and I've been assigned to you and your siblings throughout all of this."

"Hi," I say shakily. She's got perfectly straight blonde hair and light blue eyes, so light that I almost think they could be fake.

"I know this must have come as a shock."

I nod, although really, is it? Mom and Dad have been doing all sorts in our house for years. The smell of weed that permeates the air most days isn't the half of it. I guess the reality is, that this was going to happen eventually.

"Where are my brothers and sister?"

"Cooper is with my colleague, she's fantastic with babies, he's being well looked after. I was hoping that maybe you could come with me to pick Austin and Sofia up from school. It'll be a little less scary if they see a familiar face."

"Yes, yes, anything. What's going to happen to us?"

"Well," she says, her eyes still holding mine as a sadness washes through them. This must be the part of her job she hates more than any other. "We're going to need to find you all a temporary place to stay while the investigation is carried out. Then depending on what is found, you may be able to return home." She puts extra emphasis on the may, but it's pointless, I already know the outcome of this. "Or we're going to need to find the four of you a more permanent place to live."

I nod, accepting her words. They might not have just told me that everyone died in a car crash but even still, my world has just been flipped upside down.

"We're not going to be going home," I mutter sadly.

"What makes you say that?"

A bitter laugh falls from my lips. "They're guilty. Let's not talk with false hope. They're both addicts and shit parents." I slump down in the chair, suddenly feeling totally exhausted.

"Oh, okay. Well..." She looks to Principal Hartmann and then the two officers who are still standing exactly where they were when I walked in. "Shall we go and get Austin and Sofia? It will give us time to have a chat about what's to come."

What I really want to do is run. Run as fast as I can from this office, from this school, from the town and just make it all go away. But I can't. Just like before, my priority right now needs to be those three helpless kids who've just had their parents ripped from them, no matter how shit they were, I wouldn't wish that on anyone, which is why I've kept my mouth shut all this time.

"My car is in the parking lot. Is there anything you need to grab before we go?"

"Y-yes, I've got some books in my locker I need."

"Okay." She nods, pushing to stand and then holding her hand out for Hartmann.

"Poppy, take the time you need. We'll be here for you when you're ready to return."

"Assuming I'm not shipped halfway across the state?" I mutter, the reality of what's possibly about to happen slamming into me. This could be my last day at Rosewood High. It could be my last day with Harley and Ruby, with everything I've ever known.

Tears burn my eyes as Bea follows me toward my locker. I empty it out because, why shouldn't I? I may never see it again.

With a loud sigh, I push open the main entrance doors and make my way toward the Prius I'm directed to.

After dumping my bags in the trunk, I fall into her passenger seat.

"This isn't the end, Poppy. You could very well be back here in a few days and be able to return to some kind of normal life."

"Really? How many kids in this situation have done that before?"

She pales.

"Exactly."

"Before we start looking at other options. Do you have any family who might be able to help you all out temporarily?"

I think of Mom's sister, Jake's mom, and curl my lip up in disgust. Talk about out of the frying pan and into the fire. She fucked off sometime around Thanksgiving and we haven't seen or heard from her since. Something that I know Jake is more than happy about.

We've got no grandparents, or at least not any that would be interested. Dad's parents are both alive but they haven't visited us before so I can't imagine they'd jump at the chance of taking us all in.

"Dad has a sister. She lives in Maddison County. We see her a couple of times a year, she always brings us gifts. But her and Mom have never really gotten along, so it's kind of strained at best."

"Okay, do you think she'd help? I'd really rather not put you all into the system. This could be a very temporary thing."

"Bea," I sigh. "I appreciate your positivity. But please, can we cut the bullshit. This sucks. It really fucking sucks, but there is no way my parents are getting off scot-free here. They've been doing drugs and neglecting the four of us for years. Even if they do get out, you'd be stupid to allow us to return to them."

"Wow. That was... honest."

"Look," I say, keeping my eyes on the passing scenery. "I want my family together. I do. I'd love nothing more than to be a happy unit where our parents do what they're meant to and we all grow up with happy childhoods, but that is not the case. I've watched the kids miss out on so much over the years, and they deserve better."

"You've got a very mature head on your shoulders, young lady."

"Yeah, well that probably comes from basically being a mom for years. Can I just ask one thing?"

"Of course. Although I can only promise to do my best. A lot of things right now are out of our control," she says, almost as if she's sensing what I'm going to say.

"Please try to keep them together. They're family, they deserve to grow up together."

"And what about you?"

I shrug. "Do whatever, just focus on them."

"They're very lucky to have you, Poppy."

"I'd rather they had decent parents," I mutter sadly as I rest my head back and close my eyes.

Tears continue to burn my eyes, but none fall. I haven't got any for my parents. All I feel is fear for my siblings.

It's not until I see their school up ahead that it really starts to affect me. How are we supposed to tell two little kids that their parents are in prison and our lives are about to change forever?

"It'll be okay. Kids are more resilient than we expect. If they can see you being brave, they'll take strength and comfort from that."

I nod as I climb from the car when she does.

The next thirty minutes absolutely guts me. Seeing both Austin and Sofia's bottom lips tremble as we explain to them the best we can about what's going on and that, other than to go and get our stuff, we're not going to be staying at home for, well… possibly ever.

With them both huddled into my sides, we make our way out to Bea's car to go and find Cooper.

Bea's cell rings and she leaves us to get inside while she speaks to whoever is on the other end.

"Everything is going to be okay," I tell Austin and Sofia as I strap myself in and turn back to look at them.

"They're going to split us up, aren't they?" Austin asks, understanding this situation better than I hoped he would.

"I don't know, bud," I answer honestly. It's the best I can do for them right now. "They'll do everything they can not to let it happen."

Sofia remains deathly quiet although the sound of her shaky breaths fill the car where she's trying not to cry. I give Austin a sad smile as he reaches over and takes her hand in his.

I turn away from them when I'm not able to be brave any longer. Watching them break, it's too much. They can do whatever they want to our parents, but I can't cope with watching my brother and sister fall apart because of them.

I wipe at my eyes, trying desperately hard to keep the tears inside so they don't have to witness me fall apart as well as each other.

"Good news," Bea says, dropping down into the driver's seat. I look at her, she's got a smile on her face but it doesn't meet her eyes, she knows just how shit this all is. "My colleague has been in contact with your aunt. She's willing to take you in."

"Really?" I ask, disbelief laced through my voice.

"Really. She's going to meet us at the office. Said she'll be about an hour and a half."

For the first time since I left Zayn's car this morning, a small trickle of hope races through me.

Auntie Trish is wonderful. There've been many times over the years when I've wondered why we couldn't have been her kids instead. She's got her life together and is married to a great guy, although the two of them never had any kids of their own, which I always found odd because she's always been fantastic with me and my siblings.

The drive to the office is short and I soon find myself running through an office when I spot Cooper in the arms of another kind looking lady.

"Coop," I squeal, pulling him into my arms and hugging him like I haven't seen him in years.

He coos at me and I'm unable to fight the tears any longer. With him still in my arms, I drop on the couch the other woman was sitting on and sob like I've wanted to do since those ominous words fell from Hartmann's lips earlier today.

I glance up at the wall, hoping to find a clock. It takes a few seconds for my watery eyes to read it but when I do, I discover that it's only been just over an hour since my life changed forever. It already feels like a lifetime ago.

Austin and Sofia come over and cuddle into my side as the two women watch us with sympathetic expressions on their faces.

"Are you guys hungry? Thirsty?"

"Yeah," Austin says, no surprise there, he's always hungry.

"Sandwiches okay?"

"That's perfect, thank you so much."

We're all silent as they both walk away chatting to themselves, probably about us and what's going to happen next.

They bring us a huge platter of food along with cans of soda and bottles of water, but as Austin and Sofia dig in, I can't bring myself to eat any of it. My stomach is in knots, I'm pretty sure I wouldn't be able to keep it down even if I did try.

The clock ticks by slowly as we wait for Auntie Trish to arrive but as the minutes pass, I begin to wonder if she was lying and isn't coming at all. That is until a panic-stricken voice fills the air around me.

"Where are they? I need to see them now."

I look up as Bea points over to us and Auntie Trish comes barreling through the door.

I stand with a sleeping Cooper against my chest as she wraps us both in her arms.

I break once more as her floral scent surrounds me.

"Oh Poppy, everything is going to be okay. You're all coming home with me and we'll sort everything out. I promise."

I pull from her embrace and look into her kind green eyes. "T-thank you."

"Oh, sweetie. I'd do anything for you all, you know that."

"I know but this is..." I trail off not really knowing what to say about it. "An extreme circumstance."

"Maybe so, but you're my family." She kisses my temple before dropping down and pulling both Austin and Sofia into her arms. "I can't believe how much you've all grown. I've got your favorite candy in the car," she whispers, and their little eyes light up for the first time since getting escorted into their principal's office earlier.

It takes a couple of hours, but eventually we are able to make our way to Auntie Trish's car and I discover that the reason she was late is because she stopped to get a car seat for Cooper. We finally manage to figure out how to get him in it securely before climbing into the front seats.

She turns to me, a somber expression on her face. "I'm so sorry, Poppy. I can't even imagine how you're feeling right now."

"I wish I could explain it. It's a weird mix of terror and relief." She reaches over and squeezes my hand in support.

"I know this is unbelievably hard. But Evan and I will do everything we can to make it as easy as possible."

"Is he okay with this?"

"Of course he is, sweetie. He loves you all as much as I do. Now, let's go and pack you all some stuff and head home."

I nod to her, rest my head back and close my eyes.

It's dark by the time we pull up to her home, but lights illuminate the front of the building. It's an impressive Victorian home painted in a soft mint green. The huge front porch is covered in bright flowers and is the kind of house that every kid draws as their dream home and almost every adult wants for their two-point-five kids.

I look back over my shoulder to find all three of them fast asleep.

"Poor things. I bet their heads are spinning."

Just as we open our doors to step out, Uncle Evan jogs down the steps and pulls Auntie Trish into his arms before turning to me.

"Poppy, I'm so sorry it got to this, but I'm so happy we can help." He wraps his arms around me in a giant bear hug and I'm hit with the scent of paint that always follows him around.

"Thank you so much. I can't tell you how much I appreciate you both doing this."

"Don't be silly. You're family. We always look after our own."

I think of all their visits, their arguments with my parents as they tried to support them to turn things around and I let out a sigh. I really need some sleep.

The three of us take a passed-out child each and carry them into the house.

We've only stayed here a couple of times in the past, but it's enough for us to already have allocated rooms.

"Cooper can stay with me," I say as Auntie Trish and Uncle Evan lower both Austin and Sofia onto the twin beds in the room they've shared in the past.

"Are you sure? I don't mind taking him to give you a break."

"If he wakes, he's going to want someone familiar."

"You're right. I'll get the travel crib from the closet."

I sit on the edge of the bed and she's back in a flash and setting up Cooper's temporary bed.

"Come and have a drink with us before you hit the hay," Auntie Trish suggests after we stand staring at a sleeping Cooper for a few minutes. Uncle Evan has already unloaded the car and the suitcase of clothes I packed for myself sits on the bed.

"Uh... sure."

After pulling the door too, I follow Auntie Trish down to their kitchen.

"What do you want? We've got most things."

"A soda would be great."

She nods and pulls one from the refrigerator.

She pours herself a small glass of wine and together we go and join Uncle Evan in the living room.

I curl myself into the corner of the sectional and sip at my soda as the tension begins to weigh me down.

"I'm sorry, Poppy. I don't know what to say to make any of this better," Auntie Trish says with a wince.

"You can't. Let's just call a spade a spade. This is all shit."

After her initial shock has passed, both her and Uncle Evan bark out a laugh.

"That, my dear, is the truest thing I've ever heard," Auntie Trish says. "Everything is going to be okay, though. After a good night's sleep, we'll get our heads together and make a plan."

"Sounds good," I lie. Nothing about this sounds good but it's the hand I've been dealt so I just need to deal.

After finishing my soda, I excuse myself to bed. I strip out of my clothes and pull on a tank and some sleep shorts and crawl into the bed.

Hugging my knees to my chest, I allow myself to break once more in private.

24

ZAYN

I sit outside school where I agreed to meet Poppy after school for almost an hour before I finally accept that she's not coming.

I call her, message her, but I get nothing back and none of my messages even get read.

Dread fills my veins that he's done something really fucking dumb. But is he really stupid enough to do something during a school day? I'd like to think not but he's proving himself to be more and more unstable as every day passes.

I might not know the details of what he's done seeing as Poppy refuses to give them up, but I see the fear getting worse and worse in her eyes.

Climbing from the car, I jog around the buildings until I can look over the field where the guys are training.

Coach is nowhere to be seen as Jake runs the drills.

My eyes dart over each team member before they fall on Preston running up and down along with the others.

I narrow my eyes at him in the hope I'll get a clue somehow that he's behind this, but I see nothing.

I slip back into the shadows before I'm caught. The last thing I need is for my suspension to be extended because I couldn't follow a couple of simple rules.

Hoping that she just had second thoughts about me getting her, I climb back into my car and head for her house.

As I pull into the driveway, I find it sitting quiet. I look in the windows as I walk around and don't see anything untoward, although I can't shift the feeling deep down that something is wrong, very wrong here.

I try both the front and back doors, but they're both locked. Retrieving the ladder that I moved a couple of nights ago, I prop it up against the wall Poppy's balcony sits on and make quick work of climbing up.

Those doors are locked and her room looks like it did when we walked out last night.

"Where the hell are you?" I mutter as I climb down the ladder and once again hide it away.

I call her again the second I get into the car, but just like every other time I've tried this afternoon, it goes straight to voicemail.

"Motherfucker."

I sit in my car, my head spinning, trying to second guess that prick and what he might do with her. Anger burns in my belly. I know I promised her that I wouldn't take matters into my own hands again, but what the hell am I supposed to do now?

A little voice in the back of my head tells me that she's probably fine, that I'm jumping off the deep end right now thinking that he's done something. But I just can't shift the ball of dread in my stomach that's growing larger by the second.

My eyes flick to the clock. Jake's session is over. They'll be heading for Aces.

I slam the car in drive before I even really think about it.

In minutes I'm pulling my car up next to Ethan's and jumping out.

"Ah look, did mommy let you out, you bad, bad boy," one of the guys announces to the entire diner as I approach the team's table.

To my surprise, I find Jake, Mason, Ethan, and Shane all sitting with the rest of the team. Jake must see my shock because without me saying anything he replies with, "The girls have gone to the mall."

"O-okay. G-great. Could we… could we have a word?"

His brows draw together but he nods, sliding from the booth. I nod over my shoulder and he follows me out, but not before I lock eyes with Preston, who's sitting at the other end of the table.

The asshole smiles at me. Actually. Fucking. Smiles.

My fists curl with my need to beat whatever he's done to my girl out of him, but I can't. Not yet. It's going to fucking happen though. I'll just be smarter about it next time.

"What's up?" Jake asks when I come to a stop by the railing that stops us from walking directly down onto the beach.

"Er…" I hesitate, lifting my hand to rub the back of my neck.

"Zayn?" Concern covers his face, pulling his brows together and forming crease lines on his forehead.

Blowing out a breath, I just go for it. I deserve the beating for touching her anyway. "Have you spoken to Poppy today?"

"Uh… no, why?"

"Shit." I scrub at my jaw. "Things with Preston are bad, Jake. Like, really fucking bad. I don't know the details but he's after her. He thinks by using her, he can get to you and then you'll hand over captaincy to him or some bullshit."

He takes a step closer, listening to every word. "Go on."

"I was supposed to pick her up after school… a favor for Harley," I tag on, hoping it might make this just a little better. "She never showed."

"She probably just decided it was better than being in a car with you. She hates you, Hunter."

"Yeah." I squirm under his stare a little. "I know. But something's not right, man. She won't answer her calls, she's not even reading her messages. Her house is silent. She's just… gone."

He's silent for a moment. "You're really worried, aren't you?"

"Yeah. And I think you need to be too. He's got a fucking screw loose, I'm telling you."

"This why you beat the shit out of him, because you found all this out?"

I don't need to say the words, he can read them on my face.

"Why didn't you tell me?"

"She didn't want me to."

"Leading me to my next question, how the fuck do you know about all of this?" he quizzes, making guilt swirl around me like an angry storm.

"I overheard Harley on the phone with her, something sounded off so I started digging, asking questions. She's refusing to do anything about it… because of you."

"Me?"

"Yeah, she knows you'll fly at him for hurting her, and she's trying to protect you."

"Jesus, fuck," he says, running his hands through his hair and resting his back against the railing.

I follow his lead, my eyes moving to the diner window and locking directly onto a set I never want to look at again.

"He's a smug motherfucker. He knows."

"We need to be careful. Poppy has refused to go to Hartmann or the police, she knows that Hellburn's dad owns this place. He'll get any misdemeanors swept under the rug. If we want to get him, we need to be smart."

"What exactly are you suggesting?" he asks, glancing at me.

"I have no fucking idea, but we're going to destroy him."

25

POPPY

I barely get a wink of sleep. I spend the whole night tossing and turning, my imagination running wild about what could happen to us now, what my future might be like. Will my aunt and uncle keep us? Or is this just a stopgap to entering the system and Christ knows what will happen after that. We've all read the horror stories from those situations.

The sun is just waking up, but the kids are still asleep.

I heard movement not so long ago, which I assume was Uncle Evan going to work, but other than that, the house is silent.

I blow out a long breath and wipe my eyes. They're so sore from crying most of the night. Now the morning is here, I need to be stronger. This isn't just about me and my ruined life, it's about the kids. I need to be strong for them. Show them that there's nothing to be afraid of.

Feeling like I need to talk to someone, to hear a familiar voice, one who always makes me feel safe, I reach for my purse.

My cell phone is dead at the bottom, so after locating my charger and plugging it in beside the bed, I power it up.

I didn't even consider everyone else when all of this was going on yesterday, but when my cell comes to life, so do a stream of missed calls and messages.

Mostly from Zayn.

Fuck. Zayn.

He would have been waiting for me after school. "Shit."

I have message after message asking if I'm okay, wanting to know where I am, if I'm safe. Guilt swamps me that I didn't even think about him yesterday. I guess it's understandable given the circumstances but still, I feel awful.

But even still, I ignore his messages for now and focus on the one I want.

Hitting call on his name, I lift my cell to my ear.

It rings a few times before his sleepy voice croaks down the line.

"Poppy?"

"Shit, I'm sorry. What time is it?" I look around the room for the answer but find no clock. Pulling my cell away from my ear for a second, I find it's not even seven a.m. yet.

"It's okay. Where the hell are you? What's going on?" he attempts to ask calmly, but I hear the fear in his voice.

"Mom and Dad got arrested."

"Fuck. Where are you?"

"With Auntie Trish. The police and social services turned up at school. Thankfully, she agreed to take us all in otherwise..." I shudder, not wanting to think about the alternative.

"Jesus, Pops." I can imagine him rubbing his hand down his face in concern. "What's their address, I'm coming to you."

"It's okay, Jake. You've got school."

"Poppy," he warns, his voice low. It might scare other kids at school, but I know him better than that. "You need me, then I'm there. Send me the address," he demands once more.

"Okay fine. But we're fine, honestly."

"I don't care. I'm coming."

Tears burn my eyes and emotion clogs my throat at his need to come and protect us. This is why I never told him about Preston. I know he'd do anything, even at the detriment to himself, to ensure my happiness and safety.

"T-thank you."

"Aw, Pops," he breathes when he hears the crack in my voice. "I'll be there as soon as I can, okay?"

"Y-yeah. I'll tell Auntie Trish you're coming."

"Everything's going to be okay. I won't have it any other way."

I hang up the phone, engulfed by the silence of the house once more, but it feels that little bit easier to breathe now that I've spoken to Jake.

Squaring my shoulders, I leave my cell on the nightstand and rummage around in my bag for some fresh clothes and head for the bathroom and one very hot shower.

Auntie Trish and I are sitting on the porch watching the kids play when the rumble of an engine slowing down in front of the house has us both looking to the driveway.

Amalie's little red sports car pulls up before both her and Jake climb out. Amalie hovers a little, whereas Jake flies at me, opening his arms and embracing me in a huge hug. The exact thing I needed.

I bury my face in his chest, breathing in his scent and allowing it to ground me.

"It's going to be okay, Popsicle," he whispers, using the nickname I hated as a kid, but right now it feels like the most normal part of my life.

After long minutes, he finally releases me, although I don't get very far because he just tucks me into his side.

"Trish, it's good to see you," he says, nodding at my aunt. They've met a few times seeing as Jake has lived with us for years, but they've never really spent any time together seeing as they're not related.

"You too, Jake. And who is this young lady?"

"This is my girl, Amalie. Brit," he says, gesturing for her to join us. "This is Trish, Pops' aunt."

"Hey, it's so nice to meet you."

"Oh, you snagged a British, girl. Good on you, Jake." Trish laughs. "Can I get you all drinks? Coffee?"

"Please."

"We brought pastries," Amalie says, lifting a bag I hadn't noticed she was carrying. "We weren't sure if…" She trails off.

"I'll grab some plates."

As we sit down, Austin and Sofia finally notice that we have company and come running over to see Jake. In seconds they're each sitting on one of his knees and staring up at him like he hung the moon in the sky before driving over here.

We focus on the kids, laughing along with them, and ignoring the elephant in the room.

Auntie Trish brings out a tray full of coffee and plates for Amalie's pastries before telling us that she's going to leave us to it for a bit.

"Austin, Sofia, I'm going to make cookies, would you like to help?"

"Chocolate chip?" Sofia asks, jumping off Jake and following Auntie Trish.

"Can I lick the bowl?" Austin asks, trailing behind as if Auntie Trish is the Pied Piper.

"They're so cute," Amalie says, watching them disappear through the door.

"They're good kids. They don't deserve any of this." I sigh, staring down at Cooper who's happily sitting in his bouncer.

"What are you going to do?" Jake asks, sitting forward and resting his elbows on his knees.

"I would say wait and see if they get charged, but let's be honest, we both know they're guilty. Only an idiot would let them off."

"I know. Fuck," Jake barks, pushing to his feet and pacing back and forth across the porch.

Amalie reaches over and squeezes my hand in support.

"You can't stay here, Pops. You belong in Rosewood."

"I might not have a choice, Jake. I need to do what's best for them." I tilt my chin to the kitchen.

"I'll be eighteen in a few months, maybe Auntie Trish could look after them until—"

"We can," Jake shouts. "We'll take custody of them. We're old enough. Amalie has money, we've got a home."

"Jake, no. You're talking crazy. You can't do that."

"Why not? If it means you all stay together. If I get to keep the little family I have."

My heart swells for him. Standing before him, I wait for him to get to me and reach out for his hand to make him stop.

"As much as I appreciate everything you're saying. I can't let you do that. You need to be thinking about your future, college, Amalie. You don't need to be burdening yourself with my family."

"I just—"

"I know, Jake. Trust me, I know. These kids have been like my own for years. I know you're just as protective of all of us. But this isn't your fight. It's mine."

"Ours," he says, his lips twitching up into a smile.

He pulls me into his arms once more. I close my eyes for a beat, accepting his support. When I pull them open again, I find Auntie Trish watching us in the window with a smile on her face.

"Come on, the coffee is getting cold."

We walk back over to join Amalie, who's been silently watching the exchange between us.

"How'd the cops find out?" Jake asks after a few silent seconds.

"Who knows. It was going to happen sooner or later. Since Cooper was born. It's just been a disaster."

"I'm so sorry I haven't been there."

"None of this is your fault. You've been starting your life. As you should have been. They treated you like shit for years, I never expected you to hang around and play happy families once you finally got out."

"I shouldn't have just left you there."

"I'm a big girl, Jake. I can look after myself."

Something passes across his face but he tucks it away before I get a read on it.

"What?"

"Nothing. It's nothing."

I narrow my eyes at him, but he keeps his lips sealed.

Jake and Amalie end up staying almost all day. We all play in the yard with the kids and just try to be as normal as possible.

They excuse themselves when the police turn up, along with Bea, to talk to both me and Auntie Trish.

I'm hardly surprised that the police want to question me, I did openly admit that my parents were both guilty in Hartmann's office. A story that I'm more than happy to stick to. This might be hell right now with our futures up in the air but life in that house with them wasn't exactly heaven. I can't help but wonder if we're better off without them, whatever might happen to us.

Auntie Trish assures Bea that we have a home here for as long as we need it and she finally leaves happy that we're all happy and safe with a promise to be back in a few days once there's more news about our parents.

Apparently, there's a high chance they'll be bailed before a trial but we're not going to be allowed to see them or even have contact with them. No issue for me with that, but I know that Sofia especially doesn't really understand all of this and is already wondering where her parents are. Austin, however, just seems to be taking everything in his stride.

"Evan is out at his monthly poker game tonight. I wondered if you were interested in a girly night once the kids are in bed?" Auntie Trish asks me after sending Austin and Sofia to run a bath and find their pajamas.

She made them both their favorite dinner, but we have yet to eat.

"We could order whatever you want. Have cocktails, virgin of course, I'm not sure supplying you with alcohol while the social workers are sniffing around is a good idea," she says with a laugh and a wink. "Watch some chick flicks. Talk..." The way she says talk makes my heart drop. What does she need to tell me?

"Yeah, that sounds great."

Together we go through the kids' usual nighttime routine, or at least the one I try to give them before Uncle Evan excuses himself for his night out and gives Auntie Trish a kiss to her temple.

They're such a sweet couple and so good with the kids that I can't help wondering once again why they don't have any of their own.

"So what's it going to be. Pizza? Chinese? Thai?"

"Chinese," I say without a second thought. I might have only had some with Zayn two days ago, but I could eat it every night given the chance.

"Okay, here," she says, passing her cell over with a menu open. "Order whatever you like. I'm just going to change."

"But... how much..."

"Whatever you want, Poppy. No expense spared." With a soft smile, she disappears down to her room.

I order all my favorites before placing her cell on the counter and following her lead, replacing my jeans with a pair of sweats and a tank.

"Okay, here you go." Auntie Trish turns to me with a fancy looking cocktail in her hand when I return. "Margarita sans the good stuff."

"This looks awesome. You didn't need to go to all this effort though."

"Are you kidding. I usually spend poker nights alone watching crap TV. I'm thrilled to have a friend." She pulls me into her arms and kisses the top of my head.

We get ourselves comfortable on the couch as Auntie Trish pulls up Netflix and starts scrolling.

"Who do you fancy? We'll binge watch him."

I admit to my Zac Efron addiction and she immediately pulls up *High School Musical*.

"Wow, I haven't watched this in forever."

"So you like a blast from the past?"

"Anything a little newer with him a little... older?"

"Sure thing."

She flicks through until we agree on one I haven't seen before. We're only about twenty minutes in when the Chinese food arrives and we hit pause.

We lay all the containers out on the coffee table and sit crossed-legged on the floor.

"What's up, Pops?" Auntie Trish asks when she catches me looking at her.

"I just… I've never done this with my mom. It's nice. Normal."

"Aw, Poppy." She gives me a sad smile. "I'm so sorry."

"It is what it is." I shrug.

"I always wanted to do more. But it was never my place. Your mom and I, we've never got along. When my brother announced they were together, I was less than impressed. Crap, sorry. You probably don't want to hear this," she says, chastising herself.

"No, no. Carry on. I've lived with them all my life, but I don't even feel like I know them, if that makes any sense."

"It does. We've all known each other since school. Your dad and your aunt, Kate, were older whereas your mom and I were in the same year."

"Were they together in school?"

"No, your mom… she had another boyfriend in high school."

I nod, wondering why she seems to panic at that.

"This is so good," I say, focusing back down at the food in the hope of breaking the sudden tension.

"Poppy, I really mean it when I say that you can all stay here for as long as you need to. You know that, right?"

"I do. But I don't expect you to keep us forever. You've got your own life to get on with. The second I'm eighteen, I can get custody and get out of your hair."

"Is that your plan?"

"Yeah, I guess. I refuse to let them go into the system. So I guess it's down to me."

"Poppy," she says on a sigh and I know what's coming next.

"Do you think it's going to be that easy?"

"No, not at all." A sad laugh falls from my lips. "Nothing about any of this is easy. But I've been taking care of them for years. I'm more than capable."

"I know you are. I'm not doubting that. I just think that you need to be thinking about your future as well as theirs."

"It's fine. I'll get a job, find somewhere to live. I'm sure I'll figure it out."

"But what about college? What about a boyfriend, parties, and all the things you should be worrying about as you head into your senior year?"

"I don't feel like I've missed out this far." An image of hiding out with Zayn pops into my head and I remember just how incredible it had felt to have no responsibilities and just be a teenager for one night. I lock it down before I allow it to consume me.

That's gone. All of that is over.

Zayn's messages still taunt me on my cell. I know I need to reply, that he's worried about me. But right now, I don't have it in me to reach out. I just need to focus on my family, on our future.

"Evan and I have tried for almost fifteen years to have kids, Poppy," she says from out of nowhere. "We've done IVF, even a couple of adoption attempts, but it just doesn't seem to happen for us. This is why. If we'd had our own kids, then we wouldn't have been able to help like we can now."

"You really believe that?" I ask with a heavy heart. They'd have been the most incredible parents, and I hate that's been taken away from them.

"I believe that everything happens for a reason, yes. Poppy, I will do everything and anything I can for you and those three. I'd have done it for any child I was lucky enough to care for, but you're my family. There's no way I, or Evan, could turn any of you away."

Tears sting my eyes and my vision blurs.

"But your life, your job. We can't expect you to give everything up to suddenly become parents overnight because our own are useless."

"Poppy, it would be my honor to do all those things. I only work part-time at the college, they'll be flexible, I've no doubt. The schools around here are incredible. The neighborhood is fantastic. You could all be very happy here."

I look around the room we're sitting in. It's so homely, cozy. I know that what she's saying is true. But could I just up and leave Rosewood that easily?

"What about school?"

"I've got some contacts at Royal Maddison Prep. We could see about getting you in there."

"No, no. That's too much."

"Okay, well there are other options too. I just want you all to be happy, Poppy."

"I know. And I appreciate it more than you could know."

"Let's put the movie back on and forget about reality for a few hours. It'll still be there in the morning."

I nod, because sadly she's right.

26

ZAYN

"Harley, Zayn," Mom bellows up the stairs. "You've got guests."

I'm up off the bed and flying down the stairs in record time. But when I get to the bottom, I don't find who I was hoping for.

"Hey," I say, looking between Jake and Amalie.

"Have you seen her?" Harley asks the second she rounds the corner and finds them waiting.

"Yeah."

"Come on," I say, directing everyone down to my den.

Everyone drops down onto the couches, but unable to sit still, I pace back and forth. Jake's eyes follow my every move. I know he's suspicious. Hell, I would be too if someone came to me about Harley or Letty and said the things I did. He suspects there's more to this than I admitted to. But where there may have been at the time, now I have no idea.

Poppy has been gone a day, I've sent her numerous messages and called almost every hour, but despite some of my messages being read, she's not responded.

"Her parents have been arrested for possession of drugs."

"What?" Harley shrieks, making me wonder just how well Poppy had covered all this up.

"Fucking hell. Where are they all?"

"With their aunt. She's good, they're safe," he says, pinning me with a look.

"That's good."

"What's going to happen? They'll get off, right?" Harley asks.

"No, I don't think so."

"But... shit. They're druggies? No wonder she stopped inviting me over. Jesus, it's like we've just fallen back into Harrow Creek," Harley mutters, making Amalie's brows pull together. I'm not surprised she's never heard of the place. I wish I hadn't.

"They're coming back though, right?"

"Honestly, I don't think so. Trish said they can stay as long as they need to. They've got no reason to come back without their parents."

"Uh uh, no way. This isn't happening." The three of us watch as Harley marches from the room like a woman on a mission.

"Where's she going?" Jake asks.

"No idea. I gave up trying to predict her years ago."

I fall down onto the couch and tip my head back, trying to process everything Jake's just said.

"What about..."

"Preston?"

"I've got guys watching him."

I raise a brow and Amalie laughs. "He thinks he's suddenly some gangster boss or something."

"Ignore her. If I start sniffing around, he's going to get suspicious. Ethan is going to try to talk to him, Mason too. See if they can sweeten him up. If he's doing what you think he is then I'm going to fucking end him."

"Be sensible. We don't need you in prison too," I mutter, leaning forward and dropping my head between my shoulders.

"You got anything else you want to tell me, Hunter?"

I look up at him and swallow nervously. His eyes drill into mine.

"No." I could tell him that Poppy and I had a thing. What's the point if she's not coming back here?

"Are you coming to Justin's party?" Amalie asks, trying to break the tension.

My lips part. My first reaction is to say no, to go upstairs and wallow like a pussy. But what good is that going to do?

"Yep, let me go get changed and we can go and get fucked up."

I walk out to the sound of them talking behind me, but I don't pay any attention to the words. Now the idea has been planted, all I want to do is go and get trashed and forget all this shit.

Justin's house is smaller than mine or Ethan's where we usually party, but it's plenty big enough for the team and the squad, and the few others that decide to gate-crash.

The second we arrive, Jake and Amalie head off to the left, I guess in search of their other couples while I march straight down to the kitchen.

There are bottles and Solo cups covering every surface. Ignoring the cups, I go straight for a bottle and then in search of the guys.

I find most of them in Justin's study where the speakers are with the majority of the squad grinding up against them. I look around, thankfully not finding my sister. Although I do lock eyes with Ruby.

Her chin drops before she stumbles her way over to me, clearly having already had one too many drinks.

"Where is she? Is she okay?" she slurs as she crashes into me with her need for answers.

Placing my hands on her waist, I steady her, looking down into her blown eyes.

I lean into her so no one else can hear me. "She's okay. Her parents have been arrested. She's with her aunt."

"Arrested?" she shouts, causing a few people to look over.

"Keep your voice down, Rubes. I'm sure she doesn't want everyone knowing."

"Shit. She's coming back though, right. You're going to go and get her."

My fists clench with my need to do just that.

"I can't do that."

"Why not? She belongs here. With you."

My lips part to respond but I'm too thrown by her last two words to form any of my own.

"You know…"

"Yeah, don't worry. Your secret is safe with me."

"Shush, or it's not going to be secret that needs keeping."

Threading my fingers through hers, I pull her from the room in the hope of finding somewhere quieter to have this conversation.

Dragging her into the dining room, I kick the door closed behind us before twisting the cap off the bottle of vodka and swallowing a generous mouthful. The alcohol burns my throat but it's exactly what I need.

"What do you know?" I turn on Ruby.

"Share and I might tell you."

Rolling my eyes at her, I hand the bottle over and watch her as she takes a shot.

"So?"

"I know you've been banging her. I know you've been sneaking around. And, I know that Harley has no idea." She smiles wickedly at me. "Oh, I also know something else..." She taps her index finger to her lips teasingly. "Oh yeah, that's it. She fucking loves it!"

"Jesus. You need to stop," I snap, snatching the bottle from her when she goes to have more.

"What happened, Ruby? You used to be the sweet one then suddenly..." I wave my hand at her. "You're a mess."

"Yeah, well, that's what happens when bad boys sweep in and shatter our innocent little hearts." My chin drops at her words. I assumed it was something to do with a guy, but I didn't know for sure. "What? You don't think you're going to do the same to Poppy? Bad boys never change, Zayn. They might pretend to for a while. But they always screw you over eventually."

"Who was it?"

"Ah, ah, ah," she says, pushing from the wall and stalking toward me. "It's too late to defend my honor now, Hunter. You had your chance with me. Now you're fucking my friend so you, my friend," she says, tapping my nose. "Are off-limits. To both my body and my secrets. Now..." She takes my hand and pulls me toward the door, or attempts to, seeing as she doesn't weigh much more than a feather, she doesn't get very far. "Let's go dance, knowing that we won't end up in bed together tonight. Although," she stops, running her eyes down the length of my body. It wasn't so long ago that I might have been affected by her heated stare, but now, after everything with Poppy, my cock just isn't interested. "I have it on good authority that you've got skills."

"Yeah, no more drinks for you."

I give into her and allow her to pull me back down to the study and when she spins into my arms, I comply, because what she just said is true, nothing will happen between us.

Twisting my head to the side, I take another drink of my vodka as she grinds against me, but at no point do I offer her anymore. She needs to sober the fuck up before some other asshole decides they want to take advantage of her.

"Hey, I wondered when you were going to show," a sickly-sweet voice says as a warm hand brushes across my back before stopping on my bicep.

Ripping my eyes from Ruby, I find Laurie smiling at me seductively.

"Sorry, he's taken," Ruby slurs at her. "Go find yourself another player for the night."

"It didn't stop you from sharing before."

Regret fills me from that night. I shouldn't have touched Ruby, but I'm starting to learn that I don't have all that much restraint when it comes to my sister's friends, but I really shouldn't have gone near Laurie. She's a stage five clinger.

Laurie physically pushes herself between me and Ruby.

"Oh look, he's dancing with me now."

"Fucking hell," I mutter, finishing off my bottle in just a couple of huge swallows.

Laurie starts moving, her talons digging into the skin of my shoulders and her overbearing perfume filling my nose.

Groaning, I roll over onto my back but find my arm is trapped under something... fuck.

I sit bolt upright, rolling the person who was like a dead weight pinning me to the bed straight off the other side.

"Ow, what the fuck?" a croaky voice barks before a familiar head pokes above the side of the mattress.

"Ruby?" I ask, rubbing my eyes, trying to get them to focus while I attempt to remember anything about getting home last night.

Glancing down at myself, I relax a little when I find I'm fully dressed.

"Well, that wasn't exactly the thank you I was expecting for getting you home in one piece and away from Laurie's grasp."

"Uh... what... um..."

"Oh, calm down," she says, climbing back onto the bed. "Nothing happened."

"Okay, so... why are you here exactly?"

"I took your advice and sobered up, while you got shit-faced. Then before you did something really fucking stupid like suck Laurie's face off, or worse, I made you leave."

"Okay, that's... g-good. But still, why are you here?"

"I wasn't intending to stay, I had a car outside waiting to take me home but you dragged me down with you, tucked me into your side told me how much you missed me and other similar soppy shit—I assumed you thought I was Poppy, whatever." She waves it off like it's nothing before continuing. "You passed out and I couldn't get out, so I thought fuck it and went to sleep while you were still muttering crap."

"Right," I say, rubbing my hand down my face. "Jesus, this is a mess."

"Nothing happened, Zayn. Poppy is my best friend, I'd never."

"I know. I know. I didn't mean that." Scooting back, I rest my back against the headboard and rest my arms over my knees as the incessant pounding at my temples continues.

"You need to talk to her," she says, copying my position.

"Yeah, well… she'd need to answer her cell for that to happen."

"Jake knows where she is. Go to her."

"Her world's just been turned upside down, Rubes. The last thing she needs is me storming in and making it worse."

"Who says you'd make it worse? She might be waiting for you." She turns to look at me and raises a brow.

"Why is this so hard?"

"Nothing to do with relationships is meant to be easy, Zayn. That's why they're so much fun." She smiles but it doesn't meet her eyes.

"You want to talk about it?" I offer, seeing as she's been my sounding board this morning.

"Nah. Unlike you two, it's hopeless even thinking about it."

"Okay, well. The offer stands should you need it."

"I appreciate it." She scoots to the edge of the bed. "You mind if I…" She gestures to the bathroom.

"Fill your boots. You want me to call you an Uber to get home?" I call before she closes the door.

"That would be awesome, thanks."

Ignoring all my social media apps, I pull up the Uber one and call for a car. I don't have the energy to deal with high school gossip and drama right now, not when I've got enough of my own going on.

Ruby emerges a few minutes later, looking a lot more put together than I feel.

"Your car will be here in a few."

"Walk me out?"

Thankfully, we don't see Harley, the last thing I need with the reminder of last night's alcohol running around my system is to try to convince her that nothing happened with Ruby.

"Thank you," I say, trying to sound as sincere as possible as she makes her way down to the waiting car.

"You too, you probably stopped me from making a huge mistake last night too."

A warning to take care of herself is on the tip of my tongue, but I swallow it down. She's already got a dad to give her those kinds of warnings, I need to butt out.

I wave her off as her car speeds down the street before walking to the kitchen.

"Really?" Mom asks, looking over my shoulder to where Ruby just disappeared.

"Nothing like that. Promise."

"I should hope not." She narrows her eyes at me, and I immediately feel like a kid again.

I make myself a coffee and sit up on the stool next to her.

"You heard about Poppy?" Mom asks. She stares at me as if she's trying to read my reaction for some reason.

"Yeah, sounds awful."

She continues to study me.

"What?"

"Harley asked me to get involved to see if I can help, maybe see if there's a way for her to come back to Rosewood to finish school here."

"Right," I say, letting her words settle as I sip at my too hot coffee.

"How would you feel about that?" She pins me with another look that has me wondering if she's not really asking the question she's making out to be.

"Um..." Something flutters in my belly at the thought of her being about to get Poppy back to finish school. I have no idea if that's what she'd want. But I can't imagine she'd be too thrilled at having to start over. I know I'm not happy about it, but it's not my life that's just been thrown into a tailspin. "I guess that's up to Poppy. No harm in asking though, staying at Rosewood High would make life easier for her, I'm sure."

Her eyes bounce between mine. "Okay."

"Okay?"

She nods and looks back to her tablet that she was reading before I joined her.

"Zayn," she calls out when I'm at the door. "I left something on your dresser while you were out last night that I found in my laundry. I know it doesn't belong to me or your sisters." She quirks a brow, a small smile playing on her lips.

"Uh... okay, thanks."

I walk away wondering what the hell she's playing at, I'm even more confused when I walk into my room and discover what I missed last night—

not hard with how drunk I was—and this morning. Reaching out, I run my finger over the lace of Poppy's bra.

Looking back over my shoulder at my door, I wonder how much Mom knows. Is that why she was being weird asking me about Poppy downstairs.

I place her bra in my drawer and fall back down in the bed as both Ruby's and Mom's words from this morning swirl around my head.

27

POPPY

For some stupid reason, the first thing I did this morning was reach for my cell. Huge fucking mistake.

I'd hoped to find a message from Jake, Harley, Ruby, even another from Zayn so I knew they hadn't forgotten me already despite the fact I haven't replied to any of the previous ones yet.

The last thing I expected to find when I opened Instagram was my feed full of images of last night's party, with close-up photographs of Zayn with Laurie pressed against him.

Because looking at one image wasn't enough. I click on her profile and open each one. They're all selfies of them dancing, of their bodies pressed up against each other's, her lips pressed to his neck, his cheek, the corner of his mouth.

My stomach still turns over now as I think about it, my fists curling in the sheets beneath me. I was barely gone a few hours and he's already going after a cheer slut.

I don't know why I'm surprised. He's got a reputation after all.

I just thought, stupidly, that things were different. That he—we—were different.

Stupid, stupid, Poppy.

"Poppy, you've got a visitor," Auntie Trish calls down to my bedroom where I'm lying on the bed staring at the ceiling. I've got a million and one things I probably should be doing, but I can't focus on anything.

"Okay."

I swing my legs off the bed and pull my hair back into a messy bun. I washed it earlier and then had an afternoon nap with it wet, who knows what kind of mess it's in now.

I glance down at myself. Black sweats and an oversized gray hoodie. Yeah, I've never looked better. I roll my eyes at myself and head out assuming it's Bea or the police and I really don't give a crap how they think I look.

Auntie Trish's voice fills the air around me as I make my way toward the front door, but I don't hear another voice. So when I round the corner the last person I expect to find standing on the porch is the person who's been tormenting me all morning.

"What are you doing here?" I snap, marching over to where Zayn's standing.

"Uh… I think I'll leave you two to it," Auntie Trish announces, before spinning on her heels and walking toward me. "He's cute," she whispers in my ear as she passes.

"Hmm… shame he's a dick."

She gasps as Zayn's eyes narrow on me in confusion.

Nice fucking try, Hunter. I'm not falling for these games. I might not be in town right now but I see you and your manwhore ways.

"Pops," he whispers, the frown lines on his forehead deepening the closer I get.

"Don't. Don't Pops me. Not after what you've done."

"Me?" he asks, innocently pointing at himself.

"Do yourself a favor and knock off the act. It's not going to work on me, Hunter." I practically spit his last name.

"Oh, on last name terms are we now, Poore? And here I was coming to see how you were doing because I was concerned."

"Concerned? Oh yeah, you looked so concerned last night. Fun party, was it?"

"No, not really."

"You're such a fucking liar. I don't know what I was even thinking these past few weeks. It was a game, wasn't it? Some stupid pact with the team, see how far you can take things before you drop me from a great height."

"What the hell are you talking about?" He takes a step forward as if he's about to invite himself in.

Reaching out, I grab the door and close it slightly, shuffling forward so he has no choice but to stay out on the porch.

"I can't believe how easily I fell for it. I'm so fucking stupid. Was it *his* idea? Was that his way of ruining my life? He discovered my weakness and somehow convinced you to join in his sick and twisted games."

"Well?" I ask, throwing my arms up when he just stands gaping at me. "You win, okay. You fucking win," I scream as if the motherfucker is out there listening to this. "You ruined my life, well done. Everything's fucked. Congratulations."

Zayn's hand touching my forearm finally stops my rant.

"Pops, what are you talking about? I'm not playing any game. I've already told you that."

He takes a step toward me, his heat burning into my front through my baggy clothes.

"No, Zayn," I try to argue as he brushes his knuckles gently up my arm and wraps his hand around the back of my neck. He drops his forehead to mine and I have to really fight not to give in to the pull I feel toward him.

It's been easier to ignore while I've been here, knowing there's so much distance between us but now he's here, now his scent is filling my nose and the heat of his skin burning into mine, my resolve is slipping.

"No, Zayn. I can't do this."

"Why?"

"Why?" I ask, a bitter laugh falling from my lips. "Maybe because you spent most of last night grinding against Laurie, and that's only what the camera caught. I hate to think what happened after."

"Nothing happened with Laurie, Pops."

"Try telling her Instagram that."

"It's just photos. She was drunk. I was drunk."

"Yeah, exactly. Are you going to try to tell me you remember the night?"

"I—"

"Exactly. You have no fucking clue. I should have known you'd never change."

"But—"

"No, Zayn," I bark. "I'm not interested. In case you hadn't noticed, my life is already in crisis right now. I don't need your drama and lies on top of all of that. Now, did you come here for anything else or are you done?"

"I—"

Before he gets another word out, I take a huge step back and swing the door closed. The entire house rattles with the force of the slam.

The second it's closed and I can no longer see him, feel his touch, tears fill my eyes before spilling over.

"Poppy," he shouts, slamming his fists down on the door. "Poppy."

Sucking in some confidence, I take another step back in an attempt to stop myself from reaching back out, pulling the door open and falling into his arms.

I can't.

It's over.

My life as I knew it is over.

"No, you need to leave."

Spinning, I run full pelt to my room ready to lock myself inside and to spend the rest of the afternoon sobbing into my pillow, only I don't make it that far.

I'm stopped by a warm body before a pair of arms wrap around my shoulders.

"Shush now," Auntie Trish soothes in my ear as she holds me.

I have no idea how much time passes as I cry on her shoulder for everything that's happened in the last two days. But seeing Zayn, knowing that life is carrying on at home as if I was never there has reality slamming into me.

Rosewood is my home, it always has been. Who am I now?

I have no friends, no life, no future.

I'm just lost.

So fucking lost.

At some point she must move us because the softness of my bed hits my ass.

"I'm so sorry," I mutter, wiping at her soaked shirt.

"Poppy, it's okay. You have nothing to apologize for. I can't even begin to imagine how you're dealing with this right now."

I tuck myself back against her and she rocks me for long minutes as if I'm a kid. Which, I guess, I am despite the seriousness of the situation I'm trying to deal with right now.

"Do you want to talk about it... about him?" she asks after several long silent minutes.

Uncle Evan took the kids to the store a while ago to give them a change of scenery, so we've got the house to ourselves.

"His name is Zayn. He's my best friend's brother."

"Ohhh," she says with a knowing chuckle.

"He was very nice to look at. I'm not surprised you've fallen for his charms."

"He's not my boyfriend."

"No? He seemed pretty concerned about you, not to be yours."

"He didn't seem that concerned at a party last night. The evidence is all over social media."

"Poppy, you're a smart girl, I don't need to tell you how social media morphs things. It only shows you a small part of a story." Auntie Trish's voice holds a seriousness that only comes with experience, but then I guess that comes with the territory of being a student support advisor at MKU. I bet just a few of her issues stem straight from social media.

"I know," I mutter. "But seeing those images while I'm here." I blow out a breath. "It hurt, you know."

"I do, Poppy. I understand." She squeezes me tighter. "You want a giant mug of hot chocolate? I think I might even have some marshmallows in the back of the cupboard somewhere."

"That sounds really good."

She leaves me to sort myself out and after splashing my face with cold water, I risk a look out my bedroom window. The driveway where Zayn's truck was parked is now empty. My cell taunts me from the nightstand, but I ignore it. If there's anything on there from him then it's got the power to break me.

"I didn't think I'd miss Rosewood like I do," I admit once I'm curled up on the couch with a steaming mug of chocolate cradled in my hands. "I always thought getting away would be the best thing to happen to me, I know I didn't expect it to be with these circumstances but, I'm starting to wonder if maybe it wasn't so bad."

"I remember being exactly the same way when I was applying to out-of-state colleges. I thought getting out of Rosewood would open up the world to me. Turns out, I'm a total homebody. I never even made it to the first day. I ended up at MKU, and look how far I've gone since. I still work there."

"It's a good college. I've looked at it with my friends," I admit.

"Yeah? Do you have any idea what you want to do?"

I shake my head. "My plan was to just get away, but I'm starting to wonder if that's what I want."

"If you could go back to Rosewood now, would you?"

"Yes," I say before I've even registered that I've spoken. "I mean, I don't know. Things with Zayn are complicated, then this whole other issue with another guy. It would be easier to just run away."

"But you don't want to do that, do you?"

I shrug. "Better the devil you know, I guess." I think of Preston and a thought slams into me. "Have the police said how they discovered all this?" I ask as innocently as possible.

"I believe they were tipped off by someone. But I only overheard that when they were talking to each other."

"Of course they did."

"Poppy?"

"It's nothing. It doesn't matter." It's the truth. If my life is going to be here now, then none of it matters. I no longer have to fear Preston and his ever increasingly dangerous games. He'll need to find another way to get to Jake because he's just lost his pawn.

It makes me wonder what his game plan was with it all. If he even had one at all. Is he just that sick that what started as a plan soon turned into something much more sinister? Unless he turns up here now, he's got no leverage with Jake. If it was him who did this, he's handed all his information to the authorities instead of using it to blackmail me.

"Are you okay?" Auntie Trish asks, studying me where I'm lost in thought.

"Y-yeah." I sigh.

The next few days pass in a blur. We have more social worker visits, more police visits but nothing really changes. Aside from being told that Mom's been bailed as suspected and assured that any contact with us will land her straight back inside. Dad's still in custody, he has bigger issues than just possession it seems, but I zoned out when the officer was explaining it. They're both going away and will be until I'm old enough to live my own life. If it's five years to twenty-five years, it really makes no difference to me now. Our relationship was ruined years ago because of all this.

It's Tuesday afternoon and I'm walking back from the park with the kids after getting them out for some sun when I walk up the street to find a familiar car sitting in the driveway. I walk up beside it, telling Austin and Sofia to head inside while I bump Cooper's stroller up the steps.

"Jada, what are you doing here?" I don't mean it to come out accusatory, but it does, and I wince. "I mean, it's good to see you."

"You too, Poppy. How are you doing?"

"Oh, you know," I mutter, unstrapping Cooper and lifting him into my arms.

"I'll just go grab his bottle."

We both watch as my aunt disappears inside.

"You're a real cutie," Jada coos at Cooper. "Seems like a lifetime ago having babies this young around."

An awkward silence falls between us as Cooper giggles at Jada.

"Harley is missing you," she finally says.

"It's only been a few days."

"She's worried you're not going to come back."

"Well, I probably won't," I say on a sigh.

"Poppy," she says, her serious tone making me turn to look at her. "I know things are complicated and confusing right now, but if you want to come back and go to school, there is a place for you at my house."

My chin drops in shock.

"I know you've got a lot of things to think about right now and a lot of things are up in the air, but I'd never forgive myself if I didn't at least offer you the chance of keeping just one thing normal in your life. I know how hard starting over at a new school can be, especially on top of everything else."

"Wow," I breathe. "I really didn't see that coming."

She chuckles at me as Auntie Trish comes back.

"You want to feed him?" I offer to Jada, although I soon regret the offer when I glance at her pristine black pantsuit.

But she surprises me when her face lights up. "Yes, I'd love to. It's been so long since I held a baby."

I pass him over and she gets him settled before Auntie Trish hands over his bottle. Cooper greedily sucks it into his mouth the second Jada has it anywhere near, making her laugh.

The three of us chat about the weather and other nonsense subjects while avoiding the huge elephant that's staring at us.

I can only assume that Jada's already told Auntie Trish about the offer she just made me but neither of them bring it up.

Jada stays for another thirty minutes before announcing that she needs to get back.

She turns to me, a serious yet kind expression on her face. "Think about what I said, the offer is open should you want it. Oh and, Harley wanted me to let you know that there's a party at Ethan's Friday night and she'd love for you to come. You can stay at ours as long as you need."

"Thank you, I really appreciate it," I say, feeling totally blown away by her offer.

We wave her off before Auntie Trish goes to put Cooper down for a nap while the squeals of Austin and Sofia sound out from the house where they're playing.

"She's nice," Auntie Trish says when she finally joins me once more. "I'm glad you accepted her arrival better than her son." She laughs.

"Jada is an incredible mom. Harley, Zayn, and Letty are lucky to have her."

"She was serious with what she said. If you feel like you need to go back, then she's willing to make that happen."

"I know," I say, still trying to get my head around it.

"I'll leave you to it. You don't need to make any decisions right away, like she said, there's a lot up in the air right now. A lot of answers we don't have. Just take it one step at a time. School and the future can wait."

28

POPPY

Jada's offer and her mention of Harley wanting me to go back this weekend spun around my head all night. But no matter how much time passed, I was no closer to finding an answer.

Would it be easier to go back to Rosewood and return to school Monday as if nothing happened? Sure. But do I want to? I have no idea.

Going back means dealing with Zayn, and worse, Preston. I still have no idea if my suspicion about this all being down to him is warranted or not, but it still niggles away at me.

Uncle Evan and Auntie Trish's home phone rang during dinner last night, and the second she discovered it was Jake checking up on me, seeing as I was still refusing to deal with the many missed calls and messages on my cell, she immediately invited him to dinner tonight.

She's trying so hard to make things as normal as possible for me, but as each hour passes, I'm realizing that there's a bigger hole opening up inside me.

Auntie Trish and Uncle Evan are incredible, but as much as I want this place to become home, it's never going to be.

The thought of Jake coming for the night perks me up and I even find myself showering and pulling on real clothes and some makeup.

"Poppy, you look lovely." Auntie Trish beams at me when I finally leave the safety of my room. I've been spending more and more time locked up in there while slowly handing over the role of mother of the kids to our aunt and uncle.

"Thank you. It feels good to be normal."

"One step at a time, Poppy."

I give her a sad smile before offering to help her in the kitchen. I can see she wants to argue about it, but after another look in my eyes, she concedes and allows me to take over vegetable chopping. It's the perfect kind of mind-numbing job I need until our guest arrives.

I'm pulling open the front door the second the rumble of an engine vibrates through the house.

"Hey," I say, smiling wider than I'm sure I have in days when Jake climbs from the car and walks over to me. "No Amalie?"

"Nah, she's having a girls' night with Cami, Rae, and Chelsea. You're stuck with just me, I'm afraid."

"Ugh, how will I cope?" I joke as he ruffles my hair like he used to do when we were kids.

"How you holding up?"

I consider lying but I'm pretty sure it would be pointless, Jake can read me better than that. "I have no idea. Everything is just... weird."

"You homesick yet?" he asks, probably knowing that I've never actually left Rosewood for any length of time before.

"Yeah. I never thought I would be, but I actually miss the place. Jada offered for me to move in with her?" He stills at my words.

"Oh? Are you thinking about it?"

"Yeah, I guess. It would mean I could come back to school. Life could kind of carry on."

"I'd love to have you back, you know that. But you need to do what's going to make you happy. Life's too short to be miserable, Popsicle."

"Whoa, when did you get all wise and start seeing the positive side of things? Anything to do with a certain Brit?"

He laughs. "You know it. What's for dinner? It smells incredible."

We walk inside the house with me tucked under his arm and still unable to wipe the smile off my face. I know that Auntie Trish and Uncle Evan are my family, that the kids are my family. But there's something about being with Jake that just makes me feel safe, secure, loved in his own unique Jake way.

The seven of us sit around the dining room table and eat Auntie Trish's homemade pie as if we're a normal family. It's... nice. Normal.

Jake tells stories about what the team has been up to along with tales about him and Amalie moving into their new house and all the kinds of grown-up things I never expected him to do. But it seems that what they say is true, the right woman really can work wonders on a guy.

By the time we're full and the kids are sent to start getting ready for bed, Uncle Evan excuses himself to the living room after Jake and I insist that we'll do the cleaning. We're just about to get up and make a start when Auntie Trish stops us.

"That can wait, can I talk to you both first?"

I glance from her and to Jake who looks as confused as I feel before we agree and follow her down to her office.

She closes the door behind us and gestures for us to take a seat on her couch while she wheels over her desk chair. I can't help feeling like one of the students she looks after at college. I feel like I'm about to get a speech about something important that might just help change my life.

"I don't think it's really my place to explain all of this to you both, but with the circumstances as they are, I think it's only fair that you finally learned the truth."

Auntie Trish looks at me as a swarm of butterflies take flight in my stomach. What the hell is she about to tell us.

Jake reaches over and takes my hand, clearly sensing that something big is about to happen too.

"Poppy, my brother isn't your dad."

"What?" I gasp, sitting forward for a beat while that bit of information filters through my brain before falling back on the couch in shock.

"So who is?" Jake asks as my head spins.

"Yours, Jake." His hand tightens on mine as the silence in the small room becomes deafening. "So… you're saying that we have… the same dad?"

Jake looks at me for a second before turning back to Auntie Trish.

"But I've never met my dad."

"Not that you would remember, no. But he was here when both of you were born."

"Fuck," Jake mutters, running his hand down his face. "Where is he? What happened to him?"

"He went to prison when you were only one."

"And what about after that?"

Auntie Trish looks down at her hands for a beat. "I'm really sorry. He fell into the wrong crowd, prison only made it worse. He's not…"

"He's dead?" Jake asks bluntly. "Of course he is," he mutters to himself. I don't think Auntie Trish hears, but I do.

Scooting closer, I wrap my arm around his shoulders. "I'm sorry, Jake."

"Nothing to be sorry about." He drops a kiss to my head.

"You knew him?" I ask Auntie Trish.

"We all went to school together," she says, repeating her words from the other night. "He was your mom's boyfriend all through high school. Childhood sweethearts that everyone thought would go the distance."

"What happened?"

"Your mom," she says with a sigh, looking to Jake. "From as early as I can remember they had their fierce sisterly rivalry going on. Everything was a challenge, just like your dad was. In the end, he didn't stand a chance. When Kate first announced she was pregnant, she didn't say who the dad was, but it soon came out. It was a mess, as you can probably imagine. But your mom took him back and a year later, announced she was pregnant with you," she explains, looking at me.

"So why keep it a secret?"

"Your dad was gone by then and Will and your mom had got together while she was pregnant, so they just decided to raise you as theirs and let Kate get on with her life. For whatever reason I still don't fully understand, they thought it was for the best."

"Wow," I breathe, falling back against the couch once more when Jake does.

"I know. I've thought you should have known for years, forever really. I know it wasn't really for me to say but..."

"Thank you. You did the right thing."

She smiles at both of us, but it doesn't meet her eyes.

"I'll leave you two to mull all this over. Call me if you need me. Jake, you're welcome to stay as long as you like."

She leaves the room, pulling the door closed behind her. The click of the lock cutting through the silent room.

"Well, I guess that explains a lot," Jake whispers, still staring ahead as if it's not really sunk in yet.

"Yeah. I always wondered why my mom treated you the way she did, how she could shove you out in that trailer. I guess this answers all those questions."

"Yeah." He turns to me. I expect to find a haunted look on his face after all those revelations. After all, Jake just gained and lost a parent in the blink of an eye when he could really use a decent one, much like I could, I guess. But when our eyes lock, all I find staring back at me is happiness.

A shriek rips past my lips when I'm suddenly pulled into his arms.

"You're my fucking sister," he says as if it's the most incredible thing he's ever heard. "I've got a sister."

I can't help but laugh into his chest at the awe in his voice. Rosewood's king, bad-boy Jake Thorn is totally bowled over by the fact I'm his sister. Me.

When he finally releases me, I find he's still got the smile on his face but also that his eyes are full of unshed tears.

"You know what this means?" he asks me excitedly.

"Uh…" I hesitate, trying to figure out where he might be going with this.

"You're Poppy Thorn."

"Huh, I guess I am."

"Has a good ring to it, right."

"It does. Although realistically, it couldn't be any worse than Poppy Poore. What was my mother thinking giving me his name?" I'm not sure it's totally appropriate to joke about it yet but when I meet Jake's eyes, both of us burst out laughing.

It feels so good after the past week of drama to just laugh. Even if it is at my own expense.

"You should totally change that, you know?"

Our laughter eventually fades off into the distance and sadly, my reality comes creeping back in.

"What are you going to do, Pops?"

My heart clenches painfully in my chest at the concern in his eyes. Suddenly, Jada's offer doesn't seem so crazy. Yes, I'd be leaving Austin, Sofia, and Cooper here, but I'd be leaving them in a loving home where they're going to get the care they deserve, and I could be with my friends, my brother. I shake my head, still not quite able to process everything. I could return to school and pick up where I left off, there would be no starting over and being the new kid.

"I think… I think I might come back."

"Really?" he asks, hope filling his features.

"Yeah. Rosewood is my home." Reaching for his hand, I squeeze. "It's where my family is."

"You could move in with us," he blurts, clearly not thinking straight.

"No, Jake. I appreciate the offer. But that's yours and Amalie's house. If Jada is serious, and I think she is, then I'll be okay there."

"But—"

"It's okay, Jake," I say, cutting him off. "I know you only want to look out for me, and that means the world to me, it really does. But I'll be okay there. We can hang out whenever, it's not like you don't ever go to the Hunter's."

He nods, knowing that I'm right.

"Pops, can I ask you something?"

"S-sure," I say, although I'm not entirely sure I'm happy with where this could be going.

"Preston Hellburn."

I rip my eyes from his, not wanting to go down this road but also knowing that it's inevitable if I'm actually going to go back. He's going to be waiting for me.

"Hunter's right, isn't he?"

"Jake," I breathe. "He's just playing a stupid game. He's trying to get to you through me."

"I don't give a shit, Poppy. No one messes with my family. I don't give a shit who his dad is or how much money they've got. This shit ends before you start back at Rosewood. You got it?"

All I can do is nod. I can't lie, seeing Jake so fired up kinda scares me.

"Please don't do anything stupid. I can't lose you, Jake." My voice trembles at the end as my emotions get the better of me.

"I'm not going anywhere, Poppy." He pulls me into his arms once more. "But I do need you to tell me what he's been doing. Not tonight, but soon. That motherfucker is going to regret the day he ever laid a finger on you, Popsicle."

Although my stomach is heavy with dread, hearing Jake say he's going to fight for me is a huge relief. I've carried the burden of Preston around with me for long enough. It's time it comes to an end.

"Harley invited me to a party Friday night."

"Ethan's. You should come. Let your hair down. You deserve it."

"Will he be there?"

"He'll find his ass kicked to the curb if he tries to be."

"Okay. Yeah. I'll talk to Jada and see if I can come back Friday. Maybe even come back to school Monday?"

"Yes. You belong in Rosewood, Pops."

"I know."

"This place is great an' all, I know the kids will be happy here, but it's not your home."

I nod at him. "You should probably get back. Amalie will wonder where you've gone to."

"Are you kidding, they were going shopping and then for pizza, they'll be hours. I should probably head off though, let you get some rest. You look exhausted."

"I am," I say, thinking of just how little sleep I've got since being here. Something has settled inside me now I've made this decision and I wonder if it's enough to help me get some sleep.

We push from the couch but before we get to the door, Jake's voice stops me. "I can't believe you're my sister," he says, his voice laced with disbelief.

"I can. Deep down, I think a part of me has always known. We were never just cousins, Jake. Something always ran deeper than that."

"Yeah, you're right. It did."

I can't help it, when I finally crawl in bed later that night after talking to Auntie Trish and Uncle Evan, and calling Jada, I fall asleep with a wide smile on my face. Things might be well and truly fucked up, but there might just be light at the end of the tunnel for all of us.

This doesn't mean the thought of walking into Zayn's house and looking him in the eye again doesn't fill me with dread.

29

ZAYN

"Harley, get your ass out here or you're going to have to find your own way there," I shout through her door where both my sister and Ruby are getting ready for tonight's party.

I'm not sure what the occasion is but it's Ethan's first party of the year and everyone seems to be going a little crazy for it.

"All right, keep your panties on," Harley snaps, ripping the door open and marching past me in a minuscule dress.

"What the fuck are you wearing? I can see your ass."

"It's a dress, *Dad,* and no, you can't... quite."

"You should be fucking glad I'm not Dad because there is no way he'd ever let you out of the house looking like that."

"Well, then I guess it's a good thing he's not here." She storms off down the stairs, Ruby emerges soon after, dressed similarly only in a pair of shorts that do show off her ass.

I stuff down my protective brotherly instinct and keep my lips sealed about her outfit and trail behind them, shaking my head in frustration.

Mom's in the kitchen making herself some dinner as I pass.

"Please try to be sensible tonight," she calls to the three of us, but the girls are already halfway out the door so they don't even hear her. "Keep an eye on those two, and please, don't let me find some random girl in the house in the morning."

"I'll see what I can do." I salute her and head out to my car.

I don't have any intention of hooking up with anyone tonight. I fully intend on being able to drive those two back before they get themselves in any trouble.

The drive to Ethan's is short and by the time I find somewhere to park, I'm already regretting agreeing to this. The temptation to just drop Harley and Ruby off and then disappear is strong, but not wanting anything to happen to them in their nonexistent outfits, I reluctantly follow. They immediately go in search of drinks and the squad, whereas I go for Ethan's den, hoping to find the others in there away from the rest of the party.

I'm in luck because when I push through the door, I find Ethan and Rae, Jake and Amalie, Mason and Camila, and Shane and Chelsea littered around the couches.

"The party is out there, man," Ethan says with a smile, nodding to the door I just walked through.

I lift my can of Coke and fall down onto an empty bean bag. "Meh, I'm not really feeling it. I was just my sister's chaperone."

"Zayn Hunter not out partying and trying to get inside a cheer slut's panties, what the hell is happening?" Ethan barks. The others laugh along with him, apart from Shane and Jake.

Shane just has an amused, knowing smirk on his face while Jake stares daggers into me.

"What?" I mouth at him, feeling like I'm missing something.

His lips part to respond but Amalie notices and slaps his shoulder, causing him to shake his head and lift his drink to his lips.

"Well, okay then."

Now I want to be here even less than I did before, and that's really saying something.

Two hours later, I find myself in the kitchen with the team while they line up shots and dish out names for tonight's tagging.

I want to leave, I have no interest in their games tonight but the sight of Harley over Justin's shoulder grinding up against some guy I don't recognize in that ridiculous dress has me staying put.

I'm too busy watching her antics to notice the guys' attention turn to me. But that's all forgotten when Harley lets out a loud shriek that pierces through the booming music. Everyone looks her way but I'm quicker, I'm already in the room and ready to take down the guy she was with. But the second I see her run across the room on drunk unsteady legs, everything changes.

"You're here," Harley cries, throwing herself at Poppy who stands stock still in the entrance to the living room. Her eyes locked on me.

Relief, desire, and frustration engulf me as I run my eyes down the length of her. Her hair is curled and hanging in loose curls around her shoulders, her makeup is heavier than usual but flawless, and her body. Fuck. I bite down on the inside of my cheek as I take in her loose-fitted tank and the short skirt she's got wrapped around her waist.

My cock swells, my fists clench with my need to go over there and drag her out of the room so that no other guy can look at her, but the moment she rips her eyes from mine and embraces my sister, I know I can't.

Fueled by my anger, I storm out of the room and toward the pool area where there's another huge crowd of kids.

Someone, no idea who, hands me a joint and I happily take it as I fall down on the lounger.

The crowd inside continues to dance and enjoy themselves while I sit here stewing.

Why's she here? Did she take up Mom's offer? Is she staying or is this just a flying visit?

Before long, the blunt is taken by someone else and my need for a drink begins to get the better of me.

Pushing from the lounger, I make my way to the kitchen, telling myself I'm just going to grab a soda, although my need to drown everything out right now with something stronger nags at me.

I'm almost at the kitchen when her voice has a shiver racing down my spine.

"Zayn?"

I still, desperate to turn around but not wanting to look into her eyes again if she's going to dismiss me as easily as she did the last time I saw her.

"What?" I bark, without looking back, figuring it's the easiest way to deal with the situation unless we want to make a huge scene.

"We need to get Harley home."

Her words ruin whatever promises I'd just made to myself, and I find myself turning her way in an instant. Both Poppy and Ruby are holding on to a passed-out Harley.

"Fucking hell," I mutter, stepping up to them and scooping my sister up into my arms. "Let's go." I pin Ruby with a look, she might still be standing but she's in no better state.

I don't look to see if they fall in line behind me as I march from Ethan's house, I don't need to. I know her eyes are drilling into my back.

I place Harley into the back of my truck before helping Ruby inside. I don't bother assisting Poppy, instead, I just walk to the driver's side and rip the door open.

We've barely pulled away from where I'd parked when I look back to find Ruby passed out behind me.

"Why are you here?" I ask, my voice rougher, my question harsher than I was intending.

"It's good to see you too," she sasses.

"I'm sorry, but the last time I saw you, you slammed a door in my face. Apologies if I'm not all that welcoming right now." I focus on my anger, it helps my attempt to ignore how badly I want to pull her into my arms right now and never let go.

"I'm sorry," she whispers, refusing to look at me and instead keeps her eyes out the windshield.

"You're sorry for slamming the door or accusing me of going after a cheer slut the second you left?"

"Uh... both, I guess. I wasn't—I'm not—in a great place right now."

My grip on the wheel tightens, my knuckles turning white. I don't want to make her life any harder right now but fuck... having her turn me away like that. I won't lie, it was brutal.

I know I fucked up the night before letting Laurie get close, but nothing happened. I try to ignore the little voice in the back of my head that screams what I might have done had Ruby not been there. I hate that it's right. I could so easily have done something stupid that night.

I pull up outside my house and jump from the car before she has a chance to say anything, not that I'm sure she wants to.

I lift Harley into my arms once again as Poppy wakes Ruby enough for her to stagger inside.

After depositing them on Harley's bed, we both back out of the room, closing the door shut behind us.

"So what now?" Poppy asks, making me still where I was making my way to the stairs.

"Now? I need a fucking drink."

I take two steps but I don't get to descend.

"Zayn, please. We need to talk."

"Talk?" I balk. "That's what I came to do the other day. I—"

"Please, Zayn. I need..."

Blowing out a long breath, I turn around. My eyes lock on to her sad, lost ones and I cave. Only when I move for her, she retreats until she's at one of our guest bedroom doors. She pushes it open and walks inside.

I stalk toward her, my pulse thundering around my body with my need for her.

"Poppy, don't run from me."

"Zayn, we just need to..." She swallows nervously as I close the door, shutting us off from the rest of the house. "T-talk."

"I know."

She bumps up against the wall, but I don't stop. I don't stop until I'm pressed right up against her body with her heat burning into me.

"And we will talk. Right after we—"

My hand slides into her hair as my lips crash down to hers.

Fuck, I've missed this.

She stills for a few seconds, and I start to think she's going to push me away. I lean into her, my cock pressing against her stomach, trying to show her just how much I need her, and she finally caves and parts her lips for me.

A groan rumbles up my throat as her tongue glides against mine and she hooks her leg up around my waist.

Gripping on to the back of her thighs, I lift her, pinning her to the wall with my hips and pressing myself against her core.

"Zayn," she moans when I rip my lips from hers and begin kissing down her neck.

"Missed you, Pops," I breathe against her skin, causing goose bumps to break out.

Her nails scratch at my scalp as I get lower. "We shouldn't." Any attempt to actually stop me fails the second I push the straps of her top from her shoulders. "Oh God."

"You're right, Pops. We probably shouldn't. But doesn't that just make it so much hotter."

The fabric passes her nipples and I hungrily suck one into my mouth as she cries out, her head hitting the wall behind her.

"You need to be quiet," I warn, going for the other side.

"Your... your mom is o-out."

"Oh, now you tell me."

Spinning her from the wall, I throw her down on the guest bed, watching her bounce as she settles.

She props herself up on her elbows as I rip my shirt off and drop to my knees at the end of the bed.

"Well, now you've given me permission to make you scream." I reach for her hips, finding the lace of her panties and ripping them from her body before latching on to her clit.

"Zayn," she cries, her back arching, her hands twisting in the sheets beneath her. "Oh God. Oh God. Fuck."

Pushing two fingers inside her, I circle her clit before grazing it with my teeth.

"Come for me, Poppy. Show me how much you missed this."

Bending my fingers just so, she moans as I hit the spot before upping the ante on her clit.

"Come, Pops."

"Zayn," she cries, her muscles tightening around me and her body convulsing with her pleasure.

I don't stop until she's ridden out every last second, before standing, wiping my mouth with the back of my hand and dropping my pants and boxers to the floor and climbing between her legs.

Leaning over her, I capture her lips, allowing her to taste herself on me. She moans, her nails scratching down my back.

"I," I say, dropping a kiss to her lips. "Missed." Kiss. "You."

"Zayn." My name rips from her lips as half a demand for more and a warning.

"Shush, baby. Let me take care of you." Reaching down for my pants, I find a condom in my wallet and rip it open.

Poppy watches my every move with her bottom lip sucked into her mouth.

Part of me expects her to tell me to leave, that this shouldn't happen. But she never does.

Instead, the second I sweep my cock through her folds, her hips roll and she immediately sucks me deeper once I push into her.

"So fucking tight," I murmur against her lips as I slowly slide into her, inch by glorious inch.

Her hands burn a trail down my back before her nails scratch all the way back up.

"Fuck, yes," I grunt, dropping my head to the crook of her neck once I'm fully seated.

My speed increases and she meets me thrust for thrust as I chase the release we both need.

Dropping my hand down her body, I press my thumb against her clit and she detonates beneath me dragging me over the edge right along with her.

After pulling the condom off, I fall down on my back beside her and tangle my fingers with hers as our hearts return to normal and our skin cools.

"We shouldn't have done that." Her words are like a bucket of ice that is thrown over me.

Rolling onto my side, I turn to look at her. Tears pool in her eyes once more but she refuses to let them drop, or even look at me as she continues staring at the ceiling.

"If this is going to work, then this," she says, gesturing between us. "Can't happen."

I look around the room and gasp when I find her suitcase sitting open on the other side of the room.

"You're coming back?"

"Yeah but—"

"Don't do this, Poppy. Don't shut this down because you're scared. I'm scared too. Fucking terrified actually. But this," I say, scooting closer to her and wrapping my arm around her waist. "But this is right. This is how it's meant to be."

"Jake's not my cousin, he's my brother," she blurts.

"Uh... what?" I ask, my brows pulled together in confusion.

"My dad... well, he wasn't my dad. I've come back for him, for Harley and Rubes. To finish school so I can finally get the fuck out of here for good." She swallows before turning to look at me. "I didn't come back for this. You need to leave."

30

POPPY

I force the words out past the huge lump in my throat, but as much as it kills me to say them. I know I'm right.

I can't move in here, attempt to restart my life while Zayn and I continue with this dirty little secret we started.

It's never going to work. We'll get caught and it'll ruin everything. Jake won't have it. Harley will hate me for lying to her.

The best thing that can happen now, is that both of us forget it even happened in the first place.

This is time for a fresh start, for all of us.

I can't watch as he swipes his clothes angrily from the floor and storms to the door.

He's still naked and my eyes beg for me to look over at him, but I can't. One look and he'll know I'm lying. That the last thing I want right now is for him to walk away.

But it's for the best.

With the silence around me threatening to engulf me. Zayn crashes about in his room for a minute or two, before the door is ripped open once more, he storms down the stairs before the force of the front door slamming rattles the entire house.

It's not until he's left, taking a piece of me with him, that I allow myself to break.

Curling in on myself, I hug the pillow that vaguely smells like him to my chest.

I must cry myself to sleep because the next thing I know, I come to, still naked and still hugging the damn pillow. My eyes feel puffy from the crying and my throat is dry.

He didn't come back last night, that I'm pretty sure of. Where did he go? Back to the party? What did he do?

Before I've processed the thought, I sit up in bed, wrap the sheets around my body and reach for my cell, intent on torturing myself by scrolling through social media for evidence of what he got up to. Did I send him straight into the arms of a willing cheer slut? A shiver rolls down my spine at the thought and my stomach churns.

I did the right thing. I did the right thing, I tell myself over and over. But it doesn't matter how many times I hear myself say the words, my heart doesn't listen. It just continues to ache knowing I sent one of the best parts of my life away.

I knew he was going to be angry, rightly so, I did slam a door in his face. But I thought he... my thoughts trail off. I only believed what the evidence was showing me. What else could I do?

Trust him.

Irritated with the little voice inside my head, I climb out of bed, glad that I didn't drink last night, having a hangover would only have made today worse than it already is. My body aches as I move, and when I look down at my hips, I find the faintest of bruises from Zayn's tight grip.

A lump crawls up my throat and my hand comes up to cover my mouth as I attempt to keep myself together.

Coming here was the right decision. I knew that the second Jada drove me into town. Something settled inside me, and even walking into this house, I felt more at home than I did any time I was in Auntie Trish's.

Jake wanted to come and get me and drive me back himself. He wasn't happy when I told him no, but he'd already been out twice in the past week. It was Friday night, he should have been out enjoying himself, although I did swear him to secrecy.

I wanted to surprise Harley and Ruby and not have to worry about the fact that Zayn knew I was coming. In hindsight, was that the best idea I've ever had? Probably not.

The feeling that washed through me the second our eyes locked in Ethan's house is one I'll probably never forget. The regret, the need, the pull. It was all stronger than I expected, and it nearly knocked me on my ass. Add in the anger that filled his features and pulled his muscles tight and I knew I'd made a mistake.

Shaking the memories from my head, I pull off a robe that's hanging on the back of the door and head for the bathroom.

Aside from a toothbrush, I don't have any of my own toiletries. Jada offered to take me to my house today to pick up some stuff but I refused her offer, she's already done too much for me.

That house has been my home for my entire life, how can it so suddenly turn into somewhere I hate?

The image of Austin and Sofia's tear-filled eyes as I said goodbye yesterday fills my mind. They didn't want me to go, I'd expected that, but I hadn't appreciated just how much their trembling bottom lips would rip me apart.

I know I'm doing the right thing for them though. They can have a life in Maddison with Auntie Trish and Uncle Evan, that me, our parents, never could have offered them. The best thing that can happen for them now is for both our parents to go down and they never have to worry about them.

I shower with Harley's products, hoping that if I have the water hot enough and use enough soap that all my regrets will wash straight down the drain. It's wishful thinking because when I step out and wrap myself in a towel, I feel as if the weight of the world that's on my shoulders has only gotten heavier.

I just need to get through the weekend and get back to school. Get back to normal. Everything will be okay.

There's noise coming from downstairs as I walk back to my bedroom and the scent of coffee wafts up. Needing a huge mug of whatever Jada is brewing down there, I quickly pull on some clothes and go in search of some caffeine.

"Hey, sweetie. How was the party?" Jada asks, looking up from her tablet the second I join her.

"Um… it was…." I blow out a breath.

"That good?"

"Harley and Ruby got drunk. Zayn had to bring us all back," I say without thinking. Jada's cool, and with my own parents, not ones to ever really give a shit about anything, I forget that Harley might not want her mother knowing some things.

"Did they?" she asks, her eyes rolling.

"They were just excited to see me. Got a little carried away."

She nods, probably wondering why I'm so alert this morning if they were so trashed.

"You didn't want to celebrate being home?"

"Not really. I don't really drink."

Jada chuckles. "I knew there was a reason I liked you. Want to try to rub off on my kids a little while you're here?"

My cheeks burn as I think about just how closely I've been rubbing up against one of her kids.

"Help yourself to coffee. Anything. You know where most things are by now, don't hesitate to take whatever you need. This is your home now."

I make myself a coffee and join her.

"I don't know how to thank you for all of this."

"Don't be silly. I'm just happy to be able to help."

"I really appreciate it."

"I know, sweetie." She reaches out and squeezes my hand in support. "Whatever you need, Poppy. Just ask. My door is always open." She smiles at me before going to make herself another coffee. "If you need me, I'll be in my office."

She wanders off with her fresh mug and my eyes follow her, wondering if I can be like her when I grow up. She has everything together. A great life, job, kids, house. She makes everything look so easy, although I can't help wondering if that's true or if she's just a great actress.

I only know a little about the Hunter's previous life, but it doesn't sound all that great. Letty, Zayn, and Harley should be really proud of her though. She took her happiness into her own hands and made herself the life she wanted.

I can only hope that I can do that one day for myself.

Feeling like I should probably start my first day here by pulling my weight, I hop down from the stool and set about finding ingredients to make pancakes. If the smell doesn't lure the girls from bed then I'll go up there and drag them out soon.

The need for coffee and sugar must have been enough because just as I'm flipping the first batch of pancakes onto a plate, footsteps sound out before two very sleepy, hungover heads appear in the kitchen doorway.

"It wasn't a dream. You're really here," Harley says, beelining straight for me and pulling me into her arms. "I'm sorry, I got a little over-excited last night," she whispers into my ear.

"It's okay."

Seconds later, another set of arms wrap around both of us and I stand for long minutes accepting their support. I don't think I appreciated just how much I missed them in the week I was gone. They've both always been my main support network, and without them, I was drowning.

I know it was my own fault and I just should have picked up my cell, but it was easier said than done.

"Are you hungry?" I ask once they've released me.

"Starved. I'll get the coffee. Rubes, get the plates."

Not ten minutes later, Jada has rejoined us and we're sitting around the table stuffing our faces and chatting about life, mostly anything that doesn't involve my sudden arrival or my parents. I'm grateful they keep it light and keep me distracted from reality.

The second Jada has finished, she disappears to her office once more, leaving the three of us to chat about school and what I've missed.

Everything comes crashing down around my feet though when there's a rumble of an engine outside seconds before the front door slams shut.

I hold my breath waiting for him to walk around the corner, but no matter how much I think I can prepare myself for seeing him, when he emerges, it knocks the wind right out of me.

He looks a mess. His eyes are dark and bloodshot, his clothes are a crumpled mess.

"What the hell happened to you?" Harley asks, voicing the question that I'm sure is on all our lips.

"Nothing," he mutters, his angry eyes locked on mine as he makes his way to the coffee machine.

"I thought you brought us home."

"I did. Then I went back out. Problem?" he snaps.

"Um... no."

Ripping my eyes away from him, needing to sever the connection in the hope no one surrounding us notices, I stare down at my half-eaten plate of pancakes, my previous appetite suddenly gone.

"What are you all eating?" he asks, leaning back against the counter with his mug in hand.

"Poppy made pancakes. They were incredible."

"Oh, did she?" His eyes turn on me but I don't look up, instead I leave them to drill into the side of my head. "Didn't think to make any for me?"

"I would have if you were here."

"Well..."

Risking a glance up, I find him gesturing to himself.

"Here I am."

"Zayn, stop being a prick. Get your own breakfast," Harley snaps.

"It's okay, I can make more."

I push my chair out to do so, but Harley's hand lands on my shoulder. "No. Don't follow his rude demands. Enjoy your breakfast. He's big enough and ugly enough to sort himself out."

"But—" I look between Harley and Zayn, knowing that she is right but feeling that incredible pull toward him like always, despite what I said last night.

In the end, I side with Harley, refusing to bow down to Zayn when he's acting like he owns the place.

"You know where the fridge is. Excuse me," I mutter, pushing my chair out behind me and running for the stairs.

I manage to keep my sob in until I'm safely inside my bedroom. It rips from me the second I rest back against the door.

I'm not sure I can do this. Maybe coming here and believing I could live under the same roof as him was the stupidest thing I ever could have done.

My cell vibrates on the nightstand and distracts me from my meltdown.

Thinking it's probably Harley already asking if I'm okay, I rush over. But when I get there and take in the preview, my body turns to ice.

Unknown: Welcome home. Let the games begin...

My hands tremble as I stare down at his words. I haven't heard or even really seen him in over a week. I might have my suspicions about him being involved but other than that, he's been far from my mind. A part of me I think might have hoped that this was over. But it seems that his threat is still very, very real.

I look over my shoulder as someone runs up the stairs. I don't need to open the door to know it's Zayn. I can feel it.

I reach out to take my cell. I should show him. He'll know what to do about it. But I can't. I remember the way he looked at me downstairs. It was almost like I didn't even exist to him. I can't send him away one minute and then need him the next.

If I'm going to stand by my word, then I need to deal with my own issues. Even if they terrify me.

Squaring my shoulders, I delete his message and set about getting ready for my day, not that I have a clue what I'm doing, but I refuse to hide in here because of him.

I'm better than that. Stronger than that.

I'm putting my mascara on when a knock sounds out on my door. For a second my heart jumps into my throat thinking that it could be Zayn, but then I hear the girly chatter on the other side and I blow out a long breath, although I'm not sure if it's relief or disappointment.

"Come in," I call, shocked that they even waited long enough for me to respond. They don't usually have those kinds of boundaries.

They both pile in and dive on the bed.

"So what's the plan for the weekend then?" Harley asks, ignoring the elephant in the room that was me running from downstairs. I'm not sure why she lets me off, but I appreciate it.

"No idea."

"Ooh, we should go and get mani-pedis," Ruby pipes up.

"I'm easy. I do need to go back home though to get a few things."

"Okay well, why don't we swing by your place, grab what you need then we'll head for the nail place?"

"What about a spa? We could go all out," Ruby says, excitedly jumping up and down on the bed.

"Um... I can't really afford that," I say quietly.

"Oh, don't be silly. We've got you."

I shake my head, an uncomfortable feeling twisting my stomach. It's already too much that I'm living here and relying on the Hunters as much as I am. I don't need them paying for luxuries for me too. "No, I can't."

"Pops," Harley sighs.

"No," I say, holding my hand to stop her argument. "I need to focus. I need to get back to school, get a job, and start thinking about my future. You two go to the spa, but I can't waste a day or the money doing that."

They look between themselves, I can almost hear the words that are right on the tips of their tongues.

Thankfully both their cells beep, cutting off anything they were going to say.

They both pull them out and stare down.

"Ugh, Chelsea is calling us for a meeting at her place."

"On a Saturday?"

"Yup. Championships are approaching and she is like a dog with a bone."

"I guess you'd better go then."

They both complain as they climb from the bed, probably more to do with their lingering hangovers than the fact they need to go practice. I smile to myself wondering if Chelsea's demands might have something to do with the state of some of her squad last night, if her actions are really no more than a punishment for their actions.

"What are you smiling about?"

"Nothing. Can I... um... borrow your car?" I hate to ask, but I really don't want to walk or pay for an Uber to get to my house, and I really don't want to ask Zayn.

"Of course. Rubes can drive us. Let me go grab my key."

She disappears leaving me with Ruby.

"You know," she starts. "He really didn't do anything at the party last weekend." She pins me with a look I don't need.

"It doesn't matter."

"Doesn't it?"

"It's done, Rubes. It's over. It doesn't need talking about again."

She studies me for a few seconds as Harley's footsteps get closer once more.

"Sure, whatever you say." She rolls her eyes at me but ensures I can't comment because Harley throws her key over.

"Ready?" she asks Ruby.

"No, but let's go."

"We'll see you later, Pops. Be good."

I laugh at them. When aren't I good?

When you were fucking her brother behind her back.

Pushing the thought aside, I grab my purse, stuff my cell into it and pull on my sneakers.

The house is quiet as I make my way through, I have no idea where Zayn went, and I'm sure Jada is in her office as usual.

I unlock Harley's car and slide into the driver's seat. It's been a while since I've driven, I can only hope it's like riding a bike.

Just as I'm about to back out, movement in the second floor window catches my eye. I shouldn't look, I know that, but my eyes have a mind of their own and in a beat, I find them locked on a pair of dark angry ones.

He's standing at the window topless with all his olive skin and taut muscles on display. My body reacts like it always does but I force myself to ignore it. I've got to stand by my words, it's the right thing to do.

Ripping my gaze from his, I go back to what I should be doing, and drive away. Although I soon realize that despite the fact I've put some space between us, he's still in my head, driving me fucking crazy.

Pulling up to outside the house I've called home for all my life is weird. I've never really felt a huge connection to the place, but it's even less now. It's just a building.

I'm not sure what I was expecting coming back here. Maybe to feel like I was coming home, maybe some kind of nostalgia. But there's nothing.

It's weird the feeling of not belonging anywhere. I didn't belong at Auntie Trish and Uncle Evan's, I'm not sure I really belong at the Hunter's, but I don't belong here either. I don't even want to be here. There are too many memories. Too much that haunts me.

Pushing the door wide, I climb from the car, my eyes darting around the front yard.

My skin tingles with awareness as if I'm being watched. But as I look around, I don't find anyone or see any movement.

Setting my apprehension aside, I walk up to the front door and slide my key into the lock just like I've done a million times before.

The house is cold as I walk inside and I can't help but wonder what's going to happen with it when my parents are unable to come back. Others keep saying *if* to me, but I'm more realistic than that. I stand by my words the day I was told about all this. They're both guilty.

Ignoring the downstairs, for now, I make my way up to my bedroom. Only, I don't push my door open first. Instead, I walk into Sofia's room. Her scent surrounds me and I look at everything she's left behind. Her entire life is in this room. She's got baby photos on the wall, toys from over the years, shelves full of books. I drop down onto her bed and pull one of her stuffed toys into my arms.

Tears burn my eyes as I think about the fact we're now apart.

Should I have come here? Should I have stayed with them?

The decision to come here seemed so right when I was in Maddison and missing everything about this place but now I'm here, now I've already ruined whatever relationship I had with Zayn. I'm starting to wonder.

Am I just making a huge mess of everything?

Pulling my cell from my pocket, I find Auntie Trish's number, swallow down my emotion, and hit call.

"Hey, sweetie. How is it being back?"

"I-it's weird," I admit, the emotion I thought I'd banished coming back full force and I fight not to allow a sob to erupt. "How are the kids doing? I miss them."

"Would you like to talk to them?"

"Yes, please."

"Hang on, I'll grab them and put you on speaker."

I wait as she calls for both Austin and Sofia and in only a few minutes I hear their sweet little voices through the phone.

"Poppy," they both sing simultaneously. Their excitement makes my heart ache.

"Hey, you guys. How are you?"

"Good. Auntie Trish is taking us out to buy new toys later. How cool is that?"

"That's very cool, bud. Do you know what you want?"

Austin chats away about this new game he wants and I'm pleasantly surprised it doesn't involve killing anyone.

"Do you want me to send the console to you?" I ask, thinking of the old one they have sitting in Austin's bedroom.

"No, it's okay. Evan is beside himself at being able to buy a new one."

"They don't need a new one, you don't need to spend that much."

"It's okay, Poppy. We're not going to spoil them. But we want this place to be their home. Especially if it's going to be long term." She knows as well as I do that it's going to be.

"What about you, Sof? What are you going to get?"

She's silent for a beat. "I... I don't know. I don't think I need anything."

My heart breaks for my poor little sister. "Aw, well, I'm sure you'll find something once you're there. What about that new baby that you showed me on the TV?" I ask, thinking of the one she excitedly pointed out a few weeks ago.

"Maybe. But I've got Sarah," she says, referencing her beloved doll that is usually attached to her hip.

"Well, I'm sure you'll figure it out. How's Cooper?"

"Ugh, he doesn't stop crying."

"Why?" I ask, a little too quickly.

"It's okay, sweetie. I think he's just starting to teethe. He's just had a bit of a temperature. It's nothing to worry about, I'm sure. I've got a doctor's appointment for them on Monday to get them checked out and registered here."

"That's good."

"We're really all okay," Austin says.

"I know you are. I just miss you."

"We miss you too. But we want you to be happy."

"Aw, bud. I'm so sorry about all of this."

Everyone falls silent and I can imagine Austin shrugging in the way he does when our parents did something they shouldn't have and he just dealt with it.

"Are you excited to go and see your new school?" I ask, trying to turn the conversation to something a little less depressing.

"Yeah, Auntie Trish says it's got this amazing playground."

I should hope so for the cost of the tuition. I still can't believe that Auntie Trish and Uncle Evan are willing to enroll them both into the prep school, but I'm equally thrilled for the two of them. They're going to get an incredible education and great start in life despite the past few years. As shitty as this situation is, it could well be the best thing that ever happened to the three of them.

"That sounds awesome." I can tell they're starting to lose interest so I say my goodbyes and allow them to go back to whatever they were playing before I interrupted.

"They're really happy, Poppy. You don't need to worry about them."

"I can't help it. I've been the only one doing so for so long now that it's kind of ingrained."

"I know, and they will never forget what you did for them. You're way more than just a sister to them. Anyway, how was the party last night? Was it good to see your friends again?"

"Ugh, yeah... it was good." The party was... meh. I was desperate to get back and see everyone but I wasn't expecting to be so nervous and that ruined it for me. I should have just had a drink and enjoyed myself, but being in the same house as Zayn turned me into a nervous wreck and I couldn't relax at all. Then Harley and Ruby got trashed and that kind of ruined everything. "It's nice to be with friends though. I think it might just take a bit of time to get used to this new normal."

"That's to be expected, Poppy. None of what you're going through right now is easy. Just take each day as it comes. Hopefully, we'll get news sooner rather than later and we can all try to restart our lives."

"We can only hope. I should go, I've got a few things I need to do. I'll get more of the kids' stuff packed up for you soon."

"There's no rush, Poppy. They've got everything they need for now."

"Thank you, Auntie Trish."

"I'd do anything for all of you, you know that."

"I really appreciate it. Just hearing their voices, I know how happy they are."

"They're going to have a good life here, and you're welcome anytime. You've got your key. This house is your home too, Poppy."

"I know," I choke out. "Thank you."

"You're welcome. Speak soon."

We hang up and I spend a few more minutes with Sofia's teddy clutched to my chest before I push from the bed and make my way to my room.

Opening my closet, I pull out a couple of old bags and place them on the bed next to the teddy before turning around and making quick work of rummaging through my things.

I don't pack everything. I don't need or want everything. I have no idea what's going on, but there's going to be time to come back and go through the rest over the coming weeks and months I'm sure.

The last thing I want to take with me is something I'm not sure I'm going to find. My parents have never been the kind of people to keep all our important documents in any kind of sensible place.

I'm sitting on the floor rummaging through the disaster that is the filing cabinet my parents abandoned years ago hoping to find a piece of paper to confirm everything that Auntie Trish told Jake and I last week.

I've never seen my birth certificate. I've had no reason to. I was brought up believing that my parents were my parents so I didn't really need to go snooping, but now, I'm more than intrigued to see what it says.

I find the kids' ones first in a nice folder before discovering mine right at the bottom of the drawer screwed up at the back.

Gently pulling it out, I smooth the paper out before looking down at what it says.

My breath catches at seeing it before me.

Poppy Anastasia Thorn

My hand flies to my mouth as I suck in a deep breath. I didn't not believe Auntie Trish but there was a small amount of suspicion after that revelation. It all just seemed too good to be true. I'd always felt a deeper connection to Jake. I put it down to the fact that he was my family and treated like crap for no reason. I just wanted to help him, to save him. But it turns out it really was more than that.

Pulling out my cell, I snap a photo of the creased paper before sending it to Jake.

He reads it almost instantly and starts typing, only when a new message comes through, it's not from Jake.

My hands tremble as I stare at the name on the notification sitting proudly in the middle of the screen.

This shouldn't be happening.

She shouldn't be contacting me.

Standing, I pace back and forth a few times as I try to decide what to do. I should delete it without even looking. That's what I've been told to do should either of them try to contact me.

But can I do that?

She might be useless most of the time, but at the end of the day, she's still my mom.

"Fuck," I breathe, swiping the screen and tapping on her name.

Mom: I'm so sorry, baby. I've done nothing but let you down.

Shit.

My thumb moves as if I'm going to reply but then the little bouncing dots start and I halt, wanting to see what she's going to say next.

I wait a few seconds but I soon get to find out.

Mom: I've screwed everything up. I've ruined your life. Your brothers' and sister's lives. You're better off without me.

Every part of me wants to reply, to tell her that everything is going to be okay. But equally, I'm desperate to follow the rules of her bail and not contact her.

They didn't allow her back here for fear she might not be able to stay away. Good move, it seems. I'd originally thought that she'd probably like the freedom, but then I guess she always had d-*dad* previously. Now she's got no one.

Before I get to make a decision, another message comes.

Mom: It all ends today. Everything. I'm going back to where all this started and I'm going to end everything for good. I just needed you to know that I love you and I never wanted it to come to this. I'm sorry.

My eyes widen as I stare at her words. Thinking I've read it wrong, I read and reread her message but every time the same words taunt me.

It all ends today.

End everything for good.

"Fuck, fuck, fuck," I chant, spinning on the spot, not knowing what to do.

Without too much thought, my thumbs start flying over the screen.

Poppy: Where are you? I'll come now. Please. Please don't do anything stupid.

My hands tremble as I send the message and my eyes burn with tears. Surely she doesn't mean it. She's just being dramatic, wanting attention. It sure wouldn't be the first time. But she's never sounded quite this serious.

"Fuck," I bark when I see that my message has been read but she's not typing. "Oh my God. Oh my God."

My ass hits the chair before I realized that I was going to sit down as I continue staring at my screen long after it's gone dark.

I run her words over and over in my head but no matter how many seconds tick by, I don't get any closer to figuring out what to do.

Poppy: Mom please, don't do this. Let me help you. Tell me where you are.

This time when it's read, the dots start bouncing and I breathe a sigh of relief.

Mom: I'm going back to where it all began, where the mistakes started.

"That's not fucking helpful," I scream into the silence of the house.

Screenshotting our conversation, I send it to Jake. I notice that he's still not replied to my previous message and that this new one doesn't show as read before I lock my cell, drop it into my pocket, and collect the bags I'd left in the hallway.

I'm throwing everything into Harley's trunk when an idea slams into me.

Auntie Trish said that they all met at school. Her, Mom, Kate, our dad, Will.

"Fuck." I race to the driver's side and after fumbling with the seat belt, I turn the engine over and slam my foot down on the accelerator sending gravel flying into the air behind me.

My heart is in my throat as I pull the car to a stop in the school parking lot. There are a couple of others here, but I don't see anyone.

Jesus. What the fuck am I doing? I'm probably way off the mark here.

I climb from the car and begin walking around the campus.

I check my cell again, despite the fact it's not gone off and I find that I haven't received anything else from Mom and that Jake's still not read the messages.

My legs pick up the pace as I convince myself that I'm going to find something, anything that's going to help.

I find myself breaking into a run as I come toward the gym building. Just like everywhere else, it's deserted.

I come to a stop, place my hands on my knees, and drag in some much needed air into my lungs.

This is crazy. She's not here.

Standing, I look up to the sky wishing that she hadn't put me in this position when something on the roof catches my eye.

She wouldn't. Would she?

I look around, not even knowing how to get up there.

I race around the building hoping to find the answer but there is no ladder or anything to climb on, I do, however, find the main door slightly ajar when I get to it.

Assuming it's how she'd have gotten in, I pull it open and step inside.

Not being sporty in any way, I'm not exactly familiar with this building so my eyes flick from left to right trying to find the answer. And I finally do when I find another half open door.

Looking back over my shoulder, I pull it wider and step through.

My heart thunders in my chest and my blood races past my ears as I make my way up the stairs behind the door.

At the top, I find another door and after sucking in a long, calming breath, I reach out a shaky hand and push it open.

The sun blinds me for a second after the darkness of the building and I squint as my eyes water.

My vision might be blurry, but I don't see anyone.

I almost laugh to myself when I realize that I've been drawn into this wild goose chase for someone who doesn't want to be found. It must have just been a bird or something I saw. She's not here.

I'm about to turn to go back to the car and return to the Hunter's when something hard connects with my head and everything goes black.

31

ZAYN

I shouldn't have gone back to the party last night, and I really shouldn't have swiped the first bottle I found and drunk it all before finding another.

I couldn't help it.

Her words, her rejection, were on repeat in my head and I needed them gone.

I had no idea she was coming back, let alone moving in. I know Mom had broached the subject with me and asked if I'd be okay with it, but I didn't expect her to turn up just like that.

It knocked me for six and I couldn't resist taking everything I've been desperate for since she disappeared from my life.

Just for those few minutes, everything was right again. My world was back as it should be with my girl in my arms. Until she shattered it all over again.

I should have listened to her. Allowed her to talk before I claimed her as mine once more because now I've had another taste of her, felt her soft curves beneath my hands, and the burning heat of her pussy, there's no way I'm going to allow her to follow through with her words.

She's mine. End of.

She might think we're a bad idea while we're living under the same roof. But I fully intend to prove her wrong and show her just how good things could be while we're living in the same house.

I have a fleeting concern about Poppy, and whether Mom will allow her to stay once they learn the truth. But it's unlikely she'll kick her out. Not after all the effort Mom's gone to ensure she can stay here.

I remain at the window long after she's disappeared down the street in Harley's car trying to figure out how I'm going to fix this.

I should be pissed still. But now the alcohol has started to disappear from my system, determination takes its place.

I need to talk to Jake. Fuck Harley and Mom. If what she told me is true then it's time he learned the truth.

Marching back to my room, I drop my boxers before walking into my bathroom to have the shower I was intending on having before I heard her close the door and walk down the hall.

The second I'm out, I shoot Jake a message, but it doesn't matter that he doesn't read it. I know exactly where he is.

Swiping my keys from the dresser, I head out toward the other side of town where Ethan's gym is.

I've been here a few times with him in the past. It's the fanciest one in town, hence why we all make use of his guest passes.

The young girl on the reception desk soon lets me past once I flash her my panty-melting smile.

"Yo," Ethan calls out. "How's the hangover, man?"

"Yeah, I've felt better," I mutter, turning to where Jake is pounding the treadmill. "Can we talk?"

Frown lines form on his brow before he hits the buttons in front of him and slows the belt to a stop.

Stepping off, he grabs the towel that was hanging over the rail and wipes his face.

"Sure, what's up?"

I nod over to the bench at the other side of the gym and we both turn away from Ethan.

"It's fine. I didn't want to know what you were going to talk about anyway."

Jake flips him off over his shoulder before grabbing his water bottle and cell from the floor and following me over.

"What's up?" he asks, swiping at his cell and opening the messages he's got waiting for him.

"I need to talk to you about Poppy."

"Go on..." he encourages, shooting a glare in my direction.

"She told me that she's your sister."

"Yeah, man. How fucking mental is that?"

"Uh... yeah. How'd that happen, anyway?" I ask. I was desperate to find out more last night but Poppy didn't exactly give me a chance.

"Seems *daddy* wasn't able to keep it in his pants and was fucking around with both our moms."

"Whoa. Why didn't they tell you?"

"Fuck knows. They're all fucked-up. Are you really surprised by all this?"

"I... uh... guess not." I don't know all that much about Jake's mom and his past, it's something he keeps close to his chest, but I do know that she's no longer around.

"So what did you want to... fuck," he barks, bringing his cell a little closer to his face.

"What's wrong?"

"Uh... fuck. I need to go."

"Go? But I need to..."

"Talk about Poppy, I know. You should probably come with."

He's up from the bench before I have a chance to register his words.

"Savage, we're out," he calls across the gym and practically runs for the door.

"Jake, what the hell is going on?" I call after him, racing through the door he just swung open so hard it crashed back against the wall with a loud thud. As I catch up with him, I notice his shoulders are pulled tight and his fists are clenched at his sides.

"Hellburn," he barks at me. "Anything new?"

"N-no, not that I'm aware of."

"Good. Hopefully that motherfucker got the message."

"What did you do?"

"Nothing much. It's still a work in progress."

"He's still alive, you need to work quicker," I mutter, remembering how terrified Poppy was after their last encounter.

"I told you that we'll end him, and we will. We just need to be smarter than him."

"What's going on?" I ask when he comes to a stop at my truck.

"This," he tosses me his cell and I only just manage to stop it from crashing to the floor.

Flipping it over, I stare down at the screenshot that's filling the screen.

"What the..."

"It's from Poppy," he says, although it's really not necessary seeing as I can see her name at the fucking top. "They're from her mom." Again, obvious.

"She shouldn't be contacting her."

"No, and she really shouldn't be sending fucking suicide notes."

At his words, I focus on the messages.

"Fuck."

"Yeah, let's fucking go."

We climb in the car as Jake hits call on his cell and presses it to his ear. His grip on it is so tight his knuckles go white.

"It's just ringing."

"Where am I supposed to be going exactly?" I ask, sitting with the engine running and no fucking clue what we're supposed to be doing right now.

"School."

"School?"

"Yes, now fucking drive, Hunter."

"Yeah, okay." I put my truck in drive and speed out of the parking lot.

"Why school?" I ask once we're out on the main road.

"Just a hunch." His words are clipped and the way he sits in my passenger seat with his fists clenching and unclenching stops me from saying the words I wanted to. I don't think now is the time to admit to what's been going on.

We're on the other side of town to Rosewood High and seeing as it's Saturday, the traffic is busier than usual.

"Fucking hell," Jake complains when I stop at another light.

"What? I can hardly jump it."

"Can't you?"

"Jake, it'll be fine. We don't even know they're there."

He blows out a breath before saying words that turn my blood to ice.

"You really think that's really her mom?"

"T-that's what it said, wasn't it?"

"Yeah but... I don't know. Something doesn't feel right. Wendy is... a head case but sending those kinds of messages to Poppy. I don't know. It just doesn't sit right with me."

"W-what are you saying?" I ask, needing to know that we're on the same page here.

"Oh come on, you don't think this has Hellburn's name all over it."

"But how'd he..." I trail off as I realize that the details don't really matter because he's right. "Fuck." Slamming my foot on the accelerator, I do as he suggested before and jump the next few lights in my need to get to the school quicker.

"She's here. Look," I say, pointing to Harley's car that's parked haphazardly in one of the bays.

"Come on." We take off running, our eyes scanning all over trying to figure out where we're going to find her.

Time seems to slow as we run around looking for evidence. If it weren't for Harley's car sitting in the lot then I'd say it was a lost cause but I know she's here somewhere.

"Call her," I demand before Jake pulls his cell out and does as I suggest.

We stand with our chests heaving as we wait. After two seconds a cell starts ringing... above us.

I tilt my chin up, my eyes running up the bricks of the gym. "Up there," I say but when I look down I realize it wasn't necessary because Jake is already halfway to the entrance.

The door crashes back against the wall before he disappears inside. Picking up the pace, I run after him, my heart in my throat and dread lacing through my veins.

If this is as we suspect, what the hell is he playing at?

I'm not focusing on where I'm going by the time I get to the top of the stairs, being blinded by the last afternoon sun doesn't help and I almost crash into the back of Jake where he's frozen at the top of the stairs.

"Ah look, the cavalry has arrived. Are you ready to party?" His cold, evil voice sends a shiver down my spine before I get a look at the terrified set of eyes that bounce between me and Jake begging us for help.

32

POPPY

My head really fucking hurts is my first thought as I come to. The sun burns through my closed eyelids as I try to remember where I am and what the hell happened.

I try to pry my eyes open, but they resist.

Attempting to move my arms, I find them pinned together behind my back. I try my legs but find the same thing.

What the fuck is going on?

"Ah, good. My little toy is waking up."

Every single muscle in my body locks up at the sound of his voice seconds before everything that's happened this afternoon slams into me.

Being at the house.

The messages from Mom.

I'm at school on the gym roof.

But why is he here?

Finally, I find the strength to drag my eyelids open and the first thing I see is him, sitting on the edge of a chair in front of where I'm laid out on the rough roof, staring down at me like I'm a piece of shit.

"Where's my mom?" I manage to force out past the giant lump in my throat.

He laughs like a fucking maniac.

"Oh, Poppy, Poppy, Poppy. You've always been so easy to play."

I narrow my eyes at him but it just makes him laugh harder.

"You mean this?" He pulls Mom's cell from his pocket and throws it at me. It hits my shoulder before crashing to the floor beside me.

"How'd you get that?"

"I've been inside your house more times than you can probably imagine. It wasn't hard," he sneers, sending fear lacing down my spine.

"It-it was you wasn't it? You called the police?"

A wicked smile pulls at his lips, confirming what I already knew.

"I thought it was brilliant. I made you a promise, and I sat back and watched as I achieved it and you were carted off out of Rosewood like the piece of trash that you are."

"You think getting my parents locked up has ruined my life?" I ask, my own laugh falling from my lips despite the fact that any of this is funny.

His eyes hold mine for a few seconds and I use the time to try to sit up but the second I'm almost up, he pushes from his chair and his booted foot comes flying toward my stomach.

All the air is forced from my lungs with the force of the hit.

"Stay down there, bitch."

"Fuck you, Preston. You're not going to get away with this."

"Really?" he asks, an accomplished smile pulling at his lips. "Who do you think is going to find you up here? I hate to break it to you, Poppy. But no one is coming to your rescue this time. There is no Zayn, no Jake. There is no one but me and you."

"Fuck you."

Reaching out, his fingers grip my hoodie and I'm pulled from the ground as if I weigh nothing more than a feather before the knuckles of his other hand connect with my eye socket.

"Watch your fucking mouth, Poore."

I smile at him and he snarls, baring his teeth.

"Seems you didn't do your research very well, Hellburn," I spit, earning myself another punch, only this time it's to my jaw and the coppery taste of blood instantly fills my mouth.

"I've ruined your family. Your life. You have nothing."

"My parents were shit. Taking them away means nothing. They were nothing," I seethe, using the words he's spat at me time and time again.

"But—"

I shake my head at him. "Looks like you should have spent a little more time stalking me, asshole. I guess I should be thanking you though."

His brows pull together, waiting for what I could possibly want to thank him for.

"If you didn't *ruin* my life, then I wouldn't have discovered the truth."

"What the fuck are you talking about?"

"I'm not Poppy Poore. The sad and pathetic girl you seem to think I am with nothing to lose but who holds the keys to the one thing you really want." His eyes narrow. "I know for a fact that no matter what you do to me, you'll never get what you want. You'll never make captain, you'll never own the school because no matter how important you think you are, Rosewood is run by Thorns. And I, you piece of shit, am not Poppy Poore, I'm Poppy fucking Thorn. And we always win."

I don't see his fist coming this time and I go flying back toward the asphalt when he releases me.

My head ricochets off the rough roof as a blinding pain races down my spine from the hit.

"Motherfucker," I grunt.

"You're lying," he states as if he really believes that.

"Whatever, Preston. I don't have anything to prove to anyone, especially not you. He'll be here. There will be only one loser here."

"No," he states again, his eyes beginning to get a little wild as he's losing his control of reality. "No one is coming for you, Poore. You are mine."

He drops down to his haunches, his fingers threading through my hair and tugs so hard that I think he's going to pull it from my scalp.

I have no choice but to roll onto my back when he encourages me to do so.

One of his legs lifts over my body until he's pinning me to the floor with his hips.

"You. Are. Mine," he repeats, his voice more harrowing than I think I've ever heard it before.

He reaches behind his back and produces his knife that he had in the closet last week.

I swallow harshly as fear races through me, my stomach somersaulting uncomfortably, making me think I'm about to puke up my pancakes.

Lifting the knife, he runs the blade straight up the front of my hoodie. The fabric parts in an instant leaving me lying beneath him in just my black lace bra.

The point of the blade connects with my collarbone before he trails it down between the valley of my breasts and down to my belly button.

"The fun we're going to have, *Thorn,*" he seethes. "You know, that's even more perfect. I'll know that when I fuck you up, I'll be fucking him over at the same time. I thought it was good that you were that motherfucker's cousin. But his sister. It couldn't be fucking better."

"What the fuck is wrong with you?" I don't mean for the words to come out loud and when I see his eyes darken with anger, I instantly regret that I couldn't keep the question inside.

"Me? What the fuck is wrong with me? I'm fed up with that motherfucker walking around like he owns the fucking place. He owns nothing. He has nothing. He is nothing. Just like you. Pointless. Worthless. Nothing," he spits.

"This school, the team. All of it should be mine. And he is going to learn that when he finds you broken, begging for your fucking life."

Not that I've ever allowed him to see it, but I've always been scared of Preston. I learned a long time ago that he's unhinged. But no previous experience compares to this.

He's lost all control and the longer this goes on the crazier he's getting, to the point that I'm starting to believe that I'm not going to get off this roof alive.

My arms ache where they're pinned behind my back, the loose asphalt cutting into my skin. I try to move but all I achieve is to rub myself against him.

His lips curl in delight.

"I'm going to love fucking you up."

Placing the knife beside me, his hands drop to the button on my waistband.

He pops it open and wraps his hands around the fabric ready to pull.

I should be screaming, demanding that he stop but I already know it's pointless.

I might have warned him that Jake is coming, but the reality is that he's probably not. If he doesn't read that message and put two and two together as I did then I'm going to end up dying here.

He lifts his weight off me ready to remove my jeans when something catches his eye behind me.

His chin drops and he stills for a beat.

"Ah look, the cavalry has arrived. Are you ready to party?"

My head tilts so I can see who he's talking about, praying that Jake really is on the same wavelength as me and I find the most incredible sight.

Not only is Jake standing there staring daggers into Preston with his fists clenched tightly at his sides, but behind him, looking equally as furious, is Zayn.

I look between the two of them, waiting for them to move, to discover what they're going to do.

Time seems to grind to a halt as the four of us stare at each other, waiting to see what the other is going to do.

"Let her go," Jake barks, dragging his eyes from mine and drilling into Preston.

Zayn, however, doesn't take his eyes off me. Concern fills them. I understand why, everything hurts right now, I can only imagine how I must look.

"It's okay," he mouths but I just shake my head. Something tells me that this is far from over just because they've managed to find me.

I'm so glad I sent Jake that screenshot, if I hadn't... a shudder rips through me. It's not worth thinking about.

Preston's grip tightens on the fabric that's still hanging over my shoulders and I'm hauled to my feet. He presses his front against my back and wraps an arm around my waist, while the other holds the knife he'd previously discarded to my throat. The cold blade presses against my skin and I fight my need to swallow knowing that any movement is going to cause it to cut right through. I saw how easily it sliced my hoodie. Skin is going to be no problem.

I almost expect to find a gun pointing at us, the way he's using me for protection but when I drag my eyes up, I don't find any weapons. Just two angry guys' wide shoulders, puffed out chests, and curled fists.

I wouldn't want to be Preston when they get their hands on him.

"Give me what I want, and you can have the slut."

"She's not a..." Zayn barks.

"Never," Jake calls, their words melting into one. "Just let her go."

"Firstly, I think we both know that your sister means more to you than any stupid football team," Preston spits, his lips brushing my ear and turning my stomach with how close he is. "And secondly, you really need to learn what a little slut your sister is. Right, Zayn?"

Zayn's teeth grind making his jaw pop but he doesn't say anything. Jake doesn't react, making me wonder if he's actually hearing anything Preston is saying right now or if he's lost in his own red haze of anger.

"Or do I need to show you the evidence?" His hand slides up my bare stomach before roughly grasping my breast. He squeezes so tight I can't help a whimper fall from my lips, before he tugs at the lace so hard it rips, exposing me to both of them.

He drops the knife, running it over my collarbone and down to my breast. I whimper again, only I'm not sure if it's the relief that the knife is no longer at my throat or with fear that he could be about to plunge it into my chest.

He circles my nipple and I do everything I can not to react.

"Aw, see how she loves it. She's just begging for me to suck her into my mouth."

Closing my eyes, I allow my head to fall back on his shoulder. But it's not in pleasure. It's survival. I can't look at the reaction on Zayn's face right now as he watches Preston take what he thinks should be his.

"Let her fucking go," Jake repeats. "Tell me what you want. We'll figure something out, just let her go."

"Nah, not yet. I think we should have some fun first. See how far she'll go to protect you."

The knife leaves me but not before it's sliced through the other cup of my bra. His other hand continues to run over my exposed flesh. His touch burns, sending disgust straight through me. He makes me feel dirty, used, and I hate it.

He trails it down my stomach, hooking it into the waistband on my jeans. The blade cuts into my stomach and I wince in pain.

"Fuck you," I spit.

"She's feisty, I'll give her that. I do love it when they fight back, it really gets me hard."

I gag when I feel him press his cock into my ass, my eyes flying open and landing straight on Zayn.

Fury covers his face as he watches Preston touch me but the longer this goes on, the more my head pounds and the easier it's becoming to step away from my own body and just allow it to happen.

I should fight, I know that. But I don't think I have anything left.

Suddenly we're moving, my feet are being dragged across the asphalt until we're on the edge of the building.

"What are you fucking doing?" Jake barks, taking two giant steps and closing the space between us.

"Come any closer and we both go over. And I'll make sure your beloved sister is my cushion when we hit the concrete below."

Oh my God. Oh my God.

I'm going to die today and it's going to happen while I'm in this monster's arms. My body trembles with fear despite the fact I'm fighting like hell not to show him that I'm scared of him or his threats.

My heart races to the point I have no chance of breathing fast enough to drag in the air I need, and fear like I've never experienced before washes through me like a wave.

"Preston, please," Jake's voice is almost begging. I stare into his wide eyes as he tries to reason with Preston, but I don't think anyone but me realizes just how unreasonable he is. "We can come to some agreement, don't do this."

"I want the team. I want everything."

"Fine."

"What?" I bark. "Jake, no."

"I don't give a shit, Poppy. *You* are what matters here. I need you safe more than I need anything else."

Jake whispers something to Zayn but as much as I strain to hear, I can't make out any of the words.

"It's rude to whisper," Preston shouts. "Please, share your findings with the group."

Jake and Zayn share a look. Preston's grip on me tightens before everything happens at once and I start to fall.

33

ZAYN

"We're faster than him," Jake whispers to me.

On the field, this is true but I'm not sure I want to test the theory right now while Poppy's life hangs in the balance. If she goes over then... My stomach turns over at the thought. There's no way anyone would survive a fall from this building. We have to get her.

"We can't risk it."

"You got a better idea? This isn't going to end unless we end it. He's fucking deranged."

He doesn't need to say the words, I can fucking see the reality right in front of me. I had a good idea of what was going on with Preston and Poppy, but I never could have imagined it would have led to this.

I drop my eyes to his feet. His heels are hanging right over the edge. The smallest of movements is going to send them both crashing to their deaths.

My heart races, my skin is covered in a sheen of sweat as the tension of this situation gets too much to cope with.

"Preston, please." It's the first time Poppy has spoken since we arrived and the fear within her voice damn near kills me. I need to get her out of this. She's already been through hell. She doesn't deserve this.

"I was jealous of you all, you know that. The perfect lives, the perfect friends, the perfect prospects." Jake scoffs beside me.

"You clearly didn't look hard enough because our lives are shit, Hellburn.

You're the one with the money, the influential daddy, while we were scrambling to stay afloat."

I look to Jake, his eyes hold Preston's but the second he realizes he has my attention, his hand moves, urging me forward.

"You're the one with the power."

"I have nothing. This is high school. The team and the position you so desperately want mean nothing in the grand scheme of things. It's not worth risking your life for."

When I don't move as instructed, Jake glances at me. His eyes widening.

"Bullshit," Preston snaps before launching into a speech about Jake's position, just showing how delusional he really is.

But I don't hear any of the words because without putting another thought into it, I race forward.

But he sees it coming and he leans back.

The scream that rips from Poppy's throat as she realizes what's happening is one that I'm sure will haunt me for the rest of my life.

I'm in front of them before they've really started to fall and when I reach out, I manage to grip onto Poppy's arm.

Her eyes are wide in fear, her skin as white as a sheet.

"Fuck." Jake is at my side in a heartbeat and manages to get her other arm. "We've got you. It's okay. We've got you."

Preston's arms are locked around Poppy's waist but as we start to pull her up, his hands slip and he lets go.

Without his weight, Poppy flies toward us. I gather her up in my arms as her body trembles with the ferocity of her sobs.

Jake and I stand there still looking over the edge of the building and down to where Preston is now in a heap on the concrete.

"Fuck," he breathes, lifting his hands to his hair. "Fuck. Fuck." He takes a step back, spinning away from the horrifying scene as the events of the past few seconds hit me.

He just let go. He's...

I don't get to dwell on it because Poppy begins to wail against my chest.

"It's okay. It's okay," I whisper into her hair, moving us both back from the edge.

"You're safe, Poppy. He's gone. It's okay," Jake says, marching over and pulling her from my arms.

I feel cold, lost, the second she's gone but I know it would be wrong of me to fight him on this right now.

"Call 9-1-1," he instructs.

I stare at the two of them for a beat, relieved that Poppy has someone to support her right now, that she has some family but equally hating that it's not me with my arms wrapped around her. Before I drag my cell from my pocket, I reach behind me and pull my hoodie from my body.

"What are you... oh." Stepping up to the two of them, I gently pull Poppy's ruined clothes from her arms before tugging my own over her head. Jake releases her long enough to cover her up before he walks back to the wall and slides down to the floor, keeping Poppy cradled to him the whole time.

I make the call and in what feels like only minutes the sound of sirens and the flashing lights surround us.

Officer's footsteps race up the stairs before two surround us, staring down at where we're sitting back against the wall, Jake still with Poppy in his arms. She's not so much as looked up let alone said anything.

"Is she okay? Is she hurt?"

"Uh... I don't think so. Just traumatized."

"Okay, well the paramedics are on their way. I think it's probably best we get her checked over while we get to the bottom of what's happened here."

As if on cue, two paramedics appear behind them and encourage Jake to release Poppy. He's clearly not happy about it but after a little coaxing, he allows them to get on with their job.

They take her weight and direct her to the stairs.

"Where are you going?" he asks in a panic.

"Just to the ambulance so we can lie her down."

"Can we follow? Please? She's my sister," Jake begs the officers. "I need to be with her."

I've never heard him so vulnerable and lost and I hate it. "You go and I'll tell them everything I can."

The officers agree and Jake takes off after Poppy.

The next hour passes in a blur as I'm forced to recount the events of the afternoon, from how we found her here to what happened when we arrived and how it resulted with Preston dead on school grounds.

Even as I retell the story, I still don't really believe I've just lived through it. It's like something you see on TV, it's not something that happens in real life.

Only it has. This is very, very real.

I'm finally allowed to come down from the roof after walking the officers through everything, along with what I know about Preston's previous abuse toward Poppy.

As I say the words, guilt floods me. I should have done more to stop all of this from happening. I should have taken him out before this, I should have done what I promised Poppy I wouldn't do and called a couple of guys from Harrow Creek and dealt with it once and for all. It never should have got to this.

"Zayn," Mom calls, jumping from her car and running toward me. "Are you okay?" she cries, pulling me into her arms and holding me tight.

"Yeah, Mom. I'm fine."

"Where's Poppy?"

"Over there." I nod to where she's sitting in the back of a police car answering questions.

"She's okay?"

"Physically yeah. She managed to convince the paramedics not to take her to the hospital."

"Good. That's good. I'm gonna..." She gestures toward the car and marches over, pulling the door open and dropping down.

"Your mom's a bit of a whirlwind," Jake says, walking over with two cans of energy drinks in his hand. I have no clue where he's found them but I'm more than grateful as he hands one over.

"She loves all this. It's her job."

"I thought she spent her time getting kids out of juvie."

"Yeah, let's just hope there's no juvie involved in this one," I say, cracking the can open and downing half in one go. "If you didn't read into that screenshot—"

"Can we not?"

"Sure."

"Why didn't you tell me it was this bad?"

"I didn't know he was that deranged. I had no idea it was going to escalate this far. Plus, Poppy never actually told me any details. She refused, told me she could deal with him. I wasn't going to force it out of her."

He's silent for a beat. "You gonna tell me the truth yet?"

"The truth?" I ask, half choking on a mouthful of my drink.

"Yeah. There's something going on with you two, isn't there?" He drops down on the curb at our feet, bringing his knees up and resting his forearms on them.

"Uh..." I hesitate, dropping to sit beside him.

"Just tell me, Zayn. Your answer can't be any worse than anything that's happened here this afternoon."

"Um... yeah, it has."

"Fuck," he barks, his body locking up with tension.

"How long?"

"What?"

"How long has it been going on?"

"Couple of weeks, but—"

"You should have fucking told me."

"I know. But there's nothing to tell now, I don't think. She called it quits."

"You serious?"

"Yeah."

"You're fucking delusional, Hunter." As he says those words, the back of the police car opens and Poppy's legs appear before she climbs from the car.

My mom races around and pulls her into her side.

She looks tired, so fucking tired. But she's still beautiful.

A soft smile pulls at my lips when she looks up and finds Jake and I waiting for her.

"Let's go home," Mom says, looking between the two of us.

"You go with Poppy," I say to Jake. "I'll meet you back at home."

He nods, quickly rushing to Poppy's side and taking her from Mom to help her into the car.

My heart aches to watch her walk away from me but she needs Jake right now, not me. As much as that might hurt, I need to accept her wishes and take a step back.

34

POPPY

Jake's hand holds mine as we make our way through town toward the Hunter's house. It's the only thing that keeps me grounded, stops me from falling headfirst into the nightmare that was this afternoon.

How could I have been so stupid to believe that Mom was sending me those messages? I should have seen the warning signs. But even now, I know that I wouldn't have done anything differently. No matter the past, no matter how terrible of a parent she has been, I'll always jump when she says to. It's just ingrained in me.

It's my ultimate weakness. If only I'd realized that before Preston did.

A sob rips from my throat at the thought of Preston. Jake's hand tightens in mine and I feel him look over at me but my eyes remain on the headrest in front of me. I can't cope with seeing the sympathy in his eyes right now.

I didn't see him fall. I didn't see his body in a crumpled mess on the ground. By the time I got down there, the police had already set up barriers and covered the area. But I have a good enough imagination and that's enough to keep the image burned into my mind.

I didn't want him to die. I might have hated him, but I never would have wished that on him.

Why did he let go? Zayn and Jake could have got to him.

Why did he decide that was how this was all going to end?

To continue punishing me.

It might all be over for him now. But I've got to live with this for the rest of my life.

I may not have pushed him or caused what happened today in any way. But right now, the guilt is pressing down on me so hard that I'm struggling to breathe.

"You're safe, Poppy. It's over," Jake soothes, but as comforting as his voice is, I can't help wishing for another.

I glance in Jada's side-view mirror at the car that's following behind us and I suck in a breath.

Why was he there today? Why did he have to be the one to save me when I'm trying so fucking hard to put a wall up between us.

Without knowing it, he's just come in and bulldozed it because all I want right now is to be in his arms, to hear him tell me that I'm safe and ultimately, to make me forget. He's the only one who can do that.

No one says anything else the whole way back. There aren't any words to say.

I told the officers everything I knew. But only Preston knew the real reason for all of this and he's no longer able to tell his side of the story.

I shake my head, trying to get it to register that today actually happened.

Preston is gone. His threat is gone.

I can walk back into school without having to look over my shoulder wondering when the next attack is going to come.

That might be true, but all of this is going to bring me something I really don't want.

Attention.

Now I'm not just Jake Thorn's cousin who'd rather hide in the shadows. Now I'm Jake Thorn's sister and I'm responsible for the death of one of my classmates.

Silently we all climb from the car, Jake has me in his arms again the second he's jogged around to me and I welcome his warmth, his support, but I can't help thinking that I need to get away from all of this.

Jada lets us in and she immediately turns toward the kitchen, Jake follows, pulling me with him and in only seconds Zayn jogs up behind us.

"Coffee?" Jada asks, turning to look at us, her face full of concern and sympathy when her eyes find mine.

"I'm... um... I'm going to go and lie down."

Everyone watches me as I back out of the room. I can tell that both Jake and Zayn want to argue or demand they come with me. But I need to be alone. I need silence and solitude. I just need... I don't really know what I need, but it's not all of them looking at me with pity in their eyes.

Jake's lips part but I cut him off before he says a word.

"I'm okay, really. I'm just exhausted."

He nods and thankfully, allows me to walk out of the room.

It's not until I'm at the top of the stairs that I hear their voices but although I can't hear their words, my skin tingles with awareness knowing they're talking about me.

My eyes lock on my bedroom door and I step toward it, knowing I'm going to find what I need inside, but when I get flush with Zayn's room, my body takes on a life of its own and I reach out to open the door.

The second I slip inside, his scent hits me and I instantly feel better. I don't know why I've come in here until I spot his jersey left in a pile on his chair. Walking over, I swipe it up and bring the fabric to my nose. I breathe him in deeply and allow myself to get lost in him despite the fact he's not here with me.

Their voices filter through to me once more and I quickly dart for the door, not wanting to get caught snooping, not that I think Zayn would have an issue with finding me in his room.

I've seen the pain in his eyes while Jake's supported me this afternoon. He wanted to be the one to hold me, to try to help me put the pieces back together. Finding me here right now would give him everything he wants.

But I can't. I can't allow myself to go there again. I need to stay strong. To remember the reasons why I sent him away last night.

What's happened today doesn't change anything. It can't.

With his jersey held tight in my hand, I close his door once more and finally make my way down to the bathroom.

I rip Zayn's hoodie from me, before stripping out of the rest of my ruined clothes. I don't even look at my ripped bra. I don't need more images in my head reminding me what he did. How he shamed me. Used me. Abused me.

Turning the shower on as hot as it'll go, I step under the water, hoping it'll wash the memories of his touch from my body along with the evidence he's left that today really happened.

Once I've scrubbed every inch of my skin until it's red and raw, I step out and wrap myself with the towel waiting for me.

I don't want to look in the mirror. I don't want to see what he did to me. But my need to clean everything away has me reaching for a wipe and gently cleaning the cuts and bruises he left me with.

Tears burn my eyes and emotions clogs my throat. My body wants me to break but I refuse to do so yet.

Dragging on Zayn's jersey, I pad to my room, closing the door behind me and diving for the bed. I pull the covers back and slide under them, pulling them right up until I'm surrounded by darkness.

It's then that the tears I've been holding inside me come.

I cover my mouth as I sob and allow my tears to soak the pillow beneath me.

The sound of the door opening sometime later drags me from my fitful sleep. It's not until my brain starts to wake that I realize the images within it aren't from a nightmare. Today really did happen.

"Hey, Sis. It's just me."

He can't see me because I'm still totally cocooned under the duvet but my lips twitch up at the corners.

"How are you doing?"

The temptation to stay hidden and allow him to think I'm still sleeping is strong but I don't. Feeling brave, I pull the sheets down a little until the cool air hits my face. I blink a couple of times, my eyes sore from crying until the blurry image of Jake sitting on the edge of the bed comes into view.

He's still got deep frown lines on his brow and concern filling his eyes. I wish he could just look at me like this is any other normal day and that I didn't almost die a few hours ago.

"Yeah, you know."

He reaches out and brushes his hand over my hair.

"You're so fucking brave, you know that?"

I shrug, I don't think I did anything anyone wouldn't have done today. There was nothing I could do other than be the pawn in his sick games.

"Amalie wanted to come and see you, but I said that you probably weren't up for it. I hope that's okay."

I nod because he's right. I'm really not up for it right now. "Just tell her that I'm okay."

"I will." He smiles down at me. "That photo you sent me before..." He trails off, not wanting to go there. "That was pretty epic."

I have to wrack my brain for a few seconds to recall what he's talking about. I can't seem to think about anything that doesn't involve being up on that roof.

The birth certificate.

I smile with him and it makes his eyes soften.

"I'm Poppy Thorn," I whisper.

"You are. I still can't believe it. Do you know how many times I wished I had a brother or sister over the years?"

I shake my head. I always assumed he was fine on his own.

"I'm so fucking glad it's you." He cups my cheeks, his eyes getting a little watery.

"She's gone," I blurt out, causing his brows to pull together. "She died today?"

"W-who did?"

"Poppy Poore. She's done. She's fed up of being the pawn in his games, of watching her back, of hiding."

The smile that lights up his face makes my chest swell.

"When I walk out of this room tomorrow, I'm Poppy Thorn."

"Hell yes, you are."

"I'm going to get Jada to do whatever she needs to go to get my name changed, it shouldn't be too hard seeing as it's my actual name. I'm done with my past and allowing people to drag me down. It's time for a fresh start."

"That sounds like a plan, Popsicle. Can I ask you one question though?"

"Sure."

"What are you going to do about Zayn?"

My breath catches at hearing his name. "Um..."

"I know, Pops."

"You're not angry?"

"Let's just say I'm not overly thrilled, but I could never be angry with you."

"It doesn't matter. It's nothing. I don't need to do anything about him."

"Are you sure about that?"

"Positive. It was never meant to be anything more than a bit of fun." Jake winces at my words but it's the truth. Even now, I still find it hard to believe that the whole thing wasn't a game or a joke to him. It sure started off that way.

"Do I need to remind him what happens when he messes with you?"

I can't help but laugh at the serious look on his face. It feels good. "No, it's okay. I'll let you know if that changes though."

"I'm going to let you rest and go home to attempt to convince Amalie that you're okay. Call me if you need me, yeah?"

"I will."

Lowering down, he drops his lips to my head, lingering a second longer than necessary.

"I wish you'd told me about all of this when it started, Pops. But I understand why you didn't, and I really appreciate your loyalty."

"Always, Jake."

He pushes from the bed and walks to the door.

"Pops?"

"Yeah?"

"All that stuff you said about Zayn. It would be much more believable if you said it while you weren't wearing his number." He winks at me, a smirk pulling at his lips before he slips through the door, closing it behind him and I tug the covers up higher over my body.

35

ZAYN

I stay in the kitchen with Mom while Jake heads upstairs to check on Poppy before he goes home.

"You okay, Son?" she asks, her eyes searching mine.

"Yeah," I say, dropping my head to my hands. "Today was... yeah," I breathe, not really knowing what to say about it.

"Poppy was really lucky that Jake figured out where she was."

"I know, I dread to think..." A violent shudder runs down my spine. It's bad enough that I can't get the image of him lying lifeless on the concrete ground out of my head, but thinking about Poppy being laid beside him. I can't... I just can't. "Is everything going to be okay with the police and everything?"

"Yeah. They need to come back and talk to you all again but there shouldn't be an issue."

"That's good. Poppy doesn't need any more on her plate."

Silence settles between us before Mom disappears to her office after telling me that we'll order takeout when Harley's home.

I agree but right now, I don't think I could stomach eating anything.

Jake's footsteps on the stairs has me pulling my head up just as he appears in the doorway.

He smiles at me sadly. "Is she okay?"

"She will be. She's stronger than we give her credit for."

"Trust me, I know."

"Okay, I'm out. Call me if anything happens."

"Of course. Mom thinks we might need to talk to the police again."

"Sure, whatever they need." He turns to leave but stops before he disappears. "Look after her, Hunter. She might not want to admit it, but she needs you." It pains him to say that, I can see it in his eyes.

"I will. You don't need to worry about her."

"I'd better fucking not. You know that if you hurt her, I'll come for you."

"I wouldn't expect anything else, Thorn."

He nods at me before disappearing.

Every muscle in my body screams for me to go up and check on her but I don't. She wanted space, so I need to respect that.

I'm not going to stay away forever though because I fully intend on standing by that promise, I just made Jake. I'm not going to let anyone, or anything hurt her again.

Harley appeared not long after Jake left, and Mom and I told her what happened before she went running up the stairs to see that Poppy was okay with her own eyes.

She spoke to Harley, but she refused to come down for dinner and the food Harley took up was untouched.

Trish also dropped everything the second Mom called her to explain what had happened and she spent a couple of hours here to see with her own eyes that Poppy was okay, but even she couldn't lure her out of the bedroom or make her eat anything.

I wanted to take charge, to storm in there and demand she eats something, but I know it'll just end up with her chewing me out.

Restraint isn't one of my strong suits. But I'm really fucking trying.

Before heading to bed, I cave to my need to check on her despite the fact I know she's okay because both Mom and Harley have been in to see her and spoken to her, so I knock on her door.

I wait for a beat, but unable to walk away, I twist the handle and poke my head inside.

She's got the covers pulled right up to her neck, her eyes are closed and her lips slightly parted.

Something aches in my chest at the sight of her. My need to step inside and crawl in beside her is almost too much to bear. But knowing I can't, I silently slip from the room and close the door behind me.

I shower, hoping that the memories of today will disappear down the drain with the dirty water but as I lie in bed staring at the ceiling and running the events of the day through my mind, I realize it was wishful thinking.

The room is in darkness and the house is in silence. Harley and Mom went to bed hours ago.

I toss and turn for hours, the image I've conjured up of her lying lifeless beside Preston earlier won't leave.

I'm almost at the point of getting back up and putting the TV on or something seeing as sleep refuses to claim me when my door cracks open.

The hallway is in darkness so there's no extra light, but I don't need it. I already know who it is.

She doesn't say anything, Instead, she just lifts the covers once she's at the bed and she slides in beside me.

Turning on my side, I watch as she moves right up to me, her eyes catching the little light that's creeping through the curtains.

"Pop—" My word is cut off when her lips press to mine.

I hesitate for a second, not because I'm not willing, just because I'm so shocked.

My lips part when her tongue teases them, accepting her kiss. My arm snakes around her waist, pulling her up against my body.

No words are spoken as we devour each other. Her hands run over the bare skin of my back as I roll her onto hers and lock her ankles behind my waist.

Ripping my lips from hers, I kiss across her jaw and down her neck. My hands skim up her thighs until I get to the fabric covering her. Wrapping my fingers around it, I start pulling it up her body but I pause when I notice the color of it.

"Poppy?" I ask when I realize she's wearing my jersey. My cock twitches with my need for her. "Were you in bed wrapped in only my number?"

"Zayn, please. Make it stop."

"Fuck, Poppy. Anything."

She pushes up from the bed, making it easier for me to pull the fabric free from her body. The second I drop it over the side of the bed, I lower my hands to her breasts.

"I just want to remember your touch. Please, Zayn." Her words rip me open. I hate that she's suffering because of him. That he even had the power to hurt her in the first place.

Lowering her back to the bed, I brush my lips down her neck, over her collarbones, and down to her breasts. I kiss, lick and nip over every inch of her skin. I suck her nipples into my mouth until her back arches off and she moans my name.

"Zayn, more," she begs, her nails scratching across my scalp as I lick down her stomach, dipping my tongue into her belly button.

Finding the edge of her panties, I wrap my fingers around them and tug.

The sound of them ripping fills my room along with her shocked gasp.

Pushing her thighs wide, I lower myself to my belly before running one finger through her folds.

"Fuck, you're soaked."

"Zayn." Her voice holds a warning, one that I'm more than happy to hear.

"You want my mouth, baby."

"Please, Zayn. Please."

Leaning forward, I run the tip of my tongue up the length of her. Her legs tremble as her nails scratch with her need for more.

I focus on her clit, licking the little bundle of nerves over and over until she's writhing beneath me, lifting her hips from the bed, trying to get more friction.

Lifting my other hand, I circle her tight entrance. Her muscles try sucking me in, making my teeth grind wishing that it was my cock getting ready to sink deep inside her body.

"More, more, more," she chants.

Unable to ignore her demands, I push two fingers deep inside her, immediately bending them so that I'll hit that magical spot inside her that will make her scream.

I up the pressure with my tongue and in only a few seconds her pussy clamps down on my fingers as she cries out her release.

I watch as her back arches on my bed and her fingers grip the sheets beneath her as she loses herself to her pleasure.

Her release lasts for a few long seconds and I don't pull away from her until she's coming back down from her high.

"More?" I ask, wiping my mouth with the back of my hand.

"So much more."

Smiling, I lower myself over her, sweeping my tongue into her mouth and allowing her to taste herself.

Taking my cock in hand, I rub it against her swollen clit.

"Oh God," she moans.

"I need you so fucking bad," I admit on a groan. "I've missed you so fucking much."

"You only had me last night," she whispers as I drop lower, teasing her entrance with the head of my cock.

"That's not what I meant, and you know it."

"Do it," she demands when I push in ever so slightly, my eyes rolling back at the sensation of feeling her skin on skin.

"But—"

"I'm covered. I went and... ooooooh," she cries out when I see where she's going and sink deep inside her in one quick thrust. "Oh God."

"So fucking good. Fuck, you feel like heaven."

Her nails rake down my back before she grabs on to my ass, pushing me deeper.

"Oh shit, Pops."

"Fuck me, Zayn. Make me feel it for days."

A growl rumbles up my throat as I pull almost all the way back out before slamming back inside her. She shoots up the bed with my force. The headboard rattles against the wall but I don't pay it any mind as I repeat my previous action.

"I'm. Fucking. Addicted. To. You," I groan between thrusts.

One of my hands wraps around her hip, holding her to me, my fingertips digging into her skin enough that she'll have bruises tomorrow but as I watch her throw her head back in ecstasy, I can't bring myself to care while she's losing herself to the pleasure. If anything, knowing that I'm going to leave marks just makes me harder for her.

Skimming my other hand up her stomach, I pinch her nipples hard, making her cry out and for her pussy to clamp down on me every time I cause a bite of pain.

"You like that, baby?"

"Yes, Zayn. More. Give me everything."

"Fuck."

Lifting my hand higher, I wrap it around her throat. She immediately lowers her chin and her wide eyes lock on to mine, but they're not filled with panic. Just desire, heat and lust.

"You fucking slay me, Poppy." My fingers tighten around her throat, her pulse hammering against my thumb. "You're mine," I grate out as my balls begin to draw up. "Mine."

"Zayn, shit. Fuck." She tilts her hips, so her clit hit my pelvis, pushing her closer to her own release.

"Say it," I demand. "Tell me who you belong to."

"You, Zayn. You. I'm yours."

Releasing her hip, I press my thumb to her clit as I slam into her once more.

She screams out her releases as her pussy pulls my cock deeper than I thought possible.

"Fuck, Poppy. So good, so fucking good." Tingles explode around my body, and I'm just about to fall over the edge when the door swings open.

"What the... Poppy?" Harley squeals, her hand flying to her eyes to stop her from seeing what's happening.

Poppy tenses beneath me, but I fall headfirst into pleasure.

"Oh my God. Oh my God," I vaguely hear my sister mutter as I lose myself to my girl, my cock jerking violently and filling her with jets of my cum. Marking her, making her mine for good.

Once I get control of my body back, I glance over to the door to find it closed, and Harley nowhere in sight. I start to wonder if I imagined it until I look down to Poppy to find her with my jersey bunched up against her chest, trying to hide.

"Get rid of that. I'm not done with you yet." I swipe it away and throw it across the room.

Still buried inside her and my semi already starting to grow once more, I flip us so she's sitting astride my lap.

"Zayn, stop." I catch her wrists before she can climb off me.

"Too late, Pops. This is happening and there's nothing you can say right now that will stop me from giving you everything you need."

My hands land on her hip and I rock her on my length.

"You're not playing fair," she whispers, her head falling back in pleasure.

"Did I ever say that I played fair?" I ask with a smirk.

Her chin drops and her eyes run up the length of my body until she finds my eyes.

"You're done running from me, Poppy. I know you're scared. Hell, I'm scared too. But I need this. I need you."

"But—"

I press two fingers to her lips, cutting off whatever she's going to say.

"There's nothing you can say that's going to stop this from happening. You're mine, Poppy Thorn. You just said so yourself."

She still wants to fight it, I can tell by the tense set of her shoulders, but her eyes give her away. She wants this as badly as I do.

"But Harley," she whispers in spite of my fingers. "Your mom."

I shrug. "I don't care, Poppy. They're going to have to get used to it because you're it for me."

"Zayn," she sighs.

"No, hear me out. I could have lost you today. Do you have any fucking idea how terrifying it was watching you fall? If I didn't get to you in time. Fuck," I bark, startling her as that image I've been battling with all afternoon slams into me once more.

Gathering her up in my arms, I pull her down onto my chest and hold her tight.

"I'm not letting you walk away ever again. I love you, Pops."

She gasps at my admission. I thought saying those words that I realized were true quite some time ago would be scary, but after the events of today, nothing seems as daunting anymore.

Is this an ideal situation? No, probably not with her without a home or parents and us living under the same roof. But it's us. It's meant to be and somehow, we'll figure it out.

Twisting my lips to her ear when she's still not said anything or even moved, I whisper, "I'm going to fuck you again, now."

A shudder rips through her and she turns to look at me. Her eyes are filled with unshed tears.

"Zayn—"

"Shhh, not now. Just let me give you this. We've got all the time in the world to talk."

I rock into her again and a low moan rumbles up her throat.

"I can't even tell you how good this feels," I tell her, pulling her down onto me harder, needing to feel every inch of her against me.

"So good," she mutters into the crook of my neck as her hips roll with mine.

I fuck her until she passes out. I know she's hurting after the events of the day, but I can't lie, being buried in her for hours, having our bodies laced together, for that long, it's the best night of my life.

As gently as I can, I slip out from beneath her, cover her so she doesn't get cold, and pad toward my bathroom. I hate washing her scent off me, but the thought of being able to slide into bed with her again soon makes it a little easier.

I have a quick shower before pulling on a pair of sweats and slipping silently from the room.

I knock on Harley's door and after a second she barks, "What?"

Laughing to myself, I push the door open and walk inside.

The second she sees me, she climbs from the bed, stands before me at full height ready to fight.

"What the fuck, Zayn? Don't you think she'd been through enough today? She really doesn't need to be fucked and chucked by you. You know she was a virgin, right? No, you probably didn't, probably didn't give a shit either. You can't just go around taking whoever you want and ruining all my friends. It's not fair, Zayn." Her index finger pokes me harshly in the chest as she continues to rant.

"Harley. Harley…" I repeat, waiting for her to run out of steam.

"What?" she snaps, placing her hands on her waist and popping a hip out in frustration.

"It's not like that with us."

"Us?" She laughs but it's anything but amused. "There's a fucking us?"

"I'm…" I hesitate, not really wanting to tell my sister this only an hour or so after telling Poppy but I can't see any other way out of this. "I'm in love with her."

"What?" she screeches at a pitch I'm sure only dogs are meant to hear. "Can you even hear yourself right now?" She shakes her head and walks to the other side of the room, disbelief oozing from her. "You really expect me to believe that shit?"

"Yeah, actually. I do because it's true."

"But—"

"Harley, this isn't the first time."

Her shoulders drop and I hate that I'm doing this, but she needs to know the truth. Jake does and he was mostly okay with it, she needs to understand too.

"You've been going behind my back?" she asks, her brows pulling together and her bottom lip quivering. "You've both been lying to me?"

I don't say anything. What can I say other than yes, we have?

"Zayn, for fuck's sake. I told you to stay away from my friends, damn it."

"I know, but I couldn't. I've wanted Poppy for…" She looks up at me, her eyes widening in curiosity,

"For?" she prompts.

"For a long time. Since before the first time I even kissed her," I admit.

She thinks for a second. "Your birthday party?"

I nod. "Yeah."

"But you were horrible to her that night."

"I know, and I've regretted it ever since. Then New Year's Eve, she was my tag and things just..."

She gasps in horror. "You used her in another game?"

"Yeah, well... yeah. I wasn't about to pass up the chance."

"But you hate each other. You've fought like cats and dogs for years."

I shrug. She's not lying. But we didn't hate each other for the reason she thought. We hated each other because we couldn't accept how we really felt.

"You know what they say, Har. Hate sex is always the best."

"I wouldn't fucking know, asshole. Fuck it. I'm giving one of the guys from the team my V-card. Justin maybe, or Rich. Maybe both at once. See how you fucking feel."

"Harley," I growl, not amused in the slightest about her suggestion. "You go near them and I'll cut their dicks off and feed it to them."

"You're such a hypocrite."

"Are you in love with Justin or Rich?"

"Well, no, but..."

"There is no but here, Har. I love her. Love. Her. She's it for me."

"But—"

I smile at her.

"Fucking hell, Zayn." She tugs on her hair, spinning on the spot as she tries to accept that this is happening. "Where is she now?"

"Asleep in my bed."

"Well... you'd better get back. We don't want her waking up alone after everything."

I back up toward the door, not needing to be told twice to go back to my girl, especially when she's naked in my bed.

"Har?" I ask. "Don't be too hard on her. It's been killing her not to tell you. She didn't want to disappoint you."

"Damn you, Zayn Hunter. Damn you." As I close the door behind me, I don't miss the smile that twitches at her lips. "You'd better be the best boyfriend to ever walk the planet because if you hurt her, you're going to be the one choking on your own dick."

I can't help laughing as I push my bedroom door open, although it falls the second my eyes land on a pair of gray ones.

Poppy pulls the sheets back, revealing her naked body and inviting me back into bed.

My joggers are on the floor in a second and in the next she's in my arms, her lips on mine where they belong.

"I love you too, Zayn," she whispers, making my entire world tilt a few degrees.

36

POPPY

The weight of Zayn's arm resting over my waist presses me into the mattress, and despite everything, I wake with a smile on my face.

I told myself over and over last night that coming in here was a bad idea, but as I laid in my own bed, all I could think about was being in his arms. I craved the feeling of safety he brings me. I needed him and the longer I put it off, the more desperate I became until I found myself slipping from my own bed and into his.

Part of me expected him to send me away after how I've treated him, but thankfully, that wasn't what happened because it seemed that he needed me as much as I needed him.

My eyes flutter open and my breath catches when I find his dark, hungry eyes staring back at me.

"Morning, baby."

My cheeks heat as memories from our late-night antics slam into me. I'll be amazed if I'm able to walk away from this bed this morning after the number of orgasms he gave me.

"Good night, huh?" he says, running his knuckles across my heated cheek.

"I mean, it was okay."

His brows rise in amusement.

"Okay?"

"Maybe I need a reminder." I push against his chest and attempt to roll him onto his back, but he doesn't move. "What? What's wrong?" I ask, trying not to allow the hurt that wants to coil around my heart at his obvious rejection.

Dropping my hand, I skim over the muscles of his stomach, they jump at my contact until I wrap my hand around his length. His eyes shutter for a beat before he recovers, wrapping his own hand around me and stopping my movement.

"Talk to me, Poppy," he pleads, looking so deep into my eyes I swear he's staring straight into my soul.

"I was thinking actions spoke louder."

"Not right now." He lifts my hand from him and drops it around his waist before bringing his hand up to cup my jaw.

"How are you feeling?"

"Frustrated," I huff.

He chuckles, knocking his nose against mine. "Don't worry, I'll only be able to deny you for so long. But I want to know where your head is at first. Yesterday was..."

"A head fuck."

"Yeah, you could say that. I thought I was going to lose you, Pops," he says on a sigh.

"But you didn't. I'm right here."

"I know, and I couldn't be more grateful. Why did you change your mind... about me, us?"

"I..." I hesitate, trying to find the right words. "I needed you, Zayn. Jake was holding me, supporting me, and it meant so much to have him there, that he figured it out in the first place. But all I wanted was you." His breath catches at my admission.

"For real?"

"Yeah, for real."

"How did..." He blows out a breath.

"How'd I end up on the school roof?"

"Yeah. Start there."

I tell him about what Auntie Trish said to us about our parents meeting at school and how his messages took me back to that conversation, and thankfully, it seems that it did to Jake too.

"When did he steal your mom's cell?"

I shrug. "I don't know. He made out like he'd been at the house a few times. I guess that's how he knew about the drugs."

"Wait," he says. "He was the one who called the police on your parents."

"Seems so. He very proudly said about how he 'ruined my life'. He must be the worst stalker ever if he couldn't see that my life was shit."

"Jesus, Pops."

I shrug. "It is what it is. It's done now."

"I know but... fuck." He scrubs a hand down his face. "I can't believe he'd stoop to that level."

"I don't think any of us knew the real Preston. He was screwed up in so many ways."

The doorbell rings through the house, pausing Zayn's response.

"Poppy," Jada calls up the stairs. "The police are here to see you."

"Fuuuuck," Zayn groans much to my amusement.

"Regretting turning me down now?" I ask, quirking a brow at him.

"Fucking cockblockers," he mutters as we both swing our legs over the edge of his bed. "Here," he says, throwing me his jersey. "Wear this."

"I'm not sure..." My argument is halted when I get a look at the expression on his face. After a beat, my eyes drop down his naked body, following the lines of his cut abs down to the V that drops to his very hard cock.

My mouth waters as I stare at him.

"How quick do you think I could..."

"From the way you're looking at me right now, I'd say pretty damn fast. But that's probably not fast enough for the officers that are waiting for you downstairs."

"Shit, you're right." Dragging his jersey over my head, I push to stand. "I'll make it up to you later," I say over my shoulder as I walk to his door.

I make quick work of running to my room and pulling on a pair of panties and dragging some leggings up my legs.

As I make my way to the stairs, Zayn appears wearing a pair of sweats and a tight V-neck shirt.

"What are you doing?" I ask when he throws his arm over my shoulders and walks down the stairs with me.

"Coming with you."

"But your mom," I say, trying to push his arm from me.

"She knows."

"What?" I ask in horror, turning to him.

"Well, she's not said it in so many words, but she knows you mean more to me than I've ever let on."

"How?"

"I have no idea. Mother's intuition or some shit."

"I wouldn't know anything about that," I say sadly.

"You're about to learn. Nothing gets past Jada Hunter."

"Oh God. Was moving here a really bad idea?" I ask with a laugh.

"I guess that depends if you consider falling asleep every night with me a bad thing."

"Zayn, I've got my own roo—Officer, hi," I say as we round the corner and find Jada standing with a male and female office in the hallway.

Jada's eyes turn to both of us before she notices Zayn's arm over my shoulder.

This time when I push it away, he allows it to drop.

"Shall we?" she says, pointing through to the dining room. "Would you like coffee?"

"No, we're fine, thank you. Poppy, I'm Detective Archer and this is my colleague, Detective Jones. We've been looking into yesterday's incident and we're discovered a few things we'd like to speak to you about."

"Okay," I say skeptically, pulling out a chair and taking a seat as the officers do so.

"We went to Mr. Hellburn's house this morning," Detective Archer starts as Zayn drops into the chair beside me, lacing his fingers with mine. "Were you aware that Preston had an obsession with you?"

"Well, like I said yesterday, he'd been tormenting me for a while."

"Okay, but I think this might run deeper than you realized."

"Oh?"

Detective Jones pulls out some photographs and slides them across the table.

"Oh my God," I gasp, as both Zayn and Jada's breath catches.

"These are from his bedroom wall."

I stare at the images before me. There is picture after picture of me pinned to his bedroom wall. Many of which have been taken in my house along with others I recognize like him with his hand around my throat in the school's closet the other week.

"It seems he's had some interest in you for a while. Were you aware these images had been taken?"

"N-no. Jesus, this is scary," I mutter, taking in the evidence of his obsession.

"What did his dad say?" Zayn asks.

"He had no idea. But from what we gather, he wasn't around much of the time."

The detectives ask me more questions, but it seems that the evidence speaks for itself really and by the time they leave, they seem pretty confident that all of this is Preston's doing.

Jada sees them out, and after a brief chat, she closes the door behind them.

"Well that was dramatic," Harley says from behind where Zayn and I are still sitting at the dining table.

I spin around, my eyes wide as I take her in, leaning against the doorframe.

With everything that had happened, I'd forgotten about her late-night interruption.

"Zayn?" she asks.

"Yeah?"

"Fuck off, yeah?"

Zayn chuckles, but his sister's presence doesn't stop him from wrapping his hand around the back of my neck and dropping his lips to mine.

"Ugh, please," Harley whines before he releases me and walks up to her.

"It's like you don't want me to be happy, Sis." He rustles her hair and manages to dodge her fists when she tries to punch him in the stomach. "I'll be in my room," he says, shooting me a heated stare before disappearing around the door.

"You missy, have some explaining to do." She places her hand on her hip and pins me with a stare.

"You fancy going for pancakes?"

She opens her mouth as if she's about to rip me a new one but clearly thinks better of it.

"Yeah, actually. Let's go."

"I just need to tell Za—"

"No," she huffs. "If you go in there, I'm never getting you back. Sneak past his room, put on..." Her gaze drops to his jersey before she rolls her eyes. "Some of your own clothes and send him a message. You're mine for the rest of the day. He had you all night, it seems."

My cheeks burn bright red at her tone.

"Oh don't give me that innocent look, Thorn." Her eyes narrow but her lips twitch into a smile that I can't help but return. "I'm going to need the details, but I should warn you that if you so much as remind me that it was my brother you were banging, you might end up wearing your pancakes."

"I'll see what I can do. Call Ruby. See if she can meet us?"

"Sure. Be quick, and do not make me come up to find him doing... you know. I still need to bleach my eyes from last night."

As predicted, I don't manage to get past Zayn's bedroom door without him coming to find out why I didn't walk inside and come good on my promise from earlier. Instead, I forced him to sit on the end of my bed while I got ready to go out with his sister. He wasn't happy about it, but I think he kinda understood when I reminded him that she caught him balls deep inside me last night. That's not an image any little sister needs of her brother and best friend.

"Go out with the guys or something. Go and do something normal, hell knows we deserve it after yesterday," I say, dabbing at the tender bruises around my eyes and jaw in an attempt to cover them up.

"Poppy, are you ready?" Harley calls up the stairs.

"Yeah, hang on."

I turn to look at Zayn who sits with his muscles pulled tight and his eyes trained on me.

"Stop looking so worried. For the first time in... ever, I can go out without having to look over my shoulder. He's gone."

"I know, I just... worry."

"Aw, bad-boy Hunter is going all soft," I tease, stepping into his spread thighs and cupping his rough jaw in my hands.

"Trust me, Pops. There's nothing soft about me."

I glance down at his tented sweats and laugh.

"You might want to take care of that before you meet the guys. I'll see you later, yeah?" I lower down and brush my lips against his. His fingers curl around my hip but I manage to slip out of his hold before he can distract me too much.

"Finally," Harley huffs when I hit the bottom step.

"I just got dressed and tried to fix this," I say, pointing at my face.

"It makes you look like a badass. It's kinda hot."

"It's very hot. Stay away from my girl, Har. She doesn't swing that way."

"Shut the fuck up," Harley barks up the stairs before threading her arm through mine and pulling me toward the front door.

It's not until I step out that I remember I left her car at school.

"Shit, your..." I pause when I spot it parked outside the house. "How'd that get back here?"

"Jake and the guys sorted it. Seriously, I can't believe he's your brother."

"That's the most normal of the things that have happened in the past couple of weeks."

"Yeah but still, you're Jake Thorn's sister. You do realize how high up the social scale that's pushed you at school right."

"And you know I don't care about any of that stuff."

"I know, just be aware that people will probably treat you differently."

"Yeah, they'll be more obvious about trying to use me to get to the top instead of keeping it hidden."

"That wasn't quite what I meant," Harley says with a wince as we drop into her car.

"Well, whatever happens. I've got your back."

I turn to her before she puts the car in reverse. "You're not mad?"

"I..." she starts but cuts herself off. "I was... then Zayn came to talk to me."

"He did? When?"

"He said you'd fallen asleep."

"Oh."

"When he talked about you, about how much you meant to him. He looked... he looked different. Happy. He told me that..." She turns to look at me, her eyes soft and full of emotions. "He said he loved you."

"He told you that?"

"Shit, hasn't he told you?" she asks in a panic, thinking that she's just put her foot in it.

"Yeah, he has. I still can't quite get my head around it though."

"Why? It's the most normal thing out of everything that's happened," she says with a laugh, repeating my earlier words back to me.

"Playboy Zayn Hunter making declarations of love, that shit isn't normal," I say.

"Fucking hell, you've whipped him, haven't you?"

"There's been no whipping, but I can confirm the school gossip because your brother has mad skills in the bed—"

"Stop, stop, please. I take back what I said earlier. I don't want any details. You're going to have to tell that shit to Ruby."

I bark out a laugh as she hurries to reverse out of the drive and heads toward the oceanfront for Aces.

Usually, I'd avoid the place, but today, despite the gossip that I'm sure is rife around town, I want to walk in there with my head held high.

I've done nothing wrong here. I'm the survivor in all of this. It's about time people learned the truth about what's been going on in the hope it stops someone else suffering like I have.

Ruby is already waiting for us when we walk toward Aces. The second she spots us, she flies at me, wrapping her arms around my shoulders and holding me tightly.

"I'm so glad you're okay," she breathes in my ear.

"I'm good, Rubes," I say, accepting her embrace.

The three of us walk inside as if this is just a normal day, and I guess it is to everyone else. No one looks up, no one narrows their eyes at me or gives me any indication that they know what happened yesterday. I'm sure they must, I can't imagine something as dramatic as that has been kept under wraps in a gossip-hungry town like Rosewood, but I'm grateful that I'm not under the spotlight right now.

The second our asses hit the booth, Bill is there, ready to take our orders. Unlike everyone else, he studies me for a second too long, taking in the bruises that I tried to cover.

"It's good to see you, Poppy. Breakfast is on the house."

"Oh, no, no, we can't."

"You can, and you'll enjoy it," he says with a wink and a laugh. "Brave girl like you deserves nothing less."

That is all he, or anyone else, says throughout our entire visit.

It's almost... normal.

"So..." Harley announces, although not loudly enough for anyone else to hear. "She's banging Zayn."

Ruby's chin drops but a smile tugs at her lips. "I know."

Harley turns her narrowed stare on our best friend. "You know," she seethes. "You knew and you didn't tell me?"

"Not my story to tell, Har." Ruby looks at me and winks.

"But... but.... Ugh, I still can't believe it."

"You should, you walked in on the evidence," I deadpan.

"You did not?" Ruby screeches, earning a few curious looks from the other diners around us.

Harley drops her head into her hands. "I did," she mutters. "And I'm afraid I'm never going to unsee it."

"At least Zayn's got a banging body. It could have been worse, it could have been your parents," Ruby helpfully points out.

Harley's head pops up, her eyes wide. "Well, yeah, that would have been a shock seeing as they can't stand to be in the same room as each other these days. Speaking of..." She turns her eyes to me. "You coming for your first visit to the Creek?"

"Uh..."

"Don't tell me you don't know it's Zayn's eighteenth."

"Of course I know," I argue. It's been three years since he turned my world upside down in that damn closet, I've never forgotten the date. "It had just slipped my mind with everything."

Harley's face drops slightly but thankfully she doesn't say anything.

"Okay, so we need to go and see Dad before the party so you can come, yeah? I know he'll want to meet you."

"Uh..."

"You're coming," she states as Bill brings over three giant plates of breakfast for us.

I can see the questions on the very tip of Ruby's tongue, the entire time we sit there, but she doesn't ask. I assume she knows most of what happened yesterday through Harley anyway. Instead, we just hang out, talk about school and all the gossip, that doesn't involve me, that I've missed while we stuff our faces with Bill's epic breakfast.

"So are you coming back tomorrow?" Ruby asks when we walk out of the diner and come to a stop at the railing to look out over to the ocean beyond.

My stomach knots at the thought of walking back down those hallways where the ghost used to be who haunted me.

Memories from yesterday, the feeling of him letting go and knowing that while Jake and Zayn were pulling me to safety that he was falling to his death threaten to consume me, but I manage to swallow it down and push the image aside.

"Uh... I don't know. I need to talk to Jada, see what she's organized."

"Well, I hope you're back," she says, pulling me into a hug. "It's not the same without you."

Zayn's car isn't in the driveway when we get back.

"Looks like I get you to myself for a little while."

"Is this really weird for you?" I ask as we walk to the house.

"It's not normal."

"Nothing is normal anymore, Har."

"I'm just worried I'm going to lose you," she says, coming to a stop at the front door.

"Har, I live in your house. You're not going to lose me."

"But you're going to spend all your time with him."

"I'm not, I promise. You're still my best friend, Har-Har. Your brother is not going to change that."

I pull her in for a hug and hold her tight.

"If he so much as hurts a hair on your head then I'll kill him. You know that, right?"

"I wouldn't expect anything less."

Eventually, we pull apart, both a little emotional, and step inside.

"Girls, how was breakfast?" Jada asks.

"Amazing. Just what the doctor ordered," Harley says, bouncing into the room.

"Poppy, can we talk?" Jada asks, flicking her eyes over to her daughter. "It's okay. Harley can stay."

"O-okay." I take a seat beside Jada while Harley makes us all coffee.

"I've spoken to Principal Hartmann, he's happy for you to return whenever you're ready." I nod. The concern in her eyes is telling me that she wants to say more about me returning to school. "I've also lined up some appointments for you."

"Appointments?" I ask, narrowing my eyes. I swear, if she starts talking about birth control, I'm going to want the ground to swallow me up.

Thankfully, I think, she goes down a different route.

"I've managed to squeeze you in with the best counselor I know."

"A counselor?"

"Yeah. I know you think everything is okay, but Poppy, you've just been through something huge. You can put on a brave face all you want, sweetheart, but I'm afraid that you're not dealing with everything that's happened."

I open my mouth to argue, but I soon realize that I don't really have one because she's right.

"Also, I think it's time we had a conversation about my son, don't you?"

"And that's my cue to leave," Harley announces, leaving me with her mother to have the most awkward conversation of my life.

37

ZAYN

Poppy's body trembles in my hold. We all tried to tell her that she didn't need to do this yet, but she was adamant she wanted life to go back to normal—whatever normal is now—as soon as possible.

After a week of sitting at home and attending the counseling sessions that Mom organized for her, she was determined that this was happening.

Mom, Harley, and I are worried, but we could hardly lock her up in the house and refuse to let her out today. We've just got to trust that she knows what she's doing and that she's ready for this.

"It's not too late to change your mind," I say as we walk toward the benches where the team and the squad are gathered.

She turns to look up at me and despite the fear, I can feel it racing through her, her face is full of determination.

"No, I'm doing this. I'm not sitting at home wondering what they're all saying about me any longer. I'm facing it head-on."

I smile down at her, my chest aching with everything I feel for her. She's so strong. What she's been through over the past few weeks would break a weaker person, but she's standing tall with her head held high.

As we get closer, both Harley and Ruby smile over at us. Harley wanted to bring Poppy to school like they used to, but I point-blank refused, much to her irritation.

One by one, everyone starts to notice our approach. Shock covers most of their faces. Poppy was probably the last person they were expecting to see back at school today, let alone pressed against my side like she is.

"Guys," I nod to the team, and Jake, when we come to a stop before them all. "You know my girl, right?"

"What's up, Poppy?" Shane says, a shit-eating grin spreading across his face.

Poppy stiffens in my hold, but she soon relaxes when she realizes that he's just asking the same question he would any other day.

"Shane's known the whole time," I whisper in her ears.

"Oh."

"While we're making announcements," Jake says, standing up on the picnic bench he was previously sitting on.

All eyes turn on him as Poppy attempts to curl in my side, obviously guessing what's about to happen.

"I know you all know what's happened recently, but I just want to clear something up." His voice booms across the quad.

"Stop him, please."

"Baby, you know better than anyone that Jake will do as he pleases no matter what."

"Great."

"Well, hear this bit of gossip straight from me. That girl right there." He points directly at Poppy as she curls in even tighter to my side. "She's one of the strongest girls you'll ever meet. She also just so happens to be my sister. So anything you have to say to her, you had better be prepared to say it to me as well, because there is no longer just one Thorn in this school, there are two, and you will treat her with the respect she deserves."

"Jake," she barks. "Get the fuck down."

"Oh and..." he continues. "She's taken, so don't even think about it." He pins each member of the team with a look. "Unless you want both Hunter and me to beat your asses into next week."

Eyes turn on the two of us. I pull Poppy in front of me and drop my lips to the top of her head and wink at Jake.

When Poppy left with Harley to get breakfast last Sunday morning, I headed straight to Jake and Amalie's new place to tell him the truth, well after Mom collared me to talk about how she wasn't ready to be a grandmother yet.

I was fully prepared to leave with a black eye and split lip to rival my girl's, but I was pleasantly surprised when all I got from him was a harsh warning to treat her properly and to never hurt her. I'm not sure if I need to thank Amalie for him not going full throttle on me or if he had already accepted that I'd fallen head over heels for his sister.

Jake jumps down from the bench, walks over and holds his fist out to me.

I bump it before pulling Poppy from her hiding place.

"Was that really necessary?" she spits.

"Yep. Anyone says anything to you, you tell me, yeah?"

"I don't think anyone's that stupid." He raises a brow. He doesn't need to say the words, we all know that if that were actually true then we wouldn't have just lived the nightmare we have.

Poppy lets out a sad sigh. "Thank you," she whispers to Jake. "I appreciate you having my back."

"Always, Sis. It's me and you now." He drops a kiss to her forehead before going back to join the guys.

"Walk me to class?" she asks, looking up at me with her huge gray eyes.

"I'd love to. Want me to carry your books too?"

"You're such a goof. Come on," she says with a laugh, lacing her fingers through mine and pulling me toward her locker.

As expected, eyes follow us through the hallways as quiet whispers fill the space.

"Just ignore them," I say to Poppy.

"I am," she says with her head held high.

"I'm so fucking proud of you," I tell her, stepping into her body and pressing her up against the wall outside her first class of the day.

"Miss Thorn, Mr. Hunter, I'm not sure that's the way to start the day, is it?" Hartmann barks down the hall when spots us.

"S-sorry, sir," Poppy stutters, pressing her palms against my chest and trying to push me away. Her cheeks flame red and she refuses to look at him.

"You're going to get me in so much trouble," she whispers to me, still trying to put some space between us.

"Speak for yourself. I'm so hard for you right now."

"Zayn," she half warns, half moans. "You need to go to class."

"Well, it's your fault if Miss Peterson thinks it's for her."

"You're gross. She's like... five years past retirement."

"What can I say?" I shrug. "The older generation loves me."

"You're a nightmare." She shakes her head at me, a smile playing on her lips.

"Love you, Pops."

"I love you too," she says quietly as I start backing away from her.

I blow her a kiss before rounding the corner and bumping straight into

Rich and Justin who immediately set about ripping into me for my declaration. Assholes.

Thanks to Jake's warning, almost all the gossip had died out by the end of the week. Although it's been impossible to ignore the weird atmosphere around school knowing that we'd lost one of our own. He might have turned out to be even crazier than any of us had imagined, but he was still someone most of us had grown up with. It was weird, and I hate that a person who threatened the life of someone I love is able to leave that much of a hole behind. But I guess it is what it is, the best thing we can do now is look to the future.

"Are you sure you want to come? I would understand if you wanted to stay here," I say to Poppy who's sitting in my passenger seat while Harley's been relegated to the back.

"Of course. If you want me there," she adds hesitantly.

Reaching over, I lace my fingers with hers. "Of course. It's just not exactly the kind of place you belong."

"I want to see where you all grew up. I'm sure it's not as bad as you make out to be."

"Have you two about finished?" My sister sulks from the back.

"We should go before the toddler has a tantrum."

"Fuck you, Zayn. I don't think I like you all loved up and shit."

"We need to find you a boyfriend," Poppy suggests.

"It's okay. I already told Zayn that I was going to fuck Justin or Rich. I might even get them to double team me at the party tonight."

I can't help the growl that rumbles up my throat at her words. "Shut the fuck up, Harley."

"What? Tit for tat. You fuck my friend, I fuck yours."

"I'm not just fucking your friend though, am I?"

"As amusing as this little argument is, I'm right here, you know?" Poppy points out beside me with a smug grin on her face. "Harley," she says, turning to look at my sister. "Don't give it up to those assholes. Pick someone decent who's not been around half the school."

"Like you did?" she asks sarcastically.

"Fair point. Forget I said anything, screw who you like."

"Poppy," I gasp. "You're meant to be on my side."

"Sorry, babe. Chicks before dicks."

My chin drops as Harley barks a laugh behind me.

"Charming."

"Seriously though, Har. Don't just give it up to get back at us. Make it special."

"Maybe I don't want special," she sulks, staring out the window. "I just want... I don't know what I want."

"You will when you find him."

As we head farther out of town, thankfully the conversation turns away from my little sister's virginity and to safer subjects, mostly about tonight's party. Mom wasn't all that thrilled to let me throw another after the mess my New Year's one caused, but she didn't really have a leg to stand on seeing as she allowed Letty to have one, and as I pointed out, I'm only going to turn eighteen once.

In the end, she conceded and has booked herself into a hotel for the night with the strict instructions that by the time she returns tomorrow afternoon that the house will look exactly like it did when she left it. I told her it would, obviously, but we'll see how that goes.

As we get closer to Harrow Creek, the scenery begins to change. Gone are the big houses and perfect front yards from our side of Rosewood, and in their place are trailers and beat-up old cars.

When I was young, I thought this was how everyone lived. I had no idea that just a few miles away there were houses with pools and home gyms and all the other luxuries that come along with having money.

"Regretting it yet?" I ask Poppy when her and Harley's conversation comes to an end.

"Never," she says, reaching over and squeezing my hand in reassurance. "I don't care where you come from, Zayn, so stop worrying."

I smile at her, but it doesn't reach my eyes. I don't want to be ashamed of this place, but I can't help it. I know it made me the person I am today, but I don't have great memories of the place, and I'm more than happy to be away from the kinds of people who live here, and I'd more than happily never introduce Poppy to most of them.

The gravel at the entrance to our trailer park crunches under my truck's tires and we make our way toward our old home.

I glance over to see Poppy's eyes flitting around everything.

"You know, it's not as bad as you made it out to be."

"Appearances can be deceiving."

As I pull up out the front of Dad's trailer, movement in my rearview mirror catches my eye, but when I look up, I don't find anyone there.

"Ready to meet Dad?" Harley asks.

"I am," Poppy says eagerly, pushing the door open and jumping out.

I do the same and walk around the car to join them. It's not until we're all standing together that the person who was behind us shows his face.

"Shit," I mutter, my arm instinctively reaching out, my hand wrapping around Harley's so I can pull her behind me.

"Zayn, why the fuck are you... oh," she says, clearly looking over my shoulder and seeing the same thing I am. "What the hell is he doing here? I thought he left."

"Me too."

My eyes hold his angry ones as hate crackles between us.

"Um... what the hell is going on?" Poppy asks hesitantly. "Who is that?"

"No one you need to know," I bark, as Harley says, "Kane. He doesn't like us very much."

"You don't say," she whispers, clearly sensing the hostility coming off him in waves.

"Let's get inside and get out of here as soon as possible."

Ripping my stare from his, I spin around and gently push both Poppy and Harley toward the door. The last thing I want to do today is get into it with Kane and everything that happened.

"Happy Birthday," Dad shouts loudly as we walk up to the door. He jumps down the steps and pulls me in for a hug. "I can't believe you're a man now. I swear it was only yesterday you were toddling around in diapers. And you were—"

"Dad," I say, cutting off whatever embarrassing memory I'm sure was about to fall from his lips. "This is Poppy."

His eyes leave mine in favor of my girl.

"Harley's friend, right?" he asks, proving that he does listen to Harley's stories when we visit.

"Yeah, but she's..." Harley starts.

"Also, my girlfriend," I state proudly, wrapping my arm around her waist and pulling her into my side.

"Girlfriend?" Dad asks, his eyes wide. We might live in different towns now, but he's more than aware—mostly thanks to Harley—about my... ways.

"Yep. Girlfriend. Now are you going to invite us in or what?"

"Oh... yeah. Poppy," he says, turning to my girl, his eyes still as wide as saucers. "It's good to meet you at last. Harley talks about all the time, unlike this one who's just blindsided me."

"It's good to meet you too, Mr. Hunter."

"Oh, please. Call me Rob."

"Okay, will do. And don't be too hard on him, this is all new territory for him."

"Hey," I complain, following behind as we all pile inside. As I reach out to pull the door closed behind us, my eyes lock with Kane's once more. His narrow in anger but all I can do is smile. I had nothing to do with the beef he has with my family, although hell knows I'll do everything in my power to protect them if he decides he wants his revenge.

Shaking my head at him, I close the door and turn toward the living area of the trailer I used to call home.

"Whoa, Dad," I say, taking in all the banners and balloons.

"What? I couldn't let my boy's day go by without doing anything special. Here," he says, pushing a gift over the table toward me.

I take a seat beside Poppy and rip open the paper.

"This is stunning." I stare down at the Rolex in my hand. "How did you afford this?"

"That doesn't matter. Happy Birthday, Son."

"Thanks, Dad."

"Right, cake!"

38

POPPY

I've seen Rob in pictures a few times over the years, I know what to expect looks-wise, although I wasn't quite prepared for seeing another set of Zayn's eyes staring back at me. While Zayn mostly has his mom's African American features, his eyes are all his father's. And the way they light up when they looked into mine that first time warmed my heart.

I've heard stories about this place, most of which Harley and Zayn have been reluctant to tell me about, but so far, aside from the creepy guy who was staring at us outside, it seems... fine.

Okay, so there are none of the fancy houses and well-tended yards I'm sure the two of them have become accustomed to over the past few years, but it's not so bad, at least not on the surface. They gave me the impression we were driving into the center of Hell or something.

I sit back and watch as the three of them banter together while Rob cuts up the cake he bought for his son's birthday.

"So what are the plans for the big day then after visiting your old man?"

"Party!"

"Your mom's allowing that after the last one?"

"Of course."

"Jeez, you always did have her wrapped around your little finger."

"What can I say?" Zayn says with a shrug.

We chat away for over two hours before Zayn stands and announces that we need to get back. His dad's face drops and my heart aches for him that he's got to keep watching his kids walk away when he clearly cares about them so much. It makes me wonder why he would have chosen to keep this life when he could have had a better one in Rosewood. But I guess not everything is about money, and this place is where his heart is.

When we emerge from the trailer, there's no one hanging around outside this time. That doesn't stop the three of us from looking around for him though. I have no idea who he is, but just with one look, he sent a shudder of fear racing down my spine that I remember all too well.

We all say goodbye to Rob, Zayn thanks him once again for his gift and we climb into the car.

"So... thoughts?" Harley asks, leaning forward in her seat.

"It was nice?"

"Nice?"

"Yeah. From what the two of you had said, I thought it was going to be awful."

"It is."

"Well, on the surface it seemed fine. Apart from that guy, who was he?"

"No one," Zayn spits, his grip on the wheel tightening the second I so much as mention him. "And if you ever see him in Rosewood, run the other way."

His eyes meet Harley's in the rearview mirror, and she sinks back into her seat. The weird vibe going on between them doesn't make me any less suspicious about this guy.

The ride back is quieter than the journey to Harrow Creek, but it doesn't bother me. I'm more than happy to curl up on the seat and get lost in my own head. After spending a few hours with Marley, the counselor Jada set up for me, this week, things are beginning to get easier to think about.

I think I'll probably always feel to blame for what happened with Preston, I'm not sure that will ever go away, but already it's getting easier to bear. We've talked about my parents at length and although I already knew that what had happened was probably for the best, I'm really starting to understand it now.

Zayn and I spent last Saturday with Auntie Trish and the kids, and we had the best day. Seeing them so happy, the wide smiles on their faces made my entire year. They've had too much to deal with in their short lives and to see them lose the responsibility and just be kids for once meant everything to me. And just to be able to be their sister and not worry about also being a parent felt incredible.

"I can't believe Mom is letting you do this," Harley mutters as we pull up outside the house to already find her gone.

"You should be thanking me, Har. I'm leading the way to ensure you also get a party next year. You won't even have your style cramped by me or Letty, seeing as we'll be at college."

The mention of him not being here in just a few months makes my stomach twist uncomfortably. But I plaster a smile on my face when he turns to look at me after killing the engine because I don't want to dampen his excitement about college. I know through Harley that he's talked about UCLA for years. I don't want to be the one to ruin that for him.

"Ready to do this?"

"Hell yes," Harley barks. "But I'm stealing your girl to get ready."

"But—"

"I don't give a shit," she snaps, cutting off whatever argument that was about to fall from his lips. "Anyway, you'll probably be thanking me later. She's my birthday present to you."

Zayn's eyes narrow at his sister. "You can't give me my own girlfriend for my birthday." The way he says girlfriend sends a tingle racing through my body just like it did when he introduced me to his dad as such.

"I can, I am, and you will enjoy it. Come on, girl. We've got work to do," Harley says, shouldering open the door.

"Wish me luck," I say, turning to Zayn right as another car pulls up beside him.

Reaching out, he wraps the back of his hand around my neck and pulls me closer.

"You'll be fine. But if you can escape, come find me. I've just about forgotten the gift you gave me this morning?" he murmurs against my lips.

"Oh yeah?"

"Yeah." Taking control of my hand, he presses my palm against his crotch and I gasp when I find him hard and ready.

"Zayn," I moan, my own body heating up knowing just how turned on he is.

"Do you know how badly I want to pull you over the console and fuck you right here in my truck?"

"Oh God," I whimper. His tongue takes advantage of the opening and sweeps past my lips, searching out my own.

I lose myself in his kiss, leaning forward and wrapping my own hand around the nape of his neck to try to close the space between us.

That is until a fist rains down hell on the window beside my head and I shriek in fear jumping back from Zayn as if I've been burned.

Turning to the window, I find Harley staring daggers at the two of us with her hands on her hips.

"I should probably..." I point over my shoulder.

"I'll be there in a few minutes," he says, sitting back in his seat and making a show of rearranging himself.

"Down boy," Harley shouts into the car the second I push the door open.

"Fucking cockblock."

"Yeah, yeah, whatever. Come on, time to get sexed up... just not in *that* way."

Harley and Ruby each take one of my arms and physically drag me toward the house as if I'm about to run back to Zayn and finish what we started any second.

"Damn, that was hot," Ruby mutters. "I need a guy."

"Weren't you sucking face with Jamie last weekend?" Harley helpfully points out. Zayn and I might not have been at last weekend's party, but I sure heard all about it.

"Yeah, but that was as far as it got. He ended up so drunk he passed out on me."

I snort a laugh while Harley announces, "Wow, you must be one hell of a lay, Rubes."

"Wouldn't know. Talking about getting laid." Both of them turn their eyes on me.

"I'm not telling you shit."

"Ow, come on. Is he as good as everyone claims?"

"I've got no complaints."

"My ear, my ears," Harley cries dramatically as we climb the stairs.

"Chill out I'm not going to tell you just how big he is." I hold my hands out, totally exaggerating, much to Ruby's amusement and Harley's horror. Releasing me, she darts up the stairs and toward her room.

"She's going to kill you."

"She'll get used to it," I mutter, following behind where she ran like her ass was on fire.

"You've got two choices," Harley says the second we step into the room.

My stomach drops the second I look up and lock eyes on the two dresses she's holding up in front of me. Both contain hardly any fabric and don't look like anywhere near covering any part of me up.

"Um... I hope you're not expecting me to wear one of those."

"Sure am. Now pick. Red or purple?"

"Or my jeans and a tank?"

"Nope. It's Zayn's birthday. Don't you want him to enjoy himself?" She winks at me.

"I thought you wanted to keep us apart."

"Yeah, well, I might kind of like seeing him all happy and shit," she whispers, averting her eyes.

"I'm sorry, what was that?"

"I like seeing him happy, okay. You too. You both deserve it."

"Aw, Har. Are you going all soft?"

"Whatever. Red or purple?"

I run my eyes over the lack of fabric on each and after noticing that the actual sides of the red dress are missing, I opt for purple.

"I hate you for this, you know that right."

"Oh, sweetie. You won't when he locks eyes on you. You'll be thanking her. Now, get your ass in the shower then we've got work to do."

With a huff, I follow orders and make quick work of scrubbing and shaving my body, ready for my man's big night.

"Holy shit," I mutter, staring at myself in the mirror. This isn't the first time that Harley and Ruby have given me a makeover, but this is the first time I've ever looked quite like this.

"You like?"

"I... I... yeah. I look... wow."

"Exactly. Zayn is going to lose his mind."

I stare at my dark smoky eyes before dropping my gaze to my dark lips, the low cut of the strapless dress, and my cleavage that's on show above and down to my almost fully exposed legs.

A tingle of excitement races through me and pushes away my nerves about other people seeing this much of me. I don't care about them, but I sure as hell want Zayn to look at me because what Ruby said is right. He is going to lose his mind.

"I need your help with something tonight," I tell them both. They lean in and listen to my plan before smiles form on their lips and they eagerly agree.

After sucking in a deep breath, I hold my head up high and pull open Harley's door.

The party is already in full swing downstairs and has been for quite some time while we had our own little party for three in Harley's room along with a bottle of vodka or two.

Ruby can barely walk in a straight line with the amount she's drunk already. Harley and I share a concerned look. This is becoming more and more of a habit for her, and I'm beginning to worry that she's relying on it too much to deal with everything that happened over Halloween with her stepbrother. I hate that she's still dwelling on it all this time later.

Harley falls back, supporting Ruby so she doesn't go crashing down the stairs as we make our way to join the party.

All eyes turn on us as we emerge, or should I say, eyes turn on me.

My skin tingles as everyone stares at me, their chins drop and their eyes almost pop out of their heads.

"Uh... Zayn," Justin calls. "You need to get out here, man."

A weird silence falls over the house for a beat before Zayn emerges from his den.

"Yeah, what... fuuuuuck," he groans when his eyes fall on me. "All right, party's over. You all know where the door is," he calls, marching straight over to me.

"Pops, you look... wow."

"I got attacked by your sister," I say with a shrug.

His hand grazes along my jaw before his fingers grip on to the back of my neck.

Our eyes lock and everyone around us disappears as if they don't exist.

"Fuck, you're beautiful."

His lips brush against mine gently before his tongue sweeps into my mouth.

My body sags against his as his arms wrap around my body, holding me up.

"My bedroom. Now," he grates, his breath hitting my ear and sending a shudder through my entire body.

My core aches to do exactly what he just suggested, but it's his birthday party. Plus, I've got a plan.

"Later," I say, pressing my palms against his chest in an attempt to push him back.

"But..."

"I'll make sure it's worth your while later."

He finally pulls his face from my neck and looks into my eyes.

"You can't hang out down here dressed like that."

"Sure I can," I sass, walking around him, making sure I put as much sway as possible into my hips. "Come dance with me?" I hold my hand out as I walk toward the living room where the speakers have been set up.

In a heartbeat, his hand is slipping into mine and we're joining the crowd who are already grinding away to the beat of the music.

He keeps my back to his front, wraps his arms around my waist, and pulls me back against him. His length presses against my ass and I can't help but grind against him, teasing him.

"You're such trouble," he groans in my ear as his hand splays across my stomach.

"You love it."

"I love you."

A wide smile spreads across my face as I continue moving. After a few minutes, I turn to look back at him, only for him to capture my lips with a knee-weakening kiss.

I spin in his arms and throw mine over his shoulders, teasing his hairline with my nails. I smile into our kiss as he shudders under my touch.

I have no idea how many songs play or how much time passes, but then equally I don't care either. All I do know is that when Harley calls my name, it's way before I'm ready to release him.

"Pops. Now would be a really great time," she says, reminding me that I asked her to help out with something earlier. I'm surprised she agreed knowing where it's probably going to lead, but I know she's a romantic at heart and couldn't really refuse.

"Oh yeah. Sorry, I need to..." I point to Harley with a wince.

"But—" he starts to argue, but I cut him off.

"We've got all night. Enjoy your party. Go smoke a blunt with the guys and relax a little."

"While you're walking around in that dress? Not a chance."

I laugh at him as I walk toward Harley and leave Zayn behind.

39

ZAYN

I bite down on the inside of my cheek, watching Poppy's ass sway in that sinful fucking dress as she walks over to my sister.

Fucking cockblock.

Leaving the makeshift dance floor behind, I head out to the garden to do as she just suggested.

I find most of the guys out here passing a blunt around that Ethan probably supplied them with.

I drop down onto one between Justin and Jake and Amalie.

"You let her up for air, huh?" Justin asks, his voice full of amusement.

"Sadly," I mutter, snatching the joint from his fingers.

"She looks hot," Amalie points out, making Jake growl. "Oh calm down, caveman. She's almost eighteen, you can't keep up the protective big brother routine forever."

"Try me," he mutters. "What did she get you for your birthday?" Jake asks, trying to change the subject.

"Uh..." I hesitate, my cock swelling once more as I think about the wake-up call I had from her this morning. "N-nothing yet."

Amalie chuckles, giving me a knowing wink before she kisses Jake on the cheek and climbs from the lounger, heading inside.

"I can't believe this is all going to be over soon," Jake says, looking around at all the people in my backyard and spilling out from inside the house. I swallow harshly at the reality of what's coming for all of us. High school is almost done and we're all going to be heading off around the country as we start the rest of our lives. It doesn't seem all that long ago we started at Rosewood High thinking it would last forever.

We've achieved everything we dreamed of this year by winning the division and the state championships, but it's almost time to move on to new teams, new friends, new futures.

UCLA has always been my dream. I remember Mom showing me images of the campus when I was a kid. It was where she always wanted to go, and I've wanted it ever since. Only, the past few weeks, everything's changed for me. My vision for the future is suddenly totally different. I've just no idea what everyone else is going to think about it, but then, it's not their life, it's mine.

"There's still plenty of time for this. Plus, we'll all be back. Rosewood is our home."

"I guess so," Jake says, tipping his beer to his lips. Not so long ago, he was desperate to get out of this place, it's amazing how one person can change so much.

"Zayn," Harley calls. "Can you help me with something?"

"What, Har?" I bark, assuming that it's probably to carry a passed-out Ruby upstairs, she wasn't looking exactly sober when I last saw her so I have no idea what state she's in now.

She doesn't say anything, stands with her hand on her hip by the door waiting for me.

"What?" I snap again when I get to her.

"Do you know where the karaoke machine is?"

I sigh. "Really? That's what you wanted me for? It's in the closet in my den. Are we done?"

"No, could you come and get it? It's too heavy for me."

"Jesus. I knew I shouldn't have invited you tonight," I mutter, following her inside, swiping a bottle of beer from the kitchen as I pass.

I've drained it by the time we walk through the door into my den. I expect to find the rest of the team in here on the Xbox or at least with a few of the squad grinding down on their lap, but when I look up, all I find is an empty room.

"What the hell?" I mutter to myself as Harley comes to a stop in the middle of the room and gestures toward the closet.

What the fuck did her last slave die of?

With a sigh, I pull the closet door open and step inside, my hand running down the wall for the switch that I know is there somewhere. But before my hand finds it, the door slams behind me and I sense someone step up to me, a beat before her scent fills my nose.

Her body presses against my back and my breath catches in anticipation.

"You want to play seven minutes in heaven?" she breathes in my ear making my skin tingle with awareness and my cock to jerk in my pants.

"Fuck yeah." Before I even know I've moved, I've got her backed up against the wall, the entire length of my hard body pressed up against her soft one.

"Happy Birthday," she breathes.

"You planned this." It's not a question because suddenly Harley's random request and the empty room make total sense.

"I thought it was fitting. I also thought," she says, brushing her lips against mine. "That we could go all the way this time."

"Oh, hell yeah." I slam my lips down on hers in a bruising kiss. My need from earlier comes back full force and mixes with the alcohol and makes me forget any restraint I might usually have.

I soon realize I'm not the only one feeling that way because Poppy's hands slide under my shirt, lifting it and encouraging me to pull it off.

I do so without hesitation, dropping it onto the floor somewhere behind me.

"Poppy," I groan as she drops her lips to my collarbone and then lower, kissing across my chest, circling my nipples with her tongue before tracing the lines of my abs.

Her fingers make quick work of my pants and before I know it, she's pushing the fabric down my hips until they're pinning my legs at my knees.

Sliding down the wall, she stops on her haunches when her mouth is in line with my cock.

"Fuck, Pops," I grunt when her delicate fingers wrap around my length before she starts pumping slowly.

Reaching forward, I rest my forearm on the wall before me and stare down at her.

I can't see much in the darkness, but I can make out her silhouette to know exactly when she leans forward to lick at the head of my cock.

It jerks in her tight grasp as the sensation engulfs me before she leans forward further and sucks me deep into her mouth.

"Oh fuck. Fuck," I bark, already beginning to lose control despite the fact she's barely touched me.

Everything is heightened in the dark plus the knowledge that she's been planning this for who knows how long.

Her hand moves along with the burning heat of her mouth and the teasing touch of her tongue and in an embarrassingly short amount of time, my cock jerks deep in her mouth and I come down her throat.

She doesn't stop sucking or licking until I've finished.

Twisting my fingers in her hair, I gently lift her to her feet, and once again slam my lips to hers.

"Fuck, you're amazing," I murmur into her kiss.

My hands slide up her bare thighs, pushing her short dress up over her ass.

"Poppy?" I half ask, half warn when I find her bare of panties. "Tell me you haven't been walking around in front of all those assholes like this."

"Now, that would be telling," she teases before a squeal rips past her lips as I lift her, wrap her legs around my waist and pin her to the wall with my hips. My cock is already hard for her again and it teases her bare pussy. "Zayn," she moans, her needy voice almost my undoing.

Cupping her face in my hands, I kiss her once more. Tilting her head to the side so I can slide my tongue deep into her mouth, lapping at hers, showing her just how much she means to me, how much this right now means to me.

My hands drop over her shoulders and down her arms until I cup her breast in my hands, rubbing my fingertips over her already peaked nipples.

Gripping the fabric of the strapless dress, I pull it down so the whole thing is gathered around her waist and find exactly what I was expecting.

"Fuck, you're killing me," I grate out, taking her bare breasts in my hand and making her head fall back against the wall when I pinch her nipples hard between my thumb and forefinger.

"Zayn, please," she begs.

"What, Pops? Tell me what you need."

"You, Zayn. I need you to... argh," she cries out when I surge forward, filling her to the hilt in one smooth thrust. "Oh God, yes," she cries, making me understand why she thought to clear out the room.

Her nails scratch down my back until she clamps on to my shoulders as I grip her hips and start to pound into her.

Our slick skin moves together seamlessly as we chase our releases, and as she gets closer her cries and pleas for more only get louder. She doesn't drink very often, and when she does, it's still not much, but fuck does it help loosen her up even more than she is usually.

Pulling her bottom half from the wall, I change the angle to ensure my pelvis rubs at her clit with every thrust.

"Yes, yes, yes," she chants as I watch her full tits bounce with the force of my thrusts.

"Fuck," I grate out, my fingers digging into her ass as I try to get deeper, try to ensure she feels this for days, hoping that I make my mark on her, making her mine forever.

"Come, Poppy," I demand when I start to lose control of my own impending release.

Bringing one hand around to her front, I pinch her clit and send her flying over the edge.

"Zayn," she cries out as her pussy squeezes me impossibly tight, giving me no choice but to lose myself alongside her. My cock jerks, shooting jets of cum inside her. Making her mine.

Continuing to hold her up, I drop my head to her shoulder, trying to catch my breath.

"I applied to Maddison Kings," I blurt, not even realizing that I said the words out loud until she tenses in my hold.

"You what?" she asks, her voice quiet and unsure.

Pulling my head up, I stare into her lust blown eyes.

"I've applied to Maddison Kings," I repeat, sounding a little more confident this time.

"But... why? You want to go to UCLA. You've always wanted to go to UCLA. I don't..." She shakes her head, cute frown lines forming on her brow.

"Everything's changed now, Pops," I say, rubbing my thumb over her creased skin before cupping her cheek.

"But—"

"Nothing's set in stone, it's up for discussion but I wanted it to be an option."

"But... UCLA," she repeats, concern still filling her features.

"Yeah, but there's something else I want more."

Her eyes hold mine, hope shining in them for what I might be alluding to and my heart swells.

"I love you, Poppy Thorn. I don't want to move halfway across the country if it means leaving you behind. Maddison Kings is a good school, they have a good team and excellent programs. I could go for a year, and then maybe you could join me. We could get our own place off-campus together. You'd be close to your brother's and sister. Sorry, I—" I go to apologize, thinking that from the look on her face that I might have got a little carried away.

"You've really thought about this, haven't you?"

"You're it for me, Pops. I want to be wherever you are."

"And what if I want to be wherever you are?"

"Then I could do a year at Maddison and transfer to wherever you want to go."

"Oh, Zayn. I love you."

"I love you too," I mumble against her lips as she presses hers to mine and sweeps her tongue into my mouth.

I'm just about ready to fuck her once again when there's an almighty crash from outside our closet.

"What the hell?"

Poppy wriggles in my hold and I reluctantly place her back down on her feet.

There's another loud noise, this time something smashing before a cry sounds out.

"Fuck," Poppy barks, clearly recognizing the voice as she rushes to right her dress before flying out of the closet.

I make quick work of pulling my boxers and pants back up before following her out.

"Ruby," Poppy cries, running toward where she's sitting on the floor, her arms wrapped around her knees as she continues to cry.

Glancing around the room, I find liquid coating the far wall with shattered glass all over the floor beneath.

"What's wrong? What's happened? Are you hurt?" Poppy asks in a panic, dropping to her knees beside her friend and tucks her hair from her face.

"He... he's coming back. I can't see him again, Poppy. I can't. I can't live with him again. I won't survive it."

Ready for Ashton and Ruby's story?

Keep reading for Faze!

FAZE

FURY PREQUEL

1

ASHTON

Looking around the lavish house that I have never wanted to visit, anger races through my veins.

This is the last place in the world I wanted to be.

I should be home in the shitty apartment that Mom and I live in back in Seattle, but I'm not. I'm in *his* house, the asshole that ruined both of our lives.

It's been over five years since he walked away, leaving us with fuck all, just the bitter taste of his betrayal.

Mom said it was fine, that it was for the best. But it's all bullshit. She's tried to put a brave face on, tried to convince me that their relationship really was over and that he didn't shatter all of her hopes and dreams for the future.

But I know her better than she thinks. I see the shadows in her eyes. The coldness, the loneliness, that set in after he left. I also don't miss the number of bottles that sit in our recycling on a weekly basis. They seem to be multiplying week by week, and I have no fucking idea how to help her.

Getting suspended from school again for fighting probably wasn't the best thing to do to help, but that prick has had it coming for a long time.

I think of Jonathon fucking Parker and the way he looked down at us all like he was something fucking special.

My fists curl once again as if he's in touching distance. If I could take him out all over again I would.

My busted knuckles split open, the sting of pain a reminder I don't need of where I am right now.

He'd asked me time and time again over the years to come and visit his new home, his new family. But every time I refused. I had no interest in meeting the bitch that took him away from us or the girl who he got to play daddy for while he mostly forgot that I existed.

My teeth grind as I think about everything I lost the day he walked away. My best fucking friend. That's what I lost.

But this time was different. It wasn't him asking me to come. It was Mom. And as much as I wanted to refuse her request, I couldn't. One look into her tired, stressed eyes and I knew she needed the break probably as much as I did.

I haven't made it easy for her the past few years. I've been suspended more times than I can remember. I've been on my last warning at that shithole of a school for months, but the principal is a fucking pussy, so I doubt he'll ever actually kick me out. It'll give him too much paperwork to do, and we all know how much he hates doing any actual work.

"Please, Ash. Go and spend the week with him. Clear your head. It can be a fresh start when you get back." Her words ring out in my mind as if she's standing next to me having the conversation.

I couldn't say no to her. I've never been able to. Having experienced how much hurt he's caused her. I'd hate to do the same. I know I'm a constant disappointment to her, but no matter how I try not to be, it happens, nonetheless.

My temper always gets the better of me. My hate gets the better of me. My fury gets the better of me. It's only right that it does. It is my name, after all. The one and only thing I have that still connects me to the man who spends his days under this roof.

The perfect all-American family home. Wrap-around porch, the huge kitchen with an island in the center, the pristine garden and the glistening pool. It's a million miles away from the place Mom and I call home now.

I stand at the window waiting for her to pull up. Lisa, my stepmom, excitedly told me that I could expect her any time now before both her and Dad disappeared not long after picking me up from the airport. I can't fucking wait to meet my stepsister. It's been a long time coming, that's for sure.

I've seen the odd photo of her when I've needed to torture myself and looked at his Facebook. Every single time all it's done is to add to the anger that lives inside me as I see images of them together playing happy family.

He should be doing that with us. His real family. Not his replacements.

My teeth grind right as a little blue car pulls up in front of the house.

I lean toward the window a little, trying to get a better view of her before we're face to face. I need to get a read on her, try to make a game plan.

I know nothing about her aside from the fact she played a part in ruining my life. That he chose her and her mother over me and mine. His son and wife. The ones whose best intentions he should have had at heart.

Disappointment settles in my stomach when she doesn't immediately get out of the car. Instead, she looks down, I guess at her cell.

After a few minutes, she looks up at the house and blows out a long breath.

Is she nervous? Apprehensive about meeting me?

If she's not, she fucking should be.

This house, that I can only assume is her sanctuary, her home, is about to become the place of living nightmares because my darling stepsister has never met someone like me before, I can fucking guarantee it.

After what feels like a lifetime, she pushes the door open and a pair of legs emerge before she stands.

Her head barely appears above the door. She's so small, so breakable. I rub my hands together as my plan for my time here floats around in my head.

You ruined my life, I'm about to turn yours upside down, you motherfucker.

The second she slams the door, a smile twitches at the corners of my mouth.

She's wearing the smallest pair of shorts, that I can only imagine are cut high across her ass, and a crop top that shows off her tiny waist and more than ample tits.

Oh yeah, she's definitely rocking something I can work with.

Walking to the other side of the room, I wait out of sight for her to let herself in.

She does so quickly, but it's not until I hear her purse hit the table that I step from my hiding space.

2

RUBY

I stare up at the house and blow out a long breath, hoping that the nerves that are fluttering in my belly will subside.

Ashton is inside.

I had no idea he was coming, although I don't think anyone was aware until a few hours ago.

Mom and Stephen might have been together for years now, married even, yet I've never met my elusive stepbrother.

The strained relationship between him and Stephen isn't a secret, his refusal to attend the wedding was just the tip of the iceberg.

The thing I don't know is why. Why he hates his father so much. Stephen is a good man. I mean, he's not my dad, no one could ever replace him, but as far as stepdads go, I consider myself pretty lucky.

That could all be about to change though.

Sucking in a breath and hopefully a shit load of confidence with it, I push open the door and head for the house.

My muscles ache from the hard practice Chelsea just put us through. But I loved it. I love the pain, the knowledge that I pushed myself.

I've wanted to be on the squad for as long as I can remember. The day it was announced I was in was one of the best of my life. I'm determined to prove myself over the coming months, I want to show the seniors that I'm as good as them, that they were right to choose me, that I won't let them down.

Throwing my purse over my shoulder and clutching a couple of books to my chest, I make my way to the house.

It's silent as I step inside, making me wonder if he's here.

Needing to get something to eat before I start on my homework, I drop my purse to the table in the hallway and take a step to the kitchen only when I do, a dark figure emerges from the living room.

My heart plummets and a blood-curdling scream rips from my throat.

I should run, I should leave the house as fast as I entered, but my body doesn't respond to instruction. It freezes as my limbs tremble with fear and my vision blurs.

All I see is the figure before me, head to toe in black with his hood casting his face in darkness.

As my blood rushes past my ears and my heart pounds like a fucking drum, he lifts his head.

The first thing I see are his lips curled into an accomplished smirk, but that's enough to know who it is.

"What the fuck is wrong with you?" I bark, my voice betraying me and trembling slightly with every word.

He takes a step toward me and lowers his hood.

His dark, almost inky black eyes lock on mine and a shudder runs down my spine. His scent hits my nose and fuck if the smell doesn't have my mouth watering.

Damn him.

Ripping my eyes from his, I take in the rest of his face, a face I've only seen on the odd photo.

His nose is slightly crooked, he's got a scar on his cheek and his jawline is sharp, sharper than should be allowed on someone who is clearly this much of an asshole, but none of those really capture my attention, it's his lips that mesmerize me. They're full, almost too full for a dude. I bet he's a really good kisser.

It's not until he sinks his teeth into the bottom one that I manage to shake the crazy thoughts from my head and look back up to his eyes.

He closes even more space between us.

My head is a mess after almost having a freaking heart attack but no matter how distracting his lips are, my sensible side speaks up and I take a huge step back, only when I do, my back hits the wall, stopping any further retreat.

His lips twitch into a smile, knowing that he's got me.

"What do you want, Ashton?"

I try again, getting quickly fed up with his scary, broody, silent treatment.

His eyes scan over my face once more.

"I need your car keys."

"Go to hell."

His eyes widen at my refusal. Was he really expecting me to bend to his demand and hand them right over?

A laugh falls from his lips, it's low, unamused, evil even, and it makes something in my stomach clench in fear.

Is this how murderers act right before putting you out of your misery?

"Keys, little girl." He holds his hand out, but my only reaction is to raise a brow and to tilt my chin in defiance.

"Little girl? Fuck you, Ashton."

I push to move around him, but he's not having any of it. His large hand lands on my shoulder and pushes me back where I was.

"Ow," I complain when my shoulder blade connects with the wall.

His eyes prowl down the length of my body and I suddenly wish I'd changed after cheer practice. I feel naked under his stare in my tiny workout clothes.

"You really want to play this game, little girl?"

"I'm not a little girl, Ashton. I'm a few months younger than you, get over yourself."

"So I see." His eyes lock on my chest. As much as I want to cover up, I don't want him to think that his asshole attitude has any effect on me whatsoever.

His eyes lift once more, and something crackles between us. Hate? It has to be because it can't possibly be anything else. This guy is an asshole of epic proportions.

Who does he think he is standing here demanding my car keys as if he owns the place?

We've lived in this house for almost four years, not once has he ever made the effort to come and visit, to spend time with his dad and to meet his new family.

I can't really say I'm all that disappointed if this is the kind of person he is. No wonder Stephen has never put much effort into visiting his only child.

"Do you mind, I've got shit to be doing that doesn't involve hanging out in the hallway with you."

I swallow down my nerves when his hands land on either side of my head, effectively caging me in.

"Give me your keys and you can continue with your pathetic little life."

"You're an ass," I spit, ducking under his arm and racing around him.

I might have escaped, but the second he spins and notices that I look straight to my purse, he moves.

We both lunge for it at the same time, but seeing as he's not a midget, he beats me to it.

"Ashton," I warn, my voice low.

He glances at me for a beat before opening it up and rummaging around.

I stand with my hands on my hips, feeling totally violated. I would say something, but I feel at this point it would probably fall on deaf ears. Ashton clearly gives zero fucks about me, or anything, it seems, so long as he gets his way.

The sooner he fucks back off to his mom in Seattle, the better.

With a wide smile that exposes a perfectly straight set of white teeth—asshole—he waves my keys in the air.

"See now, that wasn't so hard, was it?"

"You're a dick."

"I've been called worse, little one. I'm outta here."

"Don't let the door hit you in the ass on the way out."

He leaves with the sound of his amused chuckle filling the hallway.

"Argh," I scream the second I know he's out of earshot.

For years I've wanted to meet my stepbrother. Now I'm wondering why I even spared him a thought.

Ashton Fury is a douchebag, and I think Stephen might just be better off without him.

He's only staying a few days. Only a few days, I tell myself as I pick up my discarded purse and head for the kitchen.

3

ASHTON

I fucking hate social media. All the dickheads posting random shit about their lives that no one else really gives a crap about. Although they like each post just so they look like they care.

Bullshit. All of it.

Having said that though, it's the perfect place to find exactly what I need.

As I put the address into the GPS, I half expect her to come running out of the house to attempt to drag me out of her car. But when I glance up at the front door, I find it closed as I left it.

I had no idea what to expect from my stepsister. All I knew was her name and age. Obviously, I had hopes that she might not be a complete loser, but I could have only wished for the hot little body that emerged from this very car earlier.

I like her feisty side. If I didn't hate her, I might think it was cute.

There's only one thing I feel toward my stepsister. Indignation.

She's lived the perfect little life here with my father and her whore of a mother, all the while Mom and I were forgotten.

My knuckles turn white, splitting once more with the force of my grip on the wheel as I back out of the driveway.

The address I was given online seems to be right on the other side of town. Good thing she's got a full tank of gas. It would have seriously pissed me off if I had to spend the little money I have on gas instead of something to help me get through the next few days.

The guy I'd arranged to meet was waiting for me in the deserted parking lot he'd directed me to, and after little fuss, I head back toward the house I don't want to be in with exactly what I need in my back pocket.

There are still no other cars in the driveway, not that I'm surprised. Dad said that they'd be gone most of the night. Some bullshit about going to a local golf club or something. I can't say I was really listening. I took the money he offered, nodded when he suggested I order takeout, and turned my back on him.

I didn't want him under any illusion that I actually wanted to be here. That I came because I thought his suggestion was a good idea. Fucking hardly. If I thought coming to visit would be fun then I would have done it years ago.

All I was doing was trying to make life easier for Mom. If me being away for a while gave her the space to breathe, then I'd almost willingly do it.

Anything for her. The woman who's given her entire life to look after me, to give me everything I need. It's not like the asshole in this house has helped since the day he walked away and left us high and dry.

I stare up at the house, wondering if she's heard me return and is waiting with a kitchen knife in hand. Or is she going to be hiding? Oddly, that thought is more appealing.

I got to her earlier, I know I did. I almost want to see her try to ignore me, trying to pretend that I'm not here, not driving her crazy. It'll make this game so much more entertaining for me.

I have every intention of this being my first and last visit here. My plan is to ride out the year, graduate… maybe, then get a job. I want to start earning some real money so Mom and I can get a better place, somewhere with heat that actually works in the winter and air conditioning for the summer. I want to be able to look out of at least one window and not stare directly into some other scumbag's apartment.

With a sigh, I push from the car with my purchase burning a hole in my pocket. I'm more than ready to kick back and make the most of the queen-size bed instead of the twin I'm used to.

The house is in blissful silence as I make my way via the kitchen to grab some food and up the stairs to the room Dad directed me to after picking me up from the airport earlier.

I couldn't help smiling when I discovered that he'd put me right next to his precious Ruby. I'd spent the entire house tour having happy, smiling photos of the three of them shoved in my face. Anyone who wasn't aware would think they're the perfect little family. Fuck our parents' previous lives, those who were left behind. They had been forgotten long ago and this was all they cared about.

Pushing through into my temporary room, I kick the door shut before toeing off my shoes, opening my window and diving onto the bed.

I pull the baggie of weed, my lighter, and cell from my pocket and get comfortable.

After restarting my music, I set about rolling my first blunt.

My mouth waters for a taste, for something that's going to make this hellhole that much more bearable.

The first drag hits exactly where I needed it to. I suck it deep and hold the smoke in my lungs until it begins to burn.

Fucking yes!

Slipping down the bed a little, I take hit after hit, not giving two fucks about this being his house. He didn't give any ground rules, so I take that as there not being any.

I'm just about to push from the bed in my need to find where that motherfucker's liquor cabinet is when my bedroom door flies open.

It seems tonight might have just got interesting.

4

RUBY

I'm still fuming from our earlier interaction and the fact he stole my fucking car as I lie on my bed hours later, AirPods in and my music attempting to get me out of my own head as I try to focus on what I should be doing. Sadly, the only thing I'm actually doing is replaying our short interaction from earlier.

He shouldn't intrigue me like he does. Especially after the way he spoke to me, the way he acted. The way he totally invaded my privacy by riffling through my purse like he owned the fucking thing.

Stephen has had nothing but good things to say about his ex-wife, so I find it hard to believe she's brought him up to be such an arrogant, selfish prick.

My fingers tighten on the pencil I'm holding until I'm worried it's about to snap in half.

It's just a few days. Just a few days.

No wonder he's been suspended from school if he acts like that on a normal day. I wonder what he did.

My inappropriate thoughts about the boy occupying the next room are thwarted when the vibration of the front door slamming hits me.

I sit up straight, pulling one of my AirPods from my ear to listen to what he might be doing.

After a few minutes, the sound of his footsteps pounding up the stairs has my heart beating faster than it should.

I shouldn't care that he's home. I should just be glad he made it back with my car hopefully in one piece.

Thankfully, he doesn't make it down to my door, assuming he knows which room is mine, of course. Instead, another door slams as he locks himself away in his room.

Good. And I hope you damn well stay in there. I sure have every intention of hiding in here until I absolutely have to leave.

Unfortunately, his god-awful music almost immediately starts, sending my irritation levels sky-high.

Thoughts of packing a bag and moving in with Harley for a few days flit through my mind. Her mom wouldn't care, that's if she's even there. I could make up some story about Harley needing company, Mom wouldn't even bat an eyelid.

It's a solid idea. It would get me away from this house, and more importantly, him. So why is it that I make no move to pack a bag and leave as fast as I can?

It seems I'm a glutton for punishment because there's a huge part of me that wants to find out more about my angry stepbrother. I want to know why he was the way he was earlier. I find it hard to believe it's because he's here. Stephen said he agreed happily after the suggestion was made.

I think about that for a moment. That can't be right. He refused every other time Stephen has tried to get him to visit. Why is he here now? And why was he apparently so happy to come?

My thoughts are halted when a familiar smell hits my nose.

Who the hell is smoking a joint outside my house? If Harley and Poppy have turned up to have an impromptu party, I'm going to be less than impressed after I specifically told them I was coming home to catch up on homework.

Pushing from the bed, I walk over to my window and look down. I expect to find the girls sneaking around the back of the house, trying not to get caught and stifling laughs. Only, that's not at all what I find because there's no one to be seen.

My fists curl as realization hits me.

Without thinking, I storm from my bedroom and toward his closed door. There's no way he can know I'm coming with the volume of his music. Half the freaking street probably can't hear themselves think over it.

Swinging his door open, I step inside as the strong scent of his blunt hits me despite the window being open, making me want to cough.

Resting my hands on my hips, I wait just inside his room for him to open his eyes and see me.

Long seconds pass as he continues and blows repeated rings of smoke into the room.

I'm just about to march his way and rip the joint from his fingers when he sits up.

My breath catches as I prepare for him to look at me. But when he does, I realize that no amount of time could have prepared me for looking in those dark, cold eyes once again.

A smile curls at one side of his lips as he runs his eyes down the length of my body. Tingles erupt in their wake and as my nipples tighten under his stare, I remember that I'm only wearing a thin tank and a pair of sleep shorts.

Fuck. Fuck him and his assholery.

Folding my arms over my chest in an attempt to hide what my clothes are doing a shit job of, I cock my hip and wait for him to finish.

"Are you about finished?" I sass when his eyes find mine once again.

He stands, his free hand running through his dark hair and pushing it from his forehead while the other continues to hold his joint.

"Oh, little one. I haven't even started."

I swallow, square my shoulders and straighten my back, ready to go up against him again.

"There's no smoking in this house. Of any kind."

"Oh yeah?" he asks, taking a drag and blowing the smoke right in my face.

"You'd better get rid of it before your dad gets back," I suggest, much to his amusement if his barked laugh is anything to go by.

"And tell me, little girl, what's he going to do about it, huh?" He bends at the knees, lowering down to my level.

I open my mouth to respond, but I have no words. He makes the most of my parted lips to blow a stream of smoke past them.

"Stop it," I spit.

"Why? You too much of a goody-two-shoes little girl to enjoy a hit?"

"Fuck you."

"Hmm…" His eyes roam over me once again. "Maybe. It's good to know you'd be up for it."

"Uh… what? No. That was not—" My words are cut off when he reaches over my shoulder.

My heart pounds and my head spins as I try to figure out what he's doing.

The second the door slams. I start to panic. I don't want to be stuck in a room with this asshole.

He steps forward, his body heat flowing into mine.

"Here," he says, offering me his joint. It's the first nice thing he's done or said since we met earlier. Although I'm not sure offering your younger stepsister drugs is actually considered a nice thing to do. Maybe where he's from.

Turning my face away from him, I silently refuse the offer.

"Ah, you too good for this? Don't tell me, you're also a cheerleader and on the school council campaigning for a life of abstinence and veganism."

My head snaps back to his in shock. He might be a douchebag, but I didn't have him down for a judgmental one too. "Don't pretend that you know me. You know fuck all about me."

"Oh, little girl," he says, his deep voice rumbling through me as he grasps my chin between his fingers. "I know you better than you think."

I want to shake him off, but he holds so hard that it actually starts to pinch.

"That hurts," I snap.

"And?"

He pushes me until my back collides with the door.

"I'm a cheerleader, so what?"

He smiles, it's accomplished and evil.

"Fucking knew it. You've got high school prep written all over you."

"Right now, all I've got all over me is you."

He growls, actually fucking growls right in my face.

"Oh, little one, trust me when I say that when I'm all over you, you'll feel me in more places than just your chin."

My eyes widen in shock at his words. I also don't miss the fact that he says when, not if. And I fucking hate that just the image that those words conjure up in my head has my lower stomach clenching in a way I haven't felt before.

He stares down at me as I will my brain to work properly with him so close. He smells like sexy male and weed, it's a heady combination. Although that could just be the weed that's causing that effect.

"Come on, I thought you were a good girl, *Rosy*."

"I'm pretty sure taking that." I nod at the joint he's still holding up for me. "Would make me anything but a good girl. And," I add sharply. "My name is Ruby. *Ruby*," I repeat, enunciating each syllable clearly so the asshole might have a chance at understanding it.

He takes another drag, making a show of holding it deep before once again blowing it out over me.

"Huh, look at that, it seems you're already dirty. And do you know what?"

I raise a brow, trying to appear totally uninterested in anything he might have to say, although I know deep down that I'm desperate to hear his voice again.

"I like my girls dirty."

Every muscle below my waist clenches.

With his blunt between his lips, he uses my moment of weakness to his advantage. His hot fingers wrap around my wrists and he lifts my arms above my head, pinning them there in one of his large hands.

Dropping his other arm, he runs his busted-up knuckles down my cheek. Goose bumps erupt around my body and I look to the side, not wanting him to see whatever he might be able to read in my eyes. I've no doubt my traitorous thoughts will be clear in their hazel depths.

I hate him. He's an asshole. So why does his touch feel so good? Even such a simple one.

Tucking his fingers under my chin, he forces me to face him. Only, much to his displeasure, I keep my eyes downcast.

"Look at me," he barks. His fingers wrap around my ponytail and my head is forced up. My eyes close, my need to defy him too strong to deny.

I resist for a beat, but his strength has nothing on my fast crumbling restraint.

Dragging my eyelids open, I gasp when I find his face incredibly close to mine with his dark eyes boring down into mine.

"Ashton, what are you..." He makes the most of my parted lips and places his blunt between them.

Anger explodes in my belly. Red hot fury racing through my veins. I shouldn't be fazed by this asshole, but he's getting under my skin faster than I know what to do with.

Spitting it from my lips, I watch as it hits his shoulder before falling to the ground.

His hold on my hair tightens as his other now free hand wraps around my exposed throat. He doesn't squeeze, but it doesn't stop my pulse thundering against his hold.

"You need to stay out of my way," he warns, his nose almost brushing mine, his breath racing over my face.

"Or what?" I sass, not willing to give up my fight against this asshole.

"Or... I won't be held responsible for my actions."

"What the hell is that supposed to mean?" My voice is all breathy and I hate it.

His hand releases my hair, but with his other still wrapped around my throat, I can't move. I do however let out a little shriek when he cups me between the legs.

"It means, little one, that I'll take whatever I like, when I like, and give zero fucks about the consequences."

"Y-y-you can't. You wouldn't." My head spins with both his warning and his touch. His words should be a reality check, they should put me off, but with his hand on me, all I can think about is him giving me more.

It's wrong. So fucking wrong.

He leans in, his lips brushing against the shell of my ear.

"You want more, don't you? Maybe I was wrong about you being a goody-two-shoes cheerleader, and the truth is that you're just a cheer slut."

"No," I cry, bucking against his hold. Only it doesn't shake him off, it only makes his fingers press into me harder.

Heat floods me as my temperature soars.

He glares down at me, his dark eyes full of hate and disgust. I've never felt so small and vulnerable in my life, and I fucking hate it.

He could do whatever he wants in this situation, and he knows it. It's why he's enjoying this power trip so much.

Unable to physically do anything about it, I use my words instead in the hope it'll get me kicked out of his room and away from his epic headfuck.

"Why do you want to touch me anyway? You hate me, remember?"

His teeth grind and his shoulders tense.

"And why is that exactly? Because I've been living here with *daddy* while you've been forgotten in Seattle?" It's a shot in the dark but one I'm confident in. But as his lips press into a thin line, I know that I hit the nail on the head.

His fingers clench slightly around my neck, but the warning isn't enough to make me stop.

"He treats me like his own daughter, you know. Gives me everything I could possibly want. Buys me whatever I want. He—"

"Enough," he roars, getting right in my face. His breaths are ragged, his eyes blown with anger. "Stop talking, little girl, before you say something you'll regret."

Before I get the chance to talk, his lips slam down on mine. Shock renders me motionless as his kiss bruises and his hold on me gets tighter.

"Ashton, no," I cry against him after a few brain-frazzled moments. My hands slap against his chest as I try to push him away. But it seems he has other ideas because before I even realize I've moved, I'm out of his room and tripping over my own feet.

I hold my breath as I wait for my body to collide with something, and only moments later my shoulder hits the wall in the hallway, and I slide down until I'm on my ass.

He stands above me. Anger and contempt vibrating from every inch of him.

"You're nothing, little girl. The only reason he puts up with you is because of your whore of a mother."

"No," I cry. "She's not."

"Pfft." He waves me off before lowering down on his haunches. "It seems that there's a lot you don't know, little one. You should know something, though." He looks over me as I clutch on to my smarting shoulder. "I'm going to fucking ruin you and leave them both with the broken pieces I leave behind. You know, just a little thank you for having me gift."

My head spins as his words register. Did he really just say those things to me, or is it the effects of the second-hand weed messing with my brain?

When I look up, I find that I'm alone in the hallway and that the pain in my shoulder is very real.

Fucking asshole.

5

RUBY

Ashton's music continues all freaking night.

Mom and Stephen came home sometime after midnight, although I didn't hear them arrive thanks to the booming bass on the other side of the wall. It wasn't until the loud shouts rang out as Stephen tried to get his son to be respectful and turn it down that I discovered they'd returned.

As I lay there staring at my ceiling, desperate to go to sleep in the hope it would help me to forget everything that had happened since I came home from school this afternoon, I can't help wondering why Stephen is bothering. It seems like a waste of energy to try to tell Ashton to do anything that might be considered thoughtful to others. I might have only spent a very limited time with him this evening, but I really doubt he's going to turn around and agree to do anything he's told, especially if that request comes from the mouth of his father.

There's some serious bad blood between the two of them I'm discovering, although I'm confident that it's totally one-sided.

I've seen the love that lights up Stephen's eyes when he talks about his son. It might have been years since he's spent any decent amount of time with him, but he fondly remembers the little boy he helped to bring into this world. Although after the past few hours, I wonder if that little boy no longer exists.

I think of the stories of the Lego loving boy he's fondly told us about and realize that there's a very good chance that Stephen knows nothing about his now hotheaded and very angry son.

I release a frustrated sigh as the arguing continues. One of them will win soon, and I have no doubt that when that person does, the music will continue and that none of us will be getting any sleep tonight.

As predicted, less than five minutes later, the bedroom door slams but the music doesn't turn off, in fact, I think it actually gets louder.

After having to get up early to meet the squad for a morning workout session, I spend the day half asleep. It doesn't matter what we're doing in each class I drag my exhausted body to, my eyelids just get heavier and heavier as I desperately try to concentrate.

"What's up with you?" Harley, my best friend, asks when she drops down beside me with her own lunch tray at the cheerleaders' table.

"Ugh, don't ask."

"Well, I did, so..."

Rolling my eyes at her, I push my tray away and rest my elbow on the table.

"Ashton has come to visit."

Her brows draw together as she thinks. "Ashton as in your stepbrother that you've never met but the one I lust after anytime he posts a picture on Instagram?"

I can't help but groan. "Yup, that one. I can assure you though, that beauty, it's only skin deep."

"Fine by me, I don't have any intentions of making him my new BFF."

"Jesus," I mutter. "He's... argh. He's a nightmare. His music was booming all night. He was smoking weed in his bedroom. He's been here less than a day and I want to kill him."

"Why is he here? I thought he always refused."

I shrug, not really having the answer to her question. "He was suspended from school, that's all I know."

"He'll be there after practice, right? I *need* to meet this enigma."

"No, Harley. I really don't think that's a good idea," I argue, although as I do, I can't help but wonder why I'm so against it.

She's interested, I've always known that, but just assumed that she'd never get any closer than his Insta. Now that he's under the same roof as me, the way he looked down at me last night, the way his lips pressed against mine, I'm not sure I want her anywhere near him.

Not that I want him, of course. He's an asshole. But I love Harley and I refuse to introduce her to a prick like him knowing that if anything were to happen that she'd only end up with her heart broken.

"Oh shush, I'll just come for a bit. Show him what he's missing." She winks, flicking her bright red hair over her shoulder. "You know what they say, once they go red, they never go back."

"And who exactly says that?" I ask curiously, knowing that the farthest Harley had got with a boy was a sloppy fumbled kiss at the summer formal a few months ago.

She shrugs. "Someone, I'm sure."

A few other members of the squad join us and thankfully our previous conversation is forgotten. There are only a handful of juniors on the squad, and both Harley and I were lucky enough to make the cut not so long ago.

I've spent years at both gymnastics and dance classes in the hope of making varsity. Pride washes through me as I think about all my hard work paying off.

My eyes roam over the squad, taking in their perfection before I stop on Chelsea, our captain, and Shelly, our assistant captain, sitting beside her. That's my next mission. I want to prove myself enough to have a shot at captain next year once Chelsea graduates.

Practice is killer. I'm not sure if it's just because I'm exhausted or that Chelsea is extra hard on us today, but I feel like I screw up every move I make.

"Ruby, lock your fucking knees," Chelsea barks. "If you don't straighten up and hold position, you're going to end up on your ass."

I wobble about as Krissy and Victoria try to keep me steady.

"Fucking hell, there are plenty of other JVs who'd love a shot at this. Get it together," Krissy snaps as I try to make my body respond.

I eventually manage the move to Chelsea's requirement before one of the girls below my grip slips and the world falls out from beneath me.

My cheek connects with something, someone's head maybe, an elbow, as I fall, sending burning pain through my face and down my neck before I collapse on the floor, landing on my already painful shoulder, I'm sure only making it worse.

"Fucking hell, Ruby," Chelsea says, racing over and staring down at me along with a huddle of the other girls, including Harley. "Are you okay?"

Releasing my cheek, I roll my shoulder. It hurts, but it's okay.

"Yeah."

I place my hand in Chelsea's as she reaches out to pull me up. Everyone else disperses, going back to what they were all doing before some drama kicked off.

"Is everything okay? You're not your usual self this afternoon," Chelsea asks. She's got a reputation for being an epic bitch, but while that may be true, she's an incredible captain, and every now and then, like just now, she does show that she has a softer side.

"Yeah, I'm good. Just family stuff, you know how it is."

"Sure do. But I need you to lock that shit down in here. You got that?"

I nod, despite the fact she's not looking at me.

Thankfully, the rest of practice passes without any more drama. I forgo showering in the locker room after once again declining the offer of Aces with the squad and the football team. I know I should go, not just because I need to ensure I'm fully part of the group, but more so because I don't want to go home in case he's there, but I've still got a ton of homework that's only been added to as the day's gone on.

I always thought that junior year was meant to be the calm before the storm, so to speak, but so far it's been nothing but hard work.

With my purse and duffle over my shoulder, I say my goodbyes and head out to the parking lot.

If I'm lucky, he'll have stolen someone else's car today and he won't be home.

Deciding to check my cell before showing up at home today, I pull it from my purse the second I'm in the car. My heart sinks the second I see a message from Mom. What now?

Mom: Family meal tonight. 7PM. Do not be late.

Groaning, I drop my head back on the headrest and close my eyes.

All I want to do is go home to my quiet house and sleep. Why do I get the impression that's not going to be happening anytime soon?

Blowing out a long breath, I rev the engine and make my way home to see what delights tonight might hold.

6

ASHTON

It's been a long ass day with only what's left of my weed and the memories of how she reacted to me last night filling my mind.

Fuck if her curvy little body didn't speak to me in a way it shouldn't. If her pert nipples that were hiding behind that thin fabric weren't just begging for me to take them into my mouth.

I wonder if anyone has ever touched her like I did last night. I wonder if me following through on my threat of taking whatever I want when I want might be a bigger deal to daddy's little princess than it might be to others. The way her eyes widened as I touched her sure leads me to believe that it's not something that's happened all that often.

A smile curls at my lips. Taking *that* from her sure would be a way to prove a point.

I had hopes for what my stepsister would be like. And as it's turning out, she's exactly what I was dreaming of. Hot, innocent, and totally unsuspecting.

Rubbing my hands together, I push from the bed and pull my jersey over my head. I stare at my name on the back and wonder if I'll ever be allowed to play again after this. Probably not. Football is the only thing that's kept me at that shitty school this long. Without it, I have no reason to be there when I could be working and helping provide for Mom and me.

Dropping it beside my bag, I push my sweats from my hips and walk toward the connected bathroom to shower before this lovely family meal Lisa intercepted me to talk about earlier. I only wanted a fucking sandwich, but instead I ended up having to endure my overly happy stepmother wanting to know my preferences for tonight's food. I'm an eighteen-year-old guy, put anything edible in front of me and I'll eat it. Clearly, she's not used to having boys around. The thought makes me smile and takes me back to my earlier musings about her possibly innocent daughter.

After a quick shower, I pull on a fresh set of clothes and run some gel through my hair. That's about all the effort they're going to get out of me for this inevitable shit show.

Not wanting to go downstairs early and give the impression I'm looking forward to this despite the fact I'm fucking starving, I equally don't want to sit here waiting. Deciding that I need some entertainment, I pull the door open and turn toward the one with my little toy inside.

I know she's there, she's been home a couple of hours. It's taken more restraint than I thought possible to stay locked inside my room this long, knowing that she's only on the other side of the door.

Something akin to excitement tingles in my stomach as I place my hand on her doorknob and twist.

I'm expecting her to see me immediately and for her to attempt to rip me a new one, but to my delight, the room is empty. The only evidence of where she is comes courtesy of the steam billowing from her bathroom.

I glance to her bed with all her homework strewn across it, trying to decide what my next move is going to be.

I'm just walking back from the window when she appears in the doorway, clutching a fluffy towel around her body.

"Get the fuck out," she shouts loud enough to alert our parents downstairs.

Racing over, I press my palm to her mouth to stop her from doing it again. I continue pushing her until she's backed up against the wall.

Her angry eyes stare up at me as her chest begins to heave.

"You seem to be in a vulnerable position right now, don't you think?" At my words, her grip on the towel tightens. It's amusing that she thinks she has any power right now. If I wanted to rip it from her body, I could in one swift move, I have no doubt of that.

The tension between us crackles as we stare at each other, the only sounds that can be heard is that of our increased breaths.

Breaking our connection, I run my eyes over her face. A darkening bruise on her cheek catches my eye and I lift my fingers to run over it, releasing her mouth once I'm confident that she's not going to scream again.

She flinches like it hurts despite the fact I barely make contact.

"Looks like I'm not the only one who likes to fight dirty."

Her brows draw together. "You think I…" She trails off with a shake of her head. "I've never been in a fight in my life. Although my need to hurt you is starting to get the better of me."

I can't help but smile. The thought of her unleashing her tiny fists on me is too amusing to ignore.

"Oh yeah, and how exactly do you think you're capable of hurting me?"

"I might be small, but don't underestimate me."

My jaw pops as I stare at her, wondering exactly what she's thinking, what she believes she could do to me that would cause any more pain. She's already ruined my life, taken my father away, I'm not sure there's much else she could do to make my life any worse.

"Ruby, Ashton, dinner is ready." The sound of Lisa's sweet voice is like nails on a chalkboard, and I visibly shudder as it sounds out around us.

"Uh oh, saved by the bell."

I take a step back as she breathes out a sigh of relief and drops her hands. Wrong thing to do.

In a split second, I've reached out and tugged at the fabric that's covering her body.

Shock renders her useless because by the time her brain's caught up with what I've done and she reaches for the towel, it's too late.

The fluffy fabric flutters to the ground, allowing me a few seconds to take in my fill of her naked body. It's fucking perfection. Her rosy pink nipples perk and beg to be touched. Her toned stomach, the small patch of hair before the apex of her thighs, the curve of her hips.

Fuck.

This was probably a huge mistake because where I previously wanted to get my hands on her to prove a point, now I'm damn near desperate to discover if she's just as feisty when she's on her back with her legs spread.

Long before I've had my fill, she bends and covers herself once more.

"Happy now?" she asks, trying to sound confident but failing miserably. "You've had a good look, you can stash it in your fucked-up spank bank for later or whatever it is sadistic motherfuckers like you do."

I smile at her, the fact she thinks I'm even remotely interested amuses me.

"You think I want you? Fuck off, little girl. If I need a willing pussy for the night, I'll go find a woman who knows what she's doing, thank you very much."

Her cheeks burn crimson before I move toward the door. I'm almost in the hallway when she finds her voice again.

"Who says I don't know what I'm doing?"

I leave her standing there with just my laugh filling her ears.

7

RUBY

"Ah, there you are. I thought we were going to have to send out a search party," Mom says when I eventually join them in the dining room.

My skin tingles with their stares, making me look up. I find Stephen at his usual place at the head of the table, with Mom beside him, and Ashton in what is usually my seat. Of course he fucking is. Without even knowing it, he's driving me crazy.

Ignoring him and trying to push down my embarrassment from not so long ago, I stalk toward the farthest chair away from him and sit down.

"Ruby? Have we all done something to offend you?" Stephen asks as I settle at the opposite end of the table.

"I think I'm coming down with something, I'd hate to spread it around everyone," I lie, badly.

"Don't be silly, honey. Come and sit next to Ash, I'm sure he'd love to get to know you better."

I don't look up at him, I don't need to to know that he's got a shit-eating grin on his face right now.

Reluctantly, very reluctantly, I stand back up and walk to the chair beside him. I could refuse and cause a scene about not wanting to sit beside him. But what would be the point? Our parents would want to know why and I can hardly tell them that it's because after trying to pressure me into smoking a joint with him—in the house, I might add if they've not already discovered that—that he then proceeded to kiss me, throw me out and then, only moments ago, strip me naked for his own sick pleasure. While I'm at it, I could also try to explain that some twisted part of me enjoyed every minute of it. But I decide against saying all of that and just sit silently beside him, keeping my eyes on the table and my hands in my lap.

"I suggested to your mom that we have your favorite," Stephen explains as Mom disappears from the room and Ashton stifles a groan. "We thought Ash would probably approve too," he adds, turning his gaze on his son.

Ash opens his mouth to respond, but he must have other ideas because no sooner do his lips part than they close again.

My eyes flick between the two of them as they stare at each other. Confusion and concern covers Stephen's face whereas Ashton's entire body is locked with tension and oozing with anger.

Glancing down, I spot his fists curled around the edge of the chair, his knuckles white with the force.

There's clearly a lot that's been left unsaid between these two. I can only hope that something good actually comes from Ashton's stay here and they manage to fix whatever it is that's broken between them.

Ashton might be an asshole, but he still deserves to have a relationship with his father.

My thoughts wander to mine and I can't help but smile. He might not live under the same roof as me now, but we're still pretty close, when he's in town of course. I think his regular work trips might have been one of the things that added to the many issues that put an end to his and Mom's relationship.

"Here we go," Mom sings, oblivious to the tension in the room. It's so freaking thick you could cut it with a knife, but as she lays out plates laden with everything to make tacos, she either misses it or just chooses to ignore it. "We weren't sure what you liked, Ash, so I just picked up everything I could think of."

"It's great... thanks," he says, unnervingly quietly.

Usually I'd dive straight into tacos like my life depends on it, but today, with dread sitting heavy in my stomach and the tension pressing down on my shoulders, eating is the last thing I want to be doing.

"Are you all set for the big party tomorrow night?" Stephen asks me after a long, painful minute of silence.

"Er... yeah, I guess."

"Party?" Ashton pipes up.

"Oh yes. It's Halloween. Every year the Rosewood students attend a haunted house party on the outskirts of town in an old mansion. It's a tradition that's been going for years, right?" Mom says, looking to Stephen with a soft smile as she remembers their previous life together.

When I glance to Ashton, he's staring between the two of them, the muscles in his neck and shoulders pulled tight.

"Those were some great parties, eh?"

It's no secret to me that our parents were childhood sweethearts back in the day, but it blows my mind to think of them both doing the same things I am now, believing that they were destined to spend their lives together. I guess it just goes to show that you don't know what road life will take you on. It's heartwarming to see that they've come back together now and reconnected though.

"Have you got your costume sorted?" Stephen asks, turning his eyes on me.

"Yep."

"What are you going as?" Ashton asks, speaking for the first time in forever.

"Zombie cheerleader."

"Wow, how original."

"I'm sorry, who made you the Halloween police?" I snap, turning my narrowed gaze on him.

He widens his eyes, but he doesn't respond. If it's possible, his silence annoys me more than if he were to bark back an insult.

Stephen tries to maintain some less than stimulating conversation that Ashton clearly has no interest in engaging in, it doesn't stop him trying though.

The meal is agonizing and all I can think about is escaping.

"You must be coming down with something. You've barely touched your dinner," Mom helpfully points out sometime later.

"You should have some more, it might make you feel better," Ashton says, turning his dark eyes on me. "It'll give you some energy at least."

My entire body jolts when his burning hot hand lands on my thigh.

My lips purse in frustration as I try to push it away without being obvious, not that our parents are paying any attention, they're too lost in their own conversation once again.

"Get off me," I whisper, putting more effort into pushing him off me.

Sadly, he seems to enjoy my attempt because as a smile tugs at his lips, his hand only slides higher up my thigh, his fingers dipping under the fabric of my skirt.

"Stop fighting, little one. You know you wore this to tempt me."

"Like fuck I did." Truth is that it was the first thing I found abandoned on the chair in my room after he left me earlier. I knew I was late and that Mom would start asking questions, so I just pulled on whatever and headed down, not putting any more thought into it.

"Are you even wearing panties?"

Standing abruptly, the chair squeaks on the tiled floor, turning all eyes on me.

"Is everything okay, honey?"

"I'm sorry, I really need to go and get some air."

"O-of course. I'll wrap some of this up for you in case you're hungry later."

I want to tell her not to bother, that as long as he's under this roof that I'm not sure I'll ever eat again. But instead I nod, and quickly leave the room, thankfully sucking in deep lungfuls of air now that I'm not surrounded by his scent.

Pushing through the back doors, I walk out across the deck until I get to one of the sun loungers that has its back to the house.

I rest my head back and close my eyes.

How did things get so complicated so fast?

Pulling my cell from my pocket, I ignore the message from Harley checking in on me after my fall and instead find my conversation with Dad.

Ruby: Hey, are you in town?

I hit send and wait with bated breath in the hope that he is and is willing to have a gate-crasher for a few days.

Going to stay with him isn't unheard of, I've just never done it because I've needed to escape my own house.

Dad: Sorry, kiddo. I'm in Colorado on a shoot. Everything okay?

Blowing out a breath through pursed lips, I roll my shoulders in the hope it loosens the tension pulling at them. Sadly, it does shit all, just makes the one I've now landed on hurt that much more.

I reply to say that everything is good and that I just miss him. It's not a total lie.

Placing my cell on the lounger beside me, I rest back and close my eyes.

I'm almost asleep when a shadow falls over me and a shiver of fear runs down my spine.

For fuck's sake. Just leave me alone, I want to scream but I know it would be futile.

"What?" I bark without even bothering to open my eyes. It's probably a stupid move, I should be on my guard with him at all times, but I'm just too freaking tired.

He drops down onto the lounger beside me, forcing my legs out of the way in the process.

"Sure, you can join me."

"I don't remember asking permission."

Dragging my eyes open, my lips part ready to spit some more abuse at him, but I don't get the chance, because his hot palm once again lands on my exposed thigh.

"Get your fucking hands off me."

My entire body freezes and he pushes it higher, his fingers disappearing under the fabric, heading for dangerous territory.

"You don't get to fucking touch me." I try to move away, but his fingers tighten on my thigh.

"I get to do whatever the fuck I want. And right now, I want to play with my little toy."

"I'm not a fucking toy, I'm not your little plaything, I'm a fucking person. A person who after barely twenty-four hours can't stand the fucking sight of you. So get your hands off me and leave me the hell alone."

When I've finished my little rant, it soon becomes obvious that the only effect it's had on the asshole is to amuse him.

"Are you finished?" he asks around a smirk.

"No, you're a fucking—argh." He grabs my arm before my hand can connect with his cheek.

"Careful now, little one. You don't want to cause yourself any more injuries."

"Fuck you."

"Hmm... like I said before, it's certainly an option. What do you think *daddy* would say if I corrupted his little princess? Maybe we could do it out here, make him watch. Force him to watch me break you in two, force him to watch you enjoy every last second of it."

"No, I—"

"Oh come on, little one. You know you'd enjoy it. I bet you're wet for me right now just thinking about my cock."

"Never," I seethe, but apparently my words, my anger, isn't enough for him. Before I know it, he's pushed his hand even higher and he's running his fingertip over me.

Something akin to pleasure races through me at his touch, but I refuse to acknowledge it.

"Tut, tut, tut, I'm disappointed, little one. I thought I was going to find you bare for me under here. I thought you were going to make it easy for me."

"What the fuck is wrong with you?" I push at his arm, trying to force him away from me and thankfully, after a second, he concedes and removes all contact from me.

A menacing laugh falls from his lips. "So many things, little one, that I've lost count. Have a great evening and enjoy finishing your homework." With those parting words, he pushes from the lounger and stalks off, leaving my head spinning and my body trembling.

Resting my head back once more, I stare up at the darkening sky.

What the fuck is that asshole's problem? What did I ever do to him to deserve this kind of torture?

After a few minutes, I start to feel vulnerable sitting out here alone, plus I know for a fact that he has the perfect view of me from his bedroom window if that's where he's just disappeared to.

Scooting forward on the lounger, I prepare to head back upstairs to try to get some more work done. Only, before I move, something floating in the pool catches my eyes.

Looking around at the back yard, I spot more paper littered around.

What the... oh no... No, no, no.

Racing over to the paper at the edge of the pool, I pull it out and find exactly what I feared.

My almost completed assignment, the paper soaked through and the ink running everywhere.

"You fucking asshole," I scream into the silent evening.

Spinning on my heels, I stare up at his bedroom window and sure as shit, there he stands with a proud fucking smirk firmly in place.

With my heart threatening to beat out of my chest, I race around the garden, collecting what I can before grabbing the pool net and fishing out a few other stray pieces.

I stare down at the soaked paper, it's totally ruined.

My teeth grind as I make my way up to my bedroom. I slow when I get to his door. My need to storm in and rip him a new one is almost too much to ignore, but a trickle of reality seeps in and tells me that no matter what I intend to do, he'll win. He'll make sure he always wins.

I can fight back all I like, but whatever this thing is between us is only going to end one way.

Forcing my legs to keep moving, I drop everything to my desk and smooth some of the less damaged pieces of paper out, but it's pointless. The whole thing is fucked.

As if he was waiting for me, his music starts up on the other side of the wall.

I scream against it, but I'm no match for the booming bass.

Pulling my cell back out, I send a message to my second savior.

Ruby: I'm struggling with this assignment. Wanna do it together?

Harley: Sure. Mom's out, you wanna come over? You can stay the night?

"Yes," I squeal as the exact question I was hoping for lights up on my screen.

I quickly pack a bag with everything I'm going to need for the foreseeable future, including everything for the party tomorrow night.

I figure I'll stick it all in my car just in case I can get away with not coming back here for a while.

After letting Mom know where I'm going, I leave the house as fast as I can, breathing a huge sigh of relief as I back out of the drive.

"Bye, bye, motherfucker."

8

ASHTON

Walking away from her knowing that her body was fully on board with the thoughts I had running around my head was one of the hardest things I think I've ever done.

Her skin was so soft under my hand, her panties so fucking wet when I brushed my finger over them, the floral scent of her hair. Fuck, all I could think about was pushing her panties aside and finding out exactly how wet she was for me.

Reaching down, I rub at my length that's tenting my sweats as I watch her run around the back yard collecting her homework. Every time she bends over, her skirt rises and I get just a hint at the ass she's hiding beneath it.

I could have taken more so easily. I should have.

"Fuck," I bark, slamming my hand down on the window frame in frustration.

Images of her beneath me writhing and moaning as I push her over the edge fill my mind and it only makes my cock harder for her.

I want her fucking broken so that I can hand her back to daddy and walk away knowing that I fucked him over just like he did us.

Selfish fucking cunt.

My skin tingles with awareness and when I glance back up, she's staring right at me.

Pushing my hand inside my sweats, I wrap my fingers around my length and squeeze. My eyelids flutter with pleasure.

I wonder how her tiny hand would feel. How hot her mouth might be?

"Fuuuuck," I grate out, stepping back from the window when she disappears.

The temptation to follow her into her room and discover the answer to those questions is strong, but I hold off, for now at least. Nothing good can come of me going after her when I'm so desperate that I can hardly think straight.

The second she's safely in her room—or so she might think—I turn my music on and fall down onto my bed, pushing my sweats from my hips, I take my cock in my hand with images of her hot little body filling my mind.

It takes an embarrassingly short amount of time before I feel the familiar tingles at the base of my spine. Two more pumps and I groan out as I come over my hand.

I'd hoped it might bring me some relief, but even before the high from my orgasm has faded, I know that I need more. And by more, I don't mean delivered by my own hand.

I need her.

After cleaning up, I slip out of my room and stand at hers, listening for what she might be doing inside.

My hand rests on the doorknob, but in the end, I decide against it.

I'll leave her stewing a little longer. Plus, it sounds like there's going to be a semi-decent party tomorrow night. I guess I've got a costume to organize because there is no fucking way I'm allowing her to spend the night with any other motherfucker, even if it is her boyfriend that I've yet to know exists or not.

I somehow manage to remain in my room for the rest of the night and thankfully after that forced bit of family time at dinner, my dad allows me the evening to hide. I know my time avoiding him is running out though.

He's wanted me to visit for years and the one time I do, he seems to spend his entire time working. I'm not complaining, quite the opposite in fact. If I get to do my time here hiding in this room and only coming out to torment Ruby, then I'll head home counting it as a win with no intention of coming back again anytime soon.

Hopefully, Mom will have had a few days break and we'll just be able to dive back into our normal clusterfuck of a life bouncing from one day to the next and hoping a lottery win might drag us from the hellhole we call home. We can only dream, right?

"Good morning, honey." Lisa's sweet voice sets my teeth on edge.

I put off leaving my room until as late as possible in the hope she might have left, seems I wasn't that lucky.

"Mornin'," I grunt, walking past her and straight to the coffee machine.

"I can do that if you tell me how you like it." I look over my shoulder at her and watch as her smile falters at the look on my face.

I'm not sure at what point she decided that I needed her to mommy me, but she really needs to fucking stop.

"I'm more than capable of making myself a cup of coffee."

"O-okay, well... would you like any breakfast?"

"Do you fuss around your daughter this much?" I ask.

"Um... well... no, but you're our guest."

"Pfft." And doesn't that just say it all.

This is not my home, and it never will be. My dad handed over his title as part of my family the day he walked away from us and into this irritatingly happy woman's arms.

"It won't be long and you can resume your lives as the world's happiest family without me bringing the tone down," I mutter.

"Ashton, what makes you say that? We love having you here."

I spin and rest my lower back against the counter as the coffee machine does its thing.

She swallows nervously as my eyes bore into hers. A small sense of achievement fills me. Good, I'm glad she's scared.

"Really?" I ask.

"Of course. Your dad told me to tell you that he's cleared his schedule for the weekend so that the two of you can spend some time together. He misses you terribly."

"Well he should have thought about that before he started fucking you and left me then, shouldn't he? Excuse me." I snatch my mug from the machine and march past her before she recovers from my comment and comes up with a response.

I don't put my music on to the level that I have the past two days, and I've got a very good reason. I'm expecting a delivery.

Once I know that Lisa has left and I've got the place to myself, I emerge from my bedroom and make the most of the rest of the house.

Dad's got a home gym that I use for a couple of hours before spending most of the day on the couch watching their fucking massive TV.

As it starts to creep around to the time Ruby has returned from school the past two days, I can't help but feel a little excitement start to bubble up.

Only, she never does.

Looks like I'm going to have to take matters into my own hands if I want to see her tonight.

9

RUBY

The second Harley looked at me, she knew something was wrong but no matter how much she begged, I refused to tell her what had me running from my own house.

I told her that I'd been working on the outside table and everything blew away with a gust of wind. It was totally unfeasible seeing as there wasn't so much as a breeze outside, let alone a gust, but she soon realized her pleading was falling on deaf ears before she gave up. That didn't stop her casting me worried glances every time she saw me at school today.

Thankfully, sleeping with her in the silent bedroom meant I had a night of much better sleep and I'm not walking around like a freaking zombie. I need my energy for the party.

I remember last year's, it was mental. Technically, Harley and I were too young to be invited but seeing as we were already JV cheerleaders, we managed to get our names on the guest list. Mom and Stephen weren't all that impressed until I pointed out how they delight in telling me all about the parties they'd crashed when they were younger and reminded them what good girls Harley and I were. Of course, I was laughing on the inside as I said the words. I might be somewhat of a good girl, but Harley seriously has her moments.

As predicted, during lunch, Harley announces that I should get ready for the party at hers and then stay the night again. That is more than fine by me, so once cheer practice is over, I follow her back to her house to get the party started early.

She snatches a bottle of vodka that her brother Zayn had stashed in his den and we take turns taking a shot while we get ready.

"Here," she says, walking into her bedroom with two huge pizza boxes in her hands. "I ordered food to soak up some of that."

"Oh gimmie," I say with grabby hands. My head is already spinning and we haven't even left the house yet.

"Zayn," she bellows out her bedroom door. "Dinner."

I look down at myself wearing just a tank and a tiny pair of panties.

"Har," I say in panic, pointing to myself as footsteps head our way.

"Oh shush. My brother's such a dog, he's probably immune to a pair of tits by now."

"I heard that," he calls as he steps into the doorway.

"You were supposed to, asswipe. Here." She thrusts a box in his direction, but he doesn't even notice.

"Hey, Ruby, baby. How's it going?"

Nerves erupt in my belly. It's no secret that I've crushed on Zayn for as long as I can remember. His dark eyes call to me in a way that a certain other pair don't. While he who won't even be thought about has terrifying dark eyes, Zayn's are like melted chocolate that I just want to dive into. Add that to his warm bronze skin and I can't help but want to discover more.

Sadly, he just sees me as his little sister's friend. He might flirt, but I'd be stupid to think it was anything more than banter.

I curl myself into a ball in the hope of hiding what my minimal clothing isn't.

"I-it's good. You?" I stutter like an idiot.

"All the better after seeing you, baby." He winks and my cheeks heat.

"Now you've got that, you can fuck off. We've got a party to get ready for," Harley barks at him.

"Ugh, you're really coming?"

"Um... of course we are. You're not the only one to have all the fun."

"You could wait until next year though, when I'm at college," he grumbles.

"And what would be the fun in that? You wouldn't get to disapprove of my outfit or the boys I choose to kiss."

He takes a step toward her, his finger coming out to tell her off. "Harley, there will be no kis—"

"Oh, take a day off. I know for a fact that you were doing more than kissing when you were a junior, so you don't get to comment. Unless you want me to tell Mom that I caught you fucking—"

"Enough."

Harley bursts out laughing. "So I thought. Now off you fuck."

"You're a pain in my ass, Harley Hunter."

"Yeah, yeah. The feeling is mutual, asswipe," she calls as he heads off down the hall.

Their banter is what a brother and sister relationship should be like. I think about the past forty-eight hours with Ashton. There is no sibling bond between us. But then, why should there be? We're strangers brought together by our parents. There's no reason for us to have any kind of connection.

Although there is. There's something that crackles between us every time we're in touching distance. But it's anything but fun banter. It's pure hate.

I see it in his eyes. I feel it in his touch.

No matter how much I fight him, we both know that he holds all the power and I need to keep my guard up before he achieves his mission to break me.

"Whoa, calm down. I'd like to get to the party before you pass out," Harley says, swiping the bottle that I was chugging from.

"Just letting go. It's been a long week."

"I knew it," she announces, slapping her knee. "What did he do to make you run from your own house?"

"It's just the music. We should get dressed."

Pushing from the edge of her bed while she pulls out her first slice of steaming pizza, I rummage around in the bag I packed to get my outfit out. It consists of my cheer uniform and some face paint. Ashton was right, it's not exactly creative but I hate costumes, or more specifically masks, so it's as much as I'm willing to do.

"Fuck," I mutter, rummaging to the bottom.

"What?"

"I didn't pack a white bra."

"So, just go without. Give the guys a free pass to second base tonight."

Looking at her, I narrow my eyes in her direction. My boobs might not be massive, but I prefer to have them contained. At least I'm not actually cheering tonight, I guess.

"Or borrow one of mine," she suggests with a shrug.

"That would probably be worse." I glance down at her chest.

"All right, no need to point out what I'm missing."

"Just put your top on. Any guy who's lucky to get a hand under tonight will think all his Christmases have come at once."

I think of the guys at school, of Zayn, and who I could end up with tonight, but every time I do, their faces merge into someone else's.

I shake my head. I need more fucking vodka.

10

RUBY

Much like last year, the haunted house looks creepy as fuck as we walk toward it. Thankfully, Zayn gave us a lift, although he made a point of expressing his annoyance at every turn. Not that either of us gave a shit. Harley is too ready to party and I'm too ready to have a night away from the drama and those eyes and evil words.

The second we're out of the car, Harley, dressed as Catwoman, takes my hand and drags me toward the house.

We're immediately engulfed into the crowd that's hovering by the entrance. She makes quick work of locating the drinks before we down one each and find the rest of the squad.

Most of them are on the dance floor, so without a second thought we join them.

The music pounds, my friends happy, if not already slightly drunk, surround me and I finally breathe a sigh of relief as I lift my arms above my head and grind my hips in time with the music.

One song blends into another, different members of the squad keep appearing with more drinks and as the time goes on, my head gets lighter and I begin to forget about everything and just enjoy myself. Even the masks of some of the students around me stop bothering me so much.

At some point, a warm pair of hands slide around my bare waist and a hot, firm body presses against my back.

"You really are trying to torture me tonight, aren't you, baby?" Zayn's smooth voice fills my ear as he moves against me.

The alcohol gives me confidence that I wouldn't have on a normal day and I push my ass back into him and he groans in pleasure.

"You're a tease, baby."

"Who said I only tease?" I shoot over my shoulder as his hands begin to hesitantly skim up my stomach.

He's about an inch from finding out that I'm bare beneath when he's suddenly gone

"What the—" I spin around, the room seeming to move along with me, telling me just how much I've had to drink but I don't see Zayn, I don't see anyone other than people enjoying themselves.

Two seconds pass as I try to figure out what the fuck just happened when I hear it.

"Trick or treat, little one?"

A violent shudder works its way through my body as his large hand clamps down on my hip. The other skates up my body, over my breast until it's around my throat.

I swallow and the low chuckle that fills my ear tells me that he didn't miss my fear.

The length of his body presses against my back, but unlike with Zayn, I don't immediately relax back into him.

"What? So you'll happily dance with that cocksucker, but you won't with me? If I cared, little one, I'd be offended."

Something hard hits the back of my head, but my alcohol fuzzed brain can't register what it is.

"Dance," he demands and as he rolls his hips against my ass, I have no choice but to follow the move.

I glance around at everyone surrounding us, but no one is paying us any mind, they're all too lost in enjoying themselves.

My head continues to spin, and it's not at all helped by his scent and the strength of his hold on me. It's possessive, dominant, and fuck if it doesn't make me want to submit.

His hand leaves my hip and slides up my stomach. Unlike with Zayn, there's no hesitation as his fingers disappear under the fabric.

In seconds, his fingers find my naked breasts. My nipples pebble against the fabric of my top moments before one is covered by his giant hand.

"Oh god," I moan, my head falling back against his shoulder as he squeezes.

Turning my head toward him, I expect to find his dark eyes boring down on me, only when I open my eyes, all I register is the mask and I scream bloody murder. I jump away from him, but his grip is too tight and I'm forced to stare at my worst nightmare. A fucking Jason mask. Of course that's what he chose for tonight, fitting I guess seeing as he's turning my life into a living nightmare.

"Let's go," he demands, removing his hand from my top and lacing his fingers through mine. For a second, I think the move is too sweet to belong to him, but that's soon forgotten when he tugs me harshly behind him.

No one looks our way, so no one sees the fear that is written all over my face as I follow the devil himself to wherever he's deemed suitable.

We climb two sets of stairs before he pushes a very squeaky door open and slips inside. The room is dark and dirty, one of the panes of glass on the window is broken, allowing the nighttime breeze to blow in, causing goose bumps to erupt on my skin. The moonlight is the only light, and it highlights the dust floating around in the air that we disturb as we enter.

Yeah, it's not creepy at all. I'm in a derelict house, in an abandoned room with Jason freaking Voorhees. Nothing good can come from this.

He releases me, and as much as I might want to turn and run, I don't. My sick fascination with what he's going to do next leaves me frozen on the spot. That and the vodka that's filling my veins.

Walking over to the window, he rips the mask from his head and drops it to the bare floorboards. The thud makes me jump and has my already pounding heart thumping against my ribs.

I'm sure he only has his back to me for seconds, but it feels like a lifetime has passed when he eventually turns his dark stare on me.

Something crackles and I feel it all the way down to my toes. I open my mouth to say something, but I don't get a chance to figure out what it might be because he closes the space between us. In seconds, his fingers are around my throat and his lips are on mine.

His tongue demands entrance and parts my lips in its need for more.

My brain misfires as I try to keep up with him.

One second he's seeking entrance and the next my back is up against the wall and my leg is hitched up around his waist. His already hard length presses against me and I can't help but move against him.

His tongue plunges into my mouth, tangling with my own, taking everything he needs. Although, I'm not sure if he's taking when I'm handing myself over willingly.

I was right about his lips the first time I looked at them. Fuck, can he kiss.

He utterly consumes me.

His hand squeezes my throat as he loses control but at no point does it concern me, if anything, it just makes me crave more. More of his touch, more of his taste, just more of him.

My fingers fumble with his leather jacket until I'm pushing it from his shoulders. It hits the floor with a thud, but it doesn't stop him.

His other hand slides down the underside of my thigh until he's palming my ass. When he finds it's bare, he groans into my mouth. His fingers continue down until he's running them over the small scrap of soaked fabric covering me.

Ripping my lips from his, my head falls back, banging against the wall as an unfamiliar feeling races through me.

"You can only hide what you really want for so long, little one. Tell me you want this. Tell me that you want me to watch you shatter."

"Ashton." His name is meant to be a warning, but it comes out sounding like a needy whimper.

Slipping the lace aside, he runs his fingers through my heat.

"Fuck, little one. I knew you were desperate for me, but shit."

"Oh god, oh god," I chant as he teases me.

Just as it starts to get even more intense, he stops touching me and stands back.

Even with the limited light, I can see his chest heaving.

I watch as he tips his face to the ceiling for a beat, but I only get a second to wonder what the fuck he's playing at because no sooner have I blinked than he's back.

His fingers wrap around the hem of my top and he tugs it up my body. I'm powerless but to lift my arms and allow him to expose me.

The moment I'm free of the fabric, his hands cup my breasts. He squeezes and a loud sigh falls from my lips.

So fucking good.

"Watch," he barks, and like the good little girl that I am. My head lifts of its own accord and I watch with fascination as his kiss-swollen lips part to suck on my nipple.

The second he connects with my sensitive skin, my entire body tingles with pleasure.

His eyes remain locked on mine and he sucks, licks, and bites, making me squeal with the weird mix of pain and pleasure.

I follow, totally lost in him as he moves to the other side.

Just when I think that's all he's going to do, he drops to his knees and begins kissing down my stomach.

Oh fuck, oh fuck. Is he going to...

His fingers wrap around my skirt and before I get to finish the thought he has it around my ankles, leaving me in just my white lace thong.

"Oh, little one. You're way too innocent for the likes of me. I'm going to fucking ruin you."

The tearing of fabric fills the room as he rips my panties from my body.

He stares at me for a beat and my cheeks heat knowing that he's eye level with my most intimate place.

Unable to look at him, I cast my eyes aside.

"What did I say?" My chin is in his grasp in a beat and I'm forced to look back at him. I find him standing once again, his dark hungry eyes staring into mine. "Look. At. Me."

Running his tongue along his bottom lip, he stares at me. His eyes are impossibly dark, but there's more in them than just his normal evil intentions.

"Wha—"

"No talking," he demands before ensuring that I'm unable to spit a comeback by filling my mouth with his tongue once again.

His kiss is bruising as our tongues duel and our teeth clash. I give as good as I get as his hands roam around my body as if he doesn't know where to touch first.

Needing to make some contact of my own, I slip my hands under the hem of his shirt. His abs jump under my touch, but I don't get to enjoy trailing my fingers along the indentations for long.

His fingers wrap around my wrist and I'm pulled away.

"I'll tell you when you can touch me. And trust me when I say that what you'll be touching will be somewhat lower."

I should be turned off, but fuck if every muscle south of my waist doesn't clench with desire.

Both of his hands grip onto my waist and I squeal as I'm lifted into his body and spun from the wall.

His lips trail down my neck as we move, and as he descends lower toward my breasts once again, I lose all train of thought and concern that he might be heading for the door to expose me to the entire school. Something tells me that he's not one for sharing if the way he removed Zayn earlier is anything to go by.

I tense as I think of him. I really hope Ash didn't hurt him.

Ashton coming to a stop puts an end to my worries, reaching out he moves something that sends another plume of dust into the air and when I look over my shoulder, I see he's revealed an old piano.

My brows pull together as I wonder what he's going to do, but the coldness of the instrument's wood bites into my back as he lays me out across it.

"Same rules apply. Watch. Me."

Following orders, I scramble to prop myself up on my elbows as he pushes my thighs as wide as they'll go and places my feet on the old wood.

My chin drops at the hungry expression on his face as he stares up at me.

"Anyone done this to you before, little one?" His voice is deep and rougher than normal and as it rumbles through me, I feel my center getting wetter.

I stifle a groan of frustration. I'm not entirely sure what I need him to do right now, but I know I need him to touch me, to do something instead of just stare at me.

"N-no."

A wicked smile curls up at his lips.

"Good. You'll always remember me then."

I want to tell him that he's such an asshole that it's probably not possible anyway but I don't get the chance because he wraps his hands around my hips as he fixes his lips over me.

His tongue almost immediately starts to circle my clit and I cry out at the sensation.

"Fuuuuuck."

I have no idea if I need to drag him closer or push him away, the sensation is so intense. Fuck. I don't even know my own fucking name as he licks, sucks and grazes his teeth against me.

My back arches, thrusting my breasts in the air as I fight to do as I was told and watch him.

His eyes remain on me as I fight to stay still and he ups the ante, circling my entrance with one finger.

"Ashton," I scream as he pushes the digit deep inside me. The foreign sensation too good to deny.

He shouldn't be doing this. We shouldn't be doing this.

I shouldn't want it to continue so badly.

With one finger inside me and his lips latched onto my core, he reaches out with his other hand and pinches my nipple.

"Oh god."

I fall down onto the piano with such force it cries out its own tune for a second.

My fingers of one hand curl around the wood as the other dives for Ashton's hair. I grip on to him, holding him in place and ensuring that he's not about to stop whatever it is that he's doing to me.

Everything around me disappears and I feel like I'm floating as sensations surge through my body.

Adding another finger, it only gets more and more intense and I hold on to him tighter.

"Let go," he whispers against me, the vibrations of his deep voice only adding to his ministrations.

"Oh god, oh god," I chant as the ball that's been growing inside me gets so big that all it can do is shatter. "Oh god. Ashton," I scream as it explodes.

White lights spark behind my eyes as my entire body twitches and convulses against his face.

"Oh my god, oh my god," I continue to whisper as he slows down and the feelings start to subside.

My chest heaves as I try to drag in the air I need, and my eyelids get heavy.

The room spins around me as the overwhelming need to sleep hits me like a truck.

The last thing I remember is Ashton coming to stand beside me and press his lips to mine. I remember thinking how hot it was that he tasted like me, but then everything goes black.

11

RUBY

I come to with what feels like a freaking drum pounding in my head.

Groaning, I roll over and my stomach turns.

I still immediately and try to cast my mind back to why I feel so horrendous.

Then the reason hits me full force.

Sitting up in a rush, my stomach rolls again and I grip the sheets, ready to throw them back to run toward a bathroom.

Thankfully, it subsides and I open my eyes.

"Huh?"

I'm in my bedroom.

Lifting the sheets from my body, I look down to find I'm wearing my cheer uniform once again, only I soon notice that one item of clothing is missing.

The image of Ashton ripping my panties from my body fills my mind and my traitorous body heats as I continue running the events of the night before through my head.

"Oh my god," I mutter, dropping my head into my hands.

Please tell me it's a really bad dream and I really didn't let my stepbrother eat me out on top of a piano.

Fuck. Fuck. Fuck.

But even as ashamed as I am for how I acted, I can't deny that it wasn't a serious fucking high. Screw his blunt from the other day, that was something else.

No, no, no. Don't even think about it.

Falling back down into bed, I pull the sheets over my head and will my body to go back to sleep. But I can't, I've got too many questions racing around in my head.

Like, how did I get from being naked on a piano to mostly dressed again and in my own bed? What did he do to me after I passed out? Did I even pass out or are there parts of last night that I'm forgetting? Shit, did I let him fuck me? I wiggle my hips and feel nothing unusual. Surely, I'd know if it went that far, right?

"Jesus fucking Christ, Ruby. What are you doing?" I ask myself before flipping the sheets back once more and pushing from the bed.

My head spins and pounds, and my stomach feels less than secure as I plod toward my bathroom, stripping out of my uniform as I do.

After making use of the toilet, I stand with my hands on the basin and stare at myself in the mirror.

"Shit," I gasp when I get a look at my smeared face paint, but that's nothing compared to my shock when I look at my chest. It's covered in red marks, some of which look suspiciously like bite marks. "What the fuck have I done?"

After a very long hot shower, I drag on a pair of sweats and an oversized shirt and reluctantly head out of my room, knowing that I can hardly hide in here forever.

Weirdly, there's no music coming from Ashton's room. It must be the first time since he arrived that he's not had it booming just to piss me off.

When I get downstairs, I find both Mom and Stephen sitting at the table eating breakfast.

"Hey, honey. I thought you were staying at Harley's?" she asks with her brows knitted together.

"Uh... change of plan?" She looks even more confused when what should have been a statement passes my lips as a question.

"O-okay. Well, did you have a good night?"

"Uh... yeah... it was... memorable," I mutter, unable to come up with a better word.

"Are you okay?" she asks, looking even more concerned.

"Too much vodka," I admit, much to her horror. "I'm sorry. I know. I just got a bit carried away."

"And that's the end of my sympathy. You know how I feel about you drinking so young."

"I know, Mom. It was a one-off, I promise."

"Good. And I hope it hurts. It might stop you from doing it again."

"Did one hangover stop you?" I ask, regretting it the second she turns her judgmental eyes on me.

She opens her mouth to respond but must decide against it.

"Just please be sensible, Ruby. We don't want you to regret your actions," Stephen says, covering for Mom's inability to lie about what they were like as kids.

I nod at him, just barely refraining from pointing out that it's already too late.

"I'm gonna take this back up to my room," I say, lifting my coffee mug up to show them.

"Could you knock for Ash as you pass? We're heading out in ten."

My stomach clenches uncomfortably at the thought of having to face him once again, but knowing I've got little choice, I leave the room and head for the stairs.

Coming to a stop outside his door, I blow out a long breath.

Just knock, shout, and hide back in your room.

Nodding at myself, I lift my hand and rap my knuckles against the wood.

"Ash, your dad wants you ready in ten."

Silence greets me.

Resting my ear to the door, I strain to hear any movement inside, but when there's nothing, my heart starts to race.

Stephen is waiting for him, surely he's not left without him.

Putting my hand to the doorknob, I lift it off again, undecided as to what to do, but something's telling me to push the door open.

"Ash?" I try again, knocking harder in case he's in the bathroom and couldn't hear me.

Getting frustrated, I finally twist the knob and push the door open.

Sucking in a sharp breath, I stare at the pristine and empty room before me.

I take a step inside, but I don't need to. I already know.

He's gone.

Lifting my hands, I tug on my hair, spinning around to look for evidence that he was ever even here. The only thing I find is his Jason mask sitting on the dresser. It's an unwanted creepy reminder of the night before and for some strange reason, the sight of it has tears burning my eyes.

He really has gone.

Ruby and Ashton's story continues in FURY

FURY

ROSEWOOD HIGH #6

1

ASHTON

Mom cuts me a seething look as she pulls to a stop at an intersection.

"I'm sorry, okay." It's so cold in here with a broken heater that my breath comes out in white clouds as I talk.

One of her brows lift. Disappointment comes off her in waves and I hate it. She's the only one whose opinion I care about. The only one I try to do better for. Hell knows she deserves it after all the shit I've put her through.

I promised her things would be different after I got back from Rosewood after Halloween, and I truly believed it would, but then *she* happened.

Things changed the night of that party. I took things that weren't meant for me, and I've been living with the consequences—the memories—ever since.

I never should have touched her, let alone allow myself to go as far as I did. And I really, really shouldn't have craved more so badly that the only thing I could do was leave.

I knew the second her orgasm rocked through her that we couldn't be under the same roof, let alone in the bedroom next door to each other. Everything about her was too much of a temptation.

I'd told her I wanted to ruin her for ruining my life, but it turned out there was only one person whose life was turned upside down after visiting my stepsister.

My fingers wrap around the edge of Mom's passenger seat, my nails digging into the worn leather as she pulls away slowly, the road like a sheet of ice beneath the tires.

"You promised me, Ash. You promised me that things were going to change. Yet here I am picking you up from the station. Things are getting worse, not better, Son."

I blow out a long breath.

"I know, Mom. But really, they had no reason to arrest me."

"They said you were dealing." Her anger is palpable. I've done a lot of shit over the years, but this is my first real scrape with the law. And I certainly wasn't dealing.

"But I wasn't," I answer, exasperated from giving the same argument for the past fuck knows how long. "I hadn't even smoked any today."

"Today? Ash, you shouldn't smoke any day. You're supposed to be an athlete."

"Hardly," I scoff. "I played football at school, Mom. I'm hardly an athlete."

"Well, you could play at college if you actually applied yourself."

"I'm not going to college. We can't afford it," I argue like our financial situation is the only thing stopping me. My awful GPA and the fact I don't have enough credits to graduate might also have something to do with it.

"I don't care, Ash. I want you to have everything."

"And I want us to get out of our shitty apartment and live a decent life."

"Just stop, Ash. Stop trying to fix everything."

"What's wrong with me wanting us to have a better life? One where you don't have to sleep with a sweatshirt on and turn to a bottle or two every night. And don't even think about arguing, I know exactly how much you've been drinking."

"It's not like that."

"Is it not? You need to let him go, Mom. It's been years. He's moved on, married... happy."

"Enough," she screams, her face going beet red with anger. "That's enough. It's not... shit," she squeals as the car jolts to the right as she hits a patch of ice. Her arms tense to try to control it, but she can't. Two seconds later the tires leave the road and we're falling down the bank off the side of the road.

"Mom," I cry as the car tumbles.

"Ashton." The fear in her voice is something I'll never forget for as long as I live, assuming I get out of this.

I have no idea how long the car continues moving, time seems to grind to a halt before the world goes black.

"Son." His voice is like knives as it fills the silent room around me.

He is the last person I want to see or talk to right now. I knew he was coming, the nurse told me they'd called him the second I was admitted. I'm still a minor. I need a parent here with me.

I'm sitting on a hospital bed with my thighs tucked up against my chest and my head on my knees in my attempt to process what's happened in the past few hours.

I feel empty in a way I've never experienced before and utterly exhausted. But it's the least of how I should feel after what I went through.

My eyes are closed tight, but I still know the second he approaches me. When his hand lands on my shoulder, I flinch.

"Ashton, I'm so sorry."

"Don't," I bark, still refusing to look up at him.

I don't want him. I don't need him.

I want her.

"I've signed your discharge papers. You're free to go when you're ready."

I blow out a long breath.

So that's it then, is it? After everything, I'm now supposed to walk out of here like everything's fine. Like my life hasn't just come to an end.

"Ash?"

Without so much as glancing at him, I climb from the bed. My legs shake as I try to stand strong. There might be nothing seriously wrong with me, but my head pounds like a motherfucker and I'm so dizzy it's like the entire world is moving around me.

Reaching out, I steady myself with my hand on the foot of the bed. I regret appearing so weak the second he steps up in front of me.

"It's okay, Ash," he soothes, placing his hand on my upper arm to steady me.

"No," I snap, pulling away from him. "You don't get to do this now. You don't suddenly get to care because you're all I've got."

"Ashton, you know that's not true."

"Do I?" I hiss, looking up into his eyes for the first time since he walked into this room. His eyes are so similar to the pair I see every time I look in a mirror. They're just another reason why I hate him. He forced this life on us—on me.

It never should have been like this.

"Let's get out of here. We can get some food and pack you some things. I've booked a hotel and got us on a flight back in the morning."

"A hotel? A flight? I'm not leaving here."

"Son," he sighs. "You have to. You can't stay here alone."

"But... but this is my home." I hate that I sound so vulnerable, but I have no idea which way is up right now, let alone how I'm supposed to deal with any of this.

She's... she's gone. And it's all my fault.

That in itself is enough to swallow me whole, let alone the fact I'm now expected to walk out of here with him and start my life over.

"Lisa is getting your room ready."

I pause as I lift one foot to shove in my boot and look up at him.

Does he really think it's that easy? That I can just move into his new house, join his new family, and everything will be okay?

I just lost my fucking mother.

I shake my head, unable to say the things I want to say to him.

All of this is his fault. If he'd never betrayed us, if he'd never left us, if he'd never broken her heart, then none of this would have happened. We might still have been a happy family in a nice house in a decent part of town.

But no. The selfish prick had to turn his back on us and walk away for someone else, for another family.

Grabbing my jacket from the end of my bed, I throw it over my shoulder, wincing as every bit of my body aches after being thrown around like a ragdoll and march toward the door.

"Don't touch me," I seethe when his hand shoots out in an attempt to support me. "I don't need you."

He silently follows me out of the hospital, but I'm forced to stop when I get outside.

The cold hits me but I barely feel it.

My breath clouds around me and I'm reminded of sitting in the car with Mom not so long ago when everything was almost right in my world.

Now?

Now I'm walking out of a hospital and leaving her behind.

Emotion clogs my throat and tears burn my eyes.

She's gone and it's all because of me. All because I couldn't keep my promise to her and stay out of trouble.

I look back at the building, wondering where she is and if she's finally at peace.

"Ashton?" Dad asks, concern obvious in his tone. But it doesn't reassure me, make me feel like I'm less alone. All it does is infuriate me. He's not here because he wants to be, he's here because he has to be. Because it's his fatherly duty.

"You can leave now that you've signed me out."

A bitter laugh bubbles up his throat.

"I don't think so. I've already told you, you're coming home with me."

"And you seem to be forgetting that this is my home. I belong in Seattle; I live in Seattle."

We stand staring at each other, the frigid air almost crackling with tension between us.

It never used to be like this between us. He used to be my best friend. But that was then. This is now and he doesn't get to drag me around like I'm a fucking kid and dictate my life for me.

2

RUBY

"You really should just go home and get it over with," Harley says, following me to the bathroom in Aces on Monday afternoon.

I know Harley's right, but just the thought of going home and seeing him makes me want to puke.

Stephen and Ashton flew in this afternoon, by now he should be making himself at home in the room next to mine once more. Only this time, it's not for a short stay.

He's moving in.

My mouth waters and my stomach twists. Turning away from Harley, I race into a stall and drop to my knees, dry heaving in the toilet. I haven't eaten a damn thing, so I guess I shouldn't really be surprised when nothing comes up. The only substantial thing that's passed my lips since that phone call has been alcohol. I can't stomach anything else.

"Rubes," Harley sighs, dropping down beside me and rubbing my back. "You need to go home and get this over with."

Dropping to my ass, I bring my knees up to my chest and rest my forehead on them.

"I can't, Har. I can't see him again." My heart shatters in my chest and my hands begin to shake.

"I know, but... you're kinda going to have to."

"I hate him. I hate him so fucking much."

"So tell him."

"He's just lost his mom." Pain for what he's just been through lances through me, but it doesn't stop me hating him.

"Don't make excuses for him. He was a class-A prick. If you want to lay into him when you see him, go for it, he deserves it."

I glance up at her in time to see her wince at her own words. "You know I can't do that."

"I know," she whispers, dropping down beside me and holding my hand. "I just... we need you in top form, Rubes. Nationals are only a few weeks away. We can't do it without our best flyer." She winks at me.

I nod. The nationals have been my dream for... forever. To get to attend this year as varsity. It means everything to me. But I fear he's about to fuck everything up without even knowing it.

The door to the bathroom opens and Chelsea, our pregnant captain, walks in. She does a double take when she spots us on the floor in one of the stalls.

"Is everything okay?" she asks, looking between the two of us.

Harley looks at me, her brows pulling together. I'm not sure if she's begging me to sort my shit out or to be honest with Chelsea. I go with the former because the thought of having to explain to someone else about Ashton fills me with dread.

"Yeah, we're good. I just got a bit queasy. I'm fine now."

Releasing Harley's hand, I push to my feet but as I walk toward Chelsea, she doesn't move.

Her eyes drop down the length of my body. "Are you eating right? I know I'm putting you through a lot right now, you need to be looking after yourself."

"Y-yeah, I am," I lie.

"Regionals were tough, but it's only going to get harder for nationals." She glances from me to Harley and back again. "I need all of the squad focused and prepared." Her words are all business, but I see a softness in her eyes that never used to be there.

"I've got this, Chelsea. You don't need to worry about me."

She stares at me for a beat, as if she doesn't quite believe what I'm saying. But after a second, she nods.

"Okay, that's good. But if you need me, either of you." She looks between us once more. "You know where I am, yeah?"

"Yeah. Thanks, Chels."

"Anytime. Now, I really need to pee." She races toward the stall and I can't help but laugh at her.

Our stone-cold queen bee really has softened somewhat recently.

"Want some more advice?" she calls out.

"Sure." I start washing my hands, waiting for her words of wisdom.

"Unless you want to pee every thirty seconds, keep the team away from your vag."

We both snort a laugh. "Sure thing, Chels."

My heart is in my throat as I pull my car to a stop in the driveway beside Stephen's and stare up at the house. My head spins and my hands tremble.

He's just one person. One asshole of a person. I shouldn't be this terrified to see him again.

Movement in the kitchen window catches my eye and my stomach twists once more.

I really just need to get this over with.

He's probably forgotten all about what happened at Halloween and moved on. He's certainly got bigger things to worry about right now. There's no way he's obsessing about seeing me like I am him. That asshole doesn't give a shit about anything, especially not me. He made that abundantly clear the very first time we met.

After blowing out a long breath, I grab my purse and duffle then climb from the car.

The house is silent as I walk down the hallway. I don't drop my bags like I usually would, I want to be ready to make a quick escape should I need to.

"In the kitchen, sweetie," Mom calls.

I can do this. I can do this, I repeat over and over in my head as I make my way down to them.

My temperature soars, my skin feeling like it doesn't belong on my body, and as I round the corner, I swear I stop breathing.

That is until I find a room with just Mom and Stephen in it, both of their faces pulled tight with worry.

The air I was holding comes rushing out of me as I look between the two of them.

"What's going on? Where's A-Ash?" I stutter, not really wanting to say his name out loud.

Stephen's shoulders sag before he looks to the floor. Mom races over to him and wraps her arm around his shoulder.

"B-but you said he was okay. Just cuts and bruises," I whisper, misreading Stephen's reaction.

"Oh, he is, sweetie. He's fine. He just—"

"He refused to get on the airplane," Stephen says, standing and marching to the other side of the kitchen.

Mom and I watch as he reaches into the top cupboard and pulls down a bottle of whiskey, twists the top, and takes a large drink.

My hand clenches with my need to do exactly the same thing.

"So... he's not moving here?" I ask, hating the hope that fills my voice. I know it's a pointless question. Ash isn't eighteen yet and I'm not sure he has any other options aside from Stephen—juvie, maybe.

"Y-yeah, he is. He's just... making his own way."

"W-what does that m-mean exactly?" My voice betrays me, cracking the whole way through the question.

"Said he needed some time." Stephen rests his palms on the counter and hangs his head.

"He'll be here in a few days, I'm sure," Mom says soothingly, although I'm not sure it has any effect on Stephen.

I'm right because not two seconds later does he march from the kitchen, the bottle in hand, without saying a word.

"He's hurting too. He still cared about Leanora," Mom muses.

I fall down into the chair beside her. "So, what now? We just wait for him to appear?"

"I guess so. Not sure there's much else we can do."

"What about the funeral?"

"It's next Friday. Stephen and Ash have already got things ready for it."

I nod, trying to keep my expression neutral. I shouldn't be so relieved that no sooner has he arrived then he'll be heading back for the funeral. The guy's just lost his mom, I really should be more concerned about him than I am myself.

"I'm going to fucking ruin you, little one." His words rip through me like a tsunami and I shudder from head to toe.

No, maybe I'm right to be worried about myself. I'd never wish for anyone to lose a parent. I can't even imagine how awful it must be. But at the same time, I do believe in karma. It's all I've got to latch on to right now.

"So..." Harley says on a video call later that evening. "How was it?"

"He's not here," I admit, flipping over onto my stomach and propping my cell up on my pillow.

"Oh. He's not coming now?"

"He is. He's just... taking his time." I want to say he's torturing me, but I'm sure he's not so much as thought of me once since walking out our door that night.

"Oh, well... that could be a good thing, I guess. Give him time to get his head straight."

"Yeah, maybe."

A knock sounds out on Harley's door before she calls, "Come in."

"Hey, is that Rubes?" another familiar voice says before the camera bounces as Poppy jumps on Harley's bed.

"Oh look, Zayn let you up for air?" I ask, much to Harley's disgust.

"I thought we agreed not to talk about such things," she mutters. "You two need to talk dirty details about my brother, then you do it well away from me."

"Calm your tits, I didn't come in here to tell you how he just stuck his—"

"La la la la," Harley sings with her fingers in her ears, much to Poppy's amusement.

"How's it going?" Poppy says after a beat, her face turning serious as she looks at me through the camera.

"Ugh." I recall what I just told Harley.

"It'll be fine. You'll see. He was just playing games before. He's got bigger issues to worry about now. He won't even bother you." I raise a brow at her, unable to even consider believing her words. If what went down between us was so easy to forget, then why haven't I?

Why is it that any time I've kissed a guy since then, I've thought of him? I've compared them to him. And so far, no one has come close to making me feel what he did.

"So, is he going to be starting at Rosewood?" Poppy asks.

"Please, can we talk about something else?" I groan, already fed up with how much of my headspace my illusive stepbrother is taking up.

"Sure. So, Zayn and I were talking—"

"Really?" Harley barks. I can't help but laugh at her. She might be happy for her brother and Poppy, but it's amusing as hell watching her try to come to terms with the fact one of her best friends is warming his bed at night.

I'm on edge for the next two days. Every time a door closes at home, or a car drives past, I'm on full alert expecting him to come crashing through my bedroom door and take all of this out on me. But he never does.

As I fall asleep Wednesday night, I begin to wonder if he's even going to show at all and his promise of turning up was just a way to get Stephen off his back.

For the first time all week, I don't toss and turn for hours before finally drifting off, although that could just be out of pure exhaustion. Chelsea is working us harder and harder in the lead up to nationals. We're practicing twice a day during the week and all Saturday mornings. It's hardcore, but I love it. Cheer is what I've always lived for and I'm on the cusp of great things, I can feel it.

Something stirs me awake a few hours later, dragging my eyes open, I find my room in darkness and the house in silence. But despite the lack of evidence, a shiver continues to race down my spine.

He's here.

Flicking the lamp on beside me, I almost expect to find him sitting in the chair on the other side of my room watching me sleep like a creep, but my room is empty, thankfully.

Throwing back the covers, I silently pull my door open and slip out into the hallway.

The door to the room next door is open as it was when I passed earlier and the light is off, but as I step farther into the hallway something outside catches my eye.

I walk up to the window and look down at the driveway.

A gasp falls from my lips the second my eyes lock with a dark pair I feared I might find.

3

ASHTON

My heart pounds in my chest as I stare up at the pair of eyes that have been haunting me since Halloween.

I swallow nervously and school my features. The last I need is for her to be able to read how I'm feeling before I've even stepped foot inside that fucking house.

So many times on the ride here, I almost turned around and headed in the opposite direction. I don't need the people under this roof. I could find a job, carve myself a life somewhere no one knows me.

But every time I went to do it, I couldn't.

Something always drew me here.

Her?

I like to think not, but as we stand staring at each other, something crackling between us, I can't help but wonder if she could well be the reason.

Her eyes narrow in my direction and my veins fill with fire at the hate she shoots my way.

Good. The feeling is entirely mutual, little one.

Their security light shines down on me, stopping what I hoped would be an incognito arrival.

I climb off my bike, my spur of the moment purchase with the money I'd been saving and pull the limited amount of stuff I could fit inside the top box before stepping toward the house.

My eyes shoot back up to the window as she backs away.

I wink at her and blow a kiss before she darts into the darkness and away from me.

Good idea, little one.

Run. Run as fast as you can.

The familiar scent of the house hits me the second I walk through the front door. I quietly close it behind me, not wanting to alert my dad or worse, Lisa, to my arrival. I could barely put up with her over-the-top happiness the last time I was here, it's really the last thing I need now.

I dump my bag in the hallway and walk through to the kitchen, flicking the light on as I go.

Staring inside the refrigerator, I find a six-pack of beer. Not exactly what I had in mind. Spinning, I turn toward the cupboard where I found what I required the last time I was here.

"Bingo," I breathe, pulling down a new bottle of vodka and twisting the top.

The first shot burns, but it's exactly what I need.

I fill my arms with whatever food I can find before turning to the stairs, collecting my bag and making my way up. I can only assume I'm expected to go to the same room, so I head that way.

There's no sign of Ruby as I make my way to our side of the house, but that doesn't mean I can't smell her presence. Her perfume lingers in the hall, making my mouth water and my cock swell.

I pause at my bedroom door and stare at hers for a beat.

I know she's awake and I suspect she's waiting for me.

Unlucky for her, I don't have any intentions of making it that easy for her.

Some things might have changed, but how I feel about her isn't one of them.

I still hate her, possibly even more now. If she didn't fuck with my head last year, then I might not have been such a mess that Mom had to come and pick me up from the station last week and... I force my thoughts to trail off. I'm not ready to think about it yet, let alone begin to accept it.

I'd hoped the long drive here would have helped. That by some miracle it might have been able to draw a line under my life in Seattle, ready to start a new chapter here. That somehow, I might have been able to outrun the pain, the guilt that I've been carrying around since Friday night. But being here now, I realize that nothing has changed.

She's still gone, and I'm still the one to blame for it.

She deserved better than that hand she was dealt. Better than me. But it's too late to do fuck-all about it now.

Closing the door behind me, I drop everything in my arms to the bed and kick off my boots, quickly followed by my jacket and shirt. I didn't ride non-stop here, but I didn't stop anywhere decent enough to really freshen up either.

I drop my trousers and boxers and with my bottle of vodka in hand, I walk straight into the bathroom.

Everything in here is set up for me. My usual shower gel sits on the shelf in the shower and a new razor and shaving foam is waiting for me by the sink.

I look over my shoulder as a shiver works its way down my spine.

How did they know what I use?

Tipping the bottle to my lips, I down a few shots before turning the shower on as hot as it'll go and stepping under the burning spray, allowing it to pound down on my tense shoulders.

The heat feels good but even as it burns my skin, it doesn't take away the pain, the emptiness.

I blow out a breath and tip my face up to the stream of water, allowing it to rain down over my skin and mingle with the tears I refuse to acknowledge that are streaming down my cheeks as I allow myself to go back to Friday night in that car.

I stand there until I can't feel my skin and my need for the bottle I abandoned on the basin gets too much.

Wrapping one of the fresh fluffy towels around my waist, I grab my bottle and take it back through to my bedroom.

I shove my bag off the end of the bed. It falls to the floor with a thud and I immediately regret it. I really don't want to wake anyone and be forced to have a conversation. I just want to vanish, to lose myself in the bottle and forget my reality, whatever that might be now.

I have no idea what time I finally fall into a vodka-induced coma but when I come to again, my headphones are still happily playing away, although they've fallen out of my ears and been shoved somewhere in the bed, but other than that, the house is in silence.

My head pounds and the room spins, but it's a feeling I'm beginning to get used to, welcome it even. It's how I felt after waking up inside that car. It's how I seem to have woken up most mornings since. In some weird fucked-up way, it makes me feel closer to her. If I'm still feeling the pain from that day, then maybe she's still with me. Maybe watching the life drain from her eyes was just a really fucked-up dream.

I know it's only wishful thinking but it's all I've got right now.

I throw the covers off and swing my legs over the side of the bed, the movement does nothing for my head but my need for the bathroom overrides my need to lie back down and shut it all out.

I stumble on the discarded towel I dropped over the edge of the bed at some point last night and carefully make my way naked to the bathroom.

Just like last night, the sight of all the toiletries that have been bought for me taunt me.

How did they know?

It almost looks like it could be home. Although, it far from feels like it. Home is in Seattle. Home is in our shithole apartment. Home is with her.

A lump climbs up my throat as the images I've been battling to drown with alcohol appear in my mind once more.

They're like a poison festering away inside me, eating at the small amount of light I had and ensuring that I begin to drown in the darkness.

I take a piss, brush my teeth and turn the shower back on, hoping it might rid me of the alcohol sweats and give me some courage to step outside this room.

I need coffee, but I don't need it bad enough to have to put myself through talking to anyone.

Still feeling like hell, I pull a clean pair of sweats from my bag and drag them up my legs before going for the door.

I wrap my fingers around the handle, but I don't push it down for a few seconds.

Going out there and making myself at home means this is really happening.

I don't want to. It's the reason I point-blank refused to get on that airplane with Dad when he was in Seattle.

I'd already refused his offer of a hotel. I had a home in Seattle and despite the fact the heart had been ripped out of it, it was where I wanted to be.

For as long as I could, I wanted to shut the solid door behind me and pretend that everything was normal.

Thankfully, he let me go, ensuring his Uber dropped me outside our building and he didn't even fight me on the fact he wasn't coming up. I didn't want him tainting my memories of the place with his face.

I'd hoped being at home would bring me comfort, but all it did was remind me of everything I'd lost. If I'd found solace there, then maybe I'd had argued about staying until the funeral at least. But I knew only minutes after stepping foot inside that I couldn't be there.

I spent the night there because I was exhausted. A sleepless night on a hospital bed after being told what I already knew, that she'd died, wasn't exactly what I needed after everything. But a bottle of Mom's finest whiskey, the weed I had stashed where I knew she'd never find it, and my own bed. That brought me some of what I needed, at least.

When I finally emerged the next morning, I packed a bag, pulled out the money I'd been saving from the shitty jobs I've done over the past couple of years, and I walked away, ensuring I locked the door on the way out.

I didn't have a lot of money. I'd wanted to save at least double what I had before making the purchase I'd been dreaming of since I was a kid, but it was all I had.

I walked straight to the nearest lot and bought what I could afford. After telling my dad where to go and to shove his plane ticket up his ass, I climbed on my new bike and set off.

I knew I was going to have to come here eventually. As much as I might hate it, I knew realistically that I couldn't end up anywhere else. He wouldn't allow it, and I'd eventually be dragged back kicking and screaming.

Sucking in a deep breath, I push the handle and step into the hallway. Fresh air hits my nose instantly reminding me that my room already smells like a drug den after only a few hours of being here.

I walk straight to the window and stare out at the empty driveway—well, empty aside from my bike—and breathe a sigh of relief. The house really is empty, and they really have left me to it.

Turning for the kitchen, I find my steps faltering outside her room.

I've thought of her more than I want to admit even to myself since I walked away that night.

I was meant to stay here a week, but I barely made it a few days.

I remember all too well the look on Mom's face when I walked back into our apartment, having got myself back to Seattle. She knew I was coming, Dad had warned her, but I'd never seen her so furious.

But still, her demands to know why I had run, what had happened had fallen on deaf ears because there was no way I was telling anyone about Ruby.

I could barely think about her without losing my mind, let alone allow anything about her past my lips.

My hand reaches out for her door handle without instruction from my brain and in seconds I'm standing in her open doorway.

Her room is exactly the same as it was before. Girly shit litters the countertops. There are a million photographs of her and her parents, my dad, along with her friends and her cheer squad.

Without any consideration, I step inside, my eyes running over each image before I stare into her eyes.

This is all your fault.

The reason I am standing here right now is because of you.

My eyes narrow as I move from image to image, the anger within me beginning to ignite once again.

If she didn't call to me the way she did. If she were anyone fucking else, then Halloween wouldn't have happened. I wouldn't have spent the past three months with her inside my head, and none of this shit would have happened.

My fist clenches with my need to hurt someone, to destroy something, but I can't unless I want her to know that the first thing I did this morning was rain hell down on her bedroom.

I spin around, looking at the rest of the room before walking over to her desk and lowering myself to the pink chair. Her calendar is sitting open and I can't help but stare down at her plans.

Every single day has *cheer practice* scrolled across it but there's one other entry that makes me pay attention.

Saturday night... *Party at Ethan's.*

Looks like I'll be partying this weekend. A small smile curls at my lips as I think about attending my second Rosewood party. The first one looked half decent, Halloween bullshit aside. I can only hope things get better from here on out.

I turn to leave, ensuring nothing is out of place. I might have ideas for my not-so-sweet little stepsister, but I've got time. Right now, I need coffee and food. But as I get to the door, my anger gets the better of me when my eyes land on a framed photo of her, Lisa, and my dad smiling and looking happy together. Looking at the glistening blue lake in the background, I'd guess that they're on vacation. A vacation I've never been invited to go on while in Seattle struggling to scramble together enough money to ensure both of us could eat. Lifting it from the shelf, I slam it down hard enough to smash the glass and leave it downturned.

Maybe it is time to show Ruby just how I feel about her.

4

RUBY

I spend almost all night staring at the ceiling waiting for him to show his face. But after he closed his bedroom door only minutes after entering the house, he never emerged again. I didn't even have to endure a night of his music.

I couldn't decide if his avoidance of me was a good thing or not. Of course, I was glad that I didn't have to look into his cold, evil eyes, but at the same time, I've still got our first meeting hanging over me.

Part of me wishes that he just stormed in here and had it out with me the second he arrived. Assuming he has anything to have out with me of course. While I've been here obsessing about our time together and unable to forget about him, he's probably not thought of me twice. I was probably just another notch on his bedpost because I'd be stupid to think that I wasn't just one easy girl in a line of many. He knew what he was doing that night. The way he touched me. There was no hesitation, no nerves. He knew my body almost better than I do myself. That isn't the actions of a virgin, that's for sure. He's probably even a bigger manwhore than the guys on the team I've attempted to use since to get him the fuck out of my head.

Either that or I wanted him to blast that god-awful music so loud that I had no choice but to go in there and pull the fucking plug just to get some peace.

But as it was, the voices in my head were louder than anything he did, and I fucking hated him even more for it.

All night I wondered what he was doing, and more irritatingly if he was okay. I hated that I cared, but the guy had just lost his mom. I might want to rid him from my memory, but I'm not actually a horrible person and I can't even begin to imagine what he's going through right now.

By the time I did fall asleep, it was so late that when my alarm starts blaring, I can hardly pry my eyes open.

It's still dark out when I finally do manage to rip them apart, just like it has been every other morning I've had to get up this early for practice.

Those people who think cheer is a joke of a sport, they damn well need to try this because right now, it's anything but fun.

Everything aches as I push myself up to sit on the side of the bed. I'm fit, I work out and practice daily, but right now, Chelsea is pushing my limits, although I'm sure my lack of sleep probably doesn't help in any way.

With my head still fuzzy from sleep, I throw myself into a cold shower to wake up.

My hair is still wet when I pull it into a braid down the back of my head and secure it with a Rosewood red band at the bottom. I drag on a pair of black leggings and a matching sports bra, followed by an oversized hoodie.

Everything else I might need for the day is shoved into my duffle.

I don't bother turning the hallway light on as I step out of my room, despite my need to disturb him like he did so many times to me before, swelling inside.

Be the bigger person, Ruby, I tell myself as I silently walk past. There's no light coming from the edges of his door, so I can only assume that he's in there and sleeping.

My fingers twitch to reach out and see if I'm right, but I don't. Instead, I make my way out of the house in the hope I haven't woken anyone and drop down into my car.

I might have escaped his first morning but there's no way I'm going to be able to avoid him forever.

The second I walk inside the locker room, Harley's face drops at the sight of me.

"Rubes?" she asks, concern pulling her brows together.

"He's here."

"Fuck. What happened?" she asks, taking a seat on the bench beside me after I lower myself down.

"N-nothing."

"So why do you look like you've been awake all night?"

"Because I have."

"But—"

"He turned up on a motorcycle in the middle of the night. The engine must have woke me and I went to the window..."

"And then what?" she prompts when I trail off, once again lost in its dark stare despite the fact he's not actually here.

"Then nothing. I went back to my room and he came up to his."

Her lips part to say something, but no words come out for a few seconds. "So, you haven't actually seen him?"

"No, not really."

"Not gonna lie, Rubes. That was a bit of an anti-climax."

"Fuck off," I say, slapping her shoulder lightly.

"What? I was hoping he'd come barging into your room and hate fuck the shit out of you."

"Jesus, Har. Been thinking about it much?"

She shrugs and doesn't even have the decency to look a tiny bit guilty.

"What? He's hot, do not deny that. I already know that you let him up in there." She wiggles her brows. "And you'd totally do it again."

"I would not," I grumble, standing to change my shoes.

"You so would. That's why you haven't been with anyone else."

"W-what?" I ask, my movements pausing at her statement.

"Oh, come off it, Rubes. You've had a million offers to rid you of your V-card since he left, hell knows you've flaunted it about enough."

"Again, what?" I ask, my irritation levels growing faster than usual with my lack of sleep.

"You don't need me to tell you how you've been since he left. You're not that stupid."

All the air rushes out of me as I fall down onto the bench once again, but I don't look at Harley, I can't. I know exactly what she's talking about and I'm not exactly proud of the person I've become in the last few months. But partying, drinking, guys, they all helped me numb the pain, dampen down the memories of him.

"I don't just want to lose it with a player who's been with half the girls in this school, Har. I thought you, of all people, understood that."

"I do, Rubes. I also don't think that waiting for him is a good idea."

I jump up from the bench and turn on her. "I'm not waiting for him," I snap, suddenly totally over this conversation. "I don't want him, Har. I don't want him in my house, I don't want him anywhere near me."

"I know, but—"

"No. There is not a but here. He is nothing to me." She raises a brow and stares at me. I can practically hear her thoughts though and it's as amusing as hearing the words out loud. "Stop it. Just stop it."

"Just trying to help."

"Are you though?" I mutter, shoving my hoodie into my bag and walking toward the gym where Chelsea is waiting. "How does she look so good? Shouldn't she be exhausted or whatever, growing a person?"

"No idea, but it looks good on her."

Her eyes scan over us before they lock onto mine. My heart drops knowing that she can see my exhaustion.

"Ruby, over here."

I groan as Harley walks toward the mats to start warming up.

"You still going to tell me everything is fine?" Chelsea asks, her eyes bouncing between mine.

I blow out a breath. "Everything is fine. My stepdad's ex died in a car crash on the weekend, his son has moved in," I admit, feeling like I owe her some kind of truth. She seems genuinely concerned about me, after all.

"Okay," she muses for a second and I can't help smiling that she didn't go with the standard 'I'm sorry for your loss' like everyone else seems to if I mention it. Sure, I'm gutted for Ashton, and Stephen to a point, it's clear he still cares about his ex, but I never met her. "Is he going to be an issue?" she asks, correctly guessing what—or who—kept me up last night.

Chelsea wasn't here during Halloween, she was off on her 'time out' as she puts it. But I already know she's recognized the change in me. This isn't the first time she's pulled me aside and questioned where my head is at.

I deserve the questions and judgment. I have been a mess and doing everything I can to put him behind me, but sadly it's easier said than done. Especially now.

"I hope not."

She smiles at me sadly like she already knows how much he fucks up my head. Maybe she does. We all know that she's had her fair share of drama when it comes to guys.

"Don't let him take this away from you, Ruby. You've worked too damn hard for a guy to fuck it all up."

"I know," I mutter.

"Nationals are two weeks away. Just two weeks. If you think you can't do this, then you need to tell me now."

"I've got this, Chels," I promise her.

"Okay. Good. You've got a bright cheer future ahead of you, don't let anyone take that from you."

"I won't." I hold her eyes steady. She knows what I want. The words haven't passed my lips. Only Harley and Poppy know my dream, but she senses it. I think deep down, we're the same and she sees that as much as I do.

"Good. We're gonna fucking smash nationals and I'm going to be able to hand over a winning squad at the end of the season." She nods at me and rubs her hand over her growing belly.

"We've got this."

"Good, now get out there and warm up. We're not leaving this gym for class until we've nailed this routine, ladies," she shouts louder so the entire squad hears her.

"Everything okay?" Harley asks when I stop beside her and start stretching.

"Yep, all good."

"Rubes?" Chelsea calls, coming to a stop in front of me.

"Yeah."

"You need help with that situation. You know the team is behind you should you need... any persuasion."

My stomach twists at her unspoken words. Do I want to set Jake, Ethan, and Zayn on Ashton for hurting me? Hell yeah, I do. But I won't. I fight my own battles. I refuse to cower behind anyone. Plus, I already have a feeling that the second Stephen insists on him starting here, that he's going to make his own enemies before too long. He doesn't need me to make that job any easier for him.

Practice is brutal, school is long and followed by putting my aching ass through another two hours of torture via Chelsea's orders.

By the time I stagger back into the locker room after Chelsea calls time, I'm about ready to sleep for a week. But the reality is that in just twelve hours I'll be getting up to do it all over again. I just hope I get some sleep tonight.

"So, what's the plan?" Harley asks, sounding a little too awake for my liking as she tugs off her leggings ready to head for the shower.

"The plan? I'm supposed to have a plan" I practically crawl onto the bench, more than willing to have a little nap here.

"Yeah. You need a plan."

"Well, I could move in with you and never go home ever again."

"That's it, take the pussy way out."

"Har, I'm so tired right now, I literally don't care."

"Nah, uh-uh. Not happening." I watch as she shoves her hand into her purse and pulls her cell out. "Hey, you busy? Okay, good. Meet us at Ruby's in thirty, yeah?"

I stare at Harley, hoping like hell she's talking to Poppy and not dragging anyone else into the mess that is my life.

"Har, you for real right now?" I complain the second she hangs up.

"Yep. I'm not letting you drag your sorry ass home with no fight in you. You want to go head-to-head with this asshole, then you need some backup. I'm going to shower, then we're going to yours. To chill or something."

Lying back on the bench, I watch as she grabs what she needs and heads toward the showers with most of the rest of the squad.

"Is it always this hardcore?" Stella asks once it quiets down a bit.

I crack an eye open and look at her. She's not been here all that long, but the second she auditioned to be a part of the squad, Chelsea snapped her up.

"Nah, it's just nationals. Chelsea really wants to prove herself. I get it, I'd be the same in her position."

"I guess. I've been in more squads than I care to count in the past few years, but none of them have been quite like this."

"That's because none of them are the best," Chelsea happily adds as she joins us.

"Not showering today, Ruby?" she asks with amusement.

"Nah, thought I'd just stink. You know, keep him away and all that."

"Riiight. Good luck with that. From experience, it probably won't work, but whatever. See you in the morning." She waves at the two of us before walking toward the exit.

"Chels," I call before she disappears.

"Yeah." She looks over her shoulder. Her makeup is flawless, her dark hair smooth and sleek. She really is stunning and talented to boot. A little jealousy stirs in my belly. She's also got the nicest boyfriend. I want to hate her, I just can't.

"Thank you."

"Anytime. You know where I am. Adios."

"She's... really something."

"I know, right."

"There aren't many high school girls who could train you guys as she has. I swear I've only seen Miss Kelly about three times since I started here."

"It's a good thing we've got Chelsea, or we wouldn't stand a chance."

"What's going to happen when she graduates?"

I shrug because, despite my dreams, I honestly have no idea.

It's almost an hour later when I pull up in my driveway, quickly followed by Harley. Poppy is here as promised, sitting on the front step.

"Why didn't you use the spare key?" I ask, noticing she's got her coat pulled around her in an attempt to keep her warm.

She nods toward the new addition to our driveway. "That his?"

"Uh... yeah. Fair enough. I don't want to go inside either."

"That's why we're here, we've got your back, Rubes."

"You just want to ogle him in real life," I mutter to Harley as I pull my key from my bag to let us in.

As we step inside, music booms from somewhere in the house.

"I guess he's awake now then."

Rolling my eyes at Harley's obvious statement, I swing the door closed and move toward the stairs.

I need to shower before anything else happens.

My eyes linger down the hall, but the second I start climbing, my legs start to speed up with my need to get to the safety of my bedroom.

"Order us pizza while I shower."

"Rubes, we shouldn't be—"

"Really?" I bark. I'm so tired I really don't need a lecture about what I'm eating. I just need food... carbs.

"Okay, okay, I'm ordering now." She rolls her eyes at me and pulls her cell from her pocket.

"Thank you."

The shower isn't half as relaxing as I was hoping with the knowledge that he's here somewhere. The house isn't overly big, so it's not like I'm going to be able to successfully hide from him forever.

I know I need to just pull up my big girl panties and go and get it over with, but I really, really don't want to.

"Better?" Poppy asks when I emerge from my bathroom in a pair of sweats and a crop top, my wet hair hanging around my shoulders.

"I just want to dive headfirst into that." I nod at my bed that they're both sitting on.

"Not until you've got this done. Are you really going to wear that?" Harley asks, dropping her eyes down my body.

"Um... yeah. I don't give a shit what he thinks. I don't want him, remember."

"Oh yeah, sorry." She winces but she can't wipe the smile off her face.

"You're a pain in my ass, Harley Hunter."

"What? He's hot. Hey," she complains when Poppy hits her with a pillow.

"I would say if you want him, have at it, but he's a prick and I wouldn't wish him on my worst enemy, let alone one of my best friends so..."

"I can look though, right?"

I shake my head at her. "Eat your heart out."

They both chat away as I blow-dry my hair and apply just a little makeup. I might not want to look good for him but equally, I don't really want the dark shadows under my eyes on full display either.

The doorbell rings right as I finish.

"Perfect timing, I'm starving."

I grab a zip-up hoodie to throw over my shoulders and run from the room, the prospect of hot cheesy pizza gets me moving.

I practically snatch the boxes out of the poor guy's hands before slamming the door in his face and turning to the kitchen, Harley and Poppy hot on my tail.

My stomach rumbles as I round the corner into the kitchen, but the second I look up, I come to a grinding halt, both Harley and Poppy crash into my back.

"What the... oh my God," Harley breathes as she gets a look at the scene before us.

Ashton is standing shirtless and covered in a sheen of sweat in front of the refrigerator, drinking orange juice straight from the carton.

I never saw him shirtless when he was here before, I was the only one who bared everything, but I'm starting to realize that I might just have missed out because Harley has a point, he is fine.

Despite the fact he must know he has company, he doesn't stop. Much to Harley's delight.

"Suddenly, I don't care so much if he's an asshole."

He must hear her words because he lowers the carton and places it back inside before swinging the door shut and turning his eyes on me.

My breath catches as our gazes lock. His eyes are as cold and angry as I remember, and they send the same shiver of fear down my spine as they did before.

A smirk curls at one side of his lips before his eyes drop from mine in favor of my body. My blood heats the second he begins checking me out. I hate that I react to him. My fists curl and my teeth grind.

By the time he gets back up to my eyes, his smirk is spread wide across his face and it only infuriates me further.

"Have you about finished?" I ask, suddenly finding my voice and wrapping the front of my hoodie around myself to cover up with the hand not full of pizza.

"Oh, little one, I've barely started."

Tingles erupt within me at his use of his little nickname for me. But as much as I hate it, I remember all too well how it sounded falling from his lips right before he... no. Nope. Do not go there.

After a second, he rips his eyes from mine and instead focuses on Harley over my shoulder.

His smile gets wider as he gives her the same treatment he gave me, only Harley isn't currently hiding behind oversized clothes, her curves are on full display.

"Hey, baby," he purrs, taking a step forward. "I don't think we've met before."

"I... uh... no," Harley stutters.

I roll my eyes, turning toward her. She stares up at him like he's an ice cream freaking sundae she wants to devour, and I just about manage not to groan.

"So, are you going to Ethan's party on Saturday night?" he asks Harley, his voice all deep and sexy. Damn him.

Wait... how does he know about Ethan's party.

"How do you—"

"I will be. You?"

"I am now."

"Oh my God. Harley, will you get a grip, please?" I beg, reaching out, wrapping my hand around her upper arm and pulling her toward me.

"What? I just—"

I cut her words off with a look.

"I'm starved, do you mind?" Ashton asks, plucking one of the boxes from my hand and flipping it open before I find my voice.

"Yeah, actually, I do."

"That's a shame because I don't really give a fuck." He pulls a slice from the box and takes a massive bite before winking at Harley and disappearing around the corner.

"Well... safe to say that Instagram does him absolutely no justice," Harley mutters, walking to the refrigerator and pulling it open. I half expect her to pull out the same bottle he was just drinking from. I'm about ready to kick her out when she pulls out three cans of soda and slides them over to us.

"Thanks," I mutter, collecting the pizza box back up and walking toward the stairs. Part of me doesn't want to follow him, but the other part screams that this is my house and that it's my bedroom and he shouldn't have the power to make me second guess my actions or where I want to hang out.

The second Harley and Poppy follow me inside, I kick the door shut. Hard.

I climb onto the bed and immediately open one of the boxes, diving straight into my first slice.

"I'm sorry, okay," Harley mutters. "He just took me by surprise."

"Yeah, whatever. Can we not talk about him?" I know Harley would never do anything to intentionally hurt me, and I know he's mouth-wateringly hot, so I guess I can't really blame her for losing her damn mind.

"So, Ethan's party," Poppy starts, but her face falls when she immediately realizes her mistake.

5

ASHTON

I'm still smiling to myself hours later, long after Ruby's friends have left, and the pounding bass of my music is the only thing I can hear.

The look on her face as I leaned into her friend was priceless. I couldn't have planned a better first time to meet again if I tried.

She's going to make this easier for me than I'd originally thought. After she disappeared last night, part of me wondered if she was over it. But it seems that is certainly not the case.

I blow out a stream of smoke and press my head farther into the pillow.

I might fucking hate this house, but I can't deny that Dad's home gym almost makes up for it. I spent all afternoon in there trying to outrun my demons. Pretty sure it did fuck-all for those, but my muscles are now aching nicely and reminding me that despite all the bullshit, I am alive.

My bedroom door swinging open makes me look up and when I find her standing there with her brows raised and her hands on her hips, I can't help but prop myself up on my elbows to get a better look.

A smile tugs at the corner of my lips as I watch her silently fume. Although, if she were to say something then I'd be unlikely to hear it because of the music that's rattling the walls right now.

My lips part as I watch her storm into the room and slam her hand down on the top of my speaker, silencing it in an instant.

"Problem?" I ask, my voice low.

She turns to me, her eyes narrowed in anger and her shoulders pulled tight with tension.

"You need to stay out of my bedroom and away from my friends," she warns.

"And what if I can't?" I ask, bringing my joint to my lips and taking a hit.

"What is your..." She shakes her head as if she can't compute my words. She stares at me for a few seconds before her eyes betray her and drop down my bare chest all the way to my low-hanging sweatpants, but I don't miss her lingering on the bruises that cover my ribs, the only evidence left from that night in Mom's car.

By the time she makes it back up, I've got a shit-eating grin on my face and my blood is starting to boil from her attention.

"Listen..." she starts. "I'm *really* sorry about your mom and everything you've been through. But you don't get to walk back in here like you own the place and do what you like. That is my bedroom, my space, my photos, *my* journal." My lips twitch in amusement. "You have no right to march in and do what you like with it."

Pushing so I'm sitting on the edge of my bed, I rake my eyes up the length of her body and run my thumb across my bottom lip.

"You mean, much like you're doing to me right now. You didn't even knock. I could have been doing... *anything*." I tilt my head to the side and raise a brow.

"I did knock, asshole. Your music was just so loud that you couldn't hear me." Her face begins to turn red with anger, her tiny fists curling at her sides.

"Careful, little one," I say, standing and taking a step toward her. "You look like you're about ready to blow."

"Ashton, I'm tired, I'm already bored with your bullshit, and I—" Her words are cut off by a gasp when I take her chin in my hand.

"And you, what?"

"I hate you," she seethes, despite the fact my grip tightens, and her lips pop open.

"Huh, and here I was thinking I might get a free pass, you know, with the dead mom and all." Her eyes narrow once more.

"Too soon?"

She might think I'm a cold-hearted bastard, but as the words pass my lips, my chest tightens to the point it's almost crippling. Not that I'm going to let her see that. The only person in this world that knows I might have a weakness, is me.

"You're a prick."

"Oh." I laugh. "I know, little one. Nothing you can say will be news to me. So, tell me, what did you really come in here for?" Tilting her face up to me, I lower down until our lips are a breath apart.

Her breathing falters with our distance and I fight the smile that wants to spread across my face knowing that she's affected by me.

"I... I came to tell you to fuck off."

I chuckle. "Yeah, maybe that's what you think you came for. But deep down, we both know it's not actually true, don't we?"

"You're insane."

"Maybe," I muse. "But I'm not the only one because while you stand there claiming to hate me, I know that you're wet for me."

"Fuck. You. Ashton."

I squeeze her cheeks harder and they finally touch mine, but I don't claim them. Instead, I brush mine across her cheek until they're at her ear.

"Is that why you hate me, little one? Because you were so drunk that night that you don't remember how it ended. You don't know whether you let me fuck you or not?"

Her breathing becomes more labored with every word I say but her expression remains hard.

A smile begins to tug at her lips, but it doesn't get much farther with my tight grip. "You think I'd have remembered if you did. Think you're giving yourself a little too much credit there."

A growl rumbles up my throat and my hand drops to hers as I push her back against the wall. She swallows nervously beneath my hold, her pulse thundering against my fingertips.

"Oh, little one, I can assure you that if I'd fucked you that night then you'd still be feeling it now."

Her eyes hold mine, but she doesn't react to my words.

"You're all talk, Ash. You're not man enough or you'd have done it."

I smile at her, but there's nothing happy about it as only evil intentions fill my mind.

"Ever heard of delayed gratification, little one? One thing I do have is patience and I'm more than happy to wait for the right time to ruin you for anyone else."

I release her and take a step back.

I keep my eyes on her as she sucks in a few deep breaths, her chest heaving and her breasts catching my eye.

"Your friend was cute. Any chance I could get her number?" I ask.

"Stay away from my friends, Ashton. And don't even think about turning up to Ethan's on Saturday night." She backs out of the room as she dishes out warnings that land on deaf ears. "This is my life. You don't get to turn up and stomp all over it."

I chuckle at her. "Watch me, little one."

She storms to her room and slams her door, leaving mine wide open. I assume it's to piss me off, but it has little effect.

Walking over, I close it before turning my music back on and falling down on my bed to finish off my joint in peace.

The next time I get a visitor, at least they have the decency to knock, although the second my dad pokes his head around the door, I soon realize that I'd much rather it be Ruby barging her way inside.

"How are you doing?" he asks, slipping farther into the room. His eyes land on me for a beat before they zero in on the ashtray beside my bed.

"Great." I roll my eyes at him.

"Lisa and I would prefer if you didn't smoke in the house."

"Would you?" I ask, tipping my chin up at him.

"Yeah." His lips part to say more. I know he wants to chew me out for smoking in the first place, but he wisely keeps his thoughts to himself.

"Did you want something?"

He stands awkwardly at the end of my bed looking like he has a million things he wants to say to me, but he seems to stumble over every single one of them. It's been years since we've had any kind of real relationship, and I can't see us fixing things any time soon. Too much has happened, too much betrayal and pain has happened.

"Uh... yeah... dinner is ready."

"What is it?"

"I- I don't know. Lisa cooked it. She's a fantastic cook though."

"I bet she is," I mutter, swinging my legs off the bed. I really don't want to go and have a family meal with them, but my empty stomach says other things.

"I'm just going to knock for Ruby. I'll meet you downstairs in a few."

I refrain from telling him that I'll get her. If I get anywhere close to her room, there's a chance I won't let her down for dinner. Instead, I clean up and grab a shirt, waiting until they've both disappeared downstairs to join them.

As I walk into the dining room, they look like a picture-perfect family as they smile at each other and pass the dishes around.

"Wow, this is cozy," I mutter, pulling the chair out beside Ruby and dropping down. She pauses, spooning some peas onto her plate, and I smile at her reaction to my closeness.

"Ashton, it's so good to see you," Lisa almost sings. "How are you doing?" Her eyes go all soft and sympathetic, and it makes anger bloom inside me.

"Yeah, you know," I mutter. Like fuck does she know anything. She's not had her life ripped away from her and landed in this hellhole.

"I know we said we wouldn't talk about the future until..."

"The funeral. You can say the word." I stab at a potato with my fork and shove the entire thing into my mouth.

"Okay... well... yes, the funeral. But I spoke to Principal Hartmann today about you starting at Rosewood High."

My eyes shoot to my father's but I don't miss Ruby's chin drop at his words.

"Not happening."

"Ashton, be sensible here. You don't have enough credits to graduate this year."

"How do you know that?" I bark, my irritation levels rising faster than I can control.

"I called your old principal to update him on the situation and to ask him to prepare for your transfer."

"I'm not going back to school."

"Sorry, Son, but this isn't up for discussion. If you're living under this roof, then you'll be continuing your education."

"You're fucking serious, aren't you?"

"Ashton," he admonishes as Lisa gasps at my language.

"I never wanted to live under this roof, or are you forgetting that?"

"You're still a minor, Ashton. Do you need a reminder of that?"

"I know how fucking old I am," I seethe.

"Then you know that you don't really have a choice about this."

I stand with such speed my chair goes crashing to the floor behind me.

I stare at my father, tension crackling between us.

He was my everything until the day he told me he was leaving, until the day I watched him rip my mother's heart out and walk away from both of us like we meant nothing.

He might as well have handed over his right to be my father that day because it was the day I lost all respect I had for him.

"This is bullshit." I storm from the room to the sound of Lisa trying to talk my dad down from following me. Maybe she's not a total idiot after all.

I grab my jacket and keys from the table in the hallway and march from the house.

The vibrations of my bike beneath me help to calm me a little but one look up at the house and it hits me once more.

Mom's gone and this is my life now.

Backing out of the driveway, I rev the engine and fly away from the house that holds everything I don't want right now.

Family.

I ride around town for hours, taking in what I guess is to be my new home. I might not want to be here, but deep down, I know Dad's right. I've certainly got nowhere else to go or any other family to rely on. All my grandparents have gone. Mom had a sister, but they'd not spoken for years. It's basically Rosewood or nothing.

I pull up in a parking lot by the ocean and with my fake ID burning a hole in my wallet, I head to the store and attempt to buy myself a bottle of something that will numb the pain.

Thankfully, the girl behind the register didn't bat an eyelid about serving me and in only minutes, I'm stepping down onto the beach. I walk along until I'm alone, then I twist the top off the bottle and tip it to my lips.

The vodka burns as it goes down, but it feels so fucking good. It's a sign that things are going to get easier in the coming minutes.

I swallow down more as I stare up at the huge houses that look down at the beach. Dad and Lisa's place is nice, but it's nowhere near the size of those mansions.

My eyes search the balconies and windows to see who might live in the colossal homes, but I find nothing.

With a sigh, I turn back to the ocean and drop down to my ass.

I see no one the entire time I sit there hidden in the darkness and drowning in my misery.

6

RUBY

"I'm sorry," Stephen says as the slam from the front door rattles the house.

"You don't need to apologize for him, love. He's hurting, it's understandable."

"It's not an excuse to talk to us like that."

Mom shrugs and smiles sweetly at him. "He'll be okay," she says, reaching out for Stephen's hand. "Just give him some time. Everything about his life has changed in the blink of an eye. It's going to take a while to adjust. Things might start to settle once we've got the funeral out of the way."

I want to ask what she means by the *we* in that sentence, but I don't get a chance because Mom turns her eyes on me.

"Do you have any parties this weekend? Maybe you should invite him, introduce him to your friends."

"Um..."

"Introduce him to the team. He's a brilliant quarterback, if the coach has half a brain then he's going to want him."

"Um... I really don't think that is a good idea."

"Why not? Making some friends might be just what he needs to feel at home here."

Thoughts of him joining my circle of friends sends a bolt of panic up my spine. I can't have him around me every second of the day. I just can't.

I open my mouth to argue but I soon decide that it would be better if I just shut my mouth and agreed. I really don't want Mom and Stephen digging into why I don't like my stepbrother.

"I told Principal Hartmann that he's likely to start the week after the funeral."

"Don't you think that's a little soon? He has just lost his mom, Stephen."

I know Mom's just concerned, and as much as I'd love to put Stephen off the idea of sending Ashton to Rosewood as soon as possible, I know that I'm in no position to really have an opinion about this. I know Stephen lost both his parents young, I can only go on his experience and hope that he's right.

"The distraction will be a good thing."

The conversation turns to a golf trip that Stephen has coming up and I tune out as I push my dinner around my plate. I'm not really hungry after the pizza earlier but I didn't have it in me to tell Mom after she'd already cooked. If I weren't hiding in my room after my interaction with Ash, then I might have intercepted her before she started.

After a tense as fuck dinner, I excuse myself to my room for an early night hoping that I can make the most of Ashton being out and actually get some sleep.

It works because the next thing I know, my alarm is going off once again, and I actually feel like I've had a decent night's sleep.

I push from my bed feeling more refreshed than I have in days and set about getting ready. Before I crashed last night, I'd messaged Harley asking if I could spend the weekend with her. It's pretty standard that I get ready for a party at hers and now Poppy lives there too, it makes even more sense for me to join them.

I shove everything I'm going to need for school and the entire weekend into bags before silently making my way out of the house.

It's not until I step out of the front door and the security light illuminates the driveway that I realize why I might have slept so well last night. Ashton never came home.

I look back up at the house, tempted to go and see if he's really not here, but no sooner has the thought crossed my mind do I force it back down. He wouldn't give two shits if I stayed out all night. Why should I allow even a bit of concern for him to fill my mind?

Fuck him and his mind games and evil words.

Fuck. Him.

I throw my bags into the trunk of my car and head for school ready to put myself through yet another hardcore practice knowing that a day off is right around the corner.

"You've been weirdly quiet all day, did something happen after we left last night?" Poppy asks from where she's resting back on one of the couches in Zayn's den.

The guys aren't here yet, but we've already gate-crashed their little get-together. Perks of not only being cheerleaders but also besties with one of the player's girls.

"Nah, I'm just glad to be out of the house. He stormed out during dinner and never returned. His bike was still missing this morning."

"Shit, do you think he's okay?" Harley asks, handing us both a soda each.

I look up at her with my brows raised. "No idea but it sounds like you might want to go and check him over for wounds." I don't mean for my tone to come out sounding quite so bitter, but it does.

"Okay, down, girl," Harley mutters, curling her legs under her and joining us on the couch. "He's hot, sure, but you're my girl. My loyalty is only and always with you."

"I appreciate that."

"You should, especially seeing as you two have both screwed me over by getting with my brother." She flashes a glance at me, but her eyes lock on Poppy's before a smile begins to twitch at her lips.

"Hey, I only kissed him and... touched a little bit." Poppy growls beside me. "I'm sorry, if I knew then I wouldn't have. I was desperate, you know."

"Oh nice." Poppy laughs.

The three of us laugh and joke and it feels good just to be normal after everything that's happened recently. I look at Poppy with a genuine smile on her face and something settles inside me. She's been to hell and back over the past few weeks, but she's made it out the other side. Her issues make mine with Ash pale in comparison and remind me that everything will be okay in the end.

Mom was right last night, he's just hurting. Things will settle down once he's had the chance to properly say goodbye and get into a routine. The thought of him attending school still doesn't sit right with me but it is what it is, so I guess I'm going to have to deal with it.

It's not long before the guys descend on Zayn's den. The second Zayn steps inside, he looks totally torn between being delighted that his girl is waiting for him and horrified that his sister is also here.

It's just something he's going to have to get used to.

They all bring beer with them and before long someone has cranked the music up and Harley and I are dancing around enjoying life and more importantly, forgetting about a certain someone who could or could not be home yet.

———

We only had a few drinks knowing that we had to get up for practice again this morning. While all the other Rosewood kids are soundly sleeping in their beds, Harley, the squad, and I are running drills down the length of the gym before we start on our routines in about an hour.

Chelsea stands at the front of all of us with a whistle between her lips and looking like she's enjoying torturing us a little too much.

"This gets harder every week," Stella pants beside me when Chelsea lets up.

"Just a couple of weeks to go and you can get reacquainted with your bed once again," I tell her.

"I can't wait."

"Right, huddle up, ladies."

The next few hours pass as a blur of sweat, burning muscles, and the same song on repeat over and over as we strive to get our routine bang on.

Thankfully, I'm more focused than I have been the past two days, something that Chelsea doesn't miss as she smiles at me at the top of her pyramid before I somersault through the air, landing in front of her.

"That's more like the Ruby I've come to know." She beams at me. "Things calming down a bit?"

"Yes and no. Everything will be fine though."

"Glad to hear it. I need you on form. You want to take over cool down? I really need to pee... again."

"M-me?" I ask, looking over my shoulder as if she's speaking to someone else.

"Yeah, Rubes. You. It's what you want, right?" She quirks a brow at me.

"Y-yes, I'd love to."

"Okay, Ruby is in charge. I'll see you all at Ethan's tonight, right? Remember... do not get drunk off your asses. I need you all in one piece for nationals. You can fuck shit up after we walk away with that trophy, okay?"

A few grumbles sound out around me.

"I said okay?" Chelsea booms.

I can't help smiling to myself. She used to be the ultimate party girl. It makes me laugh that now she's unable to party, she's stopping the others too.

I mean, she might have been that way anyway with or without the pregnancy, she's pretty headstrong and determined, but it still amuses me.

Everyone agrees before she spins on her heels and rushes toward the locker room to relieve herself.

"You did good, Rubes," Harley says from the driver's seat as we head to Aces after practice.

"You think?"

"Yeah, you're going to make a fantastic captain next year."

Nerves and excitement erupt at just her suggestion of it. "I might not get it, Har."

"Oh shush, you know it's yours. Chelsea loves you. Miss Kelly literally doesn't give a shit and you know all the girls will back you."

"We'll see when the time comes. Let's just worry about getting through nationals first, huh?"

"I'm totally focused, I'm just saying." She winks at me before climbing from the car as the rest of the squad descend on our chosen diner ready for some much-needed breakfast.

After stuffing our faces with more pancakes and syrup than we should ever eat, Harley and I make our way back to her place to chill out before getting ready for tonight's party. Not all that many juniors get invited to the senior parties but since we both got accepted into the varsity squad, our names are permanently on the guestlist, much to Zayn's annoyance.

"That dress is insane on you," Harley says when she walks back into her room with a towel wrapped around her from her shower.

"I thought it was bigger when I tried it on in the store," I say, pulling at the hem that sits dangerously high on my thighs. I hate to think just how short it would be on someone any taller than my pathetic five foot.

"Stop, it's perfect. The guys are going to lose their minds."

My stomach twists uncomfortably. I bought it with that exact idea in mind back before Ashton reappeared in my life. After he vanished, I was set on forcing him out of my system with some other guy. But despite me kissing a few, none of them have made me want anything else and I've been left with the shame of slutting it up and it not having the desired effect.

"I don't want them to lose their minds. I might just wear jeans." I lean over to grab my bag, but it's quickly snatched from my hand.

"Don't even think about it," she snaps, throwing it to the other side of the room. "I do think you should reconsider inviting Ashton though. You in that dress and flirting with other guys will be a lesson I think he desperately needs."

"No," I say without missing a beat.

"Oh, come on," she whines.

"I get that you want him, Har. But he's already ruining enough of my life, I don't want him fucking this up as well."

"Who says he'd ruin it. He might take one look at you and..."

"And what?" I snap when she trails off after getting a look at my face.

She shrugs. "Devour you."

"I don't want him to, Har. I hate him."

"Do you though?"

"Yes," I hiss. "And you keep going on about it like I'm suddenly going to change my mind is starting to get on my tits."

Her eyes drop to my said body part. "They look banging in that dress too."

"Argh, you're a pain in my ass, Harley Hunter."

"You love me really." She winks, spinning around and pulling out a set of underwear from her drawer. "I just want you to be happy, you know."

She makes quick work of pulling her panties on under her towel before unwrapping it and strapping her bra around her back.

I take in her flawless, glistening bronze skin and jealousy begins to bubble up inside me. She's so gorgeous it's often hard to look at her. How the guys manage to keep their hands off her, God only knows.

"This or this?" she asks holding up two identically revealing dresses, only one is copper and the other fire engine red.

"Are you trying to give Zayn a heart attack?" I ask with a laugh.

"Maybe, but I was more thinking about pulling one of his teammates to give him a taste of his own medicine." I roll my eyes at her. "You can hear that, right?" She points to the door, gesturing to where Zayn's is across the corridor as Poppy's girly giggle sounds out.

I can't help but laugh at the disgusted look on Harley's face.

"They are always at it. It's insane."

"Aw, Har Har, you jealous?"

"Damn fucking right, I am. I want someone to look at me like he does Poppy. It's sickening."

"I think it's cute."

"Yeah, well... ugh." She stomps her foot like a toddler about to have a tantrum. "I just want a nice guy who's going to treat me right," she says, stepping into the red dress.

"Then you probably need to look a little farther than the team. They're a bunch of dogs."

"I know. It's just easy when they're so willing."

I don't need to say the words for Harley to know I agree, we're both well aware of my actions the past few months.

"Sit, let me do your makeup," she demands, pulling the chair out that sits at her vanity unit.

"Have at it." I lower my ass to the seat, readjusting my dress once more.

She works in silence for a few minutes, adding primer, concealer, and then foundation to my skin before she pauses and looks at me.

"What's wrong?"

"I just... I know I'm giving you shit about Ash, but I get it, you know." She rests her ass back on the unit and lowers her eyes. "I watched Poppy hate on Zayn for years and look at them now. He affects you, like, really affects you. I'd hate to see you miss an opportunity because you're too stubborn to see past it."

"He affects me because I hate him, Har. He's certainly not my soul mate or any of that shit."

"Okay. If you're sure."

"I am." I pause before saying something I fear I might really regret. "If you want him, he's fair game."

"Ruby," she sighs, sympathy passing across her face. "He's hot, but I wouldn't... I couldn't."

"I kissed Zayn. I get it."

"I was just joking about that last night. It's totally cool." She smiles at me and I can't help but return it. I also can't help the relief that flows through me that she doesn't want to go after him.

It's over an hour later before Harley has finished making up both our faces and done our hair, and as I stare at myself in her full-length mirror, I can't deny that she's not done an astounding job. Poppy appeared not long after we heard her giggling with pink cheeks and swollen lips, much to Harley's delight, and she got ready with us, helping us drink our way through the bottle of vodka Harley had stashed ready for tonight.

"If you're not ready, I'm going without you," Zayn calls through the door not long later.

"Keep your pants on, we're ready," Harley calls back before Zayn takes that as an invitation and lets himself into her room.

His eyes zero in on Poppy who's wearing a pair of skinny jeans and a loose, low-cut tank. I swear his eyes nearly pop out of his head.

"We've already listened to you two going at it tonight, chill out for a few hours, would ya?" Harley mutters.

"Ignore her, she's jealous," I tell Zayn. "We ready then?"

"Rubes, you look hot." His eyes run the length of me and back up again.

"Um..." Poppy says, stepping into his side and forcing his eyes to her. He leans into her ear and whispers something that makes her sag into his hold and curl his shirt in her fist.

Rolling my eyes at them, I turn to Harley in time to see her fake gag before she storms past the happy couple.

"Come on, or I'm taking your car," she calls to Zayn who immediately releases Poppy and marches after her.

"How do you put up with living with those two?" I ask Poppy as we follow the bickering siblings out of the house.

"Being here comes with its advantages too."

"The orgasms, right."

"That wasn't actually what I was going to say but yeah, they sure help."

I'm still laughing at her as we join Zayn and Harley in his car.

"Are you two going to behave tonight?" he asks, looking at the two of us in the rearview mirror. "I really don't want to have to carry any of you out tonight."

"We'll do our best, right Rubes?" she says, elbowing me.

"Yeah," I mutter, staring out the window at the passing scenery. The vodka might already be having an effect, but it's nowhere near enough to block out the person I need it to.

I still don't know if he came home. I can only assume that he's fine or I'd have heard something.

In only minutes we're pulling up outside Ethan's house. It might still be early, but there are already cars everywhere and kids making their way inside, ready to start the night.

Excitement tingles in my belly. I am so ready to join them after the week I've had.

7

ASHTON

I wake up freezing my fucking ass off. This might be the warmer end of the country but spending the night passed out on a beach in January still isn't the best idea.

Every part of my body aches as I force myself to sit up, my eyes blinking against the early morning sun that crept above the horizon not so long ago.

I stare out at the calm ocean beyond.

I'm sure this should be a happy place. A place for people to think, to calm down, to get a little perspective. But while the alcohol numbed me for a few hours last night, the reality is now rushing back in faster than I'd like it to.

I reach into my pocket in the hope I've got something to take the edge off it. But I find nothing besides my lighter. I have no idea if I smoked my stash last night or if I even brought it with me. I can only hope it's still sitting in my room waiting for me. But I don't want to get my hopes up, I learned the hard way a long time ago that hopes are useless. They build you up thinking that something good might happen and then they drop you when you least expect it.

A little like last night. I'd hoped Dad might lay off me for a bit. But no, instead, Mom is barely cold and he's already forcing me to think about my future as if I've already forgotten that I had a life outside of Rosewood only days ago. It's like he expects me to just forget all about everything in Seattle, the people that were in it—not that there were many.

I drag my knees up to my chest and drop my head onto my forearm, willing it to stop spinning.

I know I need to go back there. I know that I don't have much of a choice. But I really don't want to look at his face again.

He was supposed to love her once upon a time, how can he just move on so quickly, care so little that she's gone?

Why doesn't he hate me? After all, I'm the one to blame here.

It would be easier if he were shouting at me, but he's just... not. He's just going about his life once more like she was never a part of it.

I guess she hasn't been for a few years, but she was a huge part of mine, why can't he just let me have this time to do what I need to do? I really don't give a shit about tomorrow, next week, next month right now. My head is still firmly in last week and I have no idea when I'm going to be able to drag it away.

My exhaustion and the remaining alcohol that's still pulsing around my body must drag me back under again because I wake with a start once more as a couple of guys go running past.

I watch them as they make their way across the wet sand a few feet down from me. One of them is wearing a Rosewood jersey with Hunter across the back.

My stomach twists at the thought of having to start at a new school. I barely wanted to go to my old one. But become a junior again, retake the shit I've already done in the hope of graduating. I'm not sure I have the energy.

Then of course there's the other issue with that.

Ruby.

The less time we're forced together the better.

She stirs something inside me that no other has. She awakens a need inside me that scares me. My need to hurt her, to scare her, to make her... mine?

I shake my head as an unamused laugh falls from my lips. No. That is not what this is.

Angry with myself for even going there, I stand and march back toward where I think I abandoned my bike last night.

There aren't many people around at this time of the morning, but as a guy flips the closed sign to open on a diner ahead, I find myself walking in that direction as my stomach starts to grumble.

"Mornin'," an older guy calls over the second I push the door open.

"Hey," I reply, barely sparing him a second glance before I slide into an empty booth and reach for the menu.

In a heartbeat, he's before me with a coffee pot and filling a mug for me.

"Uh... thanks."

"No offense, but you look like you need it, son. I'm Bill, by the way. I'm assuming you're Ashton Fury."

My chin drops. How does this guy know who I am?

I look up at him, his eyes crinkling with amusement at my confusion.

"I'm psychic." He winks before a smile curls at his lips. "I'm only kidding. I know everything about this town, boy. I'm sorry for your loss."

"Thanks," I mutter, already sick to death of hearing people say that. It's not their fucking fault, they didn't kill her. That guilt solely lies with me.

"I know things must be all over the place for you right now, but Rosewood is a good town. Just give this place a chance before you write it off."

"Have you spoken to my dad?"

"Not yet, no. But I will. Now, what can I get for you?"

My lips part a couple of times but no words pass. Who the hell is this guy?

"Don't worry. I know what you need. Leave it to me."

He's gone before I have a chance to argue and in only a few minutes the scent of bacon frying soon distracts me.

By the time I get back to the house the sun has long risen and, thankfully, there are no cars in the driveway.

I let myself in, get myself another coffee before heading up to my room to wash the sand off me from a night sleeping on the beach.

With nothing to do and my head still stuck in that fucking car as I watched the life drain from my mom's face, the clock ticks around slower than I've ever known.

I have no idea what I'm waiting for. It's certainly not for Dad or Lisa to come home, they're the last people I want to see, and I shoot down any ideas that I might be waiting on Ruby, because equally, I don't want to see her either.

I just... I just want to vanish.

Sadly, that's not how the evening goes, because not thirty seconds after the front door closes with someone's arrival that evening there's a knock at my door.

"Son, you back?"

I groan to myself and bite down my need to tell him to fuck off.

"Yeah," I call, not moving from my position on my bed staring at the ceiling.

He pushes the door open and steps inside. His stare burns into me, but I don't look his way. I don't want to see his face.

"Ash, I'm sorry if I pushed too hard last night." Even as the words pass his lips, I don't believe them. Something tells me that Lisa's put them in his mouth. "I know things are tough right now, but I just want you to see that what you're going through now, it won't last forever and that it's okay to think about the future."

I keep my breathing steady despite the fact there's a storm brewing inside of me. My fists clench at my sides, the only outward sign that I'm barely holding onto a slither of my restraint right now.

When I don't say anything in response to his little speech, he continues.

"I've managed to get us flights for Tuesday morning to go back to Seattle. I thought that would give you a few days to do anything you need to do, see anyone you'd like to see, before coming back here again."

I get the gesture, only he's missing one thing. The only person I would want to see in Seattle is gone.

I had friends, sure, but none of us were all that close. We might have been a team, but we were a bunch of kids in a shit school with mostly even shittier lives. We all had bigger things to worry about than becoming BFFs for life or whatever it is the kids here do.

"Okay."

"Everything is ready for the funeral, I just need to let the florist know what flowers you'd like, and also is there any music you think she'd have wanted to play?"

Emotions form in my throat as I think about his question, even if I did want to respond, I couldn't. The lump is too big, too insistent.

Instead, I shake my head, praying that he's about to leave so I can break down in peace.

Ruby never reappears Friday night which is probably a good thing—for her. I'm really in no kind of mood to have her anywhere near me.

Dad must have actually realized that last night's family meal was a bad idea because after Lisa has cooked, he brings me up a plate so I can eat alone.

I'm grateful, although at no point do I tell him that.

He does, however, inform me that both he and Lisa are heading out of town for the weekend and as I lie wide awake as the sun begins to rise

Saturday morning, I hear them begin to stir before leaving the house not long later.

A smile twitches at my lips at the prospect of having this house to myself all weekend. Or maybe Ruby will come home at some point and provide me with a little playmate.

Ideas fill my mind of just how much fun we could have together without the threat of our parents walking in at any moment and my cock swells.

It's been too long since I had any action, and even fucking longer since I had some fun with my little toy.

I sit up and grab my cell. Maybe it's time to find out exactly where Ethan lives and what time this party is starting tonight. It might just be time for me to meet my new classmates.

It takes me less time than I expected to discover that Ethan lives in one of those massive fucking mansions I was looking at last night. I spend almost all day scrolling through social media, getting to know what the Rosewood kids are like. Mostly, they're the same as the Seattle kids, there's just one difference. These kids have money. A smile twitches at my lips at the thought. Where there's money, there's alcohol, drugs, and girls.

I don't bother getting ready until I know the party is in full swing. I watch as images appear on Instagram, Ruby's friend Harley is more than willing to post my stepsister's whereabouts every two minutes or so, she also doesn't have an issue with showing off exactly how my little toy looks tonight.

I zoom in on the picture that was just uploaded and run my eyes down her body. I shake my head from side to side as I imagine what all the other guys under that roof are thinking as they lock eyes on her. *Not fucking happening, motherfuckers.*

Pulling out a Post-it note that Lisa left for me when I first arrived, I punch a number into my contacts and start to write a message.

Ashton: That dress is going to get you in trouble.

It only takes a few seconds for her to read it. I imagine her looking around whatever room she's standing in looking for the culprit but she's not going to find him. Not yet anyway.

Toy: Who is this?

I tap my finger against the side of my phone as I consider what my response is going to be.

Ashton: You'll have to wait and see.

As I picture her rolling her eyes at the screen, I climb from my bed and strip out of my clothes as I head for the shower. After all, I've got a party to attend and some of Ruby's cheer slut friends look like they could be worth a shot.

The house is even more impressive than I was expecting when I walk up the driveway. There are kids everywhere I look, drinking, smoking, and enjoying themselves. This party has already been going on a while it seems.

My mouth waters for a drink or a hit as I make my way inside with my hood up, keeping my face in the shadows. I don't want her to know I'm here yet.

I find the kitchen thanks to the stream of people walking out of it with drinks in their hands and after helping myself to a bottle of vodka I found along with an entire counter full of alcohol, I set about finding where Ruby might be.

The music booms and as I make my way through all the people, hardly anyone pays me any attention, they're all too busy with their own bullshit, privileged lives.

I know that not everyone who lives in Rosewood lives in quite this level of luxury, but the majority have it a hell of a lot better than I did in Seattle.

"Oh shit, I'm so sor—" a drunk girl slurs as she slams into me but the second her eyes lock on mine, she slams her lips shut and scurries away. I smile as I watch her disappear into the crowd.

Coming to a stop in a doorway, I lift my bottle to my lips as I take in the makeshift dance floor in the room beyond.

"Excuse me," a guy barks as he barrels past me with a girl attached to his arm before pulling her into his arms as they start moving in time to the music.

My eyes run over the bodies that are bumping and grinding in front of me before one dark head catches my eye.

There you are, little one.

I step back into the shadows and watch as she dances with some guy.

After a few minutes, the crowd moves, and they find themselves on the edge of the swarm of people, giving me the perfect view of them.

The guy lowers his face toward Ruby's and every muscle in my body tenses as I prepare for him to kiss her, only, he doesn't. Instead, he whispers something in her ear, something that has her throwing her head back and barking out a laugh.

She looks happy. And while that should probably put me off ruining her night, it doesn't. It just fuels me.

Why does she get to enjoy herself like everything is okay? If it weren't for her and her whore of a mother, then my family might still be together and alive.

My grip on the bottle tightens until I fear the glass might shatter in my hold.

Ruby gets swallowed into the crowd once more but the image of her body moving with his is burned into my brain.

I stay where I am, confident that everyone is ignoring me, and continue watching while the vodka slowly starts to fill my veins.

The girl I flirted with in the kitchen the other day appears at some point with a guy close behind and once she's got Ruby's attention, she and her guy emerge once again. Ruby throws her arms around her friend's shoulders before they start dancing together with their guys at their backs.

The guy's hands slide down her waist and come to rest on her hips as their bodies roll together in time to the music.

My teeth grind as the vodka no longer helps drown out my need to rip her from his hold.

Pulling my cell from my pocket, I find our conversation.

Ashton: And to think, you tried to convince me that you weren't a cheer slut.

I keep my cell in my hand and wait, after two seconds she pulls hers out from her minidress somewhere and stares down at the screen.

I watch as her body stills for a beat before she not so discreetly looks around the room.

Toy: Fuck off.

I can't help but laugh at her response.

Ashton: It amuses me that you think you can get rid of me that easily.

Toy: You ran pretty quickly last time.

Ashton: This time is different. I'm going nowhere...

A smile pulls at my lips as her expression hardens when she reads my message before she shoves it back inside her dress. Her eyes scan the room once more but unable to find me, despite the fact she knows I'm watching, she spins in the guy's arms and reaches up to whisper in his ear.

A shit-eating grin pulls at his lips before he takes her hand and drags her from the room. Her smile as she flicks one more look over her shoulder proves that she thinks she's winning. She's forgetting one thing though... I never lose. And this is my motherfucking game.

8

RUBY

I know he's watching me. I can feel his burning stare, but I can't fucking find him.

Justin continues to grind against my back. I was enjoying dancing with him until I felt that tingle of awareness race down my spine.

He shouldn't be here. He wasn't invited and he doesn't belong here.

Turning my back on Harley who's dancing with some cute guy that I've never seen before, I look up at Justin whose eyes sparkle with the alcohol we've both consumed and the anticipation of what's to come.

Justin is cute, hot even. We've got a little friendly before, but nothing more than a brief kiss that was cut short one night.

"Wanna find somewhere a little quieter?" I whisper-shout in his ear.

His hands tighten on my hips, giving me the answer I was expecting without him so much as parting his lips.

"Let's go," he practically growls, his hand slipping into mine as he begins pulling me from the room.

Just before we're through the door, I look back ensuring I've got a smile on my face.

You can watch me from the shadows all you want, but I can outrun you.

"Can we just grab a drink?" I say before we get to the kitchen. I have no idea where he was planning on taking me, but I do know that I'm going to need more alcohol for what he's probably got planned, especially with Ashton here somewhere stalking me like a creep.

Justin turns at the last minute and while he grabs himself a beer, I make myself a very strong vodka Red Bull. Something tells me I'm going to need it.

In seconds, my hand is clasped in his once more and he's directing me down the hallway to where I know Ethan's den is at the other end of the house.

We're almost there when a door to my left opens and an arm shoots out.

I squeal, but he's too quick. Before I know what's happening, I'm inside the dark room with my back pressed up against the door and his hard and hot body pressing into me.

"Ruby?" Justin shouts through the door, his fist raining down on the solid wood.

My heart thunders in my chest but with his body burning into mine and his scent filling my nose, I fear that with the amount of alcohol filling my veins it might not be fear that's fuelling my response to him.

"Get rid of him," Ashton demands.

I swallow down my apprehension and do as he says.

"It's fine, Justin. I'll come and find you in a bit."

Ashton growls at my words and presses harder against me.

"O-okay." Justin's voice is full of disappointment, and I hate myself that I don't care at that very moment. I was using him, I knew that. I'm pretty sure he knew that too, but clearly, he wasn't done.

"You're teasing me, little one."

"And you're stalking me. No one wants you here, Ashton."

"Is that right," he growls in my ear. "So you weren't imagining me when you were dancing with him? You weren't wishing it were my hands pinning your ass against my cock as you moved?"

I shake my head as his hands descend my body before mimicking his words, only we're face to face and his cock isn't pressed against my ass, his hard length is pressing into my stomach.

"Ashton." His name is meant to come out as a warning, but it sounds anything but, even to my own ears.

His lips brush the shell of my ear and my entire body erupts in goose bumps at his simple touch.

"Did he make you feel like this, little one? Did he make you as wet as you are for me right now?"

"I'm not—"

"You really going to argue with me?" he asks, amusement filling his voice. "You're forgetting that I know your body, little one." His lips trail down my neck until his teeth graze my collarbone. The scratch of pain does nothing to help the situation I've found myself in.

I should push him away, I know this. My brain is screaming at me to do it, but my body... my body is currently playing by an entirely different set of rules. Ones that he's in control of.

"This dress..." he murmurs as he licks across the swell of my breast. "Mmm." His eyes flash up to mine, but despite the darkness of the room, I see the anger swelling within them.

Even in my drunken, lust-filled haze, I'm with it enough to know that this isn't about Ashton's need for me, it's about his need to hurt me.

I'm under no illusion that I'm going to walk out of this room feeling satisfied and fulfilled, I already know it's going to be the opposite but right now, I'm not sure I'm strong enough to stop him.

I can battle with him as well as anyone else, but the second he lays his hands on me, all bets are off, and he damn well knows it.

"What were you trying to achieve with that cocksucker, huh?"

"N-nothing," I stutter as he wraps his fingers around the top of my dress.

"So you weren't grinding your ass into him for my benefit?"

"You shouldn't be here. What I do tonight, or any night, shouldn't be any of your concern."

"Were you going to fuck him?" His voice is low, his words cold.

"So what if I was?"

"You really are just a little cheer slut, aren't you?"

"Think what you like. I don't have to answer to you."

"Is that right?"

I gasp as he pulls the fabric of my dress down, exposing my bra.

My chest heaves, my nipples pressing against the padding covering me.

"Because the way I see it right now, is that you need something from me—"

"Bullshit. I don't need anything from you."

"Oh really?" He chuckles, it's so low that it should terrify me, and in some way I guess it does, but mostly, I just feel a rush of heat bloom between my legs.

Fucking vodka.

"Because I think right now, you need more from me than you can admit." His hand sneaks around my back and in a beat, my bra falls away from my body.

"Oh shit," I gasp as his hot mouth captures one of my nipples. His teeth bite down hard before his tongue laves at the burning pain.

My fingers curl into fists at my sides, my need to reach for him almost too much to bear.

"Hmm." His voice vibrates all the way down my body. "Exactly as I thought. Just a little cheer slut."

He takes a step back, leaving me feeling cold and used.

His eyes trail down the length of me and back up until he catches my narrowed gaze. My eyes fly up to cover myself, but his barked words stop their progress.

"No."

The light seeping in from the backyard illuminates his profile, allowing me to see the evil smirk that plays on his face.

Our stare remains as he lifts a bottle to his lips and swallows down a couple of mouthfuls.

"I should fuck you right here, prove just how worthless you really are."

His harsh words make my breathing catch.

"But I think that might be too easy, even for you. Plus, I kind of want to see that guy try to fill my shoes when I'm done with you."

"You're a prick, Ashton."

"Oh." He laughs, drinking more. "I know. I never pretended to be anything else, little one. Or did you forget about my first visit?"

Images from Halloween night flash in my mind like a movie.

"I didn't. Kind of impossible when I've got the evidence of you laid out for me like a good little girl on my cell."

"Y-you're lying," I state, possibly a little too confidently.

"You think?"

My lips part to tell him that he is, but the words die on my tongue.

What if he's not?

The room starts to spin as reality pushes its way through my drunken haze.

He might have naked pictures of me on his cell.

Holy shit.

My breathing increases as panic begins to take over, but before I allow it to consume me, he's back right in front of me with his hand around my throat.

"You want to try me, see what will happen?"

I shake my head, knowing that if he is telling the truth, I can't allow him to let them out in public. I want to be Rosewood's next cheer captain, not the laughingstock of the school and labeled as the new ultimate cheer slut.

"Good, girl." His eyes bore down into mine as our breaths mingle. His gaze lowers for a beat to my lips and for a second I think he's going to kiss me but then he totally ruins the fantasy by saying something that damn near gives me whiplash. "Take your panties off."

"W-what?" I balk.

"Take. Your. Panties. Off."

"Who says I'm wearing any? ASHTON!" I squeal as his hands slide up my thighs, taking my dress with it until his fingers wrap around the thin bit of lace at my hips and he tugs until the sound of them ripping fills my ears.

I'm still trying to get my head around what happened when he stands back, his eyes zeroing in on the juncture of my thighs.

"Good luck forgetting about me for the rest of the night."

I don't have a chance to blink before he wraps his fingers around my upper arm and pulls me into the center of the room. He rips the door open and disappears, but not before he slams his hand on the light switch, filling the room with blinding light. I squint, covering my eyes with my hand but I soon realize my mistake because he wasn't just trying to blind me, he was allowing everyone out in the backyard to see what was happening inside the room.

Multiple sets of eyes zero in on me before they start laughing. I rush to cover myself up, but I fear I'm not quick enough and end up flashing every Rosewood student who's out in Ethan's backyard right now.

"Oh my God," I mutter to myself, hiding behind the fireplace and sliding down the wall until my ass hits the floor.

It can't be two minutes later when the door to whatever room I'm inside flies open and Poppy and Harley come racing toward me.

"What the hell happened?" Harley asks in a rush, her face softening when she sees the state of my tear-stained face.

"N-nothing," I whisper, really not wanting to relive what I just went through,

"Nothing? One minute you were disappearing off with Justin, then the next we hear is that you're..." She thankfully trails off. None of us need her to reiterate what just happened.

"Where'd he go?" a deep voice demands as Zayn steps up behind Harley, his jaw tight with tension.

"Justin didn't do anything," I say with a sigh.

"Okay, so who..." Harley gasps. "Oh my God, it was him."

"Who's him?" Zayn asks. I look to Poppy and smile at her in appreciation for her not spilling everything to her boyfriend. She returns my smile and wraps her arm around my shoulders in support.

"N-no one. It doesn't matter."

"Ruby, I don't think—"

"Zayn, please," Poppy says softly. "Just leave it, yeah? If Ruby needs you to fight for her, then she'll ask for it."

"That's bullshit," he complains as more people fill the room, because I'm not already mortified enough.

"What's going on?" Ethan asks, his eyes drilling into the top of my head.

"N-nothing. It's nothing. Excuse me." I push to stand, ready to barge through all of them.

"We should go home," Harley says, slipping her hand into mine.

"No," I bark. "I refuse to cower down to that asshole." I slam my lips shut the second I realize I've just confirmed who it was, but I don't think it really matters, Harley and Poppy were already well aware.

"Who? Who's an asshole?" Ethan adds, sounding almost as protective as Zayn.

I step up to both of them and look between them. "While I appreciate your support. I can fight my own battles."

Zayn's lips part to say something he soon decides against it when Poppy steps up to me.

"Rae," Harley says. "Could you help us out?"

"Sure thing. Follow me."

Five minutes later, I find myself sitting on the edge of Rae's bed with a fresh drink in hand while Harley fixes my hair.

"You ever sleep in here?" Harley asks Rae as she works.

"Yeah, sometimes we mix it up a bit and come in here."

"So it's just your shag pad?"

Rae laughs. "Yeah, something like that."

The second I've finished my drink, Poppy refills my cup.

"You gonna tell us what he did yet?"

I shake my head. "He's just... angry."

"That's not your problem though."

"Who are we talking about here?" Rae asks.

Poppy and Harley both look at me, waiting to see if I want to confess before they say anything.

"My stepbrother," I whisper.

"Oh," she says with a laugh. "Yeah, they can be a real pain in the ass," she says with a knowing wink. Technically, she and Ethan aren't stepsiblings seeing their parents aren't married but they're as good as, so if anyone has any advice for me on this subject then I guess it would be her. "Word of advice?" she asks, and I nod, needing anything she can give me. "Don't back down. Give as good as you get and prove that you're stronger than he thinks."

I let out a sigh, unsure if I've got it in me to go up against him. He's not even started at Rosewood yet, and he's already embarrassed me in front of everyone I've grown up with.

"How?" I ask hesitantly.

"By drinking that." She nods at the cup in my hand. "Letting Harley make you look even more beautiful than you were when you first arrived and walking out there holding your head up high."

I nod at her.

"Word has it that Justin's asking about you," Poppy says.

"Like he's going to want me after that," I mutter.

"Don't be so sure. You're hot, girl. Any guy would be lucky to spend time with you," Harley says, coming around to my front to start fixing my makeup. "And if they don't, I'll dance with you." She winks and I can't help but laugh.

"Thank you," I say to the three of them.

With them flanking my sides thirty minutes later, I somehow find enough confidence to return to the party as though nothing happened. It might be their support, or it might be the copious amounts of vodka they supplied me with. But whatever it was, I walk back into that party with my head held high. So what, some of my classmates got a look at too much of me? It's nothing compared to most of the senior cheer squad and everyone still wants them so...

"Who's the cutie?" I ask Harley when the guy she was dancing with earlier notices our approach. His face lights up as he locks eyes on her, and he immediately gravitates toward us.

"Justin's cousin, Nathan. He goes to Maddison Prep. He's cute, right?"

"Really cute."

She steps into him and he leans down to whisper something in her ear.

"Hey," Justin says, stepping to me. "Wanna dance?" He smiles down at me and just like that, everything is okay again.

I slip my hand into his, and he tugs me into his body.

My front collides with his, my arms lift over his shoulders as his hands slide down my back until he grips on to my ass. I'm momentarily reminded that I'm no longer wearing any panties, but with the vodka racing through my veins and the music filling my ears, I can't find it in me to care.

I look up at Justin and he flashes me one of his winning smiles before dropping his lips to mine. I hesitate for a second, suddenly aware that he could still be watching, but then I realize that he has no power over me. I'm my own woman and I owe him nothing.

He thinks he can walk around doing whatever he wants, then so can I.

9

ASHTON

I should have left the party after walking away from her, but the second I stepped outside I walked into a cloud of weed and I found myself joining the guys who were passing around a joint.

I've no idea what happened to Ruby, but I did hear everyone talking about what happened.

Part of me felt bad. Only a small part though. Most of me just smiled as I thought back to her standing there with her dress around her waist like a little slut while her underwear was in my pocket.

My cock swells once more as I think about just how damp her panties were when I ripped them from her body.

She can tell me all she likes that she doesn't want me, but her body tells a very different story.

I take the hit when it's offered to me before passing it on and pushing from the lounger I was resting back in. I was expecting someone to at least ask who I was, but it seems no one really gives a shit.

Draining the rest of my bottle, I head inside for a new one to take with me on the walk home. I've achieved what I came for, I'm fed up with being surrounded by people now.

"Hey, gorgeous. I haven't seen you in Rosewood before." A warm hand slides down my back as I reach the kitchen counter.

"Oh yeah, what makes you say that?" I almost growl as I turn around to find a blonde standing before me in a dress that's almost smaller than Ruby's.

"I'd remember your face," she purrs, her hand now trailing up my abs.

"Why's that?" I ask, dropping my lips to her ear. "Is it one you'd want to sit on?"

If she's shocked by my words, then she doesn't show it. Instead, she pulls back to look into my eyes.

"I'm Krissy, by the way, and I think I need to dance with you."

"Is that right?" I glance down the hall to where everyone is still dancing and I spot a flash of Ruby's dress, only it's not just her dress because that motherfucker has his hands all over her.

"Sounds like a great idea, lead the way."

I smile down at her as I might actually be interested and allow her to pull me out of the kitchen and down to where everyone is grinding away.

The second she comes to a stop, her hands slide up my chest and the length of her body presses against mine. But I don't feel any of it, I'm too busy staring at Ruby who's got her tongue in that motherfucker's mouth.

A growl rumbles up my throat with my need to go and rip him away from her, but my new dance partner seems to take it a different way.

"I think me and you could get on really well tonight," she purrs, her lips only a breath from mine.

"You don't even know my name."

"Huh, I guess I do need to know what to scream."

My eyes narrow slightly at her. I guess at least she owns what kind of girl she is.

The side of my face burns and when I look over, I find exactly what I was expecting. Ruby has unattached herself from her little friend and is glaring daggers at the girl in my arms.

A smile twitches my lips at the thought of managing to find a girl that's on her squad. I really, really hope they're friends. That can only work in my favor. I saw the way she almost combusted when I spoke to the girl in our kitchen, and I didn't so much as touch her.

This girl, though. Krystal or whatever her name was, she seems more than willing to play my game.

"It's Ashton, baby. And you can scream it all night long if you wish."

She grinds her hips against mine. If she's expecting to find me turned on by her then she's about to be bitterly disappointed. She's going to need to do more than breathe around me to make me even a little interested in what she has to offer.

The girl shooting hate glares at me though, one look and she stirs something inside me she really shouldn't.

"Now that sounds like a plan I can get on board with," she whispers in my ear before licking her tongue around the edge. I shudder, but it's not for the reason she would like, I'm sure.

My hands slide down her back until I grab on to her ass, pressing her tighter to my body as we dance together.

"I'm not sure I like having all these others around. You wanna go somewhere a little quieter, get to know each other a little better?" she almost moans in my ear.

My eyes lift to Ruby once more and the second I see that fuck's tongue slip into her mouth, I step away from the blonde, take her hand in mine and drag her from the room, ensuring I lock eyes with Ruby before I disappear with my little friend.

10

RUBY

"Let's get out of here," Poppy shouts in my ear, distracting me from watching Ashton pull Krissy from the room.

"I… um…" I look to the empty doorway and up to an expectant looking Justin.

Something heavy settles in the pit of my stomach. I never should have come back after my time with Ash. I should have just gone running back to Harley's with my tail between my legs.

"Y-yeah, okay. Is Harley coming?" I look over Poppy's shoulder for our friend and eventually find her dancing with the same guy.

"Yeah, she's just saying goodbye to Nathan."

Five minutes later and I'm climbing into the back of Zayn's car, although Zayn is nowhere to be seen.

"I can't believe my brother is letting you drive his car."

"He likes me taking his things for a ride," Poppy says with a laugh while Harley groans and folds her body into the seat as if she wants it to swallow her whole.

"Please, I'm begging you. Stop."

"So, tell us about Nathan," I say, poking my slightly fuzzy head through the gap in the seats and staring at Harley, glad that they haven't turned their inquisition on me. I'm well aware that they have yet to straight-up demand to know what Ash did to me earlier, but as much as I appreciate that, I know I'm only on borrowed time.

"He was so sweet," she swoons, her eyes going all soft and pathetic. It's a look I've never seen on her before but with the smile that's playing on her lips, I quickly realize that it's one I want to see more of.

"Did you get his number?" Poppy asks.

"I did. We're going to meet tomorrow."

"Eeek!" Poppy squeals. "That's so exciting."

"Who'd have thought it, Harley Hunter with a prep boy?"

"Oh shush. He's not like that."

"Did he drag you into the nearest room and get you off minutes after you met him?"

"Well, no. But he did kiss me before I left."

"Exactly. He's a prep boy, a proper gentleman, not like the idiots we go to school with."

"You realize your boyfriend is one of the idiots we go to school with."

"I do. There isn't anything gentleman-like about Zayn, let me tell you." I spot Poppy's eyebrows wiggling in the rearview mirror before Harley starts begging her to stop.

"Tell me later, yeah," I say, slapping Poppy gently on the shoulder.

"Sure thing. He does this thing with his tongue..." Poppy bursts out laughing when Harley groans once more. "I'm kidding, I'm kidding... kind of."

"So, you're seeing him tomorrow? What's the plan? Where are you meeting him? You gonna kiss him again?"

"I don't know. He said he'd message in the morning, but he's in town until early evening. Anyway, enough about me. Are you going to tell us what went down with Ash tonight and why he ended up leaving with motormouth Krissy?"

I groan, falling back into my seat.

"I have not had enough to drink to relive it yet. But I think we all know why he willingly dragged her out of the room."

"You think he'd let her suck him off when he's blatantly only hard for you?" Harley asks, making me wince.

"Two things," I mutter, holding up two fingers, but with my blurry vodka-induced vision it looks like I'm holding up four. "One... he's not hard for me. He fucking hates me and would rather throw me out to sea and watch me drown than he would put his cock anywhere near me. And two... umm..." I hesitate when I totally forget where I was going. "Oh yeah. Krissy is a whore."

"Amen," Harley sings, lifting a bottle of vodka that I didn't know she'd snatched on the way out. "Those bitches give us cheer girls a bad name."

Poppy's eyes meet mine in the mirror once more and I read her silent thoughts loud and clear, and I can't help but agree. I haven't exactly been acting much better than them in the past few months.

The three of us pile out of Zayn's car and stumble toward the front door. Jada is home, her car is parked in the driveway and the lights are on, but as we stagger through the kitchen for snacks, we don't see any sign of her. It's probably a good thing, Poppy is the only sober one out of the three of us right now, but if the way she's tipping the bottle she's taken from Harley to her lips is anything to go by, then she won't be for long.

"Don't you have to go back and get Zayn?" I ask when she swallows down another shot.

"Nah, he's gonna make his own way home. I told him that I'm hanging with my girls. Gotta make sure lil' Rubes is okay." She wraps her arm around my shoulder as we start climbing the stairs.

"I'm good. You don't need to worry about me."

We pile into Harley's room and Poppy and Harley immediately flop onto the bed, surrounded by the bags of chips and candy we'd swiped from downstairs. I, on the other hand, go straight for my bag and pull out a pair of panties.

The girls chat away behind me until I step into them and begin pulling them up my legs.

"Rubes, what happened to the pair you left wearing?"

"Err..."

"Oh my God," Harley squeals. "*He* has them, doesn't he?"

"I wonder if Krissy has any idea that he's got another girl's panties in his pocket while she goes—"

"Whoa," I cry, not needing to hear the next words from Poppy's mouth.

"You can't not tell us what... *went down* now." Harley flashes me a shit-eating grin as she says this.

"Yeah, yeah I can," I mutter, stripping out of my dress and pulling on a tank and pair of sleep shorts.

"We not going to mention that the bra is gone too?" Poppy murmurs as I walk back over and take the bottle from her hand, downing at least four shots in one go.

"No, none of it needs talking about."

"He got you off though, right? You at least got something out of that fucked-up situation?"

"No, Harley, he didn't," I snap. "He's a sadomasochistic who seems to get off on torturing me and walking away."

"But last time he..."

"Last time I passed out and have no fucking clue how it ended." His words as he explained about having images from that night ring in my ears as if he's saying them to me right now.

"What? What's that look for?"

"It's for nothing other than how much I fucking hate him. Krissy is welcome to him."

I flop onto the bed, open a packet of chips and shove a handful into my mouth in the hope they stop asking me questions that I don't want to answer.

"Do I look hot enough?" Harley asks, spinning in front of the mirror and looking over her outfit of choice ready to go and meet Nathan down at the beach.

"Harley," I sigh. "You always look hot."

"Argh... I don't know. Am I showing enough skin, too much skin? I don't want him to think I'm a cheer slut."

"Then maybe don't drag him into the nearest dark corner and offer to suck him off." I don't mean for the words to come out sounding quite so bitter, and I hate that they give away my true feelings for what happened last night.

Harley raises a brow at me as Poppy slips into the room. She was here when I fell into a vodka-induced coma last night, but I'm assuming she slipped out to join Zayn at some point in the night.

"Hey, what's going on?" she asks, looking between Harley and me, clearly wondering what the sudden tension is about.

"Just trying to convince Harley that she's hot and that prep boy will dig her outfit."

"You are hot. He'll love it. Now go, or he won't get the chance to because he'll think you've stood him up."

"You gonna be okay?" She shoots me a look.

"Yes, Mom. I'll be fine. I've got a ton of homework to do, so I plan on hiding in my room until practice in the morning."

She rolls her eyes at me as she slips her feet into her sneakers and grabs her purse.

"Call me later, I want to know everything."

"I will. Laters."

She waves at us before disappearing out of the room and down the stairs.

"She's so nervous. It's cute."

"It is. Ugh," I groan, dropping back onto Harley's bed.

"What's wrong?"

"I want a nice boy who wants to date me and take me to the beach."

"Wanna know a secret?" Poppy asks, sliding her legs under the covers and settling in beside me.

"Sure. You can tell me all your dirty ones now Harley's gone."

"You got it," she says with a laugh. "First thing you need to know though..." She pauses, I'm assuming to build tension. "Bad boys do it better."

I can't help but snort a laugh at the seriousness of her tone.

"Because you've been with all the good ones to know this."

"Don't need to. It's a fact."

I laugh and it feels good just let go with my friend.

"What the hell am I going to do, Pops?"

She stills for a beat before turning to look at me. "Is he a real threat, you know, like..." She trails off, not wanting to say the prick's name who secretly tormented her for years without any of us knowing the severity of it.

"No, this isn't like that. He just wants to torment me. He thinks all of this is my fault or some bullshit. I mean, really, I wasn't the one who forced Stephen to leave his mom and hook up with mine, and I certainly didn't have anything to do with his car accident."

"I know you didn't but try to put yourself in his shoes. You're the easy target. He might be an asshole to both your parents, but he can't really do much to them. Plus, you're hot, any hot-blooded teenage boy would want a taste given the chance."

"He doesn't want me, Pops. He just wants to torture me."

"In the most delicious way."

"This isn't some fucked-up foreplay that's going to lead to a hot night of sex, Pops."

"Isn't it?" she asks, deadly serious.

"No. I'm not sleeping with him. He's a prick and doesn't deserve anything from me, especially not my V-card."

"So why have you held on to it this long? You've had most of the team wrapped around your little finger for months, you could have given it up to any of them, yet you haven't. You're waiting for someone, Ruby, and I think deep down it's him."

"Do you know what I think?"

"Hit me with it."

"I think that's Zayn's given you one too many orgasms and you've lost your freaking mind."

"Do you know, if that's true then I don't even care."

I laugh with her. "I'm so happy for you, Pops," I admit after a few minutes.

"Miracles do happen, right?"

"To some people, for sure. Right now, I just need to focus on cheer, on nationals and surviving Ash."

"You do what you need to do, but promise me something."

"Sure."

"Make sure you really make him work for it."

"Pops, I've already said I'm not—"

"Want to go to Aces? We can see if we can spy on the happy couple," she interrupts.

"Yes," I hiss excitedly. "Let me shower and we'll go. But then I really have to go home," I say sadly.

"You've got this, Rubes. You're stronger than you think."

We spend the rest of the morning hanging out at Aces. I was half expecting the team to show up at some point but they never did, and aside from a few others from school at another table, we were left alone to catch up or should I say mostly talk about Zayn. With Harley gone, Poppy was able to talk a little more openly about her new relationship.

The pair of them are so sweet it's sickening, but I'm incredibly happy for both of them. Hearing her talk about the future as if she actually has a shot at one is everything.

But as the time ticks on, my anxiety about having to go home grows more and more and by the time I drop Poppy off at the Hunter's, the ball of dread filling my stomach is the only thing I can think about.

When I pull up outside my house, I find Mom's car in the driveway but Stephen's is gone, telling me they're not back yet, and beside it is Ashton's bike.

"Fuck," I breathe. Any hope I had that he might not be here is shattered.

Mustering up as much courage as I can, I pull my bags from the trunk and hold my head high as I open the front door and walk inside. This is my home. I refuse to allow his presence to ruin that for me.

I only make it four steps at the most when he emerges from the kitchen, a can of soda in hand and just a pair of low-hanging sweats on his insanely ripped body.

I roll my eyes at myself.

Why couldn't he have at least been ugly?

He startles when he sees me, obviously he didn't hear my arrival. It takes me a few seconds, but I soon realize he's wearing a pair of AirPods.

His eyes drop from mine in favor of my body and one side of his lips curl up in a smirk as he stares at me as if I'm as naked as I was before him last night.

Tension crackles between us as I will my body to move but I'm frozen under his stare.

My heart pounds and my chest heaves. I hate that he can probably read every one of my reactions to him. I need to be better at covering this shit up.

As he closes the space between us, he sucks all the air out of the small space. By the time he's right in front of me, his fresh, manly scent filling my nose, I've totally stopped breathing.

His eyes hold mine for a beat before they drop to my lips. His tongue sneaks out and licks across his full bottom one, but just as I think he's going to do something, he spins on his heels and starts running up the stairs without saying a fucking word.

The second he's out of sight, I suck in a huge steadying breath and drop my bags to the floor.

Walking through to the kitchen, I grab enough drinks and snacks so that I don't have to leave my room for the rest of the afternoon before heading up to my bedroom.

As I pass his door, the first boom of his music fills the house. *Decided against the AirPods now then? Of course you have.*

I slam my door with as much force as I can muster. It rattles the house but with the volume of his music, I doubt he even realized I did it.

Fucking asshole.

The music continues all afternoon and no matter how loud I make mine, the offensive beat of his shitty rap always overrules mine.

I try to get my homework done but every few minutes my mind wanders. I think back over the night before, over our brief but intense exchange downstairs earlier, but mostly I wonder what he's doing just on the other side of the wall.

He knows no one here—aside from Krissy—he has no schoolwork or anything to do. What is he doing?

My need to know almost has me off my bed and walking to his door to find out more than once, but I know it would be stupid of me to put myself inside the lion's den again.

I just need to keep my head down, stay out of his way, and hope he finds something else to distract himself with. Once again, the image I've conjured up of Krissy on her knees before him pops into my head and I shake it away. Nothing good can come from picturing them together. I don't even know why I'm thinking about it. It's not like I really care.

The sun is just about set when my bedroom door flies open. Ripping my eyes from the paper I was working on—finally able to find some focus—I expect to find him standing there having come up with some new way to torture me but instead when my eyes land on the doorway, I find my mom standing there with her arms crossed over her chest and her face red like she's about to explode.

"Mom?"

"You've got some explaining to do, young lady," she snaps, her eyes narrowing in my direction.

I turn my music down and I swear, Ashton's also gets quieter at the same time.

"I'm sorry, I'm not sure—"

"Have a good night last night, did you?"

"Um... yeah, I guess. Why?" I ask, wracking my brain for what the hell I've done to piss her off to the point I can see a vein pulsating at her temple. I'm pretty sure I've never seen that before.

"Like you don't know," she says with an unamused laugh.

"Uh... I really don't."

"Care to come and explain this then." She disappears from my sight before I have a chance to ask her what the hell is going on.

Scrambling off my bed, I follow her down the hall, my brows pinching when I find her standing in her own bedroom doorway at the other end of the house with her hands on her hips.

"Mom, what the... oh," I breathe, taking in the sight before me.

"You had sex in our bed," Mom squeals like a woman possessed.

"What? No, no, I didn't."

"Well, that's not what this looks like."

My eyes take in the scene before me, and I can't deny that it really does look like I had sex in here. The bedsheets are a mess and half on the floor, there are condom wrappers and—ew—even a condom on the floor. In the middle of the bed is my underwear from last night.

"No, no, no. I didn't even sleep here last night. I left first thing yesterday morning and—"

"I don't want to hear your excuses. I expected more from you, Ruby. I thought you had some respect for us." Disappointment drips from her words and despite the fact I know I didn't do this, tears burn my eyes. I hate disappointing her, even when I haven't.

"Mom, I didn't. Jesus, I'm a virgin for Christ's sake." I have no idea if she hears me as she thunders down the stairs, but I don't think it really matters. She's pegged me as guilty already.

A tingle of awareness runs down my spine, telling me that although Mom might not have just heard my parting words, someone else didn't miss them.

"Virgin, huh?"

His deep voice rumbles through me and my teeth grind as I try to refrain from flying at him and gouging his eyes out.

"You think this is f-funny?" I shout, turning to look at him. I want to appear strong but the second my eyes land on inches of toned naked skin once again my words falter a little.

Fucking hell, Ruby, get it together. You are better than this asshole.

A wicked smile pulls at his lips. "Yeah, actually. It is kinda funny, even more so now I know the truth. Am I the only one who's gotten between your legs, little one?" His brow rises as his smirk grows.

"I'm not having this conversation with you."

"No? Too busy tidying up your mess."

"It's not my mess," I seethe.

"Funny, because it looks like your underwear in their bed."

"Yeah, that you stole from me."

"That I *stripped* from you," he corrects me, pushing from the doorframe and stalking toward me. "That I stripped from you when you were begging me to touch you."

I don't move, refusing to be bullied into submission by this asshole. Instead, all I do is lift my chin so I can keep eye contact with him as he crowds my small body with his huge one.

"I never begged for anything," I spit.

"Hmm... maybe I was imagining that part. I do, however, know that you were fucking soaked for me, little one. One touch, and you were like putty in my hands."

"I was drunk," I argue.

"Are you drunk now?" His hand wraps around my throat and my back collides with our parents' doorframe.

"No, and all I want you to do is leave me alone."

"Are you sure about that?"

"Fucking positive." My eyes narrow at him but all he does is laugh.

"You're such a shit liar, Ruby."

"I fucking hate you," I seethe.

"Doesn't stop you wanting me though, does it?" He takes a step back from me. "Now, tidy up your mess. It makes you look like a slut."

"Says the one who had Krissy between his legs last night," I mutter, but when his eyes light up with amusement and his smile widens, I know I made a mistake.

He cups his junk as he continues walking backward to his room.

"Yeah, and she fucking loved it."

He nods his chin at me once in dismissal before he disappears into his room, slams the door, and cranks his music up once more.

"You're a fucking asshole, Ashton Fury."

11

RUBY

Once I've tidied up Mom and Stephen's bedroom, complete with changing the sheets—despite the fact it's totally unnecessary—I lock myself in my bedroom and don't leave again.

Mom must be really pissed because she doesn't even come to offer me any dinner, despite the fact I smell it cooking. I have no idea if Ashton goes down to eat and I tell myself over and over that I don't care.

I get all my homework done before having a two-hour-long video chat with Harley where she tells me how amazing her date with Nathan was and I refrain from telling her anything that's happened over the past few hours. I don't want to think about it, let alone talk about it. I just want to focus on school and cheer and forget that anything else exists right now. He'll be heading back to Seattle in a few days and I'll get a little reprieve. Hopefully, that'll be the time he needs to get his head on straight and come back ready to start school, and more importantly, leave me alone. He needs his own life that doesn't revolve around tormenting me. As much as I hate the thought of him starting at Rosewood High and potentially trying out for the team, at least it should distract him.

I'm ready to go at the crack of dawn Monday morning, my need to get away from him and out of the house means I almost jump out of bed when my alarm goes off.

I throw myself into practice and then school, forgetting about the fact I'm going to have to face the music at some point. Mom can't exactly avoid me forever.

Her car is already in the drive when I pull up after our afternoon practice, something that doesn't happen very often.

"Hey," I say, somewhat awkwardly as I step into the kitchen.

"Good day?" she asks like normal, but there's a harshness to her tone that's not usually there. A huge part of me wants to plead my innocence, but that's going to lead to explaining why Ashton had my underwear in the first place and I am not going there. The less I say, the less Mom and Stephen will need to have a look closer at Ash's and my relationship, the better.

"Yeah, it was okay. You finish work early?" I ask, grabbing a soda from the refrigerator.

"I've got the week off for the funeral, actually."

"Ah, makes sense," I mutter. "When are you going?"

"Our flight is at six a.m. Shouldn't be an issue for you as you're used to getting up that early, but it'll be a shock for the rest of us."

"M-me?" I stutter, not liking where this is going.

"Yeah. You're coming to Seattle too."

"I-I can't. I've got cheer. Nationals are the weekend after next. I can't miss practice."

"This isn't up for discussion, Ruby. We're going as a family to support Ashton. I've already informed school that you'll be missing the rest of the week."

"But—"

"His mom died, Ruby. I expected more of you."

My lips part to argue more, but what can I say to that. She's right. No matter how I might feel about my stepbrother. He's just lost his mom and he deserves the support of his family.

Letting out a sigh, I spin and head out of the kitchen. "I'm going out."

"I'll plate up dinner and you can warm it when you're back."

"Thanks, Mom."

I don't even bother taking my bags up to my room, instead, I dump them back into my car and drop down into the driver's seat.

Resting my head back, I close my eyes and blow out a calming breath.

I don't want to miss practice so close to nationals. I don't want to go to Seattle, and I certainly don't want to spend any more time with Ashton than necessary, but it seems I have little choice in any of it.

Pulling my eyes open, I intend on starting my car and getting out of here, but the second I open my eyes, they find his in the window I was standing at the day he arrived.

Jesus, how was that only a few days ago? It feels like he's been here forever, terrorizing me.

Ripping my eyes from his haunting stare, I put my car in reverse and fly from the house.

I don't really have a destination in mind. I could go to Harley's, but I don't really want to talk, I just want silence. Something that's been eluding me since he arrived.

In the end, I pull up in the parking lot by Aces and walk down to the beach.

The sun is starting to set and there's a chill in the air, but I pull an oversized hoodie from the back of my car and wrap it around myself before I find a secluded spot on the dry sand and sit down and pull my knees up to my chest.

I sit there for the longest time enjoying the peace and quiet, lost in my own thoughts just watching the waves crash up on the beach.

"Hey," a familiar voice says, dragging my eyes from the ocean.

Looking up, I find Stella staring down at me.

"Mind if I join you?"

Part of me wants to say yes, that I came here to be alone, but there's something about her sad expression that makes me say the opposite.

"Sure, although I should warn you that I'm not much company right now."

"Me either," she says, dropping down beside me.

"Want to talk about it?" I offer, thinking that someone else's drama might just be what I need right now.

"Yes and no. I don't know," she sighs. "I think we might be moving again."

"Again? You've only been here like—"

"Two months, I know. I'm so sick of moving around," she groans, dropping her head into her hands.

"Where to this time?"

"I don't know, I stormed out the second my dad mentioned it. I just want to stay somewhere and graduate, you know?"

I nod, although, really, I've no idea. The farthest I've moved is three blocks when Mom and I moved out of the house we shared with Dad and into the house we now live in with Stephen.

"What about you? You want to talk about it?"

"Just family stuff. I've got to go to Seattle for a funeral in the morning."

"But practice..."

"Yeah, exactly. I didn't really think I'd have to go, but I can't really refuse. I'm just being selfish and sulking."

"How long are you going for?"

I shrug, realizing that I probably should have asked that question. "The funeral is Friday so all week I guess, I don't know."

"You'll be fine. You know what you're doing. You kill the routines every time."

"I want to be here though."

"I know, but you'll be back in time. Don't sweat it."

"I'm sure you're right."

We sit there a while longer before the cold starts to get the better of me.

"You hungry?"

"Uh, yeah actually."

"Aces?"

"Burger and fries? Sounds perfect."

Before I know it, my alarm clock is going off even earlier than usual, but unlike every other day, there is movement in the house as everyone else gets up ready for our flight.

I didn't see anyone when I got in last night, but I did find that Mom had forwarded me the flight itinerary so at least I know how many days I'm packing for.

"Ruby, are you ready to go?" Mom calls through as I'm zipping up my case.

"Yeah, I'm coming now."

I wait until the very last minute to emerge from the safety of my bedroom.

Mom and Stephen are waiting for me with tense expressions on their faces, but Ashton is nowhere to be seen. I could have sworn I heard him moving around this morning.

"Where's Ash?" I ask, looking between the two of them.

"In the car. Are you ready?" Mom asks.

"Y-yeah."

"Great. Give Stephen your case and get in the car."

"I-is everything okay?" I ask, feeling uneasy about the tension crackling around both of them.

"Yeah, I'm sure everything will be fine."

"Okay," I mutter, turning my back on them and doing as I'm told.

Ashton is in the back of the car when I pull the door open, but he doesn't so much as flinch when I climb in the other side of him, let alone look my way or greet me. The only thing I get is a lungful of stale, second-hand weed. I guess that answers my question about how he's feeling about all of this then.

In only a few seconds, Stephen has my case in the trunk and Mom has locked up the house.

The atmosphere in the car is horrendous as Stephen backs out of the drive. I crack my window a little despite how cold it is outside in my need for some fresh air.

The journey to the airport is only about forty-five minutes, but with the tension pressing down on us, it feels like a lifetime later when we finally pull up in the parking lot.

I have no idea that anything is wrong until we get to the front of the check-in line.

"There are going to be long delays on your flight to Tacoma, have you been watching the news?"

"Yes," Mom and Stephen say simultaneously.

"The news, what's going on?"

"There's been a terror threat."

My eyes almost bug out of my head. "At Tacoma?"

"Yeah."

"And we're still going?"

"It's Leanora's funeral, Ruby. We have to."

"It's not until Friday. Surely there are other flights, other airports?"

"These were the only seats I could get."

"Jesus," I mutter to myself. Could this trip actually get any worse?

"How long are they expecting the delays to be?" Mom asks the lady behind the desk.

"Right now, we have no idea. It could be nothing or it could be hours."

"Well, let's keep everything crossed that it's the former."

I want to protest, but much like when I found out about this trip, I can't.

We check-in and Ashton—who's been silent this entire time—and I trail behind our parents as we go through security and go to find somewhere to eat breakfast.

I keep an eye on the news app on my phone, but nothing seems to change, just that there's a bomb threat but at no point does the status of our flight change.

"How long are we really going to sit here waiting?" I finally ask almost three hours later and an hour and a half after our flight was scheduled to take off.

"As long as it takes. We have to get to Seattle," Stephen says.

"I appreciate that, but there has to be another way. Can't we get a transfer somewhere else or something? This is crazy."

"Just give it a little while longer, sweetie. I'm sure it'll all be sorted soon."

I roll my eyes at Mom's positivity and order myself another coffee, although I'm not sure any that are on offer are going to be strong enough for what I need right now.

"This is bullshit." It's the first thing Ashton has said all morning, aside from ordering food and drinks. I was starting to think he'd taken a vow of silence or something.

"I couldn't agree more," I mutter, much to my mom's horror.

"If you want to sit around here wasting time, then be my guests, but I'm done."

"Ashton, you can't go. The funeral," Stephen says in a panic.

"We're going to miss it if we keep sitting around here wasting time."

I refrain from pointing out that it's still days away, I'm not sure he'd appreciate my input right now.

He pushes to stand before locking eyes with Stephen.

"Car keys," he demands, holding his hand out.

"Son, what are you—"

"Can I have your car keys?"

"What—"

"I'm going to fucking drive, okay? I'll get there quicker than you all at this rate."

"Y-you can't drive all the way there on your own. That's crazy," Mom points out.

"Why? I drove here alone. I'm more than capable."

"I know, but you shouldn't have to."

"Are you going to volunteer to come with me?" Ashton asks, but exactly like I'm sure he was expecting, Mom's lips slam shut. "No, I didn't think so."

"Just sit down, Ash. You're talking crazy."

"No, I'm going. I can't just sit here."

"You can't go alone."

"Fine, I'll take Ruby."

"Um... w-what?" I almost spray a mouthful of coffee across the table.

"You're coming with me."

"Uh... I really don't think—"

"I wasn't asking," he warns me, his voice low and quiet enough that our parents can't hear over the noise of the airport. "You're coming with me."

I look to Stephen and Mom, but they just stare at Ashton like he's lost his mind, which of course I agree with.

"Keys," he demands of Stephen once more and this time, he reluctantly hands them over.

"Great," he says, grabbing my hand. "Let's go, enjoy your long wait."

I just have time to grab my takeout coffee cup as he drags me from my chair and pulls me toward the exit of the airport.

"Ash, what the hell are you doing? This is freaking crazy," I shriek behind him.

He abruptly stops and turns to me. His eyes are cold and hard like usual, but there's also something else in them, something that I've never seen before.

He sucks in a breath and looks away from me for a beat, but whatever he sees clearly pushes him to say whatever it is he's thinking because his eyes come back to mine and his expression softens.

"I was a disappointment all her life, I can't fuck this up and miss my last chance to say goodbye to her."

12

ASHTON

I watch the fight drain from her as the words spill from my lips, and despite being glad I got her on board—kind of—I also regret them instantly.

I don't want her to understand me, to see the level of pain this is causing me, but I couldn't fucking sit there staring at our parents' positive faces. I couldn't deal with the fact that I put my chances of attending my own mother's funeral in the hands of some airport staff and some possible terrorists at the other end.

There is no question about me being there on Friday. I'll make damn sure of it.

Squeezing Dad's keys in my hand so tightly they bite into my skin, I take Ruby's hand once again in my other and resume pulling her back out of the airport, assuming that she's now on board.

Do I want to drive all the way to Seattle with her by my side? No, not really. But if we're going to make it, then I need someone else to be able to take the wheel for a bit. And as much as she might drive me crazy, she's the lesser of the evils because there is no way I'm spending that many hours with my dad or Lisa.

At least Ruby isn't delusional. She knows how I feel about her, and she doesn't shy away from her own contempt for me.

We don't have to talk, we don't have to even look at each other. We just need to co-exist for a few hours without killing each other. I'm sure that's totally doable.

Thirty minutes later, we've both got a fresh coffee and a bag full of snacks and we're climbing back into Dad's car, only the front this time.

I look around the dash. Safe to say I've never driven anything this fancy before.

"Please tell me you know how to drive a car."

"Yes," I hiss through clenched teeth. "Yeah, I even have a license."

"Somehow that's not as reassuring as I was hoping for."

I turn to look at her but immediately wished I hadn't. Her hair is pulled back in a messy bun with tendrils falling around her clear face. All the makeup has been washed away, leaving her with flawless pale skin and a smattering of freckles over her nose. Her eyes look greener without the distraction of the makeup and if it's possible, her lips fuller.

"What?" she snaps, dragging me from my trance.

"N-nothing."

"Ash," she sighs. "I don't want to be here, so if you're just going to be a dick the entire time, tell me now and I'll find my way home." Her brow quirks in defiance and it has something igniting inside of me.

I bite down on my bottom lip in the hope of squashing it, or at least not allowing her to see it.

"You're going nowhere, little one."

She sits back with a huff and folds her arms over her chest. "As I expected. We doing this shit then?"

"Sure are. Hold on, little one. You're in for a wild ride."

She rolls her eyes at me as I start the car but she doesn't say anything else.

It's probably a good thing because the thought of getting her in the back seat of this car to shut her up could be the distraction from reality that I need right now.

With the GPS set to my old home, I floor it out of the parking lot before we hit the highway.

She silently sips her coffee beside me as my synced cell works its way through my favorite playlist. One I think she hates, based on the fact she tells me to turn it down every single time it's on.

I smile to myself at the thought of her standing in my doorway with her hands on her hips.

"Something funny?" she asks, making me realize that she's more aware of my presence beside her than I gave her credit for.

"Yeah, you."

"And here I was thinking you couldn't stand the sight of me."

"Oh, I can't." She flinches at my harsh words and it only makes me smile wider. "It doesn't mean I can't laugh at you though."

"Yeah, I bet you were fucking pissing yourself while I was picking up condoms from our parents' bedroom floor."

"Yeah, I never know quite how to dispose of those things..."

"Ugh, you are so gross," she complains. "I used gloves just in case, but please tell me you hadn't... you know..."

"Used them to fuck Krissy seven ways from Sunday?"

"Oh my God," she mutters, dropping her face into her hands. "You know, you two suit each other. She's a slut and you're a dog. Match made in heaven."

"Aw, you think I'm cute."

"W-what? Where did you get that from?"

"You called me a dog, and there is no one on the planet who doesn't think dogs are cute, so..." I trail off, gesturing to myself.

"There's something wrong with you. It was a fucking insult."

"Meh, she was worth the insult from you."

"I bet she was, she's had enough damn practice."

I can't help but bark out a laugh at Ruby's muttered words.

"Jealous, little miss virgin?"

"Of Krissy Motormouth Venter? Absolutely not. I know exactly where she's been." She runs her eyes down my body, lingering on my crotch for a few seconds too long.

My body heats at her attention. "You seem a little too intrigued for someone who's not interested."

"You're wearing sweats. It's like inviting women to stare."

"Maybe I am. Maybe I planned this whole thing just so we could drive together, and you could stare at my cock."

"Right. I think I preferred it when you were ignoring me."

"That can be arranged. You should probably get some sleep anyway, you're going to have to take over at some point."

"I never agreed to drive."

"You never disagreed. If we're going to get there in time, then we need to drive through the night."

"I should be at school right now."

"Nah, little one. I think you're exactly where you need to be right now."

"Pull in here," she says, speaking for the first time in about three hours.

I look up at the store and hit the indicator. Pulling to a stop, I climb out of the car after her and stretch my back.

"Nice of you to wait," I say, jogging to catch up with where she's almost at the entrance.

"I didn't want to."

Her tone amuses me. It must be the hours in a confined space because I know it should piss me off really.

"Are you really going to follow me?" she snaps, shooting me a death glare as we enter.

"Uh… no. I need to pee." I point to the bathroom sign.

"Me too," she mumbles, clearly pissed that she's not getting rid of me that easily.

With a frustrated sigh, she pushes open the door to the ladies restroom and storms inside.

We could still be sitting in an airport with our parents right now. Surely even she can see that my idea was better than that.

I do my thing before resting back against the wall a little down from the restrooms to wait for her, only she never appears.

I wait a little longer, thinking that maybe she's doing her makeup or some other unnecessary shit but eventually my impatience gets the better of me and without so much of a second thought, I push the door open.

"Excuse me, this is the ladies restroom," some woman snaps the second I step inside.

Ignoring her as I slam my hand down on the cubicles. "Ruby?"

I'm met with silence.

"Fuck's sake," I mutter, walking back out as fast as I entered.

Forgetting about her disappearing act, I head deeper into the store to grab a few things.

It's not until I'm walking back to the car that I find her resting on the hood of Dad's car eating Twizzlers.

"Where the fuck did you go?"

"Uh… I'm right here, asshole."

"Good to know that sugar does nothing to sweeten you up," I mutter, dropping my bag into the back and pulling the driver's door open.

"Oh, I'm plenty sweet. I thought you already knew that."

The memory of having my head between her thighs and her taste on my tongue hits me.

"No idea what you're talking about, little one." I drop down into the car with a smirk on my lips as she silently fumes.

"Are you getting the fuck in, or shall I leave you in whatever shithole town this is?"

"I really hate you," she snaps.

"I know, part of me is even starting to like it."

"You're weird."

"You're the one stuck in a car with me. What are you doing?" I ask when she avoids the passenger door and instead climbs into the back seat.

"Getting some sleep, as you suggested. I'm hoping it'll make the time go quicker so I can get away from you."

She takes her hoodie off, before rolling it up and placing it under her head like a pillow.

She's wearing a white tank beneath that does little to hide her tits, and I can't help my eyes lingering on their fullness.

"Stare all you want, you're not seeing them ever again," she snaps, proving that she knows exactly where my focus is despite the fact she's got her eyes closed.

A wicked smile pulls at my lips. "Don't need to. I've got evidence, remember?"

"The second you fall asleep, I'll find it on your cell and wipe it."

I chuckle. "You think I'm that stupid to leave it lying around for just anyone to find. You underestimate me, little one."

"Stop calling me that," she snaps. "It's annoying and I'm not little."

"You are. Well..." I say, my eyes returning to her tits in the rearview mirror. "Parts of you are."

"Just drive, Ashton." She shifts onto her side and rests her hand over her cheek.

I put my music back on as I pull out of the parking lot, but I keep the volume down seeing as I actually need her to sleep so she can take over driving in a few hours. It annoys me that I'm being thoughtful, but I'd rather we both didn't die in this car before we get to Seattle.

"I'm cold," comes from the back a little over an hour later.

I look down at the heat, it's higher than it needs to be and it's already beginning to make me sleepy. I can't turn it up any higher and Ruby doesn't look like she's going to be taking over any time soon.

Reaching behind my head, I pull my hoodie off and pass it back. "Here, use this."

She blindly reaches out and tugs the fabric over her bare arms.

"It smells like you," she whispers.

"Well, yeah. It was on me."

"I like it."

My chin drops at her admission. "Little one, are you awake?"

I get no response. With a smile, I turn the music up a notch, crack the window a little in the hope the fresh air will keep me awake, and I continue driving while she lightly snores behind me.

13

RUBY

Rustling wakes me up. I blink a couple of times against the darkness, trying to figure out where I am and why it feels like I'm moving. Then I realize that I am.

The events following our brief visit to the airport slam into me.

I sit bolt upright, hoping like hell that I'm dreaming and that I'm not really stuck in a car with Ashton.

"Ah, she's back with us."

"Who are you even talking to?" I mutter, rubbing the sleep from my eyes and setting about sorting my hair out.

"Glad you woke up in a better mood."

"I'm stuck in a car with you and your shitty music. What do you expect from me?"

"I thought you were a peppy cheerleader. I hate to say it, little one, but I'm not seeing much pep."

"Fuck you," I grumble, unfolding my hoodie and tucking it under my arm as I climb between the front seats and drop down into the passenger one.

"Is that what you were dreaming about because I swear at one point you moaned my name."

"That was probably just me saying goodbye as I killed you in your sleep."

He laughs, but despite the fact, his amusement should piss me off. It doesn't. Instead the sound of him actually happy makes something warm me from the inside out.

I turn to look at him, needing to see the smile that goes with the laugh, but my breath catches in my throat.

"W-why are you half-naked?" I splutter like a fool.

"Because," he says, looking over at me and giving my body the same treatment my eyes just did him. "I gave you my hoodie as a blanket. You're welcome, by the way."

"O-oh so that's why I woke surrounded by the scent of manwhore."

"Don't worry, it won't happen again, you clearly didn't appreciate it. Could I get it back?" He holds his hand out as if I'm going to pass it to him, but all I do is stare at him. My eyes run down his corded forearm, all the way to his chest, down his cut abs, and to the bulge I was staring at a few hours ago behind his sweats.

My mouth waters as I take him in. He might be the world's biggest douchebag, but he's certainly been gifted in the body department.

"Ruby?" he snaps.

"I think I prefer you like this," I admit. "It distracts me from the shit that comes from your mouth."

His eyes flick to my chest briefly before he focuses back on the road.

"I am more than down for a topless rule inside the car if you are."

"N-no that's not..."

"Exactly, now pass me my hoodie."

Reaching back between the seats, I stretch to grab it.

"Jesus fucking Christ, Ruby. Wanna shove that any closer to my face?" He's trying to sound pissed off, but the hint of amusement in his voice betrays him.

I try to move, aware that I really do have my ass in his face but I don't go anywhere.

"I would, but I'm stuck."

"Oh really?" He chuckles. "What an unfortunate position to be in?"

"Just focus on driv—Ashton," I shriek when his palm connects with my ass cheek.

"You really should have worn that little skirt you had on the other day."

"You're a fucking pig," I grunt, trying to twist myself free.

I finally manage to get some leverage to push myself out of the gap I was stuck in, dragging his damn hoodie and my bag of goodies from the store with me.

"Here," I bark, throwing the fabric into his lap.

"Thanks. Don't eat any of that." His words make me pause with my hand halfway to the chips I was about to open.

"Why? Are you going to try telling me that I'm fat next or something?"

He laughs. "No, little one, I can assure you that there's nothing wrong with your body."

"Oh?" I turn to look at him.

"There's a pizza place. I was going to take you for dinner."

"Oooh. Well, that's... nice of you."

"Yeah, don't get used to it. It might be the only time it happens."

"Good to know," I mutter, pulling the visor down to check my appearance before gracing other humans with my presence.

Ten minutes later, and Ashton is fully clothed once again and we're sitting in a booth at a quiet out-of-town pizza place.

I've no idea where we are, just somewhere hopefully between home and Seattle if Ashton set up the GPS right. That little screen still shows an insane amount of both miles and hours to go. But I'm finding it hard to stay mad about it when all Ash wants to do is ensure he's at his mother's funeral. Can't really fault the guy for his attempt.

I look up at him, twisting his glass of soda around on the table before running his finger through the condensation as we wait for our food to arrive. He's deep in thought with his brows pulled together and his lips pressed into a thin line.

My heart aches for him, he might be an ass, but he's hurting.

"Wanna talk about it?" He startles at my question as if he'd forgotten I was here. "Want to talk about her?" I offer.

It takes a couple of seconds, but eventually, his eyes lift from his glass. The darkness in them makes my breath catch, but something tells me that all his hate and anger isn't going to be taken out on me this time. This is different.

"No, not really."

"It... it might help," I suggest.

"Nothing is bringing her back. That's the only thing that could help right now."

I open my mouth to respond, but thankfully I don't get a chance to say anything because two huge pizzas descend on our table.

His eyes light up a little at the sight of our first real food since the airport, God knows how many hours ago now, but his sadness still lingers, and I fear that it's only going to get worse the closer we get to his home.

We eat in almost silence, just a few words passing between us.

Ashton pays the bill once we've finished and after both making use of the bathrooms, we head back out to Stephen's car.

It's significantly colder here compared to home, and I fold my arms around myself in an attempt to keep warm.

"It's okay," I say when Ash goes for the driver's door. "I can take over, you get some rest."

"It's okay, I can—"

"No," I say sternly, making his eyes widen a little. "Get in the back and get some rest."

He nods at me, but still, he doesn't move to the back of the car, instead just walks around the hood to the passenger side.

"Why do I get the feeling you don't trust my driving?" I ask when we're both in with the engine—and more importantly, the heat—running.

"Because I don't," he mutters, sliding his chair back and stretching his insanely long legs into the footwell.

"I'll have you know that I'm a very good driver."

"Just try not to kill me, I don't need—" He cuts himself off, but this time, I don't prompt him for more. I only know the basics of what happened with his mom. I know he was in the car at the time, and I can only imagine what he went through.

"You're in safe hands. Get some rest."

I sync my cell, amazed that he's not beat me to it, and find something quiet and relaxing before setting off on my first leg of the journey.

Ashton stays awake beside me for the longest time just staring out of the window. Every now and then, I feel his stare turn to me, but I don't take my eyes off the road. As much as I might like to know what he's thinking every time he does so, another part of me is happy to just let him brood. It's less exhausting than fighting with him.

Eventually, though, his breathing gets heavier and when I do risk a look over, he's fast asleep with his arms crossed over his chest and deep frown lines still marring his brow. I want to take his pain away, making it a little easier to bear, but I have no idea how I'm supposed to do that. Not that I'm sure he deserves it after what he's done to me, but the need still tugs at me. He's hurting and despite the fact I don't like him, I hate to see it.

I find myself almost in a trance as I drive through the night. I thought I'd get tired, that my eyes would get heavy, but I actually find the empty roads and the darkness weirdly relaxing.

Ashton wakes a few times, but he always drifts back to sleep and leaves me to do my thing with just my quiet music and his soft snores for company. The only time he so much as looks at me is when I pull into a gas station to refill the car.

By the time he fully wakes and puts his chair back upright, the sun is beginning to rise on the horizon.

"Shit, did I really sleep that long?" he asks, staring at the clock.

"Yup."

"Huh."

"Why's that so weird?" I ask, glancing over at him and wishing I hadn't. He looks all sleepy and sexy with soft eyes and messy hair.

"I've just barely slept since... it's just weird that the first time I do is while traveling."

"You're probably just exhausted."

"You hungry?"

"Uh..." In all honesty, I'm not. That pizza last night was freaking huge. But I could really do with getting out and stretching my legs, so I find myself agreeing. "Sure. I'll stop at the next place we find."

It turns out that we're in the middle of nowhere and that the next place isn't for another three hours, and by then, I'm starving.

"There," Ashton points out. The urgency in his voice makes me chuckle. "What? I really need a pee."

"You could have said, I'd have pulled over."

He looks at me and I have no choice but to turn to him.

"You'd do that for me?" he asks teasingly.

"Yeah, if it meant you didn't piss yourself and I had to spend the next few hours surrounded by the smell of it."

"Nice." He laughs.

"What, it's true."

"Sure, come on."

Ashton makes a beeline for the bathroom as I find us a table and order coffee. Now I've stepped out of the car, exhaustion is hitting me hard.

"Thanks," he mutters, dropping down across from me and pulling the mug toward him.

A weird tension settles over us as we sit there in silence both sipping our too hot coffees.

"So..." I say, needing to break it. "What did you want to do today?" I ask with a laugh.

He looks up at me from over the rim of his mug and my breath catches. He really shouldn't be quite so beautiful, it's disarming. Especially when I'm sure I look like a hot mess.

"I was thinking about going for a drive."

"Oh yeah? Going anywhere nice?" I regret the question the second it falls from my lips.

"No." His eyes hold mine, and I can't help the feeling that he's warning me of something. My stomach clenches and I have to fight to swallow the lump that crawls up my throat.

"I-I'm just going to go and freshen up. If the waitress comes back, just order me pancakes and bacon, yeah." I slide from the booth. "Oh, and another coffee."

He nods once and after grabbing my purse and the bag I brought in with me, I practically run for the bathroom.

I'd picked up the necessities in the store yesterday, so I make quick work of freshening up and changing my panties before attempting to do something with my hair. I debate putting some makeup on to hide my tired eyes, but in the end, I figure that there's no point. We're just getting back in the car, and I don't really give a crap if Ash thinks I look a mess.

He's still quiet and tense when I get back to the table, although that doesn't stop him running his eyes down the length of me as I approach. I hate that tingles erupt wherever his eyes touch, but it seems I have little control over it.

"You look tired," he says as I drop down, banishing the heat that had started to fill my veins under his stare.

"Thanks," I mutter. "Probably something to do with driving all night while you snored beside me."

"I don't snore."

"Right. Whatever. I assume you're taking over after this."

"Yep. The back seat is all yours."

"Great."

Things don't get much better as we eat. I'd hoped he might be in a better mood after almost a full night's sleep, but that doesn't seem to be the case.

"Where are you going?" he barks at me the second we emerge from the diner, and I bolt in the opposite direction of the car.

"The store. You want anything?"

"Fuck's sake," he mutters, turning around to follow me.

"It wasn't an invite. I could have got anything you wanted while you sulked."

"I'm not sulking."

"Oh really. You could have fooled me." I roll my eyes at him and head inside.

Thankfully, they have exactly what I wanted. A pillow and blanket. There's no way I can sleep again while surrounded by him. It just can't happen.

"Comfortable?" Ash asks, watching me in the rearview mirror as I get settled in my new bed.

"Yep, and bonus, it doesn't smell like boy."

He shakes his head at me and looks back to the road.

"Sleep tight, little one."

14

ASHTON

Seeing her wrapped up in a blanket instead of my hoodie really shouldn't matter to me, but as I force my eyes away from her, I can't deny that it pisses me off.

I blame the fact I've been stuck inside this confined space with her for the past twenty-four hours. Her constant presence is doing stupid shit to my brain. Although, I can't deny that using my imagination for all the things I want to do to her in here is a hell of a lot better than thinking about my reality and what I've got to face when we finally roll into Seattle.

Reaching down, I rearrange myself, before trying to drag my head out of the gutter and focus on what I should be doing.

My foot presses a little harder on the gas and the car shoots forward. My heart picks up pace as adrenaline surges through me. Ruby must have spent all night driving like Miss Daisy because the arrival time on our GPS that I was trying to beat has gone backward and like fuck do I want this journey to take any longer than it has to.

I pull out into the fast lane and push it harder, seeing what the engine can really do.

Hopefully, by the time she wakes, I'll have knocked a few hours off our arrival time.

I might not want to be in Seattle, or anywhere near my old life. But the thought of no longer being confined to a car makes it seem a little bit more appealing.

The miles and hours tick by, but eventually, I need to pull over to take a piss. I bring the car to a stop on the side of the road. I was hoping to make it to the next gas station but after the three cans of energy drink I've had, I know I'm not going to make it.

The gravel crunches under the tires and I jump out the second the car comes to a stop.

I do what I need to do around the side of the car before opening the back to find something to eat.

"Feel better now?" Ruby asks in an amused voice. Her sleepy eyes stare up at me and I rummage through the bag closest to me.

"Much. Where are the chips?"

She shrugs, still half asleep. "Try this one." She pokes a finger out from under the blanket and points to a bag in the footwell by her head.

"Fine." Pressing my knee beside her leg, I lean in and reach over. My hand touches the bag, but my eyes find hers as I stretch over her, and I freeze.

Her green eyes are dark as she stares up at me. Her scent fills my nose and the sight of her sinking her teeth into her bottom lip does something to me it really shouldn't.

I remember all too well what it was like to kiss her, the way she matched me move for move as our hate and lust collided. I remember exactly how she tastes and how fucking wild it made me.

Aside from her heaving chest, she's stock still beneath me for long, tense seconds as I fight an internal battle with myself.

"Ash?" she finally breathes. "How much farther do we have to go?"

Her question is like a bucket of ice water over me.

"About eight hours?"

"Eight hours?" she echoes, sitting up so fast her head collides with mine, making stars appear in my vision.

"Fucking hell," I mutter, pulling back, still without the chips I came for but now with a blinding pain above my left eyebrow.

"Shit, I'm sorry," she murmurs, pressing her palm to her own head to ease the burn.

"Whatever," I grumble, climbing from the car and slamming the door behind me. Walking around the back, I drop my hands to the trunk and lower my head.

What the fuck is wrong with me right now?

I need to remember that this is all her fault. I shouldn't be looking at her like she can take all the pain away, make me forget the reason we're heading back to Seattle.

"Fuck," I bark, slamming my hand down on the trunk so hard it stings.

Why did I think this was a good idea?

Turning my back on the car, I rest my ass against it and shove my hands into my pockets as I try to shut everything out.

I have no idea how long I stand there trying to get my head on straight, but by the time I pull the driver's door open once more, I find Ruby sitting in the passenger seat with the bag of chips I wanted in her lap.

"You okay?" she whispers as I silently lower myself to the seat and rest my head back.

"No, not even a little bit."

"Y-you want these?" She holds the bag out for me, and I look at it. Part of me is grateful that she's here and that I'm not alone, but the other part wishes no one was witnessing me teetering on the edge of losing control like I am right now.

"Maybe in a bit."

Sitting forward, I start the car and wait for the GPS to wake up.

"Wow, just how fast were you driving?" she asks, noting just how much time I've managed to knock off while she was sleeping.

"Speed limit, obviously."

"Sure, whatever you say. Want me to take over?"

"In a bit. Right now, I need something else to focus on," I admit.

"Something else?" she asks.

Turning to look at her, I can't help the smirk that pulls at my lips as I stare down at hers.

"Yeah, something else."

My fingers tighten on the wheel in an attempt to stop me from reaching for her. She's so close, it would be so easy. I already know she would submit, just like she has every other time I've touched her.

She sucks in a breath, but despite the fact I know she wants to, she can't rip her eyes away from me.

Doing us both a favor, I twist back to look out the windshield and get myself ready to eat up some more miles on our road trip.

I stop for gas at the next station, but I don't allow Ruby to take over the driving. I need to do something to expel some of the pent-up energy inside me the closer we get to Seattle. It's either I drive, or I need to find something to break a sweat, and right now, we don't have time for me to hit the gym, and we really shouldn't be even considering the other option that might help.

"Our parents are in Seattle," she says, interrupting my less than innocent thoughts about how we could make use of the back seat of my dad's car.

"Great."

"I'll tell them that we should be at the hotel in—"

"You're not going to the hotel," I bark, my grip on the wheel tightening until my knuckles turn white.

"Uh... why not? Where am I going?"

I look over at her as she stares at me like I've lost my mind—which to be fair, I probably have.

"You're coming with me."

"Why? You hate me. Just drop me at the hotel and you can go do your thing."

"You're right."

She breathes a sigh of relief at my words but I don't think she's thinking the same thing as me.

"I do hate you."

She gasps, proving me right.

"And I'm not dropping you at any fucking hotel. You're staying with me."

"W-why?"

"Do you ever just do as you're told without an argument?"

"Before you stormed into my life I did, often."

"So you're just a pain in my ass."

"I wouldn't be if you'd let me go."

"That's not happening. You might want to get used to it."

Her lips part to respond but she must decide against arguing this time because she closes them again in favor of staring out of the window at the passing scenery.

"Are you sure you don't want me to take over?" she asks again a few hours later.

"No, we're nearly there and you clearly drive too slow."

"I do not." I look over at her with a raised brow. "I just follow the speed limit, unlike some people."

"Yeah, well, I don't really want to spend longer in here than absolutely necessary."

"I can only agree with that. The company isn't exactly... friendly."

"I took you for pizza," I argue.

"Oh yeah, because pizza fixes everything," she mutters, much to my amusement.

"Are you hungry?" I ask, as my stomach grumbles once again.

"Yeah."

"We'll stop once more than we're not resting until Seattle."

"Fine. The sooner we're there, the better."

"Have you been to Seattle before?"

"No. But I've seen it on TV."

"We're not going to the part of town that's often shown on TV, little one."

"Oh."

"You might regret wanting to get there as fast as possible."

"Did you grow up in the ghetto?"

"That might be putting it lightly."

She swallows nervously and I can't help but smile. I'm glad she's feeling nervous, it makes my cock hard.

Oh little one, the things I have to show you.

"Nothing is open," Ruby helpfully points out as we drive through a sleepy little town. Okay, so it's kinda late, but I was expecting something to be open.

"I guess we'll just have to wait until the next town."

"But I really need to pee," she whines, fidgeting in the seat like she's been doing for the past thirty minutes.

"You're just going to have to go outside."

"Ashton," she spits, turning my way. "I didn't want to come on this little road trip, and I really don't want to pee outside where anything could bite my ass, or more specifically, that you could watch."

"I promise I won't watch," I say, lifting my hands in surrender. "Jeez, who do you think I am?"

"Honestly, I've no idea," she mutters, much to my amusement.

"Please, explain," I ask politely.

"I'm pretty sure that you already know you're an asshole."

I can't help but chuckle. "Yeah, little one. I'm aware."

"So why do it then?"

"Because..." I pause for a bit as my anger resurfaces. Most days it's like a living beast inside of me, but since being in this car with Ruby, for some reason, I've been able to breathe a little easier, like it's not sucking the air straight from my lungs. "Because it's so much fun." I wink at her and she huffs out in frustration.

"Well, I'm glad ruining my life amuses you so."

"How exactly am I ruining your life?"

"By moving into the room next door to mine, your music, your presence, just... you."

"Wow, I really do affect you, huh?"

She growls in response and my body instantly reacts.

"Do you lie in bed at night thinking about me?"

"Of how to kill you, yeah?"

"So you're not remembering just how it felt when I licked your—"

"Ashton," she barks, cutting off my words.

"Oh come on, you can't tell me that you didn't enjoy it, little one. I know for a fact—"

"Over there," she squeals, cutting off what I was saying and the memories of that night that were happily flooding my brain. She was so fucking sweet. "The lights are on."

Forcing myself out of my own head, I drive over to where she's pointing to find a Chinese takeout. It must be the only place open in this little town.

Killing the engine, I climb out. Ruby is already halfway there in her need for the bathroom.

"Hi, good evening, is there any chance I could use your bathroom really quick?"

I step inside the small waiting area just in time to see the middle-aged guy run his eyes down Ruby's body. A smile curls at his lips as he does so and it immediately puts me on alert, the hairs on the back of my neck standing.

"Sure thing, sweetheart. But I'm going to need something in return."

"Don't worry, we want food too," she says happily, totally ignoring the look in the guy's eyes. She sounds so much like her oblivious mother with that statement, I almost roll my eyes at her.

"Okay, well the bathroom is through here," he says, lifting the hatch to allow her through the counter. "It's right this way." He goes to follow her.

"Just give us the directions, no need for you to stop what you're doing," I say, stepping up behind Ruby and wrapping my hand around her waist. She tenses in my hold and I squeeze tight, hoping that it'll warn her about arguing.

"Down the hall, second door on the right." His eyes remain locked on Ruby as we make our way down the hall as instructed.

"What the hell is your problem?" Ruby hisses, twisting out of my hold.

"That guy is my problem."

"He was just being nice."

"No, Ruby. He really wasn't."

"Like you care," she mutters, coming to a stop at the final door.

"You think I don't care if you get attacked by the creep from this dead-ass town?"

She shrugs, pulling the door open and stepping inside.

"What are you doing?" She sulks when I follow her in and lock the door behind me.

"Just pee, Ruby, so we can get the hell out of here."

"With you watching?"

"I'm not fucking watching." I make a show of turning around so I'm facing the door that's not seen a lick of paint for far too many years.

"Just... wait outside, please?"

"No." I shove my hand in my pockets and wait.

After a few seconds, her need to pee wins out because the sound of rustling fabric fills my ears.

"You're a pain in my fucking ass, Ashton," she grumbles.

"Oh little one, is that an invitation?"

"Is it, fuck? You're not getting anywhere near me ever again."

The toilet flushes and when I glance over my shoulder, she's standing at the sink ready to wash her hands.

"Is that right?" I ask, stalking over to her, not stopping until my front is pressed against her back. She gasps, telling me everything I need to know about her previous statement. Dropping my lips to her ear, I make sure they brush her skin as I speak. "Because from where I'm standing, I think you like having me close."

"Ashton." I think it's meant to be a warning, but it comes out as a needy whimper.

"You're really lucky, you know?"

"Lucky?" she spits, her eyes lifting to the dirty mirror before us and holding mine.

"Yeah. If we were anywhere but this disgusting bathroom with that creep probably watching on a hidden camera then I'd prove just how much of a liar you are, little one."

"Liar... I'm not a liar."

"Sure thing." My fingers twitch to reach out to her, to touch her, but I resist. Instead, I walk backward so she can wash up and I can make use of the toilet.

"Just because you insisted on being in here, it doesn't mean I want to watch you."

I don't look back, but I know she's got her hand on the door and about to walk out.

"You'll regret it if you walk out of that door, little one. I can assure you."

She huffs. "He's not going to do anything with you here."

"I wasn't warning you about him this time."

"O-oh."

I finish up, wash my hands and in a heartbeat, we're standing back at the asshole's counter ordering some dinner. I'm not entirely sure how I feel about eating his food, but since we've munched through our snacks and nothing else is open in this town, we've got little choice.

The second he passes the bag over, I take it along with Ruby's hand and march from the building.

"Get off me," she hisses, pulling herself from my grip the second we're out of the door.

I let her go but catch up with her before she gets a chance to open the car door. Placing the bag on the roof, I cage her against it.

"What now?" she spits.

"Stop being a pain in the ass."

"Me? Jesus, Ashton. What do you want from me? I came on this little fucked-up trip. I've slept in the back of the car and driven through the night *for you.* What else do you want?"

15

RUBY

His eyes narrow on me as my breathing increases to an embarrassing speed. I can't help it. He's got me caged against the car with his big body mere inches from mine and his scent filling my nose. How the hell he smells so good after the number of hours we've spent in this car, God only knows. I sure don't feel all that fresh.

I can practically see the wicked thoughts flicking through his mind as our stare holds. His breath—also annoyingly fresh—fans my face and I can't help my mouth watering for a taste of him.

His mood has been up and down during the last part of our journey. I know it's because we're getting closer to Seattle and that he's freaking out. He likes to think he hides all this pain and distress inside, but I see it. I can see the storm swirling behind his dark eyes. And some sick part of me wants to help him take it away.

I shouldn't. I should let him drown. But I can't. It's not who I am. Even if he is a prick.

"Ash, what do you—"

"Get in the back of the car, Ruby," he hisses, cutting off my question.

My eyes drop to his lips as he talks, and something clenches inside me. It's been months since he's kissed me. I've almost forgotten what it was like.

Reaching up on my tiptoes, I lock my eyes on his. They've darkened since I last looked, his pupils almost swallowing the darkest of brown that's usually there.

"Don't test me, right now, little one. It won't end well for you."

"Who says I want it to?"

He closes the space between us, and I suck in a breath, thinking that he's going to kiss me, but right as my eyes start to close, his heat is gone. When I come back to myself, I find the car door open.

"Get the fuck in," he growls.

This time, I do as I'm told and crawl over my makeshift bed that's still laid out to the other side, assuming he's going to join me.

He does and I breathe a sigh of relief because a part of me is expecting him to jump in the front and speed off, forgetting that we had food. That all vanishes the second he closes the door behind him and essentially sucks all the air out of the car.

He places the bag between us and looks at me. "Eat."

"O-okay."

I open the bag and start arranging the boxes between us. He grabs what he wants along with a fork and sits back.

We eat in an uncomfortable silence for the longest time. And when a question that's been eating at me for days finally passes my lips, I regret it instantly.

"Do you really have pictures of me from that night?"

Ashton stops moving with a forkful of noodles halfway to his mouth.

My heart pounds against my ribs at asking such a stupid question. Of course he has. Why wouldn't he?

A smile twitches up at the corner of his lips before he slowly turns his attention on me.

"What do you think?" he asks before wrapping his lips around his fork and chewing slowly.

I swallow nervously as heat rushes south. How is he even hot eating? It's all kinds of wrong.

"I think you're an ass, so anything is possible."

"There you go then. You didn't need to even ask."

"What are you going to do with them?"

He shrugs. "Haven't decided yet. I didn't think I'd ever see you again, let alone move in. I'm sure I'll find a use for them at some point."

"Great, well, I'll look forward to that then."

"Don't be so worried, cheer slut. Give it a few months and I'm sure half the school will have seen what I've seen."

My blood boils at his words.

"Excuse me?"

"What? They've already had a good look. Might as well let them see everything, right? Plus, that's what cheer sluts are there for."

My teeth grind at his assumption that just because I like cheer, I also like opening my legs for every guy at school.

"Like Krissy?" I seethe.

"Mmm..." he says, making a show of readjusting himself as if the mere mention of her name turns him on. My stomach turns over, making me want to puke the dinner I've only just eaten. "Her mouth was almost worth coming to Rosewood for."

"You're a pig." Dropping the container I was eating from to the seat, I push the door open and climb out.

"Where are you going?"

"Getting away from you."

I slam the door on him before he has a chance to respond.

Thoughts of him spending time with Krissy shouldn't bother me as they do. Most of the guys at school have spent time with Krissy, and I don't give a shit about them. So why do I care about him? Why do thoughts of them together make me want to go and rip Krissy's hair clean from her scalp for touching him?

"ARGH," I scream into the silent night of wherever the hell we are in an attempt to expel the pent-up energy that's vibrating around inside me.

I need to run, cheer, get drunk. Anything. Anything to make it—and him—go away.

As I pace beside the car, I'm aware of his eyes on me, but I don't look back. It would be pointless anyway with the blacked-out window he's hiding behind.

I'm nowhere near as calm as I want to be when I pull open the driver's door and fall down into the seat. I readjust it so my little legs can reach the pedals and then start the car.

"What are you—"

"Shut up, Ashton. Just shut up," I seethe, starting the engine and turning up the radio the second it comes on to drown him out. "Go to sleep or something," I call before turning it up a few more notches.

He grumbles something but, thankfully, I can't make it out as I put the car into drive and head for Seattle on finally, the last leg of our journey.

Despite the fact my eyes remain locked on the road ahead, I feel his burn into me for the longest time.

"Can't you go to sleep or something?" I bark at him after turning the music down a few notches.

"But watching you fume is so much fun," he quips. "You want any more food?"

"What have you done to it?"

"I laced it with poison." I don't need to look back at him to know he's rolling his eyes. "Nothing, but you barely touched it."

"The company ruined my appetite. Put it in the bag, I might have more when I finally get away from you."

"You do know that's not happening, right?"

"Yeah, about that—"

"Not up for discussion."

"Our parents have my suitcase, my clothes, my everything." Or at least I hope they do, seeing as we walked out of the airport leaving everything behind.

"You'll get your stuff, don't worry."

"Great," I mutter. "Now go to sleep. You're annoying me."

He chuckles but after a few seconds, he does at least lie-down and disappear from my sight.

I keep the music low because despite the fact I want to annoy the shit out of him as he does me, I'm not an evil person and I'm aware of just how many hours he's been driving for.

The sun is beginning to come up and scenery around me changes as I make my way into central Seattle, my eyes flit around the buildings, the city coming to life as I slow my speed and begin to pay more attention to the GPS so I don't make a wrong turn.

Finally, the screen shows we're only minutes away from our destination. It's a welcome sign after all the hours it had shown when we first left.

I'm starting to believe that Ashton's admission that he lived in the ghetto was nothing more than a joke as I navigate through the city. I pass the hotel that Mom had mentioned in her message and I almost pull over and abandon Ashton in the car with my need for a shower and a comfortable bed, but I glance back at him sleeping and I realize I can't.

Instead, I keep driving, but it's only about twenty minutes later when I realize that he wasn't lying at all. I turn a corner and almost immediately the atmosphere changes. The fancy buildings vanish in favor of darker, graffiti-covered brickwork.

"Okay then," I whisper to myself as I pass a group of kids, probably our age, who look like they're dealing something they shouldn't be in the recess of a storefront.

So he wasn't lying then.

My eyes widen at everything beyond the car and unlike when I slowed in front of the hotel, now I really don't want to leave the safety of the vehicle.

The dilapidated apartment buildings, the beat-up cars, and the questionable looking characters who are loitering around at this time of the morning send fear skating down my spine.

"You have reached your destination," the GPS chirps at me. I find a space on the side of the road and pull the car to a stop, staring up at the apartment building it directed me to.

I swallow nervously. Is that why he wanted me to stay with him, to scare the shit out of me? I'd have been more than happy in that nice looking hotel with a room to myself instead of risking my life here.

Twisting in my seat, I look at Ashton who's fast asleep under my blanket. His full lips are slightly parted and his dark lashes resting down on his slightly reddened cheeks.

He looks beautiful and peaceful. So peaceful that I almost don't have it in me to wake him... almost.

"Ashton," I say slightly louder than necessary.

He stirs, but he doesn't wake.

"Ashton, we're here."

His eyes fly open and he sits up, staring out of the window as if he's in a trance. I have no idea if he's actually awake or not as he sits totally motionless for a few seconds.

"Ash?" I whisper, scared to drag him from wherever he's gone.

After a few beats, he turns to me. The look in his eyes makes my breath catch. He looks as if he's in physical pain just being here.

"T-this was a mistake," he admits quietly, ripping his eyes from mine.

"I can go back to the hotel," I offer, assuming that's what he means, but when his shoulders tense, I start to wonder what the hell he is actually talking about.

"No," he snaps harshly.

"O-okay. Well, what..." I trail off when his attention goes back out the window. He swallows, making his Adam's apple bob and the tendons in his neck tighten.

After a few more seconds, he seems to steel himself and he swings his legs from the seat and runs his fingers through his hair.

"Y-you okay?" It's a stupid question, I know that before it even passes my lips, but I don't know what else to say right now.

"No, Ruby. I'm anything but fucking okay right now. Grab your shit, we can't sit in this fucking car any longer."

I nod at him because finally, we agree on something. Killing the engine, I push the door open, breathe in a lungful of... well, not-so-clean air, and stretch out my sore muscles. I really need to sleep in a bed.

He joins me on the sidewalk after a few moments, his eyes still locked on the building before us.

"Did you live here long?" I ask, needing to break the silence.

"Yeah."

He takes off toward the entrance and I've no choice but to follow unless of course today was the day I wanted to be murdered on the street.

I rush to catch up with him as he pushes through the doors. I'm amazed—and somewhat relieved—when an elevator appears around the corner and I step toward it.

"Don't," a low voice rumbles from behind me.

My hand pauses halfway to the button and I spin to him. "You don't want to go in there. Stairs." He tips his chin toward the stairs and starts toward them.

I follow and start climbing despite the fact my leg muscles scream at me with every step I take.

"I'm too tired for this. What could be so bad about the elevator?"

"You don't want to know, trust me. We're nearly there." He looks back at me and for a moment I think he's going to stop to help me, but then he spins back around and continues forward.

Finally, he comes to a stop in front of a door with chipped green paint and a wonky number sixty-seven hanging on the front of it. The hallway itself is... depressing. There really is no other way to describe it. It also smells, but I can't quite put my finger on what the musty, stomach-churning scent consists of.

After a few seconds, Ashton slides a key into the lock and after sucking in a deep breath, he pushes the door open and steps inside.

I have no idea how he must be feeling, being back here after everything that's happened but the hard set of his shoulders and the way his head is slightly lowered as he stands in the middle of the room, I know he's struggling more than he wants to admit.

Stepping into the sparse, cold apartment behind him, I close the door and scan my eyes around the space. It's an open plan living/kitchen area with limited furniture and belongings. If he hadn't told me downstairs that it had been his home for some time, I never would have believed it. It looks like they've just moved in or are in the process of moving out.

Stepping up to him, I place my hand between his shoulder blades, my need to try to comfort him getting the better of me. I wrap my other hand around his upper arm in the hope my touch might help in some way. He startles as my heat hits him, but he doesn't move or say anything as he stares at the same spot on the wall.

"Ash? Are you—" My words cut off when his eyes cut to mine. My breath catches in my throat at the pain lacing through his dark eyes.

Before I'm even aware he's moved, his hand is around my throat, my back crashes against a wall and his tongue is forcing its way past my lips.

His kiss is bruising, wet, and dirty, and I lose myself in it almost instantly. He sucks on my tongue before biting down on my bottom lip. I swear the coppery taste of blood hits my tongue.

His fingers hold my throat tightly, but I don't miss the caress of his thumb against my pulse point as he continues to kiss me.

"Ashton," I moan into his kiss as the length of his body presses against mine, squashing me between his solid frame and the wall at my back.

Lust shoots straight between my legs the second I realize it's the length of his hard cock pressing against my stomach.

"Fuck, Ruby," he groans, dropping his lips to my jaw. "I need... I need it to go away," he admits. The pain in his voice breaks my heart. He might be an ass, but he's suffering the worst pain in the world right now having lost his mom.

"Let me," I say, shocking the hell out of myself.

"Ruby," he groans, his hand wrapping around my shoulder before he pushes slightly, showing me exactly what he wants.

My back slides down the wall until I'm face to face with his sweatpant-covered cock.

My mouth goes dry at the thought of what I'm about to do.

I hesitantly glance up at him, and the second I find his dark, haunted gaze staring down at me, I know that there's no way I can refuse.

I might not be Krissy or one of the other cheer sluts like he makes out I am, but I can do this for him. Give him the release he needs to get out of his own head right now.

My fingers wrap around the waistband of his sweatpants, but the second my knuckles brush his skin, he jumps away from me as if I burned him.

"No," he barks. As he steps away from me, his demeanor completely changes. Gone is the lost, broken boy from a few moments ago, and in his place is the vicious asshole I'm much more accustomed to. "I don't want you," he spits, looking down at me hunched on the floor like I'm nothing more than a piece of shit on his shoe.

My lips part and tears burn the backs of my eyes, but I fight them. There's no way I'm going to show this asshole that I care about him rejecting me, because I don't... it's just the exhaustion getting to me.

His eyes pin me to the spot for a few more seconds as he backs toward the door.

"Don't touch anything, and do not, under any circumstances, open the door," he warns, but before I get to ask him what the hell he's talking about, he's gone and the door is slammed behind him.

My legs give out and my ass hits the floor with a thud.

"What the fuck?" I mutter, staring at the closed door like it holds all the answers to the mystery that is Ashton Fury.

I rest my head back against the wall, my eyes full of tears from his rejection but desperate to close.

Knowing that I can't pass out on the floor—I may as well go back to the car if the fucking floor is my other choice—I climb to my feet and look around.

There are four doors leading from this main room, I already know that one of them is my escape should I need it, so I can only assume the other two are bedrooms and a bathroom.

Sucking in a breath, I prepare to go in search of the bathroom. I really don't want to be poking my nose around Ashton and his mom's home, but I feel l have little choice seeing as the prick left me alone.

I pause with my fingers wrapped around the handle, hating that I'm invading their privacy by doing this but not having any other option.

I pull the door open a little and peek through the crack. It's obviously a woman's room, so I quickly close it once more. Ashton should be the one to deal with that room first.

I try the next one and find exactly what I was after.

I make use of the toilet before stripping down and splashing cold water over myself. I want a shower and I stare at it longingly, but it just feels wrong to make myself at home like that, so I cope with the bar of soap on the side and the ice water. I squirt a little toothpaste on my finger from the tube littering the basin and attempt to brush my teeth. I'd bought a brush from the first store we stopped in, but I left everything in the car, and I can only assume that's vanished along with Ashton.

Quietly, I close the door behind me and look around the space once more. The furniture is all old, worn, and chipped. The kitchen units look like they're barely holding themselves together and the windows are small and dirty and hardly let any light in. I understand why when I walk closer and find that both of them stare directly into someone else's apartment in the next building.

There are a couple of photo frames on the dresser and I slow as I pass, staring at a younger, sweeter looking Ash with his mom's arm around his shoulders. She stares down at him like he's her world and my heart rips open for the poor boy who's lost everything.

I keep moving, looking around the place, not that there's much to see until my eyes land on his door.

I know I shouldn't but my need to know more about the boy who messes with both my head and my body is too strong.

I twist the handle and push his door open. I'm hardly surprised when a black room greets me. Music posters cover the walls, most of them I've no idea who they are, gangsta rap isn't really my thing unless you count being kept awake by it night after night as being a fan.

His bed is covered in messy black sheets and much like the main room, there's not much in the way of possessions. There's a couple of bottles of cologne, a set of headphones and a cell charger, but that's it. I sit down on the edge of his bed and try to imagine what his life was really like here, but it's hard when there's so little to go on. One thing I do know though, he's not grown up like I have, and I start to really understand why he hates me.

Stephen left him and his mom here and started a new life in Rosewood. We're not rich, not by any stretch, but we've got enough to live easily and not worry about buying food and other necessities. We certainly have hot water and heat, which this place seems to be lacking.

When my eyes get heavy and my body starts to shut down, I look over my shoulder at his bed. I really want to crawl under those sheets and drift off. But I can't.

Instead, I walk out, closing the door behind me as if I never entered, and curl up on the couch, wishing I'd gotten my blanket and pillow from the back of the car. I curl myself in a ball and try to get as comfortable as possible. Thankfully, I'm so tired that the cold and hard, lumpy couch doesn't really bother me, and in minutes I'm out.

16

ASHTON

I didn't have any plans when I stormed out of the apartment but the second I locked eyes on Dad's car sitting by the sidewalk, I knew I couldn't get back in it. Not when it's going to smell like her, remind me of her.

I ripped my eyes away from what's been our home for the past few days and started walking up the street like I have almost every day since Dad left and Mom moved us here.

This place is like what I imagine hell must be like, but it's home, in all its fucked-up glory.

The smell of weed on every corner, the dealers, the hookers, the beat-up, smashed-up cars, the screams and cries of people as they're taught whatever lesson someone thinks they're due sound out and it all just feels normal, and I feel like I can breathe properly for the first time since I rode out of this place on my bike.

I walk for hours as the sun gets higher and higher in the sky and the city comes to life.

I have nowhere to go this time in the morning. The few friends I do have will either be passed out or heading to school—probably more likely the former as they attended school about as much as I did.

When I finally feel like I've run out of energy, I turn back around, make one quick stop, and head for home, or more specifically, my bed.

Every muscle in my body aches as I climb the stairs. I might have been asleep when Ruby drove us into the city, but it couldn't have been much before that I drifted off. I laid there for hours, thoughts of where I was going and what I was going to have to do spinning through my mind, not to mention the memory of having Ruby pinned to the car only a few hours before.

I need to stay away from her, that much I know. What I can't figure out is why I'm unable to let her go. I should have taken her back to the hotel and let her get comfortable with Dad and Lisa, but instead, I took her to the one place I don't want to be, let alone have a visitor, and then I bloody left her there after she offered to...

I shake my head. I can't allow myself to think about her on her knees before me. That can't happen. Not because it's forbidden or whatever bullshit I'm sure people would spew at us if they knew, but because I don't trust myself with her. She brings out this crazy side of me, one I don't even recognize and I'm sure that if she really experiences the things I want to do to her, to hurt her, to punish her, then she'll never look at me again. Not that that would be a huge issue, but we are going to have to put up with each other somehow seeing as we now live under the same fucking roof.

I push the door open, closing my eyes as I step into the apartment. The memories that flooded me the first time I stepped in here a few hours ago threatened to floor me, I have no reason to think it'll be any different this time.

Closing the door behind me, I keep my eyes on the floor, that is until a noise has me lifting my eyes and scanning the room. I expect to find her standing somewhere staring at me with a furious expression on her face but instead, I find her curled up in a ball on the couch snoring softly.

My breath catches at the sight of her. This apartment is freezing, to the point I can see my breath in front of my face, yet she's there without so much as a blanket covering her.

Walking over, I drop down to my haunches in front of her.

"Ruby," I whisper, but she doesn't so much as stir.

Knowing that I can't leave her there freezing, I slide my arms under her body and lift her into my chest. The second she feels my heat, she curls into me and nuzzles her cheek against my shoulder.

My heart rate picks up as I stare down at her, but I don't allow myself time to really think about my reaction because I march toward my bedroom, ignoring the couple of images of Mom and me when I pass.

The second we're in my room, I lay her down on my bed, pull her sneakers off, and cover her up.

Taking a step back, I stare at her curled up in my bed. I have no idea how I feel about it. I want to hate it, but I'm not sure I do, and that only makes me want to hate it that much more.

Turning my back on her, I make my way to the bathroom and quietly close the door behind me.

I strip out of my clothes, trying to ignore the chill that bites into my skin, I know it's about to get a lot worse. I don't bother waiting after turning the shower on, I know it's not going to get any warmer. Instead, I brace myself and step under the ice-cold stream.

I make quick work of washing the last few days off me before stepping out, drying off as fast as I can.

With the towel around my waist, I head back to my room, pull on a clean pair of boxers and sweats, and crawl into bed.

Do I want to be in here with her? No, not really. But like fuck am I going to be the one shivering on the couch when there's a perfectly good bed here with thick covers.

Sleep comes easily, not that I'm surprised after the past two days. With the help of her warmth beside me, I allow the darkness to come and hopefully with it, a little peace. Being back here, seeing Mom's things, being where she used to be, it's fucking with my head. I don't want to be here. I don't want Ruby here. But at the same time, I can't imagine either of us anywhere else right now.

When I eventually wake, it's the kinds of city commotion that I'm all too used to and have almost missed in my short time away. But it's not the sound that alarms me, it's the hot little body in my arms and the burning stare I can feel.

"I know you're awake," she whispers. "So you can let go of me now."

I wish I could, but with my limbs still heavy with sleep, my arm and leg stay exactly where they are, wrapped around her, pinning her to me.

"You're warm," I murmur, keeping my eyes shut and wishing I could drift back off away from this bullshit reality.

"Ash." She chuckles, trying to pull away from me but finding herself stuck.

I should release her, I know that, but fuck.

Ripping my eyes open, I find her awake green ones staring back up at me. Seeing them is like a bucket of cold water over me.

I release her immediately and roll onto my back.

"Sorry," I mutter, staring up at the ceiling. "You were just... warm."

"Yeah," she sighs, following my move and shifting to her back. "Where'd you go?"

"Out."

"Riiight." She pushes to sit up and grabs her cell from the nightstand.

"You were really cold when I came in, so..."

"Thank you," she whispers. "Jesus, it's late." That much is obvious from the fact the sun is dropping in the sky once more.

She taps around for a bit, I assume replying to messages, but I leave her to do her thing.

"Our parents want to know if we want to meet them for dinner."

"No."

"O-oh."

"Tell them you can't either."

She glances over at me, but I don't return her stare.

"O-okay." She turns her attention back to the screen and taps away, assuming, turning down their offer. I have no idea what they must be thinking right now about all of this, but to be honest, I don't really give a shit.

I regret my actions the second I flip the covers back and the coldness of the apartment hits my skin. I shiver, but it's not enough to force me back inside. I'm almost at the door when she speaks.

"Ash?" Her voice is so soft and unsure that it makes me turn around.

"Yeah."

Her eyes drop down my bare chest, lingering on where I know my morning wood is pressing against the fabric of my sweats. She swallows nervously and it does nothing to help it go down.

"About last night..." she starts hesitantly.

"Forget it. It was..." I blow out a breath, remembering just how she looked on her knees before me. "A mistake. Won't happen again."

"O-okay. G-good." I swear I see disappointment cross her features, but I don't hang around long enough to find out. Instead, I turn my back on her and head for the bathroom for a shower that is sure to put pay to the hard-on I've had since waking to find her in my arms.

When I emerge, I find her pulling open the few cupboards we have in the kitchen.

"What are you doing?" I bark and she startles as if she's just been caught robbing the place.

"Oh shit, I... um... I'm looking for something to eat."

"Good luck with that. You might find some crackers."

I continue toward the bedroom with a towel around my waist, but I pause halfway across the room when she speaks again.

"Is this really how you lived?"

"Yeah, little one. It was," I say sadly and continue forward before she has a chance to say anymore. I'm not ashamed of how we lived, it was our reality. If I didn't want her to see it, then I could have just dropped her at the lavish hotel Dad booked and kept her away from it.

You probably should have done that, a little voice screams in my head as I walk to my dresser and pull out a pair of boxers.

I drop the towel when a gasp sounds out in the doorway. Thankfully, she waits until I've dragged them on to speak.

"I'm going out," I say, reaching for some clothes.

"Take this, please."

Not knowing what she has for me, I turn around.

"No," I spit, seeing the credit card in her hand.

"Why not? You deserve it, Ash. Your dad pays for it," she admits with a wince when my face hardens with anger. Of course he fucking pays for her credit card, why wouldn't he?

Fucking asshole.

"I don't want anything from him."

"I... I get that—"

"No, no, you fucking don't. You don't have a clue. You think seeing this place means you understand anything about my life. You fucking don't."

She backs up into the doorframe as I take a step toward her, backing away like a scared little animal.

"I don't want his fucking money. If he wanted me to have it, then he'd have done so, and this wouldn't have been my life."

"Ash, this place is freezing, there is no hot water, no food. If we are going to stay here, then we need to fix it."

"Why? Can't Princess Ruby cope with a little cold?" I raise my brows at her.

"I can cope perfectly fine. But we don't have to." She forces the card my way again. "I'm not some prissy little girl who's going to scream when I don't get my way, Ash. But why suffer when we don't have to?"

I step toward her and she once again presses her body against the doorframe in her need to keep some space between us.

"Trust me, little one. I know exactly how to make you scream." I look at her from under my lashes as I close the space between us. The heat from her body seeps into mine and for a second I almost reach out and hold her to me as if she's a fucking heater. But I don't. I hold my arms at my sides and stare into her quickly darkening eyes. "And you know I could do it again in a heartbeat if I wanted to."

"Ashton," she warns, although all I hear is a plea for me to do just exactly as I said.

"Is that what you want? You want me between your thighs again, licking your pretty little pussy until you scream my name?"

She swallows as her eyes shutter at my words.

"You're wet for me again, aren't you?"

"Ash." Her chest heaves, her breaths almost coming out as pants.

Reaching out, I slip my hand under her hoodie and tank until I find the smooth skin of her belly.

"If I were to push my hand inside your panties right now, I'd find you dripping for me, wouldn't I?"

She shakes her head almost violently in denial, and all I can do is smile at her attempt to deny what's crackling between us.

It's the perfect distraction and one I'm not sure I'm going to be able to put off diving headfirst into very, very soon.

Her entire body tenses as I slide my hand into her sweats and panties.

"Oh God," she gasps when I graze her clit.

"You're a really shit liar, little one. You feel that?" I ask, dipping my finger inside her and coating my finger in her juices.

This time she nods, her eyes closed and her head resting back against the doorframe.

Leaning forward, I brush my lips against her ear and delight in the shudder that rips through her at my simple touch.

"Soon, I'm going to fucking ruin this. I'm going to make sure you remember forever who took away your innocence, make sure every other motherfucker who dares try to take what's mine pales in comparison."

She gasps at my words but her body defies her because a flood of wetness drips down my hand.

"So fucking desperate for it too, aren't you?"

She shakes her head once more.

"Don't fucking lie to me, Ruby," I bark, making her lift her head and open her eyes.

I circle her clit once more and she has to fight to keep eye contact with me.

"Tell me you fell asleep last night thinking about what it would have been like to suck my cock into your mouth."

She drags her bottom lip into her mouth, her teeth sinking into it until I'm sure it must hurt. Then after a beat, she nods.

"Good girl. If you're lucky, you might just have to do it soon."

Ripping my hand from her, I lift my fingers to her lips.

"Open." She hesitantly does as she's told, and I push my wet fingers past her lips. "Now suck them clean."

She does as she's told, my cock weeping as her tongue laps at her juices.

Fuck me.

"Good girl," I repeat. "Now, don't even think about finishing yourself off because this..." I cup her over the fabric of her sweats. "Is mine. Your pleasure, your pain, from here on out, is mine. You understand that?"

She nods once more, and I pluck the credit card from her fingers and walk away from her.

"Code?" I call over my shoulder and she quickly rattles off the numbers before I rip the door open and storm out of the apartment.

17

RUBY

I once again find myself with my ass on the cold, hard wooden floor watching Ashton walk away from me. My chest heaves, lust races through my veins and my head spins.

I was so close. So fucking close. And then he ripped his fingers away. Asshole.

Climbing to my feet, I walk back to the kitchen on shaky legs. My core throbs with my need for release and the temptation to go against him and finish myself off in his bed, surrounded by his scent is almost too much to ignore.

But I don't. Instead, I walk toward the bathroom.

"What the hell?" I mutter as I round the couch and find something I wasn't expecting to see. My case.

I lift it onto the couch and flip it open to find all my things exactly as I packed them.

I pull out my toiletry bag and a clean set of clothes and take them through to the bathroom.

I already know there's no hot water, so as I strip down, I brace myself for the blast of ice.

"Oh my God," I squeal as I dance around under the water. If I weren't awake before then I certainly am now. I wash my hair, cursing Ash out during every second of the torture.

By the time I step out, my teeth are chattering and my skin is covered in goose bumps.

"Fuck, fuck, fuck." There's no towel.

I pull the door open and peek out, making sure he's not already returned before running across the apartment, aware that the windows look directly into someone else's. The second I'm in his bedroom, I reach for the towel he dropped earlier. It's still damp and now freezing, but it's better than nothing.

I wring out my hair and whip the towel over my body, soaking up the ice-cold droplets.

In minutes, I have my clean clothes on, but I'm still shivering despite pulling my hoodie tightly around myself.

I fill the coffee machine that's sitting on the counter in the kitchen, praying to anyone who'll listen that it works before returning to Ashton's bedroom to retrieve his sheets.

With a steaming mug of black coffee—not my favorite, but I'm not exactly in a position to complain right now—and the only packet of crackers I could find, I huddle up in his sheets and hug the mug in front of my face in the hope it'll take the chill off.

The sensible side of me knows that I should walk out and go and find our parents. But there's something that stops me from leaving. I know what it is, it's the pain in his eyes, a pain I don't want to make worse, and I have a feeling that me walking out that front door will do that. So I torture myself in here as the sun begins to set outside, turning the entire apartment a murky orange. I guess I should just be glad there's still electricity and that I have light.

I scroll my way through social media, catching up with everything I've missed while sleeping today before I shoot my dad, Harley, and Poppy a message catching them up on what Seattle is like. In other words, I lie. I also, somewhat reluctantly, return the missed call I have from Mom. I know she's worried, probably for a very good reason, but I force some happiness into my voice and convince her that everything is fine and that we'll be at the funeral in plenty of time tomorrow.

I've somewhat warmed up a few hours later when a key is pushed into the lock on the other side of the door. My heart jumps into my throat as I wait for him to slip inside.

I have no idea what kind of mood he might be in, and I brace myself for what might be about to come my way.

The second he emerges, the breath I was holding rushes out of me at the sight of the bags in his hands. He bought food.

"Well, don't just sit there, help me unpack."

I scramble out of his sheets and rush to the kitchen with him.

"We've got hot water and heating too," he says.

"Thank you."

"I didn't do it just for you," he admits, glancing at me out of the corner of his eye.

"I know, but I appreciate it. Coffee?" I ask, my lips twitching with a smile when I see him pull some cream out of one of the bags.

"Please. Black, no sugar."

"Why am I not surprised."

"Because I'm a bitter motherfucker," he jokes, making my smile grow.

"Yeah, something like that. So I can have another shower with hot water now then?"

"Yeah, but you're going to need to be quick."

"Why?"

"We're going out."

"Out?"

"Yep, and you're wearing this." He throws a bag at me that I catch while narrowing my eyes at him.

"W-what is it?"

"A dress, little one."

"I have clothes," I sulk, unsure how I feel about the fact he's been shopping for me. "Thank you for picking up my case by the way," I relent after a few seconds.

"Your mom left it at the hotel reception, I just picked it up." He shrugs like it's no big deal, which I guess it isn't really, but it shows he does actually have a heart because he thought of me and did something nice. "We're leaving in an hour. You want a sandwich?"

"I'd love one."

"You do that," he says, nodding to the bathroom. "And I'll do this."

I follow orders and with the bag in hand, I make my way to the bathroom, grabbing my case on the way for everything else I might need.

Although it damn near kills me to do it, I don't look into the bag before I get in the shower. I put off seeing what he thinks will suit me in favor of a hot shower.

The second the heat hits me, I sigh in relief. After being cold for so long, it feels incredible.

I take time washing my hair this time and scrub every inch of my body, washing the long journey off me.

I step out and wrap myself in a now warm towel thanks to the heated rack, and I set about moisturizing and spraying myself with perfume.

My need to know finally gets the better of me and I reach a hand into the bag. What I pull out can't possibly be a dress, it feels like nothing more than a scrap of fabric.

"What the..." I hold it up, my eyes almost popping out of my head.

There's no way I can wear any underwear under this thing.

"Ashton," I snap, pulling the door open an inch.

"Yeah."

"There's no way I can wear this dress."

"Why?"

"Have you seen it?"

"Uh... yeah, I picked it."

"Why? To make me look like the whore you think I am?"

"No, Ruby. Because I think you'll look hot." He quirks a brow at me. "Now, show me if I'm right or not."

"I'm not... I can't..." I huff.

"Don't make me come in there and put it on you myself."

"You wouldn't."

"Wouldn't I?"

My lips part to argue but I realize that yeah, he probably would.

"For fuck's sake." I close the door again and examine the fabric. I may as well go out naked. With a groan, I drop the towel and pull it up my body.

I secure the straps over my shoulders and look down at myself.

The fabric skims over my body perfectly. If I didn't know he'd picked it in a shop, I would think it was made for me. The swell of my breasts are more than visible with the low-hanging neck and as if it wasn't short enough, there's a split up to my hip.

I can only see the top half of myself in the cracked mirror over the sink, but I can't deny that the top half looks good, despite my wet hair that I'm not sure what I'm going to do with because I didn't bring a hairdryer or my straightener.

Sucking in a breath and hopefully some confidence, I pull the door open and step out.

Ashton has his sandwich halfway to his lips when he looks up at me, and I can't help but laugh when he drops the entire thing to the plate resting on his lap.

"Fuck."

"I'm basically naked, Ash." I lift my arms from my body in frustration.

He has to clear his throat before he says anymore. "You're wearing it."

"I can't. If I even so much as bend over then—"

"Don't bend over."

"Fucking hell."

"Here," he says, pushing a plate toward me. I look down at it and my stomach growls loudly. "Eat."

I do as I'm told but only because I'm starving.

"Mom's got a hairdryer and all kinds of shit in her room, you can use it," he says, resting back on the couch once he's finished eating and runs his eyes over my body.

"I… I'm not sure."

"It's fine, little one. I'm going to have to start packing it all up tomorrow so it may as well get one last use."

"Are you really sure, I don't want to…"

"Go, it's fine."

I put my empty plate down, grab a few things before making my way into his mom's room, and pull out the stool at the vanity unit.

He leaves me alone for ten minutes while I dry my hair, but he must get bored, or lonely because he's soon standing in the doorway watching me as I apply my makeup.

"Where are we going tonight?" I ask, suddenly feeling a little excited about discovering another part of his previous life.

"Here," he says, handing me a small bottle of vodka. "Take the edge off."

"Thanks," I mutter, lifting the already open bottle to my lips. It burns as it hits the back of my throat, but I welcome it.

"Just to our usual hangout."

"You're going to introduce me to your friends?"

"Something like that."

I narrow my eyes at him but he doesn't say anything more about it.

"You nearly ready?"

"Y-Yeah."

I make my makeup heavier than I usually would, team that with the almost obscene dress and the vodka and I'm feeling good. I don't know anyone here and I'll probably never see them again. What the hell does it matter how I look?

"Is this place far?" I ask as Ashton directs me away from his dad's car and instead, we walk down the street. Thankfully, he allowed me to pull on one of his hoodies before leaving so at least I'm not completely freezing as we make our way to his mysterious location.

"Nope." He slips his hand into mine and tugs me along behind him. I'm wearing the shoes I packed to wear tomorrow, and they were certainly not made to walk the streets of Seattle.

Thankfully though, after only five minutes, he turns me down a dark street.

Butterflies erupt in my belly. Where the hell is he taking me?

He brings me to an ominous black door before he pushes me up against the wall and stares down at me.

He hasn't touched me since he walked out earlier, yet my body is still embarrassingly aware of his every move, waiting for him to strike.

"Ash?" I ask, my nerves about where we're going evident in my voice.

"You stay by me. You don't accept a drink from anyone but me, and you don't go anywhere with anyone but me. Understood?" His eyes bore into mine, expressing just how serious he is about this.

"O-okay," I agree when what I really want to do is ask if we should even be bothering. We could just go back to his apartment and order takeout or something.

"Perfect."

He pulls me from the wall but he doesn't move, so all I end up doing is crash into him.

"Remember what I said earlier. This," he says, cupping me between the legs. The heat of his fingers burns my sensitive skin, making me damn near desperate for more of his touch. "No other fucker gets to even think they have a chance."

I nod, my words getting caught in my throat.

"Let's go."

He moves this time, his arm comes around my waist and he pulls me into his side.

After knocking on the door, it opens and after a second, whoever is at the other side must realize who it is, and it's pulled back.

Ash walks me into a dark hallway, the only two people are what seem to be guards at the doors.

"Fury," one of them says with a nod as we pass. Ash returns the gesture but he doesn't say anything as he leads me down the hallway.

The music gets louder the deeper into the building we get before we come to a set of stairs. He leads me down and that's when the party reveals itself.

"What is this place?" I shout over the music.

"A basement, little one."

There are couches everywhere, each one littered with people. There's what seems to be a makeshift dance floor in one corner with bodies grinding and gyrating against each other. There are other couples dotted around.

"Oh my God, are they having sex?" I ask, my eyes almost bugging out of my head as I take in one couple on a couch as we hit the floor.

"Probably," Ash answers without even looking at the couple who've caught my attention.

I always thought Ethan's parties were wild, but this really is something else.

Eyes turn our way as we make our way through all the people. The scent of cigarettes, weed, and whatever the fuck else people might be smoking fills my nose and I swear I get a little hit from it alone.

"Well, well, look who's decided to show his fucking face," some guy says from a couch as we approach. Ashton brings us to a stop as the guy stands. The two embrace briefly. Ashton releases my waist so he can thump this guy on the back. "It's good to see you, man."

"You too."

They part and the guy's eyes come to me.

"And who do we have here?" he asks, his hungry eyes eating me up.

"This…" Ash says, turning to look at me. "Is mine, motherfucker."

The guy chuckles. "And when does Ashton Fury refuse to share his toys?"

"From right now."

I look between the two of them, trying to figure out if they're joking or not.

"Well, that is a damn shame because she is fine." He shoves his hand in my direction. "Name's Axel, but these motherfuckers call me X." I slide my hand into his because I have no idea what else I should do in this situation. He lifts my hand as if he's going to kiss my knuckles, but before he gets the chance, he pulls me into his body and drops his lips to my ear. "But I don't care which you use when you scream my name."

"X," Ashton growls behind me before his hand grips painfully onto my hip and I'm hauled back into his body. He wraps a protective arm around my waist before sitting down on the couch after someone gets up for him.

I fall down on top of him and am forced to sit there while everyone stares at him and glares at me.

What the fuck is this place and why are we here?

"Hey, man," the guy next to us says. "Sorry to hear about your mom."

Ash nods at him, accepting his condolences but I don't miss the way his entire body tenses at the mention of her.

"I'm Cash," he says, turning his eyes on me, but unlike Axel, he doesn't strip me bare with one look, hell he looks at me like I could well be a guy. It's a relief.

"Ruby," I say with a smile.

"Got this one whipped then?"

I look to Ash who's talking to the guy on the other side of him.

"I'm not sure that's the right word."

Cash smiles at me but I can't help thinking there are things he'd love to tell me.

I look around the room once more. We're sitting in a square of four couches. Most of the seats are filled by guys, there are only two girls sitting on their own with drinks in their hands, any others who are here are on guys' laps, some sitting less innocently than others.

I watch one couple for a few minutes. I know I should look away, but I'm weirdly fascinated by their shameless public display.

She's straddling his lap, and he's quite obviously fingering her as she arches her back and throws her head back in pleasure.

I'm so engrossed watching them that I don't realize that Ashton has finished talking.

"You like watching, little one?" he growls in my ear. "It sure got you wet last week with everyone's eyes on you."

"Fuck you," I spit. "You can't compare what you did to me to... to that."

"Hmm," he groans, his grip tightening as if he's about to turn me in the same position as that girl.

"I need the bathroom," I say, pulling away from him.

"Right down there." He nods toward a door where another girl disappears.

"What? You're not going to escort me?" I ask, widening my eyes at him.

"I can watch your every move."

"But who knows what I might get up to in that stall."

"Don't test me, little one."

I smile at him, loving that I can get to him quite so easily.

I climb from him, trying to be as elegant as possible so that I don't flash anyone, and walk toward the door. His eyes follow me the entire way and when I look over my shoulder before I push the door open, my eyes lock with him instantly. Unfortunately, as I look away, I catch someone else's. Axel's. Where Ashton's cold stare might scare me somewhat, Axel's downright terrifies me.

Ripping my eyes away, I slip inside the bathroom and breathe a sigh of relief when I only find a couple of girls reapplying their makeup in the mirrors.

I spend longer inside the stall than necessary as I try to get my head together. I need more alcohol for this.

The second I pull the door open, my eyes lock with a blonde's.

I walk over to the sink to wash my hands and her stare follows me.

"You're with Ashton," she states.

"Uh... I guess."

I turn to her as her eyes drop down my body.

"You're not his type."

"Oh, is that right?" I ask, my brows lifting in shock. "And I'm assuming that you are."

"He's mine."

"Oh really? Funny because he's never mentioned you."

Her lip curls and she steps toward me. She might have a few inches on me, not that it's hard, almost everyone does. But I've no doubt I'm quicker and stronger if she wants to try something.

"Leave it, Nat," another girl warns as she emerges from the other stall. "Ash made it clear he was done with you, in case you'd forgotten."

Nat growls at whoever the new girl is. "Go and find someone else's cock to bounce on tonight to get over it."

Nat opens her mouth, I'm assuming to rip this girl a new one but at the last minute she must change her mind because instead she huffs out a breath, turns on her heels, and storms out.

"I'm. Willow. Ignore her, she's a whore who thinks she owns the Kingston boys."

"T-the Kingston boys?"

"Don't ask," she says with a roll of her eyes, turning to wash her hands.

"I'm Ruby," I say after a few seconds.

"So, you and Ash, what's the deal?"

"He's... uh... my stepbrother."

She whistles. "Stepbrother. The way he had you on his lap didn't exactly scream siblings to me."

My cheeks burn bright red.

"Hey, no judgment here. You can ride him all the way into next year for all I care."

My chin drops at her words.

"You want a drink?" she asks, taking a step to leave the bathroom.

"Y-yeah. I really think I do."

I follow her out, grateful to find someone other than Ash to talk to.

She leads me to the other side of the basement to a makeshift bar. I stand there awkwardly as she makes us both a drink. I have no idea what it is, but I need it and I decided back in those bathrooms that I trusted her.

"Thanks," I say, taking the Solo cup and immediately lifting it to my lips.

"So, from the look on your face, I'm assuming this is the first time you've been to a party quite like this." She lights up a joint as she asks the question, and my eyes widen. She seemed like a good girl. She chuckles at me as she takes a drag.

"Is it that obvious?"

"Yeah, just a little."

"Apparently, I've lived a sheltered life."

"Well, hang around Ashton long enough and he's sure to corrupt you."

My face heats at her words.

"It seems he's already started. You fucked him yet?"

My jaw drops in shock that she'd happily ask a stranger that question outright.

"Oh don't look so horrified. I've known Ash for years. He wouldn't give a shit. He certainly dressed you up like that for a reason."

"How'd you know I didn't pick this?"

"Honey, please, don't insult me."

"Princess," some guy purrs as he walks up to Willow. "Long time no see." He pulls her into a hug and she happily turns her back on me as she falls into conversation with whoever it is.

I lean back against the counter and continue watching. The temperature in the room is definitely higher than when we first walked in and the cloud of smoke that fills the space is much thicker.

There's a couple off to the side, the guy's hands are all over her, exposing her to anyone who cares to watch like they've got no care in the world that they have an audience.

There are groups of mostly guys sitting around with girls either trying to get their attention or already grinding down shamelessly on their laps.

I sip on my drink as I look around. I have no idea what I'm drinking but I do know that it's strong. Strong enough that it's already making my head spin.

I locate the couches where I left Ashton and watch in shock as he leans forward to the coffee table and snorts a line of coke.

"Holy shit," I gasp, although I don't really know why I'm shocked.

"You look lonely," a voice says to my right and it makes my spine stiffen.

"Nope, just checking the place out." I regret the words the second they fall from my lips.

"I know something I'd like to check out." Axel's eyes run down the length of me and my skin prickles, but it's not with desire like when Ash does it.

"So you're friends with Ash?" I ask, hoping to turn this back to safe territory.

"I'm not sure I'd describe us as friends. But we like to do certain... activities together." An evil smirk curls at his lips as his eyes lock on my chest. "I really think you might enjoy it too."

"I doubt that. This isn't really my—" My words are cut off when he steps closer to me, his knee pressing between my thighs. "Do you mind?" I snap at him.

"No, not really." His eyes bounce between mine. "You really should drink up." He passes me a new drink, but I refuse to take it, Ashton's warning ringing out loud in my ear.

I look up to see if I can get his attention, but Axel's frame is too big, and I can't see past his shoulder.

"You think he's going to come and rescue you? You really are a stupid little rich girl. What I can't figure out is why Fury hasn't broken you yet. You're the perfect little toy."

I tremble as he reaches out and runs his fingertip down my neck, over my collarbone, and down to the swell of my breast. I swallow and close my eyes as I prepare for him to go lower but the second I do, his touch is gone.

"Motherfucker," a low, familiar voice roars before me.

I rip my eyes open to see what happened to find Ashton standing over Axel with his chest heaving and his fists clenched. I glance at Axel to find his nose spewing out blood all over the floor.

Time seems to stop for a few seconds as I stare at the scene before me until Willow rushes to Axel's side and helps him to sit up.

"You fucking asshole," she barks at him. "Do you know who that is?"

"Fury's latest fuck toy. Ow," he complains when the feisty little redhead punches him herself. I knew I liked her.

After another second, Ashton seems to break from his trance and he turns his cold, furious eyes on me. He takes two steps forward and I press myself back into the counter in my need to keep some space between us.

I've seen Ashton angry a few times now, but never like this.

Fear skates up my spine and without realizing, my hand releases the drink Axel had pushed into it.

"Let's go," Ashton grits out. It's so low and deep I almost think I imagine it until he reaches for my arm and pulls me behind me.

"Get him to give you my number," Willow calls out behind us, but I don't dare turn to look at her for fear I'll end up on my ass with the speed he's trying to make me walk.

"Ashton, slow down," I shout behind him. His grip bites into my forearm as we make our way down the hallway we entered from. "Ashton, I can't go this fast."

The second we're through the door, Aston stops, and I breathe a sigh of relief that he's going to let up, but I soon discover that's wishful thinking.

"Ashton, put me down," I squeal as I fly over his shoulder, his ass right in my face. "Ashton." I kick my legs, hoping that I can connect with a part of him somehow. "Ow," I squeal when his palm connects with my bare ass cheeks.

The realization that I'm flashing anyone who might be watching us gives me a new lease of life and I punch his lower back.

"Put me down," I scream but still he refuses as he eats up the sidewalk, carrying me wherever the fuck he's taking me.

I breathe a sigh of relief when I feel him cover my ass with the hoodie I was wearing when we arrived. That reprieve doesn't last long though because his fingers creep up my thigh until he's palming my ass.

"Get the fuck off me."

My head is starting to spin so much I'm worried I'm about to puke down his back where the blood is rushing to it so fast.

"Ashton, I swear to Go—shit." His finger slides through my folds, finding my entrance.

He says no words as he continues forward, his grip on my legs almost painful as he continues to tease me.

"Ash... fuck," I cry out as he pushes a finger in deeper.

I look up when he pauses and realize that we're at his apartment building. In seconds we're inside and then he's jogging up the stairs as if I'm nothing more than a feather on his shoulder, his finger still inside me.

He kicks open the door to his apartment before slamming it closed once we're inside.

Releasing me, he places me on my feet and I sway, worried that I'm about to pass out, but I don't get the chance because his hand finds my throat and he's right there, in my face, his breath mingling with mine and his eyes warning me about what's to come.

"What the fuck did I tell you?" he seethes, it's so quiet I almost miss it.

When I don't answer, his grip tightens but I don't panic like I probably should, if anything it just makes me even more aware of him, of his scent, his anger, his presence.

"Answer me," he demands.

"Y-you t-told me—"

"To stay by me," he all but growls.

"But—"

"You took a drink from him. You let him touch you."

"I didn't—" He sucks in a breath through his teeth. "I didn't drink it, and I didn't let him."

His eyes flit between mine as if he's fighting some inner turmoil before his fingers twitch once more and his lips crash to mine.

His kiss is bruising, dirty, wet, wicked and I give as good as I get. My anger at him, desire for him colliding headfirst and making me spin out of control. He releases my throat, his hands dropping to my thighs so he can lift me up the door and wrap my legs around his waist.

My bare core aligns with the fly of his jeans and I can't help but rub myself against him.

"No," he barks, ripping his lips from mine, his fingers digging into my hips to stop me moving. "You don't get to just take."

"Ashton," I warn.

"Maybe if you'd listened to me, it wouldn't have been like this."

"It was always going to be like this." Disdain drips from my words. "I hate you too much for it to be any other way."

His eyes are impossibly dark, his jaw popping with frustration and the vein in his neck pulsating. He's not just angry right now, he's barely holding himself together. Part of me fucking loves it. That I can make him lose control like this.

My nails scratch at his scalp as he lifts me higher and pins me there with his hips, freeing up his hands. His huge palms skim up my sides until his fingers wrap around the thin straps over my shoulders.

His eyes hold mine as he tugs. The fabric is so flimsy that it rips immediately.

"Ash," I gasp as the cool air of the apartment surrounds my breasts.

Dropping his head to the crook of my neck, he sucks the sensitive skin below my ear into his mouth until it starts to hurt.

"Ashton," I moan as the pain causes a flush of heat to wash through me.

He moves, but only slightly before his teeth sink into my skin.

"Oh God."

He continues down my chest until he's nipping and sucking over both of my breasts and teasing my nipples with the tip of his nose as he passes them.

My back arches against the door, desperate for more. My fingers twist in his hair as I try to pull him where I need him but he's too strong and denies me what I crave.

"Bad girls don't get what they want, little one. You're at my mercy now and you're going to learn what happens when you defy me."

"Shit, Ash, Please." I have no idea what I'm begging for really, but I know I need it. And need it bad.

I squeal as he pulls me from the door. His fingers dig into the flesh of my ass as he walks us toward his bedroom.

I fight for him to put me down but his grip doesn't falter until he throws me down on his bed. My dress is already around my waist, exposing everything to him but the second I stop bouncing he reaches out and pulls my dress from my body before my shoes hit the floor with a thud.

"Much better."

He pulls his hoodie over his head, dropping it to the floor beside him before he toes off his boots as his hands go to his waistband.

My mouth waters at the thought of seeing him bare. He's had full access to my body before, but he's always kept himself hidden from me, forcing me to use my imagination where certain parts of him are concerned.

His jeans drop from his hips and he kicks them off, his eyes never leaving me.

"I think it's time to resume what you started yesterday, don't you?"

Butterflies take flight in my stomach at what he's suggesting, but despite my nerves, I don't waste any time in scooting to the edge of the bed. I'm too desperate to bring him to his knees.

I already know from the hard set of his muscles that he's right on the edge, and I can't wait to finally push him off.

18

ASHTON

Her chest heaves as she sits on the edge of my bed with her huge green eyes staring up at me. The only time I've seen them this dark and full of desire was Halloween night. The night that's been imprinted in my brain ever since.

I wanted more that night, I'm not going to deny that. I was expecting more that night. Hell knows she was up for it, but the second she came down from her high and she passed out, I knew that was the end. I also knew I wouldn't be able to hang around and look into her eyes the next morning, knowing just how badly I needed her.

That night might have actually been the only night I've ever put a girl's needs and feelings before my own. Fuck knows I don't usually give a shit after getting what I wanted from her. But Ruby was different. She was always different, and not just because she's my stepsister.

The first time I looked into her eyes, the feelings that rushed through me almost brought me to my knees. Most of it was hate. I hated her for the life she had, for everything she took from me. But there was more to just that and the revenge I craved.

My entire body flinches when she reaches out and tucks her fingers under the band of my boxers. My cock is already trying to punch its way through the fabric but it gets even harder at the thought of what's to come.

Reaching out, I thread my hands into Ruby's hair.

"You gonna keep me waiting, little one?" I grate out.

It's impossible to miss that her hands are trembling against me. I know she's a virgin, she accidentally announced that to me after I fucked her over with her mother—a little reward that I wasn't expecting after that stunt, but one I'm happy about, nonetheless.

When she still doesn't move, I lift my other hand and run my thumb along her full bottom lip.

"Anyone ever been inside this pretty little mouth before?"

She shakes her head so slowly and my breath catches in my throat at her admission.

When I looked up from doing that line earlier, the coke assaulting my senses, I thought I was hallucinating as I watched X reach out and fucking touch her. He's a stupid motherfucker, he's proven that time and time again, but I didn't think he'd do something so brazen after I warned him to stay away from her.

My fingers tighten in her hair as my anger returns full force. I might have let her go to the bathroom alone—I'd just watched Willow walk in after all—but maybe she was right to be surprised. I should have fucking escorted her.

I thought she was safe with Willow. I trusted Willow with things that Ruby doesn't need to know about. Her fucking brother though, not a fucking chance.

My knuckles ache as I tighten my fists again, moving her closer to where I need her.

"I'm not going to wait all fucking night."

I feel like a prick, but I can't help it. I fucking need her just as much as I need the memory of him touching her out of my head.

My words spur her on because she tugs at the fabric around my hips and allows them to drop down my legs and my cock to bob in front of her.

She gasps before her tongue sneaks out and runs across her bottom lip where my thumb just was.

Cupping her chin, I tilt her head up so she's forced to look into my eyes.

"Don't stop until I'm coming down your throat, little one. You owe me."

She swallows nervously and my grip tightens as my thumb caresses her cheek.

"As long as you don't use your teeth, trust me, you can't fuck this up."

She nods and I release her. She stares at me for another second before focusing back on my cock.

Her hand burns and I suck in a sharp breath as she takes me in her small fist.

"Fuck," I grunt as she begins to jack me. "Ruby, I need—" A groan rips from my lips as she leans forward and licks at my tip. "Fuck, yeah. That."

At my reaction, she gets braver, licking at me and gently sucking me into her hot little mouth.

It's fucking mind-blowing but the second she properly sucks me past her lips and to the back of her mouth my knees almost give out.

My fingers tighten in her hair as I try to stop myself from thrusting even farther and forcing myself down her throat.

I watch her as she pulls off me, her cheeks hollowed as she sucks on me, her eyes locked on mine, and her lipstick smeared over both of us.

"You need to remember this the next time you let someone else touch you."

She shakes her head, wanting to argue with me but I don't give her the chance to pull away and say anything. It wouldn't matter even if she did. X isn't exactly the kind of guy who waits to be asked before he takes what he wants.

He and I have been in competition for years. It's turned ugly more than once, and I know he wouldn't bat an eyelid to try to take Ruby from me. Anything to hurt me, to look like the big man in front of his boys.

I shake my head, forcing the thoughts out. I don't need to think about any of it. I'm not here for them. My time with them was severed the second Mom's eyes closed that day and my life here officially ended.

Needing more, I forget about my earlier promise to myself not to push her and I flex my hips until the tip of my cock fills her throat.

She gags and splutters around my length, and I let up a little.

"You want me, little one. You gotta take what I give."

She nods at me and eagerly sucks me back into her mouth.

She takes me deeper this time, relaxing her muscles and giving me everything her innocent little mouth can manage.

The image of her before me, the heat of both her mouth and hand, and I'm racing toward my release sooner than I'd like.

"Ruby," I groan, my eyes locked on her bobbing up and down on my length. It's the only warning she's going to get. If she wanted a nice boy who would pull out, then she should be sucking one of the posh boys from Rosewood, not this scumbag from the backstreets of Seattle.

"Shit, fuck," I bark a second before my cock jerks in her mouth and my fingers tighten in her hair as I empty myself down her throat, just like I promised I would.

The second I pull out of her mouth, I slide my hands around her waist and lift her into me, slamming my lips down on her and wrapping her legs around my waist.

I can taste myself on her tongue, but it doesn't put me off one bit, if anything, it just reminds me of what she just did and ensures my cock doesn't stay soft for long.

"You like sucking my cock, little one?" I groan, my words getting lost in our kiss.

"Ashton," she moans before sucking my bottom lip into her mouth and biting down hard. The taste of copper fills my mouth.

"You," I spit, narrowing my eyes at her. "You just fucking drew blood."

"Yeah?" she asks, a smirk pulling at her lips. "What the fuck are you going to do about it?"

"Oh." I chuckle. "You have no fucking idea."

She squeals as I launch her at the bed before the sound of my name echoes around the silent apartment as I walk out of the bedroom, leaving her alone.

"Where the hell are you going?"

I grab a bottle I'd left on the side, twist the top, and throw it somewhere as I make my way back to the bedroom.

My steps falter when I find her still naked in the middle of my bed. She watches me as I lift the neck of the bottle to my lips and swallow down a generous shot.

The high I'd found tonight is long gone and I need it back. I need everything I can get my hands on right now if I'm going to attempt to forget about what tomorrow is going to bring.

"You gonna share or do I have to watch you drink it all," Ruby sasses, her eyes running down the length of me and locking on my cock which is once again standing at attention for her.

Walking over, I hand her the bottle before crawling onto the bed at her feet and pushing her ankles wide.

She's clearly not expecting that because in her shock, vodka spills from the bottle and drops onto her chest. Leaning forward, I lick up her breast, collecting up the trail of liquid as I do.

"Oh God," she moans, dropping the bottle to the bed to give me better access to her body. It's at that moment I realize she's more dangerous than the alcohol in her hand or the blow I snorted earlier. She's the exact fucking distraction I need, and I'm fully prepared to make use of every second of her tonight.

I continue licking at her, sucking her sensitive skin into my mouth and nipping at her until she's covered in little red marks. Finally, I suck one of her nipples into my mouth and tug hard as she arches off the bed.

"Ashton," she cries, her fingers tightening in my hair, holding me to her. I sink my teeth into her, and she squeals as if she's already close from this alone.

"You want more?"

"Yes," she squeals as I suck on the other one.

"Why? Why didn't you listen to me tonight?"

"I'm... I'm sorry. I didn't think... shit," she moans as I start kissing down her stomach.

"No, little one. You didn't think. Those parties, they're not the good little high school parties you're used to."

"I... I noticed."

"You don't watch your back here, someone will stab you in it. It's every man for themselves. So if you want to make it back to Rosewood in one piece, I suggest you start listening." I have no idea if my threat is necessary. After the way Axel looked at her earlier, there is no way I'm letting her back into one of those parties. It was fucked up that I took her in the first place. But this place, me, we're fucked up.

I shouldn't have rubbed her in his face as I did, but he fucking deserved it after his last little stunt. I might not have given a shit about the girl he took from me, but that's not the fucking point.

"Ashton." Her voice drags me from my memories, my feud with that prick.

"You wanna come, little one?"

"Uh-huh."

"You want me to eat you again until you come all over my face just like last time."

"Yes, Ash. Yes," she begs, her back arching and her hips rolling with her need for me to touch her.

I kiss across her pelvic bone before I lift one of her thighs and sink my teeth into the soft flesh, sucking until I know I'll leave a deep red mark behind. My fucking mark.

Any other motherfucker here even gets the chance to get anywhere near her, they'll soon learn she's fucking taken.

When I pull back, I can't help but smile at the darkness of my brand.

"You see that, little one?" I ask, looking up at her.

She glances down, her wild eyes take a few seconds to focus but the moment she sees it, she gasps. "Ash," she cries.

"Mine," I state, running my finger over the angry mark before trailing it up to her pussy and sweeping it through her wetness.

My eyes hold her hooded ones as I circle her entrance.

"Say it."

She licks her lips, and my cock jumps at the sight.

"W-what?"

"Who does this pussy belong to, little one?"

"Y-you?" I'm not sure if it was meant to come out as a question but it does.

"Yes, Ruby. Fucking mine."

I reach for the bottle of vodka and swallow down some more before handing what's left to her.

"Drink. Then you're mine."

She eagerly tips it back and the second she pulls the bottle away from her lips, I latch mine around her clit.

She moans around the mouthful of vodka as her body tenses. "Oh my God," she finally cries once she's swallowed.

19

RUBY

My back hits the mattress as he circles my clit with his tongue.

My head spins with the vodka and the events of the night. Of the party, Axel, Willow, and Ashton.

He was so fucking angry.

Fear races down my spine once more at the memory, but it mixes with what he's doing to me and I cry out his name.

So good.

He slides a finger inside me, and everything apart from the two of us falls away. There is no Seattle, no bullshit between us, no hate, It's just us, this moment and pleasure. So much pleasure.

My fingers sink into his dark hair as I try to pull him closer. He's right up in my business but still, it's nowhere near enough, and I'm not sure it ever will be.

I wonder if that's how he felt while my mouth was so full of his cock. I always thought I'd hate doing that, it certainly never really appealed to me with any of the guys I've got close to before, but the second I pulled his boxers down, taking him my mouth and making him feel as good as he had me that night was all I could think about.

He pushes a second finger inside me as he continues his assault on my clit. I feel so full, but I have a feeling that it's nothing compared to where this is going.

The rational side of my brain knows I shouldn't let it go there, but the reckless girl inside of me knows that it's exactly what's going to happen. It should have happened on Halloween, we both know that, and maybe if it did, we wouldn't have ended up as we have. He might not have run, he might not have a reason to claim he has images from that night. He might care.

I shake my head. No, he still wouldn't care.

Being here, going to that party tonight, it taught me a lot about Ashton, things that explain a lot about the cold, dark person that he is. I'm pretty sure at this point in his life he's incapable of caring. He's too lost.

My skin starts to burn and my body begins to feel weightless as my orgasm builds higher and higher.

His finger bends just so and he rubs at that magical spot inside of me that makes my eyes cross with pleasure.

I'm just about to fall over the edge, the beautiful oblivion is right there, right in touching distance... and then it's gone.

"What the—" I look to find Ash between my legs, wiping the back of his hand across his mouth. His eyes are dark and his lips are parted as he heaves out his breaths.

Fuck, he's beautiful.

Dark. Dangerous, Addictive. But really fucking beautiful.

A smirk curls up at one side of his lips.

"You defied me, little one."

My chin drops in shock. "Y-you can't leave it there."

"Can't I?" His hand slides down the inside of my thighs and my core clenches.

"Such a pretty pussy. It's going to be such a shame to ruin it."

He teases me with one fingertip, ensuring my orgasm remains right there, teasing me.

"Ashton, please."

"Please, what?"

"Please..." I look down to where he's playing with me and then to his cock. "Fuck me."

If he's shocked by my words, he doesn't show it.

"Thought you'd never ask."

He throws my legs around his waist as he scoots forward. My eyes remain locked between my legs as he takes himself in hand and glides the tip through my wetness.

"Ash," I moan, my head falling back in pleasure as he lowers it to my entrance and pushes just slightly inside me.

My muscles ripple, trying to pull him in deeper, to find out just how he'll feel.

"Are you on the pill, little one?"

I nod.

"Do you trust me?"

I shake my head. "Not even a little bit, Ash."

He chuckles, reaching over me to his nightstand. After a beat, he pulls back with a little silver square between his fingers.

"I've never gone bare, Ruby. Not even this close to it."

"Bullshit," I moan as he keeps moving against me.

"No," he barks, his hand wrapping around my throat, forcing me to look at him. "Not bullshit. Not even close."

I know he's not telling me this to convince me not to use one. If he wanted to go down that route, he'd be inside me already.

My heart races as I look between him and the condom, my head screaming at me that I shouldn't be so reckless. But tonight, I don't give a shit.

Reaching out, I pluck it from his fingers and fling it across the room.

"Little one?"

"Let's have our firsts together," I whisper, already knowing that he's far from an actual virgin. I don't need his skilled touch and confident words to know that, just his aura says it all. Plus, if tonight's party is how he used to spend his time here, then... well... anything is literally possible. I watched him snort coke while a couple fucked against the wall somewhere behind him.

My thoughts vanish from my head the second his lips pull into a smile and his fingers tighten on my throat. "Yeah?"

"Yeah. Tonight, it's just me and you." I lift my hand and trace the fullness of his lips with my finger. "Nothing between us."

He drops his lips to mine and plunges his tongue into my mouth, searching for mine and forcing it to join, which it does willingly.

After long delicious minutes, he pulls back. His forehead rests against mine and his dark, haunted eyes bore into me.

"I'm not the guy you should give this to, but like fuck is that going to stop me."

His lips slam down on mine once more, his fingers twitching around my neck, but his thumb gently caresses my pulse point making my head spin. Then just when I relax into it, he thrusts his hips forward. His grip on me stops me from flying up the bed as my body tries to process what just happened.

"Oh fuck," I cry as the pain sears through me. It's like I'm being ripped in two.

Tears burn the back of my eyes and I squeeze them tight, not wanting to ruin all of this by crying.

He doesn't move, hell, I don't think he even breathes as I lie there trying to compose myself as the pain begins to subside.

"Ruby?" His voice is so soft, so at odds to all the wicked things he's said to me since... well, since we met that it makes my eyes fly open. The second they do, tears escape, trickling down my temples and soaking into my hair.

Releasing my throat, he leans down and licks my tears away before bringing his lips back to mine.

But this kiss is different. It's softer, sweeter, and does nothing for the emotion clogging my throat or the tears that are still in my eyes.

After a few minutes, he moves, and pain and sparks shoot out from my core.

"Oh," I gasp.

"You feel so good, little one. So fucking tight." His words give me the confidence I didn't even realize I needed.

"Yeah?" I breathe, running my hands up his sculpted back and resting them over his shoulders as he continues to move slowly.

He kisses across my cheek before his lips press against my ear.

"I've never taken anyone's virginity before," he admits quietly, making me gasp. "In case you wanted another of my firsts."

"Ashton," I moan when he suddenly sits up. The angle change is mind-blowing.

I rip my eyes open and look at him sitting between my thighs with his cock buried deep inside me. I look over every inch of him, every line, indent, and tense muscle, and it's when I notice just how tense he is that I recognize how torturous this must be for him right now. His restraint is way better than I'd have given him credit for.

"Fuck me," I breathe. A smile twitches at my lips when his eyes shutter at my words.

"Fuck, little one."

He slides his hands under my ass, lifting me slightly before he pulls almost all the way out before sliding straight back in.

The pain is still there, but as I take his length again, something else takes over. My lost orgasm begins to resurface and for the first time, I wonder if he left me hanging not just to torture me but in the hope it might make this better.

He repeats the action, again and again, his movements remaining slow. His fingers dig into my ass with his need for more but at no point does he give in to it.

I moan, my back arching when he pushes deeper.

"Good?" he asks, his voice strained.

"Yeah, more."

He releases my ass, bringing his fingers to my clit and pinches hard.

"Oh shit."

"Sure you're ready for this?" he asks, a smirk on his lips.

"Give me everything."

The next time he slowly pulls out, he doesn't take his time sliding back inside me, instead, he powers forward, slamming into me and making me shoot up the bed.

His other hand clamps around one of my hips and he ups his pace, slamming into me again and again.

My eyes get heavy as my release gets closer once more, but with his eyes locked on mine, I can't find it in me to close them. I want to watch him. I want to see the moment he falls over the edge again.

He pinches my clit harder once and I lose all control of every part of my body. My muscles lock up and my eyes slam shut as pleasure crashes into me. Wave after wave of white-hot, addictive, ecstasy.

At no point does he stop moving and thankfully my release subsides just in time for me to open my eyes and to witness him lose control. He throws his head back, his grip on my hips becoming impossibly tight before he roars, and his cock jerks violently inside me. Knowing what he's doing, that he's marking me, branding me, just like he did on my thigh, sends aftershocks from my orgasm racing through me.

"Holy shit," he pants, dropping down on top of me and pressing me into the mattress. Our sweat-slick skin sticks together as his fingers absently trace circles on the hip he just released.

"You okay?" he mumbles, his voice heavy with exhaustion.

I'm silent for a minute as I consider his question. My body aches, my head spins, but fuck, I feel so alive right now.

A smile, despite the fact he can't see it. "Yeah. Yeah, I am."

He doesn't say anything in response, and I can only assume he's passed out on top of me.

I run my fingers through his hair, loving the softness against my skin before I trail them down his neck and onto his back. His skin prickles under my touch and I can't help but smile that I affect him—even if he is asleep right now.

"You're making me hard again," he whispers, startling me.

"Shit, I'm... sorry."

"Don't," he snaps harshly, pulling his face from the crook of my neck. The second I look into his eyes, I relax at the heat staring back at me. "Don't ever apologize for that."

I don't get to respond because his lips find mine and I'm swept away in his kiss.

We kiss for the longest time, our hands explore everything we can reach, but at no point does he try to take it further. He's way more thoughtful than I ever expected him to be, and the polar opposite of how all of this started.

"Shower with me," he murmurs in my ear before licking up the sensitive skin of my neck.

"Okay," I breathe, knowing that I could really do with one after all of that. Although when he climbs from the bed, leaving me cold, I regret my decision instantly. That isn't until he bends down and scoops me into his arms.

"I can walk."

"You don't have to." He carries me all the way to the bathroom before turning the shower on and stepping inside once the water is warm.

I gasp when he presses my back against the tiles, the coldness biting into my flushed skin.

"I can't get enough," he admits before capturing my lips once more.

Water rains down over us, washing away the evidence of tonight and letting it swirl down the drain, I only hope it could take Ashton's anger at the world with it because even riding the high I am right now, I know that sometime soon I'm going to come crashing back to reality.

He unhooks my legs from his waist and lowers my legs to the floor before he begins kissing down my body until he's on his knees before me.

"Does it hurt?" he asks so quietly I almost miss it over the torrent of water.

"Just a bit tender," I lie. Reality is that it's more than a little tender.

Lifting one leg from the floor, he throws it over his shoulder before leaning forward and licking gently up the length of me. I'm still so sensitive from our time together that it's almost too much to bear.

My fingers tangle in his wet locks as he continues his gentle assault on me.

He doesn't let up until I'm coming against his face.

I'm still fighting to catch my breath when he stands before me, reaching out for my cheek.

"Hey," I say shyly. I'm not embarrassed, far too much has happened between us for that to be the case now, but staring at him right now, I feel like I'm finally meeting the real him. The Ashton who's put all his hate and anger to one side, the boy who—even if only for a few moments—has lowered his walls and allowed me to see the person hiding behind.

"Hey." A smile curls at his lips and I'm powerless but to step into him and reach up to feel them against mine once more.

Gentler than I thought he was capable of, he washes every inch of me before wrapping me in a towel and leading me back to his bedroom. He encourages me onto the bed and after fixing the twisted sheets he crawls in with me, pressing his front to my back and wrapping his arm around my waist, locking me in place.

"Ash?" I whisper.

"Yeah."

"Are you okay?" I know I should probably leave it and let him deal in his own way, but while he's been so open with me, I can't help digging a little more.

He thrusts his hips against my bare ass. "I've been worse, little one." He nuzzles my neck before gently biting down on my skin.

"T-that's not what I meant."

"I know. But that's all you're getting."

"Okay. But... if you want to talk, you know I'm here, right?"

"Go to sleep, Ruby. I'm trying to do the right thing here and let your body rest."

"O-okay," I say, fighting a smile that he's just admitted doing something nice for me, despite the fact my core clenches at his words and desire once again fills my veins. "I just needed you to know."

"Thank you," he whispers so quietly, I wonder if I was even meant to hear it.

I have no idea what time it is, all I know is it's dark outside and after the vodka and the exercise, I'm exhausted. Only minutes after we stop talking, I close my eyes and lose myself in the feel of him holding me so tightly.

20

RUBY

The second I wake up, I know something is wrong, and it's not just because he's not holding me any longer—like he was every time I woke up in the night—it's more than that, I can sense it.

I guess I shouldn't be surprised. Today is the day we bury his mother. I still have so many questions about her, about what happened, about how he's dealing with it. But he shuts down every attempt I've made to talk about it.

I want to be what he needs, but at the same time, I know that bottling it up isn't going to help in the long run.

He blames himself. He hates himself. That's about as much as I know, and it doesn't really give me a lot to go on to try to help.

My head gently throbs at my temples reminding me of last night's vodka and I sit up slowly so I don't upset my stomach. I pull at the sheets to cover my still naked body but they don't move. I soon discover why when I look up.

Ashton is sitting on the end of the bed with his head in his hands. His shoulders are slumped in defeat and my heart aches for him. I want to help, I want to take the pain away, but I can't. I can't do fuck-all but stand beside him while he experiences what I'm sure is about to be the worst day of his life.

If he knows I'm awake, then he shows no signs of it. Sliding forward, I push my legs off the bed and sit beside him before wrapping my arm around his shoulder and placing my other hand on his thigh.

He tenses at my touch but he doesn't do anything else.

"Tell me what you need," I say, pressing my lips to his bare shoulder, hoping that he's going to let me in, let me support him.

He waits a few seconds, then sucks in a deep breath. I start to think he's going to respond and a little hope seeps into me but instead of speaking, he jumps up from the bed with such force that his elbow flies backward and straight into my eye.

I want to cry out as my eyes water with the pain, but I don't want him to feel any worse than he already does, so I swallow it down.

"Ash, what are you doing?" I ask when my vision clears, and I find him pulling on a pair of black sweats and a black zip-up hoodie.

"I can't fucking do this," he mutters before pocketing his cell and marching from the room.

"Wait," I call, running after him, not stopping to bother covering up. No point now, he's definitely seen everything I have to offer.

He stands in the doorway ready to leave the apartment but before he disappears, he looks back at me over his shoulder.

I gasp at the look on his face. His eyes are dark and haunted, his lips are pressed into a thin line. He looks... devastated. Broken. Totally and utterly lost.

"Ash, please," I beg, surging forward in the hope I can stop him walking out and doing whatever he's planning on doing.

But before I get anywhere near him, he swings the door closed behind him.

"Ashton," I scream, but I can only imagine that he's gone and knows I can't chase him. "Fuck's sake," I bark, spinning on the spot, not knowing what to do.

I take myself to the bathroom, make use of the toilet and brush my teeth as I try to get my brain to function. I inspect my eye in the mirror, thankfully, there's no sign of what just happened. I can only hope it stays that way.

Finding the hoodie he discarded when we got in last night, I pull it on and go in search of my purse, or more importantly, my cell.

I find it by the front door where I must have dropped it when he backed me up against the door.

Images of last night threaten to play out in my mind like a freaking movie, but I push them down. The tenderness between my legs is enough of a reminder right now.

Pulling my cell out, I call Mom.

"Good morning, sweetie. Are you ready?"

"Um..." I hesitate, looking around the apartment for a clock but coming up empty. Pulling my cell from my ear, I stare at the time and panic. "Not quite. Um... we might have a problem," I admit with a wince.

"What's wrong?" Mom's voice immediately changes with my words.

"Err... Ashton just stormed out. He's... um... he's not dealing with this very well. I'm not sure what—"

"Stephen," she says away from the speaker. "Ruby said that Ashton is gone."

I can't hear his response but whatever he says, she agrees.

"Our Uber is coming in ten minutes to go to the church, we'll get you on the way through. He'll be there. He just needs..." She trails off because, quite honestly, none of us know what he needs right now.

"I'll be ready," I say, rushing to hang up so I can get ready in record time.

Thankfully, I get just over thirty minutes before the buzzer goes off. I push my feet back into the shoes I wore last night and after grabbing my purse, I make my way to the door.

I find an Uber by the sidewalk with Stephen standing beside it in a sharp black suit.

He smiles sadly at me. "You look beautiful, Ruby. Have you heard from him?" His brows pull together in concern.

"No, I'm sorry. I don't think he's in a very good place."

I take a step toward the back of the car where I can see Mom waiting for me, but Stephen's voice stops me before I reach out for the handle.

"I have no idea what's going on between the two of you, but I just wanted to say thank you for being there for him... as much as he allows, anyway."

I open my mouth to respond but I soon find I have no words. I have no idea if I'm helping Ashton in any way right now. I think of last night, if it weren't me then I'm sure he'd have found someone else willing to help him forget for a few hours.

Jealousy twists my stomach as I think of the girl from the bathroom at that party last night. I've no doubt she'd have kept him company given half the chance.

"We should go," I say in the end, reaching forward and pulling the door open.

I'm wearing a black pencil skirt. It doesn't make getting in the car all that easy, but after a few seconds I drop down into the seat beside Mom.

"Hey, Mom," I say, glancing over at her.

"Hi, sweetie. How are you?" Something about her tone seems off. I have no idea if she's still pissed because she thinks I had sex in her bed or if she's annoyed that I'm not staying at the hotel with them. Whatever it is, I really don't have the energy to worry about it right now.

I stare out of the window as the car begins to move.

"Did he say where he was going?" she asks after a few seconds of silence. "If he was going to attend?"

"I don't know, Mom. He didn't say anything. I really hope he doesn't miss it. He'll regret it."

Mom nods, shooting Stephen a concerned stare.

"He'll be there," he says, his voice full of confidence I really don't feel.

There are a few people gathered already when we arrive at the church. But when I look around, I don't see him.

"Come on, Ash," I mutter to myself as Stephen goes to talk to someone, dragging Mom with him.

I stand awkwardly on the bumpy path that leads toward the church entrance, praying that he comes. Desperate for him not to make a mistake that he's going to regret forever.

He told me he wanted to at least do this right. I really hope he meant that.

We're welcomed into the church in time for the arrival of the coffin, but still, he's not here.

I sit closest to the aisle with Mom and then Stephen beside me. My knee bounces as we wait. A handful of people fill the church behind us, and I can't help wondering who they all are and if they're as concerned about Ashton's absence as I am.

"He'll be here," Stephen whispers over to me, probably in an attempt to stop my leg annoying the crap out of him.

After long, silent, anxious minutes, the priest comes to stand at the front, and I try to swallow down the lump of emotion that's suddenly appeared in my throat.

"Could you please stand?"

We do as we're told, and the organ starts playing. My stomach twists as my eyes burn. I can't help it. I might not have ever met the woman, but she was Ashton's mom, Stephen's wife. I feel their pain, their loss right alongside them. I might not know the whole story behind her and Stephen's relationship, but I know he cared enough to marry her, to have a baby with her. No matter the outcome of them, he still cared, like I know my mom and dad do for each other.

Everyone shifts around me, the rustling of their clothes filling my ears, as I assume they look to the doors. Although I'm not sure why, this isn't a freaking wedding.

I suck in a deep breath, trying to center myself so I don't end up a blubbering mess, and I look over my shoulder.

What I find sucks all the air from my lungs.

"Ashton." His name is the faintest of whispers on my lips as I stare at him.

He's wearing the same clothes that he walked out of the apartment in, only now the hood is up.

His eyes are focused on a point at the front of the church as he walks down the aisle with his mother's coffin on his shoulder.

My vision blurs as I watch him. His expression hard, his eyes cold and his jaw tense as he moves.

I have to fight to keep a sob inside.

He came, and not only is he here, but he's doing this... for her. It's too much.

My body shakes with my need to cry, but I know I've got to fight it. I've got to be strong for him, even if he doesn't think he needs me to be.

I blow out a shaky breath as I rip my eyes from him and take in the two guys behind him that I can see. Their hoods are up, and they're dressed exactly the same as Ash, but my breath catches when I realize that I recognize them. The one directly behind him is the guy he was talking to on the couch last night, Cash, I think. And behind him, surprisingly, is Axel.

I watch as the three of them move past me. If any of them are aware that I'm here watching them, then they don't make it known as they continue to walk forward and in only a few seconds, place the coffin on the stand. Five of them step away but Ashton pauses beside the coffin.

Mom must sense that I'm about to lose control because her hand slips into mine. I squeeze it tight in the hope it might help, but nothing does. The sight of a broken, devastated Ashton standing before his mom absolutely wrecks me.

Everything he's done to me since he reappeared, his vicious words, his cruel touch, all of it drifts off until it all means nothing.

That boy. That cold, angry, merciless boy, is utterly lost, completely shattered, and drowning faster than any of us realize.

My heart aches for him. My muscles scream at me to walk over there and to pull him into my arms, to give him the kind of support that I'm sure he's desperate for right now.

But I can't. I know I can't.

He won't accept it. He barely accepts it when we're alone, there's no way he'll accept it in a room full of people. He won't allow himself to show anyone in here that kind of weakness.

After a second, he reaches out and places his hand on the smooth wood of the coffin.

His shoulders rise and fall at a rapid rate as he stares down. I swear every single person in that congregation holds their breath in those few beats as we all watch him say goodbye to the person he loved most in this world.

After another second, his hand drops along with his shoulders and he takes a step back. He doesn't turn around or look over his shoulder. He doesn't need to, he seems to know where he's going as he backs toward the pew beside where we're standing and joins the five guys he walked in with.

"Please be seated."

Everyone moves, but I'm frozen in place as I stare at Ashton's profile. I can't see a lot, he's still got his hood over his head but I see enough.

I want to walk over, slide my hand into his hand and stand—or sit—strong beside him.

"Ruby," Mom hisses, dragging me from my trance, and reluctantly, I turn back to face the front and lower my ass to the cold wood beneath me.

The service is beautiful, the way people talk about Leanora only confirm what I already know—that she was an incredible woman. Each person who speaks does so with such love in their voice, their expressions showing such loss.

By the time the priest brings this part of the funeral to a close and instructs us to head outside, I feel like my emotions have been tossed in the dryer. I barely know which way is up as I stand and walk beside Mom out of the church, knowing that I'm leaving him behind to take his mom to her final resting place.

My eyes bore into the side of his face as I pass, desperate for him to turn to me, but he doesn't so much as flinch.

Mom and I don't speak as we follow the others toward the burial ground. Stephen walks behind us, also silent.

The congregation feels smaller as we all stand around the grave. I've only ever been to one funeral before and that was a cremation. This feels so much more final seeing a hole in the ground where she's going to rest.

After only a few minutes, the coffin is before us and the hooded pallbearers join the crowd. But this time, Ashton breaks away from his little dark gang of six and he comes to stand right beside me on the edge of the semi-circle we're all standing in.

I look up at him, but he doesn't return my stare. His eyes are still locked on the coffin, his face still set in his stone mask. I think he probably hopes that means no one can see beneath it. But he's wrong. While his face might be unreadable, his expression impenetrable, his eyes tell a whole other story, and I haven't even looked into them directly. But I know that when I do, what's inside them is going to slice me open.

The priest begins the next bit of the service as the cold air of Seattle bites into our skin, our breaths coming out in white clouds around us.

I have no idea what he says. His words blur into just background noise as the heat from Ashton's arm burns through my coat and into mine.

I want to reach for him but I can't. My fists curl at my sides as I try to stop myself from doing something that he won't want, something that will push him over the edge.

I sense the ceremony is coming to an end as the priest moves around the grave with a shovel in hand ready to commit her to rest. The sight, the thought that she's about to be buried in the ground has a lump so huge in my throat that I struggle to breathe around it.

I'm not the only one with the same issue because people sniffle and shift uncomfortably around me, but I don't look at any of them, I can't, my eyes are locked on that wooden coffin as the first pile of soil rains down on it.

A gasp sounds out from beside me. It's the only reaction I have heard or seen from him since he arrived. Part of me is relieved that he's actually feeling, seeing what's going on. I was worried he'd somehow completely checked out and although he was here in body, his mind was entirely elsewhere.

The second pile is thrown in and my body startles as his hand threads through mine. His fingers grip mine impossibly tight causing pain to shoot up my arm but I can't move, I just deal with it because right now, he needs a lifeline and I refuse to cause him any more pain than he's already in.

We stand, side by side, connected, as the priest finishes whatever he's saying.

The world around me blurs as I stand beside an unmoving Ashton.

The sound of people talking fills my ears before movement around me alerts me to the fact they're walking away.

"There's a car waiting for both of you. Take your time. We'll see you at the reception," Stephen says in my ear.

Turning to look at him, I smile sadly. “Thank you,” I whisper.

“Look after my boy.”

I nod, it’s the only thing I can do as a new wave of tears burn my eyes and turn the world blurry around me.

21

ASHTON

Ruby's hand is locked in mine with a vise-like grip. I know I should release her, allow her to follow all the others to the reception Dad organized. But I can't find it in me to do so.

I need her. I need her so fucking bad right now that I just can't let her go.

I know that all I'm doing is hurting her. And although a part of me planned for it to be that way, to show her just how lucky she was with the happy little family she had with my dad. But it's morphed into something I wasn't expecting and now I'm leaning on her in a way I shouldn't, sucking the life out of her to feed my own, to keep me fucking breathing.

I stare at Mom's coffin. The one I chose specifically for her, covered in a scattering of mud. That's all she is now. Just a body. A cold body in a box that's about to be surrounded by mud.

I did that. I caused that.

"It's all my fault." I don't realize the words fall from my lips until the hold Ruby has on my hand tightens. I'm surprised she's still got any blood left in it to move.

"No, Ash. None of this is your fault." Her voice is so soft that it has a flood of tears filling my eyes. I've fought all morning to keep it down, to swallow my pain, my loss, my grief. But standing here now, just the two of us. I'm not sure I can keep it inside any longer.

I'm exhausted. Completely fucking drained.

I drop to the cold, hard ground, and because I refuse to release her hand, Ruby has no choice but to follow me.

I keep my eyes on the hole in the ground before us as I pull my knees to my chest and wrap my one free arm around my legs.

"Axel and I had been picked up on the street. We were searched there and then, but despite the fact they didn't find anything, the officers threw us in the back of their cars, nonetheless.

"They thought we were dealing, or at least in possession. But it was our lucky day, or so I thought because for once, neither of us had anything on us, and we weren't actually doing anything suspicious.

"We were taken to the station, questioned, and made to sit and wait for fucking hours.

"Axel had been arrested time and time again, I knew he'd get out scot-free. His dad has enough of Seattle PD in his back pocket to ensure he's cleared of almost anything he could get pulled in for. I, on the other hand, didn't have that luxury. I might have worked for them, but I was disposable."

"But you said you didn't do anything," she says quickly from her matching position beside me. She still hasn't looked at me, and I've never been more grateful. I don't need anyone looking at me right now. I don't even want to look at myself.

"No, but the decent cops in the city are desperate to take down the Kingstons. They've been running rings around the authorities for years, but nothing has ever stuck. They're lawless, above it all. They manage to get away with everything and get it swept under the rug.

"Anyway, we were released and when I walked out, Mom was sitting there waiting to take me home. I'd never seen her so angry. She knew I was involved in some less than legal shit, although we'd never had a conversation about it, but I was bringing home more cash than most school kids to help keep the roof over our heads and pay off some of the debts she'd got herself into over the past few years.

"She didn't say anything as she wrapped her hand around my upper arm and all but dragged me out of the station like I was a kid, not almost a fully grown man who was bigger than her." A sad smile pulls at my lips at the memory before pain lances through my heart at knowing I'm never going to experience her trying to discipline me again. She used to tell me that no matter how old I was, that I was always going to be her little boy, that I would always be submitted to her harsh words whenever I screwed up, even when I was a married man with my own kids.

"We got in the car and still she was silent. I felt like such a shit. She was so disappointed in me." I blow out a long breath, silence settling between us.

She doesn't say anything and I'm grateful. I don't need an inquisition. I don't even know why I'm really telling her this. I guess it's just festered too long inside me and finally needs to come out. Expel my sins or some shit before we lay her to rest.

"I tried apologizing, but she wouldn't have it. I understood why. I'd told her after I got back from Rosewood that I'd step away from the Kingston boys, that I'd try to make a new start. Focus on trying to graduate, on football, but it was all bullshit. One offer of some extra cash for a job with them and I jumped at the chance.

"It didn't help that I was trying to do everything I possibly could to get this girl out of my fucking head," I admit with a wince. I don't look at her but I like to think she's smiling. It gives me the encouragement I need to continue.

"When she did speak, she was furious, and I realized that her silence was her trying to keep her cool until we got home, and we could really hash it all out.

"But we never got there. She hit a patch of ice and her car skidded off the road and down the little bank until we ended up wrapped around a tree.

"I blacked out and when I came to, I found her beside me, hunched over the wheel, her hand in mine, her eyes barely open." My voice cracks as I remember it as vividly as if it happened yesterday. "She... she told me that she loved me, that she was proud of me, that... that I needed to do something better with my life. S-she made me p-promise that I wouldn't go back to them."

Ruby shifts closer, pulling our joined hands closer to her while taking one away to wrap around my upper arm.

"S-she died. Right there in front of me."

"I'm so sorry, Ash," she whispers, her voice sounding as rough as mine.

I suck in a breath and turn my head to look at her. Her cheeks are streaked with her tears and the makeup they've washed away and there are more threatening to spill.

Her breath catches as her eyes find mine. I have no idea what's staring back at her but I can't imagine I'm looking my best right now.

She releases my arm and reaches out to cup my cheek, her thumb wiping at my skin, collecting up the tears I didn't even realize had fallen.

"She sounds like an incredible woman," she whispers, her eyes holding mine. "And she was really lucky to have you."

I bite down on my bottom lip to try to keep the sob in that threatens to erupt at her words. Instead, a laugh rips from my lips.

"I caused her nothing but shit for years." I laugh again, recalling some of the things I've done to piss her off.

"You're a teenager, that's kinda what we're supposed to do."

"Little one, don't try to tell me that you've ever pissed off your parents. You're such a goodie-two-shoes."

She smiles at me, and it makes something inside me feel a little lighter.

"I've had my moments. Plus, Mom's still off with me because she thinks I had sex in her bed so..."

I laugh, dropping my head as I remember her angry little face as she tried to plead her innocence.

"That was good. You can't deny that."

"You're an ass, Ashton Fury," she says lightly, but the second she realizes what she's just said, she gasps. "Shit, I'm sorry. I didn't mean to—"

"Shush, it's okay. Insult me all you want, it's really not going to make my day any worse."

"I'm—"

"Don't. Don't tell me you're sorry again. None of this is your fault. None of this is anyone's fault but—"

Her fingers press against my lips cutting off what she knows is about to fall from my lips.

"It was an accident, Ash."

Parting my lips, I suck her fingers into my mouth, needing to think about something other than the grief that's ripping me in two.

She smiles at me, her eyes darkening as my tongue laves at her.

"Ash," she half moans, half warns, flicking a glance over at the grave before us.

I release her fingers but not because she wants me too or because she thinks it's inappropriate, she should know by now that I don't really give a shit about what everyone else thinks is okay. I release her because I can't stop the words that spill from me. "She'd have loved you."

"W-who? Your mom?"

"Yeah, my mom. She always wanted me to meet a sweet girl who was strong enough to stand up to me."

"Ash, I'm not sure—"

I cut off her words in the same way she did me earlier, only I don't leave my fingers at her lips long enough for her to do anything with them because I slide them around the back of her head and pull her lips to mine.

Pushing my tongue into her mouth, I lose myself in her kiss and she lets me take everything I need. Her hand wraps around the back of my neck and squeezes lightly, her touch warms me from the inside out and makes me realize that maybe I'm not as alone as I thought I was.

I didn't want to move to Rosewood. I didn't want to be with Dad and his new family. But things are changing faster than I know how to control.

Breaking our kiss, I rest my head against hers and stare down into her eyes. The green shines bright with a mixture of lust and emotions that are swirling within them.

"You deserve better than this," I admit quietly. It's the truth, she deserves a hell of a lot better than how I've treated her, how I'm sure I'm still going to treat her.

"Take what you need right now, Ash."

"Fuck, little one."

"We should probably go," she suggests, pulling back from me.

I look around, suddenly realizing just where we are. The coldness from the ground beneath me seeps into my bones.

"Yeah, we should."

I push to stand, taking her hand and pulling her up with me.

"They're going to be waiting for you."

I open my mouth to respond but I decide against it for now.

We both brush ourselves off before I turn to Mom's grave once more. I pull Ruby into me and kiss her hair. Even in her heels, she's so small that I can easily rest my chin on the top of her head.

"Thank you," I whisper but it's not too quiet for her to hear because she tenses in my arms.

"I'm here, Ash. Take whatever you need."

I nod, silently accepting her words as I say my final goodbye to the woman who's given the best part of her life to ensuring I have a future.

"Bye, Mom," I breathe before turning my back on the grave and walking toward the gates with my arm locked around Ruby's shoulders, her arms around my waist for support.

Once we're outside the church grounds, I pull my cell from my pocket to call a car.

She spots what I'm doing and stops me.

"Your dad said a car was waiting for us." She looks down the street until her eyes land on an idling car. "There."

I allow her to lead me toward it, but I freeze when she opens the door and checks with the driver that he is indeed waiting for us.

She steps inside, tugging on my arm for me to join her but I don't move.

"Ash?" she asks, her brows pulling together in concern.

I shake my head. "I can't."

"But—"

"Please, Ruby. Just go and... and I'll be there in a bit."

"But—" she tries again but I don't have it in me to argue about this. "I'm sorry." I close the door on her and bang my hand on the roof instructing the driver to leave.

I watch the car disappear and it feels like it takes a part of me with it.

I don't look away until it turns the corner, only when I do look away, I just find myself looking over my shoulder to where she's resting.

Dropping my head into my hands, I scream out my frustration and my pain. If any of the pedestrians are particularly concerned by my actions, then they don't show it because while I stand there bleeding out my pain all over the sidewalk, everyone just continues on with their lives.

22

RUBY

I twist in my seat and watch him on the sidewalk as he stares at the car.

My heart aches for him and everything he's going through, but I know forcing him to do anything he doesn't want to right now is wrong.

He needs to do this in his own way and in his own time. And if he needs a breather before going to the reception, then who am I to judge? It's not like I really have any experience with the kind of loss he's experiencing right now.

I don't look away until the driver turns the corner, and he disappears from my sight.

I glance at the driver and I almost demand he turn around so I can go back to him. But I don't. I told him he could take whatever he needed to help get him through this, but I'm not forcing myself on him. If he wanted me beside him right now, I would be.

Fuck, why does that thought hurt so much?

I rub the heel of my hand against my chest as a shiver rips through me.

"I'm sorry, but is there any chance you could turn the heat up a little?" He agrees as I wrap my arms around myself and stare out of the window.

My eyes feel swollen from crying with Ashton, and my insides feel like they've been tossed around in a hurricane.

The drive to the reception is only short and long before I'm ready, the car is pulling up to some kind of hall.

"Thank you," I mutter to the driver before pushing the door open and climbing out. The sun is already starting to drop behind the buildings making the city look darker than it actually is.

I smooth my coat down over my butt, appreciating that it's probably covered in mud from sitting on the ground in the graveyard, but I can't really find it in myself to care.

The second I step through the doorway, I feel like every set of eyes turns on me.

I suck in a breath as my stomach tumbles.

Stephen comes racing over, quickly followed by Mom.

"Where is he?" he asks in a rush.

"He... um... he needed a breather."

"He's coming though, right?"

I stare at him for a beat, concern for his only son bleeding from his eyes. "I don't know, Stephen. I'm sorry. He's... he's really struggling."

"Shit. Where is he?"

"I don't know," I answer honestly. "But even if I did, I think it's best you leave him to do his thing."

He nods regretfully. "I wish things were different. I wish he'd let me in. What's the secret?"

A shocked laugh falls from my lips. "You're asking me? He hates me."

Stephen shakes his head. "Ruby, come on. You're smarter than that. My son doesn't hate you, he just hates himself right now. But he's let you in."

My lips part to respond, but I'm too shocked to find any words.

"Please, just... look after him."

"Stephen, I don't think—" My words are cut off as some guy similar in age to Stephen walks over and holds his hand out to him. Both he and Mom turn the man's way and introductions begin.

I blow out a breath and turn away from them in favor of finding the bathrooms. I feel like a hot mess and I've no doubt that I look like one too.

Spotting the sign, I make my way over, keeping my head down to ensure no one attempts to spark up a conversation with me.

Thankfully, it's empty. I stop at the basin and risk looking at myself in the mirror.

My eyes are red and bloodshot, my skin is blotchy and my makeup is a disaster... well, mostly missing, to be honest.

I wipe at the black smears under my eyes before turning toward a stall and locking myself inside. I close the lid and sit down. Dropping my head into my hands and allowing myself a few quiet minutes to collect my thoughts.

Everything that Ashton told me spins around in my mind like a vortex, his pain blends with mine and his desperation makes my heart hurt.

I wish I could help, could take it all away, but there's nothing I can do right now other than what he tells me.

My cell buzzes in my lap and I pull it out to find messages from both Harley and Poppy in our group chat asking how it's going.

I've barely spoken to them since we left Rosewood, and guilt adds to what I'm already trying to deal with.

Seeing that Harley sent the most recent message, I hit call on her name and wait for it to connect. It's not until it starts ringing that I realize that she's probably at practice but as I'm about to hang up, she answers.

"Hey, how are you?"

I open my mouth to speak but no words come out, instead, a sob rips up my throat.

"Shit, Ruby. Hang on." She covers the speaker, but I hear her tell Chelsea—I assume—that it's me and that she'll be back. "Hey, I'm here. What's going on?"

"God, Har. It's so awful," I say honestly. "It's like I'm watching him shatter before my eyes."

"Ashton?"

"Yeah, who else?"

"I... I don't know. What's going on, Rubes?" A door closes but I pay it little mind and instead focus on my conversation.

"I... um... I slept with him."

"Ruby," she half sighs, half laughs.

"I've been staying at his old apartment with him. He took me to this insane party last night, and... ugh... I don't know. One thing led to another and..."

"You gave him your V-card."

"Yeah."

"How was it?" she asks curiously.

"It was..." I blow out a breath. "Amazing. But then today happened and... ugh... I don't know. This is a mess. He's a mess. I don't know what I'm doing."

"Everything will be fine, Rubes. When are you back?"

"Our flights are tomorrow but I have no idea if we're going to drive back again or what. Stephen's car is here so..."

"We... uh... we really need you back, Rubes. Nationals are next weekend."

"I know, I know." I really don't need her to tell me this. I'm well aware that time is not on my side here.

"I'm sorry, but I've got to go. Chelsea is giving me her best death stare. I'll call you later, okay?"

"Yeah. Thanks, Har."

"Anytime. Speak soon." She blows me a kiss before hanging up.

I put my cell away, make use of the toilet now I'm in here before pulling the door open with the intention of fixing my makeup and going back out there. Only I don't get that chance because when I look up, my world falls from beneath me.

"Mom?" Her brows lift. "How much of that did you hear?"

"Enough."

Disappointment and disbelief drip from that one word. My stomach clenches and I pray that the ground will swallow me whole and put an end to this whole day.

My heart races as she continues staring at me, and I replay that brief conversation with Harley over and over in my head.

"Ruby," she says slowly as if she can't even believe the words that are about to pass her lips. "Please tell me you didn't... that you haven't..." She can't even say the words.

I hate the way she's looking at me, like I've done something so dirty, so forbidden that she doesn't even want me standing in front of her.

Everything inside me screams to lie, to tell her it wasn't true that nothing has happened. But why should I cower down because she thinks it's wrong?

Yeah, things between Ash and I are... complicated. He hates me, and I'm pretty sure I still hate him... maybe. But when we're together, it's... different. He's different. He's let his walls down, he's allowed me in, even if for the briefest moment. I refuse to let her judgment ruin what's grown between us, even if it ends up being nothing.

"Yes, Mom. I slept with him."

She gasps, her eyes narrowing to the point I wonder if she can actually see me. "But... but... he's your stepbrother."

"Right, *step*." I roll my eyes at her. "We're not related. Stephen isn't my dad. Ash is just a boy I met recently just like I do with new kids at school on almost a weekly basis."

"But... you can't. He's Stephen's son."

"So because you're sleeping with his dad, Ash and I aren't allowed near each other? That's bullshit and you know it."

Her face reddens with anger.

Turning away from her, I twist the faucet with more force than necessary and wash my hands while she stands there fuming.

"Where are you going?" she snaps at me when I step toward the door.

"Back out there to support your husband."

"You need to stay away from him, Ruby. He's bad news."

"Oh come off it. You don't even know him."

"I know what Stephen has told me."

"Pfft, you think he knows Ash?" I shake my head. "You're delusional."

My hand is on the handle, ready to pull it open to storm away from her judgmental eyes when her words stop me.

"He's not a good person."

I spin on my heels and pin her with a look. "He's angry, I get that. I even understand it. He had a happy life here and then his dad left Leanora for you. He moved halfway across the country and abandoned him."

"Stephen didn't abandon him. His and Leanora's relationship was long over before he left."

"He was a child, Mom. That shit doesn't matter. In Ash's eyes, his dad left and shacked up with you, with us."

"Your dad left, and you never joined a gang."

I throw my hands up in frustration.

"Not even the same. Not even close. Dad lives on the other side of town." When he's actually in Rosewood, that is, and not away with work. "I can see him whenever I like. He can take me out, we can do things together. You two still talk, you're still friends. We have a nice house, a comfortable life. Ash didn't have any of that. He's watched Leanora struggle to keep a roof over their heads. She—"

"Was an alcoholic," Mom interrupts.

"Is it any wonder? Have you even seen where they live?"

"No, but—"

"No, Mom. I don't want your excuses and for you to tell me all the things you think you know. You don't know Ash, you don't know what it was like for him." I mean, I don't really and I'm going out on a limb here, but I refuse to allow her to judge us like she is. We did nothing wrong. We are doing nothing wrong.

So what if our parents are married?

"You're seventeen, Ruby." She tries changing tactics.

"Maybe so, but not for much longer. And in case you hadn't noticed. So is Ash, so don't pull the age card on me. And plus, are you really going to stand there and tell me that you and Stephen didn't do anything until you were both eighteen? I already know you were together at thirteen." I raise my eyebrows, reminding her that she tells anyone who'll listen that they were childhood sweethearts.

Her lips part but she has no words. She doesn't need them though, the answer is written all over her face.

"Right, so shall we continue this conversation when you can be less of a hypocrite?"

"Ruby," she warns, her voice low and angry.

"No." I hold my hand up to stop her. "All you need to know is that I know what I'm doing." I don't, I don't have a fucking clue but like fuck am I telling her that. "We're being careful, I'm on birth control, so you don't need to worry about that." I pull the door open as a thought hits me. "Oh, and... we didn't do it on your bed. That was a prank that Ash pulled on me. So don't worry, we haven't dirtied up your space."

I blow out of there before she has a chance to respond. My legs feel like jelly as I race down the small hallway and back to the party. I have never stood up to Mom like that before. To be fair, I've never had to. But there was no chance I was allowing her to look at me like that. Like I'm an idiot being corrupted by Ash. I walked into all of this with my eyes open, I can't help it if I never stood a chance against him.

I scan the room, looking for Stephen. I fully intend on giving him my apologies and getting the hell out of here. Something tells me that Ash isn't going to show his face, and I really can't deal with Mom again right now.

Spotting him across the room, I make my way over but I can't be halfway there when someone else catches my eye.

"Willow?" I breathe, my brows pulling together. Her pixie cut hair looks as perfect as it did last night and her makeup is on point, making me feel even more of a mess than I already did. And like most people in this room, she's wearing black, but I have a feeling that's not because she had any intention of attending a funeral. The rest of Ashton's friends didn't show up, so I'm assuming the church was it for them.

"You need to come with me." She reaches out and takes my hand, pulling me from the room without a second thought.

"Wait, I can't just leave," I argue, but it's weak at best.

"He needs you, Ruby. Who's more important right now? These people you've never met or him?"

My lips part to respond but she must read the answer on my face because she resumes pulling me toward the exit once more.

"What's he done?" I ask once we're outside and the noise of everyone's chatter has vanished behind us.

"Nothing yet, but it's only a matter of time. He's drowning, Ruby, and I think there's only one person who's able to keep him afloat." My brows pull together. "You, Ruby."

She opens the door of the muscle car we come to a stop by and all but pushes me inside. I drop down into the passenger seat as she races around and sits beside me, bringing the engine to life.

"This your car?" I ask, suddenly realizing this isn't the sort of thing I'd expect her to drive.

"No, it's Axel's. Probably best we don't tell him I borrowed it either."

"Your secret's safe with me." I really don't want to talk to that guy more than I have to.

Willow drives us away from this side of town toward where they live, or more specifically where the party was last night.

Dread twists in my stomach the closer we get until she pulls the car to a stop around the back of the building.

"What is this place?" I ask, looking at the old, dilapidated building before us.

"It used to be a factory, but business ceased a few years ago. It's been our hideout ever since. I'm pretty sure Dad's forgotten it even exists. Works perfectly for us." She pushes the door and twists to get out.

"Wait, who's your dad?"

"We definitely don't have time for that little history lesson. Let's just say that he's someone you probably never want to meet."

"Okay," I breathe as she closes the door behind her before I turn to do the same.

The second I'm out, she's ushering me toward the door.

She knocks and in seconds we're inside and heading back down the hallway. A hallway I kinda hoped I'd never see again.

The cigarette smoke mixes with the weed and I struggle to suck in the air I need.

We're just about to round the corner to where the party is when she suddenly turns to me, forcing me to stop if I don't want to crash into her.

"What?" I ask when her eyes search mine.

"I just... remember that he's really hurting."

My heart jumps into my throat. What the hell am I about to walk into?

I suck in a breath and nod at her.

"I know," I whisper but with the music booming in the distance, I doubt she heard me.

23

RUBY

If I thought my legs were weak when I walked away from Mom not so long ago, it's nothing compared to how I feel as I follow Willow into that party.

I look around and it feels like déjà vu. It makes me wonder if any of these people even left after we did last night or if this is just one permanent party down here. The number of cups and bottles that litter the place sure point toward the latter being the case.

I scan the people down here. There's less than last night. Maybe some of them do have lives aside from getting drunk and high.

The guys who carried the coffin earlier, well four of them, are sitting on the same couches Ash was at last night. Two of them look up and Cash smiles sadly at me before nudging the one beside him who also looks my way.

Their attention makes me nervous but not as nervous as knowing that both Ash and Axel are missing.

"Where is he?" I ask, turning to look at Willow who's standing beside me.

She tips her chin in front of us, and after a beat, I look that way.

I scan the heads looking for him but it's not until I get to the very far wall that my eyes land on him.

My stomach turns over, threatening to spill its contents over the concrete at my feet.

"Is that... is that..."

"Nat," Willow spits.

"He doesn't want her, Ruby. He's just—"

"Hurting. You said. Although I'm sure it hurts a little less with her tits in his hand," I mutter, taking in where his arm disappears under her shirt.

"He doesn't know what he's doing."

"You're really going to defend him?"

She spins me to face her. "He doesn't want her. He needs you. Go and prove it to him."

I turn back to look at him pressing that whore into the wall, his body pinned against hers, his hand disappearing and what I can only assume is his tongue in her mouth.

I think back to the kiss we shared in the graveyard earlier. It was so sweet, so full of emotion and need and the memory just shatters. He ruins it, just like he ruins everything.

My chest heaves as I continue to watch him. Betrayal flooding my veins, jealousy eating me from the inside out.

But he's not yours, a little voice says in my head.

"Ruby," Willow warns, beside me. "You can't just stand there staring. Go teach him a lesson."

The thought of walking over there and announcing my presence, seeing the smug as fuck look that I know will be on her face, fills me with dread.

Thankfully, I don't have to because as if he can feel my stare, he rips his lips from his little slut and looks over his shoulder.

His eyes don't focus for long seconds and my breath catches in my throat.

"Is he on something?"

"Yeah, although I have no idea what he's taken. Stupid motherfucker."

Just as I don't think things can get any worse, fear snakes down my spine a second before arms wrap around my waist and I'm hauled into a solid chest.

"Didn't think he'd let you back in here, baby," Axel practically growls down at me. His eyes run over me, heating with desire. "You look hot, but I gotta say, I preferred yesterday's dress."

"Axel, put her down. She's here for Ash."

"Yeah, but it seems to me that he's otherwise engaged. He fucked her yet?"

"Axel," she snaps. But he didn't need to ask the question out loud, we're all already wondering the same thing, I know that I am.

I look to Ash to find that he's pulled back from Nat a little, he's released her, but she's now wrapped around him like a fucking snake.

"My sister told you to teach him a lesson, so shall we?" he offers, his voice low and dangerous, but he doesn't give me a chance to tell him to fuck off because his grip on me tightens and before I know what's happening, my back crashes, against the wall, my head bouncing off it as pain shoots down my neck and I'm caged in by his huge body and his lips are on mine.

"No, no," I cry against his lips as his giant hand wraps around my waist, pinning me to the spot. "Get off me."

I find my fight just as his other hand drops to my leg in search of the hem of my dress and I lift my knee, but it doesn't connect because he's gone and when I open my eyes, he's no longer in front of me.

People shout, scream, and run toward me, excitement in their eyes.

"Don't fucking touch her," Ashton roars.

At hearing his voice, I look to where everyone else is and find him on top of Axel, smashing his fists into his face.

"Ashton," Willow screams, reaching for his arm but he pays her no attention as he pulls his arm back once more, his elbow connecting with her ribs and sending her stumbling back to the floor before he continues his assault.

The guys cheer him on, all hungry for blood while the few girls that are here either back away or scream.

"Fuck," I shout, ripping my eyes from Ashton's back to Willow, who's sprawled on the floor.

I rush her way because let's face it, she deserves my help more than either of those two.

"I'm okay. Go and stop him."

"Willow, I—"

"Please, Ruby. Just stop them from killing each other."

Jesus fucking Christ.

Pushing to stand, I storm over.

"Ashton," I scream at the top of my voice, not wanting to get too close after watching Willow go flying only moments ago.

But he doesn't so much as slow down.

"Ashton." I try again but the roar of the crowd and I'm sure the blood rushing in his ears right now is too loud for him to hear me.

Both his hands go around Axel's throat and I seize my opportunity.

Sucking in some strength, I take a step forward, hoping I can avoid his arms should he decide to use them and place my hand on his shoulder.

The second I touch him, his muscles relax under my touch.

"Stop," I plead, looking over his shoulder at Axel's almost unrecognizable face to find Ashton's grip on his throat hasn't lessened. "Ashton, please. You're going to kill him."

Axel splutters for breath, his fingers clawing at Ashton's forearms, desperate to get some air into his lungs.

"I should kill him. He fucking touched you... again."

"Ashton," I say much more calmly than I'm feeling. "Let him go."

After a few seconds he does before he slumps forward.

"Let's go," I demand, my voice hard once more as I try to keep my anger beneath the surface. I refuse to lose my cool in front of these many people, even if I want to wrap my hands around Ash's throat just like he did to Axel.

After a beat, he starts to climb from Axel's limp body. But he's not out of it enough because the second he can move, he sits and his fist flies toward Ashton's face.

His lip splits, bright red blood immediately begins trickling from it.

The roar that rips from Ashton's throat is like nothing I've ever heard before as he turns and with one swift punch to Axel's temple, knocks him cleanout.

"Fucking hell," I mutter, pulling at Ashton's arm to get him away from Axel in case he comes back to and tries again. It's unlikely looking at the state of him but I don't want to risk it.

As we back away, I feel his chest still rising and falling and breathe a sigh of relief. At least he hasn't killed him.

"We need to leave." He doesn't move for a beat, he plants his feet into the floor and just continues to stare at the scene he created before him.

"Ashton. Now," I bark.

Finally, he moves, but not toward the exit, instead, he turns his cold, angry eyes on me.

I gasp and he steps into my body. He stares down at me, his heat burning into me and his scent filling my nose.

The image of him with Nat slams into me and a fresh wave of anger and betrayal races through me.

Unable to control myself, my arm flies out before the soft skin of my palm connects with the roughness of his cheek.

His eyes flare in anger as he captures my wrist in a tight hold and hauls me into his chest.

"You're going to regret that, little one."

Before I even know we're moving, he's backed me up and I only realize we're in a side room when a door slams behind him and we're plunged into darkness.

"Does this hurt?" he asks, glancing at my palm which feels like it should be glowing red.

"Yes," I hiss. I'm just about to tell him that it was worth it when he roughly pushes me against whatever is behind me. A desk? A unit? I have no idea because aside from the light coming through a small, frosted window to the main room, it's completely dark in here.

"Well, allow me to help you forget about it."

His lips crash to mine, the taste of copper fills my mouth as I fight against him but he's too insistent and as his tongue slips past my lips is when I succumb to his kiss.

The kiss is the opposite of the one we shared in the graveyard only a little bit ago. There is no tenderness or concern about how the other is feeling. It's brutal, vicious, full of hate, and the need to hurt.

"Ashton," I pant as his lips rip from mine in favor of sucking on the skin of my neck.

"You drive me fucking crazy."

"See, I thought it was that whore who was driving you crazy not so long ago."

"She's nothing," he growls, his hand skimming my waist and sliding around until he's squeezing my ass, his fingers digging in until it starts to hurt.

"No? You sure seemed to be enjoying yourself with your hand up her top."

"I needed a distraction."

A bitter laugh falls from my lips. "I've heard that before. Is that all I am to you?"

He pulls back from nipping at my collarbone and looks into my eyes. He looks so fucking deep, I swear he can see right into my soul. His blown orbs flashing in the darkness surrounding us.

"No, Ruby. That is not all you are to me. You're... you're... different."

"Right. So different that it's fine to come here, get fucked off your ass, and feel up some whore. Fuck you, Ashton. I'm worth more than this."

I push from whatever it is he has me against, but I don't get very far because the second I move forward, he comes at me with more strength and I end up against the wall.

"You're everything, Ruby. Fucking everything."

One minute my feet are on the floor and the next my skirt is bunched up and my legs are wrapped around his waist.

His hard length grinds against my core and my head spins.

"You feel that? That's for you, only you."

"You're a lying shit, Ashton. Don't try to tell me you weren't hard for her only minutes ago."

"It wasn't her I was hard for. She might have been the body, but in my head, it was you. Only you."

"So you were going to fuck her, imagining it was me. That's fucked-up." He continues to grind against me, the pleasure sparking from my core making it harder and harder to think straight.

"Fuck," he groans. "Yeah. Always you in here, little one," he admits, tapping his temple. "Always fucking you."

His lips find mine again and this time, I don't fight. I can't.

"Ashton," I moan when his fingers slip inside my panties and find my core.

"So wet for me. You like fighting, huh?"

"You're an asshole," I say, my head falling back as he spears two fingers inside me.

"I know, but I think you love it."

"Oh God." He finds that spot inside me and rubs until I see stars.

His lips brush my ear. "I didn't want her, Ruby. I needed... I needed out of my head and you... you weren't here."

"Because you sent me away," I gasp as he stretches me wider.

"I... I need you."

"So take me, Ash."

His cock is pushing at my entrance in record time.

"Oh God," I whimper as my body tries pulling him in deeper.

I shouldn't need him this badly. It's dangerous. And I already know it's going to damn near kill me when it all comes crashing around my feet. Because I have no doubt it will.

24

ASHTON

The second I thrust up into her, everything in my head settles and everything feels right once again.

I knew the moment her car vanished from my sight that I'd make a huge mistake sending her away.

She was my lifeline. She was the one thing that was stopping me from drowning and I'd just let her go.

Going to the factory wasn't a conscious decision, it's ingrained in me to go there when shit gets too hard. It's been the place I've escaped to for years. Down there, no one judges, no one criticizes, everyone just lets you lose yourself in whatever poison you choose. Alcohol, drugs, pussy. Anything and everything is on offer and available at almost every hour of the day, and never have I needed to lose myself more than I did after walking away from that church and leaving Mom to rot in the ground.

The boys were already there and the second they saw me, someone shoved a bottle of vodka in my hand and I almost downed the bottle in one in my need to disappear, to drown the pain, to just make everything go away.

She was my lifeline, and she was no longer by my side. Alcohol and whatever pills someone passed me were all I had. Until Nat dropped onto my lap.

Ruby's not wrong. Nat is a whore. She's fucked her way around all the boys more than once, and time and time again tries to play us off against each other thinking that she means more to us than the easy fuck she is. She's a game. One we've played many times over the years.

I'm too lost, too far gone to think any better of what she's offering.

I know deep down I knew I shouldn't. But right and wrong were a long way from my thoughts as she ground her ass down on my cock.

Only when I tipped my head back and closed my eyes, it wasn't Nat with her blonde hair and filled lips in my mind, it was Ruby and her soft smile, her mesmerizing green eyes and sinful curves.

"Fuck, little one," I grate out as I impale her so deep on me, I feel her cervix at the tip of my cock. "This... this right here. This is fucking it." I pull out slowly.

"Yes," she cries as I thrust back in, only harder this time.

"You feel that? You feel what you fucking do to me?"

"Yes, Ashton. Yes."

My fingers dig into her hips with such force I have no doubt that I'll leave bruises but no matter how hard I try, I can't release my grip. I need her, this, too fucking bad to let up.

"Just me and you, little one. Just me and you."

I drop my fingers to her clit. I circle them a couple of times, groaning as her muscles tighten around me before I pinch hard and send her crashing into her release.

She clamps down so hard, pulling me in so tight that I have no choice but to follow her over the edge.

Her name rips from my throat with a guttural roar as I fill her, mark her, claim her.

"You're mine, Ruby. Fucking mine," I pant into the crook of her neck as we both come down from our highs.

After a few seconds, I drop her to her feet, but I don't release her right away, instead, I pull her lips back to mine, threading my fingers in her hair and holding her tight.

I try to put everything I'm feeling into that kiss, but I know I'll never be able to achieve it.

Desperate for some air, I pull back, resting my head against hers, and look deep into her eyes.

"Ash—" I press my fingers to her lips, stopping whatever she was about to say.

"I'm sorry." The words feel alien falling from my lips. The only person I've ever really apologized to before was Mom, and while I might not fully understand the reason for needing to say the words to Ruby right now, I know that I need to. "Let's go home."

She nods at me and after a beat, I release her so we can both sort out our clothing before walking back out there.

Taking her hand in mine, I lead her toward the door.

The second I pull it open and step out, almost every set of eyes turn on us.

"Oh my God," she mutters, hiding behind me.

"No point hiding now, little one. They probably heard you screaming my name." I can't help the smile that twitches at my lips, no more so than when my eyes land on Axel laying on one of the couches having his wounds tended to by a couple of girls.

Axel is a prick. We might be part of the same group and I might have been doing his and his father's dirty work for a few years but we'll never be true friends.

A couple of the guys nod at me, not one comes over to say anything as I lead Ruby out of there. I never wanted her back here, but I know I only have myself to blame.

The second we're outside, I pull her into me and wrap my arm around her shoulder. Neither of us say anything on the short walk back to the apartment.

I'm not sure what I would say even if I wanted to.

I'm just... empty. Totally and utterly empty.

"Are you hungry?" Ruby asks as I close the door behind us.

"Uh?" I try to remember the last time I ate anything. Yesterday, maybe. All I remember consuming is vodka and pills.

"I guess. Order takeout, whatever you want. I'm gonna..." I nod toward the bathroom and take off before she says any of the million things that I can read on her face.

She wants to know if I'm okay. If there's anything she can do to help. But right now, I don't have any answers for her.

I close the door behind me, turn the shower on hot and strip out of my clothes.

I stand under the scalding water hoping that it might wash the day and all of my sins off me.

Dropping my head into my hands, I think back over this morning. Of arriving at the church and seeing her in the back of the hearse surrounded by her favorite flowers, of lifting her onto my shoulder, of listening to everyone talk about what an incredible woman she was, the majority of whom didn't even know most of her beauty.

A sob erupts from me as I think about lowering her into that hole, the place she's going to lie forevermore.

Falling back against the tiles, the room spins around me, the lingering high from the alcohol and pills fading from my system and allowing reality to crash back in.

The thought of Nat, of touching her the way I did. Of almost doing more makes my stomach turn.

Fucking hell, I'm a mess.

I slide down the wall until my ass hits the old shower tray beneath me, now unable to hold all of it inside.

My body trembles as sobs wrack my body for everything I've lost and all the mistakes I've made. The guilt eats at me stronger than ever as I try to deal with the overload that has been today.

I have no idea how long I've been there when the door opens but my throat is dry and my eyes burn with the tears I've shed.

"Ash, are you... shit," she gasps when I assume her eyes land on me curled up on the floor.

"I'm okay, just leave me." The words are quiet, a whisper. I doubt she even hears them over the sound of the water.

The door closes again, and I assume she's done as she's told and left me to drown in my own misery, but a few seconds later I hear fabric rustling.

Dragging my head from where it was resting on my knees, I look up.

"Ruby," I breathe, thinking I'm seeing things.

She watches me as she shimmies her panties over her hips and then takes a step forward.

She doesn't so much as flinch as she steps under the still burning water and gently kicks my ankles. I lower my knees to allow her some space, and in a beat, she's sitting astride my lap with my face in her small hands.

"It's okay to fall apart, Ash," she says softly before leaning forward and brushing her lips against mine.

I want to tell her no, that she should leave me here alone to fight with my guilt and fucked-up decisions, but the second her tongue swoops in to find mine, I lose all sense of what I should be doing and accept what she's offering.

An escape.

My fingers slide into her wet hair, holding her to me, ensuring that she's not about to leave as fast as she entered because right now, I know I couldn't cope with that. My other hand trails down her back, wrapping around her slim waist and holding her to me as tight as I can.

Her kiss is so gentle, so passionate that it brings tears back to my eyes. But this time, with her here, with her wrapped around me, I don't sink.

She keeps me above water, just like I knew she would and just like I know she shouldn't be.

25

RUBY

I had no idea what I was going to find when I invited myself into the bathroom. But it certainly wasn't a broken, sobbing Ashton on the floor of the shower. I thought maybe he'd passed out from the drinking and drugs, but never that he was shattering on the other side of the wall.

I probably should have walked back out and left him to it.

It's what he deserved after what he did tonight. But that's not who I am.

My stomach twists violently as I think about him having his hands all over her. But I understand it... I think.

People do crazy shit when they're consumed with grief, totally overpowered by the loss they can't understand or accept.

That's the reason why I don't walk out of that door. Why instead, I strip out of my clothes and join him.

I want him to see that there is more than just pain right now. While, yes, his mom might be gone. He's not, he's here. And she'd want him to grab life with both hands and take it on headfirst. I also have a feeling that she'd want someone beside him as he does it, and it doesn't look to me like any of his so-called friends are interested in supporting him.

I know that guys and girls do things differently, but the thought of me going through this and my girls not being there to hold my hand damn near shreds me and it's not even happening.

Why is he alone in this? None of it seems fair.

The second I drop onto his lap, he grabs onto me as if I'm the air he needs to breathe, and right now, I'm happy to be that for him.

I'm aware that it might be a short-lived thing, that tomorrow might flip everything on its head once more as we decide how to get back and attempt to continue with—or in Ashton's case, restart—our lives.

We kiss for the longest time. Gone are the rough touches and vicious words from that factory and in their place are the soft caresses, the desperation from our kiss in the graveyard earlier.

"Ruby," he moans into my kiss, his voice filled with almost disbelief that I'm here.

"It's okay," I say, once again taking his cheeks in my hands. "I'm right here."

I stare down at him, our foreheads pressed together but he refuses to open his eyes.

Dropping a kiss to the end of his nose, I trail them down over his lips and across his jaw.

"Ruby," he repeats, my name almost a plea on his lips.

I kiss down his neck, my fingers trailing down his arms and chest.

"Make it go away," he begs.

My heart shatters for him. I want to do more but there is nothing.

Instead, my lips find his once more and my hips grind down on his length that's been gently pressed against me for quite some time.

A moan rumbles up his throat at my movements and I do it again, a little more insistently. His grip on my hips tightens, it stings a little but I think nothing of it as he keeps encouraging me.

After a few minutes, I push up from him. His lips rip from mine and for the first time in ages, his eyes open.

Panic fills them as I assume he thinks I'm about to leave.

I shake my head at him and reach between us, wrapping my fingers around his shaft.

"Not going anywhere," I whisper as I lift him and rub the tip through my wetness.

His eyes darken and threaten to close once more but, although hooded, they remain on me as I guide him to my entrance and slowly sink down.

Everything inside me is tender after last night, and then how he took me in the factory earlier but it's not so bad that I want to stop. Actually, the farther I sit down on him, the easier it becomes as the pleasure takes over.

A hiss passes his lips as I sit right down taking all of him inside me.

"Ruby, you're..." He trails off, his large hands skimming over my shoulders and up my neck until he takes my face in his hands much as I did to him not so long ago. "You're incredible," he breathes, his eyes widening as he says the words as if he can't believe they just passed his lips.

"Shh," I soothe, pressing two fingers against his lips. "No talking."

He nods as I lift off him before sinking back down.

His head falls back against the tiles with a thud but his eyes remain on me.

I repeat my actions, holding his stare as I do so. A smile begins to pull at his lips as I continue to move, and his touch, the gentle caress of his thumbs over my hip bones, that gives me the confidence I need to keep going.

At no point do I increase the speed. Everything remains slow, as he moves his hands and begins teasing my breasts, pinching my nipples between his fingers, I grow desperate for more. But this isn't about me.

Leaning forward once more, I take his lips on mine. He eagerly returns my kiss before pushing from the wall to shift our angle.

With both my arms and legs wrapped around him as he impales me, he's so freaking deep. I'm so full of him that I can barely breathe. Add in my compassion for how he's feeling, and I almost lose myself along with him.

His grip on me tightens, his kiss becoming more urgent and I know, that despite our slow pace, that he's close.

His cock swells even harder inside me, stretching me that little bit tighter before he slips his hand between us to find my clit.

"We do this together," he groans in my ear.

I don't need his fingers, those words along with everything else and the feel of him inside me sends me crashing over the edge in an instant. His body vibrates with a groan as his cock jerks inside me, hot sticky cum filling me, branding me, making me his.

Tears burn my eyes at the emotion of the moment, the connection I feel to him but I refuse to let them drop. I need to be the strong one right now and I'll be damned if I'm not going to be exactly what he needs.

I promise myself there and then, that until the sun rises, I'm his. Consequences be damned.

Ashton finds my lips once more and he kisses me softly as we come down from our highs. Then after a few minutes, he lifts me to my feet and sets about cleaning me up.

No words are said as he grabs the bottle of shampoo I've left on the side and squeezes some into his palm before he begins washing my hair.

He rinses it out before conditioning it and making a start on my body. His touch is so gentle as he works over every inch of my skin with the creamy bubbles.

He watches me with fascination, stares at every part of me like he can't believe I'm here with him. I gasp in half shock, half pleasure when his fingers slip between my legs to clean me.

Desire coils in my lower stomach once more making me wonder if it will ever be enough with him. If I'm always going to need more.

I bite down on my bottom lip as he continues to work me. But right before I climb the final crest of my orgasm, he stops.

But he doesn't step away, instead, he takes my hand in his, squeezes some of his shower gel into my palm, and gestures to his body. Not needing any encouragement to touch him, I rub my palms all over his chest and abs. I drop lower to his V and smile when his once again hard cock twitches. But I don't reach for it. Not yet. Instead, I slip behind him and rub at his tense shoulders, down his back, and over his ass. I squeeze lightly as he groans at my touch, pulling me back around in front of him and forcing us both back under the stream of quickly cooling water. I'm amazed it lasted as long as it did. We must have taken it from the entire building.

No sooner have the bubbles left our skin does Ashton reach out behind me and cuts the water off.

Our bodies brush against each other and my breath catches as he stares down at me, his eyes bouncing between mine. It feels like he's looking at me for the first time. It's fascinating as I try to read everything he usually keeps hidden in his dark depths.

But no sooner has he started, does he step back and the moment is broken.

Reaching behind him, he grabs a towel and wraps it around my body before doing the same to himself, only he tucks his around his waist.

I expect him to walk to the door and leave me here. The thought alone leaves me feeling cold. But that's not what he does, instead, he sweeps me into his arms and carries me out and to his bed where he lays me down, rips the towel from my body, and crawls over me.

His hands land on either side of my head and he stares down at me, droplets from his hair hitting my face and running down to the sheets beneath me.

"Ruby, I don't..." He lowers his head to mine. "I don't have the words to tell you how you make me feel, how much that just meant, so let me show you instead."

He takes my lips in the deepest kiss I've ever experienced before he sets about what he just promised.

By the time he drops down beside me and pulls the covers over both of us hours later, there's not an inch of my body he's not touched, kissed, licked, dare I say it... loved. I lost count of how many times he made me come and how many times his name rolled off my lips as I dove headfirst into pleasure. But it's safe to say that as he pulls me into his arms and drops his lips to my shoulder, that I'm well and truly exhausted.

When I finally wake, the sun is up and the bed beside me is empty.

My heart drops that he's not here. But I guess I'm not really surprised. I know that last night—or the previous one—wasn't the beginning of something for us. It was just... well... needed.

After all our time together, the growing tension. It was inevitable. And now it's over... I guess we just go back to hating each other like before, or we somehow find a way to exist around each other.

I blow out a breath and swing my legs from the bed.

My body aches and when I look down, I find red marks all over my breasts and thighs and fingerprint bruises on my hips.

A wave of heat washes through me as I think about our time together, about all the ways he made me come, about all the things he made me feel.

My heart aches once more for the broken boy I found on the shower floor.

I want to say he screwed up last night. But we weren't—we aren't—a couple. I guess he had every right to go running into someone else's arms. I just really wish the sight of the two of them together didn't hurt so damn much, didn't feel like such a betrayal.

I pull on a clean pair of underwear, sweats, and a zip-up hoodie before pulling the door open and stepping out to discover what kind of mood Ashton might be in—assuming he's here, of course.

I see him the second I step out of the bedroom and I instantly know that his walls are back up. I can tell by the hard set of his shoulders.

He's only wearing a pair of black boxer briefs as he stands with his palms on the kitchen counter, staring out of the window, I can only assume directly into the apartment opposite because there's nothing else to look at.

Walking over, I come to a stop beside him to discover what he's so fascinated with.

In the living room in the other apartment, there is a little boy doing puzzles with his dad. The boy is probably eight or so, and he looks so happy.

Ripping my eyes away from the two of them, I look toward Ashton. His expression is tight, his jaw tics, his eyes a little wet.

I open my mouth to say something but I don't get the chance because the buzzer goes off.

"Shit," he mutters, twisting away from me and slamming his hand down on the button to let whoever it is in.

I narrow my eyes at him, wondering who it is as he runs his fingers through his messy hair and looks up to the ceiling.

Whoever it is apparently doesn't need dressing up for because he doesn't make any effort to go to his room to find some clothes.

"Who is it?" I ask, finally finding my voice.

He turns to me, his eyes dark and cold in a way I remember all too well. I told myself in the bathroom last night that it was a one-night thing. I knew this, yet looking at him right now, knowing that was exactly what it was. It hurts. It really fucking hurts.

Everything in me wants to walk over and wrap my arms around his waist, to tell him that everything is going to be okay. But I don't think he'd even accept it if I tried.

His lips never so much as part to answer me, although his eyes do run the length of my body, lingering on the red marks that aren't hidden by the open hoodie and bralette I'd pulled on.

There's a knock on the door a few minutes later and he wastes no time in answering it.

I haven't looked at the time, I haven't even thought to. But the second I hear a familiar voice, I realize my mistake. My stupidity.

"Morning, are you both—" Stephen stops talking the second his eyes land on Ash, they narrow, harden, and then turn on me.

I should wrap my hoodie around myself, cover up the marks that Ashton was staring at only seconds ago, but under his angry stare—much like his son's—I'm frozen, powerless to do anything but stand there and be judged by him.

"No," Stephen says after long, excruciating seconds. "No, Ash. No."

"Stephen, it's okay," Mom says, shocking the fuck out of me. She places her hand on his shoulder and he visibly relaxes.

"It's… it's…" he stutters, looking back to Ash, who doesn't look like he really gives a shit about anything right now, let alone his father's opinions about his decisions. Then Stephen's spine goes ramrod straight and he turns on Mom. "Wait," he spits. "You knew... about this." He aimlessly waves his arm around behind, kinda pointing to the two of us. "And you never told me."

"I found out yesterday at the funeral, I thought we'd already had enough drama for one day. I was going to tell you once we got home."

"Well, it's a little late for that now, don't you think?" he barks in a tone I have never heard him use with Mom—or with anyone before.

Stephen spins back around, pinning Ash with a look as he storms over to me.

"How could you?" he spits at his son. "I trusted you, Ashton."

Stephen wraps his arm around my shoulders and holds me as if I'm his only child who's bleeding out in front of him. Only, I'm not. I'm not his, Ashton is. And Ashton looks like something possessed right now as he glances between the two of us, at his dad supporting me, not him.

"I'm sorry I fucked up your precious little Ruby, Dad."

Stephen gasps, his grip on me tightening as Ash spins on his heels and storms toward his bedroom.

"Wait," Mom cries. "Our flight is in a couple of hours. We need to know what you're doing, how we're getting Stephen's car back."

Ashton stops, the muscles in his back tense. My heart is already racing from the events of the past few minutes but as I wait for him to say something, I realize just how badly I want him to tell our parents that we're driving back together so we can have some more time, but deep down, I know. I knew when I first woke this morning. I knew when he turned to me before our parents arrived. This is it. It's over.

"I'll drive the car back, Ruby is flying with you."

"No, wait," I say, stepping out of Stephen's hold and moving toward him. "I can come with you. So you're not alone," I say quietly just to him.

He flinches at my words, but he doesn't turn to me, he doesn't even look over his shoulder at me. Instead, he just breaks my heart right there in front of our parents while not even giving me the time of day.

"I don't want you, Ruby." Then he marches forward, slamming his bedroom door behind him.

A sob erupts but I manage to catch it in my throat.

I knew this was coming. I knew when the sun came up this morning that everything would change once again. I knew, and yet I allowed myself to think—to hope—that maybe, just maybe it wouldn't end and that last night actually meant something to him.

But he just proved that he really is just the boy with the barbed words and vicious touch.

I suck in a deep breath through my nose and then blow it out through my mouth, trying to calm myself. No one needs me to fall apart right now.

I need to pick myself back up and move on like all is right in the world, that is until I get home and lock myself in my bedroom. All bets are off then.

"How long until we need to be at the airport?" I ask without looking back. I know that if I so much as glance at Mom right now, then I'll break. I can already picture the soft, sympathetic look in her eyes, that's bad enough, I don't need to look into them.

She might not have been on board with this yesterday, actually, she's probably happy about this right now, but I know that her concern for me will override that, right now at least.

"We need to be there in an hour ideally," Stephen answers.

"Okay. Um... have a seat, I won't be—"

Ashton's door opens once more and my words vanish into thin air as I stare at him. He's once again dressed head to toe in black, his hood is pulled high up on his head and his eyes are trained on the floor.

Even if I wanted to speak to him right now, I know that even trying would be pointless. He's built those walls up so high, I have no chance of scaling them. Possibly ever.

"Ashton?" Stephen says, his voice full of the concern that was missing for his only child when he first walked in.

"Don't worry, I'll get your car back. And if you're lucky, it might even be in one piece, unlike your precious *daughter,*" he spits, ripping the door open and storming through it.

The silence rings out for long seconds after he disappears.

"Right, well..." I force out through the suffocating lump in my throat. "I'd better get my stuff packed then."

I'm in the doorway of Ash's bedroom with my eyes locked on the floor, afraid to look up and see the bed or any of his belongings that are going to shatter the fraying grip I have on my emotions right now.

"Ruby, are you—"

"I'm fine, Mom," I snap, really not needing to get into this right now—or ever. "There's a coffee machine on the counter, please could you make me one?"

"S-sure, sweetie. Coming right up. Stephen?"

I don't hear his response because I kick the door shut with my foot. I want to stop, mull over what's just happened but I know that if I do so much as think about him then I'm going to fall apart faster than I can control. Right now, I just need to focus on what needs to be done. I need to get dressed, pack, and get to the airport. Real life is calling. Cheer is calling. Nationals are calling.

He doesn't want me... that's fine. I've got other, more important, things in my life besides Ashton freaking Fury.

26

ASHTON

I knew what had to be done before I even closed my eyes last night. And knowing it was coming ripped me in two. But I couldn't be selfish enough to keep her.

She's already put up with more than she should have to when it comes to me. Her place isn't here with me. It's in Rosewood with her squad, her friends, her life.

This has just been a dream... or a fucking nightmare depending on which way you look at it.

I was up before the sunrise this morning knowing that I couldn't be lying beside her when she woke and turned those huge green eyes on me.

I've let her in more than anyone, ever, and now I was going to have to pay the price.

My father's reaction to discovering what had been going on only confirmed that it was time to pull the plug. Focusing on that, helped to brush aside the way he went to her thinking that all I was capable of doing was hurting her.

Last night was the opposite of that. The kisses, the touches, the murmured words. None of that hurt. This morning though, it's fucking agony.

Yesterday, I said goodbye to the woman who gave me life, and this morning I feel like I might have just said goodbye to the one who might just have brought me back to life.

I walk for hours through the city, until I know they are all long gone. It's going to be bad enough walking back into that apartment and smelling her perfume, sensing her presence, I really don't need to see her again.

The sun is once again beginning to drop when I finally get back to the building and walk up the stairs.

I don't want to be here, but aside from Rosewood, I literally have nowhere else in the world to go.

I push the key in the lock and step inside.

Looking around, I see them both everywhere.

Mom in the kitchen cooking, singing along to her favorite music. Ruby curled up asleep on the couch the first day we arrived.

I stumble back against the door, the memories playing out in my head like a movie as I slide down and hit the floor.

I sit there for the longest time, running through different times in my life, fond memories from years ago, some more recent with a certain little brunette but while they all might bring me some kind of comfort, they're all agonizing at the same time. Just constant reminders of all the ways I've fucked up and all the things I've lost.

By the time a knock sounds out above my head, my ass is numb and my stomach growls for food.

I sigh, stand to my feet, and pull the door open. I have no idea who it is, but quite frankly if there's a guy standing at the other side with a gun ready to put a bullet through my head so he can rob the place then he can have at it for all I care.

"Willow?" My brows pull together at the sight of her standing there with takeout in her arms and a soft expression on her face.

It's not unusual for her to be here, hell, she and the boys have been here more times than I can count. But why now? Why today?

"Thought you might be hungry," she says, lifting the bag in case I hadn't already seen it.

"Come in."

She immediately makes herself at home, pulling plates down from the cupboard and dishing up the food.

"I brought this too," she says, holding up a bottle of vodka.

"Great, can we just have that?" I mutter, sitting on the couch with my elbows on my knees and my head hanging pathetically between my shoulders.

"Nope," she announces happily, making me groan.

"Here. You look like shit, you need to eat something." She thrusts a plate at me, forcing me to sit up and take it. The smell makes my stomach growl loudly, so loudly that it makes her laugh before the words "I told you so," slip from her lips.

"Whatever," I mutter, grabbing the fork and diving in.

"So..." she asks, joining me on the couch with her own plate.

"So..." I counter, really not in the mood to talk about anything but fearing that she's not going to let me get away without. Why couldn't it have been one of the guys who came with food? None of them would give a shit about how I'm feeling right now. They'd just let me get drunk and forget it all.

"You let her go."

"Yeah, she needed to go home."

"Yeah, I know that, but *home* isn't what I'm talking about, Ash." She pins me with a look that tells me that she knows exactly what I've done.

"You've spoken to her?"

She shrugs, guilt passing over her face.

"Fucking hell." I should have known those two would get along, team up against me.

"I may have found her on Instagram and sent a message or two, yeah. She's home safe, by the way, in case you were wondering."

"I wasn't," I lie.

"Sure." She raises a knowing brow at me before going back to her own dinner.

The silence is deafening but it's better than the kind of conversation she wants to have with me, so I'll take it.

Sadly, it doesn't last, and not a second after Willow slides her empty plate onto the coffee table does she curl her feet under her and turn my way.

"She cares about you, you know that, right?"

I don't respond and it pisses her off.

"For fuck's sake, Ashton. That girl could well be the best thing that's ever happened to you."

"You don't even know her," I point out.

"No, maybe not. But I know you." She narrows her eyes at me. "The way you look at her, the way you are with her. She's different. And—" she quickly adds before I get a chance to say anything. "Don't even think about lying to me."

"I... I..." I stutter, trying to come up with something to say.

"I've watched you with all those other sluts, Ash. I've seen the way you look at them, treat them as if they're nothing more than a toy for you to play with. That was not how you looked at her."

"You don't know what you're talking about," I spit, panicking that she's touching so close to the truth.

"Like fuck I don't. Pushing her away isn't going to help anyone. Least of all you right now."

"How do you know what I need right now?" I bark, not thinking any better of it.

"Nice, Ash. Real fucking nice."

Guilt swamps me as tears fill her eyes. "Fuck, I'm sorry, Low. I didn't mean."

"I know, I know," she says, pulling herself back together. "I get it, Ash. I really fucking do. I also know that you don't need to be alone right now, especially not when you've got a girl desperate to support you."

"Yeah, well... she shouldn't. I've been nothing but an ass to her since we met. I'm pretty sure these past few days were just a sympathy vote because I was grieving. She let me—"

"Seriously, Ash. You really believe that?"

No. "Yeah, what else is there. She hates me, and the feeling is fairly mutual."

"Riiight. You're a fucking idiot, Ashton, you know that?"

I shrug.

"So what's the plan?" she asks, finally steering clear of any conversation to do with Ruby. "The rent must be up on this place soon."

"End of the week," I admit. I've been trying not to think about it. This place was our life and now I'm supposed to empty it, get rid of all our stuff like it means nothing.

"Okay so..."

I shrug again and it gets her back up. "Stop it. Stop trying to act all nonchalant. It doesn't fucking suit you."

"I'm just trying to get through this, Low. I don't know how else to fucking do it."

"Where do you want to start?"

"What?"

"Where do you want to start? Her bedroom? Get the most painful bit done first."

A chill runs through my body at the thought of going through all of Mom's stuff and getting rid of it all. Low must see my reaction because she reaches out and takes my hand in hers.

"It's okay, Ash. I'll help with whatever you need."

I hold her eyes for a few seconds. "You're a good friend, Low."

A small smile twitches at her lips. "I'm glad you think so because something tells me that you need one right now."

I blow out a long breath before reaching forward and downing whatever drink it was she made me.

"I'll get the trash bags."

I push from the couch, taking both our plates through to the kitchen before grabbing the bags and the bottle of vodka and walking to Mom's bedroom door without putting much thought into it.

The thought of doing this alone terrifies me, but having Low here... well, it makes it that little bit better.

I push the door open and walk into the room, letting the scent that still lingers fill my nose.

Fuck, I miss her.

I sense Willow come to stand in the doorway behind me and I turn to look at her.

A sad smile plays on her lips as she stares back.

I appreciate her being here so much right now, but I can't help wishing she were someone else.

"You're wishing I was her, aren't you?"

My lips part but no words pass.

"It's okay to want her, to need her, Ash. It's also okay to be scared. Focus on this, get the apartment sorted and then once you've had a few days to process everything, go to her. Talk to her. Be honest with her. Show her what's really in here." She taps two fingers to my chest above my heart before wrapping her arms around my shoulders and holding me tight.

It takes me a few seconds to return her embrace, but when I do, I'm glad I did.

There's never been anything between Willow and me, aside from the fact I know her brother would castrate me if I ever were to touch her—me and any of the boys—it's just never been like that between us. To me, she is just one of the guys. Just slightly better to look at.

"Okay, let's do this. I can do this."

27

RUBY

The journey home is excruciating. Stephen's anger never leaves. Every time he pins Mom with a look, I swear she's about to go up in flames. Mom looks to be on the edge of bursting into tears every thirty seconds, regret clear to see swimming behind them. I, on the other hand, am just numb.

The farther I get from him, the more I feel like I left something behind.

As much as I suspected it was coming, his rejection hurts.

There's barely a word spoken between the three of us the entire trip. I spend the entire time with a painful knot in my stomach and a lump in my throat that stops me from eating or doing anything that might be a distraction.

It's not until we're finally home and I'm able to lock myself in my room that I pull my cell out of my purse and turn it back on.

I know that everyone is expecting me home today, but I've missed practice now so I'm hoping I'll be able to hide in here until Monday morning rolls around and I have little choice but to rejoin the world once more.

Flopping down on my bed, the familiarity of it makes me sigh and I wish I could curl up under the sheets and never emerge again.

Flipping onto my back, I turn my cell on and wait to see if I have anything from anyone.

A notification pops up with a message from a @queenwillow. Despite everything, a smile twitches at my lips. I like Willow.

Tapping the Instagram app, I find her message.

Willow: I hope you don't mind me reaching out. I'm just worried. How is he?

All the air I didn't know I was holding in rushes out of me as I press my head back into the pillow and close my eyes.

How is he? I wish I knew.

Ruby: Of course not. I just got home... without him. He made me leave. He's... not good.

I squeeze my eyes closed, willing the tears to stop as I think about the look in his eyes, the hurt, the desperation.

I tell myself that this is what he wanted, and not only that, it's the right thing to do. Just look at our parents, because of us they are now falling apart. I might not have heard anything from them yet, but I know an argument is brewing between them, and it's going to be all our fault.

Staring at my screen through blurry eyes, I read her response.

Willow: I'll go check in on him. Everything will be okay.

Ruby: Will it?

My hands shake as I lower my cell. I'm pretty sure I already know the answer to that question, and it doesn't involve any of Willow's positivity.

Not really wanting to read her answer to that question, I lift my cell again and change the subject.

Ruby: How's Axel?

Willow: Still an ugly mofo. He'll survive.

Annoyed that I'm surrounded by the scent of airplane and his lingering smell, I climb from my bed, pull out a clean set of underwear and pajamas, and head through to my bathroom in the hope I can wash the last few days off of me.

I knew going to Seattle was a bad idea. Why wouldn't anyone listen to me?

I stand under the water for so long that my skin begins to wrinkle but I know I can't hide in here forever.

Finally, I turn the water off and step out, wrapping towels around me, I turn to look at myself in the mirror above the sink.

I look tired, no, exhausted. The circles under my eyes are darker than I think I've ever seen them, and my skin is pale. I guess there's no hiding how I'm feeling on the inside.

I do everything I can to distract myself but there's not all that much I can do while in here, so I pull my pajamas on and walk back to my room.

Two people sitting on my bed scare the crap out of me, but the second my panic subsides, and I look into their eyes, I can't stop the flood of tears.

"Oh shit."

"Ruby."

I have no idea who says what, and I don't really care as both Harley and Poppy wrap their arms around me and hold tight.

"I messed up," I admit once I can get some words out.

"No, girl. You didn't. He did."

"N-no," I argue, but it's pointless because Harley pulls back and looks at me with a raised brow. "Okay, so he's partly to blame."

"Partly?"

"Yeah, it's not like he forced himself on me. I was just the stupid girl who fell for it."

"You're not stupid, Rubes," Poppy says softly. "Some boys have a way of making us lose our minds."

"Well, I'm pretty sure I left my mind here while my body fucked off to Seattle."

"We brought pizza and ice cream."

I sigh at her words because despite not really wanting to eat, my stomach is growling to be filled.

"You can tell us all about it as we stuff our faces with carbs."

"How's practice? Are we ready for the weekend?"

"Everything is good, Ruby. You don't need to worry."

Poppy opens the pizza box, allowing the scent of cheese and tomato to permeate the air, and my stomach growls louder. She offers me the first slice and I take it, eagerly. Then, I go back to the very beginning. It's only days ago that we walked out of that airport in favor of Stephen's car but right now, it feels like it was a lifetime ago.

"So when's he coming back?" Harley asks.

I shrug. "No idea. But he has Stephen's car, so I guess he'll need to at least return that at some point. If he doesn't just drive it straight off a cliff," I say with a sad laugh.

"He wouldn't, would he?" Poppy asks, concern pulling her brows together.

"Honestly, I have no idea. I'm pretty sure he's already hit the self-destruct button, I guess we just need to see how far he takes it."

I blow out a slow breath. Praying that he's not going to do something stupid, but equally not feeling all that confident about it. I think of Nat. We've been gone a good few hours now, I wonder if he's already gone to search out her *services.*

The rest of the weekend drags. I spend Sunday working out and getting ready for a week of insane practices and then nationals. I tell myself not to look at my cell because he won't have reached out, and although I'm right, it doesn't stop me from checking every hour or so just in case.

Willow messages a few times trying to reassure me that he'll be okay, that she's seen him but even her words don't make me feel any better.

I'm still a mess when I walk into the gym early Monday morning. I'm the first—seeing as I can't sleep—aside from Chelsea who's setting up.

"You're back," she says with delight when she spots me.

"Yup," I mutter.

"Is... is everything okay? Harley said—"

"Everything is fine. Nationals is this weekend, I'm ready for this."

She stares at me for long seconds. She doesn't believe a word of it.

"You don't have to lie to me, Ruby," she says softly, reaching out for my hand. "I'm here as your friend, not just your captain. Some things are more important than cheer, nationals approaching or not."

I suck in a breath, desperate not to allow the tears that are burning the back of my eyes to spill.

There's a commotion at the main doors as the others begin to arrive and Chelsea looks up.

"Go wait in the office, let me set these up."

"O-okay." I really don't want to talk, but at the same time, I really don't need the squad seeing me fall apart.

I drop down on the chair in front of what should be Miss Kelly's desk, should she ever actually be here. It's been so long since I've seen her face that

I wonder if she even still works here. Chelsea takes such good care of the squad though, it's not like we actually miss her.

I stare up at the ceiling, willing my tears to subside.

I've never been a crier. In fact, until Ashton showed up in my life, I was never really affected by anything. I've always been totally level-headed. But add him into the mix and I turn into an emotional head case.

Fucking boys.

Chelsea joins me after a few minutes and drops down into Kelly's chair, her hand instinctively going to her swollen belly.

"How's she doing?" I ask, nodding to her belly.

"Perfect, but she doesn't stop moving."

"Little cheerleader, that's why. Already somersaulting."

She laughs but it doesn't meet her eyes, she's more concerned about me right now, which I kind of understand having looked at myself in a mirror.

"I slept with him," I blurt. "He was hurting, things just... happened."

"And then..."

"Then he put his walls back up and sent me away. He's still in Seattle doing God knows what and I'm here trying to keep myself together. Our parents are at each other's throats because of it," I say, thinking of the shouting I've tried to drown out this weekend. I have no idea if Ashton and I are the full cause of the tension or if we've just piled a lot more on top of other shit they're dealing with. Mostly, I try to stay out of their business and focus on my own life, but I can't help feeling guilty that we've caused this. "It's all just a mess."

"Right..." She sits back, her hand still rubbing at her belly. "Do you love him?"

"W-what?" I ask, startled.

"Do you love him?"

"No, he's an asshole."

"Doesn't stop you from falling, Rubes. Most of the guys on the team are assholes, but look at them coupling up."

"Ash is on a different scale." I think back to that factory of him pinning Natalie up against the wall, off his head on whatever he'd taken. I shake my head.

"The worse they are, the harder we fall, Rubes."

"Do we have to talk about this? I just want to lose myself in cheer, focus on the weekend. Forget he even exists."

"And what if he turns up before the weekend?"

"I can move in with you, right?" I ask jokingly, but she doesn't return my amusement.

"Ruby," she says seriously, leaning forward and placing her elbows on the desk. "This squad needs you. This squad can be yours in only a few weeks if you want it bad enough. But none of us are going to look down on you if you need some time out. Life's hard, Ruby. I get that more than most these days. I have no doubt you'll get to nationals again next year if you want to take a step bac—"

"No," I interrupt, knowing where she's going. "No, I've worked too hard for this. I want it too badly."

"I know you do, Ruby. I wouldn't be suggesting that you could lead this squad if I didn't already know that. But I'm worried about you."

"I'm fine. I need this, Chelsea. I need a distraction."

"And if he comes back before the weekend and becomes the distraction?"

"Then I'll have to deal with that when and if it happens."

She nods. "Okay. You're going to be a good captain one day, Ruby. Cheer is in your blood. But you need to remember that the outside world exists sometimes." Her words come out sounding sad, and I know that she's talking from experience. "It's too easy to get swallowed up by this life. I refuse to allow that to happen to any of you, and I need you to be aware of it, so you can ensure it doesn't happen under your watch either."

She pushes to leave but I stop her.

"Are you really serious about me taking over?" I hate to ask. I hate the vulnerability in my tone as I do. It's what I've wanted from as early as I can remember and I'm right on the cusp of it. I'm equally as excited as I am terrified that it might actually happen.

"Yes, Ruby. I'm serious. After nationals, I need to nail Kelly down and make a plan. The girls are going to have to vote you in, so nothing is set in stone but I believe you're the only one for the job, we just have to hope they all agree with me. Then together we can start auditions for next year."

Butterflies take flight in my belly at the thought.

"But right now, nationals are our focus. You ready?" she asks, holding her hand out to me and pulling me in for a hug once I'm on my feet. "You know where I am, yeah. Don't let his asshole ruin this for you. And remember, my offer still stands. The team will take him down should it become necessary."

I can't help laughing at the thought alone. "Ash isn't a Rosewood boy, Chels. I'm not sure they'll be all that much of a threat to him."

I think of the guys he hangs around with. They make Jake and Ethan look like teddy bears.

"Okay, well, they're behind you too should you need it."

"I appreciate it, but it won't be necessary. I can fight my own battles."

"I know, but sometimes, you don't need to do it alone."

When we emerge from the office, Harley is leading the warm-up and Chelsea still has her arm slung around my shoulders.

"There's your assistant captain right there, girl," she whispers in my ear, and a wide smile curls at my lips.

Harley and I against the world... or the world of cheer at least. Hell, yeah!

I join the squad on the mats to complete the warm-up before Chelsea gets us into formation.

I slip back in as if I haven't had a week away. It's like coming home and it feels so good.

The rest of the week is like any other week at Rosewood. If we're not practicing for the weekend, then we're in class. We don't even go to Aces with the team because we're too exhausted. It's exactly what I need to try to drag my head back from Seattle and away from the boy who messes with my mind.

I've not heard anything from him and every time I've spoken to Willow, she's said a variation of "he's okay." I didn't believe her when she first said it on the weekend, and I certainly don't now. But what am I supposed to do about it?

Thankfully, Mom and Stephen seem to have sorted things out and it's once again peaceful in our house. Neither of them has tried talking to me, possibly because I keep myself hidden away as much as possible, but I know that conversation is coming. Stephen was too angry to just let it rest. And we all know that at some point, he's going to have to reappear and we're going to have to deal with what happens next.

But I'm putting all of that aside because this weekend is about me. It's about me and my dream.

28

RUBY

The weekend is everything I hoped it would be and more. The second I climbed onto the bus—driven by Miss Kelly who miraculously appeared in the hope of national success—with my best friend by my side and the rest of the squad, I put everything to do with Ashton freaking Fury behind me.

It was time to focus.

We sailed through prelims on Friday afternoon, and although the semis this evening were tighter, we won with a clear margin.

"We're almost there, girls," Chelsea says, lifting her fruit juice in the air before us.

We got back to the hotel thirty minutes ago and Kelly has given us strict instructions not to even try to find alcohol and to be in bed not a second after midnight. She then proceeded to get dressed up and fucked off, so I don't really think she cares all that much. I sure hope not as I pour vodka into my glass and take a sip.

We're all hanging out on the loungers around the pool, riding high on our success from this afternoon and trying to relax before we do it all over again in the finals tomorrow.

The finals. Tingles race through my body at the thought. The varsity finals.

I fight to contain my smile, not wanting to sit here looking like a mental case but I can't hide it when my lips curl.

"You okay?" Harley asks with a laugh when she notices the expression on my face.

"Can you believe we're in the varsity finals tomorrow?"

"No," she breathes. "I can't." She glances over at the JV team on the other side of the pool. They lost their semi-final. I'm not overly surprised. They don't have Chelsea pushing them at every turn.

A couple of the JV girls notice my attention. We all used to be good friends. After all, we've all grown up together but since Harley and I got chosen for varsity, we've been given the cold shoulder by most of them. I get it, they want to be where we are but once we get this weekend over with, we're going to be auditioning for next year's varsity squad so they're going to need to get over themselves if they want a place—assuming I get a say of course.

Someone turns up a song on the wireless speaker and a few of the girls grab us and start dancing.

"Come on, we're supposed to be enjoying ourselves," Harley says, grabbing my hand and pulling me from my lounger.

She pulls me into her body and then pushes out again. My head spins with the vodka and I laugh at her antics, feeling light for the first time in well... months.

We dance, laugh, and generally just act like idiots with the rest of the squad.

"I need to pee," I shout in her ear, releasing my hold on her and stepping away.

"I'll get more drinks."

I make my way inside the hotel, the music getting quieter with each step I take. I breathe a sigh of relief, enjoying the peace for a few minutes.

Thankfully, there's no one else in the bathroom allowing me a little time to myself to process everything that's happened today and what we've got coming tomorrow.

Still, I can't keep my smile from my face. We've got a real shot at winning tomorrow, I know we have. But I don't want to get carried away with myself. There are still a lot of things that could go wrong, now isn't the time to get complacent.

Someone comes and goes while I sit there but I don't make any attempt to move. But I know I need to get back out before Harley comes looking.

I can't help but smile as I stare at myself in the mirror. I look like my old self again. The sparkle is back in my eyes. That doesn't mean I've forgotten about him or what happened but having this weekend to focus on has helped me to shove it all into a box to deal with later.

I touch up my lipstick and wipe some stray makeup from under my eyes before adjusting my skirt and leaving the bathroom.

The vodka that the girls have been topping off my drinks with is starting to take effect and my head spins, the fresh air as I step out of the hotel doesn't help the situation. I think I might be done for the night if I want to stand any chance of being on form for the finals tomorrow.

I walk past the bushes with the sound of the squad laughing and joking in the distance but just as I'm about to round the corner to join them once more, there's some rustling behind me. I twist to look over my shoulder but I don't get a chance to move before a solid chest presses against my back and a strong arm wraps around my waist, pinning one of my arms to my side, while a huge hand covers my mouth to stop me from screaming. I try to anyway, but the sound is muffled as I try to kick and elbow whoever it is.

My attempts are futile, I make no contact with the asshole who thinks this is a good idea.

My heart pounds in my chest and I continue to try to scream as we disappear into the dark undergrowth behind the hotel.

"Keep fighting, little one. You know it only makes me want you more."

Ashton.

He spins me and presses my back against a tree.

"You fucking asshole," I spit at him. "Why are you here?"

We might be in the dark with only the moon helping us see, but I can't miss the darkness of his eyes, or the fact that both show lingering evidence of him fighting.

"What happened?" I ask, hating that I sound like I care as I reach out and run my fingertip gently across the healing cut on his bottom lip.

"Just exorcising some demons."

"Via your fists. Don't tell me. Axel."

"Yeah, him and a few others. But they don't matter." He leans into me, his hard length pressing against my stomach. His hand skims up my side until his fingers wrap around my throat, flexing a little as if to tell me something.

"You shouldn't be here." My voice is hard but my insides are having a freaking party at having him so close, at having his scent in my nose.

"Maybe not," he says, his nose running up my cheek. "But I'm here anyway."

"You should leave." I try to stay strong but with his lips so close to mine, it's getting harder and harder.

I force myself to remember how he rejected me before we left Seattle, trying to focus on the pain, not how good things had been between us.

"You don't mean that, little one," he says, lips so close they brush mine. The scent of him mixes with the alcohol on his breath.

"You've been drinking."

"So have you. I hope your coach doesn't know what you're slipping in your drinks."

"Our coach doesn't give a shit."

The hand that isn't around my throat finds the bottom of my hoodie and slips under, finding the smooth skin of my stomach.

"You looked so hot in your little uniform up on that stage earlier."

I gasp. "Y-you were watching?"

"Sure was, little one. Watching and hard as fuck imagining what it might be like to fuck you while you wear that uniform."

"N-not happening." I want to sound strong, sure, but my voice comes out all breathy.

Damn him and the effect he has on me.

He chuckles. "It's cute that you think you can deny what you really want."

His hand lifts higher until he cups my breast over my crop top, and I fight my need to moan when he pinches my nipple between his fingers.

"I've missed you, little one."

"Well, maybe you should have considered that before turning your back on me."

"I'm sorry," he whispers in my ear, sending goose bumps racing across my skin.

"No, you're not. You're just saying that to get your way."

"Am I?" His lips graze that spot under my ear and my entire body shudders.

I lift my hands to press against his chest to try to push him away from me but when he sucks that patch of sensitive skin into his mouth, instead of pushing, I find my fists curling into the fabric of his hoodie.

"Ashton." It's meant to be a warning but it's far from it when his name passes my lips. "You need to leave," I try again, but my argument is weak at best.

"You're only lying to yourself." He wraps his hand around the back of my thigh and hooks my leg around his hip, allowing his length to grind against my core.

My head falls back against the tree with a thud.

"I hate you," I groan as he presses harder against me.

"You should," he admits before sinking his teeth into my neck.

"Then why are you here?"

"Because I need you."

I tense against him. "So you just want an easy fuck?" I snap.

"No, little one. If I wanted easy, I certainly wouldn't be here."

His hand skims down my thigh until he's palming my ass. He groans into my neck when he realizes I'm just wearing a thong and my ass is bare.

"I don't want anyone, Ruby. I came for you, no one else."

"Fucking hell," I mutter to myself, squeezing my eyes closed tight. Why is it so hard to say no to him?

His fingers inch lower until he finds the edge of my panties.

"Oh little one, so wet for me." He runs his fingers over the damp fabric, teasing me.

"Ashton."

"So now you want me to stay." He laughs against my neck.

"No. I want you to leave, but if you insist on torturing me, I may as well get something out of it."

He pulls his head from my neck and stares into my eyes. I swear he stops breathing as he does, causing my stomach to knot in anticipation.

"You fucking slay me, Ruby."

He dives for my lips and I'm powerless to stop him as his tongue plunges into my mouth and licks at mine.

His taste explodes in my mouth and I suck on his tongue. A groan rumbles up his throat as his fingers slip under my panties.

"Fuck, I missed this."

"You mean you didn't run to that slut the second I got on an airplane?" I regret the words the second they pass my lips, but I can't help that I've wondered if that was where he went when he stormed out.

He pulls back, his fingers almost cutting off my air supply, his eyes boring into mine.

"Is that what you really think of me?" Anger flickers across his face, his lips pulled into a thin line.

"I can only go on previous experience, Ashton. You went running pretty quick last time."

"That was different."

"Was it?"

"Yes, it was before. Before..."

"Before?" I prompt.

But he doesn't respond, he just shakes his head before slamming his lips back on mine and plunging two fingers deep inside me.

Any fight I might have had—which admittedly wasn't a lot—disappears the second he curls his fingers inside me and finds that magical spot.

"Oh God," I moan into his mouth.

"Come for me, little one. But don't scream. Not unless you don't want my cock inside you."

I feel a wave of heat in my core at his promise of more and he doesn't miss it.

"Fuck, could you be any sexier? You're dripping down my hand, little one."

I want to be mortified by my reaction to his dirty words, but I can't find it in me to care.

"More," I plead.

His hand leaves my neck in favor of the zipper running down the length of my hoodie. He parts the fabric before pushing my crop top up and over my breasts.

The cool air surrounds them making my nipples pucker.

"Oh God," I moan when he blows a stream of warm air over my sensitive peaks.

My head crashes back against the tree again but I barely feel it.

He pushes my hoodie from my shoulders and then leans back a little to stare at me.

"If you're not quiet, everyone else is going to get to see what I see right now. Do you want that?"

I shake my head, squeezing my eyes closed in embarrassment.

"Look at me. I want you staring into my eyes as you fall over the edge so you remember who's doing it to you."

I slam my lips shut to refrain from telling him that there wouldn't be anyone else in my mind. He already knows he's the only one, and right now, I don't want to give him the satisfaction of the reminder.

He closes the space between us once more, my nipples brushing against his hoodie causing sparks to shoot down to my core and push me closer to release before his lips find mine.

He kisses me so deep it causes emotion to clog my throat but I refuse to allow myself to believe this is more than a bit of fun. He saw an opportunity to torment me and here he is.

"Come, Ruby," he demands into my mouth, and with one movement of his fingers, I crash.

"Ashton," I moan against his lips as my body convulses as wave after wave of pleasure surges through me.

Long before my release has subsided, his fingers are gone leaving me cold, but it only lasts so long because in seconds he's got me up against the tree, both of my legs around his waist and his cock pressing at my entrance.

"I need you so fucking bad, Ruby." He surges into me, and I have to bite down on the inside of my cheeks to stop me from crying out as the pleasure and bite of pain from a week without this, mix and engulf my body. "So good. So fucking tight," he groans in my ear.

His hips begin to piston, thrusting in and out of me as he kisses down my neck and one of his hands lifts to tease my nipples.

"Ashton," I moan quietly as pleasure collides with the pain of the tree trunk scratching into my back. It's a heady combination and one I'm not ready to end quite yet.

"Fuck, I'm not gonna last, little one."

His fingers find my clit and he pinches hard, encouraging my next release to come crashing forward. I fall under his spell without any warning and I cry out his name louder than necessary as I fall. His cock twitches violently inside me, filling me with his hot cum.

"Oh God," I half moan, half curse.

We really shouldn't have done this.

The music from the party I left comes back to me as I float back down from my high.

Ashton is still sucking on the skin above my collarbone. Threading my fingers in his hair, I pull him back.

"You need to leave."

"I've barely started, little one. Do you have your room key?"

"No, absolutely no way, Ash." I think of the room I'm sharing with Harley. *No, just no.*

"You need to leave, and I need to get back. Tomorrow is one of the most important days of my life and I don't need to lose myself in you."

"Aw, you get lost in me."

"Do you give me much choice?" I snap. Now I've come back to myself, I'm angry and disappointed that I let him get to me so easily.

I should be stronger than this after the way things ended between us.

"Put me down," I demand, trying to wiggle out of his hold and only successful with scratching up my back more.

"Fine," he spits. "But this isn't over."

I right my clothing before staring him dead in the eye.

"It is, Ashton. This was the last time you're getting anywhere near me. Consider it a goodbye fuck."

"Ruby?" His brows pull together as if that hurt him, but I know better. Nothing I could say to him could hurt him. He only came here to get inside my panties, well, mission accomplished, asshole. I hope you enjoyed it because it's not happening again.

"I suggest you go home, Ashton. I don't want to see you here again this weekend."

Before he gets to respond, I do exactly what he did to me in Seattle, turn my back on him and walk away as if he means nothing to me.

He doesn't need to know that my heart is shattering all over again with every step I take.

29

ASHTON

Watching her walk away is the least of what I deserve after what I've put her through. That being said though, it hurts like a motherfucker.

I stand there in the shadows for the longest time wondering if she's gone straight back to the party with the evidence of what we just did dripping out of her or if she's run straight past them and back to her room.

The temptation to see if I can follow her and find out which room is hers is strong, but I know she's right. I need to give her the space she wants. This is her big weekend; I'd never forgive myself if I ruined it for her.

I know one thing though, I'm not leaving. I'm not missing out on a chance to watch her up on stage again tomorrow.

Like most guys, I like cheerleaders for one very good reason. But I've never really paid much attention to what they do unless they're on their knees for me, so to say I was a little blown away by Ruby and her squad when they were up on stage earlier, would be an understatement.

She was utterly captivating as she defied gravity with some of those moves. I might not have hung around long enough to watch any other squads, I didn't exactly have any interest in them, but I already knew who deserved to win.

After long minutes, I turn away from the music playing from the pool area where they're all hanging out and head back toward the motel where I've booked a room for the night.

It didn't take all that much research to find out where she'd be this weekend, and after snooping through her laptop that she'd helpfully left on her bed without a password, I soon found the hotel she was in.

Thankfully, Dad and Lisa weren't in when I pulled up to the house this morning. It might have been a week since they left me in Seattle, but I have no doubt that they're still pissed at me for corrupting their good little girl.

I unloaded everything I'd packed into Dad's car before repacking a bag and heading back out. I know I'm going to have to deal with them, I've already put too much off, but I figured they could wait a few more days. Ruby was more important.

I knew I'd fucked up the moment I rejected her that morning. I didn't need Willow turning up to confirm it. But equally, I really needed this past week to attempt to put myself back together.

I'll be the first to admit that my life in Seattle was a mess and losing Mom really didn't help at all. Being back there, having to bury her. It was all just too much.

It may have taken three drunken, and high days with the Kingston boys and without Ruby but by the time I woke up Tuesday morning with the same hangover I'd been suffering with almost since she left, I knew it was time to pull my head out of my ass and attempt to put my life back together.

And the first thing I needed to do was find her. To find her and to tell her how much I appreciated everything she did for me.

Although, I already know I've fucked that up.

She didn't have to drive to Seattle with me, she didn't have to stay in the apartment and she certainly didn't have to try to hold me together while I was so insistent on falling apart.

I push the key into the lock of my motel room and swing the door closed behind me.

My bag is still sitting on the bed where I left it when I first arrived, I stare at it, knowing what's inside.

Kicking my shoes off, I crawl onto the bed and pull my bag closer, unzipping it and pulling out the book that's sitting on the top.

I found two full boxes of journals that I had no idea Mom wrote. Both of the boxes are sitting in my bedroom at Dad's house. Those, along with a few other of her things I kept needing something of hers in the hope it helps me feel closer to her even though she's gone.

I trail my fingertip over the embossed leather cover with this year's date on it. I've not read any yet. I told myself that I'd have a few days in Seattle to lose myself as I sorted through the rest of the apartment and decided what to do with all the things that made up our lives then I was going to come back here, apologize to Ruby and attempt to rebuild my life.

Well, I've been back a few hours and I'm pretty sure I've fucked up that first part of my plan for being back here already.

I blow out a breath and tip my face to the ceiling.

Things can only get better, right?

Flipping the cover open, I prepare for what I might read.

January 1st
New year. New start. New me.
That's what everyone says, right?
I guess it's fitting because this is the year everything changes. This is the year I take life by the balls and do something I've been dreaming about for years.
Ashton graduates this year, or at least I hope he will. And then we are gone. Out of this hellhole that has bled so much life out of both of us.
I thought Seattle was my chance to start over when I came here for college. I had plans, dreams. I wanted to make something of my life. Be better than what I'd seen up until that point, be better than the people I'd been forced to spend my early years with.
And it was great. It was everything I wanted it to be.
I got my degree, the job, the boy.
Everything was perfect.
Until it wasn't.
I can't pinpoint exactly when things went wrong with Stephen—although if I were to read back a few years, maybe I'd find it—and to this day, I don't think either of us did anything wrong. We just... grew apart. And through that, he found Lisa again, and I found... loneliness.
I'm happy for him. A part of me will love that man until my dying day. After all, he gave me my boy. A boy I would give my life for if I needed to.
That's why it's time for this to happen.
He thinks I don't know what he's doing. He thinks I'm oblivious that he's got himself tangled up with the Kingston boys, that, or he doesn't think I even know who they are in the first place.
Every day, I see a little bit more of the happy boy I knew drain out of him and in its place the anger, the dejection that it takes to do the kinds of things that I'm sure they're going to ask of him. If we stay here too much longer, they're going to pull him in so deep that they'll never let him go.
That's why we're leaving.

That's why I've saved every single penny, I could since the day Stephen left, to give us a new life, a good life, a life with prospects, a future. A forever.

I close the book and run my hand down my face.

She was planning on us leaving Seattle?

My brows pull together as I think back to the weeks and months before she died. I had no idea. Why didn't she tell me?

Because you would have refused to leave, asshole.

I blow out a breath and open the book back up again. Just the sight of her handwriting has me on edge, but reading her words guts me in a whole new way. Knowing she had plans for her—for our—life. I shake my head.

Fuck, I miss you.

I turn to the next page and find a photograph of a house staring back at me.

It's a stunning light gray colonial-style house with a front porch and yard. It has shutters on the windows and blooming flowers out front.

I run my finger over it as I imagine Mom standing on the porch in the sun enjoying the peace.

Needing to know more, I keep reading.

Maybe squirreling all the money away wasn't the best idea in the short term. Both Ash and I have suffered because of it. But every time my stomach rumbles and we have no food in the apartment, I tell myself it's worth it. That one day, we'll have our home, we'll have everything we could ever want.

He's probably going to hate me when I tell him my plans, that I'm taking him away from the only home he's ever really known, and I also know that he has every right to refuse. He'll be eighteen. But it's a risk I've got to take. As much as I'd have loved to do this years ago, I didn't have the money to do it properly and starting over in a new place wouldn't have been any better for us.

This way, he'll have graduated, be able to start university, or community college, depending on how the next few months go, and we can have a real shot at happiness.

Maddison County might not be where I've always dreamed of living but I know it's right for us.

It has good education opportunities for Ash. It has a thriving community, so I should be able to find a job. But most importantly, it's close to Stephen.

I hate myself every day for how the relationship has turned out between Ash and Stephen. Ash blames him for everything, and I understand it, I watched my parents go through something similar. I know it's easy to blame the person who leaves. But

Stephen isn't a bad person. Actually, he's the best. It's why I married him and had a baby with him. Things just... didn't last. That flame you hope will burn forever just... went out.
I want to fix things. I want Ashton to get to know his dad. I want Stephen to be the incredible father I know he is.
I just want everyone to be happy and safe.

I close the book again and rest my head back against the wall.

Mom was going to move us to Maddison.

She's right. There's no way I would have gone willingly. But now I'm here and my life has changed in a way she never could have predicted, I can see that she was right.

I needed to get out of Seattle. If this past week being back there with the guys has taught me anything, it's that I would have ended up dead eventually. I was only on the outskirts of the Kingston boys, but slowly, they were dragging me into the fold. My jobs were getting bigger, riskier. It was only a matter of time because my death would have been the only way out. Because once you're in and you know their secrets, that is the only way they let you out of their clutches.

I flick through the rest of the pages, staring down at Mom's words and stopping at some of the images she stuck in as she dreamed of our new life.

It's not until I get to the very back that I find an envelope with a bank name stamped on it.

With my brows drawn together, I lift the flap and pull out the contents. The bank card is still attached to the letter like the day it arrived in the mail. The only thing different about it is that Mom's written the PIN on the top.

My hand trembles as I hold it.

Is this our entire future that she'd been working toward in this bank account?

I shake my head once more, a smile pulling at my lips.

She really was giving us the chance to start over.

The temptation to go and find an ATM and discover just how much she was sitting on is high. But it's late and I have no idea where one is.

I force myself to place everything on the nightstand before stripping down to nothing and heading for the shower. Not that I really want to wash Ruby's scent off me but as much as it's comforting, it's torture at the same time.

She should be here with me right now, naked in my arms but instead, I fucked the entire thing up with my need for her and probably just proved to her once again why she does hate me as she claims to.

The scalding hot shower does little for my mood. My head is spinning with the revelations I discovered from Mom and my blood is running hot as I think about how Ruby looked up against that tree earlier.

I have a fitful night's sleep full of dreams of colonial houses and Ruby in her cheer uniform and by the time my alarm goes off to ensure I'm at the venue in time for her finals this morning, I'm nowhere near ready to wake up.

There are people—cheerleaders—everywhere when I pull up to the sports complex on my bike. I thought yesterday afternoon was busy, but it was nothing like this. I knew cheer was big across the country but our squad in Seattle was nothing more than a piece of ass to have at football games and parties. They never competed in anything. Thank God, because after what I saw yesterday, I realize that they really weren't in it for the sport, I really think they did just want to get on their knees for the players.

I park and make my way inside. Without a ticket to allow me entry, it takes a little work to get into the room where the final competition is taking place, but I soon sweet talk a cheerleader into smuggling me inside as her brother before dropping her the second I'm past the guards.

I find a seat in the shadows so I can watch her performance. I have no idea if Dad and Lisa are here. From the number of families I can see, I'd be amazed if they weren't here to support Ruby. Neither of them seems like the kind of parents that wouldn't go out of their way to be here for her moment of glory.

I have to sit and watch a few other finals—all just proving to me how good Ruby's squad is in comparison—before the varsity finalists take to the stage.

The second I see her, nerves erupt in my belly. She looks tired and nervous, although still totally breathtaking. The tiny red and white Rosewood High cheer uniform fits her like a second-skin, and I realize in that moment just how much all of this means to her.

I've teased her about being a cheer slut time and again in my time here. But none of this is about gaining the attention of any sports team at school. This is her sport.

They get in formation as the crowd around me quiets down before the music starts and they bound into action.

Girls jump, dive, and somersault everywhere, it's mesmerizing, but at no point do I take my eyes off my girl.

My girl.

My heart pounds as those words repeat in my head.

Fuck, I want them to be true.

The smile on her face as she does her thing melts my heart. I've never seen her so happy as she is right now, and it makes me determined to see her smile at me like that.

I have no fucking clue how I'll achieve it. All I know how to do to make a girl happy is to make them come, but I'm sure I'll figure a way.

My cock swells as I watch her move flawlessly across the padded stage. She's so in sync with the other girls, I literally have no idea how they manage to coordinate it so well.

I have no idea how far through the routine they are but all of a sudden, one of the spotlights that are roaming around the crowd illuminates me.

My heart jumps into my throat, but I tell myself she's too busy and focused to see me.

But when I look up, my eyes immediately lock with hers. Our connection only lasts for the briefest of moments, a nanosecond, but it's still enough for me to see her shock, her horror at my being here.

Having said that though, nothing about her movements falter. If I couldn't read her like I can, then I wouldn't have a clue anything just happened.

But as it is, I can, and it just confirms what I already know.

I fucked up last night. Hell, I've been fucking up since I first stepped foot into Rosewood. But last night might have just been the icing on the cake. Although, I'm not sure being here right now helps all that much either. But there was no way I was missing this.

As the music comes to an end and they fall into their final positions, the crowd around me explodes with applause. I join them, but I don't stand to my feet, instead, I sink down into my seat because I think my presence might not have the effect that Ruby wants right now while she hugs the rest of her squad, a huge smile plastered on her face.

I remain in my seat watching the other finalists perform, my interest in the competition waning by the second. I'm not surprised to discover that my sudden interest in cheer only exists when Ruby is bouncing around on the stage.

I almost get up and see if I can go and find her, but I don't, not yet. I figure I'll wait for the results to be announced and when they're inevitably crowned champions, hopefully, she'll be in such a good mood that she won't just turn her back on me again. Optimistic thinking? Possibly.

30

RUBY

I stand with my right hand locked in Chelsea's and my left in Harley's as we huddle on the stage beside the other finalist squad waiting to hear our fate.

My heart is in my throat as I run through our performance again and again in my head.

It was perfect. Totally fucking flawless. Until I saw him in the crowd. The second my eyes locked on him, everything started to unravel.

My counting faltered and my timing was off but no matter what I did, I couldn't get him out of my head and focus back on what I should have been doing.

Were we good enough to win this thing? The others were. They were on point, even after their late night. Harley might have seen me running across the pool area in my need to escape from Ashton, but the others stayed out there well past their midnight curfew.

I, however, fucked up and it's all his fault.

Why is he even here? I can't imagine he gives a fuck about cheer until he's got a slut on her knees for him like I'm sure he had Krissy a few weeks ago.

Red hot fury fills my veins. Did he just come here to continue ruining my life? It seems all he's done is make good on that promise since the threat first passed his lips all those months ago.

I scan the crowd, trying to see Mom and Stephen in the mass of faces but with the bright lights trained on us, it's hard to see much. I do, however, point-blank refuse to look to where I saw him earlier.

I don't care if he's still here. I hope he's not. I don't need or want him here, no matter what the result of this is going to be.

Chelsea's hand trembles in mine. She wants this so fucking bad and I'm terrified I've ruined it for her.

"And the winners of the medium varsity cheer nationals are..." The announcer pauses to build the tension as my stomach turns over. I swallow down my nerves, hoping that I'm not about to puke in front of all these people. "The Clift..." His words fade away as the blood racing past my ears gets too loud. I squeeze my eyes shut as tears fill them faster than I can control.

I try to release the hands in mine but they refuse to let go of me.

We lost. We fucking lost and it's all my fault.

No, it's all *his* fault.

My eyes spring open of their own accord and I stare at the place in the stands where I saw him earlier. I frantically search, needing him to know just what he's done to me, but I don't find him. All I find is an empty chair.

The asshole couldn't even hang around to find out if he'd successfully ruined everything.

I'm in a total daze staring at that chair when Harley tugs on my arm and pulls me into a tight hug.

"I'm sorry, I'm so sorry," I whisper in her ear. Her body tenses against me.

"What the hell are you talking about, Rubes? We just got runner up at nationals, that's fucking epic."

When she pulls back, she's got a wide smile on her face. While I can't deny that we've just done well, we have, it's just... we should have won. We were good enough. They were good enough.

"We should have won," I say sadly.

"Hey, there's always next year," she says brightly, her smile not faltering, that is until her eyes meet mine once more. "Rubes, what's wrong?"

"Chelsea doesn't have next year." I glance at where she's pulling Aria into a hug and my tears spill over.

I fucked this up. I fucked up her dream.

"Ruby," Harley screams as I run from the stage.

I crash through the door leading from the stage toward the locker rooms where all our stuff is.

My lungs burn by the time I get there and my hands tremble as I frantically pull my stuff from the locker.

I need to get out of here. I can't be here.

I pass crowds of cheerleaders, their coaches and family and friends but I don't see anyone in my need to escape.

I fly through the exit that will lead me toward the main doors and finally outside when someone grabs my arm and I'm forced to stop.

I'm pulled back and I stumble, too stunned by being caught to find my footing and I crash into a solid chest.

A familiar scent fills my nose and my entire body stiffens with anger. My teeth grind and my fists curl.

"Ruby?" he whispers as if he's talking to a scared animal.

"Why are you here?" I seethe, finally looking up into his dark eyes. But unlike I'm used to, they're not angry, they're full of... concern?

"I came to support you."

"Bullshit," I spit at him, trying to rip my wrist from his vise-like grip. "You don't care about me, about how I, or the squad, do. You're probably laughing inside right now because we came in second."

"No, you were robbed if you ask me. You were clearly the best."

"Oh just fuck off, Ash."

"What? I'm being honest."

"Honest? Honest?" I bark. "You wouldn't know honest if it bit you in the ass. Now get your fucking hands off me."

When he still holds me captive, I drop my bag off my shoulder, allowing it to fall to the ground with a thud and slam my curled fist into his chest.

"I hate you, Ash. I fucking hate you and all of this is your fault. We'd have won if you weren't here. It's all your fault."

I know I'm causing a scene and I know I look like a crazy person but all I can see is the disappointment that I know will be in Chelsea's eyes for not achieving her goal and the guilt at knowing I was the one who fucked it up. I lost my count, I lost time. And all because of him.

"I fucking hate you," I squeal again. Tears stream down my cheeks and drip from my jaw, but I don't care.

I've been bottling this up all week and it feels so good to finally get it out, to scream at him after how he hurt me.

I'm not quick enough to pull my arm back and he manages to wrap his fingers around my other wrist, successfully stopping me from hitting him. Not that I'm under any illusion that I was actually hurting him, but it was making me feel better.

He flips us and pushes me up against the wall, my hands pinned above my head. My chest heaves as I stare at him, my eyes narrowed in anger, my teeth bared.

"I know you hate me, little one. You should, but believe me, I'm here for you."

A bitter laugh falls from my lips.

Our eyes hold as we stare at each other, something crackling between us.

"Do you know how fucking hot you look in that uniform," he says, his eyes finally dropping from mine. "I've been hard since the second you came out on stage."

"Good. I hope it fucking hurts."

"Ruby, I—" His words are cut off as two others call my name and come running over.

"There you are. Are you okay?" Chelsea asks as Harley stares daggers at Ash.

"Let her go," she spits as if he's nothing more than a piece of shit on her shoe.

He glances over at her and raises his brow.

"Sorry, red. None of your business."

"Excuse me?" She wraps her fingers around his forearm and digs her red talons into his skin. I can't help but smirk at her. "You've got my best friend pinned against the wall against her will, I think it's very much my business, asshole."

Chelsea ignores the two of them and looks at me.

"Is this him?"

I nod, wishing the ground would swallow me up and take me away from all of this.

"Unless you want a bigger issue than a couple of cheerleaders, then I suggest you let her go."

"Not until she hears me out."

"No, she doesn't need to listen to anything you have to say. I'm also pretty sure you weren't invited here or even have a ticket."

Ashton swallows, confirming Chelsea's suspicions.

"So if you don't want security to haul your ass out of here, I suggest you walk away now."

Thankfully, he releases me, and all the blood races back into my arms the second I lower them once more.

"Are you threatening me?" he asks, turning on Chelsea. His eyes drop to her obvious bump and I can't help wondering what he must think about this situation.

"Yes, I fucking am, asshole. You hurt a member of my squad then you hurt me too."

He shakes his head at Chelsea.

"Go on, underestimate me. I dare you," she seethes.

He laughs, actually fucking laughs in her face.

"Looks like someone already had some fun with you, I'll leave them to the games if you don't mind."

Chelsea's lips press into a thin line but before she gets to react, I do.

"Hey, Ash?"

"Yeah." He turns to me, a little relief seeping into his features that I want to talk to him. Good, this should come as a surprise then.

My arm flies out and my palm connects with his cheek with a loud slap.

"Stay away from my captain. Stay away from my best friend, and most importantly, stay the fuck away from me." I run my eyes down his body before climbing my way back up. "I've been there, and it really wasn't all that memorable," I lie, turning away from him, swiping my bag from the floor and taking both Chelsea and Harley's hands and leading them back the way I came from.

I feel his eyes burning into me until the door closes behind us, cutting off our connection.

"Are you okay?" Chelsea asks, coming to a stop in front of me.

"I'm so sorry." My bottom lip trembles as I say the words to her.

"Sorry for what? I'll go up against the likes of him for fun any day, you don't need to apologize for that."

"No, not that. We lost and it was my fault. He was in the crowd and I—"

"Whoa, whoa," she says, holding her hand up to stop me. "We didn't lose, Rubes. We came second. At nationals. It's incredible."

"I know, but it was your dream and I fu—"

"No. You didn't fuck anything up. I watched that entire routine. It was flawless, Rubes. If you think you missed a step or miscounted, then it's in your head because I can tell you right now that you, all of you, we're spot on."

"But—"

"It wasn't our time. The other squad was incredible too. The judges must have seen a bit more spark in them or something. Us not winning is not your fault, Ruby."

My bottom lip trembles hard as she looks at me with soft yet determined eyes.

"You haven't let anyone down. I'm so fucking happy with second. We've all worked our asses off for this, and after the year I've had, it's more than I could have ever asked for. But do you know what?"

I shake my head, too cut up to speak.

"Next year, you are going to lead this squad right back here, and I'll be so fucking proud of you even if you don't get through prelims because winning doesn't matter, not really. What matters is this." She squeezes my hand and the tears filling my eyes finally get to be too much once again and spill over. "You're all my family and all I want is the best for all of you." She pulls me into her arms and holds me tight, her bump pressing against my tummy.

Harley's arms come around both of us before I feel more people surround me. When I finally look up, I find the entire squad around me, all with huge smiles on their faces.

"You okay?" Chelsea mouths and I nod because I am with my girls around me, I can take on the world, including Ashton freaking Fury.

"Good. Now we came in fucking second, ladies. Shall we go and fucking celebrate?"

A round of cheers and agreement sound out as we move as a group toward the lockers to collect everyone's things.

Chelsea pulls me into her side, wrapping her arm around my shoulder. "You're going to be a kickass captain next year, you know that, right?"

I bite down on my bottom lip to stop me from reminding her that they need to vote me in and instead nod in agreement.

"And I hate to say this, Rubes. But shit, that boy of yours is fine. Was he good?"

"Ugh... yes," I say with a groan, making her laugh.

"Make him work for it before you give it up again, yeah?"

"He ain't getting it again."

She looks down at me with her brow raised. "Girl, I love you but please, don't lie to me. You saw the way he was looking at you, he's not letting you go anywhere."

"But—"

"Trust me, Rubes. Just make him work... hard." She winks at me before walking over to the other seniors in the squad and joining in their conversation.

"What did she say?"

"She thinks Ash is hot and that I'm gonna give it up again."

Harley stares at me like I've just sprouted another head.

"What?"

"Well, she's right. He is hot and he's fucking gone for you. He has been for ages."

"He's not. He hates me as much as I hate him."

"Sure. You keep telling yourself that."

As a group, we decided against the official celebrations that were being held that Sunday evening and instead after leaving the area we saw our families and went for pizza to celebrate. Then tracked down Miss Kelly to drive us all back.

All the girls were still buzzing from our success while I was silently stewing on the argument with Ashton. I don't care what he says, or what Chelsea tries to convince me, if he didn't show his face things would have turned out differently. Although I can't deny that Chelsea does seem delighted with our second place. I still would have loved to have seen her with that winner's trophy. Maybe she's right, maybe it just wasn't our time.

I blow out a breath as I stare at the passing scenery.

"You want to talk about it?"

After Harley found me in our hotel room bathroom last night in my underwear inspecting the damage on my back, she demanded to know what had happened. I'd given her the basics but based on the state of my body it shouldn't have been hard to guess.

I'd admitted that Ash had found me but that was it.

She thought it was hot that he'd accosted me and had his way with me in the darkness under the cover of the trees and I let her have her little fantasy.

"Not really," I mutter, slumping down in my seat a little more.

"Rubes, come on. You're going to have to go home and face him soon. You need to know how you're feeling about it."

"I know how I feel about it. I hate him and never want to see him again."

"I get that, but it's not exactly practical seeing as he lives in your house. Plus, knowing that he made his way out here this weekend just to support you, I doubt he's going to allow you to avoid him for long."

"Har, you don't believe that shit, do you? He didn't come to support me, he came to torment me."

"Really? I know he's been cruel, but you really think that's what this weekend was about?"

"Yes. I really do."

"Even after everything that happened in Seattle?"

I sigh, my irritation levels with her rising. I pick at my red nails for something to do. "Nothing happened in Seattle. He used me to bury his pain, that was all it was. I was close and stupidly willing."

"I know he probably deserves it, but you've got a really low opinion of him."

"Of course he deserves it. He embarrassed me in front of everyone at Ethan's party, he's lied to me, he made it look like I'd had sex in our parents' bed." Harley's brows pull together at that but I shake my head and continue. "And, he claims to have pictures of me on his cell from Halloween."

"And you believe him?"

"Why wouldn't I? He hasn't exactly proven himself trustworthy or to have my best interests at heart ever."

"No, you're right."

"Why are you all Team Ashton all of a sudden, anyway?"

She shrugs. "It was just the way he looked at you earlier. The fact he came here. I don't know. I think you should probably just talk to him, lay it all out on the table and maybe... I don't know, start over? Things have been beyond tense for both of you. You've been stressed about this weekend, he lost his mom. It might be time to put it all behind you so you can start fresh. He's going to be at Rosewood... tomorrow?"

"Oh God," I groan, tipping my head back and staring up at the bus roof. "Did I tell you he plays football?"

She laughs beside me. "Of course he does. Ruby, like it or not, this boy is about to insert himself into every part of your life. Whether you move forward with him or attempt to cut all ties and live as separate as possible, you are going to have to have it out with him."

"I'm scared, Harley," I admit quietly.

"Scared of what?"

"Him. Being in the same room alone with him. How I feel about him."

I don't need to look at her to know she's got a shit-eating grin on her face.

"You can say it, you know... *I told you so.*"

"Me? No, never. I wouldn't do that."

I laugh at her attempt to sound innocent.

"It's a mess, Har."

"You'll figure it out. And I'll be right here beside you as you do." She bumps her shoulder against mine in support.

"So... how's Nathan?"

Harley actually squeals in excitement at the mention of his name. "He's coming over later. Wants to take me out for dinner to celebrate our success."

"He's driving all the way from Maddison on a Sunday night? Boy's got it bad!"

She swoons. "He's so sweet. I really think we could have something."

I smile at her, wishing my life was as simple with a nice, sweet guy.

"Want to come back to my house to help me pick something to wear and avoid going home?"

"Now that sounds like an offer I can't refuse."

After saying goodbye to the squad once Miss Kelly pulls up at school, I climb into Harley's car that she left in the parking lot over the weekend and we head to her house.

"Do you know where he's taking you?"

"Nope, no idea."

She chats away about him, telling me things that I already know, but I don't have the heart to tell her because she's so excited.

"Is he already here?" I ask when she pulls up at her house and there's an unfamiliar car in the driveway.

"Nah, that's not his. Maybe Zayn's got someone round."

She shrugs and climbs out, and I refrain from telling her that almost all of Zayn's friends are also our friends and we know what they drive. But she doesn't seem too bothered, so I just follow her inside.

"Mom, I'm home," she calls into the silent house.

Jada was at the arena earlier supporting us, but she had to get back for work. No surprise there, the woman is always working.

"Oh hey, girls," she says when she emerges from the hallway where her office is.

"Hey."

Another pair of footsteps sound out behind her and Jada tenses, something that I notice Harley doesn't miss.

"Mom?" she asks but Jada just swallows nervously.

"I... uh... wasn't expecting you back yet."

I'm half expecting some half-dressed man to emerge from the hallway. Harley has never said anything about her mom having a boyfriend but I'm sure she must date. She's young and hot after all. But when a guy does emerge, I have my suspicions that she isn't having a relationship with him. He's obviously older than us, but not by much.

His eyes immediately land on Harley before they narrow in anger.

Harley tenses beside me and reaches for my hand.

What the hell?

"I was just helping Kane with a few things," Jada says as a way of explanation as the tension in the room only gets heavier. She turns to him and smiles softly. "I'll call you once everything is in hand."

"Thank you," he says coldly, his voice rough and... dangerous, much like his appearance.

His eyes never leave Harley as he moves around us to the front door.

"Mom?" Harley asks the second the door closes behind us, her voice full of accusation.

"It's nothing, Harley. I'm just helping out. Everything is fine."

"Really?" she asks, a humorless laugh falling from her lips. "You really believe that after everything?"

"Yes, sweetie. I do."

"I can't believe you." She shakes her head at her mom and marches toward the stairs.

"Harley," Jada calls as my best friend bolts up the stairs. But it's too late, she's gone.

Jada turns her sad eyes on me. "I'm sorry, Ruby."

"Don't worry about it. I'm sure she'll be fine," I say, although seeing as I have no clue as to what the hell just happened, that could all be lies. "I'll just..." I trail off, pointing to the stairs and following behind Harley.

When I get to the top and turn into her room, I find her pacing back and forth in front of her bed.

"Har, what's going on?" It takes a good few seconds for her to look up at me, and when she does my breath catches at the look in her eyes. She looks terrified. "Harley?" I warn, my own heart rate picking up a notch at her obvious fear. "Who was that guy?"

She looks back down at the carpet and blows out a breath.

I start to think she's going to ignore my question and I'm getting ready to ask my next when she finally responds.

"You remember after Halloween, after what went down with Ash?"

"Yeah," I encourage.

"And no matter what Poppy or I did, you refused to talk about it."

"Yeah."

"Well... this is kinda like that."

"You let him go down on you at Halloween?"

Her eyes widen in shock. "What? No. I didn't mean like that. I meant that I didn't want to talk about it."

"Oh, I was gonna say, he's hot, I'd imagine you'd want to scream that from the roof—"

"Stop. Please, just stop."

"O-okay."

"I can tell you that he's not touched me, there's nothing like that at all here. He just..." She shakes her head. "I can't."

Her shoulders drop in defeat as she falls down onto the end of her bed.

I watch as she tries to deal with whatever it is that involves the dangerous looking guy downstairs, wishing I could do something to help, and equally appreciating for the first time how annoying it must have been for both Harley and Poppy when I refused to talk about Ash.

Deciding I need to distract her, she's got a date to look forward to after all, I turn to her wardrobe. "So... what do you want to wear?" I ask, looking back over my shoulder at her.

"I'm going to cancel," she admits quietly.

"No. Harley, you are not going to do that. Whatever is going on here, don't let it ruin your time with Nathan."

She stares at me for a beat as if she's battling with her decision.

"Y-you're right." She pushes from the bed and comes to stand beside me. "Thank you," she whispers.

"Whatever you need, Har. I'm right here." I wrap my arm around her shoulder and pull her into me.

Thirty minutes later and we're back in Harley's car so she can drop me home before going to meet Nathan. I'm pretty sure he was supposed to pick her up, but she changed her mind and insisted that she wanted to drive. Something tells me that she just needed her own company for a bit to digest whatever that was with her mom in the foyer of their house.

"Call me if you need me," Harley says before I climb out of her car, my eyes locked on Ash's bike.

My stomach twists knowing that he's inside and possibly waiting for me. But I can hardly avoid my own house.

I could go to my dad's. He's not in town, but I've got a key. I could move in with his housemate. I laugh at myself.

Man up, Ruby, a little voice says in my head as I take a step toward the front of the house.

Harley gives me a little wave as I turn back before she reverses out of the driveway.

I let myself in and drop my bags by the stairs as I make my way through to the kitchen to where I can hear Mom and Stephen talking.

"Hey, sweetie, did you enjoy the rest of your day?"

"Y-yeah, it was good. We just celebrated," I say with a wince. Not winning hurts, I can't deny that. But I know Chelsea is right, it just wasn't our time. Maybe next year.

"As you should, you were incredible. The whole squad was."

"Thanks, Mom."

"Would you like some food? I can heat up the leftovers."

"No, I'm good. We went out for pizza. I'm just gonna go and do some homework."

"Okay." I turn to leave but her voice stops me. "Ruby?"

"Yeah."

"Ashton is home."

I nod, unable to get any words past the lump that has suddenly appeared in my throat.

"I've told him to give you space. I suggest you do the same for him." She doesn't need to tell me twice.

"Sure thing."

"He's starting at school tomorrow," Stephen adds.

"Tomorrow?"

"Yeah, but don't worry, I'm not about to ask you to be his chaperone or anything."

"Good."

"Okay, well..." I back away from them both, not giving them a chance to say anything else before I lock myself in my room for the night.

They watch me leave, but they don't say anything else. I'm surprised, I was expecting a lecture about Ashton and what we can't do under their roof. Although I've been so sad and angry the past week, they're probably pretty confident that I don't want to be anywhere near him. And they'd be correct.

With a sigh, I collect up my bags and make my way to my room. My footsteps falter as I pass Ash's door. I know he's inside, I can feel it and it annoys the shit out of me.

But I keep my head high and walk straight past.

The second I step into my room, I can't help but smile at the huge bouquet of red and white—our school colors—flowers that are sitting on my dresser.

Dumping my bags on the bed, I walk over to admire them, plucking the card from the holder as I do. I find a typed message, which is odd because Mom always prefers to handwrite to make it more personal, but I figure it's Sunday and was last minute.

You'll always be my number one!

XXX

I smile at her corniness and place the card beside the vase the stems are resting in.

They're really beautiful and exactly the thing I needed to make this homecoming a little more pleasant.

A noise from the room next door stops me in my tracks to the bathroom, and I hold my breath as I wait to see if he's going to come barreling in here to have it out with me.

But after a few seconds and no more noise, I figure that he's leaving me alone and I go back to what I was doing.

31

ASHTON

My fists curl in the sheets beneath me as I listen to her quiet footsteps climb the stairs.

Every inch of me wants to pull the door open and drag her in here so we can finish what we started earlier.

She can shout, scream, hit me all she wants. I deserve it. Maybe not for showing up to support her this weekend, but for all the other shit I've pulled.

But I lie there doing nothing.

I need to let her cool off. I can't chase her. Yet.

After long painful minutes of listening to her move about in her room, a knock sounds out on my bedroom door.

After I got back, I refused to eat with, or even talk to, Dad and Lisa. I just wanted to hide. So after grabbing a couple of cans of soda and a bag of chips, that's exactly what I did. Although not before Dad called out after me that I had twelve hours to get my shit together because tomorrow the principal was expecting me at Rosewood High bright and early to start my new life.

Great. I can't fucking wait.

I thought I was nearly done with school. Okay, so I wouldn't have graduated like Mom was hoping for, but I would have been done and free to do whatever I wanted.

Now though, I'm going backward.

"The perfect opportunity to start over and make something of myself," Dad had called up the stairs as I walked away from him earlier.

I guess that could be true. I could actually attend school instead of getting wasted and high with the Kingston boys and actually give myself a future. But dropping back to being a junior fucking sucks. Even if Rosewood has a killer football team. Do I really want to do it all over again?

Whoever it is knocks again and I freeze. Did I miss her moving around and coming to my door? My heart pounds at the thought of her appearing in the doorway, but when I call out and the door swings open, it's not Ruby standing there. I almost roll my eyes at myself, of course it's not her, it's Dad coming to give me a lecture I'm sure.

"You busy?"

I raise a brow at him. I'm lying on my bed doing absolutely nothing. Do I look busy?

"No."

"Can you come down to my office? We need to have a chat."

I want to refuse, continue to be the asshole that I'm sure I've convinced him that I am since I moved here. But he's right. It's time we talked.

"Sure, lead the way."

The walk down to his office is tense as fuck, but I fight my need to turn around and hide back in my room. This chat has been a long time coming, years actually.

"Take a seat." I do as I'm told, grinding my teeth the entire time.

"I've spoken to Principal Hartmann. He's gotten your transfer papers from your old place and he's happy for you to join as a junior now ready to restart your senior year next semester. It sounds like you've had a glowing reference from your old coach, and Hartmann has already mentioned you joining the team. I really think you should consider it."

I nod at him, he's not saying anything that I don't already know. And as for the team, playing football will probably be the only thing that gets me through all of this, so yeah, I'm on board with that.

"He will introduce you to Coach and some of the team tomorrow, no doubt. But I need to warn you that I've told him that you are going to take this seriously. This is your second chance, Ashton. Not many people get the chance to right their wrongs like this. Your attendance and GPA are poor, and if it weren't for your skills on the field, I really think Hartmann would have had second thoughts about allowing you into his school. I've assured him that you're going to be an asset to both the school and the team, and I really need you to be on board."

I stare at him, unsure what he's really expecting of me. I've always hated school. Football is the only good thing about education as far as I'm concerned, so I'm finding it hard to get excited about this new start like I think he's expecting of me.

"Did you know Mom was saving all the money you've sent her since the day you left?" I blurt out, needing to change the subject away from me, having to promise something I'm already sure I can't deliver on.

"Uh... no." The frown line on his head tells me that he had no clue.

"I knew you sent money, she told me time and time again when I blamed our shitty living situation on you. So I just assumed you never sent enough."

"Ashton, every month I sent—"

"I know, I found it."

"Found it?"

"I discovered her journals in her room. I started reading this year's. She kept all your money in an account. She was waiting until I finished school and she planned to move us both to Maddison County to start over. She wanted to buy a house, give me better opportunities, and for us to be closer."

"Wow, okay," he breathes, slumping back in his chair.

"I thought you were the bad guy who wasn't looking after us—me."

"Ash, no. I know I left, but things weren't good between your mom and me. I loved her, I always will, she was such a huge part of my life, but things were long over by the time I reconnected with Lisa online. My priority was always you, making sure you were safe, looked after."

"But you saw how we lived, you left us like that."

"Your mom was a stubborn and independent woman, Ash. I'm sure you don't need me to tell you that. I tried to help, to give her more, to do what I thought you both needed but she wouldn't accept it. She wanted me to be happy here just as much as I wanted you both to be. She didn't want to drag me into your lives more than necessary because technically, I gave up that right when I left Seattle."

I blow out a long breath, dragging my eyes from his and staring down at his desk between us.

"I won't sit here and say that I did everything right, Ash, because I know that I didn't. Our relationship wouldn't have been what it has if I'd done things right. But I tried. All I wanted was for you to have the best start in life."

"You're not the only one who's fucked things up."

He shakes his head. "None of this is on you, Ash."

"I appreciate that, but it is."

He opens his mouth to say something but swiftly closes it again. After swallowing down his nerves or whatever it is that's stopping him, he finally says the words that I know are coming.

"We need to talk about Ruby."

I nod because I knew I wasn't getting out of this room without her coming up.

"I'm sorry," I say, shocking the fuck out of him if his lowered chin is anything to go by. "Honestly, I'm not sure I'd have got through the last week without her. She's a fucking angel."

He nods. "Y-yeah, she is."

"I hated her to start with. She had everything I wanted. *You.*" I slump down in my chair, not really wanting to admit these things to him but at the same time knowing that we need to get all of this out. "I can't even put into words how much I missed you when you left. And then I see pictures of you playing happy family with Lisa and Ruby. It hurt, Dad. It hurt so fucking bad."

"When I came here last year, it was with the intention of hurting her. Of hurting you. Showing you that leaving me behind and starting over with a new family wasn't going to be that easy. Only... she wasn't what I was expecting and when I got her at her weakest, she spoke to me in a way no one had before. She affected me like no other and I freaked and—"

"Left," he interrupts, nodding as if he's putting the missing pieces of a puzzle together in his head. "It was you."

"W-what was me?" I ask, my brows drawing together.

"After you left, Ruby, she... she kind of fell apart. She... changed. We thought it was just a teenage girl thing. She was acting out, getting drunk—shit, I probably shouldn't be telling you this."

"No, no go on," I say with a smirk.

"Jesus, Ash. What do you want me to say here? She's my stepdaughter. I love her almost as much as I do you."

"Say whatever you like, we both know that if I don't like it then I'll just ignore it."

"Yeah, that's what I'm worried about."

He blows out a long breath and scrubs his hand down his face. "Lisa is going to kill me for this," he mutters to himself. "Is it serious?"

"Uh..." I hesitate because how am I actually supposed to give him a serious answer. We've had a couple of angry, emotional moments together. I doubt they could be classed as serious in anyone's books.

"Is how you feel about her serious?"

I rub at my jaw wishing I was anywhere but here and having this hellish conversation with a man I feel like I don't know anymore.

"I-I think so. This is all new to me, but I can tell you that I feel differently about her then I do any other girls I've fu—" I cut myself off when his fists curl on top of the desk. "Spent time with."

"I can't stop you doing whatever it is you want to do. I'm not stupid enough to even try. But I need you to promise me something."

"Shoot."

"Go big or go home, Ash. You either want her and you're serious, in which case you need to prove yourself to her, to me—to us. Or... you walk away now before you cause any more damage, and you allow her to get on with her life while you restart yours. I want you both to be happy and I trust both of you enough to be able to choose the right thing for yourselves. But if you go after her and you hurt her, well... I might not be so nice after that. I want you here, Ash, but you're eighteen soon..." He trails off, leaving his warning about being kicked out of his house hanging in the air between us if I do anything to fuck this up or hurt Ruby.

"I get it, Dad."

"Good, because I'm serious. I want you here more than anything. I want everyone I love around me. But if you hurt either Lisa or Ruby in their own house, I'm not going to have a choice."

"I know. I'll do the right thing." *I hope.* There's got to be a first time for everything, right?

"We done?" I ask, pushing to the edge of the seat. We've just talked more than we have in years and I'm more than ready to go and hide on my own in silence once more.

"Yeah." I'm at the door before he speaks again. "I'll talk to Lisa about this but maybe don't repeat exactly what I said to you."

A smile tugs at my lips. "Sure thing." I can just imagine how his go big or go home statement would sound to Ruby's mom.

"Thanks, Dad."

"I want to trust you, Ash. Please, don't let me down."

I nod, unable to make any promises. The one thing I seem to be good at is letting people down and fucking things up.

I pause at my door when I get there. I desperately want to keep going and knock on her door to see if she'll even talk to me, but I don't.

There's going to be plenty of time to talk. I owe her a little space after everything.

I might not have made any promises out loud to Dad, but I fully intend on at least trying because she deserves it. She did everything she could for me when I was at my lowest, the least I can do is what she asks of me.

For now, at least.

"Ashton Fury, I've heard a lot about you," Principal Hartmann says after introducing himself and inviting me into his office.

I might have only walked through the admin part of Rosewood High but already the differences to my old school are glaringly obvious. For a start, the staff I've seen look like they actually want to be here, the buildings don't look like they're about to crumble to the ground and the students look... happy. It's weird.

"All good, I hope," I reply, dropping down into the chair in front of his desk and shoving my hands into the pockets of my hoodie.

"If we're talking about on the field then yes, in the classroom... not so much."

"Huh, I'm surprised the teachers noticed," I mutter, looking around his office before my eyes land on the photograph of his family sitting on his desk. My old principal didn't dare do something like that for fear one of his students would go after his kids. It just proves that this really isn't Seattle.

"Your GPA leaves something to the imagination, young man. If you think you're going to come in here and wow us with your football skills and we'll ignore your academic progress, then you've got another thing coming."

I nod, knowing that his words are right.

"I've spoken to Coach and he's more than willing to let you attend his conditioning sessions starting this afternoon if you're up for it, but getting a place on his team is going to require dedication and an improvement in your grades."

"You got it."

"Okay," he says, studying me, probably wondering why I'm making this so easy for him. It makes me wonder exactly what he has heard about me. I might not have been the best student in the past but I was far from the worst.

"I've got your schedule here, there is some flexibility should you need—"

"I'll be great, thanks." I lean forward and tug it from his fingers. My past performance might lead people to think I'm not capable of achieving anything, but that's far from the truth. I'm not stupid, just bored.

I run my eyes over the piece of paper, spotting all the usual subjects and nothing I can't cope with.

"Okay, so... do you have any questions for me?"

"Nope. Just point me in the direction of..." I glance back to the schedule to see how my week is starting. "Chemistry, and I'll get out of your hair."

"Actually, I've arranged for someone to give you the grand tour."

"Great." I just about manage to hold in my groan. I really don't need someone to hold my hand, I'm sure I can navigate my way around this place without too much effort.

Thoughts of a peppy cheerleader happily showing me around fills my mind, and I start to wonder if he's going to have arranged for Ruby to be my guide. Surely, I'm not that lucky.

"It's probably best you get to know each other, you know, captain to captain and all that." Hartmann winks at me and I push from the chair.

So not Ruby then. I try to keep my disappointment off my face.

He hits the intercom button on his desk before barking, "Can you please send Jake in?"

A polite voice agrees before the door opens and a dark-haired guy wearing a Rosewood Bears jersey steps inside.

"Jake Thorn, this is Ashton Fury. Ashton was captain of his team in Seattle. He's going to be joining you for conditioning in the hope of making the team. Jake is our current captain. He led us all the way to the championships."

"Okay, great. Shall we," I say, nodding to Jake and walking out of Hartmann's office.

"So you were captain. You win anything?"

"Nah. Our school... it wasn't like this one. The sports funding was shit but we did the best we could with what we had."

"Well, I hope you're good because our best players are about to graduate."

"I guess you'll find out soon."

"I guess so."

I trail behind Jake as he gives me a brief tour of the place, pointing out where I do and don't want to go, where the team hangs out and how things work around here.

"That's your first class down there." He points to a green door at the end of the hallway.

"Great, thanks for the tour." I turn to leave him but he stops me.

"Fury," he says, taking a step toward me so our chests are only a few inches apart. "I don't give a shit how good you are on the field. You hurt Ruby, and my boys and I will make sure you never play again. You got that."

I stare into his narrowed eyes, not standing down in any sense as a smirk pulls at one side of my mouth.

"Warning heard loud and clear, *captain.* But I should warn you that I've eaten boys bigger than you for breakfast. So I'd like to see you try."

I don't wait for him to respond. I spin and take off down the hall, ready to introduce myself to my first teacher.

"We'll see, Fury. We'll see," I hear him mutter after me.

I'm still smiling when I step into the classroom.

Silence fills the room immediately at my interruption.

"Oh hello, you must be Ashton," the teacher says softly. She's young, almost too young to be teaching high school, but whatever. It's not her who captures my attention because when I turn to my left, I lock eyes with the one person I do want to see.

My smile widens as she swallows nervously and sinks down in her chair as if she's going to be able to hide behind her desk.

Nice try, little one. Nice try.

32

RUBY

I wasn't surprised when my body woke me before the sun came up this morning. I've been doing it for so many weeks as we prepared for nationals it's become almost normal.

I tried to force myself to roll over and go back to sleep but it was pointless.

In the end, I got up and got ready as if I had somewhere to be. The sun was barely up when I pulled open the front door and made my way to my car.

I figured there was no chance of bumping into Ash if I left this early.

Mom accosted me when I escaped my bedroom last night for a snack and confirmed that he would be starting at Rosewood today and that Stephen was talking to him, warning him to give me some space.

I appreciated it, but Ashton has proved to me time and time again that he doesn't really listen to rules, especially when it comes to me.

She warned me to be careful but thankfully, she steered clear of talking about anything else to do with the two of us. I can only hope I got through to her in the bathroom at Leanora's funeral and that she's going to back off and let us make our own mistakes.

I let out a sigh as I pull open the gym doors and walk inside the dark space.

I flick a couple of the lights on, just enough to see where I'm going and to alert anyone to the fact that I'm in here.

I cross my legs and sit right in the middle of the room as I run the events of the weekend through my mind.

Chelsea was right, our routines and performances were killer. I know I was hard on myself when we didn't score first place, but it's only because I want it for all the girls who have put everything into this. I want it more for them than I do for me. I wanted it for Chelsea. She deserved it.

I rest back on my palms and tip my head up to the ceiling as I wonder what the next few months will hold.

Is Chelsea right? Will the squad want me as their next captain, and if they do, who is going to replace the seniors? Harley and Stella are obvious choices, but the rest of the JV team, they're going to need some work.

Hopefully, summer camp will help sort them out, help them see the mountain that they've got to climb if they want to match our success from the weekend, let alone exceed it.

I've no idea how much time passes while I sit there contemplating my future.

Ashton keeps trying to force his way into my thoughts, but every time his face pops into my mind, I shake it out. He's consumed enough of my time the past few weeks. I'm done with it. With him.

Eventually, the door opening behind me drags me from my thoughts. Looking over my shoulder, I find Chelsea walking in.

"Couldn't sleep either, huh?" she asks, correctly guessing why I'm sitting here like an idiot.

"Nope. You've ruined sleeping in for me," I joke.

"Sorry, about that. It was worth it though." She dumps her bag by the wall and walks over, before dropping down beside me.

"Yeah, it was," I say with a smile.

"How are... things?"

"I haven't seen him," I admit. "But he's starting here today, so I think my avoidance tactics are going to come to an abrupt end."

"You need to talk to him," she says, confirming what I already know.

"I know," I sigh. "He just makes me a little crazy when we're close."

She chuckles to herself. "I know what that's like." Her hand rubs over her bump.

"How did you get over it?"

She shrugs and leans back on her palms. "I didn't, I got under it."

I can't help but snort a laugh. "Your advice is for me to sleep with him again?"

"No, no. Honestly, I don't know, Rubes. I've barely met him. I'm not sure those few angry minutes I witnessed in the arena really showed him at his best. But I saw the way he looked at you. It wasn't a look of a guy who hates you, Rubes. Maybe just hear him out. He's been through a lot. Maybe something has changed since you left him in Seattle."

"Hmm... maybe."

"At the end of the day, Ruby. You won't ever find out if you spend your time hiding in your bedroom or in here. If he's going to end up on the team, as you suspect, you're going to need to be able to stand to be in the same room as each other. And you might need to do it fast because if he fits right in then you know he'll be at Justin's party this weekend."

I groan, thinking about the congratulation party the guys are throwing for the squad.

"I'm never going to escape his ass, am I?"

"Nope, which is why you may as well make the best of the situation." She laughs. "What's the worst that could happen?"

We sit chatting until the sound of students descending around us fills the gym and a few teachers poke their heads in to check on us.

"We should probably head out."

"It feels weird not practicing."

"You've only got a week off, make the most of it."

I stand from the floor before holding a hand out to help Chelsea up before we head out to join the others at the team benches.

I was hoping to get through at least an hour without having to see him, but it seems luck isn't on my side this morning because not twenty minutes into first period does he come marching into my chemistry class.

"Fucking hell," I mutter under my breath, much to Harley's amusement who's sitting beside me.

As if he can feel my stare, his eyes almost immediately find mine and my heart jumps into my throat.

Maybe this is going to be even harder than I expected.

My eyes don't leave him the entire time he talks to Miss Harris. I know I need to look down, look anywhere, but I can't.

By the time he turns my way, I'm in a total daze and unable to do anything but stare at him.

"Here, take my seat." Harley's words drag me back to reality.

"What?" I snap at her, in total disbelief that she'd even consider doing this to me.

"What?" she asks innocently, gathering her books and standing from her seat. "I'm doing an experiment. A chemistry experiment."

I growl at her and she bursts out laughing as she makes her way to the back of the room and to a spare chair.

She locks eyes on me as she lowers down and smiles sweetly.

"I hate you," I mouth, but all she does is shrug before going back to arranging her books.

"So… this is cozy," Ashton whispers as he sits his ass beside me.

"Is it?" I mutter, crossing my arms over my chest and letting out a huff of frustration. So much for staying out of his way.

Refusing to look at him, I keep my eyes on Miss Harris who quickly picks up where she left off, completely oblivious to the tension that's suddenly filled the room.

"Safe to say, my morning keeps getting better and better." His arm rests on the back of my chair, his thumb grazing my shoulder blade and sending tingles down my spine.

"Do you mind?" I snap, shooting forward away from his touch.

"No, little one. Not really."

"Well, I do. Keep your hands off me."

"Is that what you really want?" he all but growls.

It's so low and deep that I know no one else would have heard him and damn him because it affects me exactly as he was expecting it to. Heat floods my body and I'm immediately taken back to his room in Seattle where he growled all kinds of dirty things in my ear.

He leans forward with me, his fingertips skating down my spine and I jump up.

"Ruby, is everything okay?"

"Y-yes. I just need the bathroom. Do you mind?"

Miss Harris sighs at me and rolls her eyes. "Be quick."

I dart out of that classroom like someone set my ass on fire.

"Fucking hell," I mutter, falling back against the bathroom door and tipping my face to the ceiling.

We're not even an hour into the day and he's already driving me insane.

After giving myself a little pep talk, I make my way back to class. Apologize to Miss Harris and reluctantly return to my seat.

Thankfully, Ashton had started taking notes in the few minutes I've been gone, and he continues long after I return.

I'm glad he's turned his attention away from me, but irritatingly, I'm also disappointed.

I flash a glance behind me to Harley who's watching us curiously. A smile curls up at her lips and I just shake my head at her.

The second the bell rings, I'm out of the room. A smirk pulls at my lips when Miss Harris calls Ashton back so she can give him some extra homework to catch up. Fingers crossed all his teachers do that and keep him busy for the foreseeable future.

"What the hell was that?" I bark at Harley when she steps up to me as we head to history.

"What, I was just being nice to the new student."

"Bullshit, Har. What game are you playing?"

"Me? Actually, I wanted to see what game Ash was playing. Did you really think he'd show up here and let you ignore him?"

"I..." I'd hoped he might however I knew realistically it was never going to happen.

"He wants you, Rubes. Whether you like it or not. Which by the way, I think you do, if the way you reacted to him earlier said anything."

"What? I didn't—"

"Really?" she asks with a laugh.

"You need to talk to him."

"I really, really—"

She pins me with a look just before we get to our next class. "You really, really do. You don't want this? Tell him and stay strong. You decide you do want it? Stop playing games. It'll only end up with you being hurt worse."

Harley's words ring out in my head throughout the rest of my morning classes.

He hurt me. Walking away from me that morning in Seattle after everything that had happened between us. Doing whatever he did after we left. All of it hurt, it still hurts.

Can I just forgive him for all that?

I know he was—is—in a bad place. His mom had died, but that's no excuse to take it out on me, rip my heart out and stomp all over it.

I recall his touch this morning. How it burned, how it set my blood on fire.

I want that again, I'm not even going to try to deny that. But is it worth it? Or are we destined to destroy each other?

I don't see Harley after history, and thankfully I don't see Ashton again, well not until I walk into the cafeteria for lunch. The second I'm in the doorway, I see him.

He's standing with the team, Jake by his side, as I assume he introduces Ash to everyone.

My stomach turns over. This is really happening. He's inserting himself into every aspect of my life and there's shit all I can do about it.

Everywhere I turn—at home, at school—he's going to be right there, taunting me, reminding me, tempting me.

"Uh oh, skank, two o'clock," Harley says in my ear as she appears at my side.

Ripping my eyes away from Ashton, I find Krissy, Aria, and Victoria heading straight for him.

"Did she really suck him off at Ethan's party?"

A growl rumbles up my throat at her words.

"Alright, no need to go all cavewoman on me, I was merely inquiring as to what went down."

"I don't know. I didn't ask." But as we stand there continuing to watch the show, I think we get our answer because Krissy walks right up to him, the length of her body presses against his, absolutely zero hesitation and no shame, as she runs her palms up his chest.

"Wow, someone's about to get her eyes gouged out with your nails," Poppy mutters, joining the two of us and watching the show.

"I don't care. She can touch him all she likes." As I say this, he looks up, his eyes immediately finding mine.

"I've lost my appetite. I'll see you both later."

I don't waste another second of my time watching as Krissy shamelessly grinds up against him as if she fucking owns him and I storm off, ready to go and hide and try to forget everything about this day.

Tears burn my eyes as I fly down the hallways, my heart pounds and my hands shake as I try to contain everything that's threatening to burst out of me. The anger, the devastation, the regret.

I fly through the gym doors and find it as empty as it was first thing this morning before I push through the hidden office door around the corner.

As I expected, it's empty. Miss Kelly is nowhere to be seen as usual. I slam the door behind me but despite the bang being loud, it does little to make me feel any better.

33

ASHTON

Before I get a chance to push Krissy off me, a voice rings out through the team.

"Put the new boy down, Krissy. You don't know where he's been," the pregnant cheerleader barks, coming to stand in front of me.

She wraps her fingers around Krissy's upper arm and all but drags her from me.

"You," she says, pointing right in my face. "You are playing a very dangerous game."

My chin drops as silence surrounds us. I swear to God, the entire cafeteria is holding their breath to see what is going to happen next.

"You don't know what you're talking about."

"Don't I?" she asks as Ruby's two friends come to stand beside her. "So, Ruby didn't just run out of here because this slut decided you belong to her?"

I glance at Krissy, who doesn't even react to the insult.

"You don't know shit about me and Ruby."

The team moves over behind their girls, showing where their loyalty lies, not that I thought for a million years they'd stand with me when they've just met me, but it makes me wonder if becoming one of them is going to be a bigger mountain to climb than I first thought.

"Claim her, or let her go," she warns, her eyes boring into mine, ensuring that I'm unable to look away. "But if you hurt her, you can bet your ass we're all coming for you."

Tension crackles around us as our stare holds.

Who the hell is this bitch?

"I'm Chelsea, by the way," she says with a smirk as if she can read my mind. "And we," she says, gesturing to herself and everyone around her. "Own this place. You make one wrong move, and you are done. *Family* or not. Ruby is one of us, you never have to be."

I want to laugh at her threats. Compared to what I've lived through in Seattle, they are child's play. I'm used to guys—and girls—having knives and guns and not being afraid to use them.

But something about how she narrows her eyes at me hits deeper than having any weapon waved in my face and I know it's got everything to do with the girl they're warning me about.

"Where is she?" I ask, assuming that they're going to tell me to go to hell and leave her alone.

"I don't know for sure, but I can make a good guess. Follow me."

"Baby," one of the guys from the team calls out before walking around the others and pulling her into his side. "I'm so fucking hot for you right now," he whispers not so quietly in her ear.

"Really? Can you just fucking lead the way?"

They both turn on me, eyes narrowed.

"Thin fucking ice," Chelsea growls. "Thin fucking ice." Before she takes the guy's hand and starts marching out of the cafeteria and expecting me to follow. Which of course I do because she's about to lead me to Ruby.

"So this is where the magic happens then?" I ask as we step into the gym who is covered in cheerleading paraphernalia.

"Ashton," Chelsea growls. "I might be taking you to her right now, but don't be under any illusion that it's because I like you, because I don't. You hurt her and until you make it right, we'll never be friends whether you get your ass on the team or not. My girls are my priority, and my future captain is top of that list."

A little bit of pride washes through me as Chelsea insinuates that Ruby is going to step into her shoes in the coming months. Having watched her up on that stage over the weekend and her passion when things didn't go their way, I have no doubt that she'll be incredible.

Chelsea pokes her head around the corner and then nods at me.

"She's in there. Can we trust you with her?"

"I'd never hurt her."

Chelsea places one hand on her waist and juts her hip out.

"Not physically." I can't promise that whatever comes out of our mouths might not sting because we have a way of cutting each other down with words.

"We'll be out here."

"You don't have to babysit us."

"No, but we might need to beat your ass."

I roll my eyes at her, briefly glance at her boyfriend who mostly just looks amused and turned on by her being all fired up and I turn away from them.

The second the window to the office comes into view, I see her curled up on the office chair, hugging her legs to her chest with her head on her knees.

She looks so tiny and helpless and all I want to do is pull her into my arms and tell her that everything is going to be okay.

The click of the door opening startles her, her entire body flinches as I step inside.

"Please, just leave me alone. I'm fine."

I stare at her for a few more seconds as guilt swamps me.

I did this.

I blow out a breath as I prepare to say the words I need to say to her.

"I'm sorry, little one."

Her head snaps up so fast I'm surprised she doesn't hurt herself.

"Get out," she seethes, her eyes narrowing as she looks at me.

"No, not until we've talked." I close the door at my back to make a point. We're not leaving this office until we've either sorted things out or killed each other. I guess only time will tell which comes first.

"I've got nothing to say to you, so I suggest you walk straight back out and go and find your little slut."

"I don't want her, Ruby."

"Just like you didn't want Nat? You had a funny way of showing that too."

"I don't..." I sigh, my hands coming up to my head.

"Nothing happened with Nat."

"Aside from what I saw." She raises a brow at me, uncurling herself from the chair and standing to her feet, preparing to fight.

"Y-yeah, aside from that. I made a mistake, Ruby. I was... I was lost and needed someone."

"You had me, Ash. I was right there with you through all of it, and you pushed me away when you needed me most. You never even needed to be anywhere near her. You could have got in that car with me and we could have gone anywhere."

"I know. I fucked up," I admit, holding her gaze so she knows how serious I am.

I can make all the excuses I want about my state of mind that day, but at the end of the day, I fucked up. I sent away the one good thing in my life and fell back into old habits to drown out my bullshit.

"That's all you do, Ash. You fuck up. All you've done since we met is hurt me. I know you hate me, and I understand it, I do, but fuck, it's time to give it up. We're fucking stuck with each other now whether we like it or not."

"I don't want to hurt you, Ruby."

"Well, you're fucking good at it." She marches toward me, stopping before we're in touching distance. "Excuse me."

"No."

"No? You're going to keep me locked in here?"

"Until you hear me out, yeah, if that's what it takes. I don't want to fight with you, Rubes."

"That's all we're capable of, haven't you realized? We're toxic, Ash. A disaster waiting to happen. All we do is hurt each other, our parents are fighting. It's just..." She throws her arms out from her sides. "It's pointless, Ash. Now get out of my way and let me get on with my life."

"What if I don't want to?"

"I don't really give a shit what you want right now. I gave you what I thought you needed in Seattle, and all you did was throw it back in my face. So go and find Krissy, or one of the others, I'm sure they'd happily be your little toy until you get bored of them."

"No," I spit, stepping into her space and forcing her to back up until her ass hits the edge of the desk. My fingers grip her jaw as my body presses against hers. "I don't want them. I couldn't give a shit what they would happily do for me. I want you, Ruby. Just you." My eyes stare down into her green ones as they fill with tears. She tries to shake her head, but my grip is too hard for her to move much.

"You're lying."

"Am I?" I sneer, closing the space between us until my nose brushes hers.

"What do you want, Ash? What do I need to do for you to let me out of here?"

A smile curls up at my lips at the possibilities.

"Tell me what I need to know."

"Which is?" she asks, forcing herself to sound bored by this whole exchange but I know it's fake. I can see the heat in her eyes behind her tears, and I can feel her pulse thundering against my fingers.

I lean in closer, brushing my cheek against hers until my lips tease the shell of her ear.

"Tell me you're mine."

She tenses but no words pass her lips.

"Ruby," I growl. "We both already know it's a fact, but I need to hear you say it."

"A fact?" she spits. "To you maybe, but as far as I'm concerned, I don't belong to anyone."

Pulling back, I rest my forehead against hers, my breaths racing out past my lips and mixing with hers as I stare down at her.

"Please, Ruby, I need—"

I'm too lost in her to see her hands lift. Her palms slam against my chest and I'm so shocked by her strength that I back up, putting some space between us.

"I don't give a shit what you need right now, Ash. I care about what I need, and that's not to be anywhere near you."

Before I get a chance to respond, she's ripped the door open and flown through it.

"Fuck," I bark, tugging at my hair until it hurts. "FUCK."

I take a step back until my ass hits the desk and I rest back, tipping my face to the ceiling.

All this shit is new to me. I want to tell her how I feel, that I'm serious about all this but I've got no fucking clue how to do it.

I'm surprised to find the gym empty when I emerge sometime later, I was expecting the team to be waiting for me to teach me a lesson for hurting one of their own.

The bell rings as I'm making my way down the hall and I'm forced to abandon any lunch plans I had in favor of finding my next class.

All I can hope is that she's in it.

But it seems that's wishful thinking because I don't see her again for the rest of the day, I do, however, spend my last two classes in the firing line from the team and the squad's death stares.

As first days at a new school go, it's not been the best. Things don't get any easier either when I finally locate the locker rooms after school to join in with the team's conditioning session to discover that Coach is busy, and that Jake is in charge and that his sole intention for the session is to see how far he can push me.

By the time he lets up, my entire body aches and is covered in sweat. It's been too long since I've done that kind of a workout.

"I think I might have underestimated you," Jake admits, coming to stand beside me as I get dressed after showering off the mud and grass that covered almost every inch of me.

"Oh yeah?"

"That would have broken most guys."

"I'm not just any guy though."

"So I see." Another guy comes to join us, Ruby's friend's boyfriend, I think.

"You think he's got what it takes?" he asks Jake but stares at me.

"It's early days. Let's see if he lasts the week first. Chelsea might kill him first."

"I can hear you," the blond guy, who I can only assume is the dad to Chelsea's baby pipes up from the other side of the locker room.

"Fuck off, Dunn. Don't even pretend you were gagging for a bit of that when she went all momma bear on this guy's ass," Jake shouts much to a few of the guy's amusement.

"Not denying anything. Might go home and try to get her pregnant all over again though. Ow," he complains when someone throws something at him.

"Do we need to have another conversation about Ruby?" Jake asks me as the other guy's brow rises possessively.

"Nope. I know what I want. But if you wanted to help me out, you could put in a good word to Ruby."

"Not gonna happen, man. You gotta dig yourself out of your own shit."

"Great," I mutter, turning away from them and continuing to get dressed.

"So, same again tomorrow?"

"Can't wait."

"Coach and I are going to be picking next year's team soon. Captain too."

I don't reply and I think it pisses him off but he lets it go.

"Aces?" he asks the rest of the locker room and after a few minutes, they all start disappearing. I have no idea if that was a group invite that included me, but I make no move to follow.

By the time I'm ready, they've all disappeared, leaving me to walk to the parking lot alone. I climb on my bike and head for home, wondering if Ruby will have met the team at Aces or if she's hiding from me in her room.

I get my answer the second I show up at home because her little blue car is sitting in the driveway.

Stopping in the kitchen for a drink and some food, I make my way upstairs, marching straight past my own door and straight to hers.

I knock knowing that she's inside, but I get no response.

"Ruby?"

"Go away."

"You wanna hang out?" It's a long shot, but I figure it's worth it. "Do that chemistry assignment together?"

"No."

I can't help but smile at the bite in her tone. "Ruby?"

"What, asshole? I'm busy."

"I meant what I said earlier. You're it for me, little one."

"Whatever."

"I'll wait as long as I need to," I say quietly, resting my head against her door.

I should just storm in and take what's mine. The temptation is strong but I know in the long run it'll just make her hate me more.

"Well, if you change your mind, I'll be right next door."

I get no response this time, so I leave her to it and kick my own bedroom door closed behind me.

It's only ten minutes later that I hear her door open and her storm down the stairs. The slamming of the front door shakes the house before she disappears.

I fall back on my bed with a sigh.

What I said was true, I'll wait for her to calm down and realize that I'm serious although I don't really want to.

34

RUBY

The memory of how it felt having his body pressed up against mine in that office and the knowledge that he was only on the other side of the wall quickly became too much and not long after telling myself to just stay put and do my homework, I end up pulling my sneakers on and storming out of the house in favor of hanging out with Poppy and Harley at Aces.

I knew they were meeting the team there but I'd refused to go in case the guys dragged Ashton along. I know he's good, Stephen has bragged about Ashton being captain of his team back in Seattle, so I can only assume that Jake's going to want him to be part of next year's team, and that means he'll be dragged into the fold.

They might have all stood by me earlier but that's only because he's the new boy. I'm sure that in a blink of an eye, he'll be one of them.

I spend the evening with the girls but while they are all busy chatting away and reliving the weekend, I'm lost in my own head, although I'm not so lost not to notice that I wasn't the only one with my head in the clouds because Harley wasn't really present either. But no matter how many times I ask her what was up, she refuses to tell me. I can only assume it's that guy. And although I understand that she might not want to talk about it, I wish she'd give me something so I'd know how to help.

The sun has long set by the time I pull back up at the house, unfortunately, the second I walk into the kitchen I realize that I should have stayed out longer because I walk straight into what looks like a happy family dinner.

"Ruby, are you hungry? Come join us."

Tingles race down my spine and I rip my eyes from Mom and find exactly what I'm expecting. Ash with his gaze locked on me.

My breath catches at the heat in his dark depths as he runs them down the length of my body, lingering on my bare legs for several seconds too long seeing as he's sitting with our parents.

"Um... no, I'm good, thanks. I'm just gonna..." I take a huge step back before spinning on my heels and running from the room and up the stairs.

"Ruby," Mom calls as I make my escape, but I don't stop to find out what she wants.

Pushing through to my bedroom door, I throw my purse onto my bed and smile when I catch sight of the flowers sitting on the side.

"Ruby?" Mom calls, inviting herself inside.

"What is it, Mom? I have tons of homework."

"I just want to... wow, these are gorgeous. Who are they from?"

"Uh... you?" I ask like she's lost her mind.

"I didn't get you these, Ruby," she says, plucking the card from its clip and turning it over. "Wow, someone sure thinks highly of you."

"It... they're really not from you?"

"No, Ruby. They're really not from me."

"Stephen?"

"Baby, Stephen doesn't buy me flowers, I doubt he'd buy them for you."

"Huh. Do you think..."

"That they're from Ash?" she finishes for me when I trail off. "I think there's a good chance, sweetie."

I drop down onto the edge of my bed and she comes to sit beside me, reaching out to take my hand.

"I know I was mad, and I said some things that I probably shouldn't have in Seattle. I was shocked, stunned actually. I just didn't see it coming. I didn't even consider you'd look at Ash like that, or he you, for that matter. You're my baby girl, and it's easy to forget that you're growing up and turning into a young woman.

"I'm not going to sit here and tell you that I'm okay with what has developed between you two because, quite frankly, I'm not. Ashton isn't exactly the kind of boy I always hoped you'd end up with. He's hot-headed, angry, he's got a bad reputation, and some of the things he's done, including being arrested for possible possession of drugs. On paper, he's not exactly the kind of boy any mom wants for their daughter.

"But..." she says before I get a chance to try to defend Ash. Although, really, everything she just said is true so I'm not entirely sure what I could say. "I've seen how he looks at you. I've heard the way his voice softens when he talks about you—"

"When has he talked about me?" I interrupt, feeling like I must have missed out on something here.

"It doesn't matter." She shakes her head and gives me a smile. "He knows he messed up sending you away like he did—"

"That wasn't all he did."

"I'm sure it's not, sweetie. I can't believe I'm saying this, but maybe you should just give him a chance. Hear him out and then decide where you want to go with your relationship once you have all the information. After all, he's not going anywhere anytime soon, so you're going to have to come to some kind of truce at some point. I refuse to live in a house where people are fighting."

"I don't know, Mom."

"You don't have to decide what to do right now." She twists so she's facing me and looks into my eyes. "You're a smart girl, Ruby. If I had any doubts that you'd act before thinking of the consequences, then we wouldn't even be having this conversation, but I trust you to do what's going to make you happy. And if that's Ash, then so be it. The heart wants what it wants, and what our parents or others think doesn't really come into it."

"Talking from experience?" I ask, intrigued by her story with Stephen and Dad.

"Yeah, your grandmother hated Stephen when we started dating. Thought he was going to corrupt me."

I snort a laugh because we both know that Grandma was right.

"We've got to make our own choices and trust our own instincts. I was wise enough to choose Stephen when we were a lot younger than you are now, so I have to trust that if I knew back then, then so do you."

She gives me and smiles that I quickly return. "Thanks, Mom. I really appreciate your understanding."

"I just want you to be happy, sweetie. I hate seeing you hurting like this."

She pulls me into her arms and holds me tight.

"Having said all this though, your father is probably going to shit a brick when he finds out." I can't help but burst out laughing.

"I'll talk to him when he's back in town."

"Rather you than me, Ruby," Mom jokes. "Are you sure you don't want any dinner?"

"No thank you, I ate at Aces with the squad and Poppy."

"Okay." She squeezes my knee before standing up and walking to the door. "Ruby," she says once she has the door open.

"Yeah."

"Life's short. Leanora has just taught us that. Don't waste it."

"I'll do my best. Love you, Mom."

"Love you too, sweetie. I'll leave you to your homework."

"Thank you." She closes the door and I look down at my chemistry assignment that's still spread out across my bed where I left it before I walked out earlier.

An idea pops into my head and before I have a chance to convince myself it's a disaster waiting to happen, I gather everything up and tuck it under my arm. Maybe having some help won't be so bad. We might even get it done quicker.

There's a slight tremor to my hand as I lift it to knock, but I don't let it stop me.

"Yeah," he barks, sending the butterflies in my stomach into hysterics.

I blow out a slow breath before reaching for the handle and pushing the door open.

I'm pretty sure the last person he was expecting it to be is me because he doesn't even look up from his notebook.

"What is it? I'm busy."

I stare at him hunched over. He's wearing a white t-shirt, the fabric stretched over his wide, muscular shoulders and a pair of black sweatpants. His feet are bare and his hair is still wet from a shower.

"I... um..." I stutter, now I'm here I have no idea what to say.

"Shit," he breathes, so quietly I'm sure I'm not meant to hear it. "Hey." He looks up at me and although his eyes are softer than I've seen many times before there is still an edge to them and despite the fact his lips curl into a smile, I can see the tension within it.

I get it. I walked out on him earlier when he was trying to tell me something. But as he stood there trying to defend himself all I could see was him grinding up against Nat in that basement and then him with Krissy. If he wants to convince me that what he was saying was true, then he's going to need to rid those images from my head and replace them with something else.

"Hey." I smile at him and I hate that I must appear nervous as I lean back against his doorframe, afraid to step inside and be alone in a room with him. I remember Seattle and the time we spent together in his apartment all too well, the memories already has heat surging through my veins. "Did you... um..."

He rests back on his headboard as I stumble over my words, his eyes running the length of my body and setting my skin on fire. I might be wearing a hoodie and a pair of yoga pants now but I may as well be naked from the way he's looking at me.

"Did you send the flowers?"

His lips twitch and his eyes fly up to meet mine. I swear to God a bit of color hits his cheeks at my question and it makes the pull I feel toward him even stronger. This vicious bad boy is blushing.

"Yeah, little one. I did. Wanted you to have something nice to come home to. You deserved it."

"Ash, that's..." I shake my head, my words escaping me. "Thank you."

"You're welcome. Are you just going to stand there, or did you want to come in?"

"Err..." I suck my bottom lip into my mouth as I consider my options.

"I don't bite. Well, not unless you want me to." He winks and I groan.

"Ash, don't, or I'll..." I gesture over my shoulder to leave, although I already know that I'm probably not capable of walking away right now.

"I'm sorry. What have you got there?" he asks, nodding at the books I have under my arm.

"Chemistry," I say, holding up the books to prove that's what it is and feeling stupid for it. "Thought that maybe we could..."

"I haven't started it yet. Come sit and I'll find my books."

Sucking in a deep breath, I nod and slowly close the door behind me.

I look around the room, wondering where I should sit. My eyes land on his empty desk and chair and I'm just about to head over to keep as much space between us as possible when a box on the other side of his bed catches my eye. I look up at what he was reading when I came in and find it's not homework at all.

"What's all this?" I ask, unable to keep my nose out of his business.

"Mom's journals. I found them in her room when Willow and I sorted it." He studies me as he says her name, I guess waiting for some kind of reaction that he spent time alone with a girl. But I already know she helped him, she told me herself. We've been in touch since I left, we've messaged most days. Having seen Ash at his lowest, she understands what I—we—are going through in a way that Harley and Poppy don't. Plus, she knows him, so that helps. Well, until it doesn't, and she starts telling me just how sweet and thoughtful he really is, even though he won't ever admit it.

"Oh wow. You've been reading them?" It's a stupid question seeing as he was sitting here doing just that only minutes ago but the question falls from my lips anyway.

"Yeah, I'm learning all sorts of things about her that I didn't know."

"Oh yeah, like what?"

"Like this." My movement toward his desk is halted when he holds a piece of paper out for me, forcing me to walk toward his bed so I can take it and see what it is.

"What... oh," I breathe, seeing a bank statement with quite an impressive figure at the bottom of it.

"Turns out I was wrong about a lot of things."

"Oh?"

"Dad was sending money, a lot of it. Mom was just putting it away. We were going to move here after I graduated, apparently. Well, to Maddison. She wanted me to be close to my dad, get a fresh start."

"Wow," I breathe, not really sure what to say. "W-would you have let her uproot your life like that?" I ask, thinking of the life he had in Seattle, it might not have been ideal, but it was his life, nonetheless.

"I don't know. I've wondered that a lot the past few days, but I don't think I have the answer. Not that it really matters now. I'm here."

"I guess. What are you going to do with this?" I ask, handing the paper back to him.

"Use it for college, I guess. It's what she wanted for me, so I may as well see it through."

"You want to go to college?" I sit down on the edge of his bed, now too invested in this conversation to worry about our proximity.

"Yeah, I guess. It was never really an option before, so I just dismissed it. But now... Dad's right. This is a second chance. Going back and having to redo the year sucks but in the long run, it's probably for the best. I know I didn't have a future in Seattle. If I stuck with the boys, then I'd have ended up dragged farther into their world, or I'd have ended up dead."

My fingers tighten in his sheets as he says those final words, a move he doesn't miss.

His eyes lock on my hand for a second before it trails up my arm until he finds my eyes. I swallow nervously, waiting to see what he's going to say next.

"So, I guess it's just all about the future now."

I nod. "And what do you want for it?"

"You."

I gasp at his honesty, our eyes holding as my heart rate increases.

He reaches forward and places his hand on mine. "I meant what I said earlier, Ruby. I'll wait as long as it takes for you to realize that I'm serious."

I nod, unable to speak past the lump in my throat.

"So... chemistry," he says with a laugh, immediately breaking the suffocating tension that's filled the room with his confession. He drags his textbook over and flips it open to the page we were working on earlier and grabs a notebook.

"I was thinking..." I stare at him and it's as if I'm seeing him for the first time with his head shoved in a book like a real student, not a boy who's too consumed by his own anger to think about anything but the shitty hand life has dealt him. He doesn't notice my attention and continues to talk about our assignment like he actually cares.

I realize that he probably does and all the bad boy anger and hatred at the world was just his way of coping with the shit that had been thrown at him.

Smiling at him, I crawl up the bed toward him and sit beside him, reaching for his free hand in the process.

He doesn't say anything about my contact, his words barely falter but I hear the waver in his voice the second he feels my warmth.

Together we complete the assignment before moving on to others we were both given in our other classes.

"Let's see your schedule then. I can warn you about the teachers."

He digs it out and passes it over, but before I look at any of his teacher names, I look to see how many classes we actually share. My stomach clenches when I realize that it's not just chemistry. Today, it seems, was a one-off because we're going to be spending a lot of time together for the rest of the week. Maybe this truce really was the best thing to do.

"What?" he asks when I don't say anything for a few seconds.

"N-nothing. We have a lot of classes together," I admit.

"Oh yeah?" he asks, leaning over and tucking a lock of hair behind my ear. "Looks like I might not graduate after all then."

"W-why not?" I spin my head to him and find him staring back at me, his eyes full of heat and his bottom lip pulled into his mouth.

"Because I'll spend more time studying you than what I should be."

I can't help but laugh at him despite the deadly serious expression on his face. "Cheesy much?"

"Don't care. It's true. You're so beautiful, little one."

My cheeks flame red hot at his compliment.

"Ash," I warn, knowing that if he pushes too hard that I'll end up throwing caution to the wind and diving in with both feet again.

"You know what I want, Ruby. I'm not going to hide it from you."

"I-I know but..." I swallow down my nerves and drag my eyes from his hypnotizing ones.

"Don't hide from me, little one." His hot fingers find the edge of my jaw and he tips my face back so I have no choice but to look at him. "Tell me what you're thinking."

"I think... I'm not ready for this." I gesture between the two of us.

"I'm not asking you to marry me." He chuckles and the sound makes all my muscles south of my stomach clench with desire.

"I-I know but... there's so much I don't know about you, and you've just moved here and—"

He reaches out and as if I weigh no more than a feather, he lifts me from my place beside him and plonks me on his lap so I'm sitting astride his thighs.

His hands slip under my hoodie, but they stop at my waist, holding me in place.

"Ruby," he sighs, sitting forward until we're chest to chest. "You've seen me at my very lowest, I'd be tempted to say that you know me better than anyone. You witnessed that, you embraced that, and you helped me put the pieces back together. You're still fucking here. That tells me everything I need to know."

"That—"

"Hey," he says softly. "Look at me."

I drag my eyes back, afraid that if he looks too hard, he might find everything I'm battling to keep down.

"I'm not asking you for anything other than for you to give me a chance." His thumb caresses my stomach and despite the fabric of my pants in between us, my skin pricks with goose bumps. "Trust me when I tell you that I want you, and only you, Ruby."

"Ash," I sigh, feeling myself getting swept away with his words and the honesty in his eyes.

"We can start again. Start fresh. It seems to be my thing right now. I'll take you out, treat you properly. You don't even have to give it up again... yet." He winks at me, although his joke is kinda ruined by the fact I can feel him hard against my thigh. "I don't care how long you make me wait. I just want this. I just want you."

His lips graze my jaw and my entire body shudders with pleasure.

"Oh God," I whimper as he kisses toward my ear.

The heat of his hands, the gentle brush of his lips. They send me spiraling into a place I remember all too well.

"I missed you, little one. I hated it when you left. I've never been so alone. I hated that apartment without you. All I could think about was you." His lips trail down my neck as he keeps talking, telling me all the things that I've been desperate to hear but never thought I would.

"You saved me, Ruby. And if you'll let me, I'll spend forever trying to pay you back for what you did that week."

"Ash, I didn't do it to receive—"

My words are cut off when he licks up the column of my neck.

"I know, but I want you to have everything you deserve. I sure as shit know that I'm not it, but I'm a selfish fuck who's not going to let you go, Ruby."

"You deserve everything." My hands brush his arms until I thread my fingers into his hair and tug, successfully pulling his face from the crook of my neck. "Everything, Ash," I repeat to ensure he heard me.

His eyes shutter as he takes in my words and his head shakes slightly, but I tighten my grip on his hair and stop him from refusing to accept my words.

"Fresh start, yeah?" I ask, bumping the tip of my nose against his.

This time, he nods. "Okay, yeah. Fresh start."

Closing the space between us, I press my lips to his. We don't move for the longest time, just holding on to each other, but after a while, my need for more gets too much and my lips part, my tongue seeking entry into his mouth.

"Ruby," he groans, accepting my kiss and tangling his tongue with mine. "Fuck, I missed you."

In seconds, my back is pressed against his bed, and he's looming over me, staring down into my eyes.

"I'm sorry. I'm sorry for everything, for all the bullshit, for all the pain." The honesty in his voice, on his face, rips me wide open.

Reaching up, I cup his cheek with my palm, loving the roughness from his scruff against my skin. "It's okay."

"Fuck, I don't deserve you." He dives for my lips again, stretching his body out against mine and pinning us together so tight I have no choice but to feel his length pressing against my stomach. Heat pools in my core but I tell myself that no matter how good this is right now, we really are starting fresh, and that includes going all the way.

As desperate as I am to slide my hands under his shirt, to feel his burning skin, his hard muscles against my palms, I refrain. We've got all the time in the world for that, but we only get this chance to start over once and I want to do it right, take it slow, enjoy getting to know each other properly.

We kiss until we're both breathless and when he pulls back, he only goes as far as resting his forehead against mine.

"Ash?" I ask, a thought slamming into me. "Those photos you said you had on your cell—"

"You want to see the photos I have of you?" he asks, amusement crinkling at the corners of his eyes.

"Uh..." I'm not sure how I feel about potentially looking at images of me from that night in whatever position I might have been in.

He rolls away from me for a beat to grab his cell from the nightstand. He opens his photo app and hands it over to me.

"Go on," he encourages.

I scroll through his camera roll and in only a second I gasp in shock.

"Oh my God, you didn't." I keep scrolling, seeing image after image of myself. Only, they're not what I was expecting at all. "Ashton, this is creepy."

"Is it? I just thought you looked too beautiful not to capture it."

I shake my head as I look at all the images of me sleeping in his bed in Seattle. There's nothing dirty or seedy about the images. There's not even any nudity, just my face illuminated by a stream of sunlight from the partly closed curtains.

I keep scrolling, knowing that Halloween was a long time ago now, but I don't find anything. Just normal teenage boy drunken party pictures and a million memes.

"It was bullshit, Ruby. I don't have anything from that night other than my memories."

"Oh God, that might be almost as bad." My face flames. "I can't believe I let you do that to me that night."

"That? You mean that you let me eat you until you were screaming my name?" He brushes his nose against mine, taking his cell from my hand and discarding it on the bed somewhere. "You don't need to be embarrassed with me, little one. I've been all up in there since."

"Ashton." I slap his chest lightly.

"And..." He drops his lips to my ear. "I can promise you that I will be again too."

My thighs rub together at the thought.

"What happened after... *that* happened. I don't remember ever getting off the piano, let alone getting home."

"What do you think happened?" he asks, his eyes sparkling with amusement.

I shrug. "If I knew, I wouldn't be asking," I say with a raised brow.

"Okay, so after you came all over my face and ruined me for every other woman on the planet, I covered you up, lifted you into my arms and carried you downstairs and out to Dad's car that I'd... borrowed... and brought you home. I tucked you into bed, kissed you, and walked away knowing that my life was never going to be the same again."

His honesty makes my heart hurt.

"Why didn't you stay, the next morning we could have—"

"I knew how I felt, but there was no way I could have accepted it back then. My life was... a disaster. And I lived in Seattle, nothing would have worked, and I would have refused to have you in Seattle and around the people I hung out with for any length of time."

"What do they do, the Kingston boys?" I ask, the question has been eating at me since Willow dodged the question the night of the funeral.

"Anything illegal that happens in Seattle, you can guarantee they had a hand in it somewhere. Those you met are just the kids. Their fathers. They run that city, and the boys just do their dirty work."

"So drugs?"

"Yeah, and everything else you're probably thinking of."

"I can see why your mom wanted you to get out."

"Trust me, I understand too."

"So they just let you walk away?"

"I never got in deep enough to be a threat to them, and I've never given them a reason to worry about my loyalty. As long as I move on, keep my head down, they'll never bother me again."

"Were you actually friends with them?" I ask, thinking of his obvious distaste for Axel.

He laughs. "Yeah, there are some good guys in there."

"And girls?" I ask, broaching the subject.

"Just one. And don't think I don't know that you've been talking to her."

"Willow?"

"Yeah. I know all about your budding friendship."

"I like her," I admit. "And she cares about you."

"She's a good girl. We've had each other's backs for a few years now."

"I'm glad you had her, and the others."

"Mm-hmm... and I'm glad I've got you."

He tugs me so I'm right under his body. His hand skims up my thigh and once again disappears under my hoodie and stops at my waist.

"Thank you," he whispers against my lips.

"You already said that," I point out.

"Yeah, well... I mean it."

35

ASHTON

When I wake the next morning, I think it was a dream and the reality is that I'm in my bed alone, maybe with just my chemistry textbook for company, but then a light snore comes from beside me and my eyes fly open.

She really did spend the night in here with me.

I stare at her for a few long seconds. Her dark hair is in a mess around her face, her eyes are closed with her long lashes almost resting against her cheekbones, her full, red lips are parted slightly and she's laying with her hand propped under her cheek.

Reaching for my cell, I open the camera and take a few pictures of her. Just like that morning in my bedroom back in Seattle, I can't help myself. She's too beautiful, too perfect I feel like I need to capture it in case this is all one big joke, that this isn't my life and that she's not real.

Knowing that I woke up early for a reason, I reluctantly climb from the bed without waking her and pull on my sweats that I lost at some point last night. I know that under my covers she's dressed similar to me in just her underwear and it makes my morning wood ache for her.

But I made her a promise to start over and to take things slow—as slow as her sleeping in just her underwear in my bed, of course—and I intend on seeing it through.

She's worth it. Worth it and more.

I understand that I need to prove myself to her, and I'm more than willing to do so.

I slip from the room as quietly as I can and make my way downstairs. I grab an energy drink from the refrigerator before making my way down to Dad's home gym.

The last thing I want to do while she's almost naked in my bed is a workout, but I have a feeling that Jake isn't going to go easy on my ass in the coming weeks as he tries to prove I'm not Rosewood Bears material, but I'm determined to prove him wrong.

I sync my cell to the wireless speaker and get to work. I let things slip after the season finished on a devastating loss for my old team, so I've got some work to do to get ready for tryouts and hopefully a new season.

I push until my skin is dripping in sweat and my muscles burn. It feels good, but still nowhere near as satisfying as being with my girl right now.

I slow the treadmill, kill the music, and head upstairs, knowing that I've still got a whole day and a Jake conditioning session after school to get through.

The house is still in silence as I climb the stairs and when I push through into my bedroom, I find Ruby still fast asleep in my bed, only she's rolled over and the covers are nowhere near covering her hot little body. Her ass is out, her high-cut panties showing off the fullness before I run my eyes up to her slim waist, up to her peacefully sleeping face.

Reaching down, I palm my quickly swelling cock, but with a shake of my head, I walk toward my bathroom to wash the morning's sweat off me.

I drop my sweats and boxers and step into the shower, allowing it to blast me with ice-cold water before it begins to warm up.

Tipping my face toward the torrent of water, I try to push thoughts of her from my mind and focus on other mundane things like classes and homework.

It would be so easy to reach down and give myself the release I crave, but I don't want it to come from my hand. The next time I come, I want it to be with her... for her.

A tingle of awareness runs down my spine and my cock jerks. I don't need to look over my shoulder to know that she's just walked in and that she's watching me.

"You planning on joining me, little one?"

Her gasp of shock that I know she's there makes me laugh.

"I always know when you're close to me, Ruby. I feel it."

Finally, I twist around and look over my shoulder. My eyes almost bug out of my head at the sight of her leaning back against the basin in just her small crop top and panties.

Her eyes hold mine for a second before they drop down my body. There's not much she can't see right now, seeing as I'm standing behind just a glass door.

She bites down on her bottom lip as she lifts one hand to brush her hair away from her face.

The air in the room crackles with anticipation as I wait to see what she's going to do.

"Little one?"

After a beat, she spins on her heels, opens the cupboard above the sink, and pulls out my toothbrush and toothpaste.

She bends slightly, sticking her ass out toward me as she loads the brush up and begins brushing her teeth.

"Uh… I think that's mine, little one."

She shrugs before bending farther forward and spitting the foam out.

My fists clench with my need to drag her in here with me and have my way with her.

My cock aches as it bobs hard in front of me.

I know if I asked nice enough, she'd relieve me, but I really want to do as she asked and hold off.

I slam my hand on the shower faucet, turning the water off, and step out of the shower. I stand right behind her, her ass against my stomach and my cock brushing against her bare thigh.

I wrap my wet arm around her waist and force her to stand, bringing my lips to her ear. Her eyes find mine in the mirror and I hold them captive.

"You're playing a very dangerous game, seeing as you were the one to set the rules," I growl.

"Maybe I like breaking the rules."

I wrap my hand around hers as she lifts it to put my brush back.

I take it and hold it out for her to put some toothpaste on it before lifting it to my mouth, refusing to let her go despite the fact she tries to wriggle out of my hold.

"Ash, you're wet."

"I know. Are you?"

I can't help myself and slide my hand down her stomach. I figure if she's really set on not doing anything, then she'll stop me.

But all she does is gasp, her hand falling back against my chest as my fingers slip under the lace at her waist.

Her eyes close as my fingers part her and search out her clit.

"Eyes on me," I mumble around the toothbrush still in my mouth.

Her dark green orbs immediately find mine once more.

Dropping my fingers lower, I find her soaked and more than ready for me.

Throwing the toothbrush into the sink, I lift my now free hand to her throat, feeling her pulse thundering under my fingers.

"Fuck, little one. Woken up a little horny?"

She nods, her cheeks flushing. "But you weren't there," she whispers, making me groan.

"No, I was in here. Naked."

She whimpers as I spread some of her wetness around her clit and pinch it between my fingers.

"Shit," she gasps.

"You want to come, my little tease?"

She nods slowly, her eyes growing heavy with lust.

"You're so fucking addictive." I bite down on her ear and her hips roll.

"Ash," she moans, her body locking up as she gets closer to her release.

"You going to let me watch you come, little one? You gonna be a good girl and keep your eyes open for me?"

"Y-yes."

I drop my fingers to her entrance once more and slide two deep inside, my thumb continuing to tease her clit.

"Who do you belong to, Ruby?"

"You."

"Say it," I demand, nipping her earlobe again.

"You, Ash. I belong to youuuu..." she cries as her orgasm slams into her.

Her eyes flicker with their need to close, but she holds our connection as her body clamps down around my fingers.

"Fuck, you're sexy."

I drag my fingers from her pussy once her release has faded and trail them up her stomach and over her breasts.

"Open," I breathe, and she does without missing a beat.

I slide my fingers past her lips.

"Suck."

And she does, her tongue swirling around my digits, making my cock weep to feel the same thing.

I release her throat, pull my fingers from her mouth, and spin her around.

"Fuck, you're perfect."

I slam my lips down on hers before she has a chance to respond.

I groan when I taste her as her tongue caresses mine.

"So fucking sweet."

Lifting her into my arms, I wrap her legs around my waist and carry her out of my bathroom before ripping my lips from hers and depositing her on my bed.

I take a step back and smile as she reaches for me, her chest heaving, and her skin flushed from her release.

"You're really testing my patience, little one," I warn, taking another step back from her.

"Consider it your punishment for pushing me away."

She tilts her head to the side, I'm assuming trying to look cute but she follows it up with a leisurely perusal of my naked body so it loses its effect, especially as her eyes lock on my very ready cock.

She runs her tongue along her bottom lip as she stares, and I almost lose my damn mind.

"Ruby," I warn. I'm about three seconds to telling her to fuck her rules and taking everything I need.

She pushes to stand, her eyes lifting to mine.

"Ash," she breathes, and I almost reach for her when her lips twitch into a smile and I realize that she's playing me. "We really should get ready for school. Wouldn't want you to be late on your second day."

Before I have a chance to do anything, she bolts for the door.

"I'll be ready in thirty. Maybe you can give me a ride?" She jokes, wiggling her brows before barking out a laugh and disappearing from my room.

Fuck. That girl's gonna be the death of me.

I scrub my hand down my face, realizing my mistake almost instantly. I can smell her.

"Fuck," I bark, loud enough that I'm sure she'll hear me.

I dress and gather everything I'm going to need for the day and invite myself into Ruby's room. She can fuck right off if she thinks I'm going to knock after already being knuckles deep inside her this morning.

I drop down on her bed, taking in her room and the flowers that I dropped off in here on Sunday before she got home.

She only makes me wait a couple of minutes, and when she emerges from her bathroom—already fully dressed and ready to go—she doesn't even flinch that I'm here.

"How'd I know you'd be waiting in here?" she says with a laugh.

"Am I that predictable? I'd better up my game."

"No," she says harshly, stepping between my thighs. My hands brush up her legs before groping her ass and squeezing just enough to pinch. "We're done with games. Either we do this or we don't."

"Oh, little one," I say, pushing to stand and taking her face in my hands. "We're so doing this."

"Okay, but..." She looks away nervously.

"But what, baby." I catch her eyes again as I wait for her to say what's on her mind.

"Can we keep it on the down-low at school for now? Just until it's not so new. People are going to judge and—"

"Whatever you want." I drop a kiss to the tip of her nose.

I don't really give a shit who knows about this between us, I'd more than happily go and shout it from the rooftops if she wanted me to, but I agree because I just want her to be happy, and if she wants time, then I can give her time.

"Ready to go?"

"Yep." Hand in hand, we make our way downstairs. There are signs that our parents have been here. The scent of toast fills the air and there are two dirty plates and mugs in the sink but there is no sign of them. Not that I'm going to complain.

"What do you want to eat? We don't have much time."

"You," I say, wrapping my arms around her from behind and sucking on the skin of her neck.

"Definitely no time for that." She chuckles, breaking from my hold and pulling a cupboard open. "Here." She throws me a cereal bar before pulling out two travel mugs of coffee and kick-starting the machine.

"I can hardly take one of those on my bike."

"I can drive."

"But I've got training after school."

"Okay, well... I'll take your coffee then."

"Deal."

Only a few minutes later, Ruby slips into her car while I throw my leg over my bike and start the engine.

I follow her all the way to school, trying to wipe the smile off my face the entire way.

I take my coffee from her once we've parked, and she takes me to the benches where both the team and the squad seem to hang out.

Her friends look between the two of us suspiciously as we walk toward them, and the second Ruby breaks away from me to join them, I see them bombard her with a million questions while flicking glances my way.

"Morning," I say to Jake, who's got his arms around a pretty blonde.

"Morning. Brit, this is Ashton," he says to his girl.

"Hey, nice to meet you," she says sweetly, her British accent throwing me off for a second.

"You ready for this afternoon's session?"

"More than ready."

"Good." He turns his attention back to his girl and I look to the rest of the team. Zayn, the guy who was talking to me in the locker room last night, has his tongue down Poppy's throat while Harley continues to question my girl.

As if she can feel my stare, Ruby looks over her shoulder and directly at me. She smiles and I swear it nearly knocks me on my ass.

36

RUBY

I know the second his gaze lands on me. I feel it. My body feels like it's burning up from the inside out.

"Ruby," Harley warns when she notices why my attention has drifted off. "Stop trying to tell me nothing's happened."

I tried to play it off after we walked here side-by-side, but neither she nor Poppy are having any of it. My only saving grace is that Poppy is currently preoccupied with Zayn's tongue.

"Okay fine," I sigh. "But we're keeping it quiet."

"If that's the case, you might want to stop looking at each other like you can barely contain yourselves."

I shrug. I can't help it.

"Fucking hell," Harley moans, throwing her hands up in frustration. "I need to find new friends. I can't deal with you and Poppy both being loved up. I hate being the third-wheel." Her eyes roam over the members of the squad who are already here, as if she's choosing her victim.

"Seniors are out, they're all bitches and leaving soon. Ooooh... Stella."

"I think she might be leaving too," I say before snapping my lips shut. Was that supposed to be a secret?

"What? For real? She's amazing. We need her next year, damn it."

"I don't know for sure. I don't think she does either."

"Well, we need to keep her."

"Agreed. Have you put much thought into next year's squad?" Harley asks me, successfully distracting me from Ashton's heated gaze and onto cheer.

I shake my head at her, not wanting to get ahead of myself.

"Let's head inside, I need to go to my locker."

The morning passes, classes pass in a blur of boredom and lust-filled stares across the classrooms where Ash and I weren't able to sit together. The ones we were, however, he didn't exactly take the whole keeping it quiet thing seriously as his hand got higher and higher up on my thigh with every minute that passed.

I have no idea if anyone else noticed, but I felt like everyone knew as I damn near melted into a puddle of need on the chair.

He might have got me off this morning, but as good as it was, it wasn't enough. After the time we spent together in Seattle, that short moment between us really didn't scratch the itch I had. I knew from the moment I found him in the shower that I may have made a mistake the night before telling him that I wanted to take things slow because all I wanted to do was strip down, join him and let him do the kinds of wicked things he did to me in the shower in his apartment.

But I stood strong, knowing that I'd made the right decision.

It's just a shame I question it with every second that passes.

He's not in my class before lunch and as I sit there with my stomach rumbling, more than ready to go and discover what we're going to find in the cafeteria today, I wonder if I'm actually hungrier for food or just for him.

Thoughts of Miss Kelly's office hit me. There's no way she'll be in there, maybe we just venture down there and have a little time to ourselves...

A hand slapping my shoulder startles me. "You're doing it again," Harley snaps.

"Sorry, sorry." It's not the first time this hour that she's laughed at me for zoning out on her in favor of thoughts of Ash.

"It's been one night and you're like a lovesick puppy." She laughs.

"Do I complain when you go on about Nathan?" I ask, lifting my brows.

"Well, no, but I'm sure I've not done that." She wiggles her finger around in front of my face in accusation.

I lean into her to ensure no one else in class hears what I'm about to say. "That's because he's not made you come yet."

"Ruby!" she squeals, earning her a warning scowl from our teacher.

"Facts, Harley. Facts."

"Whatever."

"So more on that subject. You planning on giving it up to him or you just hanging out some more?"

"I'm not sure. We haven't talked about it. Plus, we haven't exactly ever met anywhere to allow much more than a kiss."

"Maybe you should plan something. Get a little one-on-one time, see where it goes."

"Yeah, maybe." Her eyes glaze over as she loses herself in her thoughts, much like I'm sure I was a few minutes ago, but I don't point that out.

Finally, the bell rings, allowing us to pack up and go in search of food.

The hallways are packed as we move with the crowd toward the cafeteria.

"Look out, lover boy is already here," Harley says, her height giving her the advantage of being able to see through the mass of bodies.

Turning, we make our way over to our usual tables as a smile starts to twitch at my lips at the thought of seeing him. I feel ridiculous, it was barely over an hour ago I saw him, but I miss him.

No wonder Harley wants new friends. I'm annoying myself.

Just as the crowd parts so we can make our way over, someone else beats me to Ash.

My teeth grind and my fists curl as I watch Krissy once again slide up to him.

Didn't she get the fucking message yesterday that he wasn't interested?

Something inside me snaps the second she lays her perfectly manicured hand on his chest.

A growl rips from my throat as Harley's hand wraps around my forearm, but I rip it away from her and storm toward them.

He doesn't have a chance to push her off, but his arms are rising to do so as I grip her upper arm as hard as I can, making sure my nails sink into her bare skin and I drag her away from him.

I swear to God the entire cafeteria sucks in a breath as they wait to see what's going to happen next.

"He's not fucking interested," I seethe so quietly that only she'll hear it before my arm flies out and my palm connects with her cheek with a loud slap. There's a collective gasp that rolls through the room as Krissy's hand comes up to cover the glowing red handprint on her cheek.

I step toward her as her tear-filled eyes meet mine. My chest heaves as I wait for what she's going to say, but she doesn't get a chance because I'm spun around and hauled into Ashton's arms.

"I'm not even sorry," he growls before slamming his lips down on mine.

His fingers thread into my hair and his arm wraps around my back to pin us together.

Silence still surrounds us as his tongue pushes past my lips to claim mine.

I have no idea how much time passes before he pulls back, his own breathing labored from our kiss. Conversations have started up again around us as he stares down at me, everyone clearly getting bored with the show.

"Fuck, I love you."

His hand grips the back of my neck and his lips capture mine once more, but I'm so stunned by his words that I don't respond.

"We need to get the fuck out of here right now."

"Uh..." Before I know what's happening, I find myself flipped over his shoulder as a round of cheers erupts from behind us. I don't look up to see them, I'm too lost in Ashton.

I stare at his ass as he marches us out of the cafeteria, and he doesn't set me down until we're in the parking lot.

"Put this on," he says, thrusting a helmet at me the second my feet are on the ground.

"W-what?" I ask, taking it from him when he gives me little choice because he releases it and climbs onto his bike.

"Put the fucking helmet on, Ruby," he growls, the roughness of it hitting exactly where it's meant to, and I squeeze my thighs together as I do as I'm told.

The engine comes to life and I climb on the back, assuming that's what I'm meant to do, and no sooner have I wrapped my arms around his waist do we fly out of the parking lot.

"Oh my God," I squeal. I've never been on the back of a bike before but I think... I think I kind of love it. Or that could just be the man I'm wrapped around like a koala bear.

The journey home is shorter than I think it's ever been in my life and before I know it, I'm on my feet beside the bike and Ashton's lips are back on mine.

"I need you, little one. I fucking need you right now," he growls into my mouth, his grip on my chin almost too tight, but I freaking love the possessiveness of it.

"Y-you've got me."

He lifts me into his arms so my legs wrap around his waist and after unlocking the door, he jogs up the stairs and crashes into his room.

We fall onto his bed in a mess of limbs and dirty kisses.

"Ashton," I moan as he rips my shirt over my head and throws it behind him somewhere.

"Ruby, fuck."

Holding himself up with one arm, his lips trail down my neck, his teeth graze my collarbone before he drags down the fabric covering my breast, and he sucks my nipple into his mouth.

"Ashton," I cry, my back arching off the bed.

"More," he groans between soft kisses and sharp nips to my sensitive skin. "I need more."

He kisses down my stomach as his fingers slip around my back to release my bra. The fabric joins my shirt on the floor before he drags my skinny jeans and panties down my legs and dropping my sneakers to the floor with a thud as he pulls each off.

He stands at the edge of the bed, still fully dressed, staring down at me.

"So fucking beautiful, Ruby." My skin burns and my core aches as his dark eyes take in every inch of me.

He drops to his knees before me and hooks both of my legs over his shoulders before kissing down my thigh toward where I need him most.

"Are you wet for me, little one?"

"Yes," I whisper without any hesitation.

"You want my mouth?"

"Yes, Ash."

He pulls his head back before he gets to my core and instead of using his tongue, he trails his finger over my sensitive skin.

"Perfect. Fucking perfect." He dips his finger inside me, just enough to tease me before he leans forward and sucks my clit hard.

"Fuck," I cry, my hips lifting from the bed, the sensation of the suction along with the tip of his tongue teasing my clit almost too much to take.

My hands thread through his hair, but I'm unsure if I want to pull him closer or push him away as his assault gets even more intense. I thought this morning was good, but that is going to pale in comparison to what's building in my core right now.

Every muscle in my body pulls tight and the only thing I can focus on is the ball of desire that's about to explode within me.

"Ash," I cry. "Ash, I'm gon—" My release slams into me, stealing both my words and my breath simultaneously.

The pleasure comes in wave after wave and he doesn't stop licking or stroking me until it's subsided to nothing more than aftershocks.

The second he pulls back, he stands, wiping his mouth with the back of his hand, and pulls his hoodie over his head. His chest and abs are immediately revealed, and my eyes eat up the inches of perfection as he works his pants off and kicks both them and his boxers off.

Just like this morning, he's deliciously hard, the tip glistening with his need for me, and my stomach clenches, more heat heading straight between my thighs.

"Shift up a bit," he demands, tilting his head to gesture for me to scoot up the bed.

I rush to do so, and he crawls in between my legs, quickly reaching out to wrap them around his waist.

His length teases my entrance, and I can't help but roll my hips to get more friction.

"Greedy girl," Ashton growls, dropping down so his hands are planted on the bed on either side of my head. "I fucking love it."

He drops his lips to mine, not giving me a chance to respond with the question that's on the tip of my tongue.

His tongue licks deep into my mouth and my lingering taste hits my tastebuds, making me moan.

He kisses me deeper than I swear he has before. It's not just a kiss, it's a claiming. He's branding himself on my soul and ensuring I'm never able to forget.

His hand skims down my body, teasing my nipples, pinching them so that I gasp, stealing his breath, but his kiss never falters.

He circles my clit, awakening another orgasm before his touch leaves me in favor of his cock. He teases me with the tip, coating himself in my juices and gently pushing inside of me but never giving me what I need.

"Ashton, please," I beg against his lips.

"Who do you belong to, Ruby?"

"You, Ashton. I'm yours. Only yours."

"Yesss," he hisses as he sinks inside me.

My walls ripple around him, adjusting to his size.

His kiss pauses but he doesn't move his lips from mine. We just stay there, frozen, breathing each other in, and absorbing the sensations of the moment.

That is until he rolls his hips and sets off an explosion of sensations within me.

"Fuck," he groans as I tighten my legs around him and scratch my nails down his back. "This... this right now. It's fucking everything, little one. Everything."

And then he moves. His hips piston as his tongue sweeps into my mouth once more. His hand slips around the back of my neck so he can tilt my head just so to seal his lips to mine as our skin begins to glisten with sweat.

Every one of his movements sends me higher, making my body pull tight as I get ready to crash.

"You feel so good, baby. I'm gonna come so fucking hard," he grates out, his eyes holding mine captive.

His fingers find my clit once more and the second he pinches it between his fingers, I fall. I fall into blissful pleasure knowing that when I get to the bottom, he's going to be right here, holding on to me.

"Ashton," I scream, my back arching, my nails digging into his shoulders as I ride out my orgasm.

"Fuuuuck," he groans. "Fuck, Ruby." His cock jerks violently inside of me, sending little aftershocks shooting around my body.

He drops his head to the crook of my neck as we both fight to catch our breaths, although he makes no move to pull out of me.

"Fuck, Ruby," he pants after long seconds of nothing but our increased breathing filling our ears. "Do you have any idea how hot that was with Krissy?"

I tense at the mention of her name. "Don't say her name. Especially while you're still inside me."

"Ah, little one. This little jealous streak is so fucking sexy. But trust me, no matter whose name I say, there's only one I'll be calling out when I come."

I slap his shoulder lightly. "This isn't funny. That bitch needs to keep her hands to herself."

"She might from now on, baby. Did you see the print you left?"

I shake my head. I was too angry to really register any of it. It all seems like a blur now.

"I was impressed. But you can't go around slapping every girl who looks at me."

"She didn't just look," I sulk.

"True. I love that you're possessive of what's yours, but I think Hartmann might have something to say about all the girls at school walking around with a Ruby-shaped handprint on their cheeks."

"You're assuming all the girls at school want to—shit," I gasp, realization slamming into me. "School. We should be in class. What time is it?"

"Too late to be worrying about going back to class. Plus, we have other things to be doing." He drops his lips to my neck and sucks my skin into his mouth hard enough to leave a mark.

I've never skipped school in my life, and the knowledge that I'm doing it right now doesn't really help me relax.

"Stop worrying. It's one afternoon."

"I know, but—"

He presses his fingers to my lips. "Relax, baby. Let me distract you."

He unhooks my leg and finally pulls his now fully hard cock from me before falling down beside me.

He hooks my leg around his waist, allowing his cock to tease me once more. His hand cups my cheek, his fingers threading into my hair as his nose brushes mine.

"Did you mean what you said?" I blurt, unable to keep the question in a second longer.

"Mean what, little one?"

"W-what you said in the cafeteria," I whisper, now feeling stupid for bringing this back up. He probably didn't mean to say the words. Hell, he probably doesn't even remember saying them in the heat of the moment.

"What did I... oh." A smile curls at his lips as his thumb tenderly caresses my cheek. He stares so deep into my eyes that I swear I'll never be the same again. "Yeah, Ruby. I meant every word."

I gasp, not really expecting for him to remember, let alone have meant it.

"You're like no one I've ever met before, little one. You're so strong, you don't take any of my shit. You're just... my number one."

I swoon so freaking hard that I can barely breathe. "I love you, little one. You brought me back to life."

My bottom lip trembles as my eyes fill with water. I try to blink them away, but every time I open my eyes, the blurrier he gets.

"I love you too, Ashton," I breathe, forcing the words out through the giant lump in my throat. "I don't know when it happened, but I do, I love you and I never want to go another day without you." A sob rips up my throat and the tears I've been fighting finally spill over when I see his own glistening at my confession.

"Ruby," he whispers, gathering me up in his arms and holding me so tight that I'm sure he's about to crack a rib, but I don't so much as flinch because it feels so good.

His lips press into my hair as he whispers again and again that he loves me, ripping me open in the very best way with every word.

When he finally allows me to pull my face from his chest, I find his own cheeks wet with tears.

"Thank you, Ruby," he says once more before capturing my lips and showing me with his body, as well as his words, just how he feels about me.

The feeling of something vibrating against my thigh forces me to rip my lips from Ashton's. I've lost track of time just like I've lost track of the number of orgasms he's given me since we fell into his bed however long ago. All I do know is that my muscles are quivering and we both really, really need to shower sometime soon.

"What the hell is... oh." I pull Ashton's cell from beneath me and see Dad across the screen. "Oh shit, did the school call him?" I ask in a panic.

"Even if they did, I'll sort it. Don't worry." He swipes the screen but the slight frown on his brow doesn't deepen as if we might be in trouble, instead a smile pulls at his lips.

"W-what is it?"

"Your mom and my dad are going to be out until late." He throws his cell back down on the sheets and rolls on top of me, pressing me into the mattress at my back. "You know what that means?" he asks with a twinkle in his eye.

"That we have to get our own dinner?" I ask, slyly.

"Hmm... that and... I get to make you scream for hours yet."

"Oh my God, Ashton," I squeal when he bites down on my nipple, his fingers dropping to my core. "I'm not sure I've got it in me."

"Baby, you'll know when you've got it in you, trust me."

"Oh my God, you did not just say that."

He smiles at me and winks and I can't help bursting out laughing.

"How about we shower, then order some food. I'm starving. Maybe we could watch a movie or something, you know something a little less—"

"Fun?"

"I was going to say energetic."

"Okay, baby. Shower, food, and a movie. Sounds like the perfect date to me."

"Hmm... it does, doesn't it?"

"You deserve better though."

"We've got the rest of our lives for that, Ash. A night in with you is everything I need right now."

"Fuck, I love you." He sits up, threads his fingers through mine, and pulls me up to him. "Let's go shower before I dirty you all up again."

He lifts me into his arms and carries me into his bathroom. He stands us under the shower and allows us to get blasted with cold water for a few seconds.

"Ashton," I squeal with a laugh.

"It's okay, little one. I promise to make it up to you. I promise to always make it up to you."

EPILOGUE

Ruby

"Oh look, here they are," Harley announces loudly to the entire team and squad when we walk toward them hand in hand the next morning.

We figured after our little show the day before, there was no point in keeping anything between us quiet. Everyone in Rosewood High knew what we went to do the moment he threw me over his shoulder and walked out.

Mom and Stephen came in long after midnight last night and thankfully, neither tried to find us to give us a speech about skipping or for slapping Krissy, so either they don't know yet, or they're saving it for when we get home later tonight. Whichever it is, I don't really care. I stand by what I did yesterday. Krissy has had it coming for a long time. I'm surprised I was the first to do it, to be honest.

"Thanks, Har," I mutter, coming to a stop in front of her. Ash stops at my back and wraps his arms around my waist and rests his chin on the top of my head.

"What? We all know what—or who—went down last night."

"Yeah, yeah, you're just jealous. How are things with Nathan?" It's a low blow, but I can't help myself. I'm too happy and high on the endorphins from the multiple orgasms I had before we even got out of bed this morning.

"Great, thanks." She rolls her eyes, telling me that maybe things aren't all that great in reality.

"Hey, look, Ashton and Ethan can start an 'I'm banging my stepsister club'," Jamie, one of the JV players, shouts. "Ow, what? I was just saying."

"Shut the fuck up, asshole, before I make you," Ethan barks at the rest of the JV members who have gathered to watch the show with his arm slung around Rae's shoulder.

"I'm just hoping it's contagious, I could do with one myself. Ow," he snaps again.

"Leave them alone," Chelsea pipes up. "They're cute. Let them do their thing."

Laughing at them, I twist in Ashton's arms.

"Hey," I say, smiling up at him.

"Hey, little one. You ready to head to English Lit?"

"Sure am. Har, you coming?"

"Yep, I'm with you." We say goodbye to Poppy who's cuddled into Zayn's side and head toward the building.

"Who's Nathan?" Ashton asks, clearly eavesdropping on our previous conversation.

"A guy from Maddison Prep that Harley met at Ethan's party. They've had a few dates," I answer for her.

"Ah, dating a prep boy, eh? I hear they don't put out until at least the tenth date," Ash says with a laugh.

"Shut up, you idiot. He's a good guy, right, Har?" I'm not looking where I'm going and I slam straight into the back of her as we walk through the doorway into our classroom. "Har?"

I step around her and take in her pale face.

"Are you okay?" I ask, looking to see what's captured her attention to find a guy with light brown hair and bright blue eyes staring right back at her like he's wishing she'll go up in flames right in front of him. "W-Who's that?" I ask, looking back to Harley who's on the verge of tears, her entire body trembling in fear.

"Y-you remember Kane, the guy from my house on Sunday?" she whispers so only Ashton and I can hear.

"Yeah." I look back at him, noticing the similarities and not just in the angry stare.

"That's his little brother, Kyle."

"Okay. And why does he look like he wants to kill you?"

"Probably because he does."

Are you ready for one final trip to Rosewood?
Keep reading for Legend!

LEGEND

ROSEWOOD HIGH #7

1

KYLE

"So how does it feel?" Kane asks as I drop down into his passenger seat after throwing the few belongings I had into the trunk.

"It's been about thirty seconds, bro."

"I know." He shrugs. "I just thought you might feel different."

"Relief?" I ask, glancing over at him.

"Fuck, bro," he growls, running his hand down his face and resting his head back on the headrest. "I'm so fucking sorry you had to go through that."

"It's not your fault," I mutter, looking out the window at the building and the barbed wire-topped fences I'm about to finally break free from.

"I should have been there. I could have stopped it." Regret laces his voice, and I know why. He thinks this happened because he got distracted and left me alone at that party. But it can only be my fault. It was my decision. It was my mistake. It's time he lets it go and moves on.

"It's okay, Kane. I don't blame you for this. It's just... it's over. Time to move on."

"Speaking of... I've got a surprise for you."

I raise a brow, waiting for him to spill the beans. I'm sure there are going to be a lot of surprises waiting for me, seeing as I mostly checked out on real life for the past twelve months.

"Go on," I encourage, already getting impatient for him to just put his car into drive and take me away from this place and the memories that I already know are going to haunt me for the rest of my life.

"What's the one thing we used to dream of?"

"Err... become millionaires and move to LA?" I ask with a laugh, knowing that there's no way he's achieved that without me knowing.

"Close, but no."

"Just tell me," I sigh, my head falling back in defeat. I'm so fucking tired. All I want to do is go home and crawl into a semi-comfortable bed for a month. My eyes fall closed and I relax for what feels like the first time in just over a year. It's a weird feeling.

"We've left Harrow Creek."

I let a second pass for him to tell me that he's joking, but when he doesn't, I rip my eyes open once more and stare straight at him.

"For real?" I ask, more hope than is probably necessary filling my voice. He's not wrong that we used to dream of leaving that shithole on almost a daily basis. But without money, and seeing as we were only kids, there was no way of that happening. Although, I didn't think it would be right now either.

"For real. I got us a new place."

"Where?"

I swear some of the color drains from his face at my question and a little guilt flickers through his eyes.

"Kane?" I warn, already assuming what's about to fall from his lips. "Don't tell me that you've—"

"Rosewood."

That one word is like a bullet to my chest. All the air drains from my lungs and my shoulders sag.

"Why, Kane? Why would you do that to me... to us? Of all the places."

He stares at me, his brow wrinkling in concern. "It wasn't very easy, and I needed help, a lot of help. We didn't have that many options, so it was Rosewood or stay in the Creek and that was not happening. After..." He gestures to the building behind me. "You needed a fresh start, and I've done everything I can to give you one. I know you might not like it, but you've got a year to make the best of it before you can go to college."

I hate that my first reaction to what he's done is anger, but I can't help it. I know I should be grateful, and I am. Not going back to the Creek is the best news I could have wished for. But going to Rosewood. The place the one person I never want to see again lives, that's not exactly what I wished for upon release from that hellhole.

She was the one that put me in there, I sure as hell don't want to see her the second I come out. My fists curl, my nails digging into the worn leather of Kane's passenger seat as I try to contain the anger she ignites within me.

"Rosewood is a big town, Kyle. You probably won't even see..." He trails off, correctly guessing where my head is at.

"Kane, this is a really fucking bad idea," I warn.

"I've got us our own house, I've got you a place at Rosewood High so you can graduate, and hopefully, we'll keep social services off our back until you turn eighteen in a few weeks."

"Yeah, then I can leave," I mutter.

"Kyle," Kane warns, his voice low and menacing. It might work on others, they might think it's scary, but I know him too well to be scared of him. He's my big brother. My best friend. The one I've always relied on, trusted with everything. I fear that I might just have to put everything I'm feeling right now aside and do those things once again.

"Fuck... Rosewood, really?"

"I've pulled a lot of fucking strings to make this work for us, bro. I need you on board."

I stare at my brother. The one person I've looked up to all my life. There's no way I can say no to him now. Not after he's supported me through this and apparently done everything in his power to help me start over.

"I guess you'd better take me home then."

The corner of Kane's mouth twitches up into a smile. "It's not much but—"

"It'll be perfect. I'm sure a huge improvement from where I've been."

Kane flashes a look back over his shoulder, but I don't. I'm done with the place, it's time to move forward, even if that has to be in Rosewood with the girl that condemned me to hell in the first place.

I keep my eyes focused out of the window as Kane takes us to our new home. Being out here, everything just feels... strange. I might have hated that place, my cell, the guys who I was forced to live with. But after so long it became normal of sorts. Being out in the open... it's weird.

"What's the first thing you want to do?"

I don't even have to think about it and the words fall from my lips in a heartbeat. "Sleep in a comfortable bed."

"Huh, and here I was thinking you'd want a girl, or even a walk on the beach."

"They can come after. Sleep and a hot shower... alone."

"Damn, I was going to come and watch as well," he mutters with a laugh as he takes a left at an intersection I've never seen before but he seems to know well.

"You're still weird, I see."

"Would you want me any other way?"

"I guess not."

It's almost two hours after we left that place that I never want to think about again when he pulls into a quiet neighborhood and then onto a driveway.

"Wow, this is… cute."

"I never promised you a mansion, Ky."

"No, but this looks like a grandmother should live inside. It's not exactly party central." My heart constricts at the mention of a grandparent. That's just one more thing that I'll never forgive *her* for.

"A good thing seeing as we're going to have a social worker on our back for the next few weeks along with your parole officer."

I twist in my seat and look at my brother where he's still holding the wheel and staring up at our blue and white bungalow.

"Thank you," I say sincerely.

I surely didn't expect any of this, and I may have sounded somewhat ungrateful when he first mentioned this place but I really do appreciate what he's trying to do.

"It's not just for you, bro."

"I-I know. I can't imagine what you've had to do to secure all this. How are you even paying for it?"

"Gran left us a bit of money, and like I said, I had some good help."

"Who the hell wanted to help us? Two scumbags from the Creek."

"Someone who understands. Shall we?" he asks, cutting off any more questions I might have.

He shoulders the door of his old Nissan Skyline and jumps out. I guess some things never change.

Following suit, I climb out and grab my stuff from the trunk.

I trail behind Kane as he heads up the stairs to the porch. There's a swing seat at the other end and a coffee table with an ashtray in the middle.

"Smoking outside only."

"Sure thing, *Mom*," I say with a laugh but as his shoulders tense before me, I realize it might have been the wrong thing to say.

He spins and pins me with a hard look.

I've never been scared of Kane… okay, maybe a few times when I was younger but I know I can hold my own now, especially after the amount of time I've spent working out and fighting off assholes in the past year but still, the look on his face makes me swallow somewhat nervously.

"All it takes is for that social worker to turn up and get a sniff of weed in this place and all of this is going to come crashing down around our feet, Ky. You think they were happy about giving me guardianship of you, even if it is for a few weeks? Let me answer that for you… No, no, they fucking didn't. I might be older than you, but not by much and my rep isn't exactly squeaky fucking clean. This," he says, holding his hands out to gesture to our granny house. "Is a fucking miracle. So for a few weeks, just a few weeks, you need to do what the fuck you're told or I'll send you back into that place myself for fucking up all my hard work. You got that, little bro."

I have to clench my jaw to stop me from saying anything in response to his patronizing tone.

"You got it," I say in the end. "Point me in the direction of my bed."

"It's not even lunchtime yet."

"I don't give a shit."

"Okay. Well, Bea is coming at four to make sure you've settled in so you need to be awake and showered and looking respectful by then."

I drop my eyes to his exposed inked arms, his ripped jeans, and battered boots. Respectful, right.

"You know what I mean," he mutters before pulling the screen open, unlocking the front door and dragging it open.

Inside is a mostly empty living space. There are two old couches with a coffee table in the middle. There's a dining table in front of what can only be described as vintage kitchen units and a couple of mismatched chairs. It's… interesting. But a hell of a lot better than where I've come from.

"You get yourself a job and hopefully we'll be able to get some better shit."

"It's fine, K."

He glances at me but he refrains from pointing out that we don't even have a TV right now. "This is your room." He swings the door open and I find something that makes me sigh in relief. A queen-size bed with what looks like fresh sheets. Heaven.

Dropping my bag, I jump on the bed and starfish in the middle of it.

"My room's at the other end of the hall. The bathroom is in between us. I bought you a new cell and a laptop with the money I had left over." He nods to the dresser where the boxes sit.

"Kane, you didn't—"

"I did. I told her that I'd take care of you, give you a fresh start. That's what I'm doing."

"But… what about you?"

"Me?" he asks with a humorless laugh. "We're out of the Creek, Ky. I'm good."

"But what about work? What about…"

"That doesn't matter right now." Walking over to the dresser, he picks up the cell phone box and throws it at me. "Maybe set an alarm, yeah?" Then he walks out and closes the door without saying another word.

His footsteps get quieter before the front screen at the front door rattles and the house falls silent.

I stare at the room I'm sitting in. It's not much to write home about. The walls are a dirty cream color, the woodwork is chipped, the floor is stained, and the window is cracked. But… it's mine.

There's one single dresser along with a nightstand beside the bed, and a door that I can only assume is a closet.

Pushing from the bed, I kick my sneakers off and pad over. Pulling it open, I find a few of my old clothes hanging inside.

I haven't seen them for a year and I'd forgotten they even existed.

I pull each of the drawers open finding brand new boxers and socks and a few new t-shirts and sweats.

Dragging a couple out, I tuck them under my arm and head out to find the bathroom. I might want to sleep, but before that happens, I need to wash the smell of that place off me.

The bathroom is… well, it's blue. Really fucking blue.

But none of that matters because the water is hot and I'm the only one in the room, in the house actually, seeing as I saw a trail of smoke in front of one of the windows as I walked here.

A lot might have changed in a year, but Kane isn't one of them. He's still as unreadable as ever. I have no clue if he's happy about this or not. I know he wants me back. That's not in question. But does he really want to be in Rosewood? He hates those who did this to us as much as I do. Of all the places in this country. Why here?

Steam billows from the stream of water and after stripping down, I stand under the torrent.

It's so hot it burns, but I relish in it. After having to wash in lukewarm water for a year, I'll take the pain. It isn't like I haven't felt worse. I drop my hand to the scar on my side, remembering the pain of the knife but I quickly push it aside, that's all in the past now and all this is, is a reminder of why I'm never going back there.

I stand there so long the water begins to run cold. I make quick work of washing with the shower gel on the side before getting out and drying off with a towel that is thicker than I've felt in a long time.

I find a brand new toothbrush in the cupboard that I make use of. There's also a new razor and shaving gel but I can't be bothered with that. Those new bedsheets are calling.

The second I step into the hallway dressed in just a pair of sweats I find Kane heading this way.

His eyes go from mine and to my body, zeroing in on the scar for a beat.

"Whoa, where'd my little brother go?"

"He went to fucking juvie, bro."

A smirk curls at his lips.

"Jailbait and cut. You're gonna be fighting the Rosewood pussy off," he jokes.

I want to join him but the second he mentions pussy, only one girl pops into my mind.

I shake my head and turn toward my room.

"What? Don't tell me they turned you in there. You still want pussy, right?"

I flip him off before I slam my door closed.

Pulling the sheets back, I fall into them, loving the feeling of the crisp, cool cotton against my skin.

"Okay, everything looks good here," Bea says, closing her folder and looking up at me with a soft smile playing on her lips.

Turns out this afternoon isn't the first time I've met my social worker. She'd been to visit me inside a couple of times. I've had so many people try to 'help' me over the past year that I stopped paying attention to who everyone was after a few months. I didn't need help. I just needed to get out and pay the girl, who put me there in the first place, a visit.

"Do you need anything else from us?" Kane asks almost nervously. It's weird seeing him take control of this situation like an adult. He's always been my fun, slightly insane older brother, seeing him act the part of my guardian, even if it is just for Bea's benefit is weird.

"Yes, you've done a great job here, Kane. I know it's not been easy but hopefully, everything will go smoothly over the next few weeks and you'll be free to continue your lives without me breathing down your neck. Have you heard from your parole officer yet?"

I nod, remembering the meeting we had before I left.

"Okay, good. I spoke to Principal Hartmann earlier, everything is ready for you to start at Rosewood High on Wednesday."

"Wednesday?" I ask, assuming that I'd at least get a week to myself.

"Yes, we thought it best you get into your new routine as soon as possible. I spoke to him about being on the team and your previous experience with tutoring."

"Great," I mutter, glaring at Kane. I really don't need any more on my plate than just restarting my life.

"It'll be fantastic, Kyle. Rosewood High is a great school with a fantastic football team should you decide to join. It'll give you fantastic opportunities for the future."

I blow out a long breath. My future. I have no idea what that looks like for me now. I'm a Harrow Creek trailer park kid with a record. Not exactly the thing dreams are made of.

"Yeah, we'll see."

"Well, you've got time to figure stuff out."

"Okay well, if that's everything, I'll see myself out. Here's my card." She slides it across the table toward me. "I'll be in touch on Wednesday evening to see how school went but if you need me in the meantime, I'm always available on my cell."

"Thanks," I mutter, glancing down at her card.

She smiles at both of us before tucking her chair away and letting herself out as she said she would.

Silence surrounds us long after the shutter has crashed shut.

I have no idea what she really thought of the whole situation but I guess it doesn't really matter. She's happy enough with it to allow it to continue.

"I met with Principal Hartmann last week," Kane says after a few minutes of silence once the shutter door had slammed shut.

"Okay."

"Bea is right. It's a good school. Nothing like Harrow Creek High."

"Is anywhere as bad as Harrow Creek High?" I ask with a laugh, stretching my legs out and slumping down in the chair a little.

"You've got me there. I know it's a lot, but the team won state last year. All their best players are about to graduate, they'd be crazy not to want you."

"I don't know, K. So much has changed."

"Has it though? Football was our thing, our way out."

I nod at him because I always allowed him to think that it was our thing, when really, it was his. He's always been so much better than me. I swear if we were lucky enough to be born somewhere different he'd already have the NFL after him. He is *that* good. But as it is, our life was—is—shit, and those kinds of opportunities don't just appear for kids like us.

They happen for Rosewood kids, not Harrow Creek kids.

"We'll see," I mutter, pushing to stand and pulling the refrigerator open to grab a soda.

"We're gonna have futures, Ky. I'm going to make sure of it."

"I'm just happy to be free. I'll worry about the rest later."

"Talking about being free… you need to get changed."

"Why?"

"Why? Because we're celebrating tonight."

"That's okay. I don't need—" He pins me with a look that cuts off my argument.

"The guys will be here in an hour or so, the girls too…" He wiggles his brows at me.

"Kane, I don't need—" I try again.

"Humor me. I want to celebrate. This is a new start for us, kid. Things can only get better from here on out."

He scrubs his hand on the top of my head like he used to when we were kids, only I'm not so small anymore. I almost match his six-foot-three and after the muscle I've gained in juvie I might even have a few pounds on him right now.

"Fine," I say. "But is it a good idea with Bea breathing down our necks?"

"She's good, she's happy. Let's enjoy ourselves for just one night, eh?"

"Okay, fine."

I wake with what feels like a drum pounding in my head.

Fucking Kane.

I roll over with a groan, hoping that my stomach stays settled and bump into a person.

My eyes fly open and my heart jumps into my throat when I find not one but two half-naked girls in my bed.

Jesus, fucking hell.

What happened last night?

Lifting the covers, I find that I'm still wearing my boxers.

"Get the fuck out," I bark, my voice rough from a lack of sleep and a raging hangover.

I shake both of the girls awake.

"Get the fuck out of my bed."

They both look as rough as I feel as they do as they're told and drag their bodies from my bed before stumbling across the room toward the door.

The sight of them with makeup down their faces, their dresses twisted up around their waists and their tits half hanging out does nothing for me and I briefly wonder if that's just because of who they are or because I got my fill last night.

I don't remember anything past drinking straight from a bottle of vodka while Kane passed me a blunt to celebrate my release. I don't know who those girls were, when they arrived or how we even all ended up in here.

"Fucking hell," I mutter, pulling the covers over my head and allowing myself to drift back off.

When I come back to hours later, it's to the sound of my brother kicking people out of our house. I have no idea who's out there but I don't care enough to go and see.

There's movement for about ten minutes before the voices fade and the footsteps disappear before engines start and fade into the distance.

"Ky, you up?" Kane asks after knocking on my bedroom door.

"Go away," I bark, rolling onto my back.

"You want food?"

I want to say no, but my stomach growls at the thought of something decent to eat and I find myself throwing the covers back and dragging on a clean pair of sweats.

"Whoa, aren't you a sight for sore eyes."

"Fuck off," I grunt, pushing past him where he's blocking my doorway and marching for the bathroom.

"You're welcome, by the way," he says with a laugh as I slam the door behind me and immediately reach for my toothbrush.

I don't look up as I take care of my mouth, hoping that as I rid myself of the putrid taste, I can remove the hangover and lack of memories from last night. But the second I'm done and I lift my eyes to the mirror, I can't help but gasp.

I've got girl's lipstick fucking everywhere.

"Fucking hell."

I scrub my hand down my face and push my hair back before turning the shower on and stripping down.

"Good night, eh?" Kane asks when I drop down to the table while he fries bacon at the stove.

"Can we not talk about it?" I slide down the chair until I can rest my head back and close my eyes as the sound of his deep chuckle fills the room.

"Tell me that you at least remember it."

Feeling his stare burning into my skin, I drag my eyes open and stare at him.

"No, I have no fucking clue what happened, although the lipstick trail was a good indication."

The fuck actually fucking belly laughs at me.

"I told you to lay off the vodka after a year off."

"Whatever. At least I don't remember most of the mistakes."

"Who says they were mistakes? Two girls are never a mistake, Ky."

"Whatever you say. That ready yet?"

He drops a plate down in front of me and my mouth waters.

"Don't get used to it. I might have sorted us a house but I'm not your keeper," he mutters, pulling out his own chair.

"Wouldn't have expected you to be."

"I have today off, but after tomorrow, you won't see me much."

"What are you doing?" I ask, thinking of the less than legal shit we both did for money before I went away. Surely he must have a better job now to even stand a chance of getting me here.

"Doesn't matter," he mutters, stuffing a piece of bacon into his mouth. *Or maybe not then.* "You should probably spend more time worrying about yourself than me. You're heading back to high school tomorrow." He winks and my stomach twists.

I want to graduate, I have always wanted to but the second I got thrown in the back of that cop car a little over a year ago, I knew that the chance was even slimmer than it was already. Not that many kids leave Harrow Creek High with a diploma, the odds were already against me, despite my ability.

"Can't wait." The enthusiasm in my tone says it all about how I feel about returning to school. I should be finishing up senior year right now, yet here I am about to start it a year later than I should have. Although I can't deny that it's all my fault.

"Just do something for me." The serious tone in his voice has me looking up at him.

"Sure."

“Stay away from *her.*”

I snort. “You’re kidding, right?”

“No. I promised… uh… I just had to promise you’d put your head down and focus on your education. No going after revenge.” His brow lifts.

“You’re fucking kidding me,” I repeat, not believing that he can ask that of me after everything.

He shrugs and all it does is piss me off further.

“Just stay away from her.”

His plate clatters into the sink before he stalks to his bedroom.

“Is that what you’ll do when you see *her* again?” I call after him but he doesn’t respond aside from slamming his door hard enough for the entire house to shake.

2

HARLEY

"Who's Nathan?" Ashton, my best friend's boyfriend asks, as we walk toward English lit.

I can't help the wide smile that pulls at my lips as I think of him.

I haven't seen him since he took me out Sunday night but we've messaged almost every moment since.

He's sweet. Really freaking sweet. And he treats me like I'm something special, something worthwhile. It's nice. Especially as both of my best friends now have boys and I'm playing the odd one out.

"A guy from Maddison Prep that Harley met at Ethan's party. They've had a few dates," Ruby answers for me while I relive my time with him.

"Ah, dating a prep boy, eh? I hear they don't put out until at least the tenth date." My breathing falters at his comment.

We kissed, he's run his hand up my thigh and wrapped it around my waist, but that's where we've stopped so far.

"Shut up, you idiot. He's a good guy. Right, Har?"

I'm lost in my own head as we walk into our class. My thoughts back on Nathan as he kissed me goodbye on Sunday night. It was... nice.

I look up at the last minute knowing I'm about to weave my way through the desks to locate my own at the back when my world comes crashing down around my feet.

I stop dead on the spot and Ruby slams into my back as my heart jumps into my throat and I swear it damn near stops beating.

"Har?" Ruby asks, concern lacing her voice as she walks around to see my face.

She gasps at whatever she finds on my face but her reaction to this isn't the one that affects me.

"Are you okay?" I rip my eyes from him to find Ruby staring right at him with a scowl on her face.

I want to laugh. She's so small and so sweet yet she stares at him like she's about to walk over there and rip him a new one.

"W-who's that?" she asks, looking back at me and taking in my tear-filled eyes.

My lips part but it takes a second for any words to come out.

"Y-you remember Kane, the guy from my house on Sunday?" I whisper, ensuring no one but the two of them can hear.

The image of walking home to find him in my house Sunday night hits me and I feel the sting of betrayal from my mother having anything to do with the Legend brothers after what happened twists my insides once more.

I know she likes to help kids who seem to be a lost cause, but I never thought she'd stoop so low to help them.

No wonder she looked so sheepish when we discovered them.

"Yeah." She nods and then looks back to him.

I do the same and find what I already know, his light blue eyes are trained right on me. Although the happy-go-lucky look I remember from our childhoods is long gone. In its place is hate like I've never witnessed before.

I swallow nervously.

I did that to him.

"That's his little brother, Kyle." My voice cracks on his name and I hate it.

What I did was right. Okay, maybe frowned upon where we grew up, and I certainly never intended for Kyle to take the rap for it, but he was still in the wrong.

"Okay. And why does he look like he wants to kill you?"

"Probably because he does."

I swallow down my fear, my nerves and suck in a stealing breath.

My instinct is to run. To get as far away from his cold, evil eyes and hide anywhere I can find where I'm safe.

But what's the point in that?

He's here, and something tells me that he'll find me no matter where I go.

"Are you going in or what?" Someone barks from the hallway, bringing me back to reality and reminding me that I stopped right in the doorway.

"Yeah, sorry," Ruby mutters, dragging me to the side a little so the others can pass. "What are you going to do?"

"I'm going to sit my ass down and do my work, Ruby. What are you going to do?" I don't mean to snap at her but I can't help it. My emotions are currently being put through a blender.

"Are you sure? If you want to sk—"

"No," I cut her off, assuming where she's going. "I'm not running from him."

A proud smile pulls at Ruby's lips.

"Good for you, Har. Let's do this."

"You want me to beat his ass, just let me know," Ashton offers, startling me. I'd forgotten he was witness to this.

"Morning everyone. Please find your seats and let's pick up where we left off last lesson," our teacher calls out over the chatter filling the room.

The three of us move toward the back of the room. The closer I get to Kyle, the harder it becomes to breathe. It's like he literally sucks the air from my lungs. I know he probably wants me dead, but I'd have put money on him making it much more painful than this.

His calculating eyes follow me as I pass him and it's not until I'm a few feet away that I finally suck in a huge breath.

Running would have been so easy. But it would only last for so long because eventually, I'd be right back here.

I find my seat beside Ruby and pull my books out.

I know she's watching my every move. I can feel her burning stare, but she doesn't say anything. Not yet.

I hoped I'd got away with putting off explaining my reaction to Kane's appearance in my house. I thought it was going to be a one-off thing and we'd all move on and forget about it. But it seems I was wrong because it wasn't a one-off. It was a warning sign. A sign that my entire life is about to turn upside down.

I wish I knew... If I thought anything like this was about to happen then I'd have... What would you have done?

I blow out a breath.

There was nothing to do.

My past. My decisions. My mistakes. They're just catching up with me in the form of a smoking hot Kyle Legend.

I run my eyes over the backward cap he's wearing. His blond hair poking out from beneath it. I take in his shoulders, which are so much wider than I ever remember them being and down his exposed arms that are hanging down beside the chair. His fists are curled in frustration causing muscles to pull his forearms tight and for his veins to pop out.

This version of Kyle Legend is definitely different to the one I remember.

My stomach twists as reality hits me.

Kyle isn't a bad person. Actually, he was always a pretty awesome person. And despite the issue between us, I'm pretty sure everyone here is going to love him.

He and Zayn were always tight, well, until we moved and carved out a better life for ourselves.

It makes me wonder what the relationship might be like between them now after what I did.

Will Kyle take it out on him too, or is his wrath going to be solely aimed at me?

Every second of English lit this morning was as painful as the moment I walked in and saw him. The only good thing about it was that we were kept busy the entire time and Ruby was unable to unload the million and one questions I could see behind her eyes.

I get two more hours of relief as we had different classes, but I know my time is running out because lunch is approaching and there's no way, no matter where I hide, that she won't find me and try to drag every single bit of information out about what happened.

Dread sits heavy in my stomach as the bell rings and kids start filing out of class toward the cafeteria. It's not until I'm out of the door that the whispers register.

I've been so lost in my own head this morning that it could have been going on for hours, but it's only now I take notice.

"I heard he went in for attempted murder."

"And only served a year. Puh-lease. That's bullshit. It was just assault."

I shake my head at the group of girls as I pass them.

"He's so fucking hot. Have you seen the size of his arms?"

"Yeah, I'd let him throw me over his shoulder any day."

Rolling my eyes, I continue as the trail of whispers get worse and even more unbelievable until I get to the cafeteria.

Ruby is already here, and I have to swallow down a groan as she jumps up and runs over to me.

I know she's only trying to help but right now, all I want to do is disappear.

"Are you okay?" she asks, looking me up and down.

"Of course."

"Have you seen him again?"

I shake my head as I follow her over to our tables. "It's only a matter of time. Have you seen Zayn?"

"Not yet. I'm sure he'll be here in a bit."

I look around the cafeteria as I sit down beside her, trying to see if he's here.

"So I'm hearing all kinds of crazy shit about this guy. Most of which I don't believe for a second. But… do you feel like telling me what I should know?" She pins me with a look and raises a brow.

"Not really," I mutter. I look to the line forming for food. Part of me wants to join it just so I've got something to do but I already know that I'm not going to be able to eat anything.

"Har," she sighs, sympathy filling her eyes as she wraps her fingers around my hand. "Let me help you."

"It's not that I don't want that. I do. I just… I really don't want to have to think about it, let alone talk about it."

"I get it." She squeezes my hand tighter "I'm here, whenever you're ready. But can I ask just one question?"

"Sure."

"He didn't actually… kill anyone, did he?"

I can't help the laugh that bubbles up my throat at the thought of Kyle actually killing anyone.

"No, Rubes. As far as I'm aware, he's never killed anyone."

"He went to juvie though, right?"

"That's two questions," I point out. "But yeah, he's done a year."

"Right, and—" I raise a brow at her in amusement that her one question is now turning into three but her words are cut off when everyone around us falls silent. "Shit," she breathes.

My entire body tenses, my temperature increases a few degrees and my need to run almost gets the better of me once more.

It's only been a few hours and he's already getting under my skin. And I swear he's not even trying.

Swallowing down my apprehension, I suck in a breath and lift my eyes.

My brother is standing before us with none other than Kyle fucking Legend by his side.

My teeth grind as the two of them stand together as if the years haven't passed and they're still close. I swear to God, if he knew about this, I'll fucking kill him. If he knew and didn't warn me. If he knew and... and is okay with this then..." My fists curl, my nails digging into my palms until it hurts so much, I'm convinced I've drawn blood.

"Guys, this is Kyle. He's a fucking kick-ass running back." He directs his words to Jake, but I don't miss his eyes very briefly flick to me. "He's starting as a junior. You're going to want him on the team next year."

"Legend, yeah, I know all about your performance," Jake says, his eyes lighting up with excitement. It's no secret that he's worried about the team who are going to proceed him and the rest of the seniors that are about to graduate.

"This is bullshit, Zayn," I snap, standing from my seat before my brain has even processed what's just happened.

Zayn's concerned eyes turn on me at the same time Kyle's amused ones do.

"Har, it's okay."

"Are you fucking kidding me? Did you know about this?" I fume as tears burn the backs of my eyes.

"No, I had no idea until this morning."

"You know Mom did this, right?"

"Do you really want to do this here?" he asks me quietly, glancing at the crowd around us.

"I can't believe you." My lips curl in disgust that he's happily accepting Kyle into his life, his team, this easily.

"You're making a bigger deal out of this than there needs to be." My jaw drops as I hear his voice for the first time since that night.

My eyes snap to his light blue ones and my teeth grind. My chest heaves as we stare at each other. Something crackles between us, something I remember from that night, but I force it aside. Nothing good came of that night and nothing will now.

"This is bullshit, Zayn. But it's good to know where your loyalties lie."

"Harley, wait," Zayn calls as I finally do what I've wanted to do all day. I run.

"Harley, what's—" I dodge Poppy as she tries to intercept my escape from the cafeteria and bolt down the half-empty hallway.

I have no idea where I'm going, but that's not important now. I just need to get away from him and my memories of that night.

It was just supposed to be a party like all the others I'd been to in Harrow Creek. Maybe it was naïve of us to think we could turn up once we've moved and to be treated like we always were... like one of them.

The main door to the football stadium is open when I get there.

The entire place is deserted, just as I hoped as I climb the steps between the bleachers and find myself a seat at the top.

I drop my ass to one of the red plastic seats and lower my head into my hands.

The tears I've been fighting all morning finally come.

He isn't supposed to be here, and my own mother shouldn't have been the one to help it happen.

Betrayal wraps around my chest, making it hard to breathe.

None of this is my fault. I was the victim that night, I still shouldn't be the one suffering now.

But it *wasn't* his fault either, was it? a little voice in my head screams. Yet, he paid the ultimate price.

By some miracle, no one finds me before the bell rings.

Math.

The last place in the world I want to be. The only thing that would make it worse would be having him in class.

Groaning, I pull a compact mirror from my purse and set about fixing my makeup.

By the time I push open my classroom door, I'm late.

All eyes turn on me but I keep my stare on the floor as I mutter my apologies to Mr. Wilson and make my way to my desk.

I pull out my books and get started on the instructions that are on the board for us without looking at or talking to anyone.

I stare at the equation in the textbook that I'm supposed to be solving and all the numbers, letters, and symbols start swirling around the page as my head begins to spin.

I fucking hate math.

I try. I try as hard as I can until my only reaction is to want to curl up in a ball and admit defeat.

I hate that I can't do this. Everyone else around me makes it seem so easy. Zayn and my older sister Letty, both make it seem so easy. I always feel like the stupid young one when we're all together.

They've both always got top grades in everything, seemingly without even trying yet I work my butt off and I'm still borderline failing.

I sigh, resting back in my chair and closing my eyes.

I hate feeling like a failure. It makes me feel weak, and I'm not weak.

Finally, after Mr. Wilson gives us all an insane amount of homework the bell rings and everyone begins to pack up their stuff and leave.

"Harley, could I speak with you a moment?" he calls across the room before I manage to escape.

The knot in my stomach grows as I walk toward him.

"What's up, sir?"

"We need to talk about your latest test." All the air whooshes from my lungs.

"That good, huh?"

"Harley, we both know you've been struggling all year. I know you hate the idea of it, but I really think you need to get some extra help."

The words I always say to him when he brings this up fall from my lips. "I'm fine, thank you."

"Harley," he sighs, sitting back in his chair and crossing one leg over the other. "That wasn't a suggestion. I'm putting your name in for tutoring. I've got some fantastic students in my AP statistics classes that would be great for you."

"It's okay. Zayn can help."

"Harley," he says a little more sternly than before. "You need some help. This is only going to get harder as we move into senior year. You can't wait any longer."

"But—"

"You'll get an invitation to meet whoever you are matched with in a few days. You can organize between yourselves how often, when and where you meet, but rest assured, I will be checking that you do so, and I will be expecting to see an improvement in this." He presses two fingers against last week's test paper that's on his desk and he slides it my way.

I try to swallow over the huge lump in my throat as I stare down at the huge F on the front right by my name.

As much as I want to argue with him right now, I know that I don't have a leg to stand on. And if Mom finds out about me failing a test, I really won't have a choice. She's offered to get me a paid tutor time and time again, but I always manage to put her off. I fear that my struggles and my avoidance is about to bite me in the ass with a sharp pair of teeth.

"I won't let you down," I mutter as I snatch up my test and bolt to the door.

"You're a good student, Harley. Don't let one grade drag you down."

His words ring out in my ears as I walk away and out to the parking lot.

We usually have cheer practice now, but seeing as we've got the week off, I make my escape knowing that everyone will probably want to go to Aces, and right now, I really don't want to be around anyone, and I certainly don't want to see my brother as he shoves his old best friend into the middle of our new lives.

Mom's car is in the driveway when I pull up, the sight of it is almost enough to make me turn around and go elsewhere but I know I can't put this off forever. It seems she may have already been keeping secrets for a little too long.

I slam the front door harder than necessary to announce my arrival and within seconds, I hear her soft footsteps on the hardwood.

The moment she rounds the corner, I close the distance between us.

"Why didn't you tell me?" I seethe, my blood boiling beneath my skin. "Why didn't you tell me you were helping him? Why? Why would you let me walk in blind to that situation?"

"Harley," she says softly, pissing me off even more. "You know I can't discuss clients with you."

"Bullshit, Mom," I spit, much to her irritation. "This is my life. Screw your job."

"Harley, I understand you're annoyed but—"

"Annoyed? Annoyed? That doesn't even come close, Mom. I walked into English lit and there he was. No freaking warning whatsoever."

"In my defense, I thought he was starting next week."

"Convenient," I mutter, spinning away from her and pulling my red hair back from my face.

"It's true. Now that Kane has guardianship, I'm not involved. Bea has taken over his case. I'm sorry, Harley."

"No," I say, staring into her dark eyes. "No. Not good enough. Why did you even agree to help them?"

"Because it's the right thing to do and you know it. You said it yourself that Kyle didn't do anything wrong that night so why wouldn't I help when Kane came to me?"

"You knew that he'd hate me when he got out. You knew that he'd blame me for ruining his life." While he may not have been the one to cause my pain that night, he was still there. He knew what was going on and he let it happen nonetheless.

She swallows as guilt passes across her face.

"It wasn't your fault, Harley."

"You think I don't know that? I'm the one who has to live with the memories of that night. He has every right to hate me."

"I'm sure he doesn't—"

"Were you there? Did you see the way he looked at me?"

"Well, no."

"This was the wrong thing to do, Mom. I know you want to save every kid out there with a messed-up life, but you should have stayed clear of this one. Does Letty know you've been helping Kane?"

She swallows nervously once more.

"Great, so at least I can rest easy knowing that you've been lying to all three of us. You need to tell her. She deserves to know as much as I did that the Legends have moved to Rosewood."

"It doesn't matter to Letty. She's off at college enjoying herself."

I shake my head at her. "If you really believe that then maybe you're not as smart as you make out."

"Harley," Mom snaps, hurt clear in her voice.

My mom has always been my hero, the only person I've ever looked up to. What she's achieved, it's... incredible. But right now, I'm struggling to even look at her.

"I'll be in my room," I mutter, stalking toward the stairs.

I throw myself on my bed after kicking my sneakers off and bury my face in my pillow to muffle the scream that rips from my throat.

Memories of that night hit me. I can smell the heavy mix of weed and cigarette smoke as if I'm right back there. I remember his hands on me and how his touch burned my skin. I remember how the room spun around me before everything started to get totally out of control. I remember the other pair of hands, the panic, the exact moment the desire thrumming beneath my skin turned into something else entirely. I remember how desperately I wanted to get away but Letty was no longer in sight and no matter how much I wanted to scream for help, I couldn't because I was losing control.

I knew making that phone call would be a death wish. People who live in Harrow Creek don't call the police. We don't rely on others—even the law—to fight our battles. So the second I hit dial, I knew it was the beginning of the end. I just wish they got the right guy.

It's not until a knock rattles my bedroom door a while later that I realize that I must have fallen asleep. So much for the homework sitting in my bag.

I flip onto my back and look up at the ceiling as Zayn calls out.

"Har? Can I come in?"

The sound of his deep voice has everything that's happened today slamming back into me.

Kyle Legend is once again part of my life.

I slam my head back against the pillow and squeeze my eyes shut.

"Yeah, come in," I shout back reluctantly.

The door cracks open and he slips inside before closing it again.

"I had no idea, Har. I swear."

I blow out a breath and continue staring at the ceiling, refusing to look at him.

"You could have fooled me the way you hyped him up to the team."

"What would you rather I did, ignore him? Kyle's not a bad person and you know it."

"Do I?"

"Har," he warns, walking closer and sitting on the edge of my bed. "He's just spent a year in juvie."

"I know," I spit. "I put him there, remember?"

"No, I'm pretty sure the blow in his pockets was what put him there," he mutters.

"I was the one who made the call. I set the events of that night into motion."

"No," he says, reaching for my hand but I snatch it away. I don't want his support or comfort right now. I just want to be alone. "None of that was your fault."

"Try telling Kyle that."

"He's fine about it, Har. He just wants to get on with his life."

My shock at his words has my eyes snapping to his.

"You're shitting me. Did you see the way he looked at me earlier?"

"He told me, Harley. He doesn't hold any of this against you."

"Then he's lying. Ask Ruby and Ashton. They'll tell you exactly how he looked at me."

"He was probably just shocked. He just wants to start over. Graduate. Move on. You need to do the same thing."

With him giving me death stares every time I see him? Yeah, *I'm* sure *that'll* be easy.

"Fine," I sigh, knowing that it's pointless arguing with him.

3

KYLE

I sit in the middle of a diner surrounded by members of the Rosewood High Bears and sitting next to my old best friend, Zayn Hunter.

When he walked over earlier with a wide smile on his face, I wasn't sure if it was a joke.

The night I ended up in the back of a cop car… he has every right to hate me for what went down before I was carted away.

That's if he knows what actually happened, of course.

But it seems it was genuine because no sooner had he accepted me into his new life, then he introduced me to the team and ensured I got my ass to their conditioning session after school.

I know Kane had talked about me joining the team, but I just wanted to keep my head down and get on with graduating, seems that isn't what's going to be happening because I've been thrust right into the center of Rosewood's royal circle.

"So you just got out of juvie?" a guy with dark hair and even darker eyes sitting opposite me asks. Everyone else has kept the gossiping about me behind my back today, although not very discreetly. But this guy doesn't seem to give a shit about beating around the bush.

"Yeah. I did a year," I say.

He nods in understanding, and I'm relieved when I find no judgment there.

"I'm Ash. I only started here on Monday."

"So I'm not the only one in this group to be adopted recently then," I say with a smirk.

"Think they'd befriend anyone who can throw a ball right now."

"Way to make me feel special," I mutter much to his amusement.

"So what's the deal with you and Harley then?" he asks, shocking the fuck out of me.

"Uh..."

"Ruby, her best friend, she's my girl." He nods toward where the cheer squad are sitting at another table and a small brunette girl's eyes light up the second she sees him.

I want to say I recognize her, but I've seen so many new people today that all the faces are blurring into one, the only clear one in my mind is hers. It's the same one I've focused on for a fucking year.

I was looking after her that night. I never would have let anything happen to her, yet she called the cops anyway and screwed me over.

"We've got history," I say with a shrug, dragging my soda closer and taking a swig.

"As in exes?"

I almost spray him with my drink. "No, nothing like that." Not really.

Images from that night before the shit hit the fan fill my mind and I shift in my seat as my cock swells at the memory of her sitting astride my lap.

Harley's beautiful, I've never been able to deny that. But more importantly, she was always my boy's little sister. Off-limits, no matter what.

But then they left, and she and Letty turned up that night and things just got a little out of control without her big brother there as the reminder I needed that I wasn't allowed to touch.

"Okay, so did she kill your cat or something because you looked like you wanted to slit her throat for whatever it was."

"Nah, it's not like that. I was just surprised to see her again," I lie. "So what's your story? Where did you move here from?"

He chats briefly about moving from Seattle, but he doesn't give me much to go on, although it's impossible to miss the shadows lingering in his eyes.

"So, what do you think?" Zayn says, dropping into the seat beside me. "You think you've still got what it takes on the field?"

"Fuck you, Hunter. Legend by name, Legend by nature."

"Always were a big-headed motherfucker," he deadpans, slugging me in the shoulder. "I gotta bounce, my girl is waiting on me. It's good to have you back, man. I think you're going to like it here."

"Yeah? I've definitely experienced worse."

He chuckles, I'm sure thinking about the hellhole that is Harrow Creek High but that place was like paradise compared to juvie and the motherfuckers I was forced to spend my time with.

"Harley..." he says somewhat hesitantly.

"It's fine, man. What's done is done. Time for us all to move on."

He claps me on the shoulder. "You got it, man. You need anything, you know where I am."

I don't. I have no fucking clue where he lives, but I'm sure it won't take me too long to find out.

Thoughts of the girl he shares a house with fill my mind. Maybe I should find out sooner rather than later.

"Sure. Thanks for today." I nod to the guys surrounding me. I wasn't expecting this, but I sure do appreciate it. I had a feeling I was going to walk into Rosewood High with a huge target printed on my back, but it seems I didn't need to worry... or maybe I still should because it's clear Zayn doesn't know the whole truth.

"Anytime. I'm glad you're here. We'll catch up for real soon. J's having a party Saturday night," he says, pointing at another of the guys sitting at the other end of the table. "You're coming, right?"

"Hell yeah."

"Sweet." He nods once more before turning his back and walking out of the diner.

"So a history with Harley and best buds with Zayn. This doesn't have disaster written all over it at all."

I narrow my eyes at Ash. I'm not sure if I'm annoyed with him or just impressed that he doesn't beat around the bush.

"Watch yourself, man. Things could get messy."

He laughs to himself and shakes his head. "Allow me to let you into a little secret." He leans over the table so he can whisper something to me, and I'm powerless but to move closer. "Those girls..." He looks to the squad again. "They might look sweet, sexy... easy to play with. But let me tell you, they've got fucking claws, man." He sits back, his face a mask of seriousness until his lips curl at the edges. "I've got the scratch marks to prove it." He winks and I can't help but laugh.

"That much fun, huh?"

"Man, you have no idea."

"And Harley is one of them?"

"My girl? She's about to become captain, and Harley is her right-hand woman. You want to go there after everything that's gone down between you, then all I can do is wish you luck, man."

"I'm not sure if this little chat is turning me on or scaring the shit out of me."

Ashton throws his head back and laughs. "Seeing as you've just spent a year locked up with a bunch of dudes, I'd bet money on the former." He reaches for his soda and downs it before pushing to stand. "I'm out, got a date with my girl." He winks. "I'll see you tomorrow."

I nod at him and watch as he turns his stare on his girl. Something swirls within me as he prowls toward her and swoops her up in his arms. I tell myself it's just been a really, really long time. My eyes scan around the rest of the cheer squad until I land on a dark pair of eyes. They're not the ones I want to stare into sure, but they're better than nothing.

A shy smile curls at her lips before her cheeks redden as I push to stand and walk over.

"Hey, I don't think I saw you around today," I say, dropping into the seat Ruby vacated beside her. "I know I'd remember if I did." I cringe at my line but as her smile gets wider, I realize it's worked a charm.

"I'm Aria, and you're..."

"Lonely."

She chuckles, her hand resting on my upper arm as I rest it around the back of her chair.

"The guys not making you feel welcome?" she asks, her fingers walking up to my shoulder. I glance at her long talons and Ashton's warning repeats in my ears.

My own smile twitches at my lips. The Creek girls of my past make these girls look like teddy bears. I'm pretty sure I can handle a Rosewood cheer slut.

"Not in the way I need," I growl. Leaning into her, I get close enough that my breath caresses her ear and she shivers. "You down for showing me around town... alone?" I whisper so no one else at the table can hear me.

"That sounds—"

"Aria," another girl snaps.

We both look over and my eyes almost pop out of my head when I find a dark-haired girl standing, staring daggers at Aria with her hands on her hips and one very round belly.

Holy shit.

"Yeah, I'm pregnant, asshole. What of it?" she barks at me when she notices what's holding my attention.

"Uh…n-nothing."

"Aria, we're going. I suggest you put jailbait down."

"Excuse me?" I ask, my brows lifting in shock.

"You heard me."

"Down, Chels." One of the guys who was sitting at the table with me only moments ago steps up behind her and slides his hands over her growing belly.

"Good to know the Bears don't shoot blanks," I deadpan.

Chels—I assume Chelsea—turns beet red, her entire body locking up in anger while the guy—who I'm sure I've been introduced to but don't remember, throws his head back.

"Damn straight, man. We're not fucking champs for nothing."

"Shane," she gasps.

"What, baby? Just having a laugh with the new boy."

My teeth grind at being called that. It's a nickname I remember all too well from when I was first locked inside that place. A shudder rolls through me at the memories from my 'initiation' by some of the longer residents who thought they owned that place.

"Whatever," she mutters, taking a step forward and out of his hold. "Stay away from my girls." Her finger points right at me before she uses it to indicate her squad, her eyes narrowed in anger.

"It looks like you've got enough on your plate, you don't need to worry about me. I'll make sure I'm gentle… ish."

She growls, actually growls at me.

"Alright, momma bear." The guy wraps his arms around her tighter and presses his lips to her neck but her hard eyes never leave mine, even as they begin to shutter with pleasure.

"Stay away from my girls," she warns again as she's directed out of the diner by her boy.

"So," Aria says, turning back to me. "What were you saying about showing you around?" Her eyes land on me and where I should probably feel some excitement about the possibility of spending time with her, I feel nothing.

"Another time maybe?" I push to stand and disappointment crosses her face.

I look over to the team but they're all lost in their own conversation.

Unnoticed, I slip out of the diner and look out at the ocean beyond.

As a kid, I always dreamed of moving to Rosewood so that we could go to the beach every day. We've driven through once and I remember looking out at the glistening ocean and seeing the happy families playing on the sand. It looked incredible, and at six or seven it was everything I wanted my life to be.

We might have had both our parents in our lives at that point, but things were far from perfect. If I'd have known just how bad things were going to get then maybe I wouldn't have been staring out the window that day hoping for better, I'd have just been happy that the four of us were together. We weren't going to get too many more chances.

With a sigh, I turn toward the parking lot.

It turns out that it wasn't only the girls I didn't remember from Kane's little party the other night because when I step out onto the porch later that afternoon, I find my car waiting for me. Clearly, I walked straight past it in my desperation to start at Rosewood High this morning. I roll my eyes at myself.

I hadn't thought much about it. I assumed that maybe Kane had sold it, I certainly didn't expect to see it again, that's for sure.

My black VW Golf looks exactly the same as the day I left her. Kane even made sure she was delivered back to me clean.

I walk over, taking in her black matte wheels and the sport bumpers I fitted in the months before I went away.

It feels like a lifetime ago now.

I tap her hood, a smile pulling at my lips although I feel pretty pathetic that I walk out of juvie and all I've got is my brother and my car waiting for me.

Aside from Kane's friends who came to the house on Monday night, I haven't seen any of the guys I used to hang around with.

I know why. I don't need to put much thought into the reason they're probably less than thrilled that I'm out but it still kind of stings to know that they really didn't give a shit. I'd grown up with those motherfuckers. Did all sorts of shit for them, hence why I found myself locked up.

I hated it when Zayn moved away. He was the only one who got me in that place.

I drop into my car and rest my head back.

I wish I could confidently say that they'll all stay away, but I know that I'm on borrowed time. When I was arrested, it wasn't just me they took. It was the majority of Gray's stash that was in my pockets.

He's not going to let that go with a stint in juvie. I owe him, and it's only a matter of time until he turns up wanting payment.

My fingers grip the wheel until my knuckles turn white.

I don't want anything to do with any of them. I might not be thrilled about being here, near her, but it's a hell of a lot better than being back in that shithole.

Kane's car isn't in the driveway when I get home. He's still not told me what he's doing but he did tell me not to expect him around much.

I find enough food to make a sandwich. I place that and a can of soda on the table before pulling out the books I was given today and making a start on my homework.

I was given tests from every single class I attended, and not just the standard homework the others got, helpfully each teacher supplied me with catch up work too.

I get it, I've got a lot to prove.

They'll have seen my reports from Harrow Creek no doubt but even I know they don't exactly fit the stereotype of a Creek kid. While everyone else was failing and set on a future without a high school diploma, my grades were always A's.

I worked hard. Harder than anyone else around me. I had a dream and staying in that hellhole and dealing either drugs, weapons or people wasn't where my interests laid.

I shake my head thinking that everyone I know from back there is probably still doing the exact same thing they were a year ago.

That creek is a place of ruin. There aren't many that get out and make anything of their lives. It seems the Hunters—and hopefully us—might be an exception to the rule.

I do the statistics work first. It's the easiest after all, then I set about doing the rest.

It's dark out by the time I've finished, and Kane still isn't home.

Packing everything away ready for another day at Rosewood High, I head for a shower then to bed.

As I lie there staring at the ceiling, the only thing I can see is her panic-filled eyes as she stared at me from the doorway.

She had no idea I was going to be there, that much was obvious. What I don't understand is why, because it seems that it was Jada Hunter who helped Kane set all of this up. Why wouldn't she warn Harley that I was going to suddenly be a part of her life once again? Surely a heads up would have been nice, although, I must admit, I did love her shock.

4

HARLEY

Nathan: I've got a surprise for you.

Excitement flutters in my belly as I stare down at his message. We've spoken every day since he dropped me home after our meal on Sunday night but I have yet to see him again and I'm desperate to. I hate that he's all the way in Maddison County.

"What are you smiling about?" Ruby asks as her and Poppy join me on the bench I'm sitting on.

"Message from Nathan."

"Oooh," Ruby sings, her brows wiggling.

"You seeing him this weekend?" Poppy asks.

"I think so. He says he's got a surprise." I shrug.

"He so wants to get between your legs," Ruby jokes.

"It's only been a few weeks," I argue, although I wonder if the words are more for me than them.

"Time doesn't matter. If it's right then it's right." Ruby shrugs.

"I'm just going with the flow," I tell them although I can't help the knot that forms in my stomach.

The first night we met, things between us were electric and when he kissed me... whoa. I'd only felt anything like that once before in my life and I latched onto it, that along with the fact he's clearly a really nice person.

He's perfect in pretty much every way, he's everything I said I wanted but as time goes on I can't help thinking something just isn't right. I keep telling myself that it's because we haven't had any time alone. We've either been at a party or in a movie theater or restaurant. What I really want is it to be just us away from prying eyes and other people. I want to get to know him properly. See if that spark that was there at the party reappears when we're alone.

Harley: I can't wait. x

"He'll be at Justin's party tomorrow night, right?" Ruby asks.

"Err… I have no idea. I'm not…" I trail off, knowing that they're not going to like what I want to say next.

"You're not what?" Ruby asks, her brow quirked.

"I don't think I'm going to go."

"What? Why not? Especially if Nathan is going to be there."

"It's not him. It's—"

"Kyle."

"Can we not?" I beg.

"What happened, Har?" Poppy asks, her warm hand landing on my thigh.

"I… uh… I was the one who had him put in juvie," I admit, staring at the concrete beneath my feet but their lack of response has me looking up at them.

"We kinda assumed that, Har."

"Oh."

"I didn't actually call the cops on him. He just happened to be there. I didn't even know he was in possession of anything. I totally screwed him over," I admit.

"You didn't know."

"I shouldn't have called the cops. It's not how things are done where we're from." They both stare at me like I have two heads. I understand why. Poppy might have been with us to Harrow Creek, she understands a little about what it's like there, but only people who live there really get it.

"You must have had a good reason to do it."

"Y-yeah, I thought so. But things didn't go as they were supposed to."

"That's not on you."

"It doesn't matter. I blame myself anyway. He didn't deserve that."

"Have you spoken to him?"

I shake my head.

"Maybe you should. Get it all out in the open. Zayn seems to think he's okay about everything. He certainly doesn't seem angry," Poppy says.

"You didn't see how he looked at me yesterday morning," I mutter.

"She's right. It was brutal," Ruby agrees.

"He was just surprised. He said so himself."

"You seem to have fallen onto Team Kyle pretty fast, Pops."

"Not at all. I've got your back always, you know that. I'm just telling you what I've seen and heard from both him and Zayn. He seems like a decent guy."

"Yeah, he was." My mind wanders back to a simpler time. A time where my biggest issue was having the most insane crush on my brother's best friend.

"OMG, you have a crush on him, don't you?" Ruby almost squeals.

"What? No. Why would you even say that?" I argue a little too insistently.

"Um... because it's obvious that you do. I mean, he's hot. I can see why you'd want him but—"

"He hates me. With good reason, I might add."

"Nothing a little blow job wouldn't fix, I'm sure."

"What?" I shriek. "Ruby, you did not just suggest that."

"She's got a point. It's amazing what you can convince a guy to do with a good su—" I hold my hand up to Poppy.

"Do not go there," I warn. "I don't need to know what gets you on your knees for my brother." I shudder at the thought.

"Just try talking to him, Har," Ruby says. "It was what you told me to do about a million times with Ash, remember? And it worked."

"You ended up in bed with him," I point out helpfully.

"See," Poppy says. "It's the answer."

"You two are no help. I need new single friends," I whine, not for the first time.

"Aw, you love it."

"Do I? Do I really?" I roll my eyes at the pair of them.

Thankfully, the bell rings before they can try convincing me to talk to him or drag me inside where I know he's hanging out with the team.

Only a few days in and he's already found his place in this school. It's not lost on me that as he fits right in, I feel like I'm losing my grip on my place.

"I've got volleyball. At least I can pretend the ball is his head."

They both laugh at me before waving me off as they head in the opposite direction to their classes.

At least in the gym with the girls, I know I'm safe from bumping into him.

It's only been a day and I'm putting more thought into my every step than I have in my entire time here at Rosewood High.

We haven't shared another class yet, but I know it's only a matter of time before I walk into a classroom and find him there waiting for me.

"You okay?" Stella asks me as she holds the locker room door open for me.

"Yeah," I mutter, but my voice is obviously lacking its usual spark.

"We missed you at Ace's last night."

"I had a ton of homework to do."

"Riiight."

"What's that supposed to mean."

"Harley, I'm not an idiot. I've heard the rumors."

"Of course you have," I breathe. "No, he didn't kill anyone, or even threaten to kill anyone."

"Oh, I didn't mean that. I meant that the two of you have history."

My head snaps up so fast I'm surprised it doesn't roll off my neck. "W-what? What's being said?"

"Nothing much but the way you're suddenly avoiding the team, him. It's been noticed and people are jumping to conclusions."

"The squad, you mean?" We all know what a bunch of gossiping bitches the seniors are. If they don't have a cock between their lips then they're spreading around some bullshit.

"There's nothing between us."

"You all grew up together though, right? And you are avoiding him?"

"Yes, yes. Stella, I—" Another group of girls come stumbling into the locker room, chatting and laughing away as they pass us. Stella waits, her eyes trained on me. "Kyle was Zayn's best friend until we all moved here. We grew up together, and I was there the night he was... he was arrested. That's all you need to know."

"Sure thing, Harley."

"Stella, I—"

"It's fine, Harley. I get it. But if you want to talk, I'm here, okay? I've been to a lot of schools over the years, I've seen a lot of shit. You need an unbiased opinion. I'm here."

"Thank you. I really appreciate it."

She nods at me and we begin getting changed.

"So, you ready for cheer to start up again next week?" she asks me, thankfully steering the conversation to something I'm happier talking about.

"Yes. I never thought I'd say it after all those crazy hours before nationals, but I miss it."

"Auditions are going to be brutal though, aren't they? Chelsea is such a perfectionist."

"Yep. But I get it, she wants to leave a good squad behind her. We've got big shoes to fill."

"That we do."

I feel a little better after expelling some of my pent-up energy during volleyball. I hadn't realized how much stopping all my exercise quite so abruptly after nationals had affected me. As I get dressed, ready to head home, I tell myself that I'm going to reset my alarm for the morning and go for a run before school. Hopefully a bit of fresh morning air will also help clear my head.

"Harley," Mr. Wilson shouts the second he spots me in the hallway.

I just about manage to bite back my groan of frustration as I make my way over.

"Yes, sir?" I say politely.

"I thought you'd want to know that I've matched you up with a tutor. I've handed over all your contact details and I'll leave it up to the two of you to arrange your sessions. I trust you not to let me down, Harley. You know how vital it is that you get those grades up."

My heart sinks at his words. A part of me had hoped he might forget and I could continue burying my head in the sand with my quickly declining math grades.

"I'll do my best, sir."

"Any issues, you know where I am."

"Great."

"I'll look forward to your next test results."

"Well, that makes one of us," I mutter to myself as I walk away and resume the journey toward my locker.

Pulling the door open, I poke my head inside and just about resist the need to scream out my frustration. My eyes land on the photos of Ruby, Poppy, and me that are pinned to the back and a smile curls at my lips.

I'm sifting through my books, pulling out the ones I need for the night when my cell buzzes in my back pocket.

Unknown: Congrats, tutor girl. Looks like you're stuck with me now! First session starts in an hour...

Another message comes through with an address.

I know Mr. Wilson said he was going to leave it up to us to organize but I kind of assumed it would happen in the library at least.

I tap my finger against the side of my cell as I try to decide what to reply with. I want to say that I'm not interested and hope that whoever's at the other end will be glad to get out of it.

Harley: Who is this?

Unknown: Your new tutor. Come meet me and find out...

Some movement at the other end of the hallway startles me and I find most of the football team, my brother and Kyle included, joking around as they emerge from the locker room where they must have just finished a conditioning session.

"Alright, sis?" Zayn calls when he spots me.

I nod at him but I don't return his delight at seeing me. I'm still annoyed with him for how he's accepted Kyle back into his life, which in turn annoys me even more because he has every right to.

My skin tingles as Kyle runs his eyes down my body, his lips curled in disgust as he does so.

In a moment of defiance, I lift my hand and flip him off.

I'm not in the mood for his bullshit. Especially now that I have to spend my night doing fucking math with some nerd.

His eyes widen at my move before he shakes his head at me.

I roll my eyes in their direction as they make their way down the hallway toward the parking lot and then probably Ace's. Good thing that's not where I'm going.

I grab what I need, before following where they disappeared a few minutes ago.

I head home to freshen up, seeing as I had no plans to see anyone after school, I didn't bother showering after volleyball and whoever my tutor is will probably appreciate me doing that before gracing them with my sweaty presence.

Mom's home when I get there, but as usual she's locked in her office. We haven't spoken since yesterday afternoon. I think she's giving me time to cool off, but right now, I don't feel like forgiving her any time soon. Keeping that from me was wrong, even if she did believe she had until Monday for him to start at school.

I take a quick shower, blow out my hair and pull on a clean shirt and Rosewood High hoodie. Not really feeling like making an effort, I brush a little mascara on my lashes and rub some balm onto my lips.

Checking myself in the mirror, I give my hair one last brush through with my fingers and grab my bag. The red is starting to grow out, I really need to get my roots done but I can't help feeling that it's time for a change. Pink, maybe. I feel like I need to make a statement. Show that his appearance doesn't affect me one bit—which of course is a big fat lie because in reality I've spent every moment since I discovered his arrival looking over my shoulder.

I plug the random address into my GPS and follow the directions. I know the area but I have no idea which street it is.

The street is lined with cars when I drive down it. I spot the house but have to park a ways down and walk up to it. All the houses are slightly run-down bungalows but it's not a bad area.

The driveway is empty when I walk up to the porch and there's no sign of anyone being home.

I look around, worried that I've got the wrong house but the number is clear on the mailbox by the sidewalk so I continue forward, pulling my bag up higher on my shoulder nervously.

The steps creak, probably announcing my arrival the second I stand on them.

I pull the screen open and knock on the door.

Silence.

I knock again.

"Hello?" I call when there is still no answer.

Blowing out a frustrated breath that this has all been one big waste of my time, I'm about to turn around to leave when I sense someone behind me.

"Surprise, Kitten."

5

KYLE

I press the length of my body against her back and I can't fight the smile that curls at my lips as a shudder rips through her.

I couldn't believe my luck when Mr. Wilson passed me her details as my new tutee.

I didn't get a say in taking part in the tutoring program. Bea had already signed me up. It was one of the things—aside from football—that I enjoyed the most during my time at Harrow Creek. I'd been tutoring freshman throughout my junior year. The boy I'd been matched with was keen to learn and soaked up everything I said. It made me feel like I was useful and actually giving something back to the shitpit that was that school.

"K-Kyle?" she breathes as if she can't really believe this is happening right now.

"I was wondering when you'd build up the courage to talk to me. I guess fate took care of that for me, huh?" My nose brushes against the shell of her ear and she trembles once again.

"I'm not scared of you, Kyle."

"And that might be your biggest mistake yet, Kitten."

"Stop calling me that," she hisses.

"Why? You like it, remember. The way you purred that night."

"Stop it," she snaps. "Just stop it."

Stepping forward, I force her to move with me as I reach out and twist the handle.

With my hand on her waist and her back still to my front, I push her inside and close the door behind us.

Before she has a chance to think, I spin her around and slam her back against the wall. She gasps in shock, her eyes going wide and her lips parting.

"You've been avoiding me, Kitten." I rest my forearms against the wall on either side of her head, caging her in. "And I don't like it."

"C-can you blame me? You're not exactly welcoming."

Her eyes hold mine, trying to appear confident but I hear the slight quiver in her voice.

"And to think, I was looking forward to us... reconnecting."

"Whatever you want to do to me, Kyle. Just get it over with."

A humorless chuckle rumbles up my throat.

"What makes you think I want to do anything?"

She growls at me, the sound makes my cock threaten to go full mast. I fucking love her attempt at defiance. It's so sexy.

The house is in silence as we stare at each other, the only noise that can be heard is that of her increased breathing.

A smile pulls at one side of my mouth knowing that my proximity affects her.

The vibrating of a cell catches my attention, I know it's not mine as it's in my pocket.

Dropping one arm, I slip it behind her and run my palm down her back until I cup her ass, finding exactly what I wanted.

"Kyle, what are you—"

"I think I'll take this. You have previous history after all." Pulling her cell from her pocket, I drop it into mine for safe keeping. "No one is coming to your rescue this time, Kitten." I drop my lips to her ear. "Even if you scream." She swallows nervously, a quiet whimper passing her lips.

Pulling back, I look her dead in the eyes.

"I think you lied to me earlier."

She shakes her head.

Lifting my hand, I brush my knuckles down her cheek. Her skin is warm and soft, exactly as I remember. Tucking my fingers under her jaw, I tilt her head up.

"W-what are you doing?" she stutters as I study her.

She looks exactly the same. Her eyes are dark, mysterious and immediately draw me in, her golden skin looks good enough to eat and I know from the sweet scent coming from her that she'll taste fucking divine too. Her lips are full, begging to be kissed and when she sucks the bottom one into her mouth and bites down on it, my urge to claim it as my own almost gets the better of me.

"Remembering that night." My voice is deep as I think back. Lust and anger colliding and sending me into a head spin. "Remembering how you felt on my lap, how you ground down on me." I lower my face to hers so my lips brush the corner of her mouth. "How desperate you were for me to touch you."

I trail my fingertips up her bare leg, her skin breaks out in goose bumps and she shudders when I get to the hem of her skirt.

"Or aren't I enough? Should I get Gray on the phone, see if he wants to come join the party?" It's a low blow and I know it hits exactly as I intended as her body stiffens beneath me.

"Fuck you, Kyle. FUCK YOU," she screams, her arm flying out like she's about to slap me but I'm quicker.

I pin her arm against the wall above her head.

My chest heaves as my anger swells.

"That's what you like though, isn't it? Two of us. Two of us touching you. Two of us making you lose your goddamn mind." My hand snakes up her body, squeezing her small breast through her hoodie as I go before wrapping my fingers around her throat. A move I remember Gray doing that night and how wild her eyes were.

"Get the hell off me," she growls.

"Kane should be home soon." Total lie, once again I have no fucking clue where he is. "Maybe he'd like a turn."

Her teeth grind as her eyes hold mine.

"Such a shame we never got to finish what we started that night, huh?"

Her eyes scan my face and a smile curls at her lips. "Did the boys in juvie finish you off? Bet they loved you. The nerd with the glasses who'll bend to their every whim. I bet the wolves fucking loved you, pretty boy," she spits.

I get right in her face, our noses touching, our breath mingling.

"You need to watch your fucking mouth," I warn.

"And you need to watch your fucking hands."

Before I've had a chance to even register her words, pain radiates out from my groin and I drop to my knees.

"You fucking bitch," I squeal, cupping my junk and my eyes water.

"Whoops," she says innocently, looking down on me with accomplishment in her eyes. "But look how easy you go down." She drops to her haunches in front of me and runs her eyes over my body. "Tell me, Ky. Just how many other boys got their chance with you inside, huh?"

"Jealous?" I ask, the pain finally starting to lessen so I can attempt to stand.

"Of them fucking you over?" She thinks for a minute. "I think I've already done that."

I straighten to full height, and at six-foot-two, that's a hell of a lot taller than her. We stand chest to chest with me staring down at her, rage barely contained behind my eyes as all the things I want to do to her play out like a movie in my head. Yet despite seeing all that, she doesn't back down. Not one little bit.

Stupid, girl. Stupid, stupid girl.

As we stand in silence waiting for who'll break first, an engine rumbles to a stop outside. I'd recognize it a mile away and a smile pulls at my lips.

"Ah, perfect timing, looks like our playmate has arrived."

Harley's throat flexes as she swallows nervously.

"You know Kane has always had a thing for Hunter girls. I'm sure he won't mind that you're the wrong one."

She takes a huge step back, her eyes wide in fear.

"Run, Kitten, and I'll tell Mr. Wilson you refused my support and that will be the easiest bit of what I'll do to you. You owe me, Kitten. So I suggest you do as you're told from here on out."

She looks back at the door when Kane's boots hit the porch.

"Let's get the party started then, shall we?"

We're still staring at each other when Kane pulls the front door open and steps inside.

"Ky—Harley?" I don't look up at him, my eyes are trained on her but I know if I did, I'd find his brows drawn together in concern. He specifically told me to stay away from her and yet here she is standing in the middle of our new little home.

I knew giving her this address was a risk. But there was no fucking way that we were having our first meeting in the library while surrounded by other kids.

Her need to be polite, finally wins out because she rips her gaze from me and turns toward Kane.

"Hey," she squeaks. "Good to see you again."

Kane's eyes shoot to me and narrow in suspicion.

"Is... everything alright here?"

"Yeah, everything is great. You wouldn't believe who I got paired up with to tutor. It's like fate or something."

"Or bad fucking karma," Harley mutters under her breath.

"Are you sure that's a good idea?" He takes a step closer, looking between the two of us.

"Of course. It's great to reconnect after all this time. Isn't that right, Kitten?" I run my hand down her spine until it lands on her ass and I squeeze hard.

"Yeah," she blurts as the pain hits her. "It's great. Making up for lost time."

"O-okay. Shouldn't you have books out or something."

"Thought we'd have a little catch up first, isn't that right, Har?"

"Sure."

"I'll just grab a drink and get out of your hair." Kane continues to look between the two of us but he must not see anything of great concern because as soon as he pulls a can of soda from the refrigerator he disappears down to his room.

I know there's no love lost between him and the two Hunter girls. After everything he's been through with Letty and then Harley getting me locked up, I'm surprised he's allowing her to stay in the house.

The second his bedroom door closes, I take a step toward the table.

"Get your shit out."

"W-what?" she asks, frozen on the spot I just left her in.

"Grab your bag and get your shit out. Where are we starting?"

An unamused laugh falls from her lips. "You're not serious, you don't actually want to do this?"

No, I really fucking don't, but like hell am I letting her know that.

"I need the extra credit for this if I'm ever going to graduate." Lie. "If you walk out right now and I have to tell Wilson that you refused my help, then you'll probably screw me over twice in as many years. So how about you do as you're fucking told and sit your pretty little ass down and get to work."

Her lips part to respond and she gazes at the door longingly but when she finally takes a step, it's toward me.

"Good little kitten."

"Fuck you, Kyle."

"Ah I do love having nice polite students, it makes it that much more of a pleasurable experience."

"Trust me, there is nothing pleasurable about this."

"Huh, maybe we need to add in some extracurricular activities then. I already know you're wet for me."

6

HARLEY

He pulls my bag toward him and drags out my textbooks as if those words didn't just fall from his lips. My mouth opens to respond but I soon close them again when I discover that I have no words.

My head is spinning, my brain is misfiring, and my body is still trembling from how close he was to me earlier.

I want to say his touch disgusted me. I want to say that the reason I didn't fight him off right away was shock, but it wasn't.

My face heats as I think about the sparks that shot around my body the second he laid a hand on me. Just like that night.

There's no doubt in my mind where that night would have gone if things didn't turn out the way they did. If I had any clue that my drink was being spiked, if I had any idea that someone else other than Kyle was getting ideas about where our night was going to go then I'd have run as fast and as far as I could.

"Did you know?" I blurt out, needing an answer to at least one of my questions from that night.

"Did I know what?" he asks, keeping his eyes on the book he's flicking through.

"Did you know he was spiking my drink?"

He pauses and sucks in a breath before dragging his light blue eyes up to mine. Only, they're not the color I was always used to, they're almost silver with his anger, his hatred of me.

"What do you think, Kitten?" he asks, throwing it back on me.

"If I knew the answer to that question then I wouldn't have fucking asked, would I?" I snap, getting beyond frustrated at this situation. I didn't want to meet anyone for a tutoring session as it was, I really, really didn't want this.

I look to the door once more, wondering if he'd actually allow me to escape should I try.

"Go on," he taunts, clearly able to read my mind. "Try it and see how far you get."

"I hate you," I seethe.

"Oh, Kitten. Trust me, how you feel about me has nothing on what I feel for you."

"So let me go, you don't have to look at me then."

"And what would be the fun in that?"

I study him as he scans the page he's selected before him. He's got his backward cap on like he has had every time I've seen him this week with his dirty blond hair poking out the sides, his jaw is covered in a light layer of scruff and his eyes are free from the glasses I teased him about earlier. It's been years since he wore them but I know how much he hated them as a kid.

There's a scar above his right eyebrow that I'm sure wasn't there before and his nose is slightly crooked. It might be my imagination, I'm not sure I've ever really spent any time looking at his nose before but I'm sure that's new. It makes me wonder what his life has actually been like the past year.

He shifts in his seat, telling me that he's aware of my attention although he doesn't look up or do anything about it.

"So, algebra?" he says, making my stomach drop. As if being stuck here with him isn't bad enough, we have to do math too.

I watch as he slides a mask over his face and focuses on what we're supposed to be doing.

"So Mr. Wilson said to start here as it's one of your main weaknesses." My stomach twists at those words. I hate that people think I'm weak because I struggle to add up a few numbers.

"Great," I mutter, reaching for my notepad and a pen.

He slides his chair closer to me as he talks through a technique that I've never been shown before but as much as I try to focus, the heat of his arm burning into mine is too distracting and I find myself zoning out despite the fact this is making much more sense to me than it usually does.

"Harley?" he snaps a few minutes later, dragging me from my own head.

"Yeah."

"I asked you a question."

"Um..." My cheeks burn as his eyes narrow at me. "I... I agree."

"You agree." He chuckles, but there's no humor there, just irritation. "Unfortunately for you, it wasn't a yes or no answer."

"Um..." I hesitate again, my heart racing.

"T-ten?"

"Fucking hell, Harley," he snaps, pushing his chair out behind him and stalking to the other side of the room. "This isn't a fucking joke, Kitten."

"You think I don't know that?" I shout back, standing from the chair and turning to watch him pace. "All of this... it's a fucking mess."

"This... mess," he says, stopping and pinning me with a look. "Is my life," he bellows. "Fucking hell, Harley." He drops his head into his hands and for a second, I actually feel sorry for him. I see the boy from the past, the vulnerable one who just wanted something better for his life. But then that image morphs with my hazy memories from that night and it vanishes almost as fast as it appeared.

"You need to get the hell out of my house." His voice is so low that I think I misheard him.

"W-what?"

"Get out. Just get the fuck out," he bellows before a door down the hallway opens and Kane steps toward me.

He's shirtless and my breathing falters when my eyes first land on him because... whoa, but when Kyle growls and I remember where I am and that I'm supposed to be leaving.

"With pleasure. This was a mistake anyway."

"Don't think that because you're about to walk away that this is over."

"It should be."

"Well, it's not," he warns as I stuff my books into my bag and head for the door.

"Wait," I say, spinning on the balls of my feet and staring right at him. "Cell?" I demand, holding my hand out. There's no way I'm leaving here without that.

He reaches into his pocket and pulls it out. He looks at the screen for a second before a smirk appears on his lips.

"Kyle," Kane warns, clearly sensing where his head is at.

I'm rooted to the spot as he marches toward me. He doesn't stop until his front crashes against mine and I stumble back until I hit the door.

"Kyle?" I breathe. It's hard to think with his heat burning into my skin and his angry eyes boring down into mine.

"Kyle," Kane growls again, but he completely ignores him, his focus solely on me.

"This. Isn't. Over," he says so low that only I can hear the warning.

"I-I'm s-sorry," I stutter, needing to say anything to get me away from him right now before I do something I'll regret. I've already got enough of those to keep me up at night.

A smile pulls at the corners of his lips but it's pure evil.

"It's a bit late for that now, don't you think, Kitten?" His hand slips around my body and he slides my cell into my back pocket where it was when he first found it.

He leans into my ear and my eyes close as his breath caresses my sensitive skin.

"I'll be in touch for our next session soon. I hope that one might be a little more…" I gasp as his hand slips under my hoodie and wraps around my ribs. "Satisfying."

Before I know what's happening, his burning touch is gone and he's opened the door at my back. With a squeal, I go stumbling back until I land on my ass.

"Whoops," Kyle says with a shrug, his eyes locked on my sprawled legs.

"Fucking hell, bro," Kane snaps, stepping forward to help me up.

I take his hand when he offers it to me and he pulls me up.

"T-thank you," I whisper when I'm on my feet again, but I'm unable to look into his eyes with him this close to me. Just his presence makes me nervous let alone being up close and personal to his bare chest.

"Just give him time. He'll come around."

I look around Kane to his little brother who's still fuming behind him. His chest heaves, his lips are pressed into a thin line, his jaw tics with frustration and his eyes are that dark grey once more.

His eyes widen a little in shock when he notices my attention but he soon schools his features so he's scowling once more.

"Yeah, we'll see." I turn away from both of them, hike my bag over my shoulder and try to walk away with as much dignity as I can muster.

I'm halfway down their driveway when Kyle's deep voice makes me pause.

"Make sure you wear those little red panties next time, Kitten."

Lifting my hand, I flip him off over my shoulder and keep walking without looking back at him.

Asshole.

The second I'm in my car, I lock the doors, rest my head back and close my eyes.

My heart continues to race and my palms sweat as I replay our time inside his house.

I knew the first time we got close would be a disaster but I didn't think it would be quite like that.

"Fucking hell," I mutter to myself.

My phone buzzes in my pocket and I'm reminded that it was going off before Kyle stole it.

Lifting my ass from the seat, I pull it out and stare down at the screen. There's one message in our group chat but all the others are from Nathan.

A knot twists in my stomach knowing that Kyle saw he was messaging me. I feel ridiculous for even thinking about it. I have every right to have a boyfriend and for him to message me. Kyle has never been anything to me. Just because my inner pre-teen crushed on him for years and we had one night that could have turned into something before his life changed forever, it means nothing.

I open his messages.

Nathan: Have you had a good day? I've got so much homework to do tonight.

Nathan: I can't wait to see you this weekend.

Nathan: I hate dorms. The music is so loud I can barely think. What are you doing right now?

"Jesus."

I close his messages and open the group chat to find Ruby demanding we all get ready at her place Saturday afternoon for Justin's party.

My thumb hovers over the screen, trying to decide how I'm going to get out of going but I don't bother because I know there's nothing I can say that will achieve what I want. Especially if Nathan is going to be there.

I go back to my conversation with him.

Harley: Sorry… was doing homework with a friend. What's the plan for this weekend? You want to do something Saturday night?

He starts typing instantly but his reply is exactly what I didn't want.

Nathan: Me and you have plans Friday night. Saturday is Justin's party. It's for you guys so you gotta be there.

I groan. The party being for the squad is just an excuse for a party, not that anyone really needs one. No one will give a crap if I'm there or not.

Harley: I'd rather just spend time with you.

A little hope washes through me that he'll happily swerve the party at the promise of something happening.

Nathan: We'll have plenty of time just the two of us.

I roll my eyes. *I'm really not going to get out of this, am I?*

Throwing my cell into the console, I start my engine and pull away from the sidewalk, more than ready to get away from Kyle and the memories of what happened inside that house this afternoon.

If only it was that easy.

7

KYLE

"How the fuck is that staying away from her?" Kane barks, turning his murderous eyes on me.

Shaking my head at him, I spin around and head for my room.

"Don't turn your back on me," he booms, making me stop in the doorway. "I've done all of this for you. Fucking all of it. The least you can do is what you're told."

"Fuck off, Kane. What do you think I'm going to do to her?"

He closes the space between us. His shoulders tense and his fists curled in frustration.

"You're pissed at her, I get it. But you need to leave her alone."

"And why is that?" I ask, taunting him. "Because you don't want to have to see Letty ever again."

His lips twist and I know I'm touching a sore spot.

"This has nothing to do with her."

"Does it not? Why the hell would you care about what I did with Harley otherwise. She's nothing to you."

"No, she's not. None of them are." He's lying, I can see it in his eyes. "You're pissed at her. You want to hurt her for what she did to you, I get it. Hell, I want to as well. But you need to move on unless you want to end up back where you just came from."

I scoff. "You think I'm going to hurt her. Don't you fucking know me at all?"

Turning away from him, I pop the button on my jeans and drop them down my legs in favor of my sweats.

"All I know is that you want revenge, but let me tell you, little brother. It won't make you feel any better."

"Careful, bro. Or you'll get close to admitting what happened with her that night."

"This isn't about me," he bellows, his face turning beet red.

"It's always about you, Kane," I fume, shoving my feet into my sneakers and storming past him.

"No, Kyle. This right now, all of it is about you and making sure you have a future ahead of you. Why the fuck do you think I searched out Jada fucking Hunter to help me with this shit when I want nothing to do with them. It was for you, asshole."

"Oh so now you admit who you went to for help."

"I didn't think you'd have taken it too well to begin with. It was bad enough we were coming here."

"Whatever, bro."

I push through the front door and take off running.

I need something to expel the energy running around my body after having her beneath my hands.

I blink away the image of her dark eyes staring up at me like a scared little mouse.

"Fuck," I scream as I take the path between a couple of the houses and pick up speed. I need to do something that doesn't involve finding out where she lives and finishing what we started.

My fists clench as I remember the way she trembled as I ran my fingertips up her thighs, how I know my words to her at the table were true. If I were to go higher, I know I'd have found those little red lace panties soaking wet for me.

Desire floods my veins and my cock threatens to swell despite the speed I'm going.

I really need to get fucking laid.

I think of those girls I woke up with the other morning. There's no way anything happened with them. I'd have felt a little relief if it had, but as it is, I'm as pent up as I have been since getting locked up and having nothing but my hand to take the edge off.

That cheerleader from the diner pops into my head. She could sure come in useful, but even as I think about it as a possibility, I lose all interest.

I run until my muscles ache and my skin is covered in sweat. I have no idea where I end up and it's only by chance that I manage to find my way back to our street.

Unsurprisingly, Kane's car is gone as I slow to a walk up our driveway. Thankfully, though, he left the front door unlocked. The last thing I need is to spend the night on the porch because the fucker locked me out.

As I make my way through the house toward the bathroom, something on the dining table catches my eye.

I pick up the small baggie of weed and stare down at the note.

Chill out a bit, yeah?

Shaking my head, I leave it where it was and continue forward.

I stand under the warm spray and allow the water to wash the day off me but as I stand there, all I can think about is her. I knew inviting her over was a bad idea but it was the only place I could see our first meeting happening, away from prying eyes.

My cock throbs as I think about how soft her body was, as I remember the little whimper that rumbled up her throat as I touched her. Then I'm back at that party over a year ago as she danced straddled across my lap in her little dress. She was wearing red panties that night too.

My fingers wrap around my shaft as I remember hooking them to one side and running my fingers through her wetness.

"Fuck," I hiss, my other hand resting on the tiles before me as I work myself to release with images of her in my head. Her fucking banging body, her bronzed skin, her dark captivating eyes and her full lips.

"Fuck." My grunt fills the small bathroom as I come into the shower tray.

I tip my head toward the torrent of water but no sooner has my heartbeat returned to normal do I realize that my run and that release have done shit all for me.

Irritated with myself and my need for her, I turn the shower off and step out.

After drying off and dragging on some clean clothes, I grab the baggie of weed and head out to the swing seat on the porch in the hope of doing as Kane suggested and chilling the fuck out.

"My place tonight. Got the house to ourselves," Zayn announces after our conditioning session after school on Friday.

A smile pulls at my lips at his words. I might have only been here a few days but I am more than ready to discover where he—and Harley—live.

"Legend, you in?" he asks, walking over with a towel around his waist.

"Damn straight. I'm ready to see how you party over here."

"Tonight is a quiet one, the real party is tomorrow night. Ain't that right, J?" he calls over to Justin, who is apparently hosting this weekend's official party.

"You got it, man. Parents are already gone but Nathan is kicking me out tonight so he can hang with your sister."

A groan rumbles up Zayn's throat at the mention of Harley but I'm sure it's nothing compared to the way my stomach twists at the mention of her being in a house alone with her boyfriend.

I want to ask about him, about them, but I swallow down my questions. I don't need Zayn looking too closely into things. As far as I know, he has no idea about what went down at that party, just that Harley called the cops and I ended up doing time because of it. I'm sure if he had any idea that I'd had my hands on his little sister then I wouldn't have been invited into his circle the second I appeared here.

"You'd better give him some fucking house rules. I ain't having some prep boy corrupting my little sister, J."

"Nah, Nathan's good people, bro. Plus, I've heard the plans for tonight. That fucker is so whipped by her it's not even funny."

"I don't want to know about my sister whipping anyone."

A few of the guys continue to tease Zayn and make a few suggestions about what Harley might be getting up to tonight but thankfully the second he pins one of them against the wall by their throat, everyone seems to stop. Thank fuck because I was two seconds away from doing something similar and I don't need anyone here looking too deep at my feelings for Zayn's little sister. Hell, even I don't want to put any thought into it. As far as I'm concerned, I want revenge and that is all.

Revenge.

Everyone begins to disappear once they're dressed but as Zayn makes a move to leave, he stops by where I'm shoving my damp, sweaty clothes into my duffel.

"Wanna head back with me now? We could order some pizza before the other fuckers turn up."

"Uh..."

"I've got weed and vodka."

"Sounds great, man." Not that I really needed a sweetener, I just didn't want to look too eager.

"You can follow me back."

The drive to Zayn's place is quick and I do a double-take when he pulls up into a driveway of a fucking massive house.

I knew that his mom had done well for herself but shit. This place is a million miles away from the shitty trailers we grew up in.

"Wow, this place is..." I say after parking behind him and stepping out, my eyes sweeping over the huge home before me.

"I know, right. Bit of a shock after the Creek."

"Fucking right."

"Come on, I'll give you the tour and we can get food."

I nod and follow him inside.

"Jesus," I mutter to myself as I walk into the huge hallway with an impressive staircase leading up to the second floor.

"Afternoon," Zayn sings as he turns left. Footsteps race toward us and when I look up I find his girl jumping into his arms.

"Zayn," another familiar voice—one that gives me tingles—warns. "What the fuck is he doing here?"

"He's just come over to hang before the boys get here. I didn't think you'd mind, you're going out with lover boy." Zayn steps aside as he says those final words and Harley's eyes find mine.

I nod at her in greeting.

"Special night planned, huh?" I ask, accepting a can of soda that Zayn grabs for me from the refrigerator.

She stares at me for a beat, her eyes narrowing in anger.

"I'm going to start getting ready."

Without another word, Harley hops down from the barstool and all but runs from the room.

"Well, that went well," I mutter, taking a seat on the stool she vacated.

"I'm just gonna..."

"Just leave her, Pops. She's going to have to get used to having him around."

Poppy's eyes find mine.

"At school, yeah, but you didn't need to bring him here and rub him in right under her nose."

"I just wanna hang out with my old friend. Is that so bad, baby?" He pulls her into his arms and nuzzles her neck.

"Do you two want to be left alone?" I ask, amusement filling my voice.

"Nope, I'm going to check on Harley. Just... be a little sensitive." Poppy turns her eyes on me and they narrow in warning.

"What? Was I anything but nice?" I ask defensively. In truth, I have no idea what Harley has told her friends about me. They're either as oblivious as Zayn as to what's gone down between us or they know everything.

The way Poppy is looking at me right now, I'd go with the latter. I guess I should expect it really. Chicks tell each other everything.

"I'll come down and find you in a bit." Poppy brushes her lips over Zayn's but pulls back before he can take what he really wants.

He watches her leave, practically drooling as she goes.

"Can't believe your mom allows you to live together," I mutter, wondering why he doesn't just follow her and take what he so clearly wants.

"It's complicated. If she didn't live here, I have no idea where she'd have ended up."

"Your mom likes helping lost kids, huh?"

"You have no idea. Shall we?" he asks, tipping his chin toward the door.

"Sure."

He makes his way through the house as if it's normal—which I guess it is —I, on the other hand, gawk at every room we pass. This place is huge and only makes me appreciate what Jada did that much more. People don't just get out of Harrow Creek, and if they're lucky enough to do so then they really don't find this level of success. It really proves that Jada Hunter is one of a kind.

This is the shit us Creek kids dream of but know in our minds it's totally out of reach. This makes me reconsider. A decent year at Rosewood High and hopefully a shot at a college somewhere and I could do something—do anything—more than the life I'd have been condemned to in the Creek.

"This is my den."

"And it's bigger than our entire house." I gaze around the room at the massive flat-screen TV that takes up almost an entire wall, the floor to ceiling windows that cover another along with two giant couches, a refrigerator and everything else a group of boys would need to entertain themselves for a while.

"You're welcome anytime, man. Mi casa es su casa."

"I'm not sure everyone under this roof would agree with that."

"Harley will get over herself. Just give her time."

I agree with him because there isn't much else to do but I'm pretty sure things are going to get better rather than worse.

I drop down onto one of the couches and prop my feet up on the coffee table.

"This is the life, man. You're a lucky motherfucker, you know that?"

"Yeah." He laughs. "Yeah, I do." He makes himself at home on the other couch, then looks over at me. "So what's the plan then? Year at Rosewood then..."

"Let's see if I survive the year first." He chuckles.

"I know it's only been three days, but that place is like a playground compared to the zoo we're used to. You won't have any problems there. Plus, you're a shoo-in for the team, and you've started tutoring again, right?"

"Uh... y-yeah. Didn't think I told you about that," I mutter, knowing full well that I didn't because I didn't want to tell him that I'd been given Harley as a tutee.

"Nah, Ash mentioned it. You wanna go to college, right?"

"Yeah, I guess. I don't even know if it's possible right now. Kane put everything we have into the house to get me here. I have no idea what the future holds."

"It's whatever you make it, man. Start looking at colleges, see what they need for scholarships, they'd be stupid not to accept you."

"We'll see. One step at a time."

A knock sounds on the door and Ashton pokes his head inside.

"Alright?" He drops down beside me. "Ruby's gone up to help Harley," he explains.

"So basically this is where you two hang out while the girls do their hair and shit?" I ask, looking between them with a smirk.

"That's basically it."

"You know they're probably upstairs right now talking about you both, right?"

"Nah, they're talking about you. Harley fucking hates you, man."

8

HARLEY

"I really fucking hate him," I whine as Ruby slips into my room while I sit at my vanity unit curling my hair.

Poppy sighs. "Focus on tonight. You can't show up to a date with your boyfriend while angry with another boy. Especially if you won't tell us why."

My lips part to tell them about the tutoring session but no words come out.

"You're right. You're right. Just think about Nathan."

"Do you know what he's planning?"

"Nope, just that we've got the house to ourselves because Justin will be here and his little brother is elsewhere."

"Is tonight the night?" Ruby asks, wiggling her hips excitedly.

I'm pretty sure butterflies are supposed to make an appearance in my belly at those words, but they don't. I feel totally flat about tonight.

All I can think about is him and our time together in his house last night and how badly I want to hurt him. To show him that he can't play me like he's trying to, that I won't fall for it.

Damn him. He's been here three freaking days and he's driving me to the brink of insanity already.

"I don't know."

"You could sound at least a little excited or nervous... or anything, to be honest."

"I will be once I get there and see what he's planning. Right now there are too many ideas spinning around my head. I don't want to assume anything and then it not happen."

"How are you so levelheaded about this? I'd be a nervous wreck."

I pin Ruby with a look over my shoulder in the mirror.

"What?"

"N-nothing. What are you wearing?"

I look over to the dress that's hanging on the door to my closet.

"That's cute."

An awkward silence descends on us as I watch the two of them exchange a worried glance behind my back.

"Do you want to fill me in on your little silent conversation?" I snap, my irritation levels growing.

"We're just worried about you. Kyle's arrival has—"

"Has what?"

"Put you in a weird mood. We're just worried about how you're dealing with it."

"There's nothing to deal with. He's here. I'm ignoring him. End of."

"That's why when I walked in you were talking about him?" Ruby raises a brow.

"He's downstairs with Zayn," I tell Ruby.

"Oh."

"Everything is fine. It's just weird seeing him here. My life in Rosewood it's… it's different from the life I had when he was a part of it."

Poppy narrows her eyes at me. "Is there something you're not telling us? He's Zayn's friend, I know you crushed on him but… is there more?"

My skin burns as they both stare at me.

My lips part to lie but I soon find no words come out.

"I freaking knew it."

"You can't tell Zayn, Pops. He'll kill me."

"Zayn doesn't have a leg to stand on, Har. He's banging your bestie so I think you should get a free pass. You've warned him that you're going to enough."

"This was before though," I mutter. "He can't know anything happened between us. It's in the past. Over."

"Which is why it's still affecting you?" Poppy helpfully points out.

"I was young. It was nothing more than that."

"But you've kissed him?"

"Enough," I bark, slamming my straightener down on the counter and standing from my stool. "It's all in the past. Yes, something happened but it was a mistake. It's over. There is nothing between us. He hates me, with good reason. What I need right now is to be as far away from him as possible and to not even be thinking about him as I get ready for a date with my boyfriend." I pin them both with a look and they back down quickly switching up the conversation to some gossip Poppy overheard in physics earlier.

I zone them out as I sit back down to do my makeup, trying like hell to focus on what tonight might hold instead of worrying about the boy downstairs.

"Okay, I'm ready." I hold my arms out at my sides once I've returned from the bathroom after shimmying my dress up my body and wait for the girls' verdict.

"Gorgeous, as always."

"Nathan's not going to know what's hit him," Ruby says. "Are you wearing a bra?" she asks when I spin away from where the two of them are sitting on my bed, showing them the open back.

"No. Is that the wrong thing to do? I don't want him to think—"

"It's perfect. He'll love it."

"Okay," I breathe, blowing out a breath and pulling the short hem down a little. Suddenly the nerves I thought I should have been feeling earlier assault me.

"Throw a jacket on and get out of here. Don't make him wait any longer," Poppy says, climbing from the bed, Ruby quickly following so they can go and find their boys.

Okay, let's do this.

The guys' voices filter up to us as we descend the stairs.

"Harley, baby, you're killing me," Justin announces, his hand over his heart as if he's in pain. "Remind me why I'm allowing him to have the night with you."

"Because if you so much as lay a finger on her, asshole, I'll gut you like a fucking fish," Zayn growls as he emerges from the kitchen, arms loaded with drinks and snacks.

Justin's eyes run the length of me, lingering on my legs longer than should be appropriate. My body heats at his interest despite the death glares he's receiving from my brother.

"Har, don't you think you should wear something a little more..."

"A little more what?" Poppy barks at her boyfriend, taking a step forward as if she's protecting me. "She looks beautiful."

"Hot," Justin scoffs before disappearing around the corner before he gets his ass beat.

Thankfully, Poppy manages to placate Zayn and the second she runs her hands up his chest, he forgets all about me.

"Go on, get the hell out while he's distracted," Ruby says with a laugh, pushing me forward.

"Are you sure this is okay?" I look down at myself, once again second-guessing my outfit choice.

"You look beyond stunning, Har. Nathan's going to love it."

"But you don't think it'll make him think..."

"Har, he's a teenage boy, he'd be thinking that if you turned up wearing a sack."

"I guess," I mutter, glancing back up at the stairs, suddenly wishing I could go and hide.

This time last week there would have been nothing I wanted more than to hang out one-on-one with Nathan. But now... now *he's* shown his face and sent my world into a tailspin I don't know what I want.

"He's a good one, Har. He won't do any more than you're happy with." She says it with so much confidence and internally I wince at myself.

I've always claimed to want a nice boy, one my dad would approve of, but I know that only stems from my past experience with the bad boys.

Without instruction, my head takes me back to Kyle's place and how it felt to be crushed between his body and the door. My heart rate increases. Given half the chance, he'd have taken exactly what he wanted. If Kane wasn't right there watching, I have no doubt it would have gone farther. The warning was right there in his eyes, his need evident in his demanding touch.

And you would have let it happen. I shake the little voice from my head but as I do, I turn back to say goodbye to Poppy and Ruby. They're standing at the bottom of the stairs where I left them but it's not them that capture my attention. That's the boy standing in the doorway to Zayn's den with the dangerous eyes.

My breath catches as our gazes lock before he rips his away in favor of my body. He's wearing his standard backward cap, a black hoodie with the sleeves pushed up to his elbows, and dark jeans with his hands stuffed in the pockets. From the tightness of the muscles in his forearms, I'd say that his fists are clenched right now and it sends a bolt of excitement through me that I can cause a reaction out of him.

"Okay, well…" I say, holding his narrowed stare. "I guess I'll see you guys later. Don't do anything I wouldn't do."

"Shouldn't we be saying that to you?" Ruby chuckles.

With a smile in Kyle's direction, I turn back around and reach for the front door to make my escape and see what my night holds, only I don't get out of the house before Poppy opens her mouth and makes me wish the ground would swallow me up whole.

"You got condoms, right?"

"Fuck my life, I can't listen to this shit," Zayn grumbles and stalks off.

"I'll see you all later." The excitement that zipped through me only seconds ago vanishes as I close the door behind me and blow out a long breath.

Tonight's going to be fun, it's what you've wanted since you first met Nathan a few weeks ago.

I force my legs to carry me to my car and drop down, resting my head back and sucking in another calming breath.

After a moment, I pull myself together, start the engine and begin backing out of the driveway, only the second I look up, I lock eyes with *him* standing at one of the hallway windows.

Not needing to get lost in his hate stare, I rip my eyes away, pretending I didn't see him, put the car into drive and slam my foot down on the pedal to get away from him.

The faster that happens, the better. My life was perfectly fine before he decided to gate crash it with his pretty face and haunting eyes.

School was good—math aside—cheer was epic, and I had a nice boy, someone who wanted to treat me right and make me smile.

Why does all of that seem so pointless now?

Damn him.

I'm at Justin's house in record time and pulling up next to his Porsche.

Nerves make my hands tremble against the wheel. Shaking my head at myself, I pull down my visor and check my hair and makeup before swinging the door open and climbing out.

I'm putting too much thought into all of this. I'm just coming to hang out.

The front door is open before I get halfway across the driveway and Nathan's eyes track down my body, just like someone else's did not so long ago.

I banish thoughts of him from my head as I climb the couple of steps up to the front door.

"Harley, you look… wow."

A smile tugs at my lips and I slip my hand into the one he's holding out for me. Wrapping our joined hands around my back, he pulls me into his body and drops his lips to mine.

"Hey," I say almost shyly when he pulls back.

"Hey, I'm so glad you're here," he says, his eyes bouncing between mine.

"Me too," I whisper honestly. Now I'm here and I can put everything that was going on at my house behind me, I'm actually excited.

He smiles at me and I'm reminded of the night at Ethan's a few weeks ago when we first met. His dark hair is styled perfectly, his hazel eyes have that same sparkle and his jaw is so sharp and square it makes me want to trace it with my fingertip.

"Come in, you must be freezing."

He doesn't release me as he drags me in and swings the door closed behind us.

"I… uh… wasn't sure what to wear."

"You could wear anything and still look beautiful, Harley." His hand wraps around the back of my neck as heat plumes in my belly.

His lips brush mine once again before his tongue trails along my bottom one. Eagerly my lips part for him and he more than willingly ramps things up. His other hand drops to my waist, pressing us tightly together until I have no choice but to feel his length between us.

"Did you cook?" I ask when he finally lets me up for air.

"Kind of. I'm not really any good in the kitchen. Come on." He laces his fingers through mine and pulls me farther into the house after allowing me to take my heeled booties off and leave them with the others in the hallway.

As we make our way down the hall, it gets darker and a twinkle starts from the very far room which I already know is Justin's living room.

"Oh wow," I breathe when I step inside the room to find fairy lights strung up and a picnic already laid out on a rug in the middle of the room.

I glance over at him as he studies me shyly, waiting for my response.

"You did all this for me?"

He shrugs. "I just wanted tonight to be something you might remember."

I swoon, I can't help it. Nathan is like the perfect boyfriend. Everything I've wished for since moving to Rosewood.

"It's perfect. What's to eat?" I ask, stepping onto the blanket and lowering down beside the basket.

"Literally everything I could think of." He laughs, coming to sit on the other side and opening the lid, allowing me to see the insane amount of food inside.

"You know it's only the two of us, right?" I ask with a laugh just to confirm that he's not planning on feeding the entire team tonight.

"I know. I just wasn't sure what you liked. We've only eaten together a couple of times and both times were pizza so..."

"Fair enough." I help him lay it all out before us, a smile playing on my lips the entire time.

"I sure hope you're hungry," he says to me once the basket is finally empty.

"Yeah, I am. I was too nervous to eat lunch," I admit. Although I keep the fact that it wasn't entirely because of him to myself. This is a Kyle Legend free zone.

"Yeah?" he asks like I've just told him that tomorrow is Christmas or something.

"Yeah. This is nice having no one else around."

"At last, right? Any preference?" he asks, holding up the TV remote.

"Music?"

"Sure."

He clicks through a few channels before deciding on one and lies back so he's on his side and rests on his elbow, giving me a chance to really check him out.

He's wearing a navy Henley with the arms pushed up to the elbows and a dark, almost black, pair of jeans. It's not all that much different to *him,* the main difference being that the clothes that are wrapped around Nathan's body are branded with labels that I'm sure might impress his prep school friends but they do very little for me. They're just clothes. I couldn't give a crap about the name on them.

I stare at the sliver of skin that is exposed around his waist and bite down on my bottom lip at the sight of the red waistband of his boxers. Nathan is fit, that much is obvious but he's much leaner than *him*. I guess that's not hard really seeing as it looks like he's spent his entire year away inside the prison gym.

My stomach clenches at the thought of him being locked up but I stuff it back down. I shouldn't be thinking about all of that right now.

I'm sitting here with an incredible guy who looks at me like I'm something special and my head is with someone else, someone I don't want it to be with.

"Are you okay? You seem a little distant." Concern fills his voice and I hate it. "I know we haven't talked much this week, I was just hoping it was because you were busy?" he suggests.

"Y-yeah, it was. I'm sorry, things have just been a bit crazy this week. I've fallen out with my mom, schools been hard work. I'm sorry, I really want to enjoy this with you."

He smiles at me, his concern thankfully dissipating.

"Just relax, yeah. You don't need to worry about any of that tonight."

I blow out a slow breath. "That sounds so good."

"Here," he says, offering me the bowl of chips that is closest to him. Reaching out, I take a couple and throw them into my mouth.

"So you've both got the house to yourself for the weekend? Don't they miss you at school?"

"Nah, no one will even notice. And it's not like my parents will care."

His expression doesn't falter but I see something flicker through his eyes. Pain.

"How come you don't want to go out of state for college?" I ask. He's already told me that he's been accepted to MKU but the way he talks about school and his parents, I wouldn't have thought he'd want to stick around.

"I don't know," he mumbles around a sausage roll. "It's home, I guess. Just feels right."

"Fair enough."

"You any closer to making any decisions?"

"Nah, not yet. I've got plenty of time," I say, although as the words fall from my lips I can hear Mom's voice in my head nagging at me to make a decision about my future.

I understand her need to ensure the three of us are all well educated but I really don't need the pressure. Right now, I need to get those damn test results up before I even think about applications.

We chat away about nonsense while we pick at the food he's laid out.

"You sure you don't want one?" he asks, knocking the top off his second bottle of beer.

"No, thank you. I need to drive home."

"Do you?" he asks, looking at me from under his long dark lashes.

My stomach flutters in anticipation.

"I… uh… I don't know. But I want the option."

"Think you're going to need to run away from me?"

"Who knows. You might turn out to be a murderer yet," I joke.

He chuckles. "I could well be. Have you finished?" He nods down to the leftover food that neither of us has touched in a while.

"Yeah, I'm good. Thank you, it was delicious."

"It was just a picnic."

"Best picnic I've ever had," I say with a wink as I help him pack it all up.

"There's no need to sweeten me, babe. I'm already all yours."

I shake my head at him and follow him through to the kitchen to dispose of everything.

"Did you get anything for dessert?" I ask, spinning to watch him move effortlessly around the kitchen as he tidies up.

I bite down on the inside of my cheek as I watch his muscles pull across his shoulders as he works.

"Yeah, I got—" His words falter when he turns and finds me staring at him. "Fuck," he breathes, lifting his hand and running his fingers through his hair as he stares back at me.

My skin heats as his eyes drop down my body, my nipples puckering against the fabric of my dress at his attention.

"What?" I ask, a shy smile pulling at my lips when he doesn't do or say anything for long seconds.

"You, you're just so… I don't even know."

"Thanks, I think. So dessert?"

"Oh, y-yeah." He clears his throat and turns toward the refrigerator but I don't miss him rearranging himself before he pulls the door open.

The knowledge that I affect a guy like Nathan makes me feel like a freaking queen.

Pushing from the counter I was leaning against, I walk up to him and wrap my arm around his waist as I peer inside.

"I got these," he says, pulling out a couple of chocolate mousse cups.

"Perfect. I just need something a little sweet."

I take one from him as he closes the door but I don't get a chance to walk away because he's faster and he spins us until my back is once again pressed against the counter, only this time, he steps right into me.

I part my legs, allowing one of his thighs to slide between as our hips meet. He stares down at me, his eyes searching mine.

"I can't get enough of you, Harley," he whispers, his hand landing on my waist and sliding up until it stops on my ribs, less than an inch from my breast which becomes heavy, desperate to feel his touch.

"I'm right here, Nathan."

"You make me lose my mind," he admits, his nose brushing against mine. "But I'm trying to do the right thing here."

I have no idea if he's been with other girls. From his looks and the fact he's one of Maddison Prep's star basketball players, I would be very surprised if he hadn't been with at least a few. He certainly seems to know the right moves and the right words to say to make me melt. But I appreciate that he's keeping things slow. I haven't told him that I'm a virgin but I think he knows. It's why he's holding back. Letting me take the lead.

"You say that like I'm a good little girl," I breathe, our lips so close that the heat of his burns into mine.

"Harley," he groans as if he's in pain as his length hardens between us.

If I were a different member of Rosewood's cheer squad then I'd probably already be on my knees for him. But I'm not, and nor do I want to be.

Our squad's reputation needs to change and once the seniors graduate, it's one of the things Ruby and I want to work on, should we both get voted to take charge that is.

"Kiss me."

His fingers tighten around my ribs a second before his lips take mine in a bruising kiss.

Unlike when I first arrived, there's no restraint on Nathan's part. His kiss is hard, wet and dirty and I soon find myself drowning in it—in him.

A groan rumbles up his throat as his tongue delves into my mouth and a rush of heat floods me.

"Harley, fuck," he grunts into our kiss.

Abandoning his dessert, his large palm wraps around the back of my thigh and he lifts my leg from the floor, wrapping it around his hip and opening me up to him.

I gasp, breaking our kiss, then his hardness presses against my sensitive core.

"Good, huh?" he asks smugly but he doesn't give me a chance to respond to how it feels because he dips his head, his lips latching onto my neck.

"Oh God," I whimper as he sucks on a sensitive spot beneath my ear. An entire body shudder rips through me at the move.

"We should probably get out of the kitchen," he mumbles against my skin after a few minutes.

"Uh... y-yeah," I agree, although I have no idea if my legs will hold me up and allow me to walk anywhere right now.

He pulls back, his eyes scanning my face but the second mine land on his lips, I can't help but laugh.

Reaching out, I run my thumb along his full bottom lip and rub at my lipstick.

"It's not really your color," I admit, holding my thumb up for him to see the dark makeup.

"I don't care what color it is as long as it's come from you. Come on."

He takes a step back and thankfully, I don't collapse to the floor on my jelly legs. He takes both of the desserts that had been abandoned on the counter in one hand than mine in the other.

Part of me wonders if he's about to lead me upstairs, and a refusal is right on the tip of my tongue when we turn back to the living room.

I don't like my initial reaction to the prospect of us taking this further, especially after just being like putty in his hands.

Maybe tonight isn't the night.

I hate that he might be disappointed if I can't go through with it, but a big part of me knows that he'll understand.

I don't realize my steps falter as I look to the stairs.

"What—oh. Did you want to..." He trails off and I look past him into the room, not wanting to see any excitement in his eyes.

"No, here's good. We could... err... find a movie or something."

"Yeah," he agrees without missing a beat and continues leading me inside.

He throws a few extra cushions down on the floor and we retake our places on the blanket as he flicks through the movie channels to find something suitable.

He finally lands on some high school rom-com and places the remote down. It's not really my kind of movie but I don't complain. I have a feeling we're not really going to be watching it anyway.

I'm still trying to get comfortable as he pulls the top of my dessert off.

"Here," he says, holding out a spoonful of chocolate goodness.

"I can feed myself, you know," I say with a laugh.

"Humor me." He gives me one of his knee-weakening smiles, dimple and all and I cave.

I part my lips and allow him to slide the spoon past them before I close my mouth around it. The sweetness almost immediately explodes on my tongue and I can't help but close my eyes and groan. It's so freaking good, and exactly what I needed.

"Fuck, babe. You're killing me."

"It's so good."

"Yeah?" he asks, lowering the spoon back to the cup but instead of trying it, he leaves the cup where it is and scoots closer. "Let's see how good."

His hand cradles the back of my head and he lowers his lips to mine.

"Mmm... I didn't think you could taste any better."

The length of his body presses against me, one of his legs threading through mine as he continues to kiss me.

"Nathan," I moan when he once again attacks my neck, licking, sucking and nipping at the skin.

My entire body grows hot and it feels like my skin is suddenly too small.

"Yeah, babe? Tell me what you need."

"I... I..." I stutter because while my body knows exactly what it needs, my head isn't entirely on board.

His hand skims down my body. I gasp when his thumb catches my nipple but he doesn't stop, instead, he descends until his palm lands on my bare thigh.

"This dress, Harley. It's sinful."

I bite down on my bottom lip, wondering once again if wearing it was a mistake.

"Do you have any idea how sexy you look right now?" My chest heaves as I watch him take in every inch of my body. "The things I want to do to you," he murmurs, and my stomach twists. But my thoughts are cut off when his lips find mine once more and I lose myself in his kiss, in his burning touch.

His hand lifts until it's under the hem of my skirt.

Heat floods me a second before his thumb brushes the fabric covering me.

"Fuck, babe. You're soaked," he whispers in my ear.

My back arches as he presses against me a little harder.

"You want me to touch you, babe? You want me to make you come?" His voice is so deep and rough in my ear and my eyes close of my own accord.

My breathing is erratic, my heart out of control in my chest as his own rapid breaths caresses my neck and shoulder.

"Nathan," I moan again when his lips latch onto my neck and he sucks hard enough to leave a mark. "Oh God," I cry out when he slips my panties aside and runs his fingers through my folds.

His body vibrates with his growl of approval at how ready he finds me.

My eyes squeeze tight and my back arches once more as my body tries to absorb the sensations he's igniting within me.

It's not the first time someone's touched me like this but it's not— "No," I cry, suddenly sitting up.

It takes a second to register what's happening but the second I do, I drop my head into my hands.

"I'm sorry," I mutter, it's muffled against my palms so I have no idea if he can hear me or not.

My face burns and my eyes fill with tears that I've just rejected him like that. And the reason… no. I can't. I can't even think about it or I'll fall off the ledge I'm already precariously balancing on.

"I'm sorry," he says softly, wrapping his fingers around my wrist and trying to pull my hands from my face but I fight him. "It's my fault. I shouldn't have pushed you. I'm sorry."

Sucking in a calming breath, I wipe at my eyes before pulling my hands away.

"I think I should go."

"No, Harley. It's okay. You don't need to—"

"I do. I'm so sorry I ruined your night. All of this," I say, gesturing to what he's done for me. "All of this was perfect. I'm sorry."

I run before he has time to stand and I'm already in the hallway shoving my feet into my booties and pushing my arms into my jacket when he finally joins me.

"Please don't run. We can watch the movie. Just chill out."

His hands land on my upper arms to stop me and when I refuse to look him in the eyes, he ducks down so I have no choice.

"I'm sorry," I whisper again, my voice full of emotion.

"Harley, stop." One of his hands cups my cheek and he catches the tear that falls with his thumb. "It doesn't matter."

I rip my eyes from his, too embarrassed to look into them, but when I look down, I find his cock still tenting his jeans and I hate myself all over again.

What the hell is wrong with me? I've got the kindest, sweetest guy standing in front of me practically begging me to spend time with him yet when I close my eyes all I see is *him.*

It's been over a year since I was anywhere near him. I shouldn't even remember that night, let alone allow it to fill my mind when I should be enjoying my time with my boyfriend.

"It… it does to me. I'm sorry."

Pulling myself from his grip, I pull the front door open and race through it.

9

KYLE

It's nice feeling part of something again and as I look around at Zayn's friends, I wonder if this was where I was supposed to be all along.

There's music playing in the background and there are football replays on the TV but no one's paying any attention to them, they're either too drunk, high or have a girl in their lap. Okay, so that's just Zayn and Ashton whose girls are here. For some reason, they've banned any others from joining us tonight. Seems a little unfair if you ask me but there we go.

"You two wanna take it upstairs. I might have missed you, bro, but I don't want to see your cock," I slur at Zayn who's got Poppy grinding down on his lap beside me. "Unless you wanted me to join. I'm sure I could teach your girl a thing or two."

"Shut the fuck up, Legend, and keep your fucking hands to yourself," he growls although he never lifts his head from his girl's neck.

"Touchy," I mock. "I bet Ash isn't so possessive."

"I wouldn't put any money on that bet, man. You want to get your dick wet, just wait until the cheer squad are off their faces tomorrow night. You'll have them lining up to welcome you to Rosewood properly."

"Zayn," Poppy squeals. "You're a pig."

"You gonna try telling him that it's not true?" He stares at his girl with his brow raised.

Her lips are swollen from his kiss, her cheeks are red and her eyes are blown with lust. Reaching down, I rearrange my semi. Fuck, I want a girl looking like that on my lap.

"Err… no, he's right. They're a bunch of whores. Just be careful, yeah. We all know where they've been." She glances around the room before training her eyes back on her boy.

"Hey, I'm a one-woman man."

"Now you are," she points out.

"Damn fucking straight and I'm about to prove it. Excuse us." Zayn stands with Poppy still in his arms and after telling everyone in the room to fuck off out of his house, they disappear out the door.

"Pussy-whipped motherfucker," someone calls after him.

"Let's get the fuck out of here. The juniors are partying at Richstone's. Shall we?"

A round of agreement sounds out and after a few minutes, everyone starts to leave.

"Fury, Rubes, you coming?"

"She's fucking coming alright."

"Ashton." If Ruby was supposed to be chastising him then it fails massively when his name leaves her lips as a moan.

"Fuck, I need to get laid," Justin mutters before he follows the others from the room.

"Right, well, I'll leave you two to it."

"Appreciated, man," Ash says as he kisses down Ruby's chest. "Work out in the morning?"

"Sure. Message me when you don't have a chick attached to you."

He flips me off behind Ruby's back and I slip out of the room, closing the door behind me to give them some privacy.

I've got my hand on the front door, about to rip it open when I look over my shoulder at the stairs. A smirk pulls at my lips as an idea hits me.

Jada's out and the two couples left in this house are most definitely preoccupied, so…

Before I've finished processing the thought, I'm halfway up the stairs that I'm hoping will lead me to Harley's bedroom.

"Oh God, Zayn," Poppy cries out when I hit the top step.

I shake my head, wondering how Jada and Harley put up with that shit on probably a daily basis before I come to a stop at the door opposite where the noise is coming from and push it open.

I know it's hers almost immediately and not just because the walls are as red as her hair but it smells like her. Everything about the space is just like her.

Closing the door behind me, I step into the middle of the room, taking everything in.

I'm standing at a bookcase on the other side of the room, running my eyes over the insane number of framed photos she has when the door opens behind me.

I was so lost staring at snippets of her life that I didn't hear any movement outside the room.

Her sobs rip through the room and when I spin around, I find her with her back to the door and her face in her hands.

Okay, this was not what I was expecting.

I open my mouth to say something but soon realize I have no words.

I watch her for long seconds as she crumbles before me.

Part of me enjoys seeing her pain after the agony she sentenced me to this past year, but there is a softer part buried somewhere deep inside me that feels for her and wants to help. Sadly, when she does realize that she's got an audience, it's not that nice part of me that emerges.

I take a step forward and the floor beneath my feet creaks loud enough to be heard over her cries.

Her head lifts from her hands and her eyes go wide as a scream rips from her throat.

I'm on her in a heartbeat, my hand wrapped around her mouth so she doesn't alert Zayn.

Her tear-filled eyes stare into mine. Confusion, shock, and misery swim in them.

"Hey, Kitten. What a surprise to see you here." I smirk down at her as she claws at my forearm, desperately trying to remove my hand from her mouth.

"Get the hell out of my room, asshole," she seethes the second I release her.

I chuckle, stepping closer and forcing her to press herself back against the door.

"I think I might hang around for a bit if it's all the same to you. It looks like you might need some company, Kitten." Lifting my hand, I reach out to wipe at her tear tracks but she snaps her head to the side before I can touch her.

"What's wrong? Couldn't he get it up for you?"

"Fuck you, Kyle."

"Ah, was that the problem?" I lean in until my lips brush the shell of her ear. "That he wasn't me?"

She gasps but at no point does she try to argue, which I find interesting.

"Get the hell away from me and out of my house."

Her palms slam down on my chest and she pushes but her strength is no match for mine.

"It's almost cute that you think you can push me around."

"If you'd just leave me alone then I'd have no reason to touch you, let alone push you."

"And what would be the fun in that. I wouldn't want you to forget me."

"Trust me, that's impossible," she spits, staring up at me with her top lip curled in disgust.

"Why's that, Kitten? Am I in here?" I tap her temple with two of my fingers.

"Will you stop touching me?"

"No. No, I don't think I will. Do you know why?"

"If I let you tell me, will you do me a solid and get out of my fucking bedroom?"

I pretend to think about it. "No."

She rolls her eyes at me, and I reach out and take her chin in my hand.

"Ow," she complains, pulling at my arm in the hope it'll make me let go.

"What happened tonight, Kitten? What did that motherfucker do to have you back here before midnight in tears?"

"N-nothing."

"Oh really? You two had the entire house to yourselves for the night so I heard, so in my mind, you should probably be naked right about now."

I step into her body, my knee pushing between hers and my hips pinning her to the wall.

"J-Just because we had an e-empty house, it doesn't mean—"

"You're trying to tell me that he wanted to play scrabble, Kitten?" She tries turning her face away from me, but my grip tightens and I hold her in place ensuring she has nowhere else to look but into my eyes.

"So what happened?"

She purses her lips shut, refusing to talk to me, although whatever it is that sent her running is still playing on her mind because her eyes are still full of unshed tears.

Tension crackles between us as I silently plead with her to tell me so I know if I need to go and knock the stupid motherfucker out for making her cry while she begs me to let it go and leave her alone.

She might not have figured it out yet, but only one of us is winning this silent battle.

"Shall I tell you what I think, if you're not going to tell me what I need to know?"

Her eyes narrow at me but still, her lips remain sealed.

"Okay." I smirk at her. "I think Prep Boy isn't who you really want. I think you know that he can't give you what you need. You think he's who you should want. You think he'll look after you with his fancy fucking car and weighty trust fund.

"But he doesn't do it for you, does he?

"See, you can take the girl out of the trailer park, Harley, but you can never take the trailer park out of the girl."

Her breathing increases as I talk, her chest heaves and her nostrils flare with her need for air where she still refuses to part her lips.

"I think..." I continue. "He touches you like you're made of glass. Like you're something precious that he needs to treasure. Whereas—"

She gasps, "Kyle," as I rip her jacket from her arms and throw it to the floor behind me.

In seconds, I have both of her wrists pressed against the door above her head in one of my hands.

"Oh, so now you have something to say. Kinda proves my point, don't you think?"

"You have no idea what you're talking about."

A smug smile pulls at my lips. "Don't I? I know you, Harley Hunter. I know you better than you think I do, and I know exactly what you need. Want me to prove it to you?"

Her eyes hold mine, shining brightly with defiance, daring me to do exactly what I just said although she's terrified to actually demand it of me.

I crowd myself against her, loving the heat of her skin against my body. It's been too fucking long since I've felt anyone's body against mine and I fucking crave more.

Skin on skin.

My cock aches at the thought of having her bare beneath me to show her just how it should be done.

"You look so beautiful when you cry." My voice is softer than it was before and her eyes narrow in suspicion.

Leaning forward, I lick up her cheek. Her salty tears coat my tongue and the need that's growing within me almost explodes.

I've no doubt I could lift her against the door right now and take her. She might want to fight me. She might hate me. But there's no denying what her body wants. She wanted it that night and she wants it now despite her spending the evening with her prissy boyfriend.

"There's just one problem though." I cup her cheek tenderly and swipe a fresh tear with my thumb. Leaning in closer so our lips are almost touching, I tell her what I'm really thinking. "I wasn't the one who made you do it. *He* did."

She gasps as my hand wraps around her throat. Her lips parting and her eyes widening.

"Now tell me, Kitten. Why did that motherfucker make you cry on your big night?"

"Leave please," she begs but there's no strength behind her words. It's what she thinks she should be saying.

"Kitten, stop trying to be a good little girl, we both know you aren't. Tell me the truth."

"Fuck you."

"Trust me. I'm about thirty seconds from doing just that."

She swallows nervously under my grip, her pulse hammering against my fingertips.

"Oh, is that what you want? You want me to fuck you, Kitten?"

"No, I—"

"Wasn't he man enough for the job? Do we need to show him just how it's done?"

I drop my lips to her neck and bite down on the sensitive skin right above where my thumb is digging into her flesh.

"Kyle," she cries, her knee lifting as if she's going to take another shot at me.

Not this time, baby.

I thread my knee between her thighs once again and ensure it pushes against her pussy, knowing that she's not going to resist the urge to grind on me if she's as turned on as I think she is.

"Fuck, you taste too good to be so bad."

I drag my teeth down her collarbone, the heat of her skin damn near burning my lips.

"Did he do this to you, Kitten? Did he kiss every inch of this sinful body before he made you cry?"

"Kyle, you need—" she whimpers but her words are cut off when I make my way down to the neckline of her dress and the swell of her breast.

"Did he get here, Kitten? Did he find out that you weren't wearing anything beneath your dress?"

She shakes her head and it's damn near impossible to contain my smile.

"What a stupid motherfucker. Right there for the taking and he didn't unwrap you and take what was his."

I drag the front of her dress down and expose her breast. Small, perfect and begging for my lips.

"Oh God," she gasps as I suck her peak into my mouth and swirl my tongue around the hard bud.

"This what you needed, Kitten?"

"Fuck, you need to stop, Kyle. We shouldn't be—"

"Fuck what we should and shouldn't do, Harley. You fucking owe me, and I want to fucking punish you for it."

"W-what are you going to do?"

I don't answer her, mainly because I don't have one.

I've pictured a million and one ways I've wanted to hurt her for what she did to me that night. But now we're here, her scent filling my nose and her taste is on my tongue, all I want to do is take.

Take everything from that stupid motherfucker who wasn't man enough to make her his.

I work my way back up to her neck and drag my lips across her cheek until they're hovering right above her full lips.

My mouth waters to kiss her. To remember exactly what it was like to lose myself in her and forget the outside world and all the bullshit in our lives.

But I don't.

Instead, I find the bottom of her dress and lift it higher, not that it's covering much as it is.

"What about here, Kitten?"

I rub my fingertips along her lace-covered seam. She trembles in my hold, her throat working on overdrive as she swallows and her pulse races.

A whimper falls from her lips but I refuse to give her anymore until she answers me.

"Kitten?"

Her eyes hold mine, narrowing in anger and frustration.

"If you want more, you're going to need to answer my question."

"I hate you," she seethes.

"And yet you're so fucking wet for me. Are you lying to me, Kitten?"

"No. I really fucking hate you."

"Good," I snap, startling her. "Because I really fucking hate you too. Now tell me, did he touch you."

Something sparkles in her eyes and her lips twitch at the corners.

"Yes," she states proudly. "Yes, he had his fingers all over my pussy. That what you wanted to hear?"

Something explodes within me and I rip my hand from her throat and slam it down on the door beside her head, startling her.

"Kyle, what the fuck?"

"This..." I say, cupping her with my entire hand, her juices coating my fingers even through the lace as her heat burns me. "This is mine. Do you understand that?"

"He's m-my boyfriend."

"Who sent you home tonight from your date crying. I really think you should reconsider, Kitten."

"F-for you?" she stutters.

A wicked chuckle falls from my lips. "No, Kitten. I already own you."

"Kyle," she squeals as I rip her panties aside and sink my fingers into her wetness.

"So fucking wet for me, Kitten. How long have you been thinking about this, about me touching you?"

Her lips part but as I push deeper into her heat, no words come out.

I press the length of my body against her as my finger continues to work her, stroking her walls as her muscles clamp down around me. Her hands wrap around my forearm, her nails digging in but at no point does she try to stop me or pull me away, just like I knew she wouldn't.

"Did he feel this good?" I groan in her ear, my cock rubbing against her hip desperate to get in on the action.

She shakes her head violently from side to side.

"Kyle," she gasps when I slide a second digit inside her. "Oh God."

I bend my fingers, searching out her sweet spot as her juices continue to drip down my hand.

"Did he make you come?" I whisper in her ear but this time she remains silent. "Answer me, or I stop. Did. He. Make. You. Come?"

She shakes her head, although a little less enthusiastically than before.

A smile tugs at one side of my lips. *Fucking prep school pussy.*

"Why, Kitten? Why couldn't he get you like this?" I pull back to watch her as she rides my hand.

The straps of her dress have fallen from her shoulders, lowering the neckline of her dress, and although her breasts are covered, it doesn't leave much to the imagination. Her chest heaves, exposing her nipples every time she sucks in a ragged breath.

Her teeth attack her bottom lip as she races toward the end, her entire face is flushed hot and her eyes are tightly closed.

"Look at me," I demand, hating that in her head she could be elsewhere right now. She could be imagining she's with *him*.

After a beat, her eyelids flicker open and her dark, lust-filled eyes find mine.

"Why didn't he make you come, Kitten?"

"B-because... shit," she gasps as I press my thumb to her clit. Her eyes shutter but they don't completely close.

"Because?"

"Oh God," she whimpers, her pussy clamping down on me as her orgasm begins to crest.

I immediately stop moving.

It takes her a few seconds to register what's happening but when she does, her expression hardens.

"You're a fucking asshole, Kyle."

"Never claimed to be anything else, Kitten. Now tell me what I need to know and I might give you what you need."

"You might?" she sasses.

"Well, I wouldn't be the first one to leave you hanging tonight it seems."

Her lips purse in anger.

"Now, Kitten, tell me why he couldn't get you off."

"Why do you care?"

"Because you came home crying. I want to know what he did to cause that so I know how badly I need to fuck him up."

"No," she cries. "No, don't touch him."

"Why not?" I growl, getting right in her face, our noses touching and our breaths mingling.

"B-because..." I stroke her G-spot encouragingly. "Because he wasn't you," she spits, her eyes going wide a beat later as she realizes what she just confessed.

A wide smile spreads across my face as my chest swells.

"Were you thinking about me, Kitten, while he was finger fucking you?"

Her lips press into a thin line, stopping herself from saying anything else she'll regret.

"Fuck, do you have any idea how hard that makes me?"

Reaching out, I peel her hand from the door and place it against my crotch.

"Kyle," she whimpers as her fingers flex around my length.

I work my jaw as I attempt to restrain myself.

"So, let me get this straight…" My fingers begin to move again. "While he was knuckles deep in your pussy, your eyes were closed and you were imagining that it was me. Fuck, Kitten."

"Kyle, Kyle, fuck," she whimpers as her lost orgasm returns.

Her body locks up and I lean into her ear as she rides out of the waves of pleasure I've allowed her to have.

"You're really going to regret admitting that to me, Kitten," I warn, my voice low and menacing.

The second her body goes limp, I remove all my contact and step away. If I don't put some space between us right now then I'm not going to be able to stop.

"Open," I demand, lifting my fingers to her lips.

She refuses and my anger ratchets up a few notches.

"I said open," I growl, my hand returning to her throat.

Her lips part in surprise and I push my fingers into her hot mouth.

She sucks my fingers, her tongue licking at my skin, tasting herself and my restraint snaps.

Pulling my fingers from her mouth, I slam my lips down on hers, needing to taste her. My tongue invades her mouth, searching for hers. I half expect her to push me away, to knee me in the nuts again but all she does is sag in my hold and kiss me back.

Reaching out, I wrap my hands around the backs of her thighs and lift her, dragging her away from the wall and carrying her deeper into her room.

The second my shins hit the edge of her bed, I release her, throwing her down in the middle and watching her bounce with her dress hitched up around her waist, showing me her tiny, soaked panties.

Lifting my hand, I run my thumb over my bottom lip, remembering just how hers felt.

"Next time," I warn. "I'm not going to walk away so easily." I spin on my heels and march to her door.

She's silent behind me aside from her heaving breaths.

"And, Harley?" I ask, keeping my eyes on the wood before me, knowing that if I look back all bets are going to be off. "Get rid of the Prep Boy before I break him."

10

HARLEY

I laid awake for hours last night, tossing and turning and trying to get the events of the evening out of my head.

I was so angry at myself as I walked away from Nathan. I felt so pathetic.

He's perfect. Literally everything about him is perfect yet when he touched me it was nothing like how it felt when *he* touched me.

Kyle's touch burns in a way I've only ever experienced with him. It might have been a little over a year since that night, but I still remember it as if it were yesterday.

I can vividly recall how every demanding touch affected me. I remember just how high my body soared when he whispered dirty things in my ear and pulled my panties aside.

Before that night, no one had ever touched me. I wasn't really expecting anyone to touch me that night either, but then I wasn't exactly planning on ending up in the state that I did.

Ripping my eyes open, I stare at my closed bedroom door, imagining how we looked last night with his hand beneath my skirt, his lips on my skin and his hand around my throat.

My hand flutters up to my neck to where his touch burned. The skin is tender, but it wasn't hard enough to leave a mark. He's not that stupid, although I'm not sure I'd have been able to stop him if he wanted to though.

His eyes, his words, his touch. All of it—as it always has—rendered me useless and as much as I might have wanted to fight him, I knew it was pointless the second he pressed his body against mine.

I blow out a slow breath as I regret every moment of last night.

I shouldn't have worn that dress. I shouldn't have let things get so far with Nathan—or, maybe I should have and fought harder to get Kyle out of my head—and I should have kicked Kyle out the second I found him in my bedroom.

My phone vibrating on my nightstand drags me from my depressing thoughts.

Reluctantly, I turn over and pull it closer.

My heart jumps into my throat at seeing Nathan's name staring back at me.

Couldn't he have just sent me a message?

I consider ignoring him. Kyle's parting words come back to me. But I don't want to dump Nathan. I really like him, and I want to see where things could go between us.

If only he hadn't shown his face, I might actually be able to focus on the right now.

Cursing myself for allowing my past to affect my present, I connect the call and put it to my ear.

"Hey." I wanted to sound excited but the reality is I just sound half asleep.

"Crap, did I wake you?"

"No, it's okay. I've been awake a while."

"I'm sorry about last night."

"There's nothing to apologize for. I'm the one who should be. I ruined your evening."

"Not possible. I spent it with you." I swoon at his words and smile to myself.

"What are you doing today?"

"I have no idea, but Justin seems to have a plan before tonight's party. Why, did you want to do something?"

"Not if you're busy. I'll see you later on."

"I can cancel," he offers.

"No, it's okay. I'll do something with the girls. I can't wait to see you later though. I want to make it up to you."

"Harley, I'm serious. It's fine. I just want to enjoy the night with you. I have no expectations. There's no rush."

My stomach twists as I picture how badly he wanted us to continue last night but then that image morphs into the memory of Kyle pressing my hand to his cock only an hour after I left Nathan.

Fuck, I'm such an awful person.

Nathan and I might not have put a label on our relationship, for all I know he could be sleeping with multiple Maddison Prep girls, although I very much doubt it. He doesn't seem like the type to do that.

I'm the only bad person here.

Guilt swamps me. I should take Kyle's advice and end things before it gets serious. But the selfish part of me doesn't want to. Things were good before *he* turned up. He shouldn't just get to show his face and send my life into a tailspin.

"O-okay. I'll see you later then, I guess."

"Yeah, I'll be waiting."

I end the call, questioning myself as to whether I did the right thing not.

As much as I might want to think Nathan and I could have a future, I fear that with Kyle around, we're doomed to fail no matter how much I attempt to put a wall up between us.

Like you did last night a little voice says in my head but I push it aside as I curl back up under my covers.

I don't even get a minute of peace before my cell starts ringing again.

Dragging it back out from under my pillow where I shoved it after I hung up on Nathan, I find Ruby's smiling face looking back at me.

"Morning."

"Are you okay?" she asks in a rush, making my heart skip a beat.

"Yeah, why?"

"Shit," she mutters to herself. "What happened last night?"

"Um… Nathan made us a romantic picnic in Justin's living room it was—"

"I don't mean that, I meant what happened after. I saw him, Har. I saw him coming down the stairs and when we left, your car was parked in the driveway. Do not tell me that he wasn't up there with you."

Now it's my turn to curse under my breath.

"How'd you know he wasn't with Zayn?"

"Because Zayn was balls deep in Poppy."

"Ew, thanks for that."

"What happened, Harley?"

"Okay, fine," I huff. "Things didn't end well with Nathan. I came home earlier than I expected and I found Kyle snooping in my room."

"And that's it? He was just snooping?"

"Yeah, I mean we... *talked* briefly." It's not a lie, there were a few words said between us.

"You talked?" she asks, not believing a word of it.

"Yeah, it was nothing," I say, trying to play it off as such so she stops digging. "So what's the plan for this afternoon, we still getting ready at your house?" I ask, hoping the subject change will distract her.

"Yeah, but I need to go to the mall, I've got nothing to wear."

"I really doubt that, Rubes."

"I want something new. I'll pick you up in an hour?"

"What time is it?" I pull my cell away from my ear to look at the same time Ruby says, "Just past eleven."

"Christ," I mutter. "Yeah okay, I'll be ready."

"Good, because I expect the full story about what happened last night, Harley Hunter."

"You did not just last name me," I gasp in mock horror.

"I did and I'll even pull out the middle one if you don't—"

"Yeah, yeah. I get it. No need to be so cruel."

"Good. Now get your ass in the shower, I'll be there soon."

"K, bye."

After a beat, I flip the covers back and head for the door, pausing on the way to the bathroom to call for Poppy who I can only assume is in my brother's bed still.

I knock. "Pops, you in there?"

It takes a couple of seconds and some rustling but eventually she answers. "Yeah, what's up?"

"I'm going to the mall with Rubes. You coming?"

"Can't, we're going to Maddison to see the kids. I'll be at hers later though to get ready."

"Okay, no worries. As you were."

Zayn's low chuckle fills the silence before Poppy squeals and I all but run for the bathroom before I hear any more.

Of all the boys in school, why did one of my best friends have to pick my brother to bump uglies with?

I shower, dress and I'm skipping down the stairs a couple of minutes before Ruby's due. Although the second I turn the corner and find Mom in the kitchen sipping on a mug of coffee and reading something on her iPad, I regret it.

"Hey, sweetie. Going somewhere nice?" she asks, taking in my outfit. It's nothing exciting, just jeans and a sweater but she seems to approve, not that I need it.

"Mall with Ruby," I reply coldly. She's tried to talk to me a couple of times about this whole Kyle thing but I'm not interested. As far as I'm concerned, she never should have agreed to help Kane.

"That will be nice. Are you getting something for the party tonight?"

"I don't know," I snap.

She lets out a long breath. "Harley, I know you're angry with me—"

"Angry? I'm more than angry, Mom. I'm angry at you for helping, but I do understand to a point. But the fact you didn't tell me..."

"I know and I was wrong. Everything's okay though, isn't it? He was here last night with Zayn from what I've heard, and he seems to be settling in okay."

"Yeah, sure. Everything's great." *If you consider him trying to ruin my life and get revenge for me sending him away in the first place then yeah, everything is just perfect.*

"He was always such a good boy, a great influence for Zayn. I'm glad they're reconnecting again."

"A good influence?" I can't keep the words in, disbelief drips from them as they pour from my lips.

Mom's eyes hold mine, waiting for me to say more, to explain myself but thankfully, the sound of Ruby's car pulling up outside is the perfect excuse I need to run.

"Ruby's here. I'll see you later."

I'm out of the door before she even has a chance to say goodbye.

"Perfect timing," I mutter, falling down into Ruby's passenger seat.

"Why, what's wrong?" She glances over, concern pulling her brows together.

"Ugh, just Mom trying to talk to me."

"You still ignoring her?"

"I'm not ignoring her, I'm just avoiding her."

"Okay, same difference. Just talk to her. Get it all out."

"I thought you'd probably figured out by now that I don't really want to talk about it."

"I know, but it might help. Your mom just wants to help."

"That's how I ended up in this mess in the first place," I mutter. If she didn't feel the need to try to bail every kid out then I wouldn't be living this nightmare.

"So go on, what happened?"

"You're really not going to let me get away with this, are you?"

"Not a chance in hell, Har. Tell all then I'll buy you one of those caramel latte macchiatos you like to make up for it."

"Nathan was really sweet. Everything he set up for last night was perfect," I confess. "But I screwed up." Ruby glances over but she doesn't say anything, she just lets me spew it all out until the events that led up to me leaving Justin's house early are out in the open.

"I think you're making a bigger deal out of it than necessary. He sounds like he understood."

"Yeah, and that makes me feel even more awful. He totally got it. All he wanted me to do was stay but I was mortified."

"The time just wasn't right."

"But how do you know when it is?" I ask, already knowing what her answer is going to be.

"No idea. You just know."

"What if he's not the one I should be giving it up to?" I whisper, not wanting to even say the words out loud for fear of them being true.

"Then you need to end it with him if that's what you really think."

"No, it's not what I think. It's just... I don't know. I like him, Rubes. I really like him. He's sweet, and kind and caring, and—"

"Not what you want," she finishes for me.

"No, he's exactly what I want," I argue.

"Okay, so he's not what you need."

My lips part to respond but I slam them shut again before I say something I could very well regret.

"So what happened after? You said he was snooping but I saw him coming down the stairs. He wasn't just up there snooping." She looks over and raises a brow at me in question.

"He may have finished what Nathan started," I admit quietly.

"Harley!" she squeals.

"I know, I know. I'm the worst person in the world." I slam my closed fists down on my thighs in frustration at myself. "He was just there and he was saying all these awful things and I just—"

"Couldn't' help yourself."

"Yeah, how'd you kn—Ash."

"Like I said before, the good ones aren't all they're made out to be. The bad ones however..."

"Man, this is a mess. I hate him, Ruby. Hate him."

"What happened, Harley? Like, what really happened that night?"

I shake my head, even after telling her everything that went down last night, I'm still not ready to go there.

"It was just a party that got out of control. I panicked and called the cops and he was the one that got caught."

"Why? What happened to everyone else?"

"They ran."

"So why didn't he?"

"B-because he was h-helping me." My voice cracks with emotion as I remember snippets from the end of that night.

"Okay so if he helped you then why do you hate him?"

"Because… because I do. I'm not going near him again though. Last night was a mistake of epic proportions."

"You know he's going to be there tonight, right?"

"Yeah, and so is my boyfriend, and I intend on making things up to him."

"Har, you can't do it just because you think you owe him."

"I'm not," I argue. "I'm doing it because I want to."

"Just please… please don't do something that you're going to regret."

"I think it might already be a little late for that."

Ruby gives me one of her hard stares before letting out a long sigh and climbing from the car. I don't blame her, I don't really want to have the conversation either.

I follow her lead and meet her at the hood of her car.

"Retail therapy fixes everything. Come on, let's go find you something killer to wear tonight to knock everyone's socks off."

"I thought we were shopping for you," I argue.

"We're shopping for everyone. Hell, we can buy a dress for Poppy if we find one."

"Sounds good." I thread my arm through hers as we make our way to the mall. "Thanks for this."

"Hey, what are best friends for if not to force you to tell all your secrets and give you bad advice."

"You haven't given me bad advice," I insist.

"Maybe not. But after what Ash and I went through, I'm surprised you're listening to me."

"Rubes, that boy loves you something fierce. I'd kill for that."

"Well, lucky for you, you might not have to. The two boys who want you, on the other hand, that could get bloody."

"Nathan's not like that. I don't think he's a fighter."

"And the other one?"

"Umm…" I think back to our childhoods in the Creek, of the many fights I'd witness that involved Zayn, Kyle, and their other friends. "Yeah, he is."

"I hope Nathan knows he needs to watch his back because a boy from the Creek is about to wipe the smile off his preppy little face."

"Rubes, is that really necessary?" I mutter, not thrilled with the visual emerging in my head of the two of them going a round over me. "There will be no fighting."

"We'll see. Oh, look, that dress is perfect," she says, changing the subject so fast I almost get whiplash as she points at a little red dress in the window of one of my favorite stores. "You have to try it on. Nathan will come in his pants just looking at you."

I snort a laugh but allow her to thread her fingers through mine and drag me to the store when she sets about finding the dress along with an armful of others for both of us to try.

We find ourselves a dressing room big enough for the both of us and set about finding the perfect dresses for tonight.

"The red one first," she demands as I pull my jeans from my ankles.

"Fine." Unsnapping my bra, because I already know there's no chance in hell of wearing one with how low cut it is, I drop the fabric to the floor and pull the dress from the hanger.

"Okay, what do you—fucking hell, Ruby," I gasp, taking in the marks on her chest. "Jesus, was he trying to actually eat you or something?"

Her cheeks flush as a wide smile pulls at her lips.

"Pretty much. I'm pretty sure I've got carpet burn on my back from the carpet in Zayn's den too." She turns around and sure as shit, there are bright red marks across her shoulder blades.

"Jesus. Can you two actually keep your hands off each other?"

"Sure can." She gives me a sly wink before looking down at the dress wrapped around me. "You're buying that," she states before continuing to pull the dress up that's hanging around her waist.

11

KYLE

"What the fuck was that for?" I bark at Ashton as the sting from his hit eases. I rub at the side of my head, wondering what the hell I ever did to him.

"You fucking cockblocked me last night," he grumbles as we set off from my house on the running route I've found myself over the past few days.

The last two people I expected to find when I got to the bottom of the Hunter's stairs last night were a satisfied looking Ash and Ruby.

Clearly, they'd made use of the empty room I'd left them in. The sight of the two of them looking so happy did nothing for my mood as I got farther and farther away from Harley.

"'Evening," I mumbled, walking straight past them and out the front door. I knew if I hung around in that house a second longer than necessary then I would turn around and walk straight back up those stairs and finish the job I'd started.

Their shocked stares burned into me as I passed them. Ruby wanted to say something, that much was obvious when she tried to step forward, but Ash gripped her tighter and kept her into his side.

"I refused to let Ruby go up and see if Harley was alright and as punishment, she wouldn't put out."

"Wow, however did you cope," I deadpan.

"What happened?"

"What do you mean, what happened?"

"Well, you went up to see her, right? We know she was back, we saw her car."

"Yeah, I saw her." He glances over at me as we continue running side by side. "We just... hashed a few things out."

"Riiiight."

"What?"

"Oh nothing, we *saw* you, remember. Whatever it was you were hashing out... well..."

"What the fuck ever, man. Harley and I... we have unfinished business."

"Yeah well, I hope you finished her business better than she did yours."

"You're an asshole."

"Takes one to know one."

Picking up my speed, I leave him behind for a bit as he chuckles at me.

"So what's the deal with you two then?" he asks when he easily catches up with me.

I blow out of breath. "Some shit went down before I got carted off that night."

"She made the call, right?"

"Yeah," I sigh. "My crew, they... they took things too far, Harley got caught up in the crossfire and I paid the price."

I slow to a stop when the ocean emerges in the distance and together we walk down onto the sand and sit our asses down in one of the secluded dunes.

"Okay. So you're hating on her for calling the cops?"

"Yeah and..." I trail off, really not wanting to talk about this.

"And..."

"I don't know, man." I pull my legs up in front of me and rest my forearms across them as I look out at the sun sparkling on the ocean before us.

It's sure not Harrow Creek.

I shake my head as images of that place fill my mind. It's really like hell compared to here.

"You want her?" His question makes my heart lurch in my chest.

Yeah, I want her. I want to fucking hurt her. But I don't tell him that.

"She's Zayn's little sister, even if I did, she's off-limits."

He looks over at me, his amused eyes holding mine for a few seconds.

"I'm the wrong person to talk to about off-limits. I'm fucking my stepsister."

I shake my head at him. "How'd that come about anyway?" I ask, glad to have a way to turn this conversation away from me.

"Pretty much the same as you right now. I hated her, wanted to hurt her. Turns out… she's pretty fucking awesome."

"I never said—"

"You didn't need to. I see it, man."

"Right," I mutter, ripping my eyes from him and back out to the horizon.

"Just… just try not to do something you're going to regret. They can only forgive so much."

"I don't want her fucking forgiveness."

"I know, I'm just saying."

We fall into an easy silence as we watch the waves crash onto the beach. The sound of kids playing in the distance filters down to us, and I wonder what it might have been like to grow up here with a decent family.

I blow out a sigh and it seems that Ashton knows exactly what I'm thinking.

"It's a different life here, eh?"

"Yeah, you could say that."

We haven't really talked much about his past but I know enough to know that it's probably why we're drawn together. We know how hard life can be. We've seen the deprivation, the desperation, the sheer hopelessness. We've also experienced the loss.

"You been back yet?" he asks, I assume about the Creek.

"Nah. I have no interest in going back. My life there was over the second I was put in the back of that cop car."

"No other family?"

I shake my head, not that he's looking at me. "Parents died when we were young. Gran died while I was away. It's just me and Kane."

"That's shit."

"It is what it is. Things can only get better, right?"

"What about those you left behind. You got busted for possession, doesn't someone want their stash back?"

His question makes my blood run cold.

I know it's not even been a week yet, but even so, I'm amazed I haven't seen or heard from anyone. Gray never was one to let things go and I went down with my pockets full of his fucking blow.

"Yeah, I can't imagine he's forgotten." I could go to the Creek and find him, save me waiting but like fuck am I willingly walking back into the lion's den.

"Well, I've got your back, man. Should you need it."

I look over at him. "Thanks. I appreciate that."

"You're coming to this party tonight, right?"

"Hell yeah, I been locked up for a fucking year. Ain't no way I'm passing up that chance, man."

After a few more minutes, I push to stand, brushing the sand from my ass.

I nod at him. "Ready to head back?"

"Yep, let's go."

Kane is gone all day. I still have no fucking idea what he's doing, not that I have a chance to ask seeing as he's never here.

I spend the afternoon doing homework before jumping in the shower again and getting ready for this party.

Memories of some of our Creek parties fill my mind, and I wonder how different these parties here will be. I hope a lot, seeing as the last one I went to ended up with me being arrested.

I'm shoving my feet into my sneakers when a car horn sounds out. Grabbing my cell, I make my way out before locking up the house and jogging down to the road.

Zayn's car is idling at the sidewalk.

"'Evening," I mutter as I drop down into his empty passenger seat.

"Where's Poppy?"

"She's getting ready with the girls. They're going to meet us there later."

I nod, excitement erupting in my belly at the thought of seeing Harley again.

It might only have been a few days, but as Zayn drives us through Rosewood, I realize that I'm already starting to get used to the place.

At first, seeing the luxurious houses set back from the roads was weird. I was used to shitty trailers that were dumped on any bit of land anyone could occupy.

"It's weird, right?" Zayn asks, clearly seeing what's capturing my attention. "It's like a different world. It's good though."

"Yeah, I'm starting to see that. I can understand why Kane thought this was a good idea."

"Anywhere would have been better than going back to the Creek."

"Too fucking true."

"You still go back to see your old man?"

"Sadly. Stupid fuck still refuses to leave."

"I guess there are people that like living like that."

"Yeah, fucking idiots."

"Any word from Gray?" he asks, and just like earlier the sound of his name gives me pause.

"No, you?"

"Nah, man. They all cut ties with me long before you went down."

Guilt swamps me because I was one of them. I cut ties the second Zayn left the Creek. Although it wasn't through choice.

"Listen… I'm so—"

"You don't need to do that, Ky. I get it."

"Yeah, well. It still sucks."

"I left. I knew I was starting over. I wasn't expecting to continue to fit in."

I blow out a breath. "I missed you, man."

"Aw, little Legend, you getting all soft on me."

"It's better than being hard for you," I deadpan.

"Save it for the fucking cheerleaders, man. Speaking of, you wanna know the best ones to play with?"

"You got it. I've been stuck with my hand for a fucking year. I need all the info, man."

He laughs beside me before starting on who I do and don't want to make a move on tonight. I make all the right noises in the right places to make him think I'm interested. But in truth, there's only one girl I'm searching out tonight and I don't give a fuck if she thinks she's there with her boyfriend. He needs to be taught a lesson as much as she does for allowing her to leave in tears last night. Fucking pussy.

There are cars already filling Justin's driveway when we pull up and Zayn parks his car.

"Right, let's get you used to partying Rosewood style."

"As long as it ends better than the last party I went to, I'm good."

Zayn claps me on the shoulder as we make our way to the front door.

There are people everywhere, most I don't recognize, but then I've only been at Rosewood High for three days, so I'm hardly surprised. I follow Zayn through to the kitchen where we find the majority of the senior year football team.

"Hunter, my man," Justin slurs, clearly having started the party earlier. "Legend." He lifts a bottle of beer toward me and I happily take it and knock the top off.

"Cheers, man," Zayn mutters, accepting his.

"This is Nathan, my cousin." He nods toward a preppy looking kid in a perfectly pressed white Henley. Exactly what I expected.

Zayn nods at him but I notice that the scowl never leaves his face as their eye contact holds.

After a few seconds, Nathan tips his drink to his lips somewhat nervously.

Yeah, I'd be scared too, motherfucker.

The beer soon turns into vodka and someone produces a baggie of weed that soon gets passed around once we've made ourselves comfortable in Justin's den.

I have no idea what it is with these kids and having their own dens. Kane and I didn't even have our own fucking bedrooms growing up. But as I bring the J to my lips and take a hit, I can't say I'm too fucking bothered right now.

"Fuck, that's good," I say to no one in particular.

"Ethan always gets the good shit," Zayn mutters from beside me.

I pass it over before pushing from the couch. "I'm going for a piss."

"Down the hall on the right," someone helpfully points out, clearly listening to our conversation.

I make my way out of the room, the vodka I've drank starts to make my head swim a little but I revel in the sensation of checking out of real life for a few hours. I fucking need it.

There are kids everywhere out here as I make my way down the hallway. Of course, there's a fucking line. Seeing a door for outside, I opt for that instead. I'm sure Justin won't give a shit if I water his flowers a little.

There are kids outside crowding around the pool, laughing and dancing as they enjoy themselves.

I slip into the darkness at the bottom of the yard and do my thing as kids splash about in the water behind me.

Once I've finished, I turn around and watch them from my hidden spot for a few minutes and wonder what it must be like to live a life where you have nothing to worry about.

Girls in bikinis flirt with the guys who are splashing about with them and others stand off to the side dancing and grinding together to the beat of the music.

My fingers twitch at my sides, desperate to have a girl moving against me like that.

I have no idea how long I stand there like some fucked-up peeping Tom, but eventually my need for another drink and another hit get the better of me.

I push through the bushes and slip back inside to locate the kitchen.

I fight my way through the crowd at the door and eventually get to the counter where the bottles of liquor were lined up earlier in the evening.

I help myself to a bottle before turning to rest back against the counter as I twist the top off.

I find Justin, Prep Boy, and a few others passing around hallucinogens.

I watch as a couple stick them straight into their mouths but Preppy and a few others hesitate.

"You want in?" Justin asks me when he notices that I'm watching.

"Nah, man. I'm good. You all have fun though." I turn to Nathan who's still holding his looking very much like the prep boy that he is. "Eat up, I hear they do wonders for your sex life," I quip. "You've got a girl, right?"

His lips pull into a smile. "Yeah, she's on her way."

My stomach clenches at his words.

"Better take that and show her a good time then," I say, hoping like fuck that I know what I'm doing.

"Come on then," he says, nodding toward Justin's hand.

"Fuck it. To a good night."

12

HARLEY

I hold my dress down as I step from Ruby's car in my attempt to not flash Ash or any of the kids that are loitering out the front of Justin's place.

"Come on, girl. I need another drink," Ruby shouts, already three sheets to the wind.

"I'm going to be carrying your ass home tonight, aren't I?" Ash mutters from behind us as Ruby and Poppy each take one of my arms and we walk toward the front door together.

"If you're lucky," she shoots over her shoulder. "You can totally take advantage of me."

I can't help but laugh when he complains because I know full well that she hasn't put out since seeing Kyle emerging from my room last night. And it's not for lack of trying on his part either as evidenced by the fact he walked straight into her bathroom while she was showering earlier. I didn't need to see her smug face to know she got hers while she left him hanging. He looked murderous after she kicked him out and forced him to return to his own room with blue balls.

He might act like a grumpy fucker, but secretly, I think he's enjoying the little game. I know that Ruby sure is.

"Hey, Ash," she says, stopping and turning to face him. "Did I tell you that I'm not wearing any panties?" She pulls her dress up her thighs a little as if she's going to flash him and anyone else who might be looking in our direction—probably every guy in earshot thanks to that little announcement.

"Don't you fucking dare," he growls.

"You'll have to find out later then. Be a good boy and go and get us all a drink."

He rolls his eyes at her but as we walk into the house and head for Justin's den, he goes for the kitchen, probably more for a drink of his own than one for Ruby. I think he's going to need one.

"At fucking last," Zayn calls the second we walk into the room. He's up off the couch in a heartbeat and has Poppy in his arms. "Fuck, you look hot," he mutters quietly, although not quietly enough for me not to hear.

"Ugh, puh-lease."

"Fuck off, Har. Go find your prep boy."

"At least he's got some class," I mutter, stepping away from them and doing as he suggests.

"Are you sure about that?" he calls from behind me, but I pay him little mind.

"Thank you," I say to Ash when he appears with four Solo cups in hand.

"Don't get used to it."

"It's amazing what guys will do for some action," I say as he walks toward where Ruby is talking to some of the squad.

I make my way through the house looking for Nathan. I get the attention of more than a few guys as I go proving that Ruby was right about this dress. And if it weren't for the fact Nathan was here, or the fear that Kyle is too, I might be revelling in the attention. But I'm not, and I wonder if once again my dress choice was a massive mistake.

"Whoa, baby Hunter, has your brother seen you?" Justin slurs, clearly off his face, the second I step into the kitchen. "You look smoking, baby girl."

"Shut up, J. And get your eyes off my tits."

He holds his hands up in defeat but his eyes never leave the low cut of my dress. Whatever.

Scanning the room, I finally find Nathan but my eyes almost bug out of my head not only when I take in the darkness in his but also who he's standing next to.

Of course fucking Kyle found him before me.

Nathan's smile lights up his face when he sees me, and just like every other guy, his eyes drop down my body, his mouth hanging open as he does.

"Hey," I say, sliding up to him and turning my back on Kyle. "You having fun?"

"Harley, fuck." I can barely make out the words, they're so slurred.

"How much have you had?" I ask with a laugh.

"Enough to tell you that you look fucking banging and to demand that you dance with me right fucking now."

He wraps his arms around my waist and pulls me into his body and without second thought, he slams his lips down on mine.

The taste of alcohol fills my mouth as his tongue plunges past my lips. I eagerly return his kiss, glad that there's no awkwardness after last night. His hands slide down from my waist until he's gripping my ass and pulling my body tight against his.

I feel him grow hard against my stomach as our kiss continues and heat surges through my body knowing that I'm turning him on right now. Well, I tell myself that it's that and not the stare that's burning into my back from the person I refused to acknowledge as I walked over here.

"Let's go dance," I whisper when he finally pulls back from my lips.

Reaching up, I rub at the lipstick on his face but it barely budges.

He wraps his arm around my waist and leads me from the room.

My skin is still tingling with Kyle's attention and just before we turn the corner, I look back over my shoulder, a smile playing on my lips.

My stomach flips at the murderous expression on his face but it doesn't stop me. Last night should never have happened, but that's on him, not me. He shouldn't have been in my room. He shouldn't have put his hands on me.

With the vodka from Ruby's warming my belly and flowing through my veins, it's easier to push it all to the back of my head and just enjoy myself. And seeing him there with the muscle in his neck pulsing and his hands curled into tight fists, I'm certainly enjoying myself.

Lifting my arm, I flip him off over my shoulder before I disappear from sight.

We move as one unit toward where the pounding bass is coming from and the second we're in what's usually Justin's parents' living room, we join the dancing crowd and Nathan pulls me into his arms.

It's a million miles from the little love shack that Nathan created for me last night and a thrill races through me that hopefully it won't end in the disastrous way either.

"I didn't think you were going to come," he slurs in my ear as he moves to the music although totally out of rhythm.

"Fashionably late," I whisper-shout back.

"And it was worth it. You look good enough to eat." He lifts his arm and encourages me to twirl for him.

The full skirt hemline of my dress flares out as I do and his eyes feast on my bare legs.

"I need you so fucking bad," he groans in my ear as he pulls me back into his body and grinds his length into my stomach.

Gone is the good boy who was concerned about my feelings last night and in his place is the kind of guy that I'm more used to handling.

I look at him, his eyes are totally blown.

"What have you taken?" I ask him.

"I dunno, but I feel fucking good right now."

"Nathan, I do—" I don't get to continue because he takes advantage of my parted lips and slips his tongue between them once again.

His kiss is wet and dirty, and I can't help but drown in it.

The alcohol surges around me and I forget that we're in a room with tons of others and I kiss him as if we're once again alone.

I have no idea what song is playing, the only thing I can focus on is him and the way he makes me feel. I might not be burning quite as hot as I was against my bedroom door last night but it's hella close and I'll take it.

"I missed you last night," he groans in my ear after kissing across my jaw. "Tell me that you'll stay longer tonight."

Draining what's left of the drink Ash gave me however long ago. I drop the empty cup to a shelf beside us as I turn to look at Nathan once again.

His eyes are hooded with lust, his cock still solid between us but he kinda looks like he's fighting to stay awake right now.

"I'll stay as long as you want me to."

The smile that pulls at his lips melt me and when the song changes, I twist in his arms and push my ass into his crotch.

I regret the move the second I look to the doorway and find that we've got an audience.

I shake my head at Kyle as I drop down low and rub all the way back up Nathan's body.

Kyle's lips purse in anger and the Solo cup that was in his hand collapses under the force of his fist.

I smile at him as I lift my hands behind me once I'm at full height and thread my fingers through Nathan's hair, twisting my head to the side to find his more than eager lips.

His hands slip up my waist until his thumbs brush over my nipples.

I gasp at the sensation, my belly clenching in desire and heat flooding my core.

My eyes are closed as I absorb the sensations zapping through me but all my muscles freeze the second a body presses against my front and another pair of hands land on my waist.

"What the—" My words are cut off as I stare into a very familiar angry pair of eyes. "Get the fuck off me."

He rips his stare from me and looks to Nathan who's still moving against my back, seemingly oblivious to the sudden tension between me and Kyle.

"Good shit, right?" Kyle asks Nathan.

"Yeah, man. I feel fucking epic."

"Hell, yeah," Kyle agrees, but his words hold no sincerity. He's lying. His eyes might be dark, but that's only anger, whatever Nathan has taken, Kyle hasn't had the same.

"What the hell are you doing?" I ask when he rolls his hips against me, moving in time with the music, unlike the guy behind me who seems to be dancing to his own song. "What have you given him?"

"Me?" he asks innocently, as if my question offends him. "Justin was the one who brought drugs to the party. I learned my lesson the hard way, Kitten."

If Nathan has any cares about me being sandwiched between him and Kyle, then he shows no sign of it. His hips continue to move as his cock grinds against my ass and his fingers dig into my hips, holding me close.

"You need to back off," I warn Kyle.

"Kitten, don't be like that. We both know how much you like two guys at once."

"Fuck you, Kyle." I slam my hands down on his chest but if it hurts at all then he doesn't so much as flinch and it pisses me off.

"Come on now. We both know you're wetter now I'm touching you instead of that pussy."

"Never. And he's right there."

"Kitten, he's so high right now he has no fucking clue what's going on."

"I can't believe you. I—" My words are cut off as he leans over me, his hard chest against my face as he whispers something in Nathan's ear.

I breathe a sigh of relief when Kyle takes a step back.

His eyes hold mine for a few seconds before they run down my body. He sucks his bottom lip into his mouth, his teeth biting down on it. The sight shouldn't affect me as much as it does but I can't stop the heat that surges through my body.

He lifts his backward cap and smooths down his hair before replacing it once more.

He blows me a kiss before looking up at Nathan and nodding.

I don't move until Kyle has left the room and disappeared from my sight.

Spinning in Nathan's arms, I stare up at him, my eyes narrowed in curiosity.

"What the hell was that?"

"Just enjoying myself, babe. Let's go get a drink, eh?"

My need for a breather means that I agree. We find our way to the kitchen and he pours me a vodka before helping himself to the rest of the bottle. Justin walks up to him and Nathan turns away from me for a few seconds but I think nothing of it as I sip at my drink and watch a few girls bounce off each other as they attempt to find the front door.

I have no idea what time it is, but I know it's late. We didn't get here until well after the party had started, taking way too much time getting ready. The bottle of vodka Ruby had went down far too easily as we did our hair and makeup, and we ended up having way too much fun at our own little party for three.

"Let's go somewhere quieter," Nathan suggests, turning back to me and wrapping his hand around the back of my neck.

"Y-yeah, okay," I agree. I came here with the intention of getting him alone and making up for last night, but I wasn't expecting him to be quite so off his head and that we'd actually be able to hold a conversation that he might remember.

"Come on." He threads his fingers through mine and drags me down the hallway and then up the stairs.

"Nathan, I'm not sure—"

"Shhh," he slurs. "It's okay. No funny business. Just me and you."

His lips curl into a knee-weakening smile, the exact one that pulled me to him that first night at Ethan's house and I follow with my half-full cup in my other hand.

He leads me to a doorway at the far end of the hall and we both slip inside the guest bedroom which I assume he's claimed as his.

"Mmmm," he mumbles as he wraps his arms around me from behind and drops his lips to my neck. "This is better. Just the two of us."

The music from downstairs vibrates the floor beneath our feet but still, he pulls his cell from his pocket and syncs it to the speaker sitting on the side.

He twists the cap on the bottle in his hand and takes a huge swig, his eyes on me the entire time. They drop down my body, eating me up and I remember why I wanted to see him tonight.

"That dress, babe. It's insane."

"Thanks." I step toward him and run my hand up his chest. "I'm really sorry about last night." I brush my lips against his and he immediately accepts my kiss.

His hand brushes down my back until he grips on to my ass. A move that I'm sure he never would have done last night without whatever influence he's under.

He walks us backward until he lowers down on the couch by the window and pulls me on top of him so I'm straddling his lap.

"I really like you, Harley," he admits, ripping his lips from mine and once again lifting the bottle to his and swallowing down a generous shot.

He offers it to me, and I take it from him. The neat vodka burns the second it hits my throat and I instantly regret it, although after a second when my stomach starts to warm, I change my mind.

"I like you too." I take another swig before handing it back and bending down to kiss his neck.

His hands slip up my thighs until he's cupping my bare ass and helping me to grind down on his crotch, the bottle of vodka abandoned on the couch.

"Fuck, babe. You keep doing that and I'm gonna come in my pants," he slurs happily.

"Can't have that, can we?" His eyes flash at my words and his lips curl in excitement as my fingers search out his waistband.

"Harley?"

"Sssh," I whisper, pressing two fingers to his lips, although I miss on my first attempt. "Let me make it up to you."

I pop the button on his jeans but before I get any farther, I hear the click of the door behind me.

I suck in a breath, knowing exactly who has just joined us. I don't need to turn to look, I can sense him. The tingles that run down my spine only exist when *he* looks at me.

"What are you doing?" I ask without even acknowledging him.

"Coming to join the party, Kitten. I'm all for having a bit of fun, but there we're a few too many people downstairs, don't you think?"

"Y-you need to l-leave," I stutter when the heat of his chest hits my bare back.

"Don't be like that, Kitten." His fingers drift around my exposed throat and my eyes involuntarily flutter closed at this familiar touch.

"Kyle." His name is no more than a warning growl as he presses his front harder against me.

"As you were, Kitten." His fingers trail down my arm and my eyes fall closed at his touch.

Damn vodka.

"You need to leave," I repeat, knowing that this situation is going to lead to disaster. "You shouldn't be in here."

"Your boy here doesn't seem to have an issue."

Ripping my eyes open, I look at Nathan. My breath catches in my throat when I see his eyes are closed.

He's passed out.

Thankfully his chest is heaving, telling me that he's still alive.

"What has he taken?"

"Just some acid. He'll be fine once he's slept it off."

His thumb caresses my pulse point and I swallow down my need to give into him.

"Kyle," I force out, trying to sound as strong as possible. "You need to leave."

"Why? I don't think your boy is very interested in what you have to offer right now. Unless you've got a thing for sucking him off when he's passed out."

"I thought it was you that was into that," I snap.

"Kitten," he growls, lifting me from Nathan's lap and putting me back on my feet, although he doesn't spin me around. "If you really believe I did anything to you while you were out of it, then you're stupider than I thought. You have no reason to hate me, Kitten. Well... not yet anyway."

"W-what are you g-going to do?" I try to twist out of his arms but the one he has locked around my waist tightens.

"We're going to have some fun, Kitten."

"But Nathan—"

"Nathan needs to learn who you belong to. Because... allow me to let you in on a little secret," he whispers in my ear, making my entire body shudder as his breath caresses my neck.

I rest my head back against his shoulder and close my eyes, the room spins with the amount I've drank but I don't focus on that. Instead, I focus on his touch. It's too good not to.

"It's me," he breathes. "You belong to me."

"Fuck you, Kyle." I fight to get out of his grip and to my surprise, he lets me. But I soon realize my mistake because my back hits the wall beside the couch and his hand wraps around my throat, pinning me in place.

"Yeah, that's exactly what I was thinking."

His eyes drop down my body, locking on the two small red triangles that cover my breasts, and I glance over at Nathan.

He's not really intending on doing this with him in the room, is he?

I don't know why I ask that question. The answer is freaking obvious and staring me in the face.

"Yeah, Kitten. I am," he answers, making me wonder if that question slipped past my lips or not. "And if he happens to wake up, he's going to learn a very important lesson."

He lifts the hand that's not around my throat and he trails it along the fabric from my collarbone all the way down over the swell of my breast and down to where it meets the waistband a little above my belly button.

"This dress," he murmurs, almost as if he's talking to himself. "It was a fucking brave move, Kitten. You walked in here tonight asking for trouble, didn't you?"

"No, I walked in intending on spending the night with my boyfriend who you've fucking drugged."

"Whoa, careful there, Kitten." His eyes find mine. "I didn't give your *boyfriend* anything. He took that shit of his own accord because he's a fucking idiot."

"No, he's not. He's just—"

"Not looking after you properly. I mean, if he was, then you wouldn't have been thinking about me a minute ago when you were grinding down on his lap."

"I wasn't—"

"Don't lie to me, Kitten." His grip on me tightens as my lips part on a gasp.

"I-I'm not."

"Suuure," he drawls. "Let's just pretend that he gets you wet, shall we? Just for the fun of it. We'll pretend that these are hard and begging to be sucked on because of him." He circles one of my nipples with his forefinger and it puckers harder for him. "And we both know your panties are ruined right now. Or are you going to try to lie about that too?"

"Kyle," I whimper as he continues teasing me.

"Beg me all you want. I'm not leaving this room until I've proved you wrong."

"Go on then," I say, holding my hands out to my sides. "Do your worst."

An evil yet hungry smirk curls at his lips.

He takes a step back, releasing my throat and allowing me to take a deep breath. My eyes dart to the door but I don't get to take a step.

"Don't even think about it."

Swallowing down my nerves, I look back to Kyle as he swipes up what's left of the bottle of vodka that Nathan abandoned.

He sits down on the edge of the bed as he twists the cap and lifts the bottle to his lips.

I can't rip my eyes away as he swallows, his Adam's apple bobs and the muscles ripple.

Without putting the cap back on, he rests his elbows on his spread legs and hangs the bottle between, looking up at me expectantly through his lashes.

"W-what?"

"You owe me, Kitten."

My fingers twitch against the wall they're pressed against as what he means dawns on my alcohol-filled brain.

"Go fuck yourself, Kyle."

"See… that's the thing. I've been locked away on my own for a long time… *because of you.*"

My lips part to respond, to tell him that it's not my fault, but it is. I made that call, I am the one to blame.

"You were more than willing to help him out a few minutes ago." He flashes a look to Nathan before bringing his eyes back to me and raising a brow. "So," he says, lowering the bottle to the floor and resting back on his palms.

My heart is like a runaway train in my chest as I stand there staring at him.

His eyes hold mine impatiently as he sucks his bottom lip into his mouth. I mimic the move, my mouth watering for a taste of him.

The kiss he gave me last night… it wasn't enough.

My fingers curl against the wall as I run my eyes over his jaw, down the fitted black t-shirt he's wearing that shows off every line of muscle he's rocking beneath, to the little sliver of skin that's exposed before the black waistband of his boxers and then his dark jeans.

My eyes linger on the bulge at this crotch and tingles erupt in my belly that he's turned on by me. Just like I am him. Our hate is addictive, thrilling. Dangerous. But that doesn't mean I'm about to walk away, if anything it just spurs me on.

"Harley?" he asks, his deep voice rumbling through me, forcing my eyes back up to his face.

I study him for a moment. He's still so much like the sweet boy I remember from my past. But the changes from the past year are obvious to me. The edge, the vicious words and barbed touches. They're all new and I know they're my fault.

I might not know what happened to him while he was in juvie. And I might never know. But I do know that it changed him. *I* changed him and I can't help but wonder if I might have entirely broken that little boy who had so much potential despite the shithole we lived in.

"My patience will only last so long, Kitten."

With my eyes locked on his, I take a step forward. An accomplished smirk appears on his lips but the sight only makes my insides flutter with anticipation.

In a heartbeat, I'm standing between his legs, drawn to him like a moth to a flame.

He sits up, bringing his chest to my stomach and runs his palms up the back of my thighs until he finds my bare ass.

"I swear to God, if you're not wearing any—" He moves his hands higher and his words are cut off when he finds the waistband of my thong. "Did he touch you?" he growls.

I'm desperate to look away from his electric gaze, but I can't and my head stays bowed so I can keep the connection with him.

I shake my head so subtly I'm not sure he can see it.

"Kitten," he says softly. "Did that motherfucker touch you tonight?"

His little fingers run down the scrap of fabric between my ass until they're right over my entrance. A growl rumbles up his throat as he discovers that the fabric is soaked.

Leaning forward, although still keeping his eyes on mine, his lips part right above my left breast and he sucks the skin into his mouth.

"Kyle," I gasp as he sucks to the point of pain before sinking his teeth into me.

"M-i-n-e."

"You're fucking crazy," I squeal, looking down at the angry mark on my breast.

"Yeah, and whose fucking fault is that, eh Kitten?" Before I get a chance to answer, his fingers wrap around my panties and they're ripped from my body.

I gasp as the fabric is peeled away from me and the cool air of the room surrounds my heated flesh.

"I think you like me a little crazy though, eh?" Lifting his hand, this time up the front of my dress, he runs a finger through my folds, rubbing my wetness around my clit.

"Oh God." Reaching out to find something to hold on to, my hand lands on his hat. Not happy with that, I knock it off his head and thread my fingers through his hair and grip tight enough that I know it'll hurt.

His eyes flash up to mine, excitement shining in them. "Give me all the pain you can muster, Kitten. It'll only make me harder."

Without thinking, I pull my other hand back and slap it across his cheek. The hit is so hard his head snaps to the side despite the fact I'm holding his hair.

A growl rumbles up his throat. "You're going to fucking pay for that."

"I already thought I was. This is a punishment after all, right?"

Before I know what's happening, he pushed on my shoulders so hard that I find myself on my knees before him.

"I was going to take it easy on you," he says softly as if he's that sweet kid I once knew, but I can see the evil intent shining in his eyes. "But you fucked up. More than once."

"W-what are you—" The vodka flowing through my system makes my brain misfire as I stare up at him.

"You look right at home on your knees begging for forgiveness, you know that, Hunter?"

"Fuck you, Legend." I narrow my eyes at him, hoping it shows just how much I hate him right now despite the desire that's burning through me.

He fucking knows it too.

He reaches out and cups my cheek, the move is almost tender, and my eyes shutter at his contact.

"You ever sucked anyone's cock before, Kitten?"

I once again shake my head so subtly I have no idea if he sees or feels it.

"Good. You'll remember this." He slips his thumb into my mouth and I can't help but wrap my lips around it and suck. "Fuck."

His eyes close for a beat and I realize just how much power I have over him right now.

I could get up and walk away and leave him here alone with his tented pants and my passed out boyfriend, or I could do something I've imagined more than once and take even more control from him.

I smile up at him. My newfound power going to my head. I might be the one on my knees right now begging for forgiveness but the second we do this, I'm the one calling the shots and he damn well knows it.

Pulling his hand from me, he rests back on his palms once more, offering himself up to me.

"Go on then. I don't have all night."

I grind my teeth as I stare at him. My head spins with the vodka, the desire, the hate. I have no idea which is the strongest but I also know that I'm not about to walk away, like I know I should.

Something in the back of my mind begs me to look over at Nathan, but I can't. If I see him lying there behind me then it'll change everything. And right now, I don't want to change a fucking thing.

13

KYLE

I stare down at her, my heart slamming against my ribs and my cock aching and she tentatively reaches out and runs her hands up my thighs.

Her touch burns like I was expecting it to and my mouth waters for what's to come.

I wasn't going to make her do this. But then she fucking slapped me. My cheek still burns from the hit and I resist the need to lift my hand to soothe it.

Hesitantly, she fumbles with the button at my waist. I know I could help her out and have it open in a heartbeat, but watching her is too fucking good.

"You're killing me, Kitten," I growl, making her eyes fly up to mine.

They're so dark they threaten to pull me in and drown me in their depths. And I can't deny that it's exactly where I want to be right now. Lost. Lost to her and everything she can give me.

That night. That party. It was never supposed to end the way it did. It was supposed to end exactly like this. With me making her mine despite the consequences of what her brother, or the rest of Harrow Creek, might think. I'd wanted her for too long to pass up the opportunity.

But Gray fucked it up.

Harley thinks it's her fault, and she's partly right. And while she was the one who made the call, I can't place all the blame on her. If Gray hadn't got carried away, thinking he was fucking God, then none of the events that followed would have happened.

My fingers curl in the sheets beneath me as anger slams into me. He's the one who did this to us. Who turned me into this.

I know I might be avoiding him right now. But I know it's not going to last forever, and I will never forget what he did. How he hurt both of us. I couldn't give a shit about his lost blow. That's nothing to me. The girl on her knees before me though. My future. That's fucking everything.

My stomach flips when she finally manages to open the button and pull down the zipper.

Lifting my hips to help her out, she pulls my jeans down. Her eyes lock onto my cock despite the fact it's still covered by my boxers.

I know she's a virgin. I know the reasons she ran from that motherfucker last night and the thought of being the first one she touches like this, it makes my chest swell. No matter what happens from here on out, she'll never fucking forget this.

"Scared, Kitten? I won't bite, well, not while you're down there."

She sucks in a breath, her dark eyes locking on mine once more as her warm finger brushes the skin beneath my waistband before she tugs. I lift up and she lowers the fabric until I'm exposed.

"Kyle, I—" Reaching out to cup her face once more, I rub my thumb over her cheek tenderly.

"No talking, Kitten," I warn, sliding right to the edge of the bed.

"O-okay." Sliding my hand up, I thread it through her hair and force her to look down at me.

My cock jerks under her stare and a smile plays at my lips as she gasps.

She hesitates for a second and I half expect her to twist out of my hold and run for the door. I brace myself for it because I know that if I've read her wrong and she really doesn't want this then I'll let her go. I'm not *that* guy.

But when she does move, it's not away from me.

Her hands skim up my bare thighs, her eyes still locked on my cock. Her fingers graze my length and the simple touch is enough to shoot electric sparks through my entire body.

There's no way I'm going to fucking last.

I push down the thought because right now, I don't think Harley gives a shit, and I sure fucking don't.

"Kitten," I grit out, my need for her to take me in her delicate hand is all-consuming. "Oh fuck." I release her hair and fall back on my elbows as her burning fingers wrap around my length.

My head falls back as she starts to pump me slowly, my teeth grinding as I try to get control of myself.

"Fuuuuck," I groan when I look forward once more to find her studying me. My lips part to say something but I lose all sense of myself when she moves her face closer to me.

"This what you wanted, Ky?" Her lips right over my tip, her hot breath rushing over my heated skin.

My fingers thread into her hair once more and she tenses, thinking that I'm going to force her down. I'm sure that one day soon I will do just that, but right now isn't it.

She might hate me but I'm not a total cunt.

"Harley, don't just fucking tease me."

"Why?" she breathes. "You deserve it." Her eyes hold mine, challenge shining bright in them.

"And you deserve me to thru—fuck." Her tongue laps at my tip, collecting up the precum that's beaded at the slit, cutting off my warning.

She licks at me like I'm a fucking popsicle before sucking me into her hot little mouth.

"Holy fuck. Shit, Harley." My fingers tighten in her hair to the point I must be on the verge of pulling some out but I can't help it.

It's too fucking good.

I watch as she lowers her head, taking more of me until I hit the back of her throat and she pulls off before she gags.

Her tiny hand continues to grip the base of my cock, the pressure she uses is fucking perfect, yet I know she has no idea.

"Feel better now you've got your cock in my mouth?" she asks, tilting her head to the side and running her tongue along her bottom lip. "Feel powerful?"

My chest heaves as she stares at me, her hand still working me slowly.

"Powerful? You have no fucking idea, Kitten," I growl. I think we both know who holds all the fucking power right now.

The image of her walking out and leaving me like this hits me, and my grip on her tightens even more. She should walk out, I think we both know that would be the right thing to do right now, but we also both know that she's not going to.

I sit up and pull her up to me, slamming my lips down on hers. My tongue plunges into her mouth and after a second hers joins in.

A soft moan rumbles up her throat and I swallow it down like it's mine. I want all her moans of pleasure and pleas for me.

Our kiss is dirty, our teeth clash and our bites sting. It's exactly as it fucking should be.

I suck her bottom lip into my mouth and sink my teeth into her soft flesh until I'm sure I break the skin.

"Suck me, Kitten. I want to come in your wicked little mouth."

I push her back down between my legs and she takes me back in her mouth without missing a beat, almost like she missed me.

"Fuck, yeah," I moan as I watch her head bob.

I want it to last forever, but after an embarrassingly short amount of time, I know it's coming to an end.

"Kitten," I groan, wanting her to know what's coming. She stills, so I know she's heard me but she doesn't stop.

She takes me farther back than she has so far and I lose control.

"Fuck. Fuck. Harley," I chant as my cock jerks and I come down her throat. A groan rips from me and fills the room around us as my body goes limp and my muscles quiver from the intense release that I've needed for so fucking long.

I don't realize that I've collapsed on the bed until she speaks and she sounds far away. Too fucking far away.

"Where are you—"

"I've paid my debt now, Ky."

I sit up as she backs toward the door.

"You think that's it? You think you get to suck my cock and I'll forget everything?" I stand, pulling my pants up and shake my head. "That was just the beginning, Kitten." I close the space between us in a heartbeat. My hand wraps around her throat and my lips crash to hers.

"Kyle, what are you—" I squeeze her throat, forcing her to stop talking so I can continue kissing her.

Resting my other arm against the wall beside her head, I press the length of my body against hers, tucking my thigh between her legs so I can feel her heat.

I kiss her until my lungs burn.

"This is far from over, Kitten," I whisper in her ear. "Now, are you going to play nice and do as you're told or am I going to have to make you?"

Her chest heaves against me, her small fists twisting my shirt. I'm not sure if she's aware of it but she's holding me to her and it tells me everything I need to know.

"Depends on what it is."

I laugh, but there's no humor in it. As much as I love her defiance, I'm not sure I have it in me to deal with it right now. I know what I want, and my patience is already running thin.

"Get on the bed, Kitten." I drop my hand and squeeze her waist as I suck on the skin of her neck, once again ensuring I leave a mark. I want her to look in the mirror tomorrow and remember exactly who was here. "Now." I twist us around and push her in the direction of the bed in the center of the room.

She stumbles on her heels but she manages to catch herself.

"On your back," I demand and she scoots back until she's laid out in the center, although her head is up so she can follow me as I make my way across the room to her.

"Spread your legs, Kitten."

"Wha—"

"Don't argue. You had your chance to run. You didn't take it."

"I… I don't think—"

"Kitten," I warn, my voice a low rumble in my throat.

She blows out a shaky breath but slowly parts her ankles.

"Wider." I run my eyes over the inches of bare, bronze skin before me but what I really want is covered by the skirt of her dress. It's cute. She looks hot in it, but it's going to look even better on the floor.

"Lift your dress."

Time seems to slow down as I wait for her to follow instructions but it damn near stops when she does.

So fucking pretty.

"Kyle, what are you—Oh my God," she squeals as I dive on the bed, wrap my hands around her thighs and latch my mouth onto her clit.

Her taste coats my tongue and I want to fucking drown in it.

Her hands find my hair and she pulls, trying to drag me closer as I lick, suck, and nip at her clit with my teeth.

"Fuck, fuck, fuck, Kyle."

Hearing my name ring out through the room makes my chest swell.

Fucking yes, Har. Scream it fucking louder.

Her back arches off the bed and I suck hard on her, her nails scratch at my scalp and my cock once again strains at my pants.

Unwrapping one of my hands, I find her entrance and begin circling it with one digit.

"Oh shit," she screams as I push just the tip in. Her muscles ripple trying to drag me deeper but I refuse her, drawing this out as long as possible.

"You gonna come, Kitten," I growl against her clit, making sure she feels the vibrations from my voice.

"Ky, fuck."

"I could eat you all fucking night, Kitten."

"Kyle," she squeals as she falls over the edge. My scalp burns as she pulls my hair harder, her back arches and throws her head back. "Oh my God," she chants as her entire body convulses in the center of the bed.

I don't stop licking at her until she's come down from her high, then I sit up, wipe my mouth with the back of my hand and launch myself over her.

My lips find her neck as I kiss, suck and bite at her sweet skin.

"Kyle," she cries, clawing at my back as I tease her.

"I'm going to fucking ruin you, Kitten," I promise before tucking my fingers under the straps of her dress and pulling the top half down to expose her tits.

I graze my teeth over her collarbone and work my way down, not wanting to leave an inch of her skin untouched by me.

Her dress ends up in a pile on the floor, followed soon after by her shoes before I go down on her again but I remain fully dressed.

With my hands wrapped around her tiny waist, I bring her to orgasm again with just my tongue speared inside her.

She fists the sheets beneath her as she rides it out, my name a plea on her lips.

"Fuck yeah, Kitten," I growl. "Who fucking owns you?"

"You do," she answers eagerly after so many orgasms at my hands—and mouth.

"Say it."

"You do, Kyle."

"I do what, Kitten?"

"You fucking own me, Kyle."

Lifting up from her pussy, I don't bother wiping my mouth, instead, my hand finds her throat and my lips slam down on hers. She moans as she tastes herself but she doesn't try to pull away, instead, she sucks my tongue into her mouth making me wish it was my cock again.

"I fucking own you, Kitten. You. Are. Mine."

"Yes, yes," she pants, her eyes barely open after the number of releases I've dragged out of her and the amount of vodka she's drank.

"And don't fucking forget it." I look to my left and find a pair of eyes trained on me, just like I knew they were. A smile curls at my lips before I dive for her once more just to nail the point home.

14

HARLEY

I roll over and the feeling of the covers tickling my skin where it usually wouldn't is my first sign that something isn't right. The second is the fucking marching band in my head. The third, that's my stomach turning over, but that's not to do with the vodka so much but with the speed of my memories from last night hit me.

I push up on my elbow, ready to run toward wherever the nearest bathroom might be but the second I open my eyes and find Nathan staring at me from the couch, I freeze.

"Fuck," I breathe.

"'Morning." He sits forward, resting his elbows on his knees, but he keeps his eyes on me.

I want the bed to swallow me whole as I pull the sheets tighter to my naked chest.

"H-how are you feeling?"

"Better than I should." His voice is cold in a way I've never heard before and it makes my stomach sink.

The silence stretches out uncomfortably between us but still, I can't find anything to say to him as shame burns through me.

"I saw you." His words make my breath catch. "I saw you... with him. I... I heard you... with him."

I swallow but my mouth is so fucking dry that I can't even do that.

"I-I'm sorry."

"Is that why you ran the other night? Because of him?"

"No, I—"

He pins me with a look. "Don't lie to me, Harley. It's too late for that. Did you run the other night because of him?"

"Y-yes. I'm sorry," I add in a rush like it might actually make any of this any better.

"Who is he?" Nathan asks, his brows furrowing as if just asking the question itself is painful.

"A boy from my past. He only arrived in town last week. I had no idea he was coming."

"He an ex?"

"N-no." I hesitate and hate myself for it. "I mean, something had happened before he went…" I trail off, for some reason not willing to share everything about Kyle with him. "But we were never together."

"I guess we weren't either."

I sit up in bed trying to keep myself covered as I move.

"Nathan, I'm so so—"

"Don't," he barks, pushing to stand. "You're right. We never said we were exclusive. I guess I just assumed—"

"I didn't mean to," I say in a rush.

"No, maybe you didn't. But you did it anyway. While I was passed out right there." He points to the couch and my entire face flames.

Of course I knew he was there, I was grinding down on his lap when Kyle walked in.

Fucking hell, Harley. You're nothing but the cheer slut everyone assumes you are.

"If you hadn't—"

"Don't turn this on me."

"I'm not, I'm just saying, that you'd taken… whatever, and you passed out on me. If you didn't, then—"

"Then what, all three of us could have had some fun? You know that was what he wanted, right?"

"No, I—"

"When he whispered in my ear when we were dancing. He was setting it up for the three of us…"

"And you agreed?" I ask, my eyes almost popping out of my head.

"I was wasted, Harley. I'd have agreed to anything last night."

"Fucking hell," I mutter as I drop my head into my hands. "I'm so sorry for dragging you into this mess."

"I just wish you'd have told me the truth. I like you, Harley, but I don't want to get in the middle of anything."

"It isn't anything," I argue.

He shakes his head as if it's the most ridiculous thing he's ever heard.

"It is though, isn't it? You wouldn't let me touch you because of him, and you let him do all that while I'm in the room without second thought."

"I was drunk."

"It doesn't matter, Harley. What you told him last night was true."

"W-what did I tell him?" I might be able to vividly picture a number of things that happened right here on this bed last night but I could have said literally anything to him during that time.

"That you're his. He's sure left enough evidence behind." He nods down to my chest and I lower the sheets a little.

"Jesus," I mutter, staring down at all the marks littering my skin.

"I'm just going to..." He trails off as he walks to the door.

"I'm sorry, Nathan. Really, sorry."

"It was fun while it lasted, Harley. Take care of yourself."

Pressure builds behind my eyes as I watch him slip from the room but I hold back my sobs until the door closes behind him and I know he's far enough away not to hear me.

I pull the covers over my head and cry for all the stupid mistakes I've made that involve Kyle freaking Legend over the past year. Last night being up there as the worst.

I have no idea how long I lie there crying to myself, but my eyes sting from my tears when there is a knock at the door.

"Harley, it's me. Can I come in?" Hearing Ruby's voice only makes me cry harder.

"Yeah," I call out, my voice cracking with emotion.

"Hey, Nathan said you were in here and that you might need a friend."

She walks over to the bed and sits on the edge, her face full of sympathy.

"What happened?"

"I fucked up. Big time."

"Too much vodka?" she asks, trying to make light of the situation.

"Way, way, way too much vodka."

"Oh sweetie. Come here." She pulls me into her arms and I cry on her shoulder.

"I really hurt him. He didn't deserve that."

She rubs my back in comfort. "He's okay, Har."

"Is... is Kyle still here?"

"I haven't seen him since early last night."

I wish my heart didn't sink like it does knowing that he snuck out after everything.

"You want to talk about it?"

"Yeah, but I really need to get dressed and get out of here."

"Okay, how about we go back to your house, you can change and then we go for breakfast?"

"Not at Ace's," I say in a rush. I don't want to see anyone.

"Okay, whatever you want."

She slides to the end of the bed and leans down.

"You need this?" she asks, handing my dress over.

"This," I say, snatching it from her. "Was a mistake."

"You can't blame the dress."

"I can and I will." I throw the fabric over my head and shimmy it down my body without flashing Ruby.

"Do I need to ask what happened to your panties?" she asks as I climb from the bed, clearly failing in my mission not to expose myself.

"Use your imagination," I mutter, walking to the other side of the room and opening a door that I really hope leads to an en suite. My entire body aches, but nowhere more so than the muscles in my inner thighs. What the hell did he do to me last night?

My cheeks burn as I remember watching him between my legs. I squeeze my thighs together as the memory of just how his tongue felt against me.

I knock my palm against my forehead, hoping that it knocks the thoughts straight out of my head.

The sight of Nathan's toiletries sitting around the sink does nothing for my regrets.

I make use of the toilet before finger brushing my teeth in the hope of freshening my mouth up and rejoining Ruby.

"Ready?"

"Any chance of sneaking me out of a back door?"

"We can try but I need to tell Ash that we're leaving."

"You do that. I'll meet you at your car."

"Okay. Here," she says, pulling her keys from her purse. "I won't be long."

"Thank you," I say sincerely.

"Always, Har." She kisses my cheek before disappearing out of the door and allowing me a few seconds to compose myself before attempting to sneak out and not get caught doing the walk of shame in last night's dress.

By some miracle, I actually make it out of the house unseen and I'm hiding in Ruby's car when she emerges from the front door—unlike me who snuck out the back—a few minutes after shutting myself inside.

"Ready to leave last night behind?" she asks me.

"So ready. Any chance I can leave my memories here too?"

"That bad?" she asks, glancing at me after starting the engine so she doesn't miss the blush that covers my face and down my neck which of course only highlights the many, many hickies I'm rocking. "Oh my God. How did I miss those upstairs?"

"Can we not?"

"Did he try to eat you?" she jokes, clearly remembering my words to her not so long ago.

"He did, a few times," I admit, much to her amusement.

"Harley Hunter, you naughty little slut."

"Like you can talk."

"Hey, I'm not denying anything." She chuckles. "Just tell me... was jailbait good?"

"Fucking hell, just drive. I need to shower and get out of this dress."

"You're right. You smell like sex."

"I'm pretty sure that's you."

"Nope, I showered."

"Great, so I guess I'm guilty then."

Ruby continues to laugh lightly at my expense as she backs out of Justin's driveway and heads for my house.

"I got out of Justin's unnoticed. I'm not going to have the same luck here, am I?" I ask, seeing both Mom and Zayn's cars sitting in the driveway.

"Only one way to find out." But instead of reaching for the door, Ruby throws herself between the seats and reaches for something. "Here, put this on. If Zayn sees you, he's gonna throw a fit."

"Thanks," I say, taking her hoodie and shoving my arms into it.

Once I've covered up as much as I can, I blow out a long, calming breath before pushing the door open and climbing out.

The house is in silence as we step in through the front door, but it only lasts so long because footsteps soon head our way.

"'Morning, girls. Good night?" Mom asks, looking between the two of us.

"Yeah," I lie. "Excuse me."

I take off for the stairs knowing that Mom's concerned eyes follow me.

After a couple of seconds, Ruby catches up with me.

"You should just speak to her, hear her out."

"I will, when I'm not hungover and drowning in regrets."

"Oh come on, it couldn't have been that bad."

"Not that bad?" I ask, turning on her the second we're in the safety of my bathroom. "The boy I hate went down on me, again and again, while my boyfriend was passed out on the couch. And the kicker… said boyfriend was apparently watching."

Ruby's chin drops.

"He watched?"

"I don't think he actually watched for entertainment, I think he came to and happened to find us doing… well, that." I walk over to my closet to pull out some clean clothes.

"Did you fuck him?" Her question stops me in my tracks.

"No. Well, I don't think so." I risk a glance over at her standing beside my bed with her hands on her hips.

"You don't think so?"

"I mean, I remember… *things.* But I don't remember that. Although I don't remember falling asleep or him sneaking out either, so…"

"You'd know if you did. You'd feel it."

"Well, that's reassuring, I guess."

"Go shower. We need pancakes before we talk about this anymore."

"I couldn't agree more. You okay while I shower?"

"Take your time."

I turn the shower on hotter than I usually have it, strip out of my dress and stand under the spray, wincing as the water stings my skin but I don't turn it down. I need it to help rid me of the memories and sensations of last night.

I scrub at every inch of my skin, trying to wash him from me, sadly it does little for what's in my head.

Once I'm done, I take off what's left of last night's makeup and pull on a pair of leggings and an oversized sweater that I can hide in. I refuse to look in the mirror at my reflection, I don't want to see the magnitude of my mistakes.

"Feel better?" Ruby asks the second I rejoin her back in my room.

"No."

She waits patiently while I blow dry my hair and apply a little makeup to make myself look less like death.

"Come on then, the syrup is calling."

"Where do you want to go?" Ruby asks as we make our way down the stairs.

"Anywhe— shit," I mutter under my breath when a very familiar voice filters up to me. "He's here."

"So? Hold your head up high and walk straight past him. Don't let him see he affects you."

"I wasn't intending to," I snap, making Ruby wince. "Sorry. He just drives me a little insane."

"I've noticed."

"Come on." I throw my hair over my shoulder and continue down, knowing that the second I look into the kitchen, I'm going to find him with Zayn.

"'Morning, sis. How's the head?" I look at Zayn, refusing to meet his burning stare but my skin tingles as Kyle leisurely checks me out.

"Fine thanks, *bro.*" I narrow my eyes at him.

"Ruby." Zayn nods at her over my shoulder. "Going somewhere nice?"

"We're going for breakfast," Ruby says over my shoulder.

"Do we need a word about where you went with your boyfriend last night?" Zayn asks me.

"Oh yeah," I hiss. "Just like we need to talk about where you and Poppy often disappear to."

"Hey, I'll tell you anything you need to know about what we get up to."

I faux gag at his words.

"I'm pretty sure he broke up with you last night, didn't he, Harley?" Kyle asks so sweetly it makes me want to jam a kitchen knife through his eye socket.

"Oh?" Zayn asks, looking between the two of us.

"I'm not discussing this with you," I mutter, turning my back on my brother and marching toward the front door and storming through it.

I rip open Ruby's passenger door and drop down onto the seat before she's even left my house.

"He looked at you like he wanted to take you against the wall."

"I don't want to know. I didn't look at him for a reason. Can we please talk about something else? What did you do last night?"

Ruby lets out a sigh before starting the engine and heading to the other side of town to ensure we don't see anyone.

15

KYLE

I'm still smiling to myself as the door slams behind a pissed off Harley. Knowing exactly what her baggy sweater was covering and who put it all there makes something flutter inside me.

"She's a bitch when she's hungover," Zayn mutters, going back to making our coffees.

I shouldn't have accepted his invitation to come and hang out today, but the thought of being here and seeing how Harley was this morning was an offer I couldn't resist.

"Most girls are," I mutter, trying to swallow down my real reaction that her feistiness made me hard. Fuck, everything about Harley Hunter makes me hard.

"How'd you know things are done with her and Preppy?"

"Uh… I overheard some of the guys talking about it, apparently, he got totally wasted last night."

"Don't tell me he cheated on her," he growls, going all protective big brother on her ass.

"I don't know, man. Don't shoot the messenger."

"Come on, we got guys to shoot." He holds out a mug for me before we head for his room and he turns his Xbox on.

"Where's your girl?"

He laughs lightly. "In bed, sleeping off a killer night."

"Oh yeah. I thought you disappeared early." It's a total lie, I was so focused on Harley last night that I have no fucking clue what anyone else got up to.

"I'm not one to kiss and tell, man." He doesn't look away from the screen but I see the massive fucking grin on his face.

"I've been fucking celibate for a year, you can give me more than that," I joke.

"You telling me that you didn't dip it in one of the cheerleaders last night?" he asks, the tone of his voice rising with shock.

"Don't kiss and tell," I tease.

"Fuck off, who was it?"

"Nah, not telling, man. She sucked fucking good though."

"Krissy," he states as if he knows all the girls' skills personally. Which, I guess he might.

"My lips are sealed."

"Unlike hers," he jokes.

Relaxing back on his couch, I stretch my legs out in front of me, enjoying the normalness of this morning. Shooting the shit with Zayn, killing a few guys on the game he's set up. It's all so... normal.

Good thing he has no idea that the girl who had my cock in her mouth last night was his little sister.

Zayn and I were always tight, but I'm pretty sure him finding out what's really going on is probably the one thing that could shatter this. But even as I sit here enjoying myself, I know that I'm not going to be able to leave her alone. I guess I'll just have to deal with the consequences when the time comes.

It's almost two hours later when his sleepy girlfriend finally emerges and finds herself a seat on Zayn's lap.

She looks almost as exhausted as Harley did earlier, although she makes no attempt to cover up the love bites running down her neck.

"'Morning, baby," Zayn purrs, slipping his hand into her hair and pulling her lips to his. She twists around on his lap, the shirt she's wearing—clearly his—rising to expose her thighs.

"So I guess I'll leave you two to it," I say, placing the controller on the coffee table and standing from the couch.

"Okay," Zayn mutters against her lips. "See you in school tomorrow, yeah?"

"Yeah. Later." I look back when I'm at the door after hearing no response but I soon discover why. "Fucking hell," I mutter to myself before slipping from Zayn's den and making my way to the front door.

I'm almost there when I get intercepted by Jada who's walking out of the kitchen with a mug in her hand.

"Kyle, it's so good to see you. How is everything going?" She smiles softly at me and it reminds me so much of Harley that I almost ignore her and continue the way I was going.

"Yeah, it's, uh… different."

"You can say that again," she says with a chuckle. "How's school? Are you settling in okay?"

"So far so good. Almost makes me glad I screwed everything up in juvie."

"Everything happens for a reason, Kyle. I was delighted when Kane reached out to me to ask for my help. I just knew that you both would do well here."

"Why did you do it? After… after everything." I have no idea how much she knows about that night, but something tells me Harley hasn't said much, so it can't look very good on me. I remember all too well the position we were in when the police stormed in.

"Because everyone deserves a second chance. If you'd have gone back to Harrow Creek, I think we both know how it would have gone." She raises a brow and my stomach drops at the thought.

Yeah, going back there would have been a bigger sentence than my time in juvie.

"It's great to see you reconnecting with Zayn, you were always such good friends, I hated the way you were forced apart."

"It's great to spend time together again."

"And… what about Harley? Have you had time to talk yet?"

"A little."

A humorless laugh falls from her lips. "She'll come around. I should have warned her sooner."

"Everything will be fine." I give her a reassuring smile which she can't help but return. "You don't need to worry about Harley."

She reaches out and squeezes my upper arm in the kind of motherly way I didn't realize I missed until her touch warms me from the inside out.

"If you need anything, you or Kane. I'm here. I can't imagine how hard things have been, for both of you."

"Thank you," I force out passed the lump in my throat. I learned long ago to push down my feelings, my grief from now not only losing our parents when we were just kids, but now our gran too. She was all we had back then and she took us in without a second though. But now she's gone too and it's just the two of us against the world. "I really appreciate everything you've done for us."

"Anytime, Kyle. We might have left the Creek behind but that doesn't mean we still don't look out for each other."

I nod at her as I take a step toward the door. Part of me wants to make all the excuses I can so that I can still be here when Harley gets back, but I know I need to leave. I know I need to give her some space. For now at least.

"Well, aren't you a sight for sore eyes," I say when Kane pushes through our front door, finding me sitting on the couch with a textbook on my lap.

"Fuck off. Good to see you're taking graduating seriously," he mutters, taking in the stack of books on the coffee table.

"Yeah well, I don't want it to take any longer than it's already going to. You out playing football?" I ask, spotting the mud covering his legs.

"Yeah," he says over his shoulder as he yanks the refrigerator open and pulls out a bottle of water.

"Was that before or after you got your ass kicked?" I ask, unable to miss the black eye and split lip he's sporting.

"How about you just get back to your schoolwork, eh?"

I push the book from my lap and stand, walking toward where he's leaning back against the counter and drinking his water.

"How about you stop talking to me like I'm a fucking kid and tell me what the fuck you're up to."

"Kyle," he breathes. "I'm not up to anything. I've been working. One of us has to keep this roof over our head."

"Nice, Kane. Real nice."

"What? That wasn't a jab, it's the truth. I'm not going to force you to get a job because I want you to settle in and sort out school before anything else."

I hold his eyes, looking for any hint that he's lying.

"Your birthday next weekend?"

"What about it?" I ask, not entirely happy with how he's diverted the conversation away from him.

"We're having a party."

"We really don't—"

"We do. It's not every year my little brother turns into a man." He rustles my hair as he passes me, heading to his room.

"Bit fucking late for that, don't you think?"

"Meh, we all grew up fast in the Creek, but still, it's an excuse for a party, and I need a fucking night off." He disappears into the bathroom before I get a chance to respond. I have a feeling though, that it doesn't matter what my opinion on it is, if Kane wants a party then we'll be having a party.

I grab myself a bottle of water and drop back down on the couch to carry on with my homework.

I grab my statistics book and pause with it on my lap. I need to arrange our next study session...

I spend the night at home working but the second Kane emerged from his room freshly showered and with clean clothes on, he fucked off leaving me to sort my own dinner.

I don't care about having to look after myself, it's not like I haven't done it before, but after being locked away and unable to see him for the best part of a year, it would actually be nice to spend a little time with him.

I'm lying on my bed long after midnight staring up at the ceiling wishing that I could fall asleep but totally unable to. I used to sleep great, until I suddenly had to constantly look over my shoulder. Then it was like I just stopped. I'd hoped that when I got out, I'd break the habit but it doesn't seem that I'm able to.

I must drift off at some point because when I open my eyes again the sky outside my open curtains is a burnt orange as the sun begins its climb for the day.

I drag on a pair of sweats and a shirt and take off. My muscles burn with my exhaustion but I don't allow it to slow me down. I push until I have nothing left to give. Exercise helped me survive up until this point, so I have no doubt it'll get me through my time in Rosewood.

By the time I get back to the house, my shirt is soaked with sweat and my muscles quiver with excessive use, but I feel better than I have in a while.

I shower, gather up my stuff and head for my car, ready to begin my first full week as a Rosewood High student.

There are kids everywhere when I pull into the lot. I find a space and just watch them.

I never used to give a shit about what other people did. Probably because I'd have ended up having my ass beat if I pried into other's business in the Creek but it's different here. No one is looking over their shoulder just waiting for their secrets to be exposed. Everyone is just living life. They don't need to worry about just trying to make the best of it. The majority here have everything they could possibly want handed to them on a platter. College is an option, they have a future that can be in or out of this place. The world is their oyster.

That's not how things were where we were brought up. College was something that happened to others. Or aspirations were restricted to which end of the trailer park we wanted to end up living on, and if we were able to work our way to a decent position with one of the gangs to allow us some sense of safety.

I blow out a breath. It all feels like it happened in another lifetime, but at the same time, I feel like I left that place only yesterday.

The bell rings out and all the kids that are hanging around start moving toward the building but I still can't find it in me to move. I try to convince myself that it's not because I haven't seen her. I'm pretty sure we don't have any classes together today and I'm already wondering how I'm going to get my hands on her.

My cell burns red-hot in my pants pocket and I pull it out, finding our previous conversation. A smile curls at my lips as I read back the short messages.

Opening up the keyboard I start to type.

Kyle: I feel like I've already taught you so much… Are you ready for another lesson?

It only takes two seconds for her to read the message and for the dots to start bouncing. I can't help but laugh when her response pops up because I expected it.

Kitten: Fuck off. WE ARE DONE.

Kyle: It amuses me that you think you get to call the shots here, Kitten. You might want to keep looking over your shoulder. I'm coming for you.

I add a little kiss emoji at the end to try to soften the blow and I smile, knowing just how her lips are going to press into a thin line as she sees it.

My cell vibrates once again and when I look down, I find a gif of someone flipping the bird staring back at me.

In response, I quickly shoot back someone blowing a kiss and shove my phone into my pocket before climbing from the car and walking toward the building before I end up too late. I don't need to give Principal Hartmann, Bea, my parole officer or Kane any reason to be on my ass.

My birthday is only days away. Bea will sign me off as an adult and I can finally take charge of my own life. The prospect should probably feel more freeing than it does in reality because until I turn my back on getting my diploma then I'm stuck here for the foreseeable future.

With the satisfaction of knowing I got to her, I walk into the building feeling a little lighter. Now all I need is to see it with my own eyes.

16

HARLEY

I don't want to do it, but I find myself doing exactly what he told me I should. I spend the entire morning looking over my shoulder trying to find him.

I know he's here. It's like I can sense his presence.

I also know that he's seen me because when I was standing in the hallway earlier with Ruby and Poppy, my skin tingled with awareness and my temperature soared, but as I looked around as desperately as I could, I couldn't find him.

"Hey, how are you doing?" Stella asks, coming to sit next to me on a bench I thankfully found empty after walking out of my last class in my need to avoid the cafeteria.

I blow out a breath. "Great," I mutter.

"Justin's party was banging, huh?"

I look over at her so fast that I swear my head almost snaps clean from my body.

"W-what?" she asks, her brows drawing together.

"N-nothing," I mutter, slumping down on the seat and remembering that just because I refuse to think about the events of that night, it doesn't mean that everyone else had one of the worst nights of their life. "I didn't see you there. Were you with the squad?"

"Yeah, Ruby invited me. It was fun. I saw you dancing with your boyfriend. He's cute."

"Ex-boyfriend."

"Oh?"

"It's okay. It wasn't meant to be." Or maybe it was and Kyle decided to steamroll the whole thing regardless. I push the thought down because as much as I might like to blame all of this on Kyle, I know that at least half of it is my fault. I didn't need to do any of that on Saturday night—hell, or Friday night—but I did, and now I need to pay the price. "You hook up with anyone?"

"I kissed some guy. I'd never seen him before, I don't think he goes here but he was decent," she says with a nod.

"Decent?" I chuckle.

"Yeah, I'm not sure he was entirely into it. He was kinda distracted, like he was looking for someone else."

"Trying to make someone jealous?"

"Maybe. I wasn't really complaining though. It's not like I was looking for anything serious."

"You still leaving?"

Her eyes widen in shock that I know.

"Shit, Ruby let it slip. Sorry, should I have—"

"It's fine. Honestly, I have no idea what's going on. I never do."

"Why do you move so much?"

"Dad's job. I hate it. I just get settled somewhere, make some friends and then I come home from school one afternoon to find the house being packed up and off we go again."

"That sucks."

"I mean, I've seen a lot, learned a lot. It has its benefits, I guess. But I just want a home and to graduate someplace I've stayed for longer than a few months, you know."

"It must be hard. Do you stay in touch with any of your friends from old schools?"

"To start with I tried, but everyone moves on, we grow up and it just fizzles. Dad is my only constant."

"Well, if it makes you feel any better, I really hope you get to stay here to graduate with us."

"Me too. I like it here."

"Yeah, it's not bad."

My stomach growls so loudly that Stella can't help but hear it.

"We should go and get you some food." She laughs.

I look over my shoulder at the building where the cafeteria sits knowing that he's probably in there finding his footing with the team and being dragged into my group. I bet even Ruby and Poppy are in there with Ash and Zayn making him feel welcome.

"Nah, it's okay. I don't—"

"Don't let him see that you're scared of him, Harley."

"What? I'm not scared. I'd just rather not have to look at him."

She raises a brow at me. "You're hiding," she states, pissing me off despite the fact it's blatantly the truth.

"I—"

"Come on. We'll stop in the bathroom, touch up your makeup, slap on some confidence, and walk into that motherfucking cafeteria like you own the place. Yeah?" She jumps up and I can't help but feel some of her excitement.

I don't want to be this girl. The weak one who hides from the boy who's making her life hell. I want to be strong. I want to hold my head up high. I'm Harley fucking Hunter after all.

"Hell yes."

I thread my arm through hers as we march toward the closest bathroom.

"Don't you have friends to be hanging out with instead of standing here being my personal cheerleader?"

Stella's face pales and for the thousandth time in the past twenty-four hours, I want the ground to swallow me right up.

"Shit," I breathe, realization hitting me that the reason she's standing with me is that she doesn't have anyone else.

"It's okay, Harley. I learned long ago that it's easier to just not connect with anyone. It hurts less when I leave and get forgotten about soon after."

"I'm sure that's not—"

"Stop," she says, holding her hand up to cut me off. "I dealt with it a long time ago. It is what it is."

"Well, I appreciate this. I just want you to know that."

She smiles at me and my heart aches for her. She's been nothing but awesome since she joined the squad and was quickly picked for varsity alongside Ruby and me, but hearing her talk like this, it makes me realize why she's kept her distance like she has. "And from now on, no more running from friends. Okay?"

"As long as you don't run from him." She pins me with a look. "You want to hate him, hate him in the same room so he knows it."

"You got it, girl. Let's go."

I pull my tank down a little, readjusting my girls, not that there's much of them, and run my fingers through my hair once more before threading my arm through Stella's and making our way toward where I know he is.

The commotion from the cafeteria can be heard long before we get to the doors and the closer we get, the more butterflies seem to take flight in my belly.

"You've got this. Show him that you don't give a fuck."

"I don't."

"Exactly."

I walk in with my head up high and the second we're inside, we head straight for the tables where the team and squad are.

His stare burns into me the second we move toward them, but I refuse to look his way, instead, I walk toward Ruby when she calls me.

"Where have you been hiding?"

I cringe at her words, knowing that it was exactly what I was doing.

"She was helping me with something," Stella pipes up to save me.

"Okay, cool. Come sit," she encourages both me and Stella, who easily fits in with our group despite the fact she's never really hung out with us before.

"Yo, baby Hunter. What happened to your prep boy? He dump your ass?" Rich shouts over. I roll my eyes at him before he shouts. "Ow," he complains as someone hits him.

"That's my cousin, you ass."

"Nah, he dumped her because she wouldn't put out."

My chin drops in shock as I turn to the owner of that comment.

"Excuse me?"

"You heard me." Kyle narrows his eyes on me, amusement dancing in them.

"Fuck you, Ky. You don't know what the fuck you're talking about."

Our eye contact holds, tension crackling between us and everyone falls silent around us waiting to see what's to come.

"I'm only going by what he said."

"Well, that's great. You believe what you like."

"It's true though, isn't it, virgin?"

"Wha—" I shake my head, not believing this is happening right now. "What's that even got to do with anything?"

"Just saying. He probably thought he'd get with a cheerleader and get his dick wet."

"You're a fucking prick, Kyle."

"So, prove us wrong."

"W-what?"

"Prove. Us. Wrong," he spits.

"What? You want me to fuck someone in the middle of the cafeteria to make you feel better about yourself? Fuck you, Kyle."

"Legend," Zayn warns, suddenly piping up. Apparently, even my fucking brother is enjoying the show. Ass.

"Pussy," Kyle breathes as I turn away from him.

"Fuck you."

I walk straight toward Rich who's totally engrossed in the drama unfolding before him, grip his chin in my hand as I straddle his lap and slam my lips down on his.

A loud gasp sounds out behind me, and I lift my spare hand to flip them all off.

His shock means he doesn't respond to me for a few seconds but the moment his brain catches up with his body, his fingers thread in my hair and he holds me tight.

Someone growls behind us and I can only assume it's Zayn. I've threatened to go after his friends more than once but other than Kyle. I've never touched one. Until today.

I grind down on him, feeling him harden beneath me before climbing off and dropping my hand to his crotch.

"You want to know why I haven't fucked any of you?" I look around at the team. "Much like your boy here." I rub him harder and he gasps. "Your cocks are all too small. Girls?" I ask looking to Ruby, Poppy, and Stella who are staring at me with a mix of pride and shock on their faces.

"Harley, wait—" Rich starts when I take a step back.

"Come after me and I'll fucking bite it off," I warn.

I lift my eyes to Kyle as I back away, a smirk playing on my lips as he shakes his head at me, anger darkening his eyes.

Right before I'm forced to turn around, I flip him off once again with both hands and then disappear around the corner.

"Girl, what the fuck was that?" Stella squeals excitedly. "I said go in there and show him you're not scared, not make Rich almost come in his pants."

I shrug like it's no biggie. In reality, my hands are trembling and my heart is racing faster than I'm sure it ever has before.

"Did you see his face? That was so his 'I'm about to come' face." Ruby laughs.

"Ugh, he's such a dog," Poppy complains. "They all are."

We all turn our eyes on her.

"What? Zayn used to be just as bad. I'm not excusing his behavior before we got together."

"Kyle looked like he was gonna pop a blood vessel. Did you see his eyes almost bug out of his head when you touched Rich's cock?" Ruby asks as we continue walking down the hallway with no destination in mind.

"Man, that felt good," I admit.

"You do realize that you're in serious trouble now, right?" Poppy says.

"How so?"

"Well, firstly, Zayn's going to lose his shit with Rich for kissing you back. Sec—"

"He was shit, in case you were wondering."

Ruby and Stella snigger as Poppy continues.

"Secondly, he's probably going to take Kyle down for the way he talked to you."

"And that's my problem because? Fucker deserves it."

"Thirdly, you're just asking for Kyle to come after you for that stunt."

"She's right. You might have just shown him that you're not scared, but you've upped the ante."

"Yeah well, he can fuck off. I'm not going anywhere near him again."

"Again," Poppy screeches, successfully spraying Ruby with a mouthful of water she was attempting to drink.

"You didn't tell her?" Ruby asks with a wince.

"No, you may not have realized it but I didn't want to talk about it."

"Whoops, my bad."

"What happened, Har?"

I look up at the shitty tiled ceiling of the hallway we've stopped in, trying to come up with the right words.

"He was right, nothing happened with Nathan…"

"Because…" Ruby encourages excitedly like she's about to explode.

"Because it happened with him."

"You fucked him?" Poppy shouts way too loudly for a school hallway.

"No, I didn't. He's right there too. I'm a virgin. But things… happened."

"But you hate him."

"Yeah well, I owed him one, so."

"You blew him to make up for the fact you sent him to juvie. Har, that's messed up."

I turn to Stella who's standing silently beside us probably being corrupted more by the second.

"I'm sorry. If you want to run now, I'll let you off the whole friends thing."

"No, no. Please continue. I'm enjoying this."

"Great. I'm glad someone is."

"Oh come on, Harley. It's not that bad. So what you sucked him off, I'm assuming you got yours too," she says, shocking the fuck out of me, I always thought she was such a good girl.

My face burns with the truth. "Um... I actually came out of it a hell of a lot better," I admit quietly making all three of them howl with laughter.

"So what happened to Nathan? That last time I saw you, you were grinding up against him," Poppy asks.

"Err..." I hesitate, mortified by the answer to that question.

"Tell her or I will."

"Ohhh... does this get even juicier?" Stella asks. "Where the hell was I when all this was going on?"

"Kissing a stranger?" I ask, hoping to take some of the heat off of me.

"Oooh... who were you kissing?" Ruby asks, momentarily forgetting that she was about to confess my mortifying secret.

"No idea. He was hot though. Rough." She wiggles her eyebrows in excitement.

"Har, you were saying..." Poppy prompts.

"Oh, um... Nathan was passed out on the couch," I whisper.

"In the same room?" she once again screeches.

"Yes."

Thankfully the bell rings putting an end to this mortifying conversation.

"What have you got last?" Ruby asks.

"Math," I groan. The last thing I need is Mr. Wilson breathing down my neck and asking about my tutoring sessions.

"I'm going that way. Walk with?" Stella asks, nodding in that direction.

"Sure."

"This isn't over," Poppy warns me.

"I didn't think I was going to be that lucky," I sass. "We'll talk later, yeah?"

"You can bet on it."

We all part ways and head to class.

"I think I might have got things wrong," Stella admits when we come to a stop outside my classroom. "I think being friends with you guys might just be worth it for the entertainment value."

"Trust me, girl. It's not usually this bad." I laugh, wondering if that's actually true when I think of the events of this year alone. Poppy and Zayn, Ruby and Ash. Yeah, maybe the boy drama really is becoming normal for us. And that can only mean one thing... we're turning into seniors.

"I'll believe it when I see it."

"You wanna hang out after school one day this week?"

"Yeah, I'd like that."

"I'll message you later."

She gives me a little wave as she twists away to go to her own class and a smile plays on my lips. Everything might be just a tad fucked-up right now but having Stella join our little threesome is a good thing. Not to mention that she's single and will give me back up against the two happy couples that mostly make me want to gag.

I'm still smiling when I walk into my classroom, although that soon falls when Mr. Wilson's concerned eyes land on me.

Great. Now what?

Class is... as hard as it always is.

I take all the notes, listen to everything he says, I even get some right answers, but no sooner have I figured it all out do I forget once again and it all goes tits up.

Tears burn the back of my eyes as I stare down at the page full of numbers. It shouldn't be this hard. I'm intelligent. I'm passing all my other classes, but math, argh.

I grip the pencil in my hand so hard I worry it's about to snap in two as Mr. Wilson brings the class to a close seconds before the bell rings.

"Harley, could you wait, please?" he asks as everyone else begins to make their way to the door.

I blow out a breath as dread settles in the pit of my stomach.

"What's up, sir?"

"Have you had your first tutoring session yet?"

I cast my mind back to going to Kyle's last week.

"Yeah."

"And, how was it?"

"It was... sir," I say, changing tactic. "I really don't think it's necessary."

"Harley," he warns. "The test we did last week." Hesitantly, I take it from him and at the sight of the big F at the top of the page, the tears that were already threatening fills my eyes.

"I'm so sorry," I whimper.

"Harley, you don't need to apologize, and please, don't get upset. We're going to make this better. I'm going to schedule some sessions at lunch and with Kyle's help, you'll get there. All of the rest of your grades are fantastic,

Harley. We just need to figure out a way to help you understand the numbers."

"O-okay," I sniffle.

"It'll be okay, Harley. We'll get you there."

"T-thank you," I whisper, wiping at my eyes and turning away from him.

I hate this. I hate feeling like I'm failing at something when I'm trying so damn hard.

"Hey, what's wrong?" Ruby asks the second I emerge from the classroom.

"It's math. What's right?"

"Come here." She pulls me into her arms to comfort me. It's a move that's happening all too often at the moment.

"I'm okay," I say, squaring my shoulders and running my finger under my eyes to wipe away the tears and stray makeup.

Movement over her shoulder catches my attention, but I don't get a chance to look up and see what's going on because Ruby tucks her arm under mine and starts walking us down the hall.

"Chelsea wants to see us."

"Oh, why?"

"To talk about next year, I assume. I don't really know."

Arm in arm, we walk to the gym before slipping down the hidden hallway to Miss Kelly's office. To both our shock, our elusive cheer coach is actually sitting behind her desk.

"'Afternoon, girls," she says when we enter and join Chelsea who's sitting rubbing her bump as she talks to Miss Kelly. "Harley, is everything okay?" she asks when she must see the remaining tears in my eyes.

"Yeah. Everything's fine."

"Okay, well. Take a seat. We need to talk about the squad's future and I have a feeling you two will want to be involved."

We both eagerly take a seat and set about listening to her plans, which in itself is comical seeing as she's never here.

"I know you want to take charge, and I think you'll probably get it. We'll put votes out as soon as auditions are done but in the meantime, I need you both to ensure your grades are stellar and your behavior is impeccable." Miss Kelly turns her eyes on me and my stomach drops. Not only am I failing math but my behavior in the cafeteria earlier wasn't exactly exemplary.

"You've got it," Ruby agrees for us.

"Brilliant. I'll see you all here after school tomorrow and we'll get started on building next year's champion squad."

Ruby and I nod before following Chelsea out and in the direction of the locker room.

"Anyone would think she gives a shit about the squad the way she just went on," Chelsea complains once we're safely inside the empty room.

"It's a bit of a joke," Ruby agrees, dropping down to the bench where Chelsea has left some of her stuff.

"You two are going to have a lot to take on, you know that, right? She won't help like she promises."

"We know. We've got it."

"I'll be around, I'm taking a year off with this one, so if you need anything I'm all in, I'll help wherever I can. You two just need to focus on those grades." She turns to me. "I saw yours, Harley. Is math going to be an issue?"

"No, I'm working on it."

"Good. Like I said, I'm here for anything, but math isn't exactly my strong point. Shane's pretty good but—"

"I've got it under control."

"Good. I trust you, Harley. I trust both of you. I know my squad will be in good hands." She pulls her cell from her pocket and stares down at the screen. "I gotta go. I'll see you both tomorrow, yeah?"

"Sure thing," Ruby agrees. "I need to head out too. You okay?" she asks me.

"Yeah, I'm just going to use the bathroom then I'm heading home."

"Okay. Call me later, yeah?"

"Will do." I watch them both walk out before pushing from the wall I was leaning against and head for the bathroom.

I sit down and tip my head up to the ceiling. Today has been a fucking disaster.

Regret fills me with what I did at lunch. I wanted to prove a point, but I think I might have taken it a bit too far.

I drop my head into my hands as the image of that F on my math test taunts me. I've got to do something. I can't have my place on the squad in jeopardy because of a stupid grade.

"Argh," I scream into the empty space around me but it doesn't make me feel any better.

I wash my hands before reluctantly looking at myself in the mirror. Tears still fill my eyes as I think about my reality. If I don't fix that grade, Miss Kelly will boot me from the squad and I'll never get to stand beside Ruby as her assistant captain.

I suck in a shaky breath before drying my hands and walking back to the locker room to grab my purse and head home—to do some math homework.

I'm not looking where I'm going, I'm too lost in my own head but that soon ends when I walk straight into a solid yet warm wall of muscle.

"K-Kyle?"

"Kitten, fancy seeing you here."

17

KYLE

"Yeah weird, seeing as this is the girl's locker room and I'm assuming you watched my ass walk in here," she sasses, making my dick harden as I close the already limited space between us.

My fingers find her throat and I push her backward until she crashes up against the lockers.

"Trying to be cute isn't going to help you right now," I warn, my eyes boring into hers.

"I'm not being cute," she seethes. "Let go of me." She pulls at my forearm with all the strength she can muster but I don't budge.

"That stunt you pulled in the cafeteria... you think I'd let you get away with that?"

"I don't really give a fuck, Kyle." She squirms in my hold, desperate to get away, but she's achieving nothing.

"You fucking kissed him." I get right in her face. My nose pressed against hers and our heaving breathes mingle as I tighten my grip on her throat and wrap my other hand around her waist. "You fucking kissed him," I repeat, my anger exploding within me as I remember watching her tongue delve past his lips. How they're still attached to him right now is a fucking miracle.

"You started it."

"I was only telling the truth, Kitten."

"Yeah, and maybe I've been dying to kiss Rich for years."

A growl rumbles up my throat.

"You're a really shit liar, Kitten."

"I. Don't. Care."

I stare at her as her chest heaves, her body trembling under my touch. I drop my eyes from hers, to her lips and then down to her chest. She's wearing a tank and zip-up hoodie, it's not an overly sexy outfit but fuck if I don't want to rip it off her and lay her out on the bench.

My cock swells against her hip, there's no way she can't feel what her defiance is doing to me right now.

"Why were you crying?" I ask, my voice softer than before.

The tears might have gone, but I can see the redness around her eyes. Not to mention that I was waiting for her after her math class and saw her come out upset.

"Why? Do you want to shout about that around the cafeteria to shame me as well?"

"Nothing shameful about being a virgin, Kitten."

"I know. If I were that bothered I'd have given it up to Rich by now."

"Don't even think about it," I growl, getting so close to her our lips brush. My mouth waters knowing that I could take her right now if I wanted to. I have no doubt she'd comply despite her anger.

"Why were you crying?" I try again, lifting my hand from her waist and running my thumb along the underside of her breast.

"None of your business."

A humorless chuckle falls from my lips. "See, now that's where you're wrong. Do you remember what you told me Saturday night?"

"No, I've blocked the entire event from my mind. No point remembering."

My brows rise as her words hit where they intended.

"Huh." I move forward, my lips against the shell of her ear. "So you don't remember screaming my name over and over as I made you come again, and again… and again."

"Nope."

"And you don't remember telling me that I fucking own you?" I drop my hand, cupping her pussy over the fabric of her jeans and she gasps.

"No. I was drunk and probably drugged knowing you."

"Careful, Kitten. Throwing accusations around isn't going to help."

"I have a right to be suspicious, you've got history."

"The only thing I handed you that night was neat vodka in a bottle that you willingly took." I pull back to look at her, hoping that she can see the truth in my eyes. "I'd never drug you, Harley. I'm not a fucking monster."

She laughs manically, throwing her head back and exposing her neck to me. Unable to resist, I lower my hand and suck her skin into my mouth.

"Kyle," she cries, her throat flexing beneath my lips.

She slaps at my shoulder trying to force me away but all I do is suck harder, leaving more evidence behind that I was here.

"Tell me, Kitten. Tell me why you were crying?"

"Fuck you." I'm still lost in the taste of her when she brings her knee up. I should be expecting it, she's got history after all.

I manage to move before she makes any real contact but the shock is enough for me to release her and she bolts to the other side of the locker room, her back to the door where she's about to escape from.

"You're playing a dangerous game, Kitten."

"Leave me the hell alone, Kyle. This little game you think we're playing… I never signed up for. I'm done. So fucking d-done." Her voice cracks on the final word and I stand back to my full height and take a step toward her. "No." She holds her hand up as her eyes fill with tears and her bottom lip trembles. "Just no. We're done."

I'm motionless as she flees from the room, leaving me alone with nothing but the scent of girl's perfume filling my nose.

"Fuck. FUCK," I bark, planting my fist into one of the red lockers beside me. The door buckles under my force but it doesn't make me feel any better.

"Fuuuuck," I groan, tipping my face to the ceiling and taking a slow breath.

I know that I should walk out before I'm caught but when my legs move, it's not toward the door, it's toward one of the benches. I drop my elbows to my knees and rest my head in my hands. I keep my eyes shut for a beat, trying to force myself to calm down. If I don't then the temptation to go and cause some damage—ideally to Rich's face—is going to be stronger than I can control.

When I finally drag my eyes open, I find a piece of paper by my feet. Swiping it up, I flip it over, and find that it's a report card. Harley's report card to be specific.

I scan my eyes down the subjects, taking in all the good grades, until I get to one.

Math.

Fail.

My shoulders drop. That's why she was crying.

Guilt twists my stomach that I should be helping her with this.

"Fuck," I mutter, pushing to stand and shoving the paper in my pocket.

I manage to exit the girl's locker room unseen and head for my car.

The second I pull to a stop on our street, I wish I'd stayed at school longer, or even better, went after Harley because the person who's leaning against the porch waiting for me is one I hoped I'd never have to see again.

Gray stands there with his boot propped up on the first step, his body clad entirely in black—much like mine—and his head bowed as he stares at his cell. From here I can see the ink adorning his fingers that never used to be there.

I was never scared of Gray although a lot of kids always were. He's the youngest of five brothers. Five brothers who taught him how to look after himself from a very young age.

He doesn't look up, but I'm not stupid enough to think that he doesn't know I'm here so after sucking in a breath, I climb from the car to find out what he's got in store for me.

I lost him a lot of money. I can't imagine he's here for a nice little catch-up chat. I'm just grateful he waited a week.

The second the car door slams behind me, he pockets his cell and looks up.

I notice instantly that the ink on his hands isn't the only new addition because he's also got something beside his eye.

"Gray," I say as I step up to him. He studies me silently for a few seconds, probably seeing if he can unnerve me, but he should know me better than that. We've been through too much, done too much shit together. A year away won't change any of that.

"Legend," he finally says with a nod of his head.

Walking past him, I take a seat on the swing sweat, rest my elbows on my knees and look up at him. There's no fucking way I'm inviting him inside. Not that he'd wait to be invited if he wanted to venture inside, I'm sure.

"What do you want, Gray?"

"Now there's a question," he mutters, almost to himself. "How was your… little break?" A smirk appears on his lips and my fists curl in my need to knock it off. It wouldn't be the first time we've fought, and it wouldn't be the first time I've won either.

"Fuck you."

"Legend, now, that's not nice."

"Not nice? You really want to talk about what's not fucking nice?" I ask, my anger getting the better of me as I push to stand once more. "Not nice is getting carted off with your fucking blow filling my pockets. Not nice is the search they did to make sure I wasn't hiding any more. Not nice, is being locked in a tiny fucking room for hours on end, not having anyone to talk to, only people who want to beat the shit out of you. Not fucking nice is not seeing the one woman who gave a fuck about me before she died and having to attend her funeral in fucking handcuffs, you motherfucker." Spittle flies onto his face at my outburst but he doesn't react.

"You know what's really not going to be nice?"

I step closer, my fists ready to break his fucking nose.

"What?" I spit.

"What's going to happen when you don't pay your debt."

"Fuck you, Gray. I owe you nothing. You'll have made that back ten times over by now."

"Not the point. You lost my gear. You. Owe. Me."

"I have nothing." I take a step back and throw my arms out. "I have fucking nothing, Gray. Everything is gone. What the fuck could you take from me?"

He thinks for a minute and something about the look on his face makes my blood run cold.

"Harley Hunter is looking good these days, huh?"

My teeth grind, my jaw popping despite the fact I don't want to react to this motherfucker.

"Come on, Legend. Don't pretend you haven't noticed." He leans in. "Because I know you have. You've wanted her longer than you'll ever admit. That night… that night I was just helping you out. Giving you the little push you needed."

I have his hoodie in my fist and him pressed against the railing of the porch before I've even realized I've moved.

"You fucking drugged her, Gray. You're fucking sick."

"You didn't look so bothered when she was getting ready to bounce around on your dick."

"Fuck you," I seethe, slamming him back against the wood.

"You're just angry because I wanted to play too. She'd have fucking loved it, and you know it. You could have been deep inside her cunt while she chok—" My fist flies, his nose crunching under the force of my hit. Blood covers both of us as an evil smile curls at his lips.

"Yeah, just as I thought."

My entire body is pulled tight ready for him to fight back, but instead, he just walks backward toward the stairs, spitting out a mouthful of blood as he does.

"You might want to keep a close eye on her, Legend. I'd hate for her to become payment."

"Don't you dare fucking touch her," I warn, but it's too late, he's already inside his car.

I watch as he wipes his nose on his sleeve before starting his car and wheelspinning down the street.

"Motherfucker," I bellow after him before pulling my cell from my pocket and opening mine and Harley's conversation.

I want to warn her. I want to tell her that he's just threatened her. But if he's just playing me...

Gray doesn't play.

But would he be stupid enough to mess with Harley knowing that he'll be going up against not only me but Kane and Zayn as well?

"Fuck," I shout into the empty street beyond.

I pull my cap from my head and pull my hair back, pulling until it hurts.

"Fuck."

Pulling out my key, I unlock the front door and storm inside.

I pace back and forth through the living room with my cell still in my hand trying to figure out what I should do.

I think about her tear-filled eyes as she fled from the locker room earlier and then the report card that's stuffed in my pocket.

Without putting much thought into it, I storm to my bedroom, flip open the textbook to the page we were working on last and I send the page and exercise number to her.

18

HARLEY

I slam my bedroom door after running up the stairs faster than my legs wanted to carry me.

I don't want to see anyone. I just want to hide from him, from math, from life.

"I fucking hate you, Kyle Legend," I bark into my empty bedroom.

Tears burn my eyes once more as I think about everything today threw at me.

The memory of kissing Rich makes my stomach turn. Nothing about him attracts me, I've only ever threatened to do anything with him to piss off my brother. But now I've kissed him, touched his cock. Ew. My lips curl in disgust but not at him, at myself. It was a stupid thing to do. But that's what he does to me. He makes me fucking stupid and drives me freaking crazy.

His scent still fills my nose from where he was so close to me in the locker room. His hard, sculpted body was pressed right up against mine, his hard cock digging into my hip reminding me of just how he tasted on Saturday night, how he looked as he lost control, how it felt when he came down my throat.

My body grows hot at the memory and annoys me even more.

Irritated with myself for allowing him to affect me even after I've walked away from him, I push from my door, turn my speakers up high and fall down onto my bed.

I've got work to do and continuing to put it off isn't going to get me anywhere.

I pull my math textbook out and flip it open.

I stare at it for a few seconds not really seeing any of it as my brain tells me not to even bother trying. But I know I need to shut that down. If I want to be on the squad for my senior year, then I need to do this. Hell, if I want to graduate then I need to do this.

"Okay, I can do this," I tell myself, leaning over and reading through the exercise I should be working on.

I'm halfway through my homework when my cell buzzes. It's face down on the sheets and I know that I really should ignore it.

It'll just be Ruby or Poppy checking in, they can wait.

But no matter how much I tell myself that, not two seconds later do I find myself reaching out and turning it over.

I groan the second I see who it really is.

Asshole: Turn to page 154 and start with exercise 3a.

"What?" I breathe.

Harley: What the hell?

Asshole: Don't argue, Kitten. Tell me how to work it out. Show me how you work it out.

I stare down at the screen, tempted to just turn it off and banish him from my life for a few hours but then I remember how he explained things to me during our first tutoring session once we called a truce and I find myself typing.

I write the sum on the page, I tell him how I think it should work and then I give him my answer once I've done the equation.

It's wrong. Obviously. But then he starts explaining why and even though he's not here, it's like I can hear his voice in my head as he spells it out in a way that I've only ever experienced with him.

Asshole: Now do the next one. Just like that.

I eagerly follow his instructions and soon discover that my next answer is right.

A little thrill goes through me as he messages back to confirm what I already know.

Asshole: Now do the rest. You've got this, Kitten.

Butterflies erupt in my belly as I stare down at his little pet name for me that I usually hate.

He just helped me. Why?

I shake my head, immediately realizing that I'm not going to figure him out quite that easily.

I quickly go through the rest of the exercises on the page and send him a list of my answers which, to my utter amazement are all correct.

An accomplished smile curls up at my lips, maybe I can do this. Just one step at a time.

I stare at his last message trying to figure out what to send back. There are a million things I want to say to him, to ask him when he's not full of anger and out for revenge but even now, I refrain.

Harley: Thank you.

Asshole: What are tutors for? What's next?

Harley: English paper. You?

Asshole: Same.

We message back and forth for the next three hours. It's nice. Weird. But I can't deny that I get a little thrill every time my cell buzzes and I see his name staring back at me.

It's when he tells me that he's done for the night and that he's going to shower that I realize I might have a problem because I almost demand we switch to video call just so I can go with him.

In the end, I go with something a little less desperate.

Harley: Thank you. I'm going to do some more math before bed.

He reads it but he doesn't respond, and my heart drops a little as I realize that he wasn't getting as carried away with our interaction as I was.

I place my cell back down, and after getting myself a snack and drink I pull my math book back onto my lap and attempt some more.

I've got another test on Wednesday; I'm determined not to fail this one.

The second I walk into class the next morning, his eyes are on me from the back of the room. His face is impassive and totally unreadable. I have no clue if he's still angry like in the locker room or if our messages last night softened him at all.

Ruby's fingers twist with mine as we make our way to our seats. I haven't told her about what happened after she and Chelsea left, and I certainly haven't told her about our impromptu tutoring session.

"Ignore him," she whispers, clearly seeing who's holding his attention.

My temperature burns red-hot as his eyes run over every inch of me as we get closer. Thankfully, our seats are far enough away that we can't talk because after everything that happened yesterday, I have no clue what to say to him, or even where to start.

Even long after turning my back on him to take my seat, I still feel his gaze on me. My skin prickles with awareness and tingles continue to race up and down my spine.

I can only hope that this is the only class we share today because he's already messing with my head.

I manage to escape him and it's not until I'm standing at my locker before heading to the cafeteria before lunch that I feel him.

Every muscle in my body screams at me to turn around and look at him, but I stand firm and instead remain staring at the back of my locker, hoping that he'll leave, or that I'm wrong and he's not there at all.

Sadly, that's not what happens.

My body startles when his large warm hand lands on my stomach and the length of him presses against my back. I only just manage to stifle the groan that threatens to rumble up my throat at his contact.

"Do I need to lock you up somewhere this lunch or are you going to be able to keep your hands to yourself, Kitten?"

I suck in a breath, unable to come up with a response as quickly as I'd like.

"What's wrong, cat got your tongue?"

His hand slips under the hem of my shirt, his touch scorching my already heated skin.

"I need to go, Rich is waiting for me," I lie, knowing it'll piss him off. "That was the best kiss I've had in quite a while."

"Harley," he growls in my ear, sending goose bumps racing across my skin. "I warned you about lying to me."

"Am I though?" I ask, fighting a smile. "Excuse me." Amazingly, when I twist out of his hold, he lets me go.

I slam my locker closed and march toward the cafeteria, my stomach growling for Taco Tuesday with every step I take.

I find Ruby, Poppy and Stella waiting for me at the entrance and together we join the queue.

"What the fuck is he playing at?" Poppy seethes, looking over my shoulder in the direction of our tables.

I don't have to turn around to know she's talking about Kyle. I can tell by the anger on their faces as they watch whatever is playing out.

My cell vibrates in my pocket. Despite knowing that nothing good can possibly come from it seeing as my girls are standing with me, not on their cells, I pull it out.

Asshole: Wanna see how it's really done? Turn around.

I fight it, I really fucking do. But when all three of them gasp, my body moves without instruction from my brain.

The second I look up, my eyes land on Kyle who's got Aria straddling his lap, his hands disappearing under her skirt and her lips on his neck while he stares right at me, a satisfied smirk playing on his lips.

"You just gonna let that happen?" Ruby asks me.

"Uh... yeah. Why wouldn't I?" I try really fucking hard not to allow the hurt I'm feeling come to transfer into my voice. But when her eyes soften in sympathy, I'm not sure I'm all that successful. "He's nothing to me. He can do whatever he wants."

"You really believe that?" Poppy asks.

"Yeah, I really do. He's just trying to get a reaction from me and he's not going to get one. I don't care," I say, turning back to him and ensuring he can read my lips.

I take my tray from the rail once we've all paid and we make our way over. I try not to look as we get closer but it's impossible to ignore the fact that Aria is now sitting beside Kyle with her hand resting high on his thigh while she looks up at him like he just hung the moon.

"He's watching you," Stella whispers to me as we pass. I don't need her to tell me though, I feel it.

I ignore her, pull out a chair and sit down doing the best I can to pretend that I don't give a shit about what he's doing behind me.

The second we finish eating, Stella and I escape in favor of... well, anywhere other than the cafeteria, and leave everyone—including Kyle and his new cheer slut—behind.

"That was brutal."

"It was nothing," I mutter, trying to play it off like it didn't hurt.

"You don't need to do that, you know."

"Do what?" I force some lightness into my tone that I really don't feel as we allow a couple of girls to leave the bathroom before we enter.

"Pretend it doesn't bother you."

"It doesn't. He can do whatever he wants."

She stares at me for a beat before disappearing into one of the stalls while I pull my makeup bag out in the hope I can cover up the truth that I'm sure she can read all over my face.

By the time she emerges, I've got a whole new layer of confidence plastered on.

"Just so you know, my dad has a cupboard full of guns, and I'm a pretty good shot." The seriousness she says this with makes me burst out laughing.

"Oh my God, you're serious, aren't you?"

"Deadly. I'm sure we could hide the body and get away with it."

"I'll keep that in mind."

"Okay, well if not, he's also got some scary-ass friends that I'm sure would do me a favor if I asked sweetly enough."

"Who the hell is your dad, the fucking mafia?"

"Honestly, I have no idea. He's secretive as fuck but I do know that whatever he does do isn't totally above board. Please don't tell anyone I said that."

"Of course not. Your secret's safe with me." I wink, shoving my makeup bag into my purse and getting ready to head to class.

We go our separate ways once we emerge from the bathroom. Stella toward her Spanish class and me history.

"Hey, how it's going?" Carl asks, dropping down into his seat beside me. The two of us have occupied this desk at the very back of the classroom all year.

"It's good. You?"

"Not bad." Carl is on the baseball team so he's mostly oblivious to the gossip surrounding the football team. He's easy to talk to and he's not bad to look at either. He's also been in love with his girlfriend for as long as I can remember which makes him even easier to talk to. "So ready for this week to be over though."

"It's only Tuesday," I say, although the way my week is going, I'd be inclined to agree with him.

"Yeah well. Misty and I have the house to ourselves this weekend so..."

"Say no more." I wink. "I hope you've got plenty of romantic shit planned."

"I'm doing my best." He starts rattling off some of his ideas, most of which make me swoon. Although the second I realize they're all the kind of things that Nathan would have done, my stomach twists painfully.

I had the sweet guy right there making all the right moves and saying all the right things, and what did I do? I fucked it all up. Epically fucked it all up.

The volume of chatting filling the room suddenly lessens and assuming our teacher has just entered to start the class, the two of us turn toward the front, only, I don't get a chance to look that far because my eyes lock on a very angry pair staring down at Carl.

"Move," Kyle demands, his voice hard, leaving no room for discussion.

"Ignore him," I say, placing my hand on Carl's shoulder without thinking.

A growl rumbles up Kyle's throat the second I make contact with him.

"I said. Move."

"Kyle, stop being an asshole," I snap. "There's like a million other seats in here. Just go sit in one of those."

He tilts his head to the side for a beat as if he's considering my words before one word falls from his lips.

"No."

"Honestly, it's fine. I'll just..." Carl begins gathering up his stuff.

"No, it's not fine. This is where you sit."

"I know but..." he shoots Kyle a concerned look and it's then I realize that he's scared. Brilliant. Fucking brilliant.

Carl disappears to the other side of the class giving Kyle the space he clearly wanted, so he could drop down beside me.

"Hey, Kitten."

"Go fuck yourself. Or better yet, go fuck Aria, if you haven't already."

"Careful, Kitten. You sound a little jealous there."

I snort a laugh. "Careful, asshole. You sound even more arrogant than usual."

He chuckles at me, sliding his chair over so it's as close to mine as physically possible.

"What the hell do you—"

"Afternoon everyone. All ready to get started?" Mr. Anderson says, effectively silencing the entire classroom as he slams the door closed behind me.

"Hmmm… I am more than ready to get started. What do you say, Kitten?" Kyle breathes in my ear, making me shudder as he sits back in his chair and rests his arms across the back of mine, his fingers brushing my shoulder blade.

"Get your hands off me," I snap, sitting forward and putting as much space between us as I can.

"What did I tell you about lying? I know you're more than ready," he whispers, his fingers ghosting down my spine until they run along the slivers of skin that's been revealed between my shirt and my jeans. "Are you wet for me, Kitten?"

I cut him a scathing look.

"I thought you wanted to graduate?"

An irritatingly stunning smile curls at his lips and something inside my tummy clenches.

His eyes drop from mine in favor of my lips. He sucks his bottom one into his mouth and all I can think about is doing the exact same thing to it.

Damn him.

I force myself to picture Aria on his lap barely an hour ago.

"Yeah, and I will. But right now, I've got more pressing issues."

His fingers move back up my spine and brush against my neck, almost massaging for a few seconds. My eyes shutter at just how good it feels before he wraps the fabric in his fist and uses it to pull me back against my seat, the neckline digging into my skin.

"Do you—" My words falter when I find his dark stare burning into mine.

He smiles once again, and I manage to snap myself out of whatever trance he had me under.

"Miss Hunter, Mr. Legend, are you following?"

We both turn toward the teacher, but his grip on my shirt doesn't lessen. Thank God we're at the back so no one can see what he's doing.

My face flushes with embarrassment that we've been caught as I stutter out, "Y-yes, sir."

"Okay good, so you'll both know exactly what I just asked you all to discuss and you'll be able to explain your conclusion to the class?"

"O-of course." I smile sweetly at him. Never before in my life have I been this distracted in class.

I've always been the good student, the one who always hits deadlines and often does extra—math is the exception to the rule, I guess I figured that if I try hard enough elsewhere then no one will notice. Fail.

"Okay, brilliant. You all have twenty minutes in your pairs to discuss and come up with an argument."

Students' chatter begins to fill the room as they embark on the task at hand, I, however, am frozen staring at the board with the instructions on it as Kyle's stare burns into the side of my face.

He turns toward me a little, as if we're actually about to discuss something of importance and he leans closer. His scent fills my nose as his knee brushes against my thigh. It's a simple touch and one that shouldn't elicit such a strong reaction within me, but I can't help it.

"W-what are you d-doing?"

He slides the textbook on the desk between us, I can only assume it's open on the right page because I can't focus on it.

My chest heaves as I try to fight the sensations washing through my body at his nearness, at the tightness around my throat and the heat of him against my skin.

"What are you thinking about, Kitten?" he asks.

My spine remains rigid as image after image assaults my mind of him pushing me back against the wall and wrapping his hand around my throat.

My body burns up at the thoughts alone and I know it's evident on my face.

"We need to get to work," I force out and thankfully, his grip on my neck lessens until it's gone completely.

"Yeah, I guess we do," he murmurs.

I breathe a sigh of relief when his touch leaves me and he turns toward the book, pen in hand, ready to write notes whatever it is we're supposed to be discussing. But the second I move to do the same, his hot hand lands on my thigh under the table. It skims higher until his little finger flicks the seam at the juncture of my thighs.

"So I was thinking..." he starts as if he was actually fucking listening to what we're supposed to be doing. "What if the outcome of this meeting went the other way..." He pushes his fingers between my thighs and forces them apart.

"What the fuck?" I hiss about ready to snap his wrist to stop him but then he pushes harder against my core. “Oh God,” I gasp, my body spiraling out of control at that one simple touch from him.

I know this shouldn’t be happening. I shouldn’t be allowing it. He just had Aria kissing him only moments ago in the cafeteria but fuck, I’m not sure I can stop.

19

KYLE

A smile twitches at my lips as I discreetly glance over at her.

Her lids are lowered, her lips parted but her jaw clenches almost in frustration. She wants to stop me. She thinks that would be the right thing to do. But I also think she knows that she's not the one in control here. I am.

My fingers continue to move against her while I write a few notes because I already know that our teacher is going to be good on his word of making us give an explanation, and like fuck am I not going to have one.

I almost laugh when she relaxes back in her chair a little and widens her legs.

She's so fucking easy to play. But I know exactly why, because I feel it too the few times she's touched me.

Powerless.

Fucking powerless.

I continue working as her breathing begins to increase. I glance over once more but the table hides what I'm doing to her.

"Why didn't you wear a skirt this morning?" I ask as seriously as if I'm talking about the work.

Her lust-filled eyes turn on me and her hand wraps around my forearm, her nails digging into my skin.

"You're an asshole," she seethes.

"Yet you're still letting me touch you."

Her nails dig in harder until I'm convinced that she'll have drawn blood when she releases me, not that I give a fuck. The thought of having her mark on me only gets me harder.

"And you're going to let me make you come, aren't you, Kitten?"

"No," she snaps, a little too loudly.

"Harley, is everything okay?" our teacher asks.

"Um… yeah… I really need to go to the bathroom."

Oh, Kitten. Do you have any idea what you've just done?

"Be quick," he grumbles, already pissed off with us.

The second she's gone, I pull my cell from my pocket and send a message.

Not four minutes later is there a knock at our classroom door and a familiar head peers inside.

"I'm sorry, sir. I just need to borrow Kyle Legend for a few minutes as per Coach's orders."

"Fine," he groans, looking at me and nodding to the door, seemingly totally unaware that I've set the whole thing up.

Leaving my books on the desk, I push my chair out and walk to the door, closing it behind me.

"Cheers, man. I appreciate it."

"Gonna tell me why you needed to get out?" Ash asks, his brows pulling together. I knew the second he looked at my message that he'd understand. We're the same, Ash and I, we grew up the same and we have a similar way of thinking, which is why I'm even surprised he's asking this question.

"Why do you think, man?" I slap him on the shoulder as I walk away. "I owe you one," I call back as I head for the closest bathroom.

The room is silent as I push the door open and step inside. Only one of the stalls is being used, and the second I rest my ass back against the basins, the flush is pressed.

My fingers curl around the counter as my heart beats steadily in my chest. If this isn't her, I could have an issue on my hands.

But something tells me it is. She wouldn't have run that far because she wouldn't have expected me to follow.

The lock on the door slides open and I wait for it to open.

The second it does, I know it's her. I recognize the dark purple nail polish that was sinking into my skin only minutes ago.

She doesn't notice me straight away, she's too busy staring at the floor.

Pushing from my resting place, I take a step toward her, totally unnoticed for two seconds. But my sneakers squeak on the floor and her head flies up, but I'm faster.

My hand wraps around her throat and I direct her back until she's against the wall.

"Surprise." I move forward until our noses are almost brushing.

"What the hell?"

"What? You really thought I'd let you run. I thought you knew me better than that, Kitten."

"W-we… we need to get back to class. Mr. Anderson will blow a fuse."

"Mr. Anderson doesn't give a shit or he wouldn't have let us both out," I growl, my lips brushing hers as my body presses her against the tiles at her back.

"Kyle," she warns as my hand lands on her waist and slips under her shirt.

"Kitten."

Our eyes hold, our breaths mingling and our chest heaving as we wait to see what the other is going to do.

Finally, her lips part, and as much as I might want to kiss her, to dirty her up before she's forced to go back to class, I'm too intrigued as to what she's going to say to make use of her open mouth.

"I hate you," she seethes. "Why won't you just leave me alone?"

"Oh, Kitten." I laugh. "If only I could."

"What do you want from me? An apology? I'm sorry I called the cops and you got locked up," she says totally insincerely, throwing her arms out from her side.

"Oh yeah, because you totally meant that."

"You and Gray—" Just the mention of his name makes my blood run cold. "You were going to—"

"We were going to do what?" I ask, needing to know what she thinks happened that night.

"You were going to—"

"What the hell? Harley, are you okay?" a voice says from behind me and I freeze.

"Y-yeah. Kyle was just going back to class, weren't you?" She smiles at me but there's no kindness there, it's full of hate and bitterness.

"We're going to talk about this, Kitten," I growl, low enough so that our little one-woman audience can't hear me.

"Then maybe you should stop being a dick," she suggests.

"I'd love to, but you just bring it out in me." I flex my hips, ensuring my length presses into her hip.

"Get the fuck off me, asshole." Her palms slam down on my chest and I take pity on her and back away ensuring that she notices when I drop my hand to rearrange myself in my jeans. Her eyes zero in on my movement and then darken with lust.

I blow her a kiss before backing out of the room. At the last second, I glance at the girl who interrupted us. Her blue eyes narrow on me and she bares her teeth in anger.

"Down girl, you can get a turn as well if you like."

"Fuck off, pig," she barks, much to my amusement as the door closes behind me.

The hallway is empty as I make my way back to class and take a seat.

Mr. Anderson watches my every move, I can feel his attention on me, but at no point do I look up at him. Instead, I make use of the time I've got until she returns to write some notes.

After a few minutes, I start to think she's not going to come back, but when I glance at the floor, I find that in her haste to get away from me, she left her purse.

I smile to myself, sitting back just as the door opens and she steps inside the room, still looking totally flustered and uncomfortable.

"Is everything okay, Miss Hunter?"

"Yes, thank you, sir."

He nods at her as she pulls her chair as far away from me as she can and retakes her seat.

I look over at her, an amused smile playing on my lips.

"Don't," she snaps. "Don't say anything, don't do anything unless you want the end of this pen embedded in your dick."

"I love it when you talk dirty to me."

A growl rumbles up her throat as Mr. Anderson announces that we've got two minutes to bring our arguments to a close and be ready to present.

The hate covering her face morphs into one of panic as she realizes that we're going to have to give our opinion on this seeing as we've already been warned and she's not so much as thought about it.

"I hope you're ready." I turn away from her and look to the teacher who's got his eyes on the two of us.

Oh yeah, we're definitely going first.

"Right. Time is up. Miss Hunter, Mr Legend, why don't you start us off."

I smile at him. He's so fucking predictable.

"Go on, you can start," I encourage, nudging Harley's arm with my elbow.

"Harley..." Mr. Anderson says.

Hesitantly, she stands. Her chair scraping across the old tiled floor, ensuring that everyone in the room turns her way.

She stares at our teacher before looking down at me. Her eyes are wide as she clenches her fists at her sides.

"I... um..." Mr. Anderson's brows rise as his patience begins to vanish. "Err..." She looks down at me as if I'm going to help her but I just smile up at her as sweetly as I can manage. "So... what we thought was..."

Her eyes flick to the board behind Mr. Anderson as if she's even forgotten what we were supposed to be talking about—assuming she even knew in the first place.

"Miss Hunter?" he asks, crossing his arms over his chest as sniggers begin to rumble around the room as she awkwardly shifts on her feet.

I fight to keep my ass in the chair as she prays for the ground to swallow her up but I can't do it. She might think I'm an asshole, and I am, to a point.

I push my chair out behind me and stand beside her. She looks at me, probably waiting for me to make this whole situation worse but to her surprise, that's not what happens.

"What Harley is trying to say is that we thought if the decision went the opposite way that the Civil War would have started that much later, but that the intensity of the fighting would have been much more significant. Also that the death count would have well surpassed what happened in reality."

Even as I'm talking, I don't miss the huge sigh of relief she lets out that I just got us off the hook.

"Interesting point, Kyle." He continues to question me and I answer him as if we were discussing this subject the whole time.

He smiles at me before turning back to Harley. "Well, it seems Mr. Legend has saved you from an afternoon in detention. You can both sit."

As our asses hit the chair, he begins to question another couple.

"How'd you do that?" Harley whispers. "How'd you know what to say?"

"I'm not just a pretty face, Kitten." I wink at her and she rolls her eyes.

The second the bell rings, she all but scoops her belongings into her purse and damn near runs from the door.

I hang back as students leave and Mr. Anderson wipes off the board and collects up the textbooks.

It's not until I stand and about to throw my bag over my shoulder when he speaks.

"I know things are done differently at Creek High but here, we don't tolerate our students trying to sabotage others."

I nod at him, not wanting to get into a discussion about Harley. "You got it, sir," I mutter as I walk through the door and join the mass of students heading toward the exits for the evening.

I head in the opposite direction of the majority as I go toward the locker rooms for a conditioning session.

Pulling out my cell, I can't resist sending her one more message.

Kyle: You're welcome!

Her response is instant, there are no words, just a hand emoji with its middle finger in the air.

I'm still smiling to myself when I walk into the locker room. The second I look up, I find a man standing in front of the team who I've only seen from a distance so far.

"Legend," Coach says to me as I come to a stop beside Ash. "I've heard good things about you from Coach West."

I nod at him, glad that something good might have come out of my few years at Creek High.

"With you, Fury, and a few of our JV team this year, we might just stand a chance of living up to this year's success. I'm going to be watching all of you over the next few weeks, Jake and the seniors too. I don't just want good players, I want decent fucking human beings on my team. So watch your backs, ladies," he says making eye contact with me, Ash, and the others who I know to be juniors. "If you play your cards right, you might just be able to call yourself a Rosewood Bear in the coming months."

Excited chatter vibrates through the group before Coach nods at Jake, who takes to the front of the crowd.

"Don't think it's going to be easy, you all have a reputation to keep. Get your asses changed and get out on the field, we want to see what you pussies are made of."

"How competitive was your old team?" Ash asks me once we've broken away from the crowd to change.

"Their biggest priorities were getting high and scoring pussy," I answer honestly. "We were never going to win fuck all unless you count collecting STDs."

Ash snorts a laugh as he rips his locker open and pulls his shirt over his head.

"What about yours?"

"Same. My old school was a fucking jungle. I'm buzzing to take this a little more seriously."

“You shooting for captain?” I ask, knowing that he held the position in his old team.

“Maybe,” he says, but a small smile twitches at his lips. “We’ll see. Why? You wanna be my assistant?”

I think for a minute. Kane was captain at Harrow Creek High. I wasn’t there long enough to even get a chance. Do I want to follow in his footsteps and take the lead with Ash? “Hell fucking yeah I do.”

“Damn right. This team is ours, man.” I hold my fist out and he bumps it before turning back to drag on a pair of shorts.

20

HARLEY

Anger swirls around me like a firestorm through our first cheer practice. Although we don't actually do much cheer because we spend most of the time listening to Chelsea and—shockingly—Miss Kelly explains what's going to happen next and the process of selecting our new varsity squad.

I find myself losing focus faster than ever thanks to *him* and his actions in history.

Did I want him touching me? I can tell myself that the answer is no until I'm blue in the face, but really, every time his fingers so much as graze my skin, I feel alive in a way I only ever have a few times in my life. And all of those times involve him—even if I thought I was going to die during one of them.

Ruby and Stella look at me with curious glances but I keep my lips firmly shut. They probably think I'm still stewing on the fact he let Aria kiss him at lunch. I guess I am a little. But so much has happened since then it's almost a distant memory. Almost.

"We heading to Ace's?" someone asks the second we're back in the locker room.

"Only if the team are going," Aria sings.

"Whore," Ruby mutters beside me. "We're going to Ace's."

"Uh… I'm not. I don't want to watch her grind her ass all over Kyle."

Both Ruby and Stella look at me with sympathy in their eyes. Stella more so after what she walked in on earlier.

She'd tried to get me to talk, but after all of that, I was in no mood. I'd attempted to convince her that it was fine and to drop it but I can already see that I'm on borrowed time.

"But—"

"No buts, Rubes. I'm not going. She can have at it." I keep my expression neutral while inside everything clenches in disgust at even the suggestion. "Come to mine, we'll order pizza."

They look at each other, the rest of the squad still discussing the team, before agreeing.

An hour later, Poppy has joined us, and we're hanging out on my bed with two giant pizzas between the four of us. We probably should be doing homework—I know I should be doing math—but it feels good to kick back after the day I've had.

"So how many high schools have you been to exactly?" Ruby asks Stella.

She sighs. "This is my fifth."

"Fifth?" the three of us echo.

"Two freshman year," she says, holding up her fingers to count. "One sophomore, and then another before I joined Rosewood."

"Jesus. And all across the country?"

"Yep, New York, Michigan, Colorado, Washington, here. And that's just high school. I've lost count of the number of schools before ninth grade."

"Fucking hell, it's amazing you know your own name after that," I say around a mouthful of pepperoni pizza.

"So where are you actually from?" Ruby asks.

"Well, I have no recollection of it, but apparently I was born in England. My dad moved us over here before I was one."

"What about your mom?"

She shrugs, a sad expression washing over her face. "Dead. I think that's why he moved. He couldn't be there without her."

"Shit."

"Meh," she says with another shrug, grabbing a slice of pizza. "It is what it is, gotta make the best of it, I guess."

"Well, I'm in awe of you," Poppy says sincerely.

"And you still have no idea where to next?"

"Nope. Just that it's coming. Dad's not said anymore but I can sense it. I know his tells. He's getting ready to move."

"We're going to miss you."

"Me too. I think Rosewood might be my favorite out of all my homes. I could see myself here."

"Shame you don't get a choice."

"Maybe I'll come back one day. Once I've finished college, I am finding myself a home and I'm staying put for a very long freaking time."

"Don't blame you."

Feeling sorry for Stella having to relive all her moves, I turn the conversation away from her and back toward cheer, much to Poppy's joy if her dramatic eye roll is anything to go by.

"You'd better get used to it," Stella tells her, clearly noticing her move. "If these two get captain and assistant, it's all they're going to talk about."

"It's fine," she says flippantly. "I can just go over the hall and bang the assistant's brother."

"Oh, you did not just say that." I launch a cushion at her head, both of us falling about laughing.

It feels good. So fucking good. But that all comes crashing down when my cell pings in my pocket.

My heart jumps into my throat. Without looking, I know who it is. I can sense it.

"You gonna get that?" Ruby asks when it goes off again a few minutes later.

"Um…" Reluctantly, I pull it from my back pocket and find exactly what I was expecting.

Asshole: Page 162 exercise 1a. Gimme the answers.

Clearly I don't cover up my feelings at seeing his words on my screen because as I'm still reading Ruby is asking who it is.

"Just my math tutor. Wants me to work."

"We can go," she offers.

"No, no. It's fine. He'll have to wait."

"Who is it?" Poppy asks. I knew the question was coming yet still, I don't have a decent response.

"Some nerd I swear I've never seen around school before."

"Is he any good?"

My head goes straight in the gutter and I'm right back in Justin's guest room with Kyle's head between my legs.

My cheeks heat as I stare down at his words on my cell.

"Ugh, yeah, he's all right."

It's probably about fifteen minutes later when another message comes through.

Asshole: Don't make me come over there.

The threat makes my heart skip a beat.

"Him again?" Poppy asks.

"Yeah," I say reluctantly.

"We should go. We know how important this is."

I don't get a chance to argue, not that I think they'd allow me to because they gather up the pizza boxes and the empty soda cans littering my bedroom and make their way to the door.

"We'll see you tomorrow," Ruby says as she and Stella slip out of my room.

"Call me if you need me. I'm just gonna do some homework," Poppy adds before following them out and leaving me alone with just the cell in my hand.

It pings again.

Asshole: You have five minutes to respond or shit's getting real, Kitten.

Rolling my eyes at him, I start typing.

Harley: I was busy, ASSHOLE. WHAT DO YOU WANT?

Asshole: I gave you my instructions, now... I want answers.

Harley: You're as demanding as my mother.

Asshole: Oh Kitten, I am so NOT like your mother...

My body flushes hot at what he could mean and my teeth sink into my bottom lip as those memories assault me once again.

Damn him.

Asshole: I'm waiting.

"Fuck's sake."

Leaning over the side of the bed, I grab my purse and pull out my textbook, my workbook and a pen.

Flipping the page open to the one he said, I groan at the sight of the exercise.

I go through the steps like he taught me last night and fire off my answers to him.

Asshole: First one is right. Others aren't. You need to go through the process again?

I fall back on my bed, tears filling my eyes faster than I can control.

I thought I had this. I thought I'd figured it out with his instructions last night.

Not wanting to admit defeat, I reply.

Harley: Let me try again.

I blow out a breath, turn to a clean page, and start over. Going through everything he told me last night. I get different answers this time but I have no idea if that's a good thing or not. They're probably still wrong.

I shoot him the new answers.

Asshole: Yes! Now, do the rest of that exercise.

I repeat the process again and again and every time he confirms that I've got it right.

I smile to myself as the latest 'well done' comes through, my confidence starting to grow. Maybe I can do this. Maybe I'm not destined to be a math idiot forever.

Asshole: Ready for more...

Jesus. Why do his messages about math send my head elsewhere?

Harley: Hit me.

Asshole: I'd rather not. I can think of something else I'd like to do though...

Harley: Focus. Unless you've already got Aria bouncing around on you right now.

Asshole: No, Kitten. I'm all yours.

An excited flutter rushes through me at his words.

"Focus, Harley. You hate him, remember," I remind myself as I look to the next exercise. I swallow my groan when I see it getting harder. My heart starts to race and the confidence I had started to build gets knocked down.

Kyle explains the next step of the process, and it sounds simple enough. I've already proved I can do the first part.

I set to work and quite quickly come up with some answers.

I send them to him full of hope that I've nailed it.

He reads my message immediately and starts typing. My heart pounds as I wait for his response. I've got a really good feeling about this, a part of me thinks that if I can nail this, then I can do all of it.

The dots bounce for ages and I start to wonder if he's writing an essay back.

My hope starts to wane when I realize that if they were right, he'd have already told me by now.

A lump forms in my throat and pressure builds behind my eyes.

Maybe I should just turn my cell off and avoid the inevitable. But just as I consider that option, it pings.

Asshole: I'm sorry, Kitten. But I think I know where you went wrong.

"FUCK," I scream into my room, throwing myself back on the bed in frustration. I really thought I had that.

Before he has a chance to say any more, I send him a message.

Harley: I can't do this. Sorry for wasting your time.

My thumb hovers over the off button but before I press it to put an end to all of this a call comes through.

A video call.

My hand trembles as I stare at his name.

I can't answer this. I've got tears running down my cheeks, makeup probably everywhere.

I can't answer—my finger swipes across the screen despite what my brain is telling me and the call connects.

"Kitten," he breathes when he gets his first look at me. "You were so close. Please don't cry."

A sob rips up my throat at the softness in his voice and more tears fall.

"I thought you wanted to make me cry," I mutter, trying to turn this away from me being a total failure.

His brows pinch as he stares at me, sympathy covering his features. He looks just like the boy I remember like this and it makes my heart ache.

I might not have intended the outcome of that night—he may have been involved, but he was far from the main player in trying to ruin my life that night—but still, the weight of what happened to him falls on my shoulders. The reason this is the first time I'm seeing the old Kyle, the fun loving, intelligent boy who had the world at his feet, is me.

"Not like this, Harley." The sincerity in his voice makes my breath catch.

We stare at each other in silence, only the sound of my shaky breathing filling my ears. No words are being said but I feel like a line is being drawn.

"I'm… I'm sorry, Ky."

He smiles at me, lifting his arm to run his fingers through what I now notice is damp hair. The second he drops his hand, his hair falls straight back over his brow and I smile, liking him without the ball cap that's constantly attached to his head.

His ice-blue eyes pierce mine and I swear I don't breathe as I wait for him to say something.

"Me too, Kitten. Me too."

"So…" he starts. "Did you want to try those again?"

His question damn near gives me whiplash. I was so lost in his eyes and my memories.

"Uh… not really." I laugh.

"Well, that's a real shame because I'm not hanging up until you've smashed it."

"You know I could just hang up on you, right?"

"Yeah, but you won't," he states confidently.

"Is that right?"

"Yep. Unless you want me there in person." He raises a brow and leans closer to the camera making me wonder if that is exactly what I do want.

"Never," I spit, hoping that it sounds like I mean it.

"You didn't seem so concerned that last time I was there."

"So math," I say, making him chuckle down the line. An easy smile curls at his lips and I have the urge to screenshot it because it's so beautiful and so at odds with the anger I've become used to since he appeared.

"Prop your cell up somewhere and let's do it."

I shift around, grabbing the holder that's on my nightstand and setting it up on the bed.

"Harley," he growls the second I place my cell in the holder and point it toward me. "What the hell are you wearing?"

I look down at myself and my cheeks heat. Shit.

"Um… we had practice. I've… um… not showered yet," I admit with a wince. We hardly did any actual practice so I didn't bother changing after, just threw on a zip-up hoodie over my booty shorts and sports bra. Ruby and Stella were similar so I didn't think anything of it when I was with them.

Now though with his eyes drilling into my barely clad body, I'm regretting the fuck out of it.

"O-okay," he says, clearing his throat as I release the stand and wrap my hoodie around me to cover up. "Don't feel like you have to."

"This is a tutoring session, Kyle, not—" I slam my lips.

"Not what?" he asks, amusement dancing in his blue eyes.

"Not anything else. So this exercise, you said you thought you knew what I did wrong." I never thought I'd willingly be encouraging a conversation about math, but there we go.

I pull my workbook and pen onto my lap as Kyle starts talking through the process.

In only seconds, I can see the obvious mistake I'd made and I feel a little better about the whole thing.

"Okay, so do the next exercise. I'm just gonna grab a drink."

"Okay," I say without even looking at the screen as a thud sounds out where he must have put his cell down before his footsteps get farther away.

I make quick work of going through each exercise and by the time he comes back, I've got all the answers staring back at me.

"Done?" he asks, settling himself back against his headboard and staring at me through the screen.

"Yep." I hold up my workbook so he can see. He's silent as I assume he looks at the answers and the longer he doesn't say anything the more butterflies erupt in my belly.

I really don't want to have failed again.

"Smashed it," he finally says and I drop my workbook so I can see him.

"Really?" I ask, a wide smile splitting my face.

"Yeah. Let's do one more exercise and then we can celebrate."

"Celebrate?" I ask, unsure as to whether or not I like the sound of that.

"Yeah, you wanna have some fun with me, Kitten?" His voice is low and gravelly and it does weird things to my insides let alone what's going on between my thighs.

"Um… it's probably better that I don't. Fun with you doesn't always end up so… pleasurable," I breathe that one word and have to fight a laugh when his eyes widen in shock.

"Is that right? I seem to remember things being very pleasurable when we have fun."

"That's because your idea of fun is…" I hesitate, trying to come up with the right word. "More like torture."

"Torture?" He almost spits out the mouthful of soda he'd not yet swallowed. "Oh Kitten, I don't remember you complaining."

My body heats to uncomfortable temperatures as I remember just how willingly I got between his legs at Justin's.

Jesus, I was a damn slut that night.

Alcohol. It was the alcohol.

"With your hand around my throat, it makes it kinda hard to say anything."

He throws his head back and laughs. It was not the reaction I was expecting but the sound of his joy sure makes up for it.

"Harley?" he says, dragging his head forward and holding my eyes captive through the screen.

"Y-yeah?" The stuttered word comes out as no more than a whisper.

"Take your hoodie off."

"Um… I really don't think—"

"Harley," he growls and it sends shivers racing down my spine. "Be a good girl and do what you're told."

I hold his stare, my need to refuse is right on the tip of my tongue. But instead of parting my lips to do just that, I find myself shrugging out of my hoodie as he demanded.

Ripping his eyes from mine, he drops them down my torso. My sports bra is small. I've not got all that much that needs controlling so I can get away with cute little ones.

"Go on then. I want the rest of the answers."

"And what about you?" I tilt my head to the side and drop my eyes to the bottom of the screen but I can't see anything past his neck.

"Get the answers right and it might just be your lucky day, Kitten."

"Fucking hell," I mutter to myself, looking down at the workbook in my lap and snatching up my pen.

How the hell did I end up here?

"Nothing good happens to me when I'm around you," I say quietly, unsure if he'll hear it, not that it matters if it does.

"Is that right? I guess it's a good thing you're not actually near me right now then."

"Do you mind? I'm busy working."

"Sure, you carry on. I'll just enjoy the view."

His words make me look up and the second I do they collide with his sparkling blue-grey ones.

Shaking my head at him, I look back down and try to focus on what I should be doing.

He's silent as I work through each question but I can feel his stare despite the fact it's through a screen.

It's better this way. He might be infuriating but he's easier to manage when there's space between us. His presence is less suffocating.

"Done?" he asks when I straighten my back and drop my pen.

"Yep."

"And how confident are you?"

"Hmm… I don't know. I guess it depends on what I get in return."

He thinks for a beat. "I'll show you mine if you show me yours." He wiggles his brows and I bark a laugh at his craziness.

It's nice to laugh and joke like things between us are okay. I'm not stupid enough to think it's our reality though. The second I see him at school tomorrow, I know the scowl that seems to be constantly on his face will be back and he'll look at me like he wants to kill me. It seems to be our thing, like this right now is our little secret.

And I hate that I like it as much as I do.

"You're serious, aren't you?"

I haven't forgotten that while he had me totally naked on Saturday night that he barely showed me any skin and I'm damn near desperate to see those muscles that I've run my hands over, traced with my fingertips.

"I never joke about getting naked, Kitten."

"Fuck off, why don't you. That whole thing Saturday night was a game and you know it."

"Game? No. Revenge, Kitten. It's all about revenge."

"And what about this right now. How do I know you're not going to use this against me somehow? Shame me in front of the entire school for my extracurricular activities with my math tutor."

His eyes harden as he thinks about my words. "You think I'd allow any other fucker to see you like I see you?"

I shrug because I honestly have no idea. He clearly has a game plan here. This push and pull between us. This need for revenge mixed with the sweet guy I remember, he's playing me. There's no other excuse for it. "I have no idea, Ky. You tell me."

He sits up and lifts the screen, all I can see is his face and his captivating eyes.

"Never," he says slowly. "This thing between us. It's exactly that. Between us."

"That's why you had Aria grinding on your cock earlier, was it?" I know I shouldn't say the words, I know it's only going to piss him off and ruin the light banter we've had going but the words slip past my lips without permission.

"And why you kissed Rich and damn near made him come in his pants in the cafeteria."

"You're a prick. You started all this."

"If you count me coming on to you that night a year ago, me starting all this, then yeah, okay, guilty."

I swallow down the emotion that night threatens to drag up. "Y-you were going to—"

"Bullshit," he barks, making me jump. "You don't really believe any of that was to do with me, do you?"

I shrug, unable to talk through the lump clogging my throat.

"I just wanted you that night, Kitten. I'd wanted you for a fucking long time," he admits, but if the small gasp after is anything to go by then I don't think he was supposed to.

"Y-you wanted me before that night?" My brows draw together in confusion. "But you never—"

"How could I? Zayn would have fucking gutted me alive if I touched you."

"So what was different that night?"

He shrugs. "He wasn't there. You were, and my restraint snapped."

"Did you go after me knowing what he'd done? Did you know how the night was going to end?"

He chuckles and drops his head into his hand, scrubbing his fingers against his jaw.

When his eyes come back to mine, they're damn near silver.

"No, Kitten. If I'd have fucking knew I'd have got you out of there. I fucking wish I had."

I have no words as I stare at him after that confession. I knew deep down that Kyle had nothing to do with what happened that night. It's why I never said it was him, why he didn't end up in any more shit than he already was. Gray was the dealer, the one with the connections, we all knew that. Even if Kyle did slip me something, it would have come from Gray, without a doubt, but I really wanted to believe he didn't.

He might not have got me out of there fast enough, he might have got himself a little too drunk and allowed things to get out of hand, but he never left me and it's why he ended up where he did.

I blow out a long breath, knowing that I'm potentially about to get myself in a lot of shit. If he does what he just promised he wouldn't do and Zayn sees this. The thought is almost enough to stop me. Almost.

Crossing my arms in front of me, my fingers grip the bottom of my sports bra and I peel it up my body.

"Harley, what are you—shit." His voice is so fucking low that it makes heat explode between my legs.

"Your turn," I sass, trying to keep my embarrassment at bay and appear as confident with my body as I'd like.

21

KYLE

"Shit," I growl, my cell slipping from my grip the second I see her pull her top over her head revealing her breasts to me.

I was joking when I dared her. Well, I think I was.

"Your turn," I hear her say from where my cell's landed on the sheets.

I swipe it up and flip the camera around as I swing my legs from my bed. I aim the camera right at the mirrored closed door in front of me.

Her gasp of shock does nothing for the raging hard-on I've had since I first saw her through the screen.

I knew she was freaking out about failing at this and the second she told me she was done, I knew she wasn't. Not if I had anything to say about it.

I'd hit call before I'd registered the move but I'm so fucking glad I did. The moment I saw the tears on her cheeks, I knew I did the right thing.

Was she right, did I want to make her cry? Hell yeah, but I was hoping those tears would come while she had my cock in her mouth, not because she couldn't do a math equation.

I never wanted her to feel useless, I just wanted her to understand what I went through because of what she did. Even though I know deep down that she was right to do it. I'm just pissed the wrong guy went down that night. Even more pissed he's still prowling about and threatening her.

"Holy shit, Kyle," she breathes as her eyes run down my body.

I'm only wearing a pair of boxer briefs, I have been this entire time, I just didn't let her see that.

"Yeah?" I say, cockily running my hand down over my abs, a pathetic attempt to hide the scar to avoid the inevitable questions about it.

A lot of shit might have gone down in juvie. I ended up in one too many fights, found myself being punished for them all too often. But the amount of time I had to work out isn't something I can regret when she looks at me like she is right now.

I was always too skinny. Too skinny for the kind of football I wanted to play like my big brother. I was fast though, so I was always picked for the team because of it. Bulking up was always my mission and juvie helped with that.

"You look… really fucking good."

"You're not looking so bad yourself."

She smiles shyly, making me want to get in my car right now and drive my ass to her house. My fingers clench around my cell as the temptation almost gets the better of me.

I drop my hand to my length that's tenting my boxers and she doesn't miss it.

"Touch yourself for me, Kitten."

"Um…" she hesitates.

"Too late to be shy now. You started this after all."

"Uh… no. I didn't start—"

"You took your top off first."

"Actually, it looks to me like you were half-naked first."

"Not my fault you didn't ask to see lower." I wink and she rolls her eyes at me.

"My head wasn't in the gutter like yours."

"Liar."

"What? I'm not—"

"You are. Your eye twitches when you lie to me."

"It does not."

"Want me to prove it?"

"How are you—"

"Want me to come over right now?"

"What? No," she shrieks, her eye twitching as she does.

"Right. So you don't want me to sneak into your bedroom, spread your thighs and eat you like I did Saturday night?" Her entire face flushes with embarrassment as her eye continues to twitch.

"No."

"Are you wet for me?"

"No." Twitch.

"Do you like math?"

"No, I fucking hate it." No twitch.

I laugh at her as she stares at me like I've lost my mind.

"See, I'm right."

"How does that prove anything?"

"Trust me, Kitten. It really does. Now, how about a little more proof."

"Depends on what it is."

"Lie back."

I flip my camera around and do the same, holding it as far away from me as possible so she can see all the way down to my waist.

Her eyes feast on me through the screen and I don't miss her gasp of shock when she finds the raised, rough skin of my scar.

"Not now." I growl, knowing that she's going to make a bigger deal out of it than necessary.

She stares at me for a beat, and I think she's about to ignore me and ask when she moves.

I watch her as she gets comfortable against her pillows. She's so fucking perfect. Her face is flawless, even with the smeared makeup around her eyes from where she was crying. Her long, slim neck makes my mouth water to sink my teeth in and her breasts. They might be on the smaller side, but fuck. They're round, full, the perfect fucking handful.

My fists clench, knowing that I can't fucking touch them right now.

This was a really fucking stupid idea.

"Now what?"

"Play with yourself, Kitten. Let me watch."

A surprised laugh falls from her lips at my request. "That is so not happening."

"Why? I am." I move my camera so she can see where my hand is still in my boxers, my fingers wrapped around my length.

"Kyle," she gasps, her voice full of lust.

"Don't be shy, Kitten. I've already tasted every inch of you."

"That doesn't—shit, Ky."

"Fucking love it when you say my name."

"You're serious right now, aren't you?"

I don't answer her with words, instead, I lift my hips and shove my boxers down.

"Holy fuck."

"That impressive?"

"Well, I've not exactly—" She slams her lips shut and a smile twitches at my lips.

"You've not exactly what, Kitten?"

"Do we really have to do this? Can't we go back to doing math?"

"You'd rather be doing math right now?"

Her eye twitches as she prepares her words.

"You'd rather do math than get yourself off while listening to my voice and knowing I'm gonna come for you."

"You're wicked."

"Too fucking right, Kitten. Be wicked with me."

She pauses for a second before her hand skims down her stomach and her fingers disappear into her shorts.

"I lied to you," she admits.

"I know, Kitten. You're fucking soaked for me right now, aren't you?"

Her eyes flutter closed and her full lips part as she touches herself. A little gasp of pleasure sounds out down the phone and I damn near come just hearing it.

"Yes," she breathes.

"Fuck. My dirty little kitten."

"Kyle, you've got a visitor," my brother's voice booms through the house. He's so loud that Harley's eyes fly open in panic.

"It's okay, he's not in the room," I say with a laugh, although I can't deny that my heart isn't beating hard enough to crack a rib.

"Did you forget your meeting with Bea?" he calls when he gets no response.

"Fuck. FUCK," I bark. "My fucking social worker is here."

Harley bursts out laughing. "Serves you right for trying to corrupt me," she mutters.

"Oh Kitten, I corrupted your ass on the weekend, and there's only more to come. I'll call you later, I need to deal with my boner before this bitch sees it."

She stifles a laugh before I reluctantly hang up.

"I'm coming."

I suck in a breath, willing my cock to stand down as I drag on some clothes—jeans, not sweats—and head out to meet Bea.

"Kyle, it's good to see you," she says sweetly from her position at the dining table.

"Uh, yeah, you too," I lie.

Kane studies me as I make my way over.

"You okay? Got a girl in there or something?"

"No," I snap, hating how fucking perceptive he is.

His eyes don't leave me as I pull a soda from the refrigerator and take a seat opposite Bea.

"I've heard good things from Principal Hartmann about you," she starts. "I knew that place would be a good fit for you."

"Do you need me?" Kane asks when she pauses.

"Nope, this is just an informal catch-up. You're eighteen in a few days and I can let you be free. You might be my shortest case ever."

"And easiest I hope," I mutter.

"Well, if you mean once you got here. The behind the scenes while you were in juvie wasn't quite so straight forward."

"Okay, well... I'm gonna..." Kane points over his shoulder before disappearing to his room.

"You're really lucky, you know," Bea says the second Kane's bedroom door shuts and he's out of earshot.

"I know."

"He'd have raised hell to get you here. He almost did."

I smile at her knowing the lengths Kane will go to to get what he wants.

"I'm not surprised. He's a force to be reckoned with."

"I know you don't need it, but he'll take good care of you."

"We look after each other. It's how it's always been."

"You're lucky to have each other," she says again. "Anyway, I just wanted to pop by, make sure everything was okay and to say happy birthday really."

"I really appreciate everything you've all done for me. I know granting Kane guardianship, even for a few days, couldn't have been the easiest thing to do. He's not exactly—"

"A model citizen?" she offers.

"Yeah, something like that." I think of some of the shit he was involved in back in Harrow Creek and I can't help but wonder if he's still got a hand in all that. He's certainly up to something with all the hours he's out of the house.

Bea stays for a good twenty minutes chatting away. She talks about my future, about college options. I listen, but I don't really dwell on it. I'm not ready to be making those kinds of decisions yet. I'm barely used to being back in the real world, the future seems like a long way off right now. I've got more pressing things to worry about, like when Gray is going to reappear and where Kane goes almost every hour of the day.

"I know our time is almost up," Bea says as she stands in the doorway ready to leave. "But if you need anything, either of you, you've got my number."

"Thank you, but I think we've got this."

"I expect big things from you, Kyle."

"We'll see what the future holds."

I close the door behind her and head for my room. I fall down onto my bed, the entire thing creaking with my weight.

I close my eyes for a few seconds as I process all the things Bea said about the future and the next thing I know it's dark and there are voices coming from the kitchen.

"Fuck," I mutter, sitting up and rubbing the sleep from my eyes.

Standing from my bed, I pull my bedroom door open to see who's here, but I instantly regret it.

"Fucking hell, bro. You don't live here alone," I bark, finding him with a girl pressed up against the wall a few feet down from my door. He's got her skirt up around her waist, her ass on full display.

"Hey, sweetie." She winks at me after pulling her face from Kane's neck. "Who's this K, baby?"

Her voice is so sickly sweet it actually turns my stomach.

Kane reaches out and grips her chin in his hands.

"My kid brother. Eyes off."

"Aww, I'm sure we could have some fun."

"As tempting as that is, I'm gonna have to pass this time, thanks," I mutter, not able to think of anything worse than going anywhere fucking near her.

Kane's got weird fucking taste when it comes to women. I'm all for enjoying them but that fucker has zero standards.

Thankfully, before I close the bathroom door on them, he's pulled her from the wall and carries her down to his room.

Fucking dog.

I make myself some dinner to the sounds of my brother fucking his slut into next week before returning to my bedroom. But despite there being a bathroom between us and music playing, I can hear every single one of her moans and cries for God.

I stare at the ceiling trying to convince myself to stay put and when my phone buzzes beside me, I hope it's Harley to distract me but as I bring the screen in front of me, my blood runs cold.

Unknown: It's time to pay your debts.

Below the message is a photo and it's that image that terrifies me more than his words because it's a photo of Harley… in her house.

"Fuck." I sit up so fast my head spins. My heart races as I find her number and hit call.

It rings and rings but never connects.

"Fuck."

22

HARLEY

The second he hangs up, reality crashes over me like a bucket of ice-cold water.

Reaching out, I grab my hoodie and cover myself up.

What the hell was I thinking letting him talk me into that?

Although, he didn't really have to talk me into anything, did he? I went down that road quite willingly.

"Fuck, fuck." *You're an idiot, Harley Hunter.*

I slam my math book closed, irritated with myself at how crazy he makes me.

I wanted to kill him at school earlier when he continually acted like a total prick, but then on the phone, he was so sweet. He's the boy I remember and, gah, I can't help latching onto that and forgetting all the other bullshit surrounding us.

"Harley, dinner is in thirty," Mom calls up the stairs.

"Okay. I'll be there."

Mom and I still haven't talked properly but as each day passes the tension lessens. I know we need to sit down though. It's time I talked about that night, got it all out in the open and tried to move on. It's held me back for long enough. It's literally held Kyle back and it's time to put it behind us where it belongs.

He's got too bright a future for the anger he's harboring inside. If he wants revenge, I'll let him take what he needs so that we can both move on.

It's time.

I grab a change of clothes and head for the bathroom to shower before going down to find Mom. I have no idea if the others are here, but if they are, then we can talk after. Hell, I should probably just say what I need to say in front of them, they deserve the truth too, Zayn especially.

When I get down to the kitchen a little over thirty minutes later, I find Mom alone and three plates of lasagne at the counter.

"Hey sweetie, it's just me, you, and Poppy tonight," Mom says as I take a seat.

"Where's Zayn?"

"Out with the team, I think."

Poppy joins us a few minutes later and the three of us sit in an uncomfortable silence for a few minutes.

"Mom, can we talk?" I ask, the words eating at me from the inside out.

"Sure."

"Do you want me to leave?" Poppy offers.

"No." I look over and meet her eyes. "We're sisters now." I smile at her.

"Mom, I'm... I'm disappointed that you didn't tell me about Kyle—" She opens her mouth to argue, but I beat her to it. "But I understand. I know how seriously you take your job and I know how badly you want to help those who need it. I trust that you thought you had my best interests at heart. I also know that I never quite told the whole truth about that night."

Mom's eyes narrow at me. "Go on."

"Kyle did more that night than I let on at the time."

Her brows rise for me to continue.

"It was Gray who drugged me, of that I'm positive, but I don't think Kyle was aware for quite a while. Things went farther than I admitted."

"I know," she says softly.

"What do you mean *you know*?"

"I know what happened that night, sweetie."

"But... why didn't you say anything?"

"It's your story, Harley. I trusted that you would tell me when you were ready."

"Does Zayn know?" I ask, although I think the fact he's not broken Kyle's nose yet that the answer is no.

"It's your story," Mom repeats.

Silence settles over us once again, as my mind goes back to that night.

I really want to wish that Letty didn't make me go but the more I think about it, about the time I spent with Kyle before the drug I'd been slipped started to kick into action, the more I wonder if it was worth it. For me, anyway. None of that night was worth Kyle being sent to juvie though.

I blow out a slow breath.

"Everything will be okay, sweetie. Have you two talked about that night yet?"

Poppy helpfully scoffs beside me but tries to cover it up as a cough.

"No, we haven't done much talking." Mom raises an eyebrow in suspicion.

"Right, well... can I suggest that maybe you find some time to do that. And also, talk to your brother. If what happened that night is something, then he'll want to hear about it from you."

"Like he did with me when he decided to scr—get with my best friend."

"The past is in the past, Harley. We can't change it, all we can do is try to do better in the future and only you have the power to make the right decisions."

I nod at her, her words circling around in my head.

"If you need me, you know I'm always here for you. If you want to talk about that night, I'm all ears but I trust you, Harley, to make the right decision. I trust all of you to know the best things for you and your futures."

She places her empty plate in the sink and heads for the door.

"Have you heard from Letty recently?" she asks before disappearing.

"Um..." I think back to the last time I spoke to my sister. It's been weeks, at least. "No. Is everything okay?"

"I'm sure she's just busy with classes. If you hear from her, let her know I'm still alive, yeah?"

I chuckle. "Will do." She's almost gone when I call her back. "Mom?"

"Yeah, sweetie."

"Thank you."

"Always." She smiles at me before disappearing around the corner.

"So..." Poppy starts once we're alone. "What really did happen that night?"

A couple of hours later, I'm curled up in bed in the dark with the speaker beside me playing softly. There's a storm brewing outside and the rain is lashing against my window, the wind beginning to howl around the side of the house.

I love watching the rain and if I weren't so comfortable, I'd head down to the porch and curl up on the swing seat.

It's late, I should be asleep, but I can't switch off. My head is still stuck in that video call with Kyle. If he weren't called away, how far would that have gone?

I want to say that I'd have put a stop to it before it went too far, but it had already gone past that point.

I was topless on a video call with my hand in my…

Jesus, what was I thinking?

I roll onto my back, wondering if I should have messaged again after he hung up.

I kind of expected him to want us to pick up where we left off. He certainly looked like he was into it. Part of me is disappointed that he didn't. The other part knows it was right.

Finally, my body starts to get heavier and I begin to drift off, but that all comes to an abrupt end when the side of my mattress compresses and a warm hand covers my mouth.

I try to scream, my body lashing around, my arms trying to hit whoever the fuck it is but although I make contact, they don't fucking move.

Although in my panic I can make out the figure, with tears filling my eyes and the darkness surrounding us, I can't make out any features.

My heart pounds as if it's about to explode from my ribs as I continue trying to fight, although it's pointless.

Whoever it is might not have done anything—yet—but they could. Clearly they're stronger than me.

I try to scream again as the figure looms over me.

"Calm down, Kitten. It's just me."

Every inch of my body relaxes for a second as Kyle's voice washes through me.

Then the anger hits.

"What the fuck do you think you're doing?" I hiss at him.

I blink away the tears and he becomes clearer. He's right in front of me, his nose almost brushing mine and staring right into my eyes.

His intensity is overwhelming, and my mouth goes dry.

He doesn't move for long seconds, but when he does, he makes my world spin again.

His fingers grip my chin in a painful, vise-like grip as his lips crash down on mine.

I resist for longer than he's happy with.

"Kitten," he growls against my lips. His hand slips under my sheets and he pinches my nipple through my tank. I gasp, exactly as he was intending and plunges his tongue into my mouth.

I buck against his hold, but he fully climbs on the bed and presses his entire body against mine, keeping me still.

"Careful, Kitten. I'll start thinking you don't want me here," he murmurs into our kiss before continuing before I get a chance to respond.

Pinned to the bed with only my arms free and Kyle kissing me like he needs it to live, I do the only thing I can.

I kiss him back.

His tongue licks deep into my mouth, twisting with mine. His grip on my chin loosens as our kiss continues in favor of wrapping his fingers around my neck.

I swallow against his hold, loving how it makes me feel.

Lifting my hands, I knock his hat from his head, allowing it to tumble to the bed before threading my fingers into his hair.

"Fuck, Harley," he groans, kissing along my jaw until he bites down on my ear, making me squeal in shock and for heat to surge down between my thighs.

"W-what are you doing here, Ky?" I whisper, my back arching as he once again finds my breast beneath the sheets.

"Finishing what we started, Kitten. I'm so fucking hard for you," he growls in my ear, making every hair on my body stand on end.

"Oh God."

"Don't tell me that you weren't lying here thinking about earlier, about how badly you wished I was in the same room as you. Kissing you, touching you, giving you everything you needed."

"Kyle." I wanted it to come out as a warning but when his name leaves my lips it's nothing but a plea.

Lifting his weight from me, he throws the sheets from my body, leaving me covered in nothing but my tank and sleep shorts.

It might be almost too dark to see him, but I don't miss the way his gaze sweeps down my body. I feel it, feeling the heat of his stare as it connects with my skin.

He sits up higher before pulling his hoodie over his head and dropping it to the floor, when he comes back to me, the heat of his naked chest damn near burns me.

"Couldn't think of anything else," he admits, seconds before he latches onto the skin of my neck and sucks until it hurts.

My hand finds his shoulder and my nails dig in as he continues.

"Try to hurt me as much as you like, Kitten. It won't stop me," he warns, brushing his lips over my collarbone and pulling the fabric of my tank down so he has access to my breast.

"Oh God," I moan when his teeth sink into the sensitive flesh.

"Shhh," he warns. "I really don't want to deal with your brother right now."

I slam my hand over my mouth as he sucks on my nipple, circling his tongue around the tip before biting down, ensuring a bolt of pleasure shoots straight to my core.

"You like biting me." It's not a question I don't need to ask. That much is obvious.

"I want to hurt you, Kitten. I want to hurt you so fucking bad." His eyes find mine, the silver catching in the small amount of light in the room and a shiver runs through me.

He means it.

He should. I condemned him to a year of hell.

But I shouldn't want him to do it so badly.

"You ruined my life," he continues, moving to the other side. "You need to pay."

"Oh God." His touch, his words, they're like fuel on my already simmering fire.

He lifts up, takes my tank in both of his hands and the next thing I know, the sound of the fabric ripping hits my ears before it falls to my side. I sit up so fast my head spins.

"Oh my God, did you just—"

"You don't get to hide from me, Kitten. Not now, not ever."

"Fuck," I breathe as he begins his descent down my stomach, kissing and biting every bit of skin he can. Each bite sends shockwaves through my body and every kiss is like a salve for the skin.

It's really fucking addictive.

The second he's at my hips, his fingers wrap around the waistband of my shorts and he pulls them down my legs, leaving me bare for him.

"Are you wet for me, Harley?" he asks, pushing my thighs wide and blowing a stream of air across my heated skin.

"Yes."

"Good girl. You know how I hate it when you lie to me."

My chest heaves, my fingers curling in the sheet beneath me as I wait for him to do something, to touch me, anything but he's frozen.

I wish I could see him properly, read the expression on his face and take in every inch of his body. But he's cloaked in darkness, almost as if he's a figment of my imagination. But I know he's not. His touch burns too hot, his bites sting too much.

After long seconds, he finally moves but it's not in the direction I was hoping for.

Instead, he climbs off the bed, lifts his hands to his head and paces the room.

"What's wrong?" I ask, watching his movements in the shadows.

Part of me wants to reach for the light, but another part loves the darkness.

He comes to a stop at the window and stares out for the longest time, although I have no idea what he's trying to find. It's pitch black out there with the moon covered in a thick layer of rain clouds.

"Kyle, what's—"

At my words, he turns and drops his hands to his waistband, tugging at the fabric until it drops from his hips.

Oh God, this is happening.

Every muscle in my body clenches as he closes the space between us.

Without another word, he drops to his knees at the end of my bed, wraps his hands around my ankles and drags me to him, throwing my legs over his shoulders and sucking my clit into his mouth.

"Oh my—" I slam my lips shut, reaching for a pillow to cover my face with and he continues his delicious assault on my body.

My back arches, my hips lift, my heels dig into his back, my fingers tug at his hair but he never lets up. Not even for a second.

His attack is brutal. Each swipe of his tongue and graze of his teeth send me closer to an intense release that is almost in touching distance.

"Kyle, Kyle, Kyle," I chant as he slides a finger inside me, adding to the sensations that are already driving me crazy. "Oh my God, oh my God."

This is so much better than the last time—and I thought that was good.

"Come for me, Kitten," he growls against my clit and I'm powerless but to do as I'm told.

My body quakes as pleasure like I've never known crashes over me in wave after wave of delicious ecstasy.

He doesn't stop until I've come back down, and even then he only moves as far as my inner thigh where he bites down so hard, I have no doubt he draws blood.

"Oh shit," I moan, the pain setting off aftershocks of pleasure.

I really fucking hope this isn't over yet because I already know that I need more.

23

KYLE

The taste of copper fills my mouth, but I don't stop. I need her to remember that I was here for a long time after I walk back out of her door.

Should I have come over here in the middle of the night and broken into her house? No, probably not. But I really don't give a shit.

Seeing that photo on my phone. Knowing that Gray is close to her. It fucked me up, and I needed to know that she was safe.

I want to say that my initial intentions were purely innocent. Make sure she's safe and leave. But I'm pretty sure I'd be lying.

After the way we were forced to end things earlier. This needed to happen.

I release my grip on her thigh and swipe my tongue over the bite mark as she shudders beneath me.

"Kyle?" Her voice is nervous and unsure, but it's deep and gravelly thanks to the orgasm she came down from only seconds ago, and I fucking love it.

Climbing up, I wrap her legs around my waist and fall over her, taking her lips on mine and allowing her to taste herself on me.

I kiss her like I might die without it, and I realize that actually, I might. I've craved this for so fucking long. I've dreamed of this for so fucking long.

Everything about Harley Hunter, even when we were kids, spoke to me on another level. It wasn't just because Zayn was my best friend that I basically lived in their trailer as we were growing up. I had to be there. Then when she walked into that party a year ago looking like my every fantasy and her big brother nowhere to be seen, I knew it was my chance.

If only things happened differently.

I wonder where we'd be now.

My hand runs down her thigh until I grip onto her ass, rubbing my cock against her burning pussy.

"You're mine, Harley Hunter. You belong to me," I say against her cheek.

"Yes, Ky, yes."

Fuck.

My chest swells at her words as I reach down between us and take myself in hand so I can find her entrance.

I tease her with just the tip and she greedily tries to suck me deeper. She's so wet, so fucking hot, it takes every ounce of restraint I have not to just sink right into her.

"You want my cock, Kitten?" I ask her, half expecting her to freak out because I know she's a virgin.

But instead, when she rips her eyes open and locks her stare on mine the only word that falls from her lips is, "Yes."

My lips crash to hers as my free hand skates up her body until I find her throat. Her pulse thunders under my fingertips and her pussy gets wetter as she feels the pressure of my hold.

Kinky little kitten.

I pull back and look into her dark, addicting eyes. "You on birth control?"

She sucks her bottom lip into her mouth and nods.

"You remember I said I wanted to hurt you?"

She nods again.

"Get ready."

I thrust forward, filling her as much as I can in this position.

"Holy fucking—" My hand lifts from her throat to cover her mouth. This really isn't the position to be in when Zayn comes crashing through the door. I know I'm due a beating for this, and I'll take it, but not right now.

She stills beneath me and my teeth grind as I force myself to remain motionless inside her as she gets used to my invasion.

After long seconds, her eyelids finally flutter open and I drag my hand down from her mouth.

Something crackles between us as the only sound that can be heard is the faint music from her speaker and our heaving breaths.

"I'm okay," she finally whispers, reaching up and wrapping her hand around the back of my neck so she can pull me down to her lips.

My tongue plunges into her mouth as my hips move and her pussy ripples around my length in the most incredible way.

This… this right here is why I didn't fuck anyone else after getting out.

"Fuck, Harley."

"Make it feel good, Ky," she begs, clearly still in pain.

I drop my forehead to hers as I fight with my restraint.

I want to fuck her. I want to fuck her so hard that her eyes cross and I brand myself on her soul forevermore.

But I can't. Not yet anyway.

Next time.

I smile to myself as I realize that this is just the first of many times I'm going to get this.

She might think otherwise, but I already know who's going to win.

With my fingers back where they belong around her throat, I bring my lips to hers at the same time I flex my hips slowly.

Her kiss doesn't falter as I keep moving, so I take that as the sign that she's okay and lose myself in her.

"Kitten," I growl into her mouth. "You're so fucking tight."

She gasps as I push into her a little harder.

"Ky," she moans as I release her throat and drop my hand down her body to pinch her swollen clit. "Oh fuck."

"Good?"

"I… I think so." I chuckle against her neck.

"It's more than fucking good, Kitten."

I work her until her skin is damp with sweat and her legs are trembling around my hips.

"You gonna come on my cock, Kitten."

"I… I…"

"Let go," I demand in her ear before biting down on her and circling my hips in a way I've discovered makes her purr.

"Oh God, oh God, oh fuck." She slams her own hand over her mouth as her pussy clamps down around me. Her back arches as her entire body convulses beneath me.

Even in the darkness, it's fucking breathtaking.

"Fuck, you're sexy, Kitten." I thrust two more times before I lose control and my cock jerks violently inside of her. "Harley," I groan into her neck.

Still inside her, I grab her chin, forcing her to look at me before claiming her lips once again.

By the time I let her up for air, her eyes are almost closed with her exhaustion and my cock is hard and ready for another round. But I already know I can't act on it.

"So sleepy," she whispers, curling into my side as if she belongs there.

My heart pounds and she snuggles against my chest and I wrap my arm around her waist.

It feels... right.

Lifting my hand, I thread my fingers into her hair and pull her head back a little so I can press my lips to her head.

"Thank you," I whisper, knowing that she's already succumbed to sleep.

I hold her for the longest time. It would be so easy to fall asleep and then maybe take her again first thing in the morning. But that's not what this is and we both know it.

I have no idea how much time passes, but eventually I manage to convince myself that I need to move.

I slip from beneath her without waking her and stand before picking up the sheets from the floor ready to cover her up, only something hits my foot and when I look down to see what it is, it gives me a wicked idea that I can't ignore.

Draping the sheets over her feet, I gently wrap my hand around the back of her knee, exposing the bite mark I left on her thigh and set to work.

Only minutes later, I'm dressed and standing with my hand on her doorknob ready to leave.

My body begs me to stay, to get undressed and slide back under the sheets with her. But my head tells me to leave. She's going to regret this in the morning, I already know that, and I don't want to be here to witness it.

With one more look at her sleeping peacefully in the darkness, I slip out of her room and soon after her house.

It's a decision I regret the second I strip out of my clothes and slide into my own cold bed. I might have showered when I got in but I can still smell her, still feel her hot body pressed up against mine and hear the little noises she made when I was inside her.

My cock tents the sheets, taunting me and telling me that I should have stayed.

"Fuck," I hiss into the night as I turn over and attempt to get some sleep. I already know it's pointless. If it does come, it's going to be full of images of her laid out naked beneath me.

I know the house isn't empty like usual long before I pull my bedroom door open. Not only did I wake to the sound of that woman's irritating sex squeals, but the pair of them are now crashing around in the kitchen.

I hesitantly step from my bedroom and toward the kitchen. I might have been gone a year, but I can't imagine that Kane makes a regular thing of having breakfast with his hook-ups.

"'Morning, sweetie," she sings the second she sees me, her eyes running down my body as if she wants to eat me for breakfast.

"'Morning."

"Bro," Kane grunts when he turns from his place at the stove where he's cooking fucking bacon.

"You're cooking... for her?" I ask as if it's the most insane thing I've ever said.

"Yeah. Problem?"

"Nope. Please continue. I'll be gone in a few."

"There's plenty," he offers. I look from him and to the woman.

"Nah, you're all good. I've already had my fill." I nod my head toward his friend and Kane barks out a laugh.

"You know I like it when they scream." He winks before turning back to the bacon.

"I also know that you're a dog."

I don't bother hanging around or even picking up something to eat, the second I've made use of the bathroom, I grab my school bag and get the hell out of the house.

I'm too early for school, so after parking, I head for the locker room and the gym that's beside it.

The hallways are silent as I walk through them and the locker room is empty, as is the gym.

Shoving my headphones in, I hit play on a running playlist I made the other night and get to work.

Eventually, a few others join me. Guys I recognize from our conditioning practices but no one stops to talk to me. Fine by me.

My shirt is damp and my hair is wet by the time I come to a stop and pull my cell from my pocket.

The second I see a message from her on the screen, a smile pulls at my lips and my heart skips a beat. But when I read what she's sent, I can't help but bark out a laugh.

"What's—whoa, dude. You do that?" Ash asks, coming to a stop behind me and staring at my cell over my shoulder.

"Gotta stake your claim, right?" I say, putting the screen to sleep before he sees any more.

"That who I think it is."

"I don't kiss and tell, man."

"Didn't look like you were kissing, bro. You a secret fucking vampire or what?"

I suck my bottom lip into my mouth as I remember the taste of her blood on my tongue last night.

I laugh. "Yeah, I might just be."

"You gonna shower before class? You stink."

"Fuck you." I laugh, walking through the gym and heading for the showers.

24

HARLEY

The muscles in my thighs pull as I roll over and everything down there feels really sore. My brows pull together for a second before everything hits me and my eyes fly open and I sit bolt upright, clutching the sheets to my bare chest.

Is he still here?

I look around not knowing what I really want the answer to that question to be, but as I find the other side of my bed empty and cold and no evidence of him even being here, disappointment floods me.

I wanted him to be here.

Fuck.

I drop my head into my hands. What the hell did I do last night? Why was he even here?

Did someone let him in? Does someone know he was here?

A million and one questions run around my head as my alarm starts blaring again.

"Alright, alright," I mutter, switching the thing off and climbing from my bed, my muscles protesting with every move.

I grab my robe and wrap it around me before going to the bathroom. I need to wash his scent off me and hopefully with it, the memories from my head because already I know that if I think about it too much then I'm going to want to do it again.

I should be regretting handing my V-card to a guy who can barely stand to look at me, but I'm not.

I push aside memories of vicious Kyle and focus on the sweet boy that I catch glimpses of when we're alone. When we're playing our little tutoring game and forgetting about our reality.

After brushing my teeth, I turn the shower on, drop my robe and step under the torrent of water.

It's not until I stand rubbing my sponge around my body that I realize anything is wrong.

I lift my leg and my eyes almost pop out of my head at what I find on my inner thigh.

I remember him biting me, I remember the pain as I stare at the mark as if it's happening right now, and damn, if it doesn't get me hot thinking about it. But fuck, I do not remember him doing anything else.

I run my finger over the black ink on my skin but it doesn't fucking move.

Owned by a Legend.

"You fucking..." I seethe, my teeth grinding as I stare at his handwriting.

I make quick work of finishing up my shower and after wrapping a towel around my body, I stand in front of the mirror, quickly wiping away the steam covering it. The second my eyes lock on my neck and chest, I gasp.

There is no fucking way I can cover all this up.

My hand lifts without instruction and I run my fingertips over each and every mark he left behind and I suddenly have the urge not to cover up any of them. Part of me really quite likes them.

Jesus, I'm fucked-up.

It takes me longer than usual to decide what to wear to school, my need to cover up almost every inch of my body makes it a challenge. It gets so late that Zayn ends up knocking on my door to ensure I'm alive and going to school.

"Yeah, I'm coming," I call back before he opens the door. The less he looks at me today the better.

I don't have time to think about what I need for cheer after school, so shove an outfit in my duffel bag and swing it over my shoulder in my need to not be late.

By the time I get downstairs, Zayn and Poppy have already left and I don't have time to eat anything, so I'm forced to grab a coffee in a travel mug and a cereal bar.

The hallway is packed as I make my way to my locker, keeping my head down as I go in fear that everyone will take one look at me and know exactly what I'm trying to hide.

I switch out my books and get what I need for my first class before taking off in that direction. Unfortunately, to get to English lit, I have to go by the team's lockers.

I suck in a steeling breath before I turn the corner. I spot them instantly, it's impossible not to with their god-like presence.

"Good to see you made it," Zayn shouts over when he spots me heading toward their group.

I lift my hand and flip him off.

"Watch out, lil' sis is touchy today. Rich, you should go cheer her up. We all know how much she likes your little cock," Ethan barks, laughing at his own terrible joke. But I don't bother to even look at him, I'm too busy trying not to look at the person standing beside Zayn with a smirk playing on his lips.

Fuck him.

My irritation levels grow knowing that he's getting to me by literally doing nothing other than breathing.

"You cold or something, sis?" Zayn asks, his gaze dropping to the scarf I have wrapped around my neck.

I don't need to look at Kyle to know his smirk has just got wider at my brother's comment.

"Yeah," I say slowly, nodding as I do. Then I rip my eyes from his and stare right into Kyle's ice-blue ones. "We need to talk."

Zayn's curious gaze flicks between the two of us as we stare at each other. My face burns every time he looks at me.

"Why? You wanna compare my cock size to Rich's?"

A round of jeers and dirty remarks sound out behind me.

"Fuck off, my little sister ain't going anywhere near this motherfucker's cock, ain't that right, bro?" he asks Kyle.

"Too fucking right." Kyle's eyes burn down the length of my body "Why would I go there when my brother brings home women every night."

"Oh hell yeah, bro," someone calls out, probably Rich and I fight the hurt that threatens to bubble up within me.

I want to say he's lying. He spent the night with me. But not the whole night.

You stupid, stupid, naïve bitch, Harley Hunter.

He told you he wanted to hurt you and you fucking let him.

"Great, well now we've got that cleared up." I put as much sass into my words as possible as I hold Kyle's eyes hoping like hell he can't see how fast I'm crumbling on the inside.

"I've got nothing to say to you," he spits as if last night didn't even fucking happen.

Asshole.

"Bro, I said don't touch her not insult her," Zayn mutters in an attempt to soften the blow. "I know you two got issues but shit."

"Whatever. It wasn't important anyway." I wave them both off and continue down toward my first class, my heart in my throat and tears burning my eyes the whole way.

Thankfully, the bell has not rung and when I push through into my classroom, I'm the only one in there.

I take my seat at the back of the room and suck in a shaky breath.

Last night didn't change anything and I hate that I'm being such a girl about it, thinking that he might have suddenly treated me differently today.

By the time others start filing in, I've somewhat got control of my emotions.

"'Morning," Ruby sings, dropping down in her seat next to mine. "How's it—what's wrong?" she asks the second she looks at my face.

Damn her.

"Nothing, everything is fine," I lie and the guilt of doing so to one of my best friends threatens to eat me whole. But I can't admit what happened last night, how stupid I was. I fell for every single word he said and it was all a lie.

Every touch, every kiss, every whispered word. All lies.

Pressure builds behind my eyes once again but thankfully, our teacher arrives and Ruby is forced to look away from me as he asks her a question.

Behind him, the door opens and the one person I don't want to have to even look at walks into the classroom.

He holds his head high as he makes his way to his seat. Right before he turns to sit down, he looks right at me. My entire body jolts at the look in his eyes but I'm too shocked and the contact is too brief to really decipher what he's trying to tell me.

I'm still staring at the back of his head when Ruby turns her attention back to me.

"Did something happen, you're shooting more hate at him than usual?"

"I don't want to talk about it," I seethe.

"I'll take that as a yes then," she says lightly. "You know where I am." She places her hand on my forearm and squeezes in support as our teacher gets the lesson started.

My cell buzzes in my pocket, I know exactly who it is, I've been watching him type for the last few seconds. I knew it was coming but it doesn't stop my heart rate increasing to dangerous levels the second I feel it. Knowing that his words are sitting there waiting almost gets the better of me. Especially when he sends me another three that also all go unread.

But at no point does he attempt to turn to look at me. I know this because while our teacher talks, my eyes are stuck on him and my head is firmly still back in the events of last night.

I breathe a sigh of relief the second the bell rings out and everyone around me begins to pack up and move toward the door. That was my one and only class with him today. If I avoid the cafeteria at lunch then I shouldn't have to look at him again with any luck.

He disappears from the room before I'm even off my chair. Good to know he doesn't actually want to talk to me then.

"Are you sure you're okay?" Ruby asks as we finally make our way out and toward our next class that, thankfully, we share.

"Yeah, I'm good." My voice gives me away because it sounds broken even to my own ears.

"You wanna skip and go and get ice cream."

I laugh, it's either that or I'm going to cry. "I can't. If Mom found out…"

"What if she wouldn't?"

"I can't." I shake my head at her. I so badly want to say yes and throw caution to the wind, but I can't. I'm not that girl, I'm not that student. Plus, I've got math later and we all know that I need to be present for that class.

Second period is uneventful although I spent the entire class with my head in the clouds while my heart continues to ache inside my chest.

I gave him too much last night. I gave him things that I can't get back and I'm starting to wonder if that's something I'm going to regret after not feeling that way in the slightest this morning.

I knew it wasn't going to be all hearts and flowers today. But the reality was so much worse than anything I could have imagined.

"What are you hiding?" Stella says the second I join her in our art class.

"Um…"

"Oh come on, you never wear scarves." She raises a brow knowingly.

"Do we really have to do this?"

"We certainly do, girl."

We both grab the paintings we started last time and take our seats as someone puts some music on and our teacher doesn't even bother to stand from her chair. Fine by me.

"Show me." She reaches for my scarf and I keep my hands at my sides, allowing her a peek at my neck.

"Whoa, girl. Someone had a fun night."

"You've no idea," I mutter, dropping my head into my hands.

"Tell me all."

So I do, much to her delight. I feel bad not confessing to Ruby earlier and instead trusting Stella with the events of the night before, but with her being outside of our circle, and more importantly, not close to Zayn, I feel a little safer talking about it.

"He just turned up in the middle of the night and…" She wiggles her eyebrows. "That's really fucking hot, Harley. Does he have any friends who might be up for doing the same thing but you know, at my house."

I make a show of gasping in shock. "Stella Doukas, are you a secret little slut?" I whisper.

She shrugs and tries to look innocent but seeing as she expressed her desire to have a bad boy sneak into her bedroom under the cloak of darkness, she fails massively.

"Don't judge," she says lightly. "I've met a lot of different… boys over the years."

"Okay, I think it might be time to turn the tables on this conversation. Tell me all…" I encourage, dropping my brush into the water pot between us and resting forward with my elbow on the table and my chin in my hand, ready for story time.

"Christ, where do I even start?"

"Well, this is getting better by the second," I joke, glad to be able to focus on someone else's bad choices for a while.

Stella and I end up staying in our art classroom over lunch, continuing our riveting conversation about her past conquests and slowly but surely working on our paintings. She slips out at one point to grab us both some lunch, totally understanding my need to remain hidden and when I get to math, I do so without seeing *him.*

I think I'm winning until Mr. Wilson's first words to the class are, "Surprise test."

I groan as I pull my pens out and wait for him to place the paper on my desk.

"You've got this, Harley," he says encouragingly as he passes.

I roll my eyes, knowing that there's no way that can possibly be true. But then I look down at the questions before me and I find equations exactly like Kyle and I were doing last night.

I tap my pen against my desk for a couple of seconds as I recall everything he told me while we were on video chat and I get to work, actually feeling confident about a math test for the first time in… well, ever.

"Okay, time is up," Mr. Wilson calls right as I'm finishing off the last question on the paper. "Grab a different color pen, let's self-grade them. Here are the answers…"

He projects the answers onto the screen and the second I realize the first one is exactly the same as what I've got written on my piece of paper, I can't fight my smile.

Holy shit, I did it.

I laugh to myself before covering my mouth with my hand before anyone notices my little freak out.

I go down the rest of the answers and those tears from this morning return but this time, it's with joy.

I did it. I fucking did it.

Noticing that something isn't right, Mr. Wilson walks over. "Is everything okay, Harley?"

I look up at him, my eyes full of unshed tears. I must look like I'm on the verge of a breakdown.

"I got them all right," I whisper, not able to believe it despite marking them myself.

"That's great, Harley. Well done." He smiles down at me and my chest damn near bursts with pride for myself.

He moves on to another student while I squeal internally at myself.

In a moment of madness, I reach for my cell and before I know what I'm doing, I'm staring down at the messages from Kyle that I've ignored all day.

"Shit," I mutter to myself, feeling stupid for my sudden need to tell him that I nailed this.

He won't care.

He got what he wanted.

He *hurt* me.

I let out a sigh as I stare at his words from earlier.

Asshole: I'm sorry.

Asshole: Talk to me.

Asshole: Kitten.

I can hear his growl of frustration in the last one and it makes goose bumps prick my skin.

When I start typing a second later, it's not to Kyle, but instead, Stella.

Harley: Wanna do something tonight after cheer?

She doesn't see the message straight away—as she shouldn't, she's in class as well after all—so I pocket my cell and try to force myself not to feel bad for ignoring his requests.

I spend the rest of class hanging on Mr. Wilson's every word as he explains what we're moving on to next, my confidence at an all-time high and ready to attack the next challenge sent my way.

Before I know it, class is over and I'm making my way down the packed hallway ready for cheer practice.

"Hey, sorry, I didn't reply. Miss Ash was on us all class," Stella says as we walk into the locker room together.

"No worries. You up for it?"

"Yes, I need to go home first though."

"Sure, I'm good with whatever."

"Do I get the feeling you might be avoiding going home?"

"Whatever might give you that impression?" I ask innocently.

"He was in my last class. He looked pissed."

"Good, he should. He's a dick."

"You mean you want his dick," she deadpans as we drop our bags to the bench and start getting changed.

The others join us, and after a few minutes, Ruby and Chelsea come marching through. I watch Ruby as she listens to whatever Chelsea says.

I smile at the two of them, I'm so damn proud of my girl. She's about to be an incredible captain.

"Harley Hunter," Stella gasps. "You did not tell me about that." Her eyes almost bug out of her head as she stares at my thigh.

Reaching out, I cover the bite mark and writing with my hand.

"Oh no, no-no." She knocks my hand out of the way and stares down at my skin. "He fucking branded you. That's so hot."

"He made me bleed, Stel. And then wrote all over me."

"You know why, don't you?"

"To piss me off?" I suggest.

"No, he's claiming you. That boy wants you, Har. He wants you bad."

"Oh yeah, and that's why he acted like he did this morning."

"Boys are douchebags, Har. They do all sorts of stupid shit in front of their friends—in front of the brother of the girl they're fucking."

"I'm not fucking him," I hiss quietly, trying to argue with her.

"Evidence would suggest otherwise." She nods down to my thigh and raises a brow knowingly.

"Let's just get changed, eh?"

Stella laughs at me as I pull a pair of shorts out of my bag and stare at them in horror. I thought I'd stuffed yoga pants in there this morning.

"Shit."

"Here, swap," Stella offers, taking my shorts and handing me her pants.

"Thank you."

"I'm sure I'll figure out a way to pay you back." She winks at me and I hurriedly step into the fabric to cover up the evidence from last night, hoping that the hoodie I opted for does the job on my top half.

"Wow, your house is gorgeous," I say, climbing out of my car after following Stella here after school.

"Thanks," she mutters, slamming the door of her Porsche and coming to join me.

I knew she was wealthy, you only need to look at her car, her clothes and the way she wears them to know that, but I wasn't quite expecting this, or for her to live quite so far out of town.

It's great though. Perfect, actually. Kyle will never find me here.

She leads us to a huge hallway. The walls are white, the floor tiles are white—probably some expensive marble or something—and all the fittings are matte black. It's really quite something.

"Okay wow. This is… wow."

"My dad has a thing about interior design."

"Well, he's certainly got an eye for it."

She leads me through to her kitchen which is similar to the hallway, the units are all white with black countertops, tiles and handles. Even the faucet is black.

"What did you say your dad did again?" I ask, looking around and taking it all in. There's a huge canvas at the other end of the dining room which is similarly just black and white but it looks like it's probably hella expensive.

She shrugs as she pulls open one of the doors to reveal a refrigerator enclosed behind it. "No idea. Soda?"

"Please." She passes one over before grabbing a bag of chips and tipping them into a bowl. "You've really no idea what he does?"

"Security of some sort, but that's about all I know."

"And you don't ask?" I ask, finding it odd how she can really have no idea.

"I used to. I gave up after a while when he wouldn't tell me anything. Apparently, it's better I don't know. Whatever." She throws a chip in her mouth and chews. "So what did you want to do? We've probably got the house to ourselves. There's a pool and jacuzzi, and sauna in the basement if you're down for it."

My chin drops, although I don't know why I'm surprised. Ethan's house is similar, although less modern. I guess I just didn't think there were any other houses around Rosewood that were this… big. But then after driving up the long-ass driveway that allows this place to be hidden in the trees, I shouldn't be surprised.

"Sure, if you've got a suit I can borrow."

"You got it. Shall we?" she asks, grabbing her soda and the bowl and heading for the door.

My cell starts buzzing almost the second I place it on the coffee table in Stella's bedroom—she has a full on living area at one end of her ginormous room. It's insane.

"Is that him?" she asks, glancing over at where it's flashing.

"Sure is."

"You gonna reply?"

"Nope." Picking it up, I go into the settings and turn the vibrate off because I have a feeling he's not going to stop at a few messages.

"He's gonna kill you for that."

"I'd like to see him try."

"Girl, he branded you on your first time. He's not going to have second thoughts about spanking your ass for ignoring him."

I can't deny that a flash of heat races through me at her words and the image they conjure up.

"O-oh, is that your plan?"

"What? No. I don't have a plan aside from showing him that he can't order me around and talk to me like shit and expect me to roll over and accept it. That's not who I am."

"Damn right, girl," she says, snapping her fingers and giving it all the attitude before she falls about in a fit of giggles. "Okay, this is for you." She hands me a tiny fire engine red swimsuit.

Bathroom is through there. She points toward a closed door and I take the scrap of fabric with me to change into.

Unlike the rest of the house, Stella's bedroom and bathroom is all cream and golds. It's stunning and much softer than the harsh black and white everywhere else.

In only a few minutes I'm attempting to make the swimsuit cover some of my marked skin but I soon decide that it's pointless even trying.

"Whoa, I think that might have been made for you," Stella says when I emerge. While I was gone, she changed into a silver suit that fits her like a second skin. "You want me to send him a photo, show him what he's missing."

"No," I say in a panic as she takes a step toward where my cell is.

She laughs at me as she picks up her soda.

"Let's go chill. I think you need it."

25

KYLE

I stare down at my cell, my teeth grinding.

Usually, I wouldn't give a shit if a girl doesn't text me back.

But Gray is on the prowl and the thought of him putting his hands on her makes me murderous.

Kyle: Where are you?

I know barking at her probably isn't going to get me the result I need. But I need to fucking know she's safe.

Twenty minutes later, I still have no response. She hasn't even fucking read it.

Throwing the book off my lap, I jump from the bed and shove my feet into my sneakers.

"Where are you going?" Kane asks as I storm past where he's curled up with the same woman—Alana—from yesterday. It's weird seeing him here, let alone seeing him with a woman.

"Out," I bark, ripping the door open and marching out into the rain.

I'm at the Hunter's in record time, but unlike last night, the lights are on and I fear I'm not going to be so successful sneaking in. Her car isn't here, which should tell me everything I need to know, but I'm not risking finding out for sure.

I push the door open and poke my head inside. The hallway is empty but there's music playing from somewhere.

Darting toward the stairs, I run up two at a time and fly through her bedroom door.

I don't need to look up, I know she's not here. The lack of response to me barging in tells me everything.

I look around the room, finding it tidy as if she's not even been back here and my heart thunders.

If that motherfucker has her, I'm going to fucking kill him.

I blink back the images I have from that night of his hands on her body, my fists curling in anger.

Needing to get out of the house before I'm caught, I slip back out and head down the stairs.

"Kyle, are you looking for Zayn?" Jada asks, scaring the shit out of me as I turn the corner.

My hand lifts to cover my pounding heart as my head spins a little.

"Uh… yeah?" I don't mean for it to come out as a question, and from the way Jada's brow lifts I fear she didn't miss it.

Nervously, I look behind me at the stairs. Does she know I just came from Harley's room?

"He's down in his den." She steps aside, allowing me to walk down toward the room.

"Um… I guess I should have tried there first, huh?"

She studies me, but she doesn't say anything as I step past her toward the den.

I don't want to go down there. But he might know where she is…

"Hey, man. How's it going?" Zayn asks the second I push inside the room.

I find the other seniors hanging out on the couches, amazingly without any girls on their laps for once.

"Yeah, good. Alright?" I ask them all, tipping my chin up in greeting.

"You joining us or what?" Zayn asks when I hover in the doorway. "I'm sure Jake wants to talk to you about next year," he says, looking toward his captain.

"Uh… actually, have you seen Harley?"

"Harley?" he asks, his eyes widening for a beat.

"Yeah." An excuse for why I might want to talk to her sits on the edge of my tongue, but I hold it in and wait to see what his response is going to be.

"No, not since this morning. She's probably with Ruby and Poppy. Everything all right?" he asks, his eyes narrowing on mine.

"Of course."

"Great, now come hang with us." He nods to an empty seat and other than turning my back and walking out on them, I don't really feel like I have much of a choice.

Their previous conversation continues around me as I take a seat and open the soda Zayn throws at me.

"So, the Harriers," Jake starts, leaning forward and resting his elbows on his knees. "Your old team doesn't exactly have a good rep. You any good?" he asks, although from what he's said previously, he's well aware of my skills.

I might have kept up with his conditioning sessions but he's yet to see me play any actual football. And I'm fully aware of my old team's rep.

"Yeah," I state confidently. "I am."

"Well." He rests back once more. "I hope you're as sure of your skills as you are your confidence."

"You don't need to worry about me."

"I'm about to leave my team in someone else's hands. I'm fucking worried."

"You'll forget all about it the second you join your college team."

Silence ripples around the room at my words and I fear I might have said something I shouldn't.

"Yeah, I'm sure you're right," he finally says after clearing his voice.

"Legend, come get some more drinks with me," Zayn barks as he stands and collects up a few empties.

"Sure."

I can tell by the set of his shoulders as he moves in front of me that he's about to grill me about Harley.

"What's going on?" he asks the second we're in the kitchen and out of earshot of everyone else.

"Nothing," I lie. "I just had a question about our English lit assignment. Didn't know who else to ask."

"Bullshit, Ky. Wanna try telling me the truth?"

My stomach knots. I can hardly tell him that Gray is threatening to do something to her to get to me. The hot-headed motherfucker will get straight in his car and drive to Harrow Creek to find him. He'll probably end up getting himself fucking killed.

"That is the truth. Jeez, can you lay off the big brother thing?" I try to make it sound like a joke but I'm pretty sure I fail.

"You didn't even want to look at her this morning, now you want her help. If I find out you're lying to me, I'll fucking take you out, Ky."

I put my hands up in surrender.

"I'm just going to use your bathroom."

I back out of the room with him watching my every move. The second I'm out of sight, I pull my cell out and find Ash's number.

He answers the moment I close the bathroom door behind me.

"Hey, how's it going?"

"Is Harley with Ruby?" I whisper-shout, ignoring any niceties.

"Um… no. Ruby is with me, why?"

"Can you ask her if she knows where Harley is?"

"S-sure." There's some rustling before he does as I ask. "No, she doesn't know."

"Call her," I demand.

"What the fuck is going on?" Ash asks.

"Put me on speaker." There's movement as he does as I ask. "Ruby, please can you call Harley and find out where she is?" There's a hardness to my voice which has the desired effect.

"Okay, calling now. Is everything okay?" she asks in a much softer tone than Ash did, although I can hear the concern in it.

"Yeah, probably."

"It just keeps ringing. I'll message her and let you know when I find out."

I blow out a long breath. "That's great, thank you."

"You gonna tell us what the big drama is now?"

"She just ran off, wanted to make sure she's okay."

"What did you do to her?" Ruby growls down the line.

"N-nothing." We all know it's a lie, but I say the word anyway. I've no idea if Harley has confessed to her girls about what happened last night. The fact Ruby isn't ripping me a new one right now for it makes me think she might not have. She certainly wanted to cover up the evidence if the scarf was anything to go by this morning.

"Riiight. Well, if you decide you wanna tell us the truth, we're at home. But we'll tell you if we hear anything," Ruby says softly, but I don't miss the edge of anger in her voice. Understandable, I've hurt her girl. I'm sure it won't be the last time either.

We hang up and I'm forced to rejoin Zayn to carry the cans back through to the den and spend my night talking football while I wait for my cell to ring.

It's almost three hours later when that finally happens.

I excuse myself from the room and slip out into the hall.

"Yes."

"It's nice to hear from you too," Ash deadpans.

"Do you know where she is?"

"Yes, she's staying at Stella's tonight."

The breath I didn't know I was holding comes rushing out of me.

"Okay, thanks, I appreciate it, man."

"You gonna tell me what all of this is about yet?"

"It's nothing. I... I was just worried."

"Okay well... I'll see you tomorrow then."

The second I return from that phone call, I make my excuses and get out of the Hunter's house.

———

My place is empty once again when I get back and I breathe a sigh of relief that I'm not going to have to put up with Kane and Alana going at it all night.

I grab myself a soda from the refrigerator and fall down onto my bed.

I've got a ton of homework to do but I can't focus on any of it. Instead, I stare at the ceiling, wondering what she's doing and praying that she's safe.

Right before I decide to actually get into bed and attempt to get some sleep, my cell pings. My heart skips a beat thinking that it might be her, but deep down, I know it's not.

Unknown: Our girl looks good in red.

My hand trembles as I stare at his words. His threat.

If he so much as touches a fucking hair on her head, I'll...

My thoughts trail off as I consider if I'm already in too deep in this.

I tell myself that it's just because I don't want her hurt because of me. I might blame her, want to hurt her for what she did to me. But I want to be the one to do it.

Plus, I wouldn't wish that motherfucker on anyone.

I close down his message, not wanting to give him any clue that he's getting to me. It's bad enough he'll know that I've read it.

I silence my cell and throw it to the other side of the bed in frustration and close my eyes, not that I think sleep will come anytime soon. Especially not when he's out there watching her.

Our girl looks good in red.

He just means her hair... right?

The sun was almost up by the time I actually fell asleep last night, but as I lay there thinking about a million and one things that Gray could do to Harley, I refused to allow myself to look at my cell.

If I found another photo of him watching her and I had no clue where she was I knew I'd freak out. I decided it was better not to know and trust that she was safe with Stella.

When my alarm goes off, my body refuses to wake up, it's so heavy with sleep, but I know I have no choice.

The second I open my eyes, I reach for my cell, my restraint long vanished.

My stomach clenches when I find a message from another unknown number. But when I look closer, I see that it's a different number.

Intrigued, I swipe the screen and open it up.

Unknown: You're welcome!

My chin drops as I scroll up and enlarge the image I've been sent.

"Holy shit." My cock swells as I stare at the image of Harley in the smallest red swimsuit I think I've ever…

Red.

Fuck. She's wearing red.

Without thinking, I hit call on the number.

"Good morning," a familiar voice sings. "Did you like your little gift?"

"Where is she?" I ask, totally ignoring her question.

"Um… in the shower. Don't tell me you want me to sneak in and get another? She's going to kill me when she realizes I sent that, let alone—"

"No. I just want to know she's safe."

"Of course she's safe, she's with me. Why wouldn't she be?"

"No reason. Don't tell her I called or say anything about this."

"Trust me, I—"

I hang up before she can finish that sentence and blow out a relieved breath.

She's safe… for now.

"Fuck."

I need to figure out what I'm going to do and how I'm going to get Gray off her back.

I'd like to say that I could find a load of money and that it'll make him go away, but something tells me that wouldn't be enough. He wants my blood, not my dollar bills.

I shove my hair from my brow, tugging on the strands until it burns with pain. Pain that I deserve for all of this bullshit. For putting her in danger.

I'm in the parking lot long before the rest of the school once again. I have no idea what class Harley has first, so I figure I'll just sit here until her car appears.

Only, it never does and I have no clue what Stella drives.

The bell rings out and I'm forced to either get out or skip.

I go with the former and climb from the car in favor of my statistics class.

I see no sign of her, and by the time lunch rolls around, I'm damn near losing my mind.

I've messaged her over and over again but still, she refuses to read them.

My lips twist as I think about getting my hands on her and showing her just how infuriating her defiance is.

"Kyle, did you hear that?" Miss Harper asks pointedly.

"Um… yes."

"Good, so you'll know exactly what the homework task entails then."

"Of course. Don't sweat it." I give her my best smile and after blushing a little she turns away to terrorize someone else.

The bell sounds out and we all jump into action ready to go and find out what the cafeteria is offering up today, only when I get out into the hallway, something—or someone—else catches my attention.

There's a flash of red ahead that can only belong to Harley Hunter as she tries to make her escape.

While everyone else moves toward the cafeteria, I head for her.

She keeps her head down as she moves as fast as her legs will carry her. It's cute that she thinks she can outrun me. She should know by now that I'll always get her in the end.

I catch up with her right in front of a classroom door. A classroom that I pray to fucking God is empty.

I wrap one hand around her mouth and the other around her waist as I lift her from the floor and the pair of us crash through the door and into the classroom, which, thankfully, is deserted. Not only is it deserted but the blinds are all shut and it's dark. Bingo.

Twisting her around, I press her up against the wall but keep my hand over my mouth.

I lean in close to her, so close that our noses brush.

"Nice try, Hunter."

Her jaw flexes as she prepares to say something but my hand tightens around her mouth, stopping her.

"I've messaged you. I've called you," I seethe. "You fucking ignored me."

Her nostrils flare with her need to argue with me.

"That's rude. Don't you think?"

She doesn't react so I make her nod, much to her annoyance if her narrowed eyes are anything to go by.

"Now the question is… what should I do about it? How should I punish you for thinking you could ignore me?"

Her jaw flexes again but I don't let up.

Reaching around her, I pull her bag from her shoulder and throw it across the room before reaching into the back pocket of her denim skirt, knowing that her cell is going to be there.

Her entire body jolts when I make contact with her, and I have to fight the smile that threatens to curl at my lips.

"Oh look," I say, waking it up and showing her the screen that is full of notifications of messages from me. "It works. Next time I try to contact you, you reply. You got that?"

Finally, I drop my hand from her mouth, finding her lips pursed in anger.

"Fuck you, Kyle. Fuck. You."

Grasping her chin in my fingers, I press the length of my body against hers.

"I hate you."

"Oh, I know. Feels fucking great, doesn't it?"

I drop my hand to her throat and my sudden movement makes her gasp, exactly what I was hoping for as I force my tongue into her mouth and tease hers.

Her hands lift to my chest and she tries, unsuccessfully, to push me away.

She resists kissing me to the point she bites my tongue but the second I turn the tables on her, suck her bottom lip into my mouth and sink my teeth into it, her body starts to relax. Her nails, that she was trying to claw my skin off with, suddenly vanish in favor of fisting my shirt in her small hands so she can cling onto me.

"See," I whisper into her mouth. "You can do as you're told."

"Fuck. You."

"Yeah, Kitten. I was thinking the same."

Dropping my hands to her thighs, I push her skirt up around her waist and lift her so she has no choice but to wrap her legs around my waist.

I grind into her forcing a moan to rip from her lips as my length aligns perfectly with her core.

"You feel that, Kitten?" She nods. "You fucking do that to me."

"Kyle," she cries as I reach around her, slip her panties aside and run my finger through her folds.

"So fucking wet, Kitten."

"Oh God," she gasps as I push one digit inside her.

"You want to get fucked right here in this classroom?" I drop my lips to her ear. "Where anyone could walk in and see that I fucking own you?"

I continue working her, knowing that she's long past the point of refusing anything I say to her. Her juices run down my fingers as she thinks about my words.

"You like belonging to me, don't you, Kitten?"

"No," she argues. I don't need to look at her to know her eye is twitching as she says it.

"Well, your pussy seems to disagree with you."

26

HARLEY

"Oh fuck, Kyle," I cry as he spears his fingers inside me before pulling them out and leaving me feeling bereft without him.

I shouldn't be doing this.

We *really* shouldn't be doing this.

I told myself that when I saw him next, I would rip him a new one and walk away from him for being such an arrogant, demanding prick. But then he put his hands on me and I forgot everything but how it feels when he touches me.

He drops me lower, with one hand gripping my ass while the other lifts the hem of his shirt.

"Go on then," he encourages, nodding down to his waistband.

"Ky, you're not serious?" I ask. He can't really be suggesting that we do this… here.

"I'm deadly fucking serious, Kitten."

I stare into his sparkling silver eyes, the blue vanished with his hunger. His abs jump when my knuckles brush them as I undo his button and help push his pants down over his hips.

One second he has his length in his hand and the next I've been lifted higher against the wall at my back and I feel him pressing against my entrance.

I brace myself for his invasion, knowing that it's probably going to hurt like last time, although I hope not quite as bad.

"Relax, Kitten. It's just me," he says softly, his palm cupping my cheek and his thumb gently caressing my skin. It's totally at odds with his attitude only moments ago. I guess being on the verge of sex does that to a guy.

I take a deep breath and slide my fingers into his hair, knocking his backward cap to the floor in the process.

His lips find mine at the same time he drops me down onto him.

It burns, but it's nowhere near as bad as I remember.

A groan rumbles up from the back of Kyle's throat, the sound is so damn sexy and mixed with the knowledge that I'm the one who caused it helps me to forget the bite of pain as he pulls out.

"Okay?" he asks through gritted teeth, and I can't help but swoon.

He likes to make out he's all vicious and demanding, but once you peel back that hard outer shell, he's just the sweet boy I remember. The one who would always share his chocolate with me when my own brother would scoff, leaving me with nothing.

"Yeah." My fingers twist in his hair and I drag his lips to mine as he begins to fuck me.

It's rougher than last time, my shoulder blades smarting against the rough wall behind me, but feeling him moving inside me, hearing the quiet groans of pleasure that rumbled up his throat, is fucking everything.

"Oh God, Kyle," I moan, tipping my head back as I begin to get closer. His lips attack my neck, sucking and biting, the pain only adding to the pleasure shooting around my body.

"Come, Kitten. Let me hear you scream my name."

"Oh shit."

He slips his hand between us and pinches my clit, that extra sensation is exactly what I need to send me flying over the edge.

Seconds later, he drops his head into the crook of my neck before his cock jerks violently inside me.

His hot breath fans across my collarbones and sends goose bumps racing across my skin.

"Come to mine after school. We'll do your next tutoring session."

"You want me to come to yours to do math?" I ask incredulously.

"That, and other things."

"I should say no," I tell him honestly.

"Yeah, you probably should. Hell, you can if you want, but you're still going to find yourself in my bedroom after school with your clothes on my floor."

"Jesus, Ky."

"Go on," he encourages. "Tell me no. Tell me you don't want that."

"I... um..." His hand wraps around my throat once again and I have to fight not to sigh with contentment. It's fucked-up, but I've never felt safer than when I'm in his hands like this.

His eyes widen and his brows rise as he waits.

"I passed a math test yesterday," I blurt out, no longer able to contain my smile.

"Okay, wow. That wasn't what I was expecting but... well done."

"I... I couldn't have done it without you," I admit. "Mr. Wilson put the questions in front of me and it was like I could hear you telling me how to do it."

"Yeah?" he asks, his own smile beginning to emerge.

"Yeah, so... thank you."

Suddenly the silence around us is broken by the sound of a group of kids walking past the classroom door and it's like a bucket of ice water is thrown over both of us.

Kyle lowers me to the floor before pulling his pants up and reaching for his cap.

"We should go and get food," I say, aware that I've still not answered him about after school. Part of me doesn't want to, just to see what he's going to do.

We walk toward the cafeteria together side by side. No words are said, but I guess that's an improvement on most of the time we've spent together while under this roof so I'll take it. He waits for me when I take a detour to the bathroom to clean up and gives me a killer smile which makes desire curl in my belly when I emerge.

We grab a tray each and get some lunch before dropping down on opposite sides of the team's table.

"You found her at last then?" Zayn asks Kyle, which immediately piques my interest.

"You were looking for me?" I ask, hoping to make him sweat under my brother's scrutiny. Mean? Maybe. But I don't give a shit. He's sure done worse to me.

"What?" I hiss at Ruby when she elbows me to get my attention.

My eyes meet hers but she doesn't say anything, instead, she flicks a look to my neck before covering her own with her hand.

My brows pinch together in confusion. But then the image of Kyle sucking on my neck only minutes ago in that classroom hit me and I immediately copy her move, covering my neck.

I twist away from Zayn a little more before lifting my wrap to my mouth.

"Yeah," he finally says. "I needed to know something about that English lit paper we were given."

"Oh yeah, what was that?"

A knowing smirk plays on his lips. He knows exactly what I'm doing.

"It's fine. I found someone else to ask. I... uh... can't remember her name, but that really hot blonde that sits at the front of class. She was more than willing to help."

I smile at him, hoping to hell that my true feelings aren't written all over my face as I say, "Oh, yeah. I bet she did," and roll my eyes so hard they actually hurt.

I swear everyone sitting at the table holds their breath as they wait for him to say something in response.

"Yeah, she had a real tight—ow," he complains, reaching under the table to rub at whatever that was, from the smirk on Ruby's face I'm assuming it was her shoe. "I was going to say understanding of what we had to do."

"Course you were." I roll my eyes and turn to Ruby, severing our connection. For now at least.

Sitting so far away from him for the rest of lunch but feeling his stare burning into me makes the time drag. It's no different as I sit in chemistry watching Ruby and Ash flirt in front of me knowing that I've got history with him next period.

I know he's going to bug me about going to his place after school, and although I already know that it's going to happen, I've come to terms with the fact I'm not going to be able to refuse, he doesn't need to know that.

He's already in his seat waiting for me when I finally make it to the other side of the school to our history class.

"I thought you were skipping on me," he whispers as Mr. Anderson starts the class.

"I considered it."

"Oh yeah?"

"Yeah. I like playing hide and seek." I flip my book open ready to get started, refusing to look at him despite the fact I know he's staring at me.

His hand skims down my back before his fingers tuck under the waistband of my skirt, the heat of his skin burning mine.

He leans over, his breath tickling down my neck.

"You seem to forget that I always win."

"Who said that wasn't my intention?"

His growl makes my entire body tingle.

"Oh, Kitten, we're going to have such fun tonight."

"I've got cheer practice." My argument is weak, I know that, but it's all I have.

"And I've got a conditioning session. It's like fate."

"Yeah, if you believe in that shit."

"You don't?" he asks, shocking me so much I actually turn to look at him.

"You do?"

"Maybe. We'll just have to wait and see if fate lands you in my lap later."

"Fucking hell," I mutter, trying not to show how much I like the banter between us when we're not trying to kill each other.

"So... tonight, my bed, you in?"

"You're going to need to make it sound a little more tempting than that."

"Hmmm... okay." He shifts his chair a little closer, so he can whisper in my ear and his hand slips around to grip onto my hip. "My bed, me naked, you coming... again, and again... and again."

Holy shit.

My thighs clench as he growls out those words so roughly all my hairs stand on end.

"I'll think about it."

He chuckles, sitting back in his seat before we get caught and end up in detention together instead of his bed.

"You have got some explaining to do. The scarf yesterday and then that fresh one at lunch," Ruby says, helpfully pointing out the love bite in question, just in case Stella or any other member of the squad who care to be listening to us as they get ready for practice.

"Do we really have to do this now?"

"Just tell me it was him?" Ruby raises a knowing brow. She really doesn't need me to tell her the answer, she already knows.

"Yes. It was him."

"Oh my God," she squeals and starts clapping like a baby seal. "This is so exciting. He was freaking out when he couldn't find you yesterday."

"What? Why?" I ask, my brow furrowing.

"No idea, he wouldn't say."

"Come on, ladies. Get moving," Chelsea barks when she walks in and sees us standing around gossiping.

Ruby winks at me before turning around to get changed telling me that this is only the beginning of this discussion.

Thankfully, since we were runner-up at nationals a few weeks ago, Chelsea has let up on practice and we're spending our time perfecting new routines and moves. We've still got a few weeks until tryouts and welcoming new members to our squad so mostly we're just enjoying ourselves.

"Ace's?" Ruby asks hopefully once we're back in the locker room getting showered and dressed.

"I… err… can't. I've got a tutoring session."

"Oh right, is that what we're calling it these days?" she says, smothering a laugh.

"Well, no, actually Kyle *is* my tutor."

"Okay, when did this happen?"

"Last week, I just didn't confess."

"Harley Hunter, have you been keeping secrets from me?"

Guilt covers my face and my temperature picks up as she stares at me.

"A little," I whisper, lifting my hand and holding my thumb and forefinger just a little apart.

She places her hand on her hip and tries her best to look angry but she only lasts a few seconds before she bursts out laughing.

"You gonna spill all before you leave to meet him?"

"Nope," I say with a smile. "But know this… I'm probably making a huge mistake."

"Well," she says, deep in thought. "At least you're going into it with your eyes open."

"Yeah, although I have a feeling I'm still about to run face-first into a brick wall."

"You might not. Look at me and Ash. I'm sure there are plenty that would say we were making a huge mistake."

"I think your parents probably still are," I deadpan.

"Oh shush yourself." She laughs. "Seriously though, you know where I am, yeah? My ears are open."

"Thank you. Good news though, I passed a math test."

Ruby's face lights up, much like I'm sure mine did when I realized that I'd nailed it.

"OMG! That's awesome. See, maybe all of this might just work out. Crazier things have happened."

"Yeah, we'll see."

"Rubes, can I borrow you?" Chelsea shouts, successfully ending our conversation.

"Coming, boss."

"Call me, yes?" Ruby's eyes widen with her demand.

"If I can."

"On second thought, don't. Just enjoy him and give me all the details later." She winks before skipping over to Chelsea.

Knowing that Kyle is with the team right now means I'm in no rush to be ready. We finished early tonight so I know I'm going to have to wait for him.

"You coming to get your car, or are you going straight to his?"

"Straight there. Is it okay if I pick up my car tomorrow maybe?"

"Of course."

"Thank you. I wasn't really expecting to be going to his."

"Really?" she asks with a laugh.

"I hoped I'd be able to put up more of a fight."

"Girl, sometimes, it's just not worth it. Reap the reward for putting up with his ass."

"You're nuts," I say, dragging my skirt on.

"Only way to be." I shake my head at her craziness. Who am I to judge on how she gets by after being forced to move so much. "Have you found out why he was so freaked out about not knowing where you were yesterday?"

"Other than him being an asshole and a control freak?" I ask.

"Yeah, other than that."

"Nah. He was just being… Kyle." I shrug, not thinking anymore into it.

"Okay. Ready to head out?" Most of the girls have already left, thanks to my slow ass, but Stella hung back with me. For someone who claims to not make friends, she's a pretty good one.

"Yep, let's go."

A couple of the guys from the team walk ahead of us down the hallway and I can't help looking over my shoulder to see if Kyle is about to sneak up on me any minute. But he never does.

The second we're in the lot though, I know he's still here because his car is one of the only ones left.

"You want me to wait with you," Stella offers.

"No, you take off. I'm sure he won't be long."

"Sure?"

"Yes, go."

"See you tomorrow."

I wave her off and watch as she walks to her car. I do the same but toward Kyle's Volkswagen.

I find myself a seat on the hood and pull out my cell.

I'm scrolling through Instagram when some movement in the trees to my right catches my eye. I half expect Kyle to jump out and scare me half to death. But as I keep scanning the tree line, I don't see anything or anyone.

Feeling ridiculous, it was probably just a cat or something, I focus back on the post I was reading and forget the world around me exists.

The other few cars that were out here are long gone, leaving me alone with Kyle's car and what I'm assuming is Ash's bike.

I might not be looking up when the pair of them exit the building, but I don't need to be. I feel it.

My skin prickles with awareness and my stomach flutters in anticipation.

Lifting my eyes from my cell, I find him staring right at me as he walks this way. Ashton is talking to him, but I've got a feeling that Kyle isn't hearing a word of it.

When they get to Ash's bike, he slaps Kyle on the shoulder and says something. Kyle nods but his footsteps don't falter as he continues to close the space between us.

"Hmm… you on the hood of my car. This is a nice surprise."

"I do aim to please, Mr. Legend."

A growl rumbles low in his throat as he parts my knees and steps between them, sliding my ass down the hood to get us closer.

"Fuck, Kitten. What am I going to do with you?"

27

KYLE

"Holy shit," I gasp the second I push the door open and Ash and I step out toward the parking lot.

"Wha—oooooh? Something you need to tell me, man?"

"Something with her waiting for me like that doesn't already give away?"

"You're a lucky motherfucker."

"Err… have you seen your girl?"

"Yes, and I'd prefer it if you didn't *see* my girl."

"Oh fuck off. She's hot and you love it."

"Yeah, man. I fucking do. Now you gonna go over there and rock her fucking world, or what?"

"We've got a tutoring session."

I don't look over at him, my eyes are glued on Harley but I know he throws his head back laughing.

"Sure you have. Why do I get the feeling that the only thing you're studying tonight is her body?"

"Because she needs to not fail math."

"Damn bro, you're serious, aren't you?" he asks as if I might just have sprouted a new head.

I can't keep a straight face and bark out a laugh. "Partly. We'll do the math when we're having a rest."

"Fuck yeah, man." He slaps my shoulder and turns to his bike. "Have a good night. Don't do anything I wouldn't do."

"Which is fucking nothing, so I'm safe."

"Bro, that hurts."

"Fucking truth though, ain't it?"

"Meh." He mutters something under his breath as I walk away, but with Harley waiting for me like she is, I really don't care about whatever it is.

The second I'm in front of her, I force her knees apart and slide her down the hood until her legs wrap around my hips.

"Zayn's already left," she whispers as I stare down into her dark eyes.

"Don't care."

One of my hands slides into her hair and my fingers twist in the length as I pull her head back and capture her lips with mine.

Fuck, she's too addictive.

My cock hardens against her as I plunge my tongue into her mouth.

I shouldn't do this here out in the open. It might be empty but there are always eyes in a school just waiting to spread the next bit of gossip, but I can't stop myself.

I kiss her until we're both breathless and my need to rip her panties aside and take her right here is almost too much to ignore.

Dragging my lips from her, I trail them across her jaw and down her neck, sucking on the same bit of skin I did earlier, brightening my mark.

"You smell like strawberries," I whisper against her throat.

It flexes as she swallows. "M-my shower gel."

I pull back and look at her. Her eyes are hooded with lust, her cheeks bright and her lips swollen from my kiss.

"Wanna see my bedroom?" I ask with a smile.

"I'm not that kind of girl," she quips. Resting back on her palms and running her eyes down the length of me until she finds the bulge in my pants. She sucks her bottom lip into her mouth and bites down.

"I've got news for you, Harley Hunter. You are that girl and you're about to do some wicked things to prove me right."

Her lips part once again but she doesn't say anything.

"Get in the car before I fuck you right here."

I've barely finished the words and she's scrambling from the hood and racing toward the passenger door.

"Is the prospect that bad?"

"You want anyone watching?"

"As long as I'm the one inside you, I don't give a fuck, Kitten."

Her chin drops like she's about to argue, but she must change her mind because in the end all she does is rip the door open and drop into the seat.

I stare at her for a beat, appreciating just how good she looks in my car.

"Ready?" I ask once I've joined her.

"Honestly? No, I don't think I am."

I laugh at her as I start the car.

"Well, I hate to break it to you, but it's too late to back out now." I press the button to lock the doors, showing her just how serious I am.

"Pretty sure this is classed as kidnapping right now."

"Nah, Kitten. You're going to enjoy yourself way too much for it to be that." I smirk, starting the engine and pulling out of the space.

"This is... um... bare," Harley says as she walks into my room ahead of me. Thankfully, the place is empty but I don't have any intention of hanging out in the living room in case Kane comes back. He might be okay with flaunting his conquests but like fuck are his eyes getting on Harley.

"Yeah, well not all of us become the princess in the castle," I mutter, kicking the door closed behind me and stepping right into her.

Now I've had her again, I'm fucking addicted.

A year of only looking at guys and I need to be buried deep inside her again more than I need my next breath.

Sweeping her hair to the side, I press my lips to the skin where her neck meets her shoulder and smile when a shudder runs through her.

"That's not what I meant. I'm not judging."

"Sure you're not," I breathe, making my way up her smooth neck.

But she tenses in my hold, and I know she's about to pull away from me.

"I'm not," she snaps, her hands going to her waist as her hip pops. "I don't give a shit where you live, Ky. We grew up in shithole, damp and cold trailers. This is like a fucking castle compared to that.

"So what, I live in a big house. It doesn't change who I am. I'm the girl from Harrow Creek. I'll always be the girl from Harrow Creek, just like you'll always be the boy—shit," she gasps as my body crashes against hers and we both stumble until her back hits the wall.

My lips find hers as I wrap her legs around my waist.

"You're wrong," I whisper, my heart pounding so hard in my chest I worry it's about to come out. "You're not just a girl from the Creek. You're my fucking girl from the Creek."

I stare into wide eyes as my words settle around us both.

"Fuck, I need you now."

With one hand on her ass to hold her up, the other threads into her hair and I carry her to my bed, my mouth attached to her the whole time, too afraid to pull away again in case some other scary shit falls from my lips.

Her back hits the mattress and I wrap my hands around the bottom of her hoodie, pulling the fabric up her body, releasing her lips for the briefest moment as it passes between us.

The second I drop it to the floor, I slip my hand around her back to release her bra and peel that away from her body as well, my hands moving so I can squeeze them both.

A moan rips up her throat as I do it.

"Fuck, Harley. You're so fucking sexy."

"Ky," she moans as I kiss and suck on the skin of her neck before grazing my teeth over her collarbones before making my way to her breasts so I can pull her nipples into my mouth.

"Good, Kitten?" I growl when her back arches from the bed. I kiss across to the other side and give it the same treatment.

"Kyle," she moans again. "I need—"

"I know what you need. Trust me?"

I look up at her and my eyes lock with hers. Something crackles between us but it gives me no clue as to what kind of answer to expect.

"D-do I trust you?" she asks between heaving breaths.

"Yeah, Kitten. Do you trust me?"

She searches my eyes as if she's going to find the answer she needs within them as she tries to find the word she needs.

I wait with my lips hovering right over her breast, my breath teasing her and keeping her nipple pert for me.

"Y-yes," she whispers finally.

"Yeah?" I confirm, a smile twitching at my lips.

"I shouldn't. But I do."

"Right answer, Kitten."

Instead of going back to her breast, I kiss down her stomach, undo the button on her waistband and pull her skirt and panties down her legs until she's bare before me.

"So beautiful."

She lifts her arms as if she's going to attempt to hide from me, but the second our eyes lock, she must read my warning because she drops them back to the bed.

"Why am I naked and you're fully dressed?" She lifts a brow as her eyes drop to my clothed body.

"Good question. What are you going to do about it?" I stare at her, daring her to move and she does, in the blink of an eye.

Her hands fist the bottom of my hoodie, pulling it up my body and revealing my bare torso beneath. Her fingers tickle down my skin, tracing my abs before finding the scar on my side. My muscles tense as she brushes the raised mark.

"H-how you'd get this?"

"Juvie initiation. It was nothing."

Guilt flashes through her eyes, her lips pressing into a thin line as she stares at it.

"You got hurt?"

"Kitten," I whisper, reaching out and cupping her chin, tilting her face up so she has no choice but to look at me. "That place was like a jungle. You've got to do what you've got to do, to survive."

"Ky, I'm so, so—"

"No," I bark. "We're not doing this now."

Her eyes fill with tears at my harsh tone but she quickly blinks them away.

"Now, you were about to do something," I remind her, rolling my hips to get her attention.

She reaches out and fumbles with my fly and shoves the fabric down my hips, allowing my cock to spring free.

"Fuck, Kitten," I bark as the sensation of her hand wrapping around me stops me in my tracks.

"Good?" she asks, much like I did earlier.

"Like you wouldn't believe." I quickly toe my sneakers off before kicking my pants from my legs.

"Kitten," I growl, my hand finding the back of her head as she sucks me deep into her mouth.

She takes me all the way back until I feel the back of her throat at the tip.

"Oh shit." My grip on her hair tightens as pleasure shoots through me.

She works me like a fucking pro, her hot wet mouth better than I could have ever imagined. Tears leak from her eyes as she fights her need to gag until I come down her throat.

"How are you so fucking perfect?" I ask, pushing her back on the bed and crawling over her, wiping the tears from her cheeks once she's settled.

She wipes her mouth with the back of her hand and smiles shyly up at me.

"I think we both know I'm far from that."

“Don’t think about it,” I demand, not wanting to give the past a second thought right now.

We’ve got a lot to talk about. The most pressing is the truth about Gray’s threats that I’m keeping from her. But right now, I just want to enjoy this because I have no doubt that all too soon something will fuck it up.

“But we—” I cut her off with my kiss. I’m not interested in talking right now, that can come later, much, much later.

“I’d probably be able to concentrate on this better if you let me get dressed,” Harley complains from her spot on my bed. She’s got her math book on her thighs and that is it. Just as she should be. “And I’m cold.”

“I can warm you up, Kitten.”

She pins me with a look.

“We are doing this.” She nods toward the book on her lap. “Nothing, and I mean nothing, else is happening until I’ve nailed this.”

“I’d rather nail you.”

“You already have. Twice,” she reminds me.

“Yeah, well. I’m not doing it right now,” I sulk.

Her eyes narrow as she thinks and my stomach clenches. I’m not going to like what she’s about to say.

“Spit it out, Kitten,” I encourage when she remains silent.

“I thought you hated me,” she blurts before her eyes go wide as if she didn’t actually mean to say the words.

“Yeah, well… turns out I like fucking you more than I do hating you.”

“So you still hate me, fucking me softens the blow?”

She asks the question so seriously that I can’t help but laugh.

“Yeah, Kitten. Something like that.”

“Do that again?”

“Do what again?” My brows pinch at her request, unaware that I just did anything.

“Laugh again.”

“Make me.”

She throws the book to the other end of the bed and launches herself at me, her red nails going to my sides before she starts tickling.

I laugh, not because she demanded I do so but because I can’t not.

This right now. This is fucking everything.

28

HARLEY

"You're not running this time, Hunter," Ruby says as she, Poppy and Stella approach me in the cafeteria the next morning, "We already know that you didn't sleep in your own bed last night." She looks at Poppy, ratting her out for snitching on me. "And we know you didn't stay at Stella's like you lead your mother to believe." She looks at Stella.

I shake my head at the three of them. "Looks like you've got me all figured out," I concede. Not that I really had a leg to stand on.

With most of the team elsewhere and the squad having their usual bitch fest at our normal table, we find another just the four of us so we can thankfully have this conversation in private.

"So..." Ruby starts, looking entirely too excited by what I might have to say. "Are you like... together now?"

"What? No. I'm pretty sure he still hates me."

"But you spent the night with him." Her words force me back to last night when he basically told me that I wasn't leaving before physically pinning me to his bed to stop it from happening. I'm also reminded of how I woke up multiple times in the night, and this morning to him asleep at my back with his arm thrown protectively over my waist.

It felt nice. No. It was better than nice. It felt incredible.

But I'm not stupid. I know this is nothing more than him taking what he thinks I owe him. And right when I allow myself to believe it could be more, he's going to force me to watch him turn his back on me, on this, and smile as I drown.

I push the depressing thought away because it's not going to happen. I'm not going to fall for him and he's not going to break my heart.

It's not going to happen.

"He doesn't have to like her to fuck her, I thought you of all people would know that," Poppy says, pinning Ruby with a knowing look.

"I know but—"

"There is no but there, just like there is no *us.* He's helping me out with my math and taking what he thinks he's owed after that night."

"Yeah and about that. When are you going to tell us what happened *that* night?"

"Um…" I glance at Poppy, aware that she already knows and grateful she's not told Ruby. "Fine," I huff, really not wanting to go back there but knowing my time is running out. "I went to a party that Letty dragged me along to. She'd not been back to Harrow Creek for ages seeing as she was at college, and she wanted to see some old friends.

"I didn't want to go. She'd had some… issues, shall we say, with Kane, Kyle's older brother, and I had a feeling he'd be there despite her protests that he wouldn't. Well, not an hour into the party and they both turned up.

"Kyle was already drunk and he made a beeline for me. Zayn wasn't there, so I guess he thought he had something of a free pass. I wasn't complaining. I'd crushed on him since forever."

"Rightly so," Stella adds with a nod, making me look up at her. "What? He's hot."

"Yeah, whatever. We were drinking, one thing led to another and…"

"And…" Ruby encourages.

"We kissed and stuff."

"And stuff."

"Yeah, touched a bit. Nothing crazy. Anyway, the rest of his crew were there, Kane and Letty had vanished, Christ knows where and I was enjoying life. But after a while, things started getting a little hazy. I knew I was drunk, but I hadn't had that much, you know.

"But then Kyle's friend Gray joined us, and I mean like… *joined us.*

"Kyle seemed up for it. He was wasted, mind you. So I played along. I felt safe with Kyle so I wasn't too concerned. I knew Gray was different… dangerous, but then most guys from the Creek are, it wasn't anything new to me.

"But things started to escalate, his touches more insistent, the things he whispered in my ear sent a shiver down my spine and I realized what he had done.

"I barely remember the call. Hell, until the cops turned up I didn't even really know if the call had connected or if they cared. I certainly wasn't going to lift my cell to my ear for him to see. I just knew that I needed to get out of that situation before something really bad happened because one look in Gray's eyes and I knew it was coming.

"He drugged me for a reason. He wasn't stopping."

"Jesus," Ruby mutters. She's leaning forward with her elbows on the table and her chin resting on her knuckles, totally invested in my story.

"So what happened next?" Stella asks, her jaw ticcing like she wants to go and physically hurt someone—Gray—for this. I'm not going to tell her so, but since seeing her house and hearing her previous threats, I'm kinda scared she actually has it in her to do it too.

"Things got really hazy. I remember leaning into Kyle, telling him to help me, and then I blacked out.

"I vaguely remember the commotion of the place emptying, I assume the second they discovered the cops had arrived. Then I remember an officer talking to me. Kyle was there. I remember that he was holding my hand and it made me feel safe.

"But the next time I came back to, he was gone, and I was in the hospital."

"Had he hurt you?" Poppy asks.

"No. And there was no evidence that Gray actually did anything. I knew it was him who did it, and as much as I wanted to believe Kyle wasn't involved, I couldn't be sure. They were best friends. It would have made sense for him to know."

"Did he?" Stella all but growls.

"I don't think so. He stayed while all the others ran despite the fact his pockets were full of Gray's gear."

"But he was drunk," she argues.

"Not drunk enough to sit beside me and hold my hand. Something tells me he sobered up pretty fast when reality came crashing down."

"So..." Poppy starts, looking totally confused. "If he was the one who helped you, why do you hate him."

I chuckle to myself. "I blamed him for allowing it to happen, and until he turned up here and acted the way he has, I convinced myself that he was a part of the plan."

"But you don't know?"

I shake my head. "No, I know he wasn't in on it."

"Has he said so?" Ruby asks.

"No, but he doesn't need to."

"Christ, okay. So this Gray guy…" Stella discretely cracks her knuckles under the table like she's gunning for a fight, which is hilarious because she's the small blonde girl who looks about as scary as a teddy bear.

I shrug. "Dead I hope."

Ruby gasps in shock.

"What? He'd have raped me that night, I have no doubt. He doesn't deserve to breathe the same air as us."

"True."

"So he's gone?" Stella asks with a scowl on her face.

"I mean, I guess. I haven't heard from him or seen him since that night so…"

"Okay," she says, deep in thought.

"What? What are you thinking?" I ask her.

"You said Kyle was arrested because of Gray's drugs. I assume they got seized."

"Yeah, I guess."

"Gray's going to want payment for the lost revenue."

"Uh… um… who are you?"

She laughs. "I've probably just seen too many movies," she argues, but I don't buy it.

"So you think he'll come for Kyle?" Ruby asks the words that I'm afraid to.

"I have no idea, but surely you've all seen the movies."

Silence settles over our table for a few seconds as my stomach knots uncomfortably. I don't want to be anywhere near him ever again, and I certainly don't want him anywhere near Kyle. He's already got him in enough shit.

"You going to his birthday party tonight?" Ruby suddenly asks.

"Whose?"

"Kyle's." She rolls her eyes like it should be totally obvious.

"It's his birthday?" I ask, horrified that I didn't already know this. I woke up in his bed this morning and I didn't know.

"Yeah, his brother is throwing him a party at their house. We're all going, right?"

"Uh…" Why didn't he tell me? Hell, why didn't he invite me?

"We're going," Stella states, putting an end to whatever I was going to say. That and the fact the bell rings.

"We'll all get ready at Harley's," Poppy announces, still unable to claim our house as her own.

"I've got some stuff to do after school," Stella says. "But I'll be there."

We clear away our trays and all head in different directions for our classes.

Ruby excuses herself to meet Ash and I make my way alone, crossing to a different building to our English lit class.

I'm almost there when a storage closet door opens beside me and someone wraps their hand around my arm and drags me inside.

"What the hell are you doing?" I hiss as Kyle crowds me against the wall. There's a dirty bulb hanging overhead that gives out just enough light to see each other. His hand skims up my body before it finds its home around my throat.

My heart thunders in my chest but I must admit that I'm starting to get used to him 'abducting' me when I least expect it. Hell, I'm starting to enjoy it.

"I needed something."

"Oh yeah. That's a coincidence because I need something too."

"Yeah?" he growls, pressing me harder into the wall. "Ow, what was that for?" he asks, rubbing the side of his head where I gently hit it.

"It's your fucking birthday. Why didn't you tell me?"

He shrugs. "Not important."

"Ky, you're eighteen. It's really important," I argue.

He shakes his head at me, a soft smile playing on his lips.

"I got to wake up and sink inside you, what could be more important than that?" he murmurs.

"Oh, I don't know, how about... tell me about your party?" I pin him with a look.

"How'd you... Ruby." He correctly guesses.

"Yeah, so am I not invited then, or what?"

"I don't know what Kane's got planned and I didn't want..." He trails off.

"How about you let me decide that?"

"I'm assuming he's invited the Creek group and..."

"Still you thought it was okay to decide for me?"

The truth is, I don't really have any intention of hanging out with his Creek buddies. After *that* night, I turned my back on that place, aside from visiting my dad.

He smiles at me and damn him because it makes my insides melt.

"Kitten," he breathes, making my insides quiver. "Would you like to come to my party?"

"I think I might be busy tonight, thanks for the invite though," I deadpan and he throws his head back and laughs.

His gaze is so intense when it comes back to mine that it makes my heart skip a beat, I swear.

"W-we should get to class."

"Yeah, in a minute."

His lips find mine and his hand slips under my shirt so he can wrap his hand around my waist, skin on skin.

The second his tongue slips into my mouth, I sag in his hold, grateful that he'll hold me up.

"I really want to fuck you," he admits after kissing across my jaw, his lips brushing my ears.

"B-but English," I force out, making him laugh.

"I know, Kitten. Is there anything I can do to make you skip with me?"

A million and one things that he could say to make me agree run through my mind, but I don't say any of them because I know I can't allow it to happen.

"Nope."

"Everyone else thinks you're such a good girl, don't they?"

"Ky," I warn, his deep voice and desire-filled words making my refusal to stay locked in here for our entire class harder and harder to stick to.

English lit was hell after I finally managed to slip out from Kyle and escape the storage closet.

I can't deny that I'd have been more than happy to stay in there for the entire time, but I can't risk missing class, and I certainly can't risk the chance of Mom finding out. She might let us get away with a lot when it comes to parties and drinking but school is another matter entirely.

She's not stupid, she knows from experience the kind of upbringing we had in the Creek, and she knows the things we got up to way before we were old enough to be doing them. Hell, she is a Creek girl. But she also got out, and education is the only way to make that happen. And she wants better for us. I totally understand that.

Kyle's touch barely leaves my body throughout the entire class while he sits there trying to prove that what I did was wrong.

My skin tingles with awareness, my panties still damp from his kiss.

I know I probably made the wrong decision but it's too late to go back on it now.

"Come home with me now," he growls in my ear as he stands a little too close to me besides my locker as the rest of the students make a beeline for the exit to start their weekend plans. "We can start the party early."

"You've got a conditioning session," I say, poking him in the chest a little harder than necessary. "And I promised the girls that I'd get ready with them."

"What are you wearing?"

"I have no idea," I say honestly because I haven't even thought about it.

"Wrong answer, Kitten."

"Okay." I pause trying to come up with the right answer. "Something sexy?"

"Bingo."

"I'm assuming Zayn is coming?"

"Fuuuck. I'm just going to have to tell him that I'm banging his hot as fuck sister," he says with a shrug and my heart rate picks up a few notches.

"And get your ass kicked on your birthday?"

"Ow," I complain when he reaches out and twists my nipple through my shirt. "I can take your brother, Kitten."

"Riiight. Sure."

He stares at me with his brow furrowed.

"Okay fine. But not tonight. You're supposed to be enjoying yourself."

"Exactly, which means I need a free pass to your pussy."

"Jesus, were you always this insufferable?"

"Yep, you just never noticed."

"Not sure how because I spent a lot of time looking," I mutter but instantly regret it when an intrigued smile lights up his face.

"Oh really? Tell me more."

"I'd love to," I say, looking over my shoulder and finding the perfect excuse why I can't. "But I think your new team has come to collect you." I nod in their direction and he turns to find Jake, Ethan, Mason and Zayn heading this way.

"More issues with your homework, Legend?" Zayn asks suspiciously, his eyes flicking between the two of us.

"Yeah," Kyle mutters. "Something like that."

"Right well, as fun as this has been. We've got somewhere to be," Jake pipes up. "And just because it's your birthday, don't think that means I'm going to go easy on you. You've got a reputation to uphold, Legend," he warns.

I narrow my eyes at Kyle.

Was I the only one who didn't know it was his birthday?

"Let's go then. Seems I need to remind you of just how good I am."

"Arrogant much?" I mutter, feeling Kyle's eyes on me as I stare into my locker to get my books.

"You know you love it." I don't need to look over my shoulder to know he's got a shit-eating grin on his face.

"Let's go, asshole," Zayn mutters. "Before you make her want to claw your eyes out more than she already does."

A smile twitches at my lips at the hope in that statement. My brother isn't stupid, he knows something is going on here. I'm just hoping he's happy enough to live in denial about it a while longer. I'm not ready for the shitshow that would ensue when he finds out the truth.

Hopefully by the time that happens, Kyle will have had his fun and we can all return to our normal lives where he hates me and can barely look at me, and I can go on pretending that I want to screw any other member of the team just to piss off my brother.

My stomach twists painfully, reminding me that my head and my heart are already at war with this situation.

29

KYLE

"Whoa, cover your tiny cocks boys, there's a lady in da house," Ethan barks as we're all getting dressed after Jake's brutal session.

Glancing up after buttoning up my jeans, I find Stella walking through the boy's locker room as if it's normal. Her eyes flick around all the guys in the room, a small smile playing on her face.

"Afternoon boys. It's so good to *see* you," she jokes.

Once she's happy she's got her fill, her eyes land on me.

"Me and you need to talk," she states matter-of-factly.

"Err... we do?"

"We do," she confirms. "Get your shit together."

"Looks like Legend's getting a birthday treat," someone shouts behind me.

"Woohoo, get in there, boy," someone else jeers.

I flip them off over my shoulder because despite how this looks, I already know that isn't why Stella is here.

"He should be so lucky," she sasses, throwing her white-blonde hair over her shoulder and batting her eyelashes.

After another second, her eyes find me again.

"I'll be outside. Don't make me wait too long." With that said, she spins on her heel and marches back out as fast as she marched in.

"What the fuck was that?" Zayn asks as Ash's curious eyes drill into the side of my head.

"Fuck knows, but I think I'm about to find out."

"Need company?" Ash asks. "There's something kinda scary about her."

"I'm pretty sure I can handle her."

"Wish I could fucking handle her," someone shouts.

I shake my head, laughing to myself. I might be in a better part of the country now, but the banter in the boy's locker room never changes.

"I'll see you later, yeah?" I say to Ash and Zayn.

"You got it, man," Zayn agrees. "Gonna party like we trailer park trash," he jokes.

I haven't invited the rest of the team, although I have my suspicions that they might just turn up anyway.

I'm assuming that Kane has invited some of our old crew and I'm not entirely sure how I feel about my past and my present colliding. Not to mention that the Harriers are loose rivals of the Bears. I say loose because the Bears would smash the Harriers even in their sleep so they're not exactly a threat to the Bears' success.

After shoving everything into my duffel, I throw it over my shoulder and head out to find out what Stella wants.

"Alright?" I nod at her as I approach.

"I guess that all depends on what you've got to tell me."

"Um..."

"Your car?"

"Uh... sure."

She pushes from the wall she was resting back against and marches toward the exit, leaving me to follow her.

The guys were right in the locker room. She's got a banging body, but she's not doing it for me. The girl I suspect she's come to talk to me about, on the other hand, is very much doing it for me right now.

I shove down the little voice in my head that tries to tell me that it's not just about the revenge it started out as because I'm not ready to deal with any of that.

I'm just going to get my fill of her. Get her out of my system and hope that I can then move on with my life.

She's been in my head since that night, and not for all the right reasons, it's time to purge her back out.

I press the unlock button for my car and Stella wastes no time in dropping down into the passenger seat, after throwing my bags in the trunk, I join her.

"So to what do I owe this pleasure?"

"Gray," she says, and my blood runs cold as her blue eyes hold mine.

"W-what about him?"

"Harley told us what happened that night. She said the drugs you got busted with were his."

"Right..."

"He's why you were freaking out about not knowing where Harley was the other night, wasn't he?"

My chin drops but I don't find the words to confirm her suspicions.

"Yeah, I thought so. So, what's the plan? What are you going to do about this motherfucker?"

My lips part like a fucking fish as my head spins.

"Who are you?" Is the question that finally falls from my lips when I manage to form some words.

"A girl who's worried about her friend. You're worried, which means she should be worried, but from what I see, she's no fucking idea he's even a threat. Why is that?"

"I don't want to worry her."

"Okay, I get that. I do. But she needs to know. If you think he's as big a threat as you seem to, then don't you think she deserves the heads up so she can keep an eye out, keep herself safe?"

"And if he's bluffing? Then I'll scare her for nothing."

"Is he bluffing?"

I blow out a long breath, twisting back into my seat and resting my head back.

"I don't know," I admit quietly.

Just saying the words makes me feel physically sick. The thought of him catching up with her and forcing her to pay my debt.

My stomach turns over.

"What are you doing about it?" Her stare burns into the side of my face while I keep my eyes focused on the license plate of the car in front of us.

"Umm..."

She groans in frustration. "Umm isn't an answer, Kyle. Not if she's in danger, which I'm assuming she is."

"I don't know what to do, okay?" I bark in frustration. "I don't want to scare her. I don't want her to think I've put her in danger. I don't want him anywhere near her."

"Huh," she says, sitting back and staring out the windshield.

"Huh, what?" I ask, more curious about the one small noise than anything else she's said during this strange conversation.

"You really like her, don't you." It's not a question. She's stating a fact and it makes my heart race and my palms sweat.

"N-no," I stutter.

"Right. So you're really going to sit there and tell me that all of this is just to get back at her for what happened? If you really wanted me to believe that you truly just want revenge then you wouldn't be so concerned about this. You wouldn't care what he might have in store for her."

My lips part to respond but I soon realize that I have no words.

The silence in the car is almost deafening as blood rushes past my ears so fast it makes my head spin.

I was quickly becoming aware that Harley was wriggling her way in deeper than I wanted her to, but it was easy to lock down when it was just my own crazy thoughts.

But being so obvious that others are noticing my feelings. That shit is scary.

"I can't let him get to her, Stella. I can't. What he was going to do that night, it..." A shudder rips through me at the thought. "It can't happen."

"I agree. But what I need to know is what you're doing about it. I'll help with whatever you need but I—Oh, don't give me that look, I'm more capable than you think."

"Are you about to tell me that you're a black belt in some martial art I've never heard or something?"

"Or something." She laughs. "Look." She turns to me. "Whatever you need to make this go away, just tell me. I've got... contacts who can help." I narrow my eyes at her, getting more and more confused as the conversation progresses. "Is he coming tonight?"

"I fucking hope not."

"If he is, point me in his direction."

She turns away and reaches out for the handle.

"Oh and Kyle?"

"Yeah?" I ask, wondering what on earth she might have to add.

"Tell her how you really feel."

Before I get a chance to respond, she's out of the car and the door slams closed behind her.

"Wow," I breathe, resting my head back and closing my eyes.

The rumble of an engine vibrates through me and when I open my eyes, I find Stella flying past me in a matte black Porsche 911.

"I didn't think you were going to come back," Kane mutters from his spot in the kitchen where he's arranging bottles of alcohol.

"I took the long route home," I say, swiping one of the bottles of beer and knocking the top off.

Truth is, I just drove. I didn't have any destination in mind. I just needed to clear my head and the best way to do that is to turn my music up, drop the windows down and floor the gas. Before I knew it, I was on the other side of town on roads I've never driven before.

"You all ready for tonight?"

"It's just a party." *I've been to plenty.*

"Maybe but it's not every day that it's your eighteenth."

"Why are you making such a big deal out of this?"

"Because, lil' bro, we've had a shitty twelve months and it's time to put it all behind us and look toward the future. You're a man now and you're here. All the fighting I did to get you here paid off and now we can do as we wish without social workers breathing down our necks. It's time to live, bro. It's time to enjoy ourselves. Here," he says, bringing his little speech to an end and passing over a small wrapped box.

"You didn't have to do this."

"I did," he insists. "Go on then, open it."

I eagerly rip at the paper. I kinda assumed I wouldn't be opening anything this year, so it's quite a nice surprise.

"Holy shit," I gasp when I see the logo on the leather box in my hand. "Tell me this is fake."

"Just open it."

I do, and I find the most stunning timepiece staring back at me. "Kane. Tell me this is fake."

"Bro, I'm not going to fob you off with a fake Rolex. Is it still the one you wanted?"

A lump climbs up my throat as I remember pointing out as a kid and telling him that one day I'd own one. That I'd get out of the Creek and make something of my life.

"How'd you—I don't deserve—"

"Stop, Kyle. The words you're looking for are thank you." He lifts his brows and I take a step forward until I crash against him. We share a brief brotherly hug before I pull back and stare down at the watch once more.

"I can't believe this. Thank you so much."

"Should help you pull tonight, don't you think?" he asks as I pluck the watch from its box and stare down at it in disbelief.

"Turn it over," he instructs, clearly forgetting that I ignored his last question.

Owned by a Legend.

I can't help it, I burst out laughing.

"What's so funny?"

"Nothing, it's nothing. Seriously, bro, this is everything. I can't believe—"

"Things are looking up for us from here on out. I've got a good feeling."

"I really fucking hope you're right."

"Well, let's be honest, we don't have much left to lose."

"I guess you're right." But as I say the words, the fear I was feeling while talking to Stella not so long ago about Gray reappears.

Suddenly, I feel like I might have more to lose than ever before knowing that he's intending on going after Harley.

I think of Stella's demand to know what my plan was. I wish I had one.

"Here, take this and go and get yourself sorted. They'll be here soon." Kane passes me over a ready rolled J. "It's the good stuff," he adds with a wink.

"Who is they?" I ask, needing to know if Gray's been invited.

"Just some of our old crew, the decent ones," he tags on. "And those you've invited from school. It's not going to be anything too crazy." He smiles at me but unfortunately, I don't believe a word that falls from his lips. Anytime he's had a 'small' party, it's basically turned into an insane night of lost inhibitions and debauchery.

"Yeah, we'll see," I mutter as I turn my back on him and take my joint, my beer and new watch to my room.

Sitting on the edge of my bed, I stare down at my gift, a smile curling at my lips.

I can't believe he did this.

Thoughts run through my mind about how he could afford it, but I shove them down. He clearly doesn't want me to know what he's up to or he'd have told me by now. I guess, I just have to trust him.

I set it down, drain my beer and head for the bathroom.

30

HARLEY

"Ah-ha, finally," I call out, already feeling the buzz of the vodka that Ruby brought with her when Stella finally joins us in my room to get ready for tonight's party.

"Sorry, I've got this though." She holds up a bottle of Grey Goose and I make a beeline for her. "You look like you might have had enough," she says, watching as I sway a little on my feet.

"Pizza's on its way, it'll soak it up. Plus, I'm going to a party potentially full of Creek kids. I need it."

"Fair enough." She hands over the bottle and watches as I twist the top off and swallow a shot.

I'm not lying. The thought of walking into a party with some of the same people as that night scares the shit out of me. I probably should lay off the alcohol and go in with a clear head, but I'm too nervous for that. Plus, I'll have my girls by my side and I trust them to ensure the night doesn't end up anything like *that* night.

A knock on the door sounds out and Stella twists around to open it.

"Delivery," Zayn mutters, handing over a stack of pizza boxes.

"Thanks, bro."

"Lay off the vodka, Har. I actually want to enjoy tonight, not have to drag your sorry ass home early."

"Oooh touchy," I sing, rolling my eyes at his big brother act.

Stella swings the door shut on him and I howl with laughter at the look on his face right as it slams.

"Food, give me food," Poppy calls, hopping from the bed and taking the top box from Stella.

She wobbles and sways a little too.

"I know I'm late but how much have you three had?"

"Enough to get us in the mood," Ruby says. "Now come join us. We eat then we get ready. We need to make sure Harley looks kick-ass for her boy."

My stomach twists painfully at her words.

"He's not my boy. And, my brother is going to be there so nothing is going to happen."

"Just tell him," Poppy encourages "It won't be that bad. He's already suspicious."

"Have you said anything?" I pin her with a look, hoping like fuck she's not broken girl code and spilled all my secrets to my brother aka her boyfriend.

"What? No, I wouldn't. But he's not an idiot and he's seen the looks between you."

"Shit," I mutter. "I don't want them fighting over nothing."

"It wouldn't be nothing, it would be over you," Ruby points out.

"Same thing. I don't want it to happen. Especially when this thing between us isn't really a thing,"

"Isn't it though?" Stella helpfully adds, joining us on my bed and flipping open the last pizza box.

"No, it's not. He might already be bored of me and hook up with some other girl tonight."

Pain slices through my chest at the thought, but it damn near cracks open forcing the words out of my mouth.

"And you'd be okay with that?" Ruby asks.

"Of course," I lie. "I know what this is between us. I went in with my eyes open. Hell, I might even pull tonight."

The three of them stare at me like I've suddenly sprouted an extra head.

"What?" I bark, stuffing a slice of pizza into my mouth.

"He invited you. He wants you there."

"I didn't exactly give him a lot of choice," I mumble around a mouthful of meat feast.

"Trust me, he wants you there." My eyes narrow on Stella wondering how she sounds so confident about that comment.

"That's it," I declare. "Boy talk is banned from here on out."

"What the hell are we going to talk about then?" Ruby mutters.

"Umm..." I jump up and pull open my closet. "Which dress should I wear?"

The street Kyle lives on is lined with cars when we pull up almost three hours later.

The party is in full swing and we are very fashionably late.

I am also suitably drunk and almost prepared for whatever we might be about to walk into. Or at least I tell myself that.

The reality could prove very different.

Music booms from the house as we walk past Kyle's car and join the crowd of people loitering, drinking and smoking on the porch.

There are faces I recognize from the Creek, and more than one nod in my direction as we make our way to the front door.

"We're no longer in Kansas," Poppy mutters behind me as we pass a couple practically going at it against the side of the house.

Ethan and the guys throw some wild parties, but without even stepping foot inside this house, it already feels different. Darker. More dangerous.

A shiver runs down my spine as I remember my last Creek party and one face in particular.

He won't be here, I tell myself.

I might be acting naïve but I'm happy with believing that Kyle has severed ties with Gray after that night. But I know the reality of the situation is probably very different. I'd just rather shove my head in the sand right now than consider the alternatives.

I push the door open to find the space full of people.

Bodies grind and gyrate to the heavy bass, the air is thick with smoke, the scent of nicotine, weed and whatever else might be getting inhaled is so strong that it burns my lungs.

We push through the crowd and immediately my eyes land on Kyle who's sitting on the sofa, only he's not alone.

"What the fuck?" Stella barks loud enough to be heard over the music as she comes to stand beside me and stares in the same direction. "Has he got a fucking death wish?"

I'm completely frozen as I stand there watching some brunette girl in Kyle's lap. She's got her lips attached to his neck while he downs a bottle of beer.

My fists curl as pain swirls around my heart.

It shouldn't hurt. I shouldn't care.

But I do. And I fucking hate myself for it.

Tears burn the back of my eyes as I watch his hand leisurely run up and down her back.

Bile rushes up my throat and for a few seconds, I wonder if I'm actually about to cover their living room floor with tonight's vodka and pizza.

Ruby and Poppy appear in front of me, Solo cups in their hands.

"What's—oh fuck," Ruby gasps when she follows our line of sight. "That motherfucking—"

"Leave it," I growl, reaching out to grab her arm when it looks like she's about to go marching over there.

"But he's—"

"More than welcome to her. Give me that." I snatch the drink from her hand and down it in one. Needing the extra alcohol in my system if I'm going to deal with this.

My heart tells me to leave, to stop it from getting battered any more than it already is. But my alcohol-laced brain tells me to stay put and play him at his own game.

Ash, Zayn, and a few of the other guys appear, joining our circle before Poppy and Ruby are dragged off to dance with their boys.

Neither Rich or Justin hide the fact they're checking both Stella and me out as they drop their eyes down our scantily clad bodies.

"Dance?" I ask Rich, whose face lights up like a freaking Christmas tree. Any sensible guy would tell me where to go after what happened in the cafeteria earlier in the week. But Rich is no sensible guy and he only thinks with his cock, especially after a few drinks and a J or two.

"What the hell are you doing?" Stella hisses in my ear.

"Enjoying the party. I suggest you get in the spirit of it too. Justin is a good dancer." I nod to him as Stella shakes her head at me. "You're playing with fire, girl."

"I just so happen to like getting burned," I shout back, stepping into Rich's body and running my free hand up his chest and wrapping it around the back of his neck.

When I look up into his blown, bloodshot eyes, I realize just how out of it he is.

"You look sexy as hell, Har," he groans in my ear as both his hands drop to my ass, pulling me so tight against his body that I have no choice but to feel his hard length pressing against my stomach.

I feel nothing. Absolutely nothing about the fact I've turned him on.

There are no tingles. No excitement. No desire for more.

All I really want to do is crawl back home, curl up in bed, and forget tonight even exists.

But I can't do that.

I'm here now and I refuse to show that motherfucker that he affects me in any way.

I knew this was coming.

Now I just have to deal with it.

Tipping my cup to my lips, I find it's empty.

Fuck. I need more alcohol for this.

I lose track of time, but Stella helpfully supplies me with two more drinks after refusing to accept any from anyone who isn't one of my girls.

Rich's hands get more and more adventurous and desperate as the songs change and as the alcohol continues to lower my inhibitions, I probably encourage him a little too much but I can't help hoping that at some point, Kyle will see me and have something to say about this.

The reality though is probably that he's already seen me and doesn't give a shit. He seemed more than entertained by the brunette.

Everything is… almost bearable until I hear a voice that sends a violent shudder down my spine. It's a voice I could happily live the rest of my life never hearing again.

"Baby Hunter, long time no see."

My eyes lock on Rich's in the hope he can read the fear within them, but soon realize that he's too far gone to even know his own name right now, let alone that I need him to help me.

A warm, hard body presses against my back and I fight the need to ram my elbow into his ribs.

I need to see how he wants to play this before I allow him to see that I'm scared of him.

His fingers brush against my neck and I jolt at the contact as he brushes my hair from my it.

"I missed you, girl," he breathes as bile burns up my throat and pressure builds behind my eyes. I've never hated anyone as intensely as I do him.

For the things he did—or intended to do—to me that night.

How he's ruined Kyle's life by letting him take the fall.

For the way he walks around Harrow Creek like he owns the place when all he is is a jumped-up, asshat who's hungry for money, power and respect. He might somewhat have achieved the first two, but the final one he'll never gain.

"What do you want, Gray? I'm busy." I press myself closer to Rich in the hope of creating some space between me and the devil himself, but he just moves forward with me.

"You," he growls in my ear. Every single muscle in my body locks up at the warning laced through that one word.

His hand drops down my body and once again the vodka churning in my stomach threatens to make a reappearance.

"Well, you're too late. I'm dancing with Rich."

"I'm more than happy to share, Princess. I thought you already knew this."

"Harley, is everything—You." Stella pins Gray with a look. "What are you doing here?"

My chin drops.

"You know this asshole?" I ask her, picking my chin up off the floor.

"Yeah, I met him at Justin's party. He was the guy I told you about."

"Oh no. No, no, no." I shake my head.

Gray was at Justin's. He was kissing Stella.

Why?

That one word spins around my head as my hands tremble against Rich's waist.

Why is he anywhere near me, let alone trying to insert himself into my life?

The next few seconds happen so fast, I almost start to wonder if I'm imagining them. One second, my front is plastered against Rich, and the next I'm spinning around to face Gray.

I squeeze my eyes closed, not wanting to look into his evil pits of darkness, but the second his hand wraps around my throat and squeezes tight enough to stop my airflow, they pop open.

"We have unfinished business, Harley Hunter." He lifts me with only that hand, my feet leaving the floor as he scowls at me.

"No." I try to scream but with his tight grip, I can't breathe let alone make a sound.

Everything around me blurs, the music seems to get louder and he backs me somewhere, toward the door maybe, I have no idea.

Then, in the blink of an eye, everything changes once again.

His fingers release my throat with no warning and I crash to the ground, landing hard on my ass, pain shooting up my spine.

"What the—" I breathe, my hand coming up to my sore throat as my vision clears.

Girls scream and guys call for more, overtake the pounding music as I take in the scene before me.

"Kyle, no," I scream, trying to scramble to my feet as Gray lands a punch in Kyle's face.

It doesn't matter that Gray is already covered in blood, the sight of his fists connecting with Kyle's cheek will be more permanently imprinted in my brain.

I race forward in an attempt to stop them before Kyle ends up hurt, but a pair of strong arms wrap around my waist and I'm hauled back against a solid chest.

"He can handle himself," Ash breathes in my ear.

Thankfully, he's right and after taking that one hit, Kyle starts to get the better of Gray. He's got an even bigger advantage when my brother throws himself into the mix.

I might never have confessed the whole truth to him about that night, but deep down, he knows. He always had. I'd be stupid to think that the Creek rumor mill about that night hadn't got to him even if I never wanted to talk about it.

Despite the fact it's now two on one, Gray doesn't back down and before long Zayn is also bleeding, both his lip and eyebrow split.

"No," I cry once again when Gray's knee lands in my brother's stomach, forcing him to the ground so he can use his boot instead.

I thrash against Ash's tight hold, my need to go and help them the only thing I can think about despite the fact I'd probably be the one killed if I ran in the middle of the carnage right now.

Zayn gets to his feet once Gray turns his attention on Kyle and he manages to wrap his arms around Gray's torso, pinning his arms to his sides to allow Kyle a free shot.

The fury that Kyle unleashes scares the shit out of me as his fists rain down on Gray's bloodied face again and again.

It's not until he starts screaming at him that I realize someone has turned the music off.

"I'm going to fucking kill you, motherfucker," he bellows as kids start moving to allow someone else to run into the center of the circle that's formed in the Legend's living area so they can watch the fight.

The second Kane steps in, a silence ripples through the crowd.

"Ky," is the only thing he says, and it's enough because Kyle lowers his fist and takes a step back, although his eyes remain trained on a barely standing Gray. If it weren't for Zayn, he'd be on his ass now.

Kyle takes another step back as Kane takes one forward so he's almost nose to nose with Gray.

"You're a stupid motherfucker for coming here. Now get the fuck. Out. Of. My. House." He pulls his arm back and punches him so hard that Gray's body goes limp in Zayn's arms. But he's done holding him up and he allows him to drop to the floor.

"Someone get that cunt out of here," Kane orders to no one in particular, but three guys instantly come running through the crowd to follow orders.

Poppy steps up to Zayn and spits a few choice words at him before the two of them disappear into the crowd while everyone else must decide the entertainment is over because they turn back to continue with their evening.

Kyle spins on his heels and his eyes immediately find mine.

They're so dark and his jaw is clenched painfully tight as something zaps between us.

Ash's arms loosen around my middle but I don't move.

"Everyone out of my fucking house," Kane booms, and kids immediately begin to move around me.

But neither Kyle or I so much as blink as we remain in our stare-off.

He's got blood trickling down his cheek from a cut on his eyebrow, his right eye is swelling and he's got a split lip.

He looks a mess, yet I can't look away from the devastation.

The commotion around us begins to lessen. But still, we remain immobile.

"Poppy has taken Zayn home," Ruby whispers in my ear. "Ash can take us. Are you coming?"

"I... um..."

Apparently, Ruby's whisper wasn't quiet enough because Kyle answers for me.

"No. She's not going anywhere," Kyle barks, speaking for the first time in what feels like forever. His rough, deep voice vibrates through me and affects me more than anything Rich did to me earlier.

Damn him.

"I really don't think—"

"I don't give a fuck what you think,"

"Don't talk to her like that," I snap, my own anger getting the better of me.

Kyle's eyes continue to hold mine, he's not even given Ruby the decency of a glance to apologize for his tone.

"It's okay, Rubes. You go. Kyle and I need to talk." I cringe as I hear my slurred voice. I wish I sounded stronger and more in control right now.

"Are you sure?" she whispers, quieter this time so only I can hear.

"Yeah, it's fine. Kane is here to stop me from killing him," I say loud enough for whoever is left in the house to hear me.

A smile twitches at Kyle's lips but I refuse to acknowledge it or to return it.

I'm too fucking mad. Although right now, I'm finding it hard to put my anger and thoughts into any sensible order and I have no idea what I'm more pissed off with.

"Okay," Ruby breathes. She hesitates by my side for a few seconds but she soon disappears.

"Call me if you need anything," Ash tells Kyle before they disappear from the house, leaving me alone with just the two Legend brothers.

Most might be intimidated. They're more than a force to be reckoned with. But I know them better than to cower down to them.

"Kane," Kyle growls.

"What? I want to see her attempt to follow through on her threat," he quips.

"Kane," he repeats, his voice low and haunting.

"Fine. Ruin my party and all my fun why don't you," he mutters, swiping a couple of beers from the side before crashing through the front door and slamming it behind him.

"And then there were two," Kyle muses.

"Don't try to be cute. What the hell was that?" I ask, my arm flying out and sweeping around the room behind me. I have no idea what specific part of tonight's clusterfuck I'm referring too, I don't even really care where he starts, I just need some fucking explanations.

"I didn't know he was coming."

"I should fucking hope not. Kyle, that fuck ruined your life, he almost rap…" I trail off, not wanting to say the words, it makes it feel too real and I prefer to live in ignorant bliss as much as I can. "You should have warned me. I wouldn't have come."

He takes a step forward and the scent of alcohol and weed that surrounds him like a fog fills my nose.

"Don't," I warn, holding my hand up between us. I can't let him get close to me. And I certainly can't allow him to touch me. Even when I'm sober I do shit I shouldn't when that happens.

"You should have told me," I repeat.

"But I wanted you here."

"Why? So he could do that to me? Ohhh," I say, an idea hitting me so hard it makes my head spin. "Did you want a repeat too? I know I fucked up that night, but have you been lying all this time? You were in on it and you did want to see it through. To fuck me at the same time he did."

"No," he states, stepping closer. "Never. You're fucking mine, Harley. Not that cunt's or anyone else's."

"Right," I say, a manic laugh falling from my lips. "I'm so *yours* that you had some other chick grinding down on your cock when I arrived earlier. Miss me, did you?"

"You know I fucking did. But I didn't want her."

"It certainly fucking looked like it as you touched her. As you let her touch you. Kiss you."

"Jealous, Kitten? Did you want to be the one grinding down on my cock?"

"Fuck you," I seethe, taking my own step toward him, my fists curling at my sides ready to land my own punch on his annoyingly pretty face.

"I wanted to show him that you didn't mean anything to me. I wanted him to back the fuck off," he growls, making my brows pinch.

"Why? Why do you need that?"

"B-because… fuck," he barks, lifting his hands to his hair and tugging. When I first saw him tonight he was wearing his standard ball cap but that vanished sometime during the fight, probably at a similar time to when his shirt got ripped at the neck.

"What? What aren't you telling me, Kyle?"

"Nothing."

"Bull. Shit," I snap. "Tell me, Kyle. Tell me whatever the fuck is going on. I deserve to know."

"Do you? You're nothing but a fucking snitch. All of this is your fault. All of it."

"Really?" I ask incredulously. "You really believe that? Because while I might blame myself for what happened to you, I think we both know whose fault this whole thing is, and it's neither of us. It's that fucking cunt. Why was he at your birthday party, Kyle?"

His chest heaves, his nostrils flare as he stares at me, fighting with whatever words are on the tip of his tongue.

"Fuck."

His chest collides with mine before I've even realized he's moved. I crash back against the wall but my head doesn't slam into it like I was expecting because at the last minute he cradles the back of my skull with his hand.

His lips crash to mine in a bruising kiss that I have no chance of backing away from.

My hands slam against his chest, but my efforts are futile. He's too strong. And, if I'm being honest with myself, I don't want him to stop.

I want him to claim me. Prove to me with actions that whatever that was with that brunette earlier was nothing.

I want him to show me that he means what he says. That I'm his.

My fingers twist in his shirt, holding him against me as his tongue devours my mouth as if he's going to die without my kiss. The taste of copper fills my mouth from his split lip but it only spurs me on and I suck hard on his tongue making him groan and his hips roll against me.

"Kyle," I pant when he finally pulls back. "Tell me…" I force out between heaving breaths. "Tell me the truth," I demand.

"Damn it, Harley." He slams his hand against the wall beside me.

"What? I have a right to know. Who was the girl? Why was Gray here?"

"I… fuck." He pulls away from me and backs away until he's at the other side of the room.

"Fine. Fuck you, Kyle. You can't tell me the truth then we're done here."

His eyes widen in shock but I don't give a crap. I refuse to allow him to lie to me.

"I'm leaving."

"You can't," he says in a rush, racing toward me but I'm faster and at the door in a flash.

"Watch me." I push through the door, slamming the screen against the side of the house with my force.

"What the hell?" Kane is up off the swing seat and walking toward me before I get to the stairs.

"She thinks she's leaving," Kyle spits at his brother.

"I don't fucking think anything, asshole. I *am* leaving."

Flipping him the bird, I race down the steps on wobbly legs.

"Wait," Kane calls out. "Let me take you."

"What?" Kyle barks. "She's not fucking leaving."

Kane pins his brother with a hard stare. "She's not staying."

Kane throws his car keys at me. "Get in my car, Harley."

The second they're in my hand, I take off. Needing to be away from Kyle as quickly as possible. The more he begs, the more he pisses me off, but I can't deny that my restraint is slipping.

Even when I hate him, I want him.

Asshole.

"You've been drinking, you can't drive her home."

"Get in the house, Kyle, before I fucking make you."

"I'd like to see you fucking try."

Slamming the passenger door behind me, I watch through the driver's window as the two brothers stare at each other.

I brace myself, waiting to see who's going to throw the first punch. It wouldn't be the first time the two of them had got into it. But before that happens, Kyle spins on his heels, slams the front door so hard I can only imagine that the entire house rattles, and disappears from my sight.

"I'm sorry," Kane says cooly as he drops into the driver's side.

"You don't have to drive me. I can walk," I offer. I know the last thing Kane Legend wants to be doing tonight is play taxi for me.

"No."

He starts the engine and backs out of the driveway. Neither of us saying anything else.

A million and one questions spin around my head as the silence stretches on. I want to ask about Kyle, about Gray, about tonight and so many other things about his life, but more than anything, I want to ask about Letty, but even with the amount of vodka flowing through my veins, I'm not that stupid. So I keep my lips zipped as he flies through the streets of Rosewood until he pulls up in front of my house.

Everyone else is home and the only light in the house is that of Zayn's bedroom where Poppy is probably tending to his wounds, among other things.

I'm almost sick in my mouth at the thought.

"Are you going to be okay?" I give him a double-take when I hear the concern in his voice. It's so at odds with the anger and tension that's usually rolling off him in waves.

"I'll be nowhere near you two, I'm sure I'll be fine."

Kane doesn't respond, although I do feel his stare burning into the side of my face.

I bite back the questions that are once again on the tip of my tongue and push open the door.

"Thank you," I say before slamming it on him and making my way to the house.

The front door is unlocked. Zayn probably left it that way knowing I'd be following soon after them.

I grab myself some pills and a glass of water from the kitchen, knowing that this is going to hurt like hell in the morning, and I make my way up to my room.

I kick my shoes off the second I'm inside before letting my dress slide down my body and discard it on the floor as I continue to my bed. I find a tank that I pull over my head to sleep in before curling up under the covers and willing the alcohol to drag me under.

But as I lie there, I can only picture one thing.

Kyle with that brunette grinding on his lap.

I know all of this is just a game of revenge to him. This is what he wants, me hurting and regretting what I did to him.

It shouldn't hurt this much. But I know I don't have the power to stop it.

Because I've already fallen. And he's already shattering my heart.

31

HARLEY

Eventually, I fall asleep with the events of the night playing out in my mind. Kyle's demands that I stay along with the state of him, make me wonder if I did the right thing.

Should I have stayed and cleaned him up? He was fighting for me after all.

My sleep is fitful and broken but I know it's just my mind that's stopping me from fully drifting off.

That is until I come too once again and the scuff of someone's shoe on my carpet hits my ears.

My eyes fly open, my heart in my throat that he's come after me. I should have known better than to assume he'd let me walk away like that.

Part of me is excited that he's broken in to get to me again, although I know I should still be mad at him. But I also know that the second he touches me, all bets are going to be off because I can only fight for so long when his touch burns me from the inside like it always does.

The side of the bed dips and I prepare to look into his blue depths and to submit to whatever he's come over here to take from me.

But when a hand wraps around my mouth and a pair of eyes pierce mine, they're not blue and I realize my mistake. His other hand wraps around my hip, pinning me to the bed and stopping me from bucking to get him off me.

This isn't Kyle coming to prove how good it is when we come together.

A scream rips up my throat but with his giant hand covering half of my face, no noise leaves me.

My heart thrashes against my ribs as my panic begins to get the better of me.

Why is he here? Why is Gray in my bedroom?

My eyes are wide as he closes the space between us, his nose bumping against mine.

His face is swollen and still covered in blood and I can't help hoping that it's as painful as it looks.

"You're a stupid fucking bitch, Harley."

I try to shake my head but it barely moves under his painful grip.

"He's not going to protect you this time," he breathes in my ear, sending goose bumps racing across my skin. Unable to hide my reaction to him being so close, my body trembles against his hold. "You are all mine. All. Night. The fun we're going to have, Princess."

"Fuck you," I growl against his hand. There's no way he could have deciphered the words, but I'm sure he could have a good guess at what I want to say to him. His fingers bite into my jaw in punishment anyway.

As if I weigh nothing more than a feather, he lifts me from the bed and holds me tight to his body, my back to his front.

I fight him. My elbows flying, trying to make contact with his already bruised and broken ribs.

"We can do this the hard way, Harley, or the really fucking hard way."

A moan of frustration rips up my throat as I continue to try to fight him, but I'm no match for his size and strength, and by the time my muscles begin to grow weary, he's already carried me down the stairs and out the front door.

There's a black SUV parked at the sidewalk. He marches us right up to it and pops the trunk.

"No, No. Noooo," I scream behind his hand as he slams me against the car, pinning me there with his weight and reaches for a reel of tape before pulling a length off.

"You need to learn your place, Princess," he growls, momentarily releasing his hand and replacing it with the tape.

My scream pierces the air for less than a second before I'm muted once more.

My eyes narrow at him as he turns me to look at him, trying to show him just how much I despise him with just one look.

You won't get away with this, motherfucker.

He might be right. Kyle might not fight for me. But Zayn will. And the second he discovers I'm not in my bed where I should be, he'll raise hell to get me back.

He leans in closer and I twist my face away, not wanting to look at him for a second longer.

His fingers grip my chin and he drags me back to him.

My teeth grind with my need to hurt him but with his hips pressing me into the car and only my arms free, I doubt I'm going to achieve much. I lift one, in a brief moment of confidence but he sees it coming a mile off and his hand captures my wrist, bringing it around to my back.

"Don't even think about it," he seethes, his eyes bouncing between mine before they drop to my chest. "I almost couldn't ask for more," He lifts his free hand and pinches my nipple between his thumb and forefinger until it burns in pain. I don't so much as flinch as bile churns in my stomach at having his disgusting hands on me.

"We're going to have so much fun," he promises again, making me want to turn my head and puke on the ground. He leans in so his vile breath races over my face.

He flips me around, pressing me so hard against the back of the SUV that it cuts into my stomach. Both of my arms are wrenched behind my back before he wraps rope around my wrists, binding them together.

"Get in."

I make no attempt to move which makes the vein in his temple pulsate with irritation, but I figure the longer I can remain standing out on the street with tape over my mouth the more chance I have of this being over soon.

Sadly, that's not how it happens because, after a second, he lifts me from my feet once more and throws me into the trunk like I'm no more than a piece of trash.

My shoulder smarts as it hits the floor first, quickly followed by my head. Lights flash behind my eyes from the force, a beat before all the lights go out.

"Motherfucker," I scream against the tape as the engine rumbles to life beneath me.

My eyes burn, tears threatening but I have no idea how long I'm going to be in here for and I have no intention of him seeing my tears.

I close my eyes, trying to keep them at bay and think of Kyle.

He'll notice I'm missing and find me, won't he?

I have no idea how much time passes, I drift in and out of sleep—or consciousness, I'm not really sure—but finally, the car comes to a stop and only a few seconds later the trunk opens.

He looms over me, a dark figure in front of the early morning sky. It should be the sign of a new day, of exciting unknowns, but I don't think I've ever been less excited and more terrified in my life.

"It's playtime, Princess."

He reaches in, wraps his fingers around my upper arm so tight, I have no doubt it'll leave bruises and hauls me out. My bare feet land on the sharp gravel and I wince in pain.

Gray slams the trunk closed before dragging me toward a dark, ominous-looking building.

I want to cry with every step I take, it's like walking on shards of glass and by the time he pulls me to the door and onto a concrete floor, I almost sigh with relief.

The door is unlocked and he pulls me right inside.

The first thing I notice is the smell. It's rancid. I wouldn't be surprised to find some kind of animal decaying in a corner.

My stomach turns over and I retch as he walks me further into the dark and damp space.

There are bottles littered everywhere, along with dirty needles and other drug paraphernalia. Clearly, it's not just an abandoned warehouse then.

The Creek kids used to party in old buildings almost every weekend, or whenever they found a new location. I wonder if this is one of those places. Maybe that smell is some party-goer who took things a little too far and was left in the darkness.

A violent shudder runs through me as he brings me to a stop by a giant hook-like thing that's in the ground.

"Welcome to your new home. I made it nice and comfortable for you."

I stare at the thin sheet covering the cold concrete on the other side of the hook and any fight I had in me seems to vanish.

I'm not getting out of this. And if he's right and Kyle doesn't care then there's a chance no one will find me, at least, not until it's too late.

He tugs harshly on the rope hanging from my wrists and I stumble to the floor, the rough ground scraping my knees as I scramble forward to save being dragged.

I don't need to look over my shoulder to know that he's attaching me to the hook.

"Perfect," he mutters, taking a step back to appreciate his handiwork.

He drops down on his haunches and stares me straight in the eyes. His are almost black with his anger and hatred.

"I've waited a long time for this, Princess."

In a surprise move, he reaches out and rips the tape from my mouth. It stings like a motherfucker, almost like he's just taken a few layers of skin with it and my teeth grind, stopping me from screaming out.

"Fuck you," I spit.

"All in good time."

"You're a fucking monster. Kyle should have killed you when he had the chance."

He laughs as if the idea of Kyle being able to is actually amusing to him.

His face turns serious once more before he pushes to stand and begins pacing back and forth in front of me.

"He's really got you fucking brainwashed, hasn't he? That cunt isn't capable of anything. He couldn't even keep my fucking gear safe."

"So this is about money?" I ask, the pieces starting to fit together.

Everything Kyle had on him that night would have been seized. Gray wants payback. But why me?

"I can get you money if that's what you want," I offer, although it's a total bluff. I'm not giving this fuck anything.

He laughs once more, a manic smile curling at his lips, splitting the cuts once more and allowing a trickle of blood to run down his chin.

"I don't want fucking money, Hunter, but Kyle owes me and it's time he learns that I'm serious."

"He doesn't care about me. You've already said so yourself that he's not going to rescue me, so what's the point in this?"

"Maybe I'm wrong. Or maybe I'm not and I just get to spend the next few days teaching you a lesson for my own amusement."

"You're sick. He's going to find me and he's going to fucking kill you." I put as much conviction into my words as possible, but deep down, I fear he might be right.

Kyle wanted revenge. He might not be the one dishing it out right now, but was this always where it was meant to end?

He studies me for a few more seconds before he disappears into the shadows.

The sun might be starting to rise outside but in the middle of this massive space, it's hardly noticeable from the cracks of light coming from the boarded-up windows around the edge of the building.

He crashes about a little before reappearing but the sight of him with a bottle of water in his hand makes my entire body tremble.

"No," I cry, assuming what's been dissolved into that liquid.

"I'm sorry, Princess, but I think you'll find that you don't get a say anymore."

He drops down before me and grips my chin between his fingers. My skin is already tender from the last time he held me this way and he knows it, digging his fingers in even deeper.

"Drink."

I press my lips together with as much pressure as I can muster and his eyes flash with anger.

I know I shouldn't provoke him, but there's no way in hell I'll voluntarily drink anything he gives me.

"Stupid fucking bitch. I don't even know why he wanted to fuck you that night. You're nothing special."

"You seemed up for it. I remember how hard your cock was as you rubbed it against my ass."

I don't see his arm move until it's too late. The sound of skin on skin rings out in the silent space around us a moment before the sting burns my cheek.

"Now. Fucking. Drink."

Still, I keep my lips closed when he tips the bottle to my mouth, sloshing the water down my chin and over my thin tank.

"You look like a cheap fucking whore."

"Then it's a good thing I don't give a shit about what you think, isn't it?"

He makes use of my open mouth and shoves his thumb inside allowing him to keep my lips parted so he can pour the water inside.

I push out as much as I can, but there's too much not to swallow any. I just have to hope it's not enough to affect me.

"Get some sleep, whore. The fun will commence in a few hours." With those words, he spins on his heels and disappears into the shadows.

Once he's gone, I succumb to the tears although I refuse to make a noise.

I sit there with tears cascading down my cheeks, my body trembling from the cold and praying that I'm not about to pass out, allowing him to do whatever sick and twisted shit I'm sure he's thought up.

32

KYLE

"What the fuck was that?" I bellow at Kane when he crashes back into the house after taking Harley home. "I thought you were supposed to be on my fucking side." My palms slam against his chest but he doesn't so much as take a step back.

"I'm always on your fucking side, Ky," he growls, his voice dangerously low.

"Then why did you take her? And fucking drunk."

"Not that I have to answer to you, but I'm not fucking drunk. I've had two fucking beers because I knew the second that cunt showed his face that someone would need to be in-fucking-control."

"Why didn't you just throw him out to start with?" I seethe.

"Because he clearly had the balls to show up after—"

"After?" I prompt, desperate to know if something has gone down between the two of them since I went away.

"Nothing. He shouldn't have fucking been here. But seeing as he thought it was a good idea, I wanted to see what his game was."

"And how did that work out for you?"

"Meh," he says, shrugging his shoulders.

"He had his hands on her, Kane. He shouldn't be anywhere near her, let alone touching her. He's already threaten—"

"He's spoken to you?"

I swallow nervously. I hadn't meant to admit that. I don't want to drag Kane into this mess more than he already is. He's done enough for me.

"Yeah. He threatened Harley."

"And you didn't think to tell me this?" he booms.

"What would you have done? You can't risk killing him and ending up inside as well."

His teeth grind as he thinks of all the ways he probably wants to end Gray for that stunt a year ago.

He lifts his hands to his hair and takes a few steps back from me, cooling off a little.

"You know, I told you to stay away from her for a reason," he almost whispers.

"Yeah well, I couldn't. Fucking sue me."

"She's it for you, huh?"

My lips part to agree but I catch the words at the last minute.

"She's fun for right now."

"Kyle," he breathes. "Lie to yourself all you want, hell, lie to her. But me? Nah, bro. You never fucking lie to me, you got that?"

We stare at each other in a silent standoff.

"We can't let him get to her. He wants me to pay and he wants to hit where it'll hurt the most."

"No fucking shit. It's one of the reasons I told you to stay away. I fucking knew you'd fall for her all over again."

"I never... I haven't..." He pins me with a knowing look. "Those Hunter girls are like fucking kryptonite, right?" I say, spinning the tables on him.

"Don't," he snaps. "Don't fucking bring me into this. It's got nothing to do with me."

"You moved us here. If you thought this was going to happen why not move us across the country."

"Because... because I couldn't."

I narrow my eyes at his cryptic answer but I don't try to dig for anymore. I know my brother and I know that I'm not getting any of his secrets out of him tonight.

"Why take her? Why take her if you know I need her?"

"Because," he sighs, his shoulders dropping and the fight leaving him. "It was the right thing to do. She doesn't need to witness you in this mood."

"Trust me, it would be fucking better right now if she was here."

"Why? Because you'd have used her to make you feel better? Don't forget, lil' bro, I saw you with Zoe on your lap earlier. You didn't seem to care so much about Harley's feelings while her lips were attached to your neck."

"That was for his benefit," I shout, throwing my hands up in despair. "I didn't want him to see how much I wanted her."

A smile twitches at his lips as I confess my feelings but he doesn't say anything. "I thought if he saw me with someone else, he'd think I don't give a shit about her and move on."

"You're a fucking idiot, Ky. The second you've slept off your hangover, you need to go over there and have this out with her. Tell her the fucking truth. Let her deal with all this alongside you, not keep her in the shadows. The Hunter girls, they're not weak and you'll only offend them if you treat them as such."

"Said by an expert," I quip.

His jaw pops with frustration and a little thrill goes through me that I'm not the only one who gets weak at the knees at just the mention of a Hunter girl.

"This isn't about me."

"Not right now, but we sure need to find the time to talk about you."

"Nothing to talk about."

"Sure."

He takes a step toward me, but if he thinks I'm going to be threatened by his stance then he's got another thing coming.

"Get your ass to bed and sleep tonight off. First thing, get your ass to the Hunter's and talk to her."

"So much for wanting me to stay away from her."

"Sometimes you just have to embrace it instead of fighting."

I narrow my eyes at him.

"That what you're doing?"

"Go to fucking bed. You can tidy up this mess after you've groveled your way out of the shit."

Before I get to say anything else, he marches down the hallway and disappears into his bedroom.

The house is fucking trashed, but I'm too angry, drunk, high, and horny to care right now. Turning my back on it, I follow orders and fall headfirst into my bed.

Before I succumb to my exhaustion, I find her contact in my cell and call her number.

It rings and rings.

I shouldn't be surprised, she's probably either long asleep or ignoring me. Or maybe both.

I wake when my cell starts vibrating in my hand, apparently, I fell asleep still clutching it.

"Harley?" I ask, pressing it to my ear without looking at the screen. My entire face aches as I speak reminding me of the night before.

"Stella," the voice says. "But speaking of, I'm assuming from your greeting that she's not with you?"

I push so I'm sitting against the headboard, my head spinning from last night's alcohol.

"N-no, she's not here. Kane took her home after things got a bit—Why, what's wrong?" I ask, realizing that she probably doesn't care about all this right now.

"We had plans to meet for breakfast but she didn't show up and her cell just keeps ringing."

"Probably still sleeping or stabbing a little voodoo doll of me."

"You fucked up last night," she confirms, not that I needed to hear it. "I'll head to hers then, if she's not with you."

"I'll be there after I've showered. I've got some groveling to do."

"Bring food, it might sweeten the apology."

"You're serious, aren't you?"

"Sure am. The way to a woman's heart, big cock, plenty of O's and good food."

"Thanks for that," I force out through the shock. "Message me when you find her."

"Will do. Later."

She hangs up before I get a chance to say goodbye. I laugh as I pull my cell from my ear. Whoever is lucky enough to snag her is in for a wild ride.

Tipping my face to the ceiling, I give myself two minutes before pushing from the bed and heading for the shower to wash last night off me.

One look in the mirror and I'm reminded of everything I'd rather forget from last night. I—we—might have won the showdown but I'm still sporting the evidence that it happened, I'm sure Zayn is too.

My eye is a pleasant shade of purple and barely opens and the split in my lip has opened up once again thanks to my conversation with Stella.

I reach up to wipe away a droplet of blood and wince.

Motherfucker.

He shouldn't have even been here, let alone had his hands on my girl.

My girl.

Hell yeah. I think Kane might just be right and it's time to lay all my cards on the table.

I shower, dress, grab an energy drink from the refrigerator and leave the chaos that is our house behind. As far as I know, Kane is still in his bedroom. Although knowing what he's been like since I've been back, I wouldn't put it past him to have snuck out already.

I'm at Harley's in record time, the journey is a total blur, my focus solely on what I need to say to her. The truths I need to confess.

I push my car door open after pulling up on the driveway and as I step out, Stella comes running down the steps from the house, quickly followed by Zayn.

"What's wrong?" I ask, the stricken looks on their faces making my stomach drop.

"She's not here," Stella says. Her voice is cool and calm but her eyes give away how she really feels.

"But she was. I heard her come home," Zayn adds. "No one has seen her. She's not with anyone we know."

"Fuck," I breathe, lifting my hand to my hair, irritated when I find my cap.

"H-he wouldn't. Would he?" Zayn asks, mirroring my concerns.

"I really fucking hope not."

My cell buzzes in my pocket and I reach to pull it out.

The unknown number that stares back at me makes my stomach drop into my feet.

"What is it?" Stella asks, obviously seeing my reaction.

"I-I don't know."

She comes to stand beside me and watches as I open the message.

"Holy fuck," I bark as Stella gasps beside me. "Fucking cunt."

"Wha—" Zayn grabs my cell from my hand, his eyes going wide as he stares down at the photo of his sister.

His sister, bound, gagged, barely clothed, and passed out.

"Kane," I bellow, running through the house with Zayn hot on my heels. I don't bother knocking, I crash straight through his bedroom door.

Thankfully, he's still passed out in bed, although he sits up fucking fast as we fly into his room. "He's got her. Gray fucking has her."

"W-what?" he asks, groggily sitting up and pushing hair from his eyes.

"Gray has Harley," I say much more calmly than I feel. "You need to get up now."

It takes two seconds for the words to register in his head before he barks 'fuck,' throws the sheets back and stands.

"Where are they?"

"No idea, but he sent this."

I pass my cell over and he studies it for long, silent seconds.

"I know where this is."

"How?" I ask in utter disbelief. "How could you possibly know that?"

Okay so, I didn't study every inch of the image, my eyes were mostly trained on Harley, but I didn't see anything that would give her location away.

"I just do. Meet me at my car," he demands, pulling a pair of sweats from the floor and tugging them on as we leave.

"But..."

"Do you really want to get into this right now?" He pins me with a look that brings me to my senses.

"No. Hurry," I call over my shoulder as I rush from the house, pushing Zayn along in front of me.

I swipe Kane's car keys from the side and we let ourselves in. Me in the front and Zayn in the back.

Every muscle in my body is pulled tight as I focus on that image that's burned into my retinas.

She looks so weak, so broken, so vulnerable.

If that motherfucker touches her and tries to take—a violent shiver races down my entire body, a mix of anger and devastation that I let this happen.

"Fucking hurry up," I mutter under my breath to no one.

"I hope you know that once we've got her out of this, I'm going to fucking kill you," Zayn quietly seethes from the back.

My lips part to tell him to fuck off, but swallow the words, because he's right.

"As you should."

"You're fucking her, aren't you?"

"Yeah, bro."

"If you've treated her like a piece of shit, I swear to God I'll—"

I twist around in my seat to look at him, my eyes narrowed in curiosity.

"Fucking asshole," he mutters, the fight leaving his voice as Kane drops down into the driver's seat and revs the engine.

"Ready to put this bitch down once and for all?"

"Less talking, bro."

I don't need to be looking at him to know he just rolled his eyes at me.

He flies down our street and turns toward Harrow Creek.

The entire journey to our hometown is silent and tense.

I'm still baffled as to how Kane knows where she is from just a dark picture but I'm not about to question it. I just need to hope that he's right because if we turn up there and she's not, I'm not sure what I'm going to fucking do.

I shift in my seat, rubbing my palms down my thighs in my need to do something.

"Chill. I need you on point."

"On point for what?"

"Getting your girl back."

A low growl rumbles from the back of the car but we both ignore it. I knew Zayn would be fucking livid when he discovered that I've gone after his little sister. But right now, I don't give a fuck about his opinion. We just need to get her. We can fight it out later.

I mumble some kind of agreement as I clench my fists over and over, watching the cracks in my knuckles opening up and remembering just how good it felt to hit that fucker last night.

Thanks to Kane's more than reckless driving, we're at the Creek in record time and rolling toward an abandoned warehouse that I've never been to before on the other side of the town from where we grew up.

I know Gray has Harrow Creek High and the surrounding trailer parks under his control but I had no idea his reach stretched this far. Clearly things have changed in my year away.

I don't have a chance to put too much thought into it, not that I really care if he's currently hanging out on someone else's turf, it just means there's more chance of him dying tonight.

"Bingo," Kane says as he turns a corner and finds Gray's car parked half in the bushes. If he's attempting to hide it then he's doing a shit job.

"Okay, so what's the plan?" Zayn asks.

"We go in there and take his fucking head off," I announce.

"Oh, and how are you going to do that, bro? You packing?"

"Well, no but—"

"Fucking hell. I've got this, follow me, and don't do anything unless I tell you to."

He's out of the car before either of us get to agree, and we hurry to catch up with him as he begins to stride toward the warehouse.

The place is silent, only distant birdsong and the movement of the trees overhead dancing in the wind.

Kane comes to a door and peers inside as Zayn and I share a look. He might be furious at me, but his concern for his sister shines brighter in his eyes.

"We'll get her," I assure him. He nods but I know my words aren't all that helpful. We're all aware of what Gray is capable of, so we know how risky this really is.

One second Kane is standing right there, and the next he's gone, disappeared in the darkness inside the building.

"Fuck," I breathe, racing after him.

The place is dark and it smells like death, which doesn't help the dread that is sitting heavy in my stomach.

A single light illuminates a spot on the floor as I come up behind Kane and the second I step aside to get a look at the scene before us, my blood runs cold.

"Get the fuck off her," I bark before I've even realized I've spoken.

Kane growls in frustration that I've just alerted him to our presence but it's soon drowned out by the blood racing past my ears.

That motherfucker is on top of my girl.

My fists clench as I move my leg to race forward.

Kane throws his arm out, stopping me.

"Wait," he demands and I immediately follow orders, assuming he knows more than I do.

And he's right because, after a beat, he stands, moving behind her, and dragging her limp body from the floor, the knife in his spare hand glinting in the spotlight trained on Harley.

My eyes drop to her and my entire chest burns in pain. Her entire body and the few clothes covering her are dirty, her skin covered in cuts and grazes.

She just about manages to lift her head and her eyes lock with mine.

"Kyle," she mouths but she's too weak to make an actual noise.

"Don't fucking move," Kane growls once more as Gray presses his knife against her throat.

"Move and I'll kill her right now," he warns as Harley whimpers.

"Fucking shoot him," I whisper-shout to my brother, knowing he didn't walk into this unarmed like I did.

"Not risking it, not yet. He'll move quicker."

"Fuck."

Time seems to stand still as we all remain motionless staring at each other.

That is until three footsteps sound out behind us. Something whips past my ear and Gray cries out, stumbling back and releasing Harley.

I race forward without even thinking, needing to catch her before she hits the hard floor while Gray groans in pain.

"I've got you," I say softly. "I've got you. It's okay."

I pull her fragile body onto my lap and hold her tight as she trembles and sobs in my arms.

"Kyle," she whimpers, pain splinters my chest at the brokenness of her voice.

I hold her tighter, hoping she can take some strength from me as more footsteps sound out.

"Holy shit, Stella," I gasp. My chin damn near hitting the floor when she emerges from the shadows, a pistol hanging by her side with a silencer attached to the end.

She looks around the scene before her eyes drop to Harley in my arms.

Her lips part to say something but someone else beats her to it.

"Good shot, baby," an older man says as he wraps his arm around her shoulder and kisses the top of her hair.

As I stare at the two of them, a few more guys come rushing in and go straight to Gray, hauling him from the floor, ignoring his screams of pain, and they drag him from the warehouse.

"What the fuck is going on here?" Kane barks, looking between Stella, the man I can only assume is her father, and Harley and me.

"How did you know where we were?"

"I followed him last night after you kicked him out. His guys brought him back to Harrow Creek and left him in his trailer. I put a tracker on his car."

"You put a… right, of course you did," I mutter.

"Then when you unceremoniously abandoned me in the Hunter's driveway earlier, I took matters into my own hands. And aren't you fucking glad I did."

"But… how'd you… who are you?" Kane stutters, much to Stella and her dad's amusement.

"No one you need to worry about, son," the man says.

I focus on him. He's wearing a sharp black suit, shirt and tie. His hair is almost as dark with just a few flecks of grey at the sides. But his face is a stone mask. It actually sends a shiver of fear down my spine. Whoever he is, you don't want to be on the wrong side of him, I know that for a fact.

"I'm going to deal with that cunt. You good?" he asks Stella.

"Yeah, we've got this."

He nods once, squeezes her shoulder, and walks away.

We're all silent as he disappears into the darkness and no one speaks until his footsteps have vanished and a car speeds off in the distance.

"Okay, what the fuck just happened?" Zayn asks.

"I saved her ass from that sick fuck. Now let's get the fuck out of this shithole, yeah?"

33

HARLEY

I thrash about, trying to get his hands off me. His fingers are like tiny knives against my skin, and I wish he'd just carved it all off so I didn't have to feel it.

I lost all sense of time only moments after being abandoned in that dark space with no idea when he was going to reappear again.

I wanted to stay awake, stay alert, but it was impossible to fight the darkness that clawed at me.

I drifted in and out of reality, each time I woke, more terrified than the last.

"No," I cry when I wake again and he's there, looming over me with a deadly expression covering his face.

"It's time to play, whore."

"NOOOO," I scream.

"Kitten, it's okay. It's just me," a familiar voice says in my ear.

I continue for a few more seconds until my drug-fuzzed brain registers who it is.

"Kyle?" I cry, my entire body relaxing in his hold. I try to curl up in a ball on his lap to stop the cold assaulting my bones.

"Here, wrap this around her," another familiar voice says.

"Z-Zayn?"

"It's okay, sis," he says gently as a warm, soft fabric wraps around my arms.

Kyle's arms hold me tighter and I succumb to the exhaustion trying to claim my body.

I'm safe now. I can let go.

The next thing I know, I'm being lifted out of the car, still in Kyle's arms. While I'm here, I know that no one can hurt me and I don't so much as bother opening my eyes.

I know we're in our house the second we walk through the front door, the familiar scent of Mom's favorite candles almost makes me sigh with relief.

"Mom," I say in a rush. She can't see me like this.

"It's okay, she's not here, Har," Zayn says as Kyle begins carrying me up the stairs.

"I'll go run a bath," Stella says, her small footsteps pounding ahead of us.

I don't open my eyes even as Kyle walks us into my bedroom. I don't want to look at my bed.

This is a place I should feel safe, but knowing he got to me so easily makes me feel the opposite.

What if he comes back?

What if this isn't over?

"It is, Harley," Stella says softly, making me realize I must have said those thoughts out loud. "My dad has him. He won't come after you again."

At hearing her words, I rip my eyes open, my gaze landing on her. Her eyes soften as she crouches down on her haunches beside where I'm on Kyle's lap on the edge of my bed.

"But—"

"You don't need to worry. He's not coming back for you," she says again, her eyes pleading with me to believe her.

"O-okay," I breathe, needing to trust her.

"I've run you a bath, Harley. Would you like me to—"

"No, Kyle can." A growl rumbles at the other side of the room and when I look over, I find Zayn standing in my doorway, a murderous expression on his face and a concerned looking Poppy in his arms. His lips are pressed into a thin line and there's a vein I'm sure I've never seen before pulsating at his temple.

"It's okay, Z."

"No, it's not, Har. It's really fucking not," he fumes before turning his back and marching away. His angry footsteps pound down the stairs leaving Poppy behind.

"He'll be okay. Just worry about you," she says, walking over, sitting down beside us and taking my hand. "Let Kyle look after you, I'll sort Zayn out."

"T-thank you."

"No need to thank me, Har." She leans forward and presses a kiss to my forehead. "It's what sisters do."

A sob rumbles up my throat at her words.

"Yeah."

She squeezes my hand a little. "I'll go find him. He's probably taking it out on the treehouse."

"Biding his time until he can get to my face."

"Yeah," Poppy mutters. "You might want to watch your back."

"I'll take whatever is coming to me. I deserve it." Kyle shrugs as Poppy leaves.

"Where's Kane?" I ask, noticing his absence for the first time.

"Don't know. He took off the second he dropped us off."

"Har, would you like me to stay?" Stella asks after a few minutes of silence.

"Umm..." I hesitate.

"It's okay. I can just go and hang out downstairs for a bit. Ruby and Ash are coming over."

"O-okay. Thank you, Stella. I don't even—"

"Shush," she soothes. "All in a day's work, girl."

"I don't even—"

"It's okay. We'll talk later, yeah?"

She brushes a lock of my hair from my face before standing and walking out of the room, leaving the two of us alone for the first time.

"I'm so fucking sorry, Har."

A sob erupts and this time I can't contain my tears. I curl into his chest and cry wishing the tears would wash away the memories of this night from my head permanently.

"Let's get you cleaned up then you can sleep," he whispers, standing with me still in his arms and walking toward the bathroom.

The scent of my favorite bubbles fill the air and I sigh, needing to sink into that hot water and wash the dirt away.

"I'm going to put you down, okay?" I nod and Kyle drops my feet to the ground.

My legs feel weak and unstable but I manage to stand with the support of the basin as he peels my ruined tank up my torso and drags my panties down my legs.

I watch as his eyes track over all the cuts and scrapes. None are serious but they still look bad enough.

"Did he—" Kyle cuts himself off. "I'm sorry. Don't answer that." His blue eyes search out mine and I gasp when I find them full of unshed tears.

He stands, his chest brushing against my bare nipples causing a spark of lust to shoot down my body. It's a welcome feeling after the hopelessness the last few hours have brought.

I was sure the only thing I'd feel would be the slow painful death that Gray granted me.

His hands cup my cheeks, his thumbs brushing away the silent tears that continue to track down my cheeks.

"Fuck, Harley. I thought—"

"Shush, not now, okay. I just need... I just need you to hold me."

"O-okay." his voice cracks on that one word and a tear finally drops from his eyes.

My heart shatters at the sight of it.

My poor broken boy.

"I'm okay," I say, wrapping my hand around the back of his neck, reaching up and pressing my brow to his. "I'm okay. You saved me."

"Fuck, Kitten. You never should have—" I press two fingers to his lips, cutting off his words.

"Off," I demand, dropping my hand once more and tugging at his shirt.

"Are you sure?" I stare at him for a second and lift my brow. "O-okay."

He sweeps me off my feet and carries me to the tub. The second the hot water engulfs my skin, I groan in relief.

"Good?" he asks, the first hint of the humor I love so much about him in that one word.

"Like you wouldn't believe."

He lowers me right down, the water and bubbles swallowing my broken and battered body.

Gray might not have had me captive all that long but he certainly left his mark.

I wrap my arms around my knees and rest my chin on top as I watch Kyle strip down.

His body is in a similar state to mine after his fight last night. His face is a mess and he's got bruises forming on his ribs. He's still the most beautiful man I've ever seen though. His muscles ripple as he moves, giving me a nice show to make me forget reality for a few seconds.

"Scoot forward, Kitten."

I do as I'm told and in seconds, he sinks down behind me and is pulling me back into his arms.

His lips come to the top of my head and his lips press down as he holds me tight.

"I can't lose you, Har. I fucking can't."

His words echo around my head for the longest time. I want to return the sentiment, but my head is too messed up to talk about something as serious as that right now. I haven't forgotten the events of last night or the girl.

But right now, I need him. I need to be in his arms and soak up his strength. I'll worry about the rest and where we go from here later.

He slides us back, his legs trapping my body in and his arms wrapped around my chest, holding so tightly it's actually hard to breathe, not that I'm going to tell him that.

Eventually, he reaches for my sponge, pours a ton of shower gel onto it and begins lathering it onto my skin.

It feels incredible as he washes away all the dirt of my unforgettable few hours.

I groan, leaning back into him harder and feel his length press into my lower back.

My fingers dig into his thighs as he continues his trail around my body, setting my skin on fire with his gentle touch.

"Ky," I moan as he brushes across my breasts.

"Don't tempt me, Kitten."

"Make me forget, Ky."

"Kitten," he growls, clearly not happy with my request. "You've just been through hell."

"Right? So take me to heaven."

"Fucking hell, Har."

He places the sponge on the side of the tub and ghosts his fingers down my stomach, parting my folds and finding my clit.

"Oh God," I moan as his fingers drop lower to my entrance while his thumb circles my clit.

"Enjoy it, Kitten. It's all you're getting until you're healed," he warns, although his cock poking me in the back says otherwise.

If I weren't so exhausted, I might take it as a challenge to see how quickly I could break him.

His other hand comes up to my breast, pinching and pulling at my nipple, adding to the pleasure that's assaulting my body.

"Come for me, Kitten. Show me how good my fingers feel inside your pussy."

"Kyle, fuck. Kyle," I cry as I crash over the edge. Everything slips away as my pleasure engulfs the fear and the hopelessness that consumed me last night.

He continues working me until my body stops pulsating around his fingers before he pulls them out of me and rests his palm possessively over my stomach as my chest heaves and my heart rate begins to return to normal.

The silence returns along with my memories and I shiver against him.

"The water's getting cold, we should get out."

I swallow down my disappointment. I'm not ready for this to end yet.

"Will you... will you wash my hair?" I ask almost nervously.

"Anything for you, Kitten."

I sink down lower, allowing him to wet my hair before he begins massaging my scalp with shampoo.

It feels incredible and I almost demand he continues when he encourages my head back so he can wash the bubbles away.

"Come on, time to get out."

I sit forward, allowing him to climb out of the tub first and watch his ass as he walks to the towel rack.

Even with the towel wrapped around his waist, his erection is obvious.

He notices what's holding my attention as he steps up to me, slips his hands under my arms and lifts me so I'm standing.

"Let me look after you, Kitten."

He leans forward and brushes his lips against mine in the sweetest kiss I think I've ever received, and just when I'm ready for him to deepen it, he pulls away, lifts me out, and wraps me in a warm towel.

After once again sweeping me off my feet, he carries me to my bedroom and sets about getting me dried and dressed for bed before encouraging me to crawl under the sheets.

"Don't leave me," I demand in a panic, reaching out to grab his hand, when he moves toward the door.

"I'm just taking the towels back and getting my clothes."

"O-okay," I whisper, feeling silly but still not wanting him to leave me alone.

"There's food and drink if you need it." He nods to my nightstand and I find a little picnic waiting for me. I have no idea who did it while we were in the bath but I've never been more grateful to see a glass of water.

"I probably should have thought about that sooner, huh?"

"You've been everything, Ky," I tell him honestly.

"I'll be back," he promises, and less than two minutes later he is crawling into bed with me, pulling me into his arms and encouraging me to sleep.

Seconds later, I do exactly as I'm told and allow sleep to claim me.

34

KYLE

Slipping from beneath a sleeping Harley, I sit on the edge of the bed and watch her for a few seconds, ensuring that she's not going to wake with my movement. My eyes flick over the bruises and cuts on her face and my fists curl in my need to find wherever that fucker has been taken to and put an end to him for good. A bullet in the shoulder isn't good enough.

Happy that she's in a deep enough sleep, I drag on my clothes and slip from the room.

"How is she?" Stella and Poppy ask simultaneously as I step into the Hunter's kitchen.

"Sleeping. Thanks for the food."

"It was the least we could do," Poppy says softly, sympathy for her friend oozing from her eyes.

"That was pretty badass of you," I say, pinning Stella with a look.

"It was nothing." She shrugs.

"When did you learn to shoot like that?"

"My dad had me at target practice when I could barely lift a gun. He's big on self-defense."

"Who exactly is your dad?"

"I don't have all the answers, but I do know that his men will make sure Gray regrets ever even breathing the same air as Harley, let alone putting his hands on her."

"They'll kill him?" I ask, needing to know that he's going to be wiped off the planet.

"They won't be that kind."

My eyes narrow on her but she just shakes her head, telling me that's all I'm going to get out of her.

I don't believe her denial for a second. She knows exactly what her father does. There's no way she'd have access to guns and trackers as easily as she does if she didn't.

"Is Zayn around?"

"You got a death wish?" Poppy asks, forcing out a laugh.

"I don't know, from what I've heard, he got off pretty lightly from your brother so he can't go too hard on me."

"Yeah, you keep telling yourself that," she mutters. "He's out in the garden."

"Okay, wish me luck."

"Here, take a coffee as a peace offering," Poppy says, jumping up and making him a mug.

"Do I get one?"

"Sure thing."

With two mugs of strong black coffee in hand, I make my way toward the back of the house.

I know where he is before I see him, the smoke floating up from the other side of the lounger a dead giveaway, the bitter scent of the weed another.

"Here," I say, placing the mugs on the table between his lounger and an empty one.

He doesn't say anything but I notice his entire body lock up tight at the sound of my voice.

When I glance over at him, I find his hard eyes trained on me, that same muscle in his temple pulsating to the point I'm worried he might be about to have a coronary.

I blink and he's no longer resting back with his joint between his lips but instead, he's right in my face, his nose brushing mine and my shirt twisted in his fist.

His breath coats my face as his angry, dark eyes hold mine.

"Go on," I say, holding my hands out at my sides. "Hit me. Do whatever you think will make this better."

"She was supposed to be off-limits, man," he seethes, his grip on my shirt tightening.

"I know, and trust me, I held back for a long time."

"That night. She was with you, wasn't she?" he asks, but I know he already knows the answer. "Did you fuck her?"

"N-no. We just kissed." He growls in warning, but I keep going, it's time this was all out in the open. "I wanted to though, and I thought it was our time at last. I'd watched her, wanted her from a distance for a long time. But there she was, and you weren't and… she was as interested as I was. I just fucking wish I took her away sooner. If I'd have dragged her out of there that night then…"

He nods. "I fucking hate him."

"You and me both. If it weren't for Har calling the cops, I dread to think what would have happened that night."

"Fuck," he barks, releasing me and rubbing his hands over his short-cropped hair, his face twisted as if he's in physical pain.

"I really want to fucking hurt you," he admits, turning his back on me.

"You've got a free pass. I deserve it."

He looks over his shoulder, his eyes hold mine. The knowledge of what could have happened to Harley that night, along with what almost did happen last night darkens them even more than usual and before I know what's happening, his fist isn't flying toward my face but he's pulled me into a hug, his curled fists slamming down on my back.

"You'd better fucking look after her. If you so much as hurt—"

"I won't," I say, my voice full of a confidence in myself that I don't feel.

I think he knows it too because a laugh vibrates in his chest.

"What fucking bullshit," he says with a laugh as he pulls back from me. "We're both Harrow Creek boys, it's in our fucking DNA."

"I don't know," I say, dropping down to the lounger beside the one he's now in again. "You seem to be doing a pretty good job with Poppy."

He laughs. "You've met her brother, right? My life wouldn't be worth living."

"Know that feeling," I joke.

"There's still time for me to take you out for this, you know?"

"Yeah, and I'm sure one day you will."

He falls silent for a few seconds. "Who was the chick last night?"

"Fuck knows. It was a stupid way to make Gray think I didn't want Har. He saw the move a mile away."

"I hope you know you're fucking up before you've even started."

"I know. I should have told her the truth about him. I thought I was protecting her. It was naïve of me to think she needed that."

"Fucking right. Harley doesn't need protection from anything. Aside from

Poppy, she's the strongest girl I know. Don't patronize her by making her think you underestimate her strength."

I nod at him, accepting the joint when he offers it to me.

"How's she doing?"

"Sleeping."

"Did he..." He trails off, not wanting to say the words that I equally don't want to hear.

"No, I don't think so. But I truly believe he would have if we didn't get there when we did."

He nods, and it makes my stomach drop into my feet, knowing that he agrees with me. It's no surprise. We know he's a monster. I just hate that he was part of our lives—our friend—for as long as he was.

Silence descends leaving us sitting there with just the sound of the birdsong overheard filling our ears.

There's so much more we both want to say, but neither of us vocalizes any of it. It's too painful.

"I'm going to cancel going away this week. She needs me here," he confesses, staring off into the distance.

"I think we both know that she'll hate you for doing that."

"I don't really give a shit what she thinks. She was just kidnapped and nearly fucking... again. I'm not leaving her for a week to be at some senior team booze fest."

Jake's girlfriend, Amalie, has rented a huge house for their winter break, and almost the entire varsity team are heading there with their girlfriends to celebrate the season.

"She won't want you babying her. Just go, Z."

"So you can stay here and look after her."

"No, that's not my reason." Although I can't deny that it sounds like a fantastic idea.

"You should go, you've already been invited along with Ash and Ruby so you can talk tactics with Jake all week."

"I'm not gate crashing your thing."

"You're going to be a big part of the team we leave behind, you have every right to be there."

"To get me away from Harley?" I ask, finally twisting in my lounger to look at him.

"No, I..." He blows out a long breath and turns to meet my stare. "Do you... do you love her?"

My heart tumbles in my chest as his eyes hold mine, drilling me for an answer.

"I… um… I think it might be a bit soon for that," I mumble, trying to get out of answering for real. I wanted to have this conversation with Harley first, not her older brother.

"Bullshit. You just told me you've wanted her for a long time. You know exactly how you feel about her." His brows rise and he sips at his coffee while he waits for me to find my balls.

"Fine. Yeah, yeah, I do. Happy now?"

"Nowhere fucking near, man. Now you need to go and tell her." His voice leaves no room for argument and after a beat, I push from the lounger intending to do just that.

The kitchen is quiet as I drop off my mug and as I climb the stairs, I realize why.

"Hey," I say, slipping into Harley's room where all the chatter is coming from. "How are you feeling?" I ask, zeroing in on Harley who's sitting up against her headboard with the covers pulled up to her neck.

The second her eyes find mine, I know something is wrong.

My heart beats a little fast as our connection holds, but I already know what's coming before she opens her mouth. I sense it.

"I need you to leave," she says coldly, her features hard and unwavering as if she actually believes the words.

Pain coils around my chest as I think about the words I intended to say to her when I got up here.

"Can we just talk, please? Alone."

"No. I'm done, and you need to leave."

"But—" At my argument, there's movement off the end of the bed and Stella comes to stand in front of me.

"She's in shock. Just give her some time."

"But I—"

"I know, Kyle. I know," she soothes. "But she just needs a little space to get her head around everything."

She holds my eyes, silently begging me to do as Harley wishes and not to make this any harder and my heart shatters in my chest.

"Fine," I bark, gritting my teeth and turning away from all of them before I make the mistake of showing them just how much this fucking hurts.

35

HARLEY

Watching Kyle turn his back on me and walk away like I just asked is the most painful thing I've ever experienced.

Part of me hoped that he'd fight. That he'd tell me that I was wrong and force me to change my mind. But he didn't.

He just turned and walked away, ripping my heart out and taking it with him for shits and giggles.

"Oh my God," I sob the second I know he can't hear me.

Stella and Poppy are there immediately, wrapping their arms around me and holding me tight. A few seconds later, my bedroom door opens. I panic at first, thinking that he's come back and about to witness my meltdown until I see Ruby running full pelt toward my bed and joining the huddle.

I cry until my eyes burn and I feel like I have no more tears to shed.

My body is weak and exhausted, and all I want to do is crawl under my covers and hide away from the world.

When I finally pull back, three sets of sympathetic eyes search mine.

"Are you sure that was the right thing to do?" Poppy whispers, probably expecting me to lash out at her question. I might if I had the energy.

"He lied to me. If he'd had just told me the truth instead of playing these stupid fucking games then none of this would have happened."

"He was trying to protect you," Ruby unhelpfully adds.

"Yeah, and how did that work out for him?" I mutter, gesturing to my face.

"I'm done. I'm so fucking done with him, with all of it. He never should have moved here."

Another tear drops on to my cheek as I imagine him not coming back into my life but I can't allow that to consume me. Everything has gone wrong since he walked into Rosewood.

I just want my old life back. Not this one where I feel like I can barely breathe with the searing pain in my heart.

"You need to eat," Stella says, always the levelheaded one. "What do you fancy and we'll order it."

"Thank you," I mouth to her. I have no idea if Poppy and Ruby know all the details about what happened in that warehouse only a few hours ago. But I have a feeling I might owe my life to that girl. And I sure as hell know I've got a million and one questions for her about how all of that went down.

Stella squeezes my hand in acceptance.

The three of them barely leave me all weekend, they must have come up with some kind of schedule while I was sleeping because they seem to come and go like a well-oiled machine ensuring that I'm never alone.

We order all the bad food we can get our hands on and watch sickly sweet rom-coms back to back, if it weren't for the reality of the situation, it would be a pretty sweet weekend. But as it is, it's probably one of the worst of my life.

Zayn pops in regularly to check on me and he intercepts Mom when she reappears after her business trip to save me having to relive everything to her all over again.

When she finally makes her way into my room, the girls all leave for the first time since they arrived and Mom pulls me into her arms.

"I wish you'd called," she whispers in my ear, her voice cracking with emotion.

"I'm okay. Zayn and the girls have looked after me."

"I know but—"

"It's okay, Mom."

She blows out a long breath.

"I'm so sorry, Harley. This is all my fault. I never should have offered to help Kane. I brought this on all of us."

I shake my head. "No, Mom. This isn't on you."

"But—" I pull back from her embrace and pin her with a look that stops whatever she was about to say. "Okay," she concedes, clearly seeing that I don't want to get into this right now. "I'm taking the night off, what would you like to do?"

Poppy and Zayn are sitting on my bed with me when Ruby appears the next morning, a sullen look on her face. I know both she and Poppy feel guilty about going away for the week while I'm here still recovering, but I point blank refused to allow them to miss the time away. They both deserve the break, and I'll be fine here with Mom and Stella.

Mostly I'm just glad I didn't have to go to school this morning and face the rest of our class looking like this.

"We really don't have to go."

"Stop please, I'm begging you. Just go and enjoy yourselves."

"You should come," Zayn suggests. But just like every other time he's suggested it, I turn him down. "Come on, he's not even going to be there."

"Don't whine, bro. It doesn't suit you."

It takes ten minutes, but I finally convince them all that I'm going to be fine. I've got Mom and Stella to keep me company, but mostly, I plan on locking myself in my bedroom doing homework and hiding from the real world.

I stand at my bedroom window and watch the four of them load up Zayn's car before disappearing for their trip.

My heart aches. Of course I want to be there. But I know that I'm in no mood to be around people, and I know that the second the team takes one look at me, they're going to get all annoyingly protective and want to seek revenge on my behalf. And while I appreciate their support, it's really not necessary.

"Hey girl, your mom said to come straight up," Stella says over an hour later, her arms full of books. When I told her to get my homework, she happily agreed.

"Sure, come in, make yourself at home." She dumps the books on my desk and drops a couple of bags to the floor.

"Staying all week?" I comment.

"If you need me."

"Won't your dad want you at home?"

She shakes her head. "He's out of town all week."

"And you've come here? Shouldn't we be at yours with the pool and jacuzzi?"

"We can if you want," she says sadly, making me wonder if she doesn't actually want to be there herself.

"I'm easy. We just don't have the kind of luxuries you do."

"Maybe not, but this place feels like a home." I open my mouth to respond but I find I have no words, and I can hardly argue. For as incredible as her home is, I know exactly what she means.

She gets herself set up with a couple of textbooks on the other side of the bed to get started, but I have other ideas.

"Are you ready to start talking yet?" I ask her, addressing the elephant in the room.

"I... um..."

"You don't have to tell me anything you're not happy sharing, Stel."

"Everything I've told you is true. But it's just the tip of the iceberg. Dad works with some very bad people."

"Like gangs?" I ask.

"Yeah, that kind of thing. He—I—pretty much have access to anything we could want or need at any hour of the day. But sadly, that means I don't get him all that often. He's always away, probably scouting out our next location, I don't know," she mutters with a shrug.

"That sucks." Mom works a lot but at least she's in the house doing so most of the time. "It must be lonely."

"Yeah, then add in being scared to make friends because I know I'll just leave them in a few months. It really sucks."

"We should do something fun this week," I suggest.

"I thought you wanted to do homework."

"Yeah, but it sounds a little too depressing after everything, don't you think?"

"Yes, leave it to me."

She pulls her cell from her purse and starts tapping away.

"I just need to go and speak to your mom," Stella says, hopping up and running from my room before I have a chance to ask what the hell is going on.

Only ten minutes pass before she comes flouncing back in.

"Okay all sorted," she sings, hopping back up on my bed like nothing just happened.

"Uh... care to explain?"

"Nope. It's a surprise."

"Hmph. I don't see how that is fair." I cross my arms over my chest and pout.

"It'll be worth it, I promise."

"I hope you're right."

"Don't you trust me?"

"The girl who's pretty hot with a gun? Can I say anything other than yes right now?"

She barks out a laugh and pulls her textbook back onto her lap. "Get as much done as you can, after today, homework is banned."

"Now that sounds like a plan I can get on board with."

With music playing in the background, we spend the day working, stopping for drinks and snacks every couple of hours. Mom pops in to check on us a few times and delivers more food. All things considered, it's a good day. I mean, I'm not in a mansion in the mountains with my friends, but I'm happy. Kind of.

"Ugh, I hate this," I complain, throwing my pen across the room in frustration.

"Can I help?" Stella asks, looking at the book on my lap and pulling a face when she spots my math equations.

I sigh. "It's okay. It just drives me crazy." I refrain from pointing out that for some fucked-up reason, the only person I want to help me with my math is Kyle, but after sending him away yesterday, I'm pretty sure I've put an end to all of that.

"Missing your tutor?" she asks, a smile twitching at her lips that she's found a way to make me talk about him without mentioning his name again. She got shot down earlier when she tried.

"No," I spit out way too quickly for it to actually be true.

"It's okay, you know. You can miss him."

"Well, I don't. He lied to me and because of it I found myself in that monster's clutches. He can rot in hell for all I care." She stares at me, her eyes softening as my voice cracks and I blink back the tears that threaten to fall.

"Harley, I really think—"

"No," I say, putting my hand up and cutting off whatever it is she feels the need to say. "I don't want to hear it. We are done. Not that we were ever anything more than a bad decision in the first place."

"You don't really believe that, do you?"

"Yeah, actually, I do. I never should have gone anywhere near him, let alone allow him into my bed. What was I even thinking? It was all a game of revenge for him. He doesn't care about me, he never did."

"Harley," she breathes. "Have you seen the way he looks at you? That boy more than cares about you, and I think he always has."

"No, no," I say, shaking my head, refusing to allow her words into my brain otherwise they'll just fester and cause me to start doubting myself.

"Okay," she concedes before placing her own homework to the side and insisting on helping me with mine. She's a good teacher, although not quite as skillful as Kyle, but I'll take all the help I can get right now.

It's almost midnight when she finally gets up to leave.

"You could just stay the night," I offer.

"I need to go home to pack anyway, so I may as well go now."

"Pack? I thought you were hanging around Rosewood all week?" I ask, trying not to sound too disappointed because the thought of being alone terrifies me. I know she's promised that her dad has taken care of Gray, and I believe her, but that's not going to stop me looking over my shoulder for a while expecting him to reappear.

"I know, but I've made other plans."

"Oh… okay. Anything fun?"

"I guess we'll find out tomorrow," she says with a smirk.

"We?"

"Yep, pack a bag, girl. We're heading out of town for a few days."

"Oh my God, are you serious?" I ask, the prospect of leaving this place behind is almost too much to wish for.

"Yep. Just me, you, and a whole lot of nothing else. Pretty sure there's no cell service or anything so we'll get complete peace."

"That sounds incredible."

"I'm glad you agree. I'll be back at eight in the morning. Make sure you're ready."

I nod eagerly. "Anything I need to pack?"

"Your bikini."

"Done." I squeal. "I'm so excited. Thank you."

"You're more than welcome. I need this almost as much as you do."

36

KYLE

"Get in the fucking car, Ky."

"No." I stand my ground on the porch of mine and Kane's house while I have a stare-off with Ashton and Zayn.

"Stop being such a pussy, man." Ash shoulder barges me, storming into the house and soon after my bedroom.

"What the fuck?" I bark. By the time I get to him, he's already stuffing items of clothing into my duffel bag.

"You're coming. You need to get out of town and get her out of your head for a few days."

"She's not in my—" He turns and pins me with a look. "You're a pain in my ass, Fury."

"Yeah, yeah. You'll be thanking me when you sink your ass into the hot tub I've seen pictures of."

"Yeah, well, I'm sure you'll be sinking into more than just your tub this weekend."

A smug smirk covers his face and I can't help but roll my eyes.

"Sorry, man. This is exactly why you should come."

"So I can watch all you cozy couples getting it on? Oh yeah, sounds like a winning plan," I sulk.

"Not everyone will be coupled up," he argues. "You need to relax, man. Come on, agree already. I'm not really in the mood for abduction."

My face drops at his words.

"Shit, no. I didn't mean… fuck."

"It's fine. Forget it."

Knowing I have no chance of winning this argument with both Ash and Zayn on the opposing team, I take over my own packing and in less than five minutes, I'm throwing my duffel over my shoulders and striding from the room, much to Ash's delight.

"Don't make me regret this," I mutter to Zayn, who irritatingly just smiles at me in accomplishment.

"Would I?" he asks innocently.

I stare at him for a beat, registering the tension that's still evident in his features. He still wants to hurt me for going after Harley. I get it. I kinda wanna hurt myself for it too, hence why I was more than happy to be alone this week and drown in my own misery while hoping she might reach out but knowing she won't.

He blinks, breaking our silent conversation, and I throw my bag into his trunk before pulling open the back door and sitting my ass down before I change my mind.

"Alright?" I ask Ruby who's patiently waited this whole time in the middle seat. "Poppy." I nod at Zayn's girl when I find her eyes on me in the mirror.

Both girls stare at me, tension oozing from them.

"I'm sor—" My apology is cut off when the doors open once more and both Ash and Zayn climb in. "Where exactly are we going?" I ask once we're heading out of Rosewood, the atmosphere in the car getting heavier by the second.

It's obvious that it was the guy's idea for me to tag along because clearly the girls are still firmly on Harley's side and would happily throw me out of the moving car at any moment.

"The mountains."

"That's fucking hours away."

"Yup. Get comfortable, man." Zayn's eyes find mine for a beat before he focuses back on the road.

Great.

Zayn and Poppy take charge of the music while the couple beside me whisper fuck knows what to each other. All I do know is that Ash's hand has been getting higher and higher up Ruby's skirt the longer we've been sitting here.

"Ash," Ruby gasps, her hand wrapping around his wrist to stop him. "Kyle's right there."

"Kyle's also not deaf," I mutter, shifting over so there's as much space between Ruby and me as possible.

"Jealous, man?"

"Fuck off," I grumble, wondering why I let them force me into this.

Thankfully, he takes a hint and doesn't say any more, unfortunately, that's only because he's otherwise engaged with his tongue down Ruby's throat. The sound of their lip-smacking is louder than the music thumping through the speakers.

His hand pushes higher and she squirms.

"Just climb on his lap and let him fuck you. It'll put us all out of our misery quicker," I snap when a moan rips up Ruby's throat.

"No sex in my car," Zayn snaps. "The only girl who gets fucked in here is Poppy."

"Fucking hell," I mutter, twisting away from the horny couple beside me and allowing them to continue doing their thing. It's not like they're going to stop anytime soon.

I stare at the passing scenery and the low groans continue, my cock hard as I imagine being here right now with Harley like that.

Shifting in my seat, I pull my cell from the pocket and pull up our conversation.

It's not the first time since she sent me away that I've caved and sent her a message. I scroll up through my unread apologies.

I blow out a breath, my chest deflating in disappointment.

I'm not disappointed with her. She's acting as she should. Cutting me out of her life as she should. I'm disappointed in myself for thinking that the best way to handle Gray was to keep his threats a secret.

I don't know what else to say to her to prove how much I regret it. To tell her how I really feel and how much this is ripping me apart.

I hate that we're driving farther away from her, that my all-consuming need to drive to her house and demand she speaks to me is going to be impossible.

I guess that was Zayn's intention. Take me with them and keep me away from her.

Can't say I blame him. If I had a little sister, I'd want her away from me too.

We stop a couple of times and each time I race from the car like my ass is on fire in my need to get away from the happy couples and tense atmosphere for a few minutes.

My cell vibrates in my pocket as I walk out of the men's restroom. My heart jumps into my throat thinking that it could be Harley, even though I know it's not.

Disappointment still floods me when I look at the screen, although I can't deny that the person's name staring back at me is the next best thing right now.

"How is she?"

"She's okay. Sad."

Pain grips my chest at her words. Hurting Harley was the last thing I wanted in all of this.

"I've messaged her."

"She's refusing to check her cell." I'm not surprised by this, seeing as all the messages have gone unread.

"Can you try to get her to read them?"

"I can't make any promises, Ky."

"I know."

"Ky, I—" she says, but quickly cuts herself off.

"Yes, what is it?"

"It's… it's nothing. Forget it."

"No, Stella. Whatever it is, yes. Whatever I can do to make this better, I'm all ears."

"Did Zayn and Ash convince you to go with them?" she asks, her subject change giving me whiplash.

"Yeah, we're currently…" I look around at the gas station we've stopped at. "Fuck knows where."

She chuckles.

"Try to enjoy yourself, yeah. I've got your girl. You don't need to worry about her."

"No shit, she's got Little Miss Rambo as her personal protection."

"You're just scared I could beat your ass."

"Uh… yeah, that's it," I mutter, but I fear she could be right.

"Anyway… I'll call you if anything changes—"

"What's likely to change? She is okay, right? The drugs he slipped her are they—"

"Yes, Kyle. She's fine. She admitted that she didn't have much. They'll be out of her system by now, and yes, he's being dealt with, I promise you."

"Okay."

"Please, just try to enjoy yourself."

"Unlikely."

"Well, try. Speak soon."

She hangs up on me before I get to say goodbye and I pull my cell from my ear and stare at it in disbelief.

"Everything okay?" Ruby asks, finally unattached from Ash's side.

"Yeah. How much do you know about Stella?"

"Her name," she deadpans.

"I think she's got an interesting story."

"You think?" Ruby asks sarcastically, looking over at me and raising a brow. "I doubt we'll ever find out. She'll be gone before we get a chance to dig too deep."

"She's leaving?"

"I think so. Much like everything else, I don't really know. Come on, the guys are waiting."

"Oh goodie, back to the front row seat of my very own porno," I mutter, trailing behind her.

"We're not that bad."

"I guess I deserve the torture after everything."

"For hurting my girl? You sure fucking do." She pins me with a look that tells me she's still not all that happy about me being here.

I shoot her the best smile I can muster before we climb into the back of the car for the final leg of our long-ass journey. This place had better be fucking worth it.

It's almost three hours later—thanks to Zayn taking a wrong turn—when we finally pull up to a massive cabin.

It looks like something off a postcard. And it's by far the most expensive place I've ever stepped foot inside, let alone stayed.

"This is beautiful," Poppy breathes as the car comes to a stop.

"Makes the drive almost worth it," I mutter.

"Oh, it was very worth it."

"Says the one who spent most of the time with his finger inside his girl's—"

"O-okay," Zayn interrupts, killing the engine and swinging his door open.

As I follow his lead, the front door to the place opens, and Jake, Mason, and Ethan spill out, all dressed in board shorts and already looking three sheets to the wind.

"About time motherfuckers," Ethan barks.

"Blame the driver," Ruby shouts as she helps Ash to pull the bags out of the trunk.

"Not my fucking fault," Zayn sulks.

"We all told you to turn left."

"I didn't see the turnoff." He drags his and Poppy's bags from the gravel driveway, throws them over his shoulder, and stalks toward the cabin.

"I should probably go cheer him up."

"I'm sure it won't take much," Ash calls suggestively.

"Point me in the direction of an empty bedroom, I need some peace," I say to Amalie when she emerges.

"Follow me," she says with a chuckle.

"Rubes, you wanna see your room too?"

"Damn right we do."

"Fucking sex addict," I mutter, loud enough for him to hear.

"Aw, little Legend is jealous."

"Leave him alone," Amalie snaps, pinning him with a warning look.

It's easy to think that Amalie could be vulnerable and weak with her tall, slim body and soft English accent but I dare anyone to cross the woman who's tamed Jake Thorn. There can't be anything weak about her. I might not know Jake all that well but I know enough to know it must take one hell of a strong woman to keep him in line.

"Jake," she calls, spinning on her heels and walking backward toward the front door. "You coming to show the guys their rooms?"

"Uh... I was gonna..." She raises a brow at him. "Again?" he asks, the delight is clear in his tone. "Coming."

I chuckle at the pair of them as he sweeps her off her feet and jogs with her up the stairs.

"Legend," he says, pointing to another set of stairs. Right at the top, the final door on your left.

"Ruby, you and Fury are there," he says, pointing to a door on this floor. Thank fuck. "If you need anything, ask the others, we're going to be busy for a while." They disappear through another door before Amalie's squeal pierces the air.

Great, just what I feared. A house full of loved up, sexed-up couples. This week shouldn't be frustrating at all.

Following instruction, I find a small room with a twin bed at the top floor of the house. The bed is tucked into the eaves and I have to damn near bend in half to get into it without taking my head off, but at least it's quiet.

I kick my sneakers off and crawl onto it, desperate for a few hours of peace before I go and find the others.

"Tell me you snuck in a few single chicks," Rich calls to me when I walk through the living area later that night with a beer in hand.

"Sorry, I was stuck with Ash fingering Ruby the whole way here."

The guys snort a laugh while Ash's face lights up in delight.

"Yeah, what of it? Don't tell me you weren't getting hard listening to my girl get off."

"Nothing about what you do gets me hard, Fury." I flip him the bird before falling down on one of the massive worn leather couches and tipping my bottle to my lips.

"This fucking blows," Rich says, leaning forward and resting his elbows on his knees. "Whose idea was it not to invite the rest of the fucking squad."

"Mine," Chelsea announces as she waddles into the room with her hand on her round belly. "This vacation isn't a fucking orgy." She flicks a deadly look between Justin and Rich. "We're here to enjoy ourselves to chill out."

"We could enjoy ourselves just fine with Aria and Marissa here."

"You're a dog."

"Says the pregnant cheer captain."

Shane shifts to the edge of the couch he's sitting on, ready to jump to his girl's defense but it seems it's not necessary. I guess Chelsea doesn't have the rep she does for nothing.

"At least I'm getting some."

"Oh burn," Ethan booms.

Despite Justin and Rich's almost constant moaning about the lack of girls, we have a pretty good night.

The place is stocked with everything all of us could need for the week, and as much as I hate to admit it, I think Zayn and Ash might have had a point about getting out of Rosewood and clearing my head.

We spend our days working out in the state-of-the-art gym in the basement and hanging with the girls around the pool. Even the guys stop moaning eventually, finally getting bored of their own voices.

Ash and I sit down with Jake to talk through next year, it seems that Jake has Ash pinned for next year's captain and he talks to me as if I'm going to be in a position to be worried about this shit. But I learned long ago not to count my chickens before they've hatched, so I'll just take each day as it comes and roll with the punches.

Hanging out with these guys, it's easy to forget where I've come from or what I've been through but the reality is that I have a record and a parole officer keeping an eye on everything I do. My life is a world away from the privilege most of these guys know.

I get daily updates from Stella to let me know that Harley is okay. But with every day that passes my hope of being able to salvage anything between us lessens as she still refuses to even read my messages.

My feelings about it must be obvious because even Poppy and Ruby start being nice to me by day three at the cabin. I know I look like a miserable motherfucker but the fact they're taking pity on me after what I did tells me it could be worse than I thought.

"You really like her, don't you?" Ruby asks when we find ourselves alone in the living area.

I scrub my hand over my face, sweep my fingers through my hair before placing my cap back on my head. "Is it that obvious?"

"Just a bit. You miss her." This time, it's not a question. There's no point.

"Yeah. I'm kinda used to it though. I've always been on the periphery when it comes to her. I stayed at arm's length because of Zayn and then... well..." I trail off because I know they know the truth about everything. "I stupidly thought that night was my chance. If I'd have known how badly it would have fucked everything up, I might have thought differently about it."

"You weren't to know."

"I guess not. But still, I'll blame myself for the rest of my life for what went down that night. I should have known what he'd done. I should have got her out of there before it got out of hand."

She reaches over and squeezes my forearm.

"It wasn't your fault. Just give her some time. Something tells me that she'll come around."

"Really?" I ask, sounding a little too hopeful.

"Ky," she sighs. "I'm sure I don't need to tell you that my best friend can be as stubborn as an ox when she wants to be. Just bide your time. The perfect moment to tell her how you really feel will present itself. And, it might even be sooner than you think." As she says the words, I watch guilt pass over her face.

"What are you hiding?" I ask, not wanting to beat around the bush when it comes to Harley.

"N-nothing," she stutters, looking anywhere but in my eyes.

"Is she coming here?" My heart rate picks up at the thought of seeing her walk through the door to join her friends.

"No. Forget I said anything." Before I get a chance to start begging her for information, she's up and out of the room.

Pulling my cell from my pocket, I shoot Stella a message to check in before shoving it back in my pants. I've stopped messaging Harley. Each one goes unread so I've decided that until she allows me to talk to her face to face then I'm going to hold back on everything else I want to say to her.

We're all sitting in the living room later that night shooting the shit, but while everyone else seems to be relaxed and enjoying themselves, I'm wound up like a fucking spring.

I can't help thinking that everyone knows something I don't. Not only does Ruby keep shooting me weird looks, but Ash, Zayn, Poppy, and even Amalie and the other girls are doing the same, not to mention that when someone goes to the kitchen to grab drinks, no fucker gets one for me.

I'm starting to think that either they've decided I'm not welcome anymore or there's something going on that I'm not privy to.

I'm just about to get up to get my own fucking beer when the front door crashes open.

A couple of sets of eyes turn to me before everyone looks to the door.

My heart is in my throat as I wait for whoever it is to emerge.

Heels click on the polished wooden floor and my need to get up and go and find out the truth for myself damn near gets the better of me.

I'm on the edge of my seat with my heart pounding in my chest when a shadow falls over the doorway and then a familiar body appears.

The breath I didn't know I was holding rushes out of me as I lock eyes with a blue pair I wasn't expecting.

"Stella? Is she here?" I ask, not caring what everyone around me will think about my desperation for my girl.

"Fuck yeah, get your ass over here, baby girl," Rich shouts, holding his arms out and making grabby gestures with his hands.

Stella rips her eyes from mine and pins him with a look that he really should be scared of.

"I'd probably snap your tiny cock in half, *bro*," she sasses as everyone in the room except me and Rich fall about laughing.

"It's not actually small. Chels, tell them," he whines.

A ripple of tension flows through the room as Shane curls his fists at his sides, but all Chelsea does is throw her head back and laughs harder for a few seconds.

"You're asking the wrong girl to come to your defense, tiny." She winks, holding her forefinger and thumb a couple of centimeters apart. "You need advice on which one of the singles will show you a good time, you come and see me, girl." She smiles at Stella before planting her lips on Shane to try to placate him. It clearly works because not two seconds later does he relax under her kiss and his unclenched hands slip under her tank.

Shaking my head at the two of them, I turn back to Stella.

"Shall we?" she asks, her eyes trained on mine for a beat before she turns and disappears from sight.

I look at Ruby, needing to know if this was what she was talking about earlier but all she does is smile sweetly as I walk through the room.

Stella's leaning back against the counter with a bottle of water in her hand, making herself at home, when I find her a few seconds later in the kitchen.

"What the fuck is going on?"

37

HARLEY

I wake from probably the best night's sleep I've ever had. I have no idea what time it is but the bedroom is still totally dark and the cabin is in blissful silence.

It's safe to say that I freaked the fuck out when she started heading toward the mountains.

But as promised, we didn't head to where the team was.

Although I'd tried to avoid my cell, or more so the messages that are sitting on it from Kyle, I'd caved to my need to look at Instagram, although I regretted it the second I did because I discovered that while I turned down the invitation to join them in their giant cabin, that Kyle hadn't because while I was miserable and missing him more than I'd ever admit, he was there enjoying himself. He was smiling in every single picture I found of him and it made my heart hurt worse with every one I saw.

I want him to be happy, of course I do. But I'm not sure I want him to find that happiness with my group of friends when I've been left behind.

I blow out a slow breath.

I have no idea where the location of their cabin is, I've refrained from looking up how close we might be to each other right now. I don't need that kind of temptation.

Reaching for my cell, I wake it up and check the time.

It's past lunch. Jesus.

The two days we've had here have been beyond perfect.

I have no idea how she managed it, but the kitchen was fully stocked with all the food and drink we could possibly need and the log fire in the living area was already burning when we arrived.

This place really is a slice of heaven with its huge couches, massive wraparound porch complete with day bed, and hot tub overlooking the forest below.

When I get downstairs, I find that despite the silence, Stella is already awake and reading her Kindle in front of the fire with a mug of coffee.

"Morning, sleepyhead," she says when I drop down onto the couch opposite her. "How are you feeling?"

"So much better." The wounds from my ordeal are still there and will be for a few days yet, but they're healing and my body is aching less with every day that passes. Even my head is beginning to feel a little more stable thanks to Stella.

"Good, I'm glad." She smiles softly at me, and I'm once again reminded of how grateful I am that she gave me a chance when she usually runs away from making friends.

"It's this place. It's like it has magical healing powers."

"Yeah?" she asks, a hopeful look appearing in her gorgeous blue eyes.

"How couldn't it? You've seen it." I gesture around the cozy interior.

"Yeah, I never want to leave."

"You and me both. You want another coffee?"

"Please."

I take her mug before walking through to the kitchen and making us both a fresh one.

"What's the plan for the day?" I ask when I rejoin her. I don't know why I ask, we agreed on the journey here that we were going to do absolutely nothing, and that was more than fine by me.

"I need to pop out, we've almost run out of logs." She flicks a look to the fire.

When we first arrived, the alcove beside it was full of wood, but it's all almost gone.

"I thought you said there was enough for our entire stay," I enquire. She had organized everything so well that it surprises me that we've just run out.

"There's more outside, but it's damp. The welcome pack gives an address for a place for dry stuff. Thought I'd go check it out."

"Okay. I can come."

"Nope. You are staying put."

I open my mouth to argue, but Stella pins me with one of her looks and my lips slam shut instantly.

"You can cook. There are ingredients in the fridge for lasagna."

"Okay, I can do that," I concede, although I'm not happy about it.

It's hours later when Stella finally makes a move to leave the cabin. She insisted on showering and applying a full face of makeup before stepping foot out the front door. I started to wonder if she was sneaking out on a hot date not just heading for wood.

"I'll leave the front door unlocked," she says when she comes to a stop in the living room.

"Okay. Once I've finished dinner, I might jump into the hot tub."

"I won't be too long."

Only minutes later she's gone and the cabin becomes even quieter.

I grab my AirPods from the table, press play on my favorite playlist, and I make a start on the lasagna.

I wiggle my hips in time with the music and sing my heart out, feeling lighter than I have in a long time.

Once the lasagna is assembled and just needs a blast in the oven, I clean up the kitchen, still rolling my hips in time with the music before heading to my room to change into my bikini to hit the tub.

I wasn't as organized as Stella—partly due to not knowing where we were going—so I don't have my Kindle, but I found a healthy supply of smutty romance books on the bookcase in the dining room, so I grab the one I'm halfway through along with my cell and I make my way down toward the porch to watch the sun go down behind the trees.

I glance at the clock on the wall as I pass the kitchen and notice just how much time has passed since Stella left.

Concern washes through me, and I check my cell to see if she's tried to call.

Finding nothing, I hit call on her number.

"Hey," she answers immediately. "I'll be back soon. I got lost and then started chatting to the guy at the wood place."

"Stell, have you snagged yourself a mountain man?" I tease.

"I haven't been gone *that* long."

"Long enough," I mutter jokingly. "Seriously, if he's that hot, stay longer. I'm good here."

"I appreciate that, but seriously, I'll be there soon. Dinner done?"

"Yep, just waiting for its diners. I'm just about to hit the tub."

"So get off the phone, and go and enjoy."

"Okay, okay, I'm going. See you soon."

I'm just about to hang up when she stops me. "Har?"

"Yeah?"

"Uh… nothing. I'll see you soon."

My brows pull together as I repeat our short conversation in my head. Something doesn't feel right about this.

Telling myself that I'm just reading into everything too much, I pull the refrigerator open and grab myself a soda.

I'm almost at the door when I notice that the fire has almost gone out.

Placing everything down on the side, I head over to put a couple more logs on.

I'm still poking at the embers, trying to get it to take when car tires crunch against the gravel out the front of the cabin.

"Come on, you fucker," I moan at the fire.

It's been mostly Stella's job since we got here and she makes keeping it going look so easy, but I'm thinking that might just be another of her hidden skills because it's clearly not that simple.

The front door opens and footsteps head my way, although I'm too distracted to realize they don't sound the same as the ones that left a few hours ago.

"How do you keep this fucking thing alight? I swear it hates me."

When she doesn't answer, I push from the floor and turn around to see what's the issue.

I gasp in shock when I don't find Stella looking back at me but the one person I've been fighting to get out of my head.

"What are you doing here?" I snap, my fingers curling into fists at my sides. But I can't deny the heat that floods my body as I stare at him. As always, his cap is sitting on his head, his angular face still showing signs of the fight, but it's his eyes that capture me. They are their usual light blue but there are shadows lingering behind them, regret maybe, and he looks like he hasn't slept since I turned him away.

Shaking my head, I push all those thoughts away. No good can come from thinking of that night.

His lips part to respond but no words come out.

"Stella set me up, didn't she?" I seethe, disbelief flowing through me. I fucking trusted her.

"Yeah, but don't be mad at her. She's trying to help."

"Where is she?" I ask, forcing my concern for my friend to the forefront.

"She's at the cabin with the guys. We've swapped."

I rush to the window and look out at the driveway, finding Stella's Porsche parked exactly where it was earlier.

"She's… you've… fuck."

He watches me warily as I pace the short length of the living room.

"Kyle, I—"

"No," he says, stepping up to me and forcing me to stop marching.

I try to move away but he reaches out and wraps his hands around my upper arms.

"I need you to hear me out."

"No, I don't need to do anything. I told you, we're done. You shouldn't be here. You should go back to the cabin. I don't want you here."

"You're lying," he states, stepping closer until the heat of his body seeps through the robe that's loosely tied around my middle.

"I told you, Kitten, I always know when you're lying." A smirk pulls at his lips.

"Not this time."

He stares at me, tension crackling between us. My body is desperate to lean into his heat, his touch. But I fight it.

He chuckles and all it does is kick my irritation levels up a notch.

I swallow, allowing myself a second or two to gather my thoughts. With him so close and his scent filling my nose, it makes it hard to form a thought, let alone conjure up an argument.

He releases my arm before I get to say a word, and for the briefest moment, I wonder if he's going to concede.

I should know better.

"Your eye twitches," he says softly, pressing one fingertip to the side of my eye.

I flinch at his burning touch and move to take a step back, but his fingers tighten on my arm, keeping me in place.

His finger trails down my cheek until it traces over my bottom lip. I want to pull away, but with the way his eyes are fixated on me, I can't find the strength to do it.

"I've missed you so fucking much," he whispers.

"It's been a couple of days," I sass, forcing myself to ignore the fact that I feel exactly the same about the situation.

A growl rips from his mouth at my words. His hand releases my arm but it's only for a beat because he's not letting me go.

His fingers wrap around my throat and I'm forced backward.

"Ky," I gasp, my back hitting the wall. He steps right into me as the intensity in his eyes makes a violent shudder roll down my spine.

"An hour was too fucking long, Har."

His chest heaves, his minty breath fanning over my face as our eyes hold in a battle of wills.

He wants me to submit, to admit my feelings, and risk putting my heart on the line for him.

But am I strong enough to do that after everything?

My pulse thunders under his light grip, and he feels it because his thumb starts caressing the spot I know where it's pounding against my skin.

"I'm so fucking sorry, Kitten. I thought I was doing the right thing by not telling you. I thought I was protecting you."

"You thought wrong," I growl, my memories of what his lies led to hitting me full force once again.

My stomach turns over as I remember the putrid stench from that warehouse, Gray's vile touch, his murderous promises, and dark intent.

"You left me unarmed and allowed him to get to me."

Guilt darkens his eyes, pain leaking from them.

I feel it, I feel it as if it's my own.

But is that enough?

"You lied to me, Kyle."

"I know, and I'm sorry. I thought I could keep him away from you. I thought if I tried to show him that I didn't want you—" I think of that brunette girl wiggling around on his lap. My chest splinters as I picture his hands on her body. "I thought it was safer that way."

"Why was he even there? Did you invite him?"

"Fuck knows. I never wanted to look at him again after that night." He swallows and my eyes drop to his throat as the muscles pull and his Adam's apple bobs. My mouth waters, wanting to taste his skin, to keep the roughness of his jaw against my lips.

Damn him.

"I only ever wanted to protect you, Har." He steps closer, crushing my body against the wall in the most delicious way. "I only ever wanted you."

"Ky, I—" I try to argue but he presses two fingers to my lips to stop me.

He stares at me with so much emotion swimming in his eyes, it's all I can do to remember to take a breath.

"Shhh... I'm talking," he whispers, brushing his nose against mine and sending my body into overdrive. His hand drops and he wraps it possessively around my ribs. "I'm sorry, Har. For everything. For not taking you away that night, for being so drunk I let it go on too long. For the way I treated you when I came back. I spent a year locked away and you were the only thing I could think about. I wanted you, I hated you. I was a fucking mess.

"Then I saw you again, and fuck. You fucking slayed me, Kitten.

"You were everything I didn't want to remember but was desperate for.

"I'm sorry for keeping shit from you when I should have trusted you. I'm sorry I didn't protect you in the way I should, and I'm sorry I hurt you, I'm even more sorry he got the chance to. But mostly, I'm sorry for not telling you this earlier." His hand releases my throat in favor of my cheek. "I..." He hesitates, his eyes filling with tears. "I love you, Harley."

"Kyle," I breathe, a frown marring my brow.

"Shush," he soothes. "I don't expect you to say anything. I just... I needed you to know."

His watery eyes plead with me to give him a chance, to say that I'll try.

But my head and heart are at war.

My heart feels like it's about to explode, like it no longer fits inside my chest after watching him rip himself open for me. But my head... my head wants to protect me from even more pain.

"I want to make it up to you, Kitten. Let me prove to you how I feel, how serious I am."

"But—"

"Trust me, Har, I know all the buts. I know all the reasons you should say no and turn me away. But I'm begging you, please, don't. I suffered through a year without you, it's our time now."

My lips part but I find that I can't dig up an answer as my body continues its silent battle.

"I love you, Kitten. I love you so fucking much." He drops his palm, slipping his hand inside my robe and pressing it over my heart. "I know you feel something too."

There's no way he can't feel how hard my heart is beating under his hand and my cheeks bloom knowing that he knows how hard I'm fighting for sanity right now.

"W-what will you do if I say no?" I ask, forcing the words out past the giant ball of emotions clogging my throat.

Pain slices through his eyes, but I stay strong.

"Then I turn around and walk back out the way I came in and send Stella back."

"Just like that?"

"I want to be what you need, Har. And if that's not me, then I'll just have to deal with that."

He presses his forearm against the wall behind me, caging me in. Although I know I'm free to run if I so wish.

"A-and… what if I say yes?"

Heat flashes through his eyes for a beat before he schools his features and leans in so close that our lips brush.

Liquid lust floods my body sending heat straight to my already simmering core.

"Then I'd never let you go ever again."

I sag against the wall, the conviction in his words making my knees weak.

"Okay," I whisper so quietly I'm not even sure I said the word, but the second the corner of his lip twitches up into the beginning of a smile.

"Harley," he warns as if he's worried that I'm playing him.

"I…" I bite down on my bottom lip, still battling with the argument raging but ultimately knowing that my heart is going to win out.

How can it not when he's basically bleeding out in front of me right now?

"Yes," I breathe. "Yes, Ky. I want—" My words are cut off as his lips slam down on mine and his tongue plunges into my mouth.

His kiss is all-consuming, and he steals all the breath from my lungs as he devours me.

His hands slide up to my cheeks so he can angle my head just so and deepen our kiss.

My toes curl in desire and my heart tumbles as I finally allow it to take full control of the situation.

I let my walls down and fall hard and fast as he consumes me, claims me.

His fingers thread into my hair and he tugs my head up, ripping my lips from his so he can kiss across my jaw and down my neck.

"Ky, I…" I pant, trying to get control of my breathing to be able to say the words. "I… I think I love you too."

He pauses with his lips pressed against my throat and I panic.

Was I not supposed to say that?

But then I feel his lips move and I know he's smiling.

"Look at me," I demand, knowing that I can't miss this moment.

He hesitates for a second, but the wait is worth it when he finally moves and looks into my eyes.

Tears swim in his silvery-blue depths and he has the goofiest smile on his face.

I can't help but bark out a laugh at how ridiculously happy he looks. It's an incredible sight and my chest swells knowing how much he needs this kind of happiness in his life after everything he's been through.

"I can't offer you much, Har. I come complete with a parole officer and a record, but fuck, I promise to always put you first and do my best to make you the happiest woman on the planet."

"Oh Ky, I don't need anything aside from you. We can build the rest of it together."

"Fuck," he barks, slamming his lips to mine once more. "I need you so fucking bad, Kitten."

"The feeling is certainly mutual."

His fingers make quick work of the tie around my waist and in seconds, my robe is pooling at my feet.

"Holy shit," he gasps when he takes in my gold bikini. "Stella *is* straight, right?" he asks, his voice deadly serious.

I throw my head back and laugh. "You're an idiot."

"Apparently so." His face twists with regrets.

"Hey, don't do that," I say, reaching for his rough cheeks and pulling him closer once again.

"We've got so much to talk about, I've got so much more to apologize for."

"That may be true, but I'm not really in the mood for talking and rehashing all that shit right now."

His eyes light up as he steps into my body once more. His clothes tickling against my bare skin and the roughness of his tented jeans scratching at my stomach.

"What did you have in mind, Kitten?" he asks, his head dipped so our lips are only a breath apart.

"I… I was heading for the hot tub. Join me?"

"Fuck yeah."

My fingers grip the bottom of his shirt and I pull it up his body. He assists when I get it stuck on his head.

Trailing my fingers over his chest, I linger on a bruised patch of skin on his ribs. "This still hurt?"

"No," he says, I suspect he's lying as he reaches for my thighs and lifts me up the wall, his lips pressing into a thin line as if in pain. My legs automatically wrap around his waist, my core lining up with his hard length, figuring that he wouldn't do it if it were too much.

"Ky," I moan, flexing my hips against him.

"Fuck."

His lips find mine as he rips me from the wall and carries me across the room.

The right side of my body heats as he lowers me down and when I look over, I find my fire roaring away as my back lands on the rug before it.

"Your fire looks perfect to me, Kitten," he says, staring down at me as if I'm the most precious thing in the world.

"I missed you," I admit, needing him to know that everything he's felt since I sent him away wasn't one-sided.

"Why'd you do it?" he asks, rubbing his hands up and down my thighs, his thumbs getting dangerously close to my damp bikini bottoms.

"B-because you hurt me."

"Fuck, I wish I hadn't."

"Me too. Can you promise me something?"

"Anything." The honesty shining in his eyes tells me that he means it.

"Never lie to me again—"

"Ne—" I reach up and press my fingers to his lips, cutting off his words.

"I'm not finished." He nods and I continue. "Never lie to me again and never think that I can't handle the truth. I'm a Harrow Creek girl, I can handle anything."

"I know, Har. You're so fucking strong. I'm so sorry."

"Show me."

His hands drop to either side of my head, his fingers digging into the shaggy rug beneath me as he drops his lips to mine and rolls his hips in a way that makes me moan.

"Fuck, Har. You're so fucking sexy," he growls against my lips. "I'm never going to get enough of you."

"I hope not."

My nails scratch down his back until I find the waistband on his jeans and slip my fingers beneath them and his boxers, gripping onto his ass and pulling him tighter against me.

He kisses me as if I'm the air he needs to breathe, and I know without a doubt that I made the right choice. My heart couldn't cope with watching him walk away from me again.

"Kyle," I gasp when he pulls the small triangle of fabric away and pinches my nipple. My back arches off the rug with my need for more.

Ripping his lips from mine, he trails wet sloppy kisses down my neck and chest until he reveals my other breast and sucks the hard peak into his hot mouth.

"Oh God," I moan as his tongue laves at me.

"Missed you. Missed you so much," he mumbles against my skin as he descends my stomach, pulling at the ties at my hips.

The fabric falls away and his hands press on the inside of my thighs as he lowers himself to his stomach. He moves his face forward but he doesn't stop where I want him to. Instead, he latches on to the soft skin of my thigh and sucks until I swear the skin is about to break, rebranding me as his.

"So fucking perfect," he whispers, his fingertip tracing his mark, his hot breath sends a shiver of desire racing across my skin.

"Kyle," I moan, reaching for him.

I knock his cap off his head and thread my fingers in his long locks, pulling him toward where I need him.

"Horny, Kitten?"

"Kyle, yes," I cry, hoping it'll encourage him to stop teasing me. "Please."

"My pleasure."

He leans forward and sucks hard on my clit.

"Oh my God," I squeal, thrashing around on the rug.

He releases me after a second and his tongue sets to work making me lose my goddamn mind.

"Yes, yes," I cry as my release begins to crest.

One of his fingers circles my entrance, my muscles contracting, desperate to pull him deep inside me.

I pull at his hair harder, trying to tell him what I need without finding the words.

My head spins, my body flies, and my chest heaves as I climb higher and higher.

Finally, he pushes two fingers deep inside me and bends them in the perfect way that makes me detonate.

"Kyle," I scream as my body shatters into a million pieces.

Wave after wave of red-hot pleasure courses through my body, leaving me heaving for breath and my limbs heavy with exhaustion.

He doesn't pull back until he's squeezed the last ounce of ecstasy out of me.

Sitting up, his lips pull into an accomplished smirk as his chin glistens with the evidence of my release.

Every muscle south of my waist clenches with the sight, to the point that I almost push him back down to do it all over again.

Clearly able to read my mind, he chuckles and wipes the back of his hand across his face before he stands.

I panic for a second that he's about to walk away, but then his hands drop to his waistband and he pops the button, pushing both his jeans and his boxers down his thighs.

"Oh God," I whimper as his hard length springs free.

He smiles down at me as he kicks the fabric from his legs and drops his hand to his length, stroking a few times as he trails his eyes leisurely down my body.

His gaze scorches every place it touches until I'm squirming with desire once more.

"Ky," I warn, hoping it'll break him out of his trance.

Hearing my voice, he drops to his knees between my parted thighs before rubbing the head of his cock through my folds, coating himself in my wetness.

Our eyes hold as silent promises pass back and forth between us.

"I love you," he mouths, dropping lower and pushing the tip inside me.

My body tenses at the invasion, but the second his hand skims up my body and comes to stop in its home around my throat, I relax.

Taking his weight on his elbow beside my head, he pushes the whole way in, and his tongue parts my lips, teasing mine with the same gentleness.

"Kyle," I moan, pleasure rippling through me as tears burn my eyes.

"I'm so sorry. I'm so sorry," he says between kisses as he loves me.

"Ky." I pull his head up so he can look into my eyes. "It's okay. I understand. What's done is done."

He stares at me for a beat, his body stills.

"I..." he starts, but soon shakes his head before dropping his lips back to mine for a life-changing kiss.

I cling on to him, clawing at his back as he ups his speed. Wrapping his hand around my thigh, he presses it against my chest, allowing him to take me deeper and hit the perfect spot with every thrust.

"You feel so incredible," he murmurs when he's forced to break our kiss to drag in a few deep breaths. "So fucking tight."

"Kyle, I'm gonna—"

"I know, Kitten. I can feel it." He drops his fingers between our bodies and pinches my clit. "Let go, baby. Come all over my cock."

"Ky," I cry as I do exactly as I'm told thanks to another sharp pinch and strong thrust.

My body snaps and my pussy sucks him in deeper a second before he throws his head back and roars out his release.

The muscles in his neck, chest, and stomach ripple and pull, the sight sends aftershocks shooting around my body.

Dropping my leg, I slam my hands down on his chest. He's not expecting it and as I hoped, he falls back on his ass, allowing me to crawl onto his lap.

"Hey, Kitten." He smirks, his eyes sparkling in delight as he comes down from his high.

"Hey."

"I think I need to do that again," he admits, but it's not necessary, I can already feel him growing hard against me.

"Want to take this to the hot tub?" I ask as his hands trail up my back to undo my bikini top so it falls from my body.

"Hmm… I can't think of anything I want more." He balls up the scrap of fabric and throws it across the room.

"Okay but I'm going to need that." My eyes follow the movement of my top.

"Like fuck you are."

He stands with me in his arms as if I weigh nothing, and he carries me toward the door he entered through.

"We can't go in na—"

"Says who, Kitten?"

"The welcome pack," I admit, my cheeks heating at my rule-following.

"Fuck the welcome pack, you're not wearing clothes again until we're forced to leave this place."

His hands squeeze my ass until the bite of pain mixes with my desire and my core floods with heat.

"Fuck, I can feel that."

"Yeah, then you'd better do something about it."

Before I've realized he's released me, I'm on my feet, the top half of my body bent over the hot tub.

His hand lands on my bare ass cheek with a loud slap and I squeal in shock, my heat zeroing in on my pussy.

"My girl loves it a bit rough, huh?"

His hand skims up my spine, threading into my hair and pulling my head up, forcing my back to arch.

"Ready?"

"Hell yeaaaaah," I scream as he slams into me with each thrust. "Oh shit."

Gone is the gentle lover from beside the fire and in his place is the hot-headed, bad boy that I know so well.

"Kyle," I scream into the silent forest as he pounds into me so hard that my feet start to leave the floor.

His grip on my hair tightens, the pain so fucking addicting as he pushes me closer and closer to another release.

"Give it to me, Kitten. Give me everything."

"Kyle," I cry, my body quaking with the strength of my release.

"Who do you belong to, Kitten?" he asks between powerful thrusts as he chases his own orgasm.

"You, Kyle. Only ever you."

"Fuck yes," he booms as his cock jerks violently inside me.

He falls forward, his hot chest pressed against my sweat covered back.

Wrapping one hand around my neck and the other around my waist, he holds me tightly to him.

"Never fucking forget it," he whispers in my ear. "I'll go to the ends of the earth to find you, Kitten."

I nod, too overwhelmed by him and my intense release to respond.

"I love you. I love you so fucking much."

Standing, he pulls me up with him and drops his hand down my stomach until he finds my swollen folds.

I want to tell him no more, but he bypasses my clit and drops straight to my entrance, dipping his finger into the evidence of our multiple releases that I can feel beginning to run down my thighs.

"Me and you, Kitten. Me and you."

His lips find the side of my neck and he presses them there for the longest time as the fresh early evening air cools our heated skin.

"Ready to relax?" he whispers in my ear when I shiver in his arms.

"I should probably go clean up first."

"Be quick."

He swats me on the ass as I walk away, my skin tingling with his attention until I disappear into the cabin and all but run to the bathroom so I can get back to him quicker.

38

KYLE

I can't stop the smile that splits my face as I watch her slip into the cabin.

I knew going along with Stella's crazy plan was a risk and I told myself over and over on the drive here that being sent away again was the most likely outcome to this little stunt. But even with repeating that in my head, I couldn't stop my hopes from rising.

Stella thought she was ready to talk, to clear the air and consider the future. I had to trust she was right.

The moment Harley's shocked and angry eyes locked on mine, my heart dropped and I knew that Stella was wrong.

Fuck knows how I managed to change her mind, but I'll be forever grateful for whatever it was.

Unable to wipe the smile off my face, I flip the lid on the hot tub and climb in, allowing the hot water to soothe my muscles.

I rest back, looking out over the sea of trees before me, and rest my head back, wondering how I've managed to land myself here.

You're a lucky motherfucker, a little voice says in my head as I hear footsteps heading my way.

Looking to the side, I find my girl, still fully naked and with two bottles of beer in both hands.

"I've died and gone to heaven," I say, my eyes feasting on her bronzed, beautiful skin.

"This place is pretty insane."

"I'm not talking about the place, Kitten. You could be walking to me like that in my old trailer and I'd still be in paradise."

A shy smile curls at her lips.

"Too late for that, Kitten. I've already had you twice tonight, and I can tell you now that there's more yet to come."

"Oh yeah?" Fire burns bright in her dark eyes as she steps up to the tub and drops her gaze to my body. It's hidden by the water but I'm sure she sees enough to know I'm hard again.

Reaching for myself, I wrap my fingers around my length and start jerking off.

Her teeth sink into her bottom lips as she watches my movement.

"You're insatiable."

"I've been waiting for you for a long time, Harley."

"It's been a few days," she mutters, placing the beers in the drink holders and climbs in with me.

"Harley," I say with a smile, dragging her over by her hips and planting her on my lap. "I've wanted you for as long as I can remember. You were the first girl I ever really saw. No one else has ever compared to you."

"Ky," she breathes, snuggling into my side as I wrap my arms around her and hold her tight.

"It's always been you, Kitten."

She falls silent in my arms, probably remembering all the things I've done to prove the words I just said aren't true. But none of my actions were not because I didn't want her.

"I always thought you deserved better," I whisper, answering her unspoken questions. "I always knew that you'd get out of the Creek one day and make a better life for yourself. I knew that if anything happened between us, that I'd always hold you back. And of course there was always the little issue of Zayn digging me an early grave if I even looked at you a little too long."

She tenses against me as I mention her brother.

"It's okay, Har. He knows everything."

"And you're still breathing?"

"He's screwing one of your best friends. He didn't really have a leg to stand on."

"It's true but I didn't think he'd let that stand in his way."

"I talked him around to it. I have a way with words."

"It seems you do because when I first found you here earlier, I wanted to stab you with a blunt knife and look at me now."

She wiggles on my lap and I groan in frustration.

I twist her in my arms so she straddles my lap and I can look into her eyes. "I meant every word I said to you, you know that, right?"

"I do…"

"But?" I prompt when she loses herself in her thoughts once again.

"You still hurt me, Kyle. Just because I've accepted your apology, it doesn't mean I've forgotten."

"I know, Kitten," I say, reaching up and cupping her cheek. She leans into my touch and it's all I need to know that there really is a future for us from here on out. "I don't expect you to forget just like that, but I can't tell you enough how much I appreciate you giving me a chance."

She nods at me, sucking her bottom lip into her mouth.

"Spit it out, Har. No more secrets, remember."

"That's just it," she says almost nervously. "Is there anything else I need to know?"

"No, the only thing I was hiding was Gr—" Her hand lands over my mouth and she shakes her head. "Okay," I agree, not saying his name out loud.

"You're not… you're not… involved with anything from the Creek, are you?" she asks hesitantly.

"No, Kitten. The other night was the first time I'd been back there. I have no intention of ever doing so again either."

She nods, accepting my answer.

"What about Kane?"

Unease zips through me at the mention of my brother. We've yet to have a decent conversation about how he knew where she was so fast because he's barely been at the house since. I already had my suspicions about what he's doing and it only made them worse.

I know who he was involved with before I went away, and I'm terrified that he's only got in deeper since being gone and losing Gran.

"I… I don't know. He won't tell me fuck all but honestly… I'm scared."

"Shit," she mutters. "He needs to leave all that bullshit behind."

"I couldn't agree more. But you know as well as I do that it's easier said than done if what we're both thinking is true."

"We need to help. We need to do something. We need—"

"Har," I say, cutting off her words. "I agree, of course I do. But we can't get involved. Kane will do whatever he wants, no matter what we think or do about it. And interfering will only make whatever he's doing more dangerous. We need to leave him to it and trust that he knows what he's doing.

"He's a good person beneath it all. We've got to believe that will win in the end."

We both fall silent, only the sounds of our breathing and the jets beneath us filling my ears.

"Does Letty know we're in Rosewood?" I ask, needing to break the silence and the concern that's coming off her in waves. Not that I think my question will alleviate any of that.

"Not that I know of. I haven't spoken to her in weeks, and I know Mom hasn't either. I'm worried about her," she admits.

"I'm sure she's fine. She's off at college enjoying herself. Isn't forgetting home and your family what you're supposed to do?"

She shrugs and falls forward into my chest.

"Everything will be fine, Har. I promise." Granted, it's a pretty lofty promise to make, but with her by my side, I'm pretty confident I can keep it. And ultimately, our siblings' lives have nothing to do with us really. It won't be long and we'll be heading off to college and embarking on the beginning of the rest of our lives. We're better off focusing on that than things we have zero control over.

The rest of our stay at the cabin was more than I ever could have wished for.

We spent hours talking about our childhoods, opening up about how we felt about each other and we've discussed what happens from here on out.

I'm not stupid, I know I'm still in the doghouse and have a lot of things to make up for, but I fully intend on doing so.

After we got out of the hot tub that first night, I stayed. Harley called Stella and ripped her a new one for her stunt. I could barely hold it together as she faked being angry with her friend. Credit where credit's due, she's a better actress than I ever gave her credit for, even I almost believed she was still angry.

When she finally came clean, she could barely stand she was laughing so hard. Seeing the pure delight on her face as she roared with laughter made my entire year. I pulled her into my arms and held her tight as tears of joy streamed down her face.

By the time we both climb into Stella's Porsche to drive back to Rosewood, I'm happier than I ever remember being.

"This is one sweet ride," I say, flooring the accelerator and throwing us both back into our seats with the force. "Makes this whole trip worth it," I deadpan.

"Keep going it'll be the last ride you get," she sasses, sliding her hand up my thigh until she's cupping my semi. She traces the outline through my sweats ensuring it's at full mast in seconds.

"Kitten," I growl. "We've got a long-ass drive, and unless you intend on following through, then I suggest you stop."

"I'd rather not have to grovel to Stella because you crashed her baby," she says, pulling her hand away from me.

I snatch it up before she drops it back in her own lap and I place it back on my thigh.

"I didn't say stop touching me." I glance over at her and give her one of my killer smiles that I already know will make her squirm in her seat.

"I'm not ready to go home," she admits, changing the subject.

"What do you think your mom is going to say?"

She shrugs. "It's all her fault. She can't really say anything."

"You need to give her a break. If it weren't for her then this might not have happened," I say threading my fingers through hers and lifting her hand to my lips, kissing her knuckles.

"I'm not mad she did it, I'm mad she didn't tell me."

"I know, but like you said, it's time to focus on the future now."

"You're right," she breathes.

We spend the journey back talking about our futures, what colleges we might want to go to and the things we want from life. It's incredible.

Not long ago, I didn't think I had any kind of future ahead of me, certainly not a chance at a decent college. But thanks to Jada, Kane, and the amazing girl beside me. I might just get everything I ever wanted.

We go straight to the Hunter's house when we finally get back later that night. We walk inside with our hands locked together and wide smiles on our faces. Zayn's already back, his car was outside but I don't let it bother me.

We dump our bags in the hallway and make our way down to the den where they're waiting for us.

Harley pushes the door open and every set of eyes in the room turns toward us.

I pull Harley into my arms and drop my lips to hers, bending her backward as if we're in an old movie and making a show of claiming her as mine.

Whoops and hollers sound out around the room but they're soon drowned out when I pull her back up and she slips her tongue into my mouth, deepening the kiss.

I'm powerless to resist her and meet her move for move, holding her flush against my body. That is until something soft hits my head.

"Alright. Just because I said you could, it doesn't mean you get to rub it in my face, fucker," Zayn grumps.

"What? Like you don't do it to me with Poppy." Harley pins her brother with a death stare after ripping her lips from mine.

"Okay children, calm down," Stella says, taking control of the situation. She pushes from the couch she was sitting on, walks over and takes Harley off me, wrapping her up in a hug.

"Thank you," Harley whispers in her ear.

"I got your back, girl. Plus, I had fun with the guys."

"Hell yeah, she did. Justin and Rich didn't know what hit them," Ash announces, making Harley's eyes almost pop out of her head.

"Tell me you didn't," she begs her friend.

"It was just a bit of fun. You're right about his cock though." She holds her fingers up, mimicking the size much like Chelsea did as everyone falls over laughing.

"Come and sit down," Ruby encourages, forcing Ash to shift over on their couch.

"You want sodas?" Poppy asks, walking over to the small refrigerator in here.

"Please," we say in unison as I drop down onto the couch and pull her onto my lap.

The guys eagerly catch us both up on all the gossip we missed while in our private slice of heaven and the nine of us laugh and enjoy ourselves.

Back in the Creek, I hung out with a group of guys, all of whom I called friends, but it wasn't until I was locked away that I realized how little we really meant to each other. They never bothered reaching out to me or visiting, and I never invited them.

But this, this feels different. These people surrounding me make me feel like I belong for the first time in my life. They prove to me that things can be better and that I don't just have to be the guy from the Creek who ended up in juvie. Yes, that might always be a part of who I am, but it's only a small part.

I smile to myself as I sit back and enjoy the easy banter between the other three couples and Stella, who's more than capable of holding her own by herself.

Eventually, someone suggests ordering pizza and without planning it, we all spend the entire evening hanging out in Zayn's den. But as fun as it is, I'm already craving alone time with my girl. I've been spoiled this week, it's going to take a bit of time to get used to sharing her again.

"Wanna get out of here?" I whisper in her ear while the others are distracted.

"Sure. We're gonna head out," she announces to the room without even asking me what I had in mind.

She hops up from my lap and I take her hand when she offers it.

We walk down the hallway and when we get to the stairs, she moves as if we're going to head up.

"Not yet," I whisper in her ear, pushing her toward the front door.

"Where are we going?" she asks as we walk from her driveway.

"Wait and see."

It's not an overly long walk, although more time has passed than I was expecting by the time we step down onto the sand.

"You wanted to come to the beach?" she asks, her brows knitting together.

"Yeah, I thought it might be romantic."

"You don't need to make gestures to try to convince me of anything, Ky," she says, looking up at me.

"I know, and this isn't a gesture. I just thought it would be nice. Plus, I was getting annoyed with sharing you."

"Aaand there's the truth," she jokes.

"What can I say, I'm a selfish guy." I shrug like it's nothing and she laughs at me.

"You're right, this is nice."

We walk hand in hand along the damp sand in silence, lost in our own thoughts. A lot has changed for both of us in a very short amount of time, but I wouldn't have it any other way.

Even with the pain and heartache, we've ended up exactly where we should be.

When we're between two dunes and hidden from the few other locals out on an evening walk, I pull her to a stop and twist her into my body.

"Hey," she says, looking up at me with her eyes full of love and happiness.

"Hey, Kitten."

"What is it?" she asks, clearly sensing that I want to say something important.

"I just want you to know that I'd go through all of that again time and time again if it meant it ended with having you in my arms."

A goofy smile curls at her lips.

"You're the only thing I ever really wanted and the one thing I knew I couldn't have. I don't know what I did to get this chance with you, but I promise you that I'm never going to ruin it or take it for granted."

"Hey," she says, running her thumb across my bottom lip. "You don't need to—"

"I do, Har. Everything we talked about at the cabin, I meant it. I want everything with you, Harley Hunter. I always have."

"Kyle," she swoons.

"I love you, Kitten."

"I love you too."

I drop my lips to her and hold her tight as I kiss her as if it's our first and last rolled into one.

"How's it feel?" I ask when I finally let her up for air, both our chests heaving and desire darkening our eyes.

"How's what feel?"

"To be owned by a Legend?"

EPILOGUE

Harley
Three months later...

"Are you disappointed that you're not up there like you should have been?" I ask Kyle as we sit in the bleachers at school waiting for the graduation ceremony to start.

I'm sandwiched between him and Ruby. I have no clue how she and Ash managed to score tickets for today, but they're here supporting our graduating friends.

A wave of sadness washes over me that so many of the people who have been a part of our everyday lives for so long are going to be heading off to college soon and leaving us behind to endure another year at Rosewood High.

"Nah. If I were graduating now, it would have been from Creek High, and no one wants their diploma from there. It's better this way," he says, smiling down at me and squeezing my hand.

I know he's telling the truth, but still a part of me wonders how much he hates having to do another year.

"Plus," he adds. "I could never begrudge spending more time with you even if it means more high school."

Tingles race through me as I think about what our senior year is going to entail, and I can't fight my smile.

As expected, both Ruby and Ash have been promoted to captains of the cheer squad and the football team, with Kyle and I as their assistants.

Our new senior team might not quite match up to the ones who are down there with their caps and gowns on, but with a few more months of hard work, Ash and Kyle are confident that they'll see some success this year and do Jake and the boys proud.

Ruby and I are equally as positive when it comes to our new squad.

We were both blown away by the standard of the girls who turned up to tryouts a few weeks ago, even Chelsea was stunned.

And despite the fact we're now missing one of our key players, I'm pretty confident that nationals could be in our future once more.

I really fucking hope so because I'll give anything to see Rubes lift that trophy. Hell knows she's worked hard enough for it.

Pulling my cell from my pocket, I quickly snap a picture of all the graduates sitting in the rows in front of the stage and send it to Stella.

Only a couple of weeks after our break in the mountains, she showed up at school bearing the news we were all dreading.

She was leaving.

And she wasn't just hopping across the country this time, she was leaving the country and heading to England like she feared she might be.

"How's she doing?" Kyle asks, noticing who I'm messaging.

"She's good. Bored. She's not starting at her new school until September and she's beginning to lose her mind I think."

"Can't she come back for the summer?"

I open my mouth to reply, but think better of it and shoot her another message making the suggestion, but I don't get to wait to see her response because Principal Hartmann takes to the stage to begin the ceremony.

He talks through this year's graduating class's successes. He reminisces on the team's incredible season before discussing other teams and other events that deserve celebrating until he gets to our impressive second chance at nationals the other month.

When he starts inviting the students up to get their diplomas and to individually congratulate them, I begin to get emotional.

Because he can read me like a book, Kyle turns to me and places a kiss on my cheek.

"I fucking love you," he whispers in my ear.

"This is ridiculous," I mutter, wiping my eyes with the back of my hand as

I watch my brother take to the stage. I glance over at Poppy who's sitting beside Mom and notice that I'm not the only one in tears.

She notices my attention and looks over, giving me a sad smile.

I know that Zayn is only going to MKU—after a very long discussion with Mom about his change of plans—and it's not far away, but the two of them have become very used to being in each other's pockets every minute of the day. It's going to be another huge adjustment for Pops. But I've got every confidence that she can handle it. Even if it means she takes over my place as the gooseberry of the group. I have a feeling that Zayn will be home any chance he gets, or he'll be sneaking her into his dorm at every possible opportunity. He tried to convince Mom to get him an apartment, but she drew the line at that, although I can't help thinking that she's just holding off until Poppy joins him in a year's time—because we all know that's what she's going to do.

"What are you thinking about?" Kyle whispers in my ear.

"The future."

"Ah, and what does that look like?"

I shrug. We've both said we want to go to college, but we haven't talked much more about it since our drive back from the mountains. It's something we really need to sit down and discuss as senior year rolls around. I have no huge desire to go anywhere specific, Letty and Zayn—not that he's following his, since he found love—were the ones with the college dreams, I'd just be happy to get in after my struggle with math.

"I'm not sure other than we'll be together."

"Hell yeah, we will," he agrees with a smile, lifting my hand to his mouth.

I was worried the ceremony would take forever, but all too soon, the final students make their way up to the stage and we're listening to Hartmann close the ceremony.

"I can't believe my last baby will be up there next year," Mom muses as we make our way down to go and find the graduates.

"Don't go getting all emosh on me, Mom," I joke, earning an amused smirk from Kyle. We both know I was the one fighting with my emotions the last hour.

"I'm not. I'm good," she lies. "I'm so proud of you all, you know that, right?" she asks, pulling me to a stop, forcing others to swerve around us. "I know I've been hard on you all about your education and your future, but it's only because I want you to have all the options that your father and I didn't have." Dad stands awkwardly behind us, obviously hearing Mom's words.

"We know, Mom, and we appreciate it." I reach out and squeeze her hand when I see a little sadness creep in.

She's worried about Letty, we all are after her radio silence the past few weeks. It's not like her and the longer she ignores us, the more concerned I'm getting.

She was more than just my sister when we were kids, she was one of my best friends and I can't help feeling abandoned. It's ridiculous, I know. She's probably just off living her best life, but there's a heaviness in my gut that tells me it's not that at all. Her Instagram is empty, whereas before it was full of nights out and her laughing with her new college friends.

Something is wrong. I know it is.

We take off again, searching for Zayn through the crowd.

Unsurprisingly, Poppy is the first to spot him and she flies at him. He catches her and spins her around with a wide smile on his face before slowing to a stop and planting his lips on hers.

"They're not going to cope well, are they?" Mom mutters, clearly having similar thoughts to me earlier.

"They'll be fine. Plus, it's only for a few months then she can join him."

"And what about you two?"

"We're going together," Kyle states, wrapping his arm around my shoulder.

She shakes her head at us and turns back to congratulate Zayn.

The others surround us, all the seniors have wide smiles on their faces as the team and the squad congregates together, the guys all pulling their girls into their sides.

"We fucking did it, motherfuckers," Jake booms over our group as a round of cheers sound out.

"Time to fucking celebrate," Ethan adds, slamming his lips down on Rae's and crushing her against his body.

"Too fucking right." Amalie is the next to be molested before Mason drags Cami into his arms, and Shane rubs his hand lovingly over Chelsea's bulging stomach. She's due any day now and I swear she's never looked more beautiful.

I look around at my friends, that lump back, clogging my throat as I think about having a year here without them all. I glance at Justin and Rich who are both laughing, I'll probably even miss those idiots.

"You okay, Kitten?" Kyle asks, pressing his front against my back and wrapping his arms around my waist.

"Yeah," I force out as Ash and Ruby join us. "It's just the end of an era, you know."

"It is," Ruby agrees. "But next year is our year."

"Fucking right it is," Ash booms. "We've got it in the bag. Rosewood High doesn't know what's about to hit them."

We watch the celebrations unfold for a few more minutes before everyone begins to disperse to celebrate with their families before the party at Ethan's this evening.

Excitement races through me as I think about the wild night we've all got ahead of us.

"Right, I've got him, let's go," Mom says, dragging Zayn along behind her.

We head to Zayn's favorite restaurant for a meal to celebrate, just like we did two years ago for Letty.

I glance at the empty chair, a heaviness I'm beginning to get used to pressing down on my shoulders.

She should have been here today, and although Zayn hasn't said anything about her absence, I know it's hurt him. I can see it in his eyes.

"To Zayn," Mom says, dragging me from my thoughts and holding her drink up in a toast. "Congrats, baby. I can't wait to see what the future holds for you."

Dad sits awkwardly at the other end of the table not saying a word as Zayn reaches over and takes Poppy's hand under the table.

"Thanks, Mom. For everything. We couldn't have done any of this without you."

"Always." She nods, her own eyes looking a little glassy.

"Now let's eat before you all want to leave to get drunk." She rolls her eyes in mock annoyance.

The food is incredible, and both Zayn and Kyle eat more than I thought possible.

We say goodbye to Dad in the parking lot, all of us promise to come and visit soon. It's been a few weeks since we all ventured back to the Creek and I feel bad about not seeing him more, but the truth is, all of us hate that place, and aside from big events like this, he refuses to leave. It makes things hella awkward.

The drive back with Mom and Kyle is in silence. Tension comes off her in waves showing what an effort she's put in to appear so positive and put together in front of my dad.

She'd never admit it, but I'm pretty sure she still loves him deep down. Hell knows she begged him enough to start this new life with us.

Kyle squeezes my hand in support, and I smile over at him, glad he was able to come today.

My mood instantly changes though when Mom pulls up to the house beside a car I feel like I haven't seen in forever.

"Letty is here."

I fly from the car and toward the house as Zayn pulls in behind us and screeches to a halt before he also jumps out, following me inside.

There are bags in the hallway and I take off toward the kitchen when I hear a noise but I soon come to a grinding halt when I get a look at my older sister.

She's got tears cascading down her cheeks, and when I drop my eyes down her body, I find her thinner than I think I've ever seen.

"Letty," I gasp, racing toward her as Mom steps into the doorway.

"Scarlett, what's wrong?"

"I'm so sorry, Mom," she sobs as Mom pushes past Zayn to wrap her oldest daughter in her arms. "I'm so sorry, I've totally let you down."

Lifting my head from Letty's shoulder, Zayn and I exchange concerned glances as Kyle comes to stand beside him watching Letty break in our arms.

Guilt covers his face but somehow I don't think this has anything to do with Kane. Or at least, I hope not.

Letty & Kane's story is now available in the Maddison Kings University series. Keep reading for a sneak peek of The Revenge You Seek.

Grab the prequel,
THE MISTAKES YOU MAKE,
for FREE NOW.

DOWNLOAD BOOK 1,
THE REVENGE YOU SEEK, NOW

Are you craving more of Stella?
You can read her story in the KNIGHT'S RIDGE EMPIRE series! Start the series for FREE with Wicked Summer Knight
DOWNLOAD your free prequel NOW!

SNEAK PEEK - THE REVENGE YOU SEEK

CHAPTER ONE

Letty

I sit on my bed, staring down at the fabric in my hands.

This wasn't how it was supposed to happen.

This wasn't part of my plan.

I let out a sigh, squeezing my eyes tight, willing the tears away.

I've cried enough. I thought I'd have run out by now.

A commotion on the other side of the door has me looking up in a panic, but just like yesterday, no one comes knocking.

I think I proved that I don't want to hang with my new roommates the first time someone knocked and asked if I wanted to go for breakfast with them.

I don't.

I don't even want to be here.

I just want to hide.

And that thought makes it all a million times worse.

I'm not a hider. I'm a fighter. I'm a fucking Hunter.

But this is what I've been reduced to.

This pathetic, weak mess.

And all because of *him.*

He shouldn't have this power over me. But even now, he does.

The dorm falls silent once again, and I pray that they've all headed off for their first class of the semester so I can slip out unnoticed.

I know it's ridiculous. I know I should just go out there with my head held high and dig up the confidence I know I do possess.

But I can't.

I figure that I'll just get through today—my first day—and everything will be alright.

I can somewhat pick up where I left off, almost as if the last eighteen months never happened.

Wishful thinking.

I glance down at the hoodie in my hands once more.

Mom bought them for Zayn, my younger brother, and me.

The navy fabric is soft between my fingers, but the text staring back at me doesn't feel right.

Maddison Kings University.

A knot twists my stomach and I swear my whole body sags with my new reality.

I was at my dream school. I beat the odds and I got into Columbia. And everything was good. No, everything was fucking fantastic.

Until it wasn't.

Now here I am. Sitting in a dorm at what was always my backup plan school having to start over.

Throwing the hoodie onto my bed, I angrily push to my feet.

I'm fed up with myself.

I should be better than this, stronger than this.

But I'm just... I'm broken.

And as much as I want to see the positives in this situation. I'm struggling.

Shoving my feet into my Vans, I swing my purse over my shoulder and scoop up the couple of books on my desk for the two classes I have today.

My heart drops when I step out into the communal kitchen and find a slim blonde-haired girl hunched over a mug and a textbook.

The scent of coffee fills my nose and my mouth waters.

My shoes squeak against the floor and she immediately looks up.

"Sorry, I didn't mean to disrupt you."

"Are you kidding?" she says excitedly, her southern accent making a smile twitch at my lips.

Her smile lights up her pretty face and for some reason, something settles inside me.

I knew hiding was wrong. It's just been my coping method for... quite a while.

"We wondered when our new roommate was going to show her face. The guys have been having bets on you being an alien or something."

A laugh falls from my lips. "No, no alien. Just..." I sigh, not really knowing what to say.

"You transferred in, right? From Columbia?"

"Ugh... yeah. How'd you know—"

"Girl, I know everything." She winks at me, but it doesn't make me feel any better. "West and Brax are on the team, they spent the summer with your brother."

A rush of air passes my lips in relief. Although I'm not overly thrilled that my brother has been gossiping about me.

"So, what classes do you have today?" she asks when I stand there gaping at her.

"Umm... American lit and psychology."

"I've got psych later too. Professor Collins?"

"Uh..." I drag my schedule from my purse and stare down at it. "Y-yes."

"Awesome. We can sit together."

"S-sure," I stutter, sounding unsure, but the smile I give her is totally genuine. "I'm Letty, by the way." Although I'm pretty sure she already knows that.

"Ella."

"Okay, I'll... uh... see you later."

"Sure. Have a great morning."

She smiles at me and I wonder why I was so scared to come out and meet my new roommates.

I'd wanted Mom to organize an apartment for me so that I could be alone, but—probably wisely—she refused. She knew that I'd use it to hide in and the point of me restarting college is to try to put everything behind me and start fresh.

After swiping an apple from the bowl in the middle of the table, I hug my books tighter to my chest and head out, ready to embark on my new life.

The morning sun burns my eyes and the scent of freshly cut grass fills my nose as I step out of our building. The summer heat hits my skin, and it makes everything feel that little bit better.

So what if I'm starting over. I managed to transfer the credits I earned from Columbia, and MKU is a good school. I'll still get a good degree and be able to make something of my life.

Things could be worse.

It could be this time last year...

I shake the thought from my head and force my feet to keep moving.

I pass students meeting up with their friends for the start of the new semester as they excitedly tell them all about their summers and the incredible things they did, or they compare schedules.

My lungs grow tight as I drag in the air I need. I think of the friends I left behind in Columbia. We didn't have all that much time together, but we'd bonded before my life imploded on me.

Glancing around, I find myself searching for familiar faces. I know there are plenty of people here who know me. A couple of my closest friends came here after high school.

Mom tried to convince me to reach out over the summer, but my anxiety kept me from doing so. I don't want anyone to look at me like I'm a failure. That I got into one of the best schools in the country, fucked it up and ended up crawling back to Rosewood. I'm not sure what's worse, them assuming I couldn't cope or the truth.

Focusing on where I'm going, I put my head down and ignore the excited chatter around me as I head for the coffee shop, desperately in need of my daily fix before I even consider walking into a lecture.

I find the Westerfield Building where my first class of the day is and thank the girl who holds the heavy door open for me before following her toward the elevator.

"Holy fucking shit," a voice booms as I turn the corner, following the signs to the room on my schedule.

Before I know what's happening, my coffee is falling from my hand and my feet are leaving the floor.

"What the—" The second I get a look at the guy standing behind the one who has me in his arms, I know exactly who I've just walked into.

Forgetting about the coffee that's now a puddle on the floor, I release my books and wrap my arms around my old friend.

His familiar woodsy scent flows through me, and suddenly, I feel like me again. Like the past two years haven't existed.

"What the hell are you doing here?" Luca asks, a huge smile on his face when he pulls back and studies me.

His brows draw together when he runs his eyes down my body, and I know why. I've been working on it over the summer, but I know I'm still way skinnier than I ever have been in my life.

"I transferred," I admit, forcing the words out past the lump in my throat.

His smile widens more before he pulls me into his body again.

"It's so good to see you."

I relax into his hold, squeezing him tight, absorbing his strength. And that's one thing that Luca Dunn has in spades. He's a rock, always has been and I didn't realize how much I needed that right now.

Mom was right. I should have reached out.

"You too," I whisper honestly, trying to keep the tears at bay that are threatening just from seeing him—them.

"Hey, it's good to see you," Leon says, slightly more subdued than his twin brother as he hands me my discarded books.

"Thank you."

I look between the two of them, noticing all the things that have changed since I last saw them in person. I keep up with them on Instagram and TikTok, sure, but nothing is quite like standing before the two of them.

Both of them are bigger than I ever remember, showing just how hard their coach is working them now they're both first string for the Panthers. And if it's possible, they're both hotter than they were in high school, which is really saying something because they'd turn even the most confident of girls into quivering wrecks with one look back then. I can only imagine the kind of rep they have around here.

The sound of a door opening behind us and the shuffling of feet cuts off our little reunion.

"You in Professor Whitman's American lit class?" Luca asks, his eyes dropping from mine to the book in my hands.

"Yeah. Are you?"

"We are. Walk you to class?" A smirk appears on his lips that I remember all too well. A flutter of the butterflies he used to give me threaten to take flight as he watches me intently.

Luca was one of my best friends in high school, and I spent almost all our time together with the biggest crush on him. It seems that maybe the teenage girl inside me still thinks that he could be it for me.

"I'd love you to."

"Come on then, Princess," Leon says and my entire body jolts at hearing that pet name for me. He's never called me that before and I really hope he's not about to start now.

Clearly not noticing my reaction, he once again takes my books from me and threads his arm through mine as the pair of them lead me into the lecture hall.

I glance at both of them, a smile pulling at my lips and hope building inside me.

Maybe this was where I was meant to be this whole time.

Maybe Columbia and I were never meant to be.

More than a few heads turn our way as we climb the stairs to find some free seats. Mostly it's the females in the huge space and I can't help but inwardly laugh at their reaction.

I get it.

The Dunn twins are two of the Kings around here and I'm currently sandwiched between them. It's a place that nearly every female in this college, hell, this state, would kill to be in.

"Dude, shift the fuck over," Luca barks at another guy when he pulls to a stop a few rows from the back.

The guy who's got dark hair and even darker eyes immediately picks up his bag, books, and pen and moves over a space.

"This is Colt," Luca explains, nodding to the guy who's studying me with interest.

"Hey," I squeak, feeling a little intimidated.

"Hey." His low, deep voice licks over me. "Ow, what the fuck, man?" he barks, rubbing at the back of his head where Luca just slapped him.

"Letty's off-limits. Get your fucking eyes off her."

"Dude, I was just saying hi."

"Yeah, and we all know what that usually leads to," Leon growls behind me.

The three of us take our seats and just about manage to pull our books out before our professor begins explaining the syllabus for the semester.

"Sorry about the coffee," Luca whispers after a few minutes. "Here." He places a bottle of water on my desk. "I know it's not exactly a replacement, but it's the best I can do."

The reminder of the mess I left out in the hallway hits me.

"I should go and—"

"Chill," he says, placing his hand on my thigh. His touch instantly relaxes me as much as it sends a shock through my body. "I'll get you a replacement after class. Might even treat you to a cupcake."

I smile up at him, swooning at the fact he remembers my favorite treat.

Why did I ever think coming here was a bad idea?

LOCKE

1

ALYSSA

With a quick hug to Lisa and Cami, I turn toward my car, ready for my last drive home from school for a while, if not ever.

None of us saw this coming, and it's far from the end of the senior year we'd all imagined, but there's not a lot we can do about it now. The world is kinda falling apart and if all it takes is staying at home to do our bit to help, then that is what I'll do.

I can catch up with all the work I'm falling behind on, watch a few classes online from the comfort of my bed, and video chat with my friends like everything's normal.

It'll be easy.

"Hey, sweetie. How was your last day?" Mom asks when I walk into the kitchen and find her cooking dinner.

"Fine. Weird. Do you think we'll get to go back?"

"I have no idea. We've got to trust that those who control this country know what they're doing."

"I guess so." Walking up to the pan she's stirring, I peer in. "Cooking for five thousand?"

I know crazy people have been out panic-buying as if the apocalypse is really upon us, but batch cooking seems a little extreme. We've got a pantry full of food at the best of times thanks to Mom's coupon addiction. We're not going to go hungry for a few years yet, I'm sure.

"Your brother's on his way home from college."

"Right?" This isn't a shock. She told me this two days ago when it was announced that all schools and colleges were closing because of this pandemic.

"Emerson's coming with him." At just hearing his name, my heart damn near stops.

"Why isn't he going to his house?"

"His dad is refusing to let him in."

"That's nice of him," I mutter. Emerson is a prick, so I'm not all that surprised his parents don't want him on lockdown with them.

"It's not through choice, Alyssa. They're worried about his mom's condition and with their older age."

Regret sits heavy in my stomach. I should have realized. "What does she have again?"

"Cystic fibrosis."

"I know that makes her high risk, but why can't he go home?"

"They've taken all the advice very seriously and are refusing anything that could be contaminated inside."

"And that includes their son who has nowhere else to go?"

"They think it's too big of a risk."

"So where is he… oh, no, no, no. Mom, please tell me he's not."

"What was I supposed to do, Lys? They've been our neighbors since we moved here over twenty years ago and he's been your brother's best friend since they were in diapers. I could hardly turn him away at a time like this."

"So you're happy for him to come and infect us?"

"He's no bigger risk to our family as you, me, your dad, or brother. We've all got to pull together at a time like this."

"I understand that, Mom. I was fully prepared for distance learning and only seeing friends through a screen. But does he really have to stay here? Doesn't he have an aunt or uncle or something? What about his older brothers and sisters?"

"I don't know, Lys. I didn't ask. I just offered to take him in when Fred called and expressed his concerns."

"Well, that was very generous of you." I pull the refrigerator open in a huff and reach for a can of soda.

"I know things are stressful right now, but it will be fine. He'll be in the guest room or with your brother. You'll be able to ignore him. Plus, a little birdie told me just how much work you've got to do, so you, madam, are going to be too busy to worry about what he's doing." She narrows her eyes at me in disappointment.

"Miss Richards called you?" I ask with a wince.

"She sure did. She suggested we sit down and work out a schedule so you can make the best of this time because it might work in your favor as far as graduating is concerned."

"Jesus, I'm not that far behind," I mutter.

"Really?"

"Really. I know what I'm doing, Mom. I've got this."

"Well, you better had because Maddison won't want you if you fail. That offer they gave you is dependent on you graduating."

"I know, I know."

Her eyebrow lifts in warning, but she doesn't say any more. That doesn't mean I'm unaware that this isn't the last I'm going to hear of it.

"How long until dinner?"

"Levi said they'd be about an hour."

"Great," I mutter, my voice flat. "I'll go and get some work done then while I wait."

"Start as you mean to go on, Lys."

I utter words of agreement as I walk away, but really, all I feel is dread. Weeks locked in this house with them tormenting me at every turn is the last thing I need.

2

EMERSON

"I get it. I do. But still, don't you think it's kinda fucked up? They could just strip you naked and spray you down with Lysol."

"Oh yeah, because that's less fucked up," I mutter, staring out of Levi's passenger window at the familiar surroundings as we head for home.

I didn't give it two thoughts when we got word that the university was closing and sending us all home. I thought I'd just return to my childhood bedroom and wait out the next few weeks while trying not to get into a fight with my dad, and shooting hoops in the driveway like the good old days. What I wasn't expecting was the teary phone call from my mom telling me that I couldn't come back.

I knew she was at risk, I'm not stupid. I've lived with her illness my entire life. And my parents are older, having my siblings long before I was born. We're doing this to protect the vulnerable and she is most definitely one of them. I just didn't think the imposed self-isolation they put themselves into when the first cases were announced early last week would extend to not allowing me inside the house with them.

She told me that my brothers and sister had offered to have me, but like fuck do I want to go and put myself in the middle of their growing families. Being the youngest by quite a few years meant I've never had a great relationship with any of them. We've always been at totally different stages of our lives and right now is no different. They all seem to be scoring as many babies as I am hoops these days, and I have no desire to go and be a live-in nanny for any of them.

When Levi's mom got wind of what was going on, thankfully, she wasted no time in demanding that Levi invite me to stay with them.

I was grateful; of course, I was. I'd much rather be stuck with Levi than my siblings. But moving into the Perkins' house came with one issue I really didn't need while we're all locked up inside like a bunch of dysfunctional inmates.

His sister.

Alyssa Perkins has been under my skin since the moment my hormones started racing as a pre-teen, and no matter what, no matter who I fuck, she's always fucking there. Her big, innocent blue eyes, her sinful curves, and her sharp mouth. She calls to me in the exact way she shouldn't.

I've managed to stay away from her over the years. I've snapped at her, belittled her, told her she was young and stupid—which is laughable at best seeing as really there are only a few months between us. I've done everything I can to make her hate me in the hope she becomes less tempting. But as I sit here approaching the house, I can't help my cock swelling with excitement that she's going to be in touching distance for weeks, if not months, if this plays out like the experts are saying.

It's wrong. So fucking wrong. Levi would kill me if he knew I'd been pining after her for all these years. But fuck. I want her.

My eyes lock onto my own home the moment Levi turns the car up our street. I wonder how the two people inside are really coping right now. Dad's always wrapped Mom up in a protective bubble. I can only imagine what he's like right now. A part of me is glad that I'm not about to find out, but then guilt washes that away. That is until Levi brings the car to a stop around the side of his house and movement in the window above catches my eye.

It's her usual spot on her window seat. The one that looks out directly into my bedroom and has a great view of Levi's homemade court.

I blow out a long breath. I don't need to be able to see her to know she's looking at me right now. I feel it.

"I know it sucks, man. We've just got to make the best of it. You can shout at them through the window from a distance, maybe."

"It's fine. We'll just chat on the phone. They're doing the right thing." I don't want him to think it's something else that's bothering me, so I pretend to be pissed at my parents. In reality, I understand, and had it occurred to me first, I probably would have offered to go elsewhere to protect Mom myself. I just didn't get the chance.

"Come on then. Mom's cooking her specialty." The thought of Leah's homemade chili makes my stomach rumble.

The smell assaults me the second I follow Levi in through the back door and directly into the kitchen. It's going to be the first homemade food I've had in months. Living in dorms with a load of other guys who only want to play ball, drink, or fuck doesn't really lend itself to much culinary experimentation.

"You're here," Leah says, bouncing over and wrapping her arms around Levi. "Emerson, it's so good to see you," she says over his shoulder when she finds me standing somewhat awkwardly in the doorway.

This house has been like a second home to me. I've always felt relaxed here, but then again, I've never been locked inside for an unknown amount of time before.

"Thank you so much for having me."

"Don't be silly. You're almost as much a part of this house as this one." She roughs up Levi's hair, much to his annoyance, before walking back to the kitchen. "I've made up the guest room for you. Why don't you go and drop your stuff there? Dinner will be in ten minutes. Your dad's just washing up from work."

"Sounds good, Mom."

Levi bends over to collect his bags before heading for the hallway. I go to do the same, but Leah stops me.

"They're both okay over there, you know. I've been doing their shopping and leaving it on the porch. They're just doing what they think is best."

"I know. It's the sensible thing to do. I can take over from here on out with shopping for them. You don't need any more on your plate."

"It's really no problem."

I smile at her. I know she's stretching the truth. Both her and Gary are going to be working from home as of now, so the last thing she needs to do is run around town trying to find toilet paper for two households.

"I want to pull my weight while I'm here. Just tell me what you need and put me to work. Levi too."

"That would be really great. Thank you. Now get out of here while I dish up."

I nod and collect my things before climbing the stairs toward where I know *she* is.

Pushing the door to the guest room open, I'm hit with memories of my childhood. This used to be Levi's room until he used his 'I'm the oldest so I get the best room card' and moved across the hall to the bedroom with the private bathroom. I can't blame him, but right now I could really do without being in the room with the connecting bathroom to *her* bedroom. As if temptation isn't going to be enough, she's only a door away.

Images of walking into our adjoining bathroom and finding her standing under the shower, her curves on display for me to feast on, fill my mind, and my cock swells once more. What would she do? Would she scream and ensure Levi put an end to the situation with his fists, or would she allow me to join her?

I'm lost in my dirty imagination when a knock sounds on the door and Levi pokes his head inside, efficiently killing my semi with one look.

"Locke, you coming?"

I jump from the bed and follow him from the room. I'm more than ready to see her in person for the first time in months.

3

ALYSSA

The deep rumble of their voices echoes through the house the second they walk in and my stomach drops with the realization that Mom wasn't lying. Not that I thought she was, but a girl can hope.

As I walked to my room, I saw that the guest bedroom, the one next to mine, was all set up for our visitor. The first thing I did when I got to my own space was to twist the lock that allowed him access to the adjoining bathroom. Like fuck was I sharing my private space with him.

"Did you manage to get some work done?" Mom asks hopefully as I enter the living room. I keep my eyes on her as she places the serving spoons into the huge pan sitting in the center of the table. I refuse to give him any of my attention despite the fact his eyes are practically burning into my skin.

"Sure did," I lie. In reality, I sat on my window seat and reminisced on all the dickhead things he and my brother have done to me over the years. Locking me out of my bedroom; damn, even the house one time. Reading my diary when I was at dance class and telling the entire school who I had a crush on. Stealing my toys, giving my dolls an unwanted haircut. The list of bullshit pranks was endless. I was never going to beat them, no matter how hard I tried. They were two legends of the basketball team; no one could touch them. And me? I was just the little sister. The little sister who was no good at sports and mostly had zero coordination. My skills lie in the art department, and while they were both ruling the school along with the football team, I was more than happy to hide behind a canvas.

I take the empty seat at the other end of the table and reach out for a spoonful of rice.

"It's nice to see you, sis," Levi says with what I assume would be a roll of his eyes if I were to look up.

"You too."

I love my brother, I do. But usually when he's alone. He's never quite himself when he has company, whether that's Emerson or anyone else.

"Thank you so much for having me, Gary. I really appreciate it." His deep rumbling voice vibrates through me and my hand stills on its way toward the chili spoon. My eyes defy me, and I find myself looking up and straight at him.

He might have just spoken to my dad who's sitting beside me, but his eyes are firmly fixed on me.

My mouth goes dry and I fight to swallow.

"It's no problem, son," Dad mumbles around a mouthful of food.

"How are you, Lys? School good?" he asks, but I can't imagine he really gives a shit.

"Fantastic." I give him a fake smile and force my eyes away from his intense light-blue ones.

Butterflies erupt in my belly as his stare remains on me. It might be the case that I hate him for all the dickhead moves he's made over the years, but the fact remains that he's drop-dead fucking gorgeous and is the only guy who's ever really interested me.

I used to spend hours sitting on my window seat watching the two of them shoot hoops down the driveway, or keep my light off and peer around the drapes directly into his bedroom at him when he'd forgotten to close his own.

There are two very good reasons that the girls at Rosewood High used to chase him around like a lost puppy: the six-pack and the V lines I've had the pleasure of running my eyes over on many occasions.

My temperature starts to increase as I picture him jogging around the driveway with his shirt off, his skin glistening with sweat.

Fucking hell, Alyssa. Fantasizing over him while he's living in the room next door is the last thing I need to be doing.

"So how was your last week of college?" Mom asks, turning all attention away from me. Both Levi and Emerson chat away about what they've been up to and the work they've been assigned while they're here. I hardly listen to any of it. Instead, I eat my dinner and make my excuse of having work to do so I can run away.

"Lys, you've got weeks to be doing all that. Why don't you spend the night with us? We can have a movie night or something," Dad says, halting my escape.

"Yes," Mom chirps up. "I bought popcorn and ice cream. It'll be like old times."

The excitement on her face means I don't have much of a choice. "Sounds great. I'm just going to change and I'll be back down in a bit. Don't let Levi choose the movie," I warn, knowing his addiction to scary movies.

Everyone laughs, but no one agrees. Bunch of weirdos; they all love having the shit scared out of them. I, however, prefer to be able to sleep after watching a movie and not sit in the middle of my bed with the light on, scared out of my wits.

By the time I return, all four of them are sitting on the couches, the drapes are pulled shut and there are bowls of snacks adorning the coffee table, despite the fact we all just ate our body weight in Mom's chili.

I glance around at my options. Mom and Dad are on their usual couch and Levi seems to have taken control of the love seat I usually curl up in.

My lips purse in anger and I storm over.

"Get out of my seat, asswipe."

"Um…" He moves slightly as if he's actually going to do something I say, and I start to wonder if Hell has frozen over. But before his ass leaves the cushion, he looks up at me and laughs. "No. Sit over there." He nods his head over my shoulder toward the couch Emerson is currently sitting on alone.

"No. He's your friend. You sit with him." My hands land on my hips as I wait.

"This is my seat. It was mine before I went to college and now I'm back, it's mine again. So suck it the fuck up."

"Levi," Mom chastises.

"You're serious?"

"Deadly. Now sit your ass down; the movie *I* chose is about to start."

"I fucking hate you," I mutter, quietly enough that our parents don't hear.

"Aw, I'm so glad to be spending time with you too, sis."

Sulking, I fall down on the other end of the couch that Emerson has made himself at home on, keeping as much space between us as possible. It's not all that easy, seeing as it's the smaller of the two couches and he's fucking huge.

I sit ramrod straight as the movie starts. It's barely begun and we're trailing some figure through a darkened room. The music is eerie and I'm instantly on edge.

Despite knowing that it's about to scare the living shit out of me, I can't tear my eyes away from the screen.

"ARGH, my god," I scream when something jumps out of the shadows and launches themselves at the person holding the camera.

My brother barks out a laugh as I lift my feet up onto the couch, pulling a cushion onto my lap to hug as if it might protect me.

"You're a fucking pussy."

"Levi, language."

It's only been a few hours and already Levi looks about ready to head back to college. He ignores our parents and turns his attention back to the TV.

"It scared the crap out of me too," comes quietly from beside me.

"You don't need to try to make me feel better."

"I'm not."

Suddenly the movie has stopped, and Levi is pushing from *my* seat. "I need a beer. Please, tell me you've got beer."

"Of course," Dad says like it's the most ridiculous question in the world.

"Locke?"

"Please."

Levi's at the door before I clear my throat.

"What?" he asks, reluctantly turning back to me.

"I'll have one too please."

"You can't, you're too young."

"I'm eighteen. You're only nineteen," I point out just to piss him off.

"Right. As in, older than you."

"Just get her one," Dad orders, much to my satisfaction.

"You still sure you want to stay here?" Mom asks Emerson.

He chuckles. "Yeah. It might be fun."

I scoff, successfully causing his eyes to turn to me.

"What?" I bark, spinning to look at him. His eyes drop from mine in favor of my chest. I'm only wearing a tank with inbuilt support, so as his stare holds and my nipples begin to pebble under his attention it's instantly obvious.

"Emerson," I whisper. "My eyes are up here."

"Huh. Yeah, I know. You're looking really good these days, Lys."

"You've got to be kidding me. You're actually hitting on me while Levi's in the kitchen? Jesus."

"What? No. I was just pointing out that being a senior looks good on you."

"Whatever," I say, turning back toward the TV that I don't really want to watch. But his stare is doing things to me. Butterflies are erupting in my belly faster than I can control and like hell do I want him to know that his words are affecting me in any way.

4

EMERSON

The movie was shit. It was meant to be scary, but it fell a little short of the mark; well for me at least. It was another story entirely for Alyssa, who jumped at every loud noise, let alone anything that was meant to be even a little terrifying.

I found myself watching her more than I did the movie. Her pink tank hugged her full tits and when she hugged the cushion to her stomach, it pushed them up in the most incredible way. All I could think about was dropping my lips to them and seeing if she tasted as sweet as I always imagined she might.

When she got to her fourth beer that she'd managed to sneak in after her parents cut her off at two, she started to relax. She curled her legs up beneath her and as time passed, she seemed to get closer to me and the temptation to reach out to touch her was all I could think about.

"Who wants another?" Levi asks when the end credits start to roll.

"I think it's bedtime for us oldies," Leah says, pushing up from the couch and collecting the empty glasses and bottles. When she picks up four from beside Alyssa, she gives her a hard stare, but instead of chastising her, she just whispers, "Don't let your dad find out."

With a laugh and a knowing wink, she leaves us to it.

"If you think I'm sitting through another one of those, then you must be even stupider than I thought," Alyssa barks at Levi who innocently selects the horror section and starts searching through options. "I have no idea how I'm supposed to put up with you all this time."

She pushes herself from the couch but much to my surprise, using my thigh as her hand rest. My muscles tense as her fingers grip slightly.

"I'm done. Don't mind, do you?" She looks to me and then at my new bottle of beer that's sitting on the coffee table. I don't get a chance to answer because she has it to her lips, taking a long drag before giving me one last look and disappearing, but that's not before I get a chance to check out her ass in her yoga pants.

"You about finished?" Levi asks, noticing what's caught my attention.

"What?" I ask innocently. I've caught him checking out my sister on more than one occasion before she moved out and got married. Granted, there was not a chance in hell of him ever banging her seeing as there's a six-year age gap, but still.

He forces me to endure another less than scary movie before I call it a night and head up to my new bedroom.

The second I step foot in the room, I know she's still awake because the sound of soft music coming from her room filters in and there's a light coming from the gap under the bathroom door.

Closing the door, I pull my shirt over my head and drop my jeans. I throw them both on the chair in the corner of the room beside my small bag, telling myself that I'll unpack it tomorrow.

I walk over to the bathroom door, stop and listen to see if she's inside but I can't hear anything over the beat of her music, so trying my luck, I push the handle down.

Locked.

Finding something to pick the lock with, I open it as quietly as I can and once again push down on the handle, only this time the door opens.

I find her standing at the sink, toothbrush in hand, and much to my delight she's only in her tank and a tiny pair of panties.

"I thought I locked that."

"You did."

She turns from looking at me in the mirror over her shoulder, but her eyes don't stay on mine, instead, they drop down my naked torso, lingering on my abs before dropping down to my cock that's threatening to go full mast.

"Well, then you should have taken it as a hint that I didn't want you in here. There's a perfectly good bathroom for you to use down the hall."

"But I wanted to use this one."

"Why?" One hand lands on her hip and her back straightens. I think it's meant to be in defiance, but all I notice is how her breasts push out, her nipples tightening behind the thin fabric.

"Because it has something in it that I want."

"Oh yeah, what's that? My girly shower gel?"

"As much as I like that sweet smell, that wasn't what I had in mind."

"Oh?"

I take a step toward her and her breath catches.

"Emerson?" she asks, her voice cracking as I close the space between us.

I come to a stop right in front of her. Her chest heaves, her breasts swelling even more with her arousal. Fuck, I'd love to know how wet she is for me right now.

"Yeah. It seems I forgot my toothbrush. Do you mind?" Before she has a chance to answer, I've plucked the pink brush from her hand and I've got it in my mouth.

"Ew, there's something fucking wrong with you. You do know that, right?"

I shrug.

"Ugh, you're infuriating. What's it going to take to make you leave me alone?"

I finish brushing and rinse out her brush before dropping it into the little tumbler I assume it belongs in.

I turn on her and step closer. She stumbles back a little but doesn't get very far because she hits the doorjamb to her room. "Oh, baby. You're not getting rid of me that easily." Lifting a hand, I trail one fingertip along the strap of her tank before moving across the front, loving the softness of the swell of her breasts.

She gasps as I make contact, her nipples fighting against the fabric.

"And I don't think you want me to leave you alone." I lean forward, resting one hand on the wall beside her so I can whisper my next words in her ear. "I could make you come so much better than you could alone."

"I highly doubt that. Anyone with an ego the size of yours is clearly hiding something. Maybe it's your incredibly tiny cock."

Taking her wrist, I press her hand to my fully erect cock.

"Fuck," she gasps, but to my delight she doesn't immediately pull away. Instead, her fingers wrap around me ever so slightly.

"Mmm," I moan into her ear. She shudders as my breath tickles over her skin. "Don't deny what you really want, Lys. When you're ready to admit it, I'll be in that room right there. And, I won't even lock the door."

"Well, rest assured, I'll be barricading mine shut."

"You know you don't mean that." Reluctantly, I release her wrist and she almost immediately pulls it away. I miss her touch instantly.

Pulling back, I look into her eyes. The usual dark blue is almost black with desire. My palm brushes over her hip, then pushes the fabric of her tank up so we're skin on skin, coming to rest on her waist.

I search her eyes, trying to find if there's any part of her that's actually against this. Thankfully, I find none. She might be fighting me this time, but it's only the beginning, because before my time here is done, she's going to find herself writhing beneath me and crying out my name.

Releasing my hold on her, I back out of the room. But at no point do I take my eyes from hers.

"Just remember, I'm only on the other side of the door when you're unable to satisfy yourself in a few minutes."

"You're deluded."

"What? You think I don't know you're wet for me right now?" Her cheeks heat a bright red, telling me what I already knew. "Exactly. 'Night, baby."

I turn, hook my thumbs into the waistband of my boxers and push the fabric down until it pools at my ankles. Kicking them away, I leave the door wide open and look back over my shoulder before climbing into my temporary bed. She's still standing exactly where I left her with her lips parted and her chest heaving.

5

ALYSSA

Oh my god. Oh my god. Oh my fucking god.

My head spins and my heart pounds in my chest almost as much as my clit does between my legs.

That was not what I was expecting when I discovered the news about our new lodger earlier. In all honesty, I thought he'd mostly ignore me aside from a few well-timed insults. It's how it usually works when Levi and Emerson are together. And I guess that was true when we were downstairs. But when we were alone... fuck.

I cast my mind back, trying to pinpoint a time when we might have been left alone previously, but nothing comes to mind.

Angry with myself for how he basically just had me eating from the palm of his hands, I step forward and slam the door shut, effectively ending our little moment of... whatever that was.

My skin tingles as I recall how it felt having his fingers on me. How I immediately reacted to his touch, and how he's totally right. I'm so wet for him right now it's not even funny.

I make use of the toilet before shutting the door to my room, hoping that having two between us will help block out memories of what just happened.

Despite being exhausted, I toss and turn for hours, unable to get images of him lying in bed just on the other side of the bathroom out of my head. Is he touching himself and thinking of me? Or was all of that a joke?

By the time I wake the next morning, the sun is streaming through my too thin drapes and the sound of a ball bouncing outside my window takes me back a year or two. I almost missed it when Levi moved to college. But as I lay here listening to the incessant banging, I remember just how annoying it is.

Throwing the covers off, I push myself from the bed and walk over to the window. I pull the curtains open and look down at the driveway, expecting to find my brother practicing his already pretty impressive skills. He didn't get a fully paid ride at Maddison for nothing. But I don't find Levi hitting hoop after hoop. Instead, it's Emerson moving around our makeshift basketball court wearing only a pair of shorts and his sneakers. He dribbles the ball for a few seconds before making a shot. He barely even looks up. Oh, to make something seem quite so easy.

Enthralled, watching his body move so elegantly and the sun shining off his sweat-damp skin, I take a seat and get my fill of him.

I lose track of time as I watch, but eventually, as if he knows I'm here, he looks directly up at me, a cocky smirk playing on his lips. Lifting his hand, he pulls his cap from his head and replaces it after smoothing his hair back.

I'm tempted to open the window and say something, but not wanting to look like he's affecting me, I stand and walk away. It pains me to do so, especially when the sound of the bouncing ball rings through the room.

After making use of the bathroom, and once again locking his door from the inside—not that it'll stop him, but hopefully it'll piss him off a little—I pull on my yoga pants and make my way downstairs for a much-needed coffee.

I spot Mom and Dad sitting on the swing seat in the yard. From some of the conversations I've overheard recently, they're planning on digging some new flowerbeds and putting a deck area at the bottom of the lawn or something. I watch as Dad points down the yard while the coffee machine does its thing. I'm grateful they get along so well, even after all the years they've been together. I can't imagine what it must be like to be stuck inside your house right now with fighting parents.

I grab a croissant from the bag sitting on the counter and take that and my coffee up to my room. I might have a load of schoolwork to do, but I plan on spending the day working on my art project. I probably should leave it until last as a kind of reward for getting caught up, but losing myself with my paint, especially after the events of last night, is too tempting.

I don't look out the window as I pass, but I do notice the continuous bounce of the ball outside has ceased. Placing my mug and plate down, I head for the bathroom to shower while my coffee cools.

I'm busy pulling my tank over my head as I walk into the bathroom, so I don't notice that someone is standing in the middle of the room with only a towel wrapped around his waist.

"And to think, I thought you were going to make it harder on me to get what I want."

My mouth opens and closes, much like a fish as I clutch my tank to my chest, hiding my breasts from him as my eyes take on a life of their own and drop to his still shower-damp chest.

"I… uh…"

"Not content with the little show you were watching outside then, huh? Wanted a closer look?"

"What? No. I didn't know you were in here."

"Really? I wasn't hiding, baby." A warmth spreads through me at his use of that nickname once again.

"Really. I have no interest in… this." I point to his body and he laughs.

"You're a really bad liar, do you know that?"

I fume, my lips pursing in frustration, anger starting to lick at my insides and mingle with the desire that I'm trying to ignore.

"Can you get out of my bathroom, please?"

"Our bathroom, you mean?"

"No. I mean mine. I already told you there is a perfectly good one down the hall for you to use. There is no reason for you to be in here."

"I disagree. I've got one very big reason to be in here." He takes a step closer and the scent of his shower gel fills my nose and makes my mouth water.

He lifts one hand. I almost expect him to rip my top from my body, but much to my surprise, instead he gently tucks a lock of my hair behind my ear. His fingers tickle against my skin and I'm powerless to do anything else but shudder at his contact.

"I know today wasn't the first time you've watched me from your window. I've felt your stare every time you've done it. I always know when you're looking at me. Just like I know that you know when I'm looking at you. There's always been something here, Lys. You can't tell me that you haven't felt it."

My chin drops. "But you don't like me." I hate that I sound vulnerable. I don't need to look at his face to know I've just given too much away with that one statement.

He chuckles, and the sound hits me right in the chest. "I was only lying to myself, baby."

I gasp and he makes the most of my reaction.

His lips brush so gently against mine that my hands almost forget about covering myself up in my need to grab him and pull him against me.

His fingers that were still lingering on my neck, slip up into my hair as he deepens the kiss. A moan rumbles up his throat and it's my undoing.

I release the fabric my hands are clinging to, but it doesn't drop; our bodies are too tightly pressed together.

I find the damp skin of his back as his tongue slips between my lips.

Pushing me backward, I bump up against the wall. He continues forward until every possible inch of us is touching. His hard length pushes against my stomach and a wave of heat rushes south at knowing I turn him on like this.

His lips leave mine and trail across my jaw and down my neck. He sucks and nips at the sensitive skin and I moan in pleasure.

"Emerson, is this a joke?"

He stills for a beat and I worry that I've just hit the nail on the head. He hasn't even been here twenty-four hours yet, and he's driven me to this already. Is it a bet? Am I a challenge? Did he think it might entertain him for a few weeks to see if he could seduce me? Well, that failed because apparently I'm easy when it comes to the boy I've had a crush on for as long as I can remember.

He pulls back and looks at me. Really looks at me.

"What makes you think that?"

"Because you've never come anywhere near me before. Yet one day here and... well." I gesture at our current position and laugh.

"I've imagined doing this a million times, Lys. But time's up. I can't ignore it any longer."

My brow furrows.

"You don't believe me?"

"Why would I? You've gone out of your way for years to make it well known you can't stand me."

"I had to."

"Why?"

"You think Levi would be happy with this?"

"It doesn't seem to be bothering you right now, while you're living in the same house as him."

"Maybe I've decided that it's worth the risk."

"What if he kicks you out? What if he walks away from you?"

"Then that's his decision. I can't influence how he feels. The only thing I can do is act on how I feel, and right now, I'm fed up of pretending. Bored of convincing him that I think you're his annoying little sister, when in reality I spend most of my nights wishing you were beside me."

Lost for words, the silence rings out between us.

"Prove it."

His fingers wrap around my wrists and he removes my hands from him and places them back on the fabric covering my chest. Then he takes a huge step back.

His cock tents the towel and my fingers twitch to rip it from his waist and experience all of him. I've watched him for years running around topless, but I've yet to discover what he's hiding down there.

"W- what are you doing?"

"Proving it. I'm walking away. Showing you that you mean more to me than a quick fuck to waste some time."

"But—"

"No buts. I could take you right now, hard and fast against that wall, and you know it. But that's not what this is about. I want you, Lys. Not just your body for my pleasure. I. Just. Want. You." With those final words, he walks from the bathroom and closes the door behind him.

Holy shit.

6

ALYSSA

It's been five days since he made me that promise in the bathroom and five long days since we've been alone together. Every morning I wake to the sound of him outside with a ball while I stay locked in my bedroom attempting to do as I said I would and catch up on my schoolwork, alongside doing all the new stuff my teachers are putting up online.

That's not to say he's allowed me to forget those two moments we've had. Every time he walks past me, he trails his fingertips across my skin. Whether it be the small of my back or to very briefly twist our fingers together, he makes it known that he's not forgotten his promise.

When we had another family movie night last night, he even managed to hold my hand behind the cushion I was hugging. It was the sweetest thing and it had me thinking that maybe it was the beginning of something else. But when I excused myself up to bed, he didn't join me, and it was hours later when I heard him come to his room.

It's driving me crazy knowing that he's right there every night, but I'm not yet desperate enough to go walking in in the middle of the night.

A soft knock sounds at my door. Pulling my earbuds out, I call for whoever it is to enter. I want it to be him, but I know that he wouldn't have knocked, he'd have just barged his way inside.

"Hey, sweetie. You've been up here all day. Why don't you come and get some fresh air with me? I made smoothies," my mom says.

"Sure." Pushing my laptop onto the bed, I climb off.

"How's it going?"

"Pretty well. I'm not going to fail, Mom. If that's what you're worried about."

"I know you won't. You're too stubborn to allow that to happen. You just make me panic at times."

I follow her down to the yard and we take a seat at the table where she's laid out her promised smoothie and a huge bowl of fruit. But that's not the most incredible sight. At the end of the garden, Dad, Levi, and more importantly, Emerson are all topless and digging Mom's new flowerbed.

"Not a bad view from here, eh?" she asks, looking over at them. Dad might have a few years on Levi and Emerson, but as a PT he's still very much in shape.

"Ew, Mom. One's my dad and the other my brother." I grimace.

"There's a third, you know?" Something in her tone has me turning to look at her.

"What?"

"Don't think I don't know there's something going on there."

My chin drops. "Mom, I don't know what—"

"I saw him holding your hand last night."

My cheeks heat and I cast my eyes to the patio, too embarrassed to meet her eyes. "Oh."

"So how long has something been going on?"

"There isn't anything going on," I say, almost honestly. At that moment, he looks over his shoulder and the smile that brightens up his face when he sees me makes me melt.

"Oh yeah, nothing's going on." Mom chuckles. "That's not the look of a guy who's not interested, Lys."

"Mom," I squeal. Not all that impressed with the topic of this conversation.

"What? I'm just saying."

"Yeah, well don't."

"What are you so worried about?"

I stare at her. Is she really encouraging this?

"Um… everything. Levi for a start. The fact we've been forced into isolation together. You and Dad."

"Levi just wants the two of you to be happy. If he has a problem with it, then he'll just have to get over it. Your dad and I don't have an issue as long as you're discreet and sensible." She winks and I want the ground to swallow me up. "Our house isn't a knocking shop, you know."

I groan. "Mom, seriously."

"I am being serious. I think he really likes you. We're all in a shit situation right now, especially Emerson with his concern about his mom. I don't see something positive coming out of it all as a bad thing. Plus, who knows where it could lead. One day he could be an official part of this family."

I drop my head into my hands. We've only had one kiss and Mom's here talking about marriage.

"He's a good boy, Lys. You could do a lot worse is all I'm saying."

"If you'd heard some of the stories I have, then you might have a different opinion on him."

"Boys will be boys. Your dad was one of the guys back in the day too, so I know exactly what they're like."

Lifting my smoothie, I sit back and rest my feet on the table leg as I take a sip, my eyes wandering to Emerson once again. The weather is gorgeous. The sun reflects off his sweat-damp skin and his muscles flex as he forces the shovel into the pile of mud he's shifting. I bite down on my bottom lip, remembering just how he tasted when his tongue danced with mine.

"Oh, you are so gone for him," Mom jokes, much to my horror.

"What? No. I'm not..."

"Oh, come off it. Give him a chance. You never know what could come of it."

Regrets and heartbreak?

I manage to keep the words inside, but I can't help but feel the weight of them pressing down on me. He's at college and I'm just a high school kid, not to mention his best friend's little sister. It's a recipe for disaster.

"I'm going to do some work. Enjoy the view," she says with a wink, and after collecting what's left of her own smoothie, she disappears inside.

Pulling my cell from my pocket, I lift it up and zoom in on Emerson. I snap a picture and immediately send it to the group chat I've got with the girls.

Jealous?

I've told them that he's staying here for the foreseeable when we had a video chat the other night, but I haven't mentioned anything happening.

I get a series of staring and drooling gifs back before Lisa asks for another of my brother.

Shaking my head and smiling, I take a sip of my drink when a shadow falls over me.

"Something funny?"

"Yeah, I just sent a picture of you to my friends."

"And that's funny, why?"

"Because all they really want is a picture of Levi." A smirk spreads across my lips when his brow furrows.

"Good."

My eyes widen in shock, I thought that was going to hit his giant ego on its ass.

"That means I'm all yours."

"Um..."

"Are you busy after dinner?" he asks, his blue eyes sparkling with excitement.

"Oh... let me think. I was going to spend a little time in the living room, then maybe have a trip around the garden, before visiting my bedroom."

"Smartass. You're mine after dinner so cancel all those crazy plans."

Every muscle south of my waist clenches in desire.

"O- okay."

He's gone as fast as he arrived and when I look up, I find that Dad and Levi have vanished as well.

I sit in the sun a while longer messaging with the girls and when I hear Mom start preparing dinner, I head inside to help.

"What's on the menu tonight?"

"Enchiladas."

My stomach rumbles at the thought alone.

"Awesome, put me to work then."

Mom has me chopping veggies and grating cheese. It's almost enough to distract me from Levi and Emerson's voices filtering down from the living room where they're hanging out, but I can't help straining to hear what they're talking about.

"I think that's done, Lys," Mom says with a laugh. When I look down, I notice that I've chopped the onion so finely it could be called paste soon.

"You said fine," I mutter with a shrug.

"It's perfect. Here, want to make a jug of margaritas to go with?"

"Yes," I say a little over excitedly.

"Not too strong though."

I pull up a recipe on my cell and follow the instructions.

"I'm going to put this out on the table and quickly check my emails. The enchiladas only have ten minutes to go. Could you take them out for me?"

"Of course."

Mom disappears, leaving me in the empty kitchen. I bend over, resting my elbows on the counter, and stare down at my cell. I'm scrolling through

Instagram, looking at various pictures of my school friends out in their yards, enjoying lockdown in the sun while working on their tans or splashing around in their pools. Living in Florida right now sure does have its advantages. I briefly think about people who are stuck inside due to cold and wet weather outside. It must make all of this so much harder to deal with.

We're lucky; aside from school being canceled and being stuck in the house, not all that much has changed for me. Mom can still work, Dad is doing virtual PT sessions with his clients, and aside from Emerson's mom and dad, who we're keeping an eye on, we don't have any relatives to worry about. We lost all our grandparents over the past ten years, and both Mom and Dad's siblings live their own lives in different states.

Something tickling up the back of my thigh startles me and when I turn around, I find Emerson staring down at me with a smile on his face.

"Well that was some sight to walk into. You've got a fine ass, baby."

My cheeks heat as I push up on tiptoes to look over his shoulder to ensure no one's looking.

"He's upstairs. It's just you and me right now."

I bite down on my bottom lip, but it doesn't remain there as Emerson lifts his thumb and frees it.

"Mine," he whispers, brushing his lips against mine.

"We can't. Anyone could..." I don't get to say anymore as he presses me back against the counter and steals a sweet kiss.

He steps away just in time for Mom to breeze into the room.

"Everything okay in here?" She looks between the two of us with amusement.

"Uh... y- yeah. I was just going to get—"

"It's fine. I've got it. You two go and sit down."

Reaching down, Emerson interlinks our fingers and pulls me from the room.

"Thanks, Mom," I call, although I'm not sure if I'm thanking her for dinner or for being so cool about this.

Dinner is torturous at best. Emerson ensures he sits right beside me, and so close that his thigh rests against mine the entire meal. Every time he's not eating, his fingers tickle and tease the skin that's not covered by my denim skirt. A couple of times he got so high that I thought he was going to go all the way in front of my entire family, but just as my breath caught each time, he'd lower his fingers once again.

I refused to look at him but that didn't mean that I couldn't sense his amusement. He chatted away to my parents and brother like all was normal, but I'm sure they'd think very differently if they knew what was happening only feet from them.

"Meet me at the gate in the yard in thirty minutes."

"We can't. We can't go out."

"We're not going out out. Trust me."

I race up to my room and spend the entire thirty minutes redoing my hair and makeup while debating what I should wear.

In the end, I leave on my skirt and tank, but I do replace the underwear that's beneath for something a little sexier. I've no idea if he's intending on seeing it, but I want to be prepared just in case.

Slipping my feet into my sneakers, I drop my cell into my pocket and take a breath. Butterflies flutter around my stomach at not knowing what he has planned, but I fully trust him.

I don't see anyone as I make my way out of the house and my heart drops when I get to the back gate and find that he's not there.

I'm just about to run back inside and hide in my room to pretend I never showed up when I hear footsteps on the other side.

Suddenly the gate opens and standing in the gap is Emerson. He's dressed exactly as he was earlier in a pair of grey sweats and his Maddison basketball jersey.

"Hey," I say shyly.

He reaches out and tugs me through the gap before shutting the gate like we were never there.

My chest presses against his and his arm comes around my waist. He pulls me even tighter to him. His warmth seeps into me and the nerves and anticipation that have been running rampant in my body the last few days settles immediately.

"Are you ready for your night out?"

I stare up at him; gazing at the same gorgeous face I've looked at most of my life, but seeing him for what feels like the first time. His own nerves are obvious—something I've never seen on him before—and it makes me wonder if the Emerson I've experienced before has all been an act.

"I am," I whisper eventually, remembering that he asked me a question.

Finding my hand, he tugs me into the trees behind our house. As kids we spent hours in here, making dens and playing hide and seek. It was our place.

I smile as we make our way through, twigs snapping underfoot and dry leaves rustling.

"Where are we going?" I know these woods like the back of my hand but as he maneuvers us to an unknown location, it seems that I'm not the only one, because he clearly has a destination in mind.

Some light shines through the trees beyond and I narrow my eyes to see what it might be. But as we get closer and I see what he's done for the first time, I realize that no amount of imagination could have conjured this up.

Somehow, he's tied up a sheet between a few trees to make it look like a tent. There are fairy lights everywhere and the floor is littered with what looks like hundreds of candles.

"Emerson," I breathe, not able to take my eyes off the small piece of paradise in the woods he's created. "You did all this?"

"Yes and no. I had a little help," he admits.

I'm about to ask who when it dawns on me. "My mom."

"She supplied me with all the props. I just did the leg work."

"It's incredible."

"Coming in?" he asks, holding his hand out for me and walking toward our makeshift tent.

I allow him to pull me inside before I drop to my knees and crawl so I can lay down beside him.

"I- I can't believe all of this."

"Do you know how many times I've imagined sneaking off with you in here and having my wicked way with you?"

"No, I really don't."

"Hmmm," he says, leaning toward me and brushing his nose against mine. "Maybe I should show you then."

He moves closer still until I fall onto my back on the blankets he laid out under here. His palm cups my cheek before he lowers his lips to mine.

It starts out slow, sweet, tender, but as nice as it is, I need more. I need the man who cornered me in the bathroom the other night. I need the bad boy as well as the sweet guy who made us a little den.

Reaching out, I find the hem of his jersey and push the fabric up so I can run my hand up his bare back. His skin erupts in goose bumps and I can't help but smile as our kiss continues.

I pull my nails down his back lightly and he growls, encouraging me to go further.

"Off," I mutter against his lips.

I regret it the second he pulls his lips from mine, but it's only for a brief moment as the fabric passes between us, because then he's back. His tongue sweeps into my mouth and his hand skims up from my waist until he's palming my breast. My back arches, trying to get more of his touch.

Moving over me, he drops one knee between my thighs, but it's not close enough for me to get anywhere near the friction I need.

"Emerson," I moan when he pulls his lips from mine in favor of my neck.

"Yes, baby?"

"I need…" My words trail off, not really knowing what it is I actually need.

"Tell me. It's yours."

"More. I need more."

"My pleasure," he says with a chuckle.

His fingers slide under my tank, the fabric pushing up my stomach until it's over my bra. My breasts feel heavy and swollen in the confines of my bra and I almost beg for him to remove it.

He looks up at me. His usually light-blue eyes are dark with desire. "If you need me to stop, all you've got to do is say the word."

I nod, unable to say anything. I'm too lost in his dark stare.

"Lift your arms."

I do as I'm told and in moments my tank is on the ground and his kiss is brushing across the swell of my breasts.

"So sweet," he murmurs, kissing lower and along the lace trim of each cup.

My fingers thread into his hair, holding him in place as his lips drive me crazy.

His eyes find mine. His eyelids are heavy with lust and I feel a bolt of electricity race through me knowing that I caused it. Fingers tickle along my bra strap and he mouths, "Okay?" before I lift enough for him to undo the clasp.

I want to sigh with relief when the fabric is pulled away from me, but the look of pure adoration on Emerson's face as he stares down at me from his seated position distracts me from anything but this moment between us.

"You're so beautiful," he whispers, the emotion in his voice hitting me right in the chest.

I don't get a chance to respond because no sooner has he said the words, does he lean forward once again. He circles his tongue around one of my nipples and my back arches from the blanket in pleasure.

"Oh fuck," I moan as he ups the ante and sucks it into his hot mouth.

Moving to the other side, he gives that one the same treatment until I'm moaning and writhing beneath him.

"Emerson," I moan, pulling at his hair impossibly hard when he moves to pull back.

"Anyone ever done that to you before?"

My cheeks heat, but I doubt he can see as I'm flushed from head to toe right now. Shaking my head, a huge smile spreads across his lips.

"Do I get to give you your firsts?"

I stare at him sitting astride my thighs, his chest heaving, his incredible torso on display, and the huge bulge in his sweats more than obvious.

I do that to him. Me. The annoying little sister I always thought he hated.

"Y- yes," I admit.

"I don't fucking deserve this."

"Says who?"

"A lot of people. Most of which I hope you never meet," he says with a laugh. "Now, where were we?" He shimmies down my body a little, dropping sweet kisses down my stomach until he reaches the waistband of my skirt. I expect him to undo the button and pull it down my legs, but when I lift my hips he just pushes it up.

"Fuck," he groans, staring down at my white lace panties. "Could you be any more perfect?"

"I don't know. I guess you'd better find out." The words shock me. I thought I'd be nervous in this situation, but being here with Emerson, I'm totally relaxed about what's about to happen. There's only excitement, with maybe a little apprehension. But I'm not at all scared or worried about what's to come. I already know he's going to treat me right.

His fingers brush the outside of my thighs before they wrap around the thin sides of my panties and tug.

Nerves shoot up my spine, but the moment he parts my knees, looks down at my core and licks his lips, I forget about my lack of experience and just focus on the hands-on lesson I'm about to get.

"Jesus, I want to taste you so fucking bad." His voice is rough and deep and it pulls at things inside me I didn't know existed.

"Do it."

I've barely got the words out, and he's flat on his belly, sliding his hands under my ass and teasing at my folds with the tip of his tongue.

"Emerson. Fuck. Shit."

"Oh, baby. That's nothing yet." His voice vibrates through, making my pussy flutter with need.

"Oh fuck," I squeal as he flattens his tongue against my clit. He teases, circles, nips, and sucks, and it drives me fucking crazy. My hips lift in my need for more, but he never lets up. Not once.

When I feel like my body is about to shatter into a million pieces, he slows his pace, drops a little lower and gently pushes his tongue inside.

"Oh. Oh. Oh," I chant as he slowly circles before heading back for my clit. Only a moment later, his hand leaves my ass and his fingers push inside me. The feeling of him is incredible. My pussy convulses as it tries to suck him in deeper.

"Oh, that's so hot, baby. I can't wait until you're dragging my cock in like that."

The image of him moving inside me is the last piece of the puzzle I needed to push me over the edge.

"Emerson," I cry as lights flash behind my eyes and my body takes on a life of its own as I thrash about completely consumed by pleasure.

When I come back to myself, I find him sitting between my legs with a shit-eating grin on his face.

"Proud of yourself?"

"You have no fucking idea, baby."

He looms over me, slips his hand under the back of my neck, and fixes his lips over mine. His tongue sweeps into my mouth, and the taste of myself on his tongue mixes with his own and sends aftershocks of pleasure through my body.

"See how sweet you taste?"

All I can do is smile. It seems like it might now be a permanent fixture on my face. It certainly will be if he plans on doing that to me often.

"Here," he says, passing me my discarded clothing. "We should get back."

"Uh… what?"

"We don't want Levi to come looking for us."

I glance down at my mostly naked body and realize he's probably right.

"But…" My eyes drop to his tented sweats.

"We've got all the time in the world, baby. This was about you."

My heart swells. "Have you always been this sweet guy?"

"I hide him well."

"You don't say. I thought you were a bit of a dick."

"I thought you had the hots for me," he jokes.

"Don't you know what they say about the bad boys?" I ask, my eyebrows wiggling.

"Yeah, they give the best orgasms."

I bark out a laugh. "God, I was right about one thing."

His eyebrow lifts.

"Your ego knows no bounds."

“Baby, when you squeal like that, how could it not?”

I sigh.

“Don’t pout, it doesn’t suit you.”

“I feel bad.”

“Why?”

“Because I didn’t get to return the favor.”

“See, this is why I love you. I—” His eyes go wide as he realizes what he just said. “I mean… uh…”

Sitting myself up, I wrap my hands around the back of his neck and pull his lips to mine. Tonight has been so perfect. The last thing I want is for him to ruin it by regretting what he just said.

7

EMERSON

Holy shit, did I just say that?

I accept her kiss when she presses her lips to mine but inside I'm freaking out. Did I really just tell her I love her? Do I?

Shit.

"Thank you for tonight. It was beyond perfect."

"I'm glad you liked it."

"Can we keep it up and maybe visit again?"

"Sure."

I help her into her clothes and then with our hands locked together we make our way back to the house. Leah might know where we've both disappeared off to, but Gary and Levi have no clue and I really don't want either of them suspecting anything. Not yet at least.

I know that sometime in the near future I'm going to need to come clean about my feelings for Alyssa, but I'll quite happily put that off for a little longer yet while I get to enjoy our little secret.

I pull her to me once we're at the gate and give her a sweet kiss to hopefully see her through the night. What I really want to do is follow her to her bedroom and climb into bed with her, but I'm worried about taking this too fast. She's already admitted tonight that it's been her first experiences, so I need to allow her to take the lead—as much as it's going to kill me to do so.

My cock is still threatening to fight its way out of my sweats when we eventually part.

"You go, I need a few minutes."

She glances down at my not-so-little issue and smiles. As much as I might want her to drop to her knees in front of me and finish off from where we left things, the innocent little smile she gives me as she pushes through the gate is almost as good.

Fuck, when did I get so pussy whipped?

I think back and I remember the moment I walked into the Perkins' back yard when I was fifteen and Alyssa was fourteen. She was sunbathing in the tiniest of swimsuits. I'm pretty sure it was in that moment that she ruined me for anyone else. I tried like hell to get her out of my system, but it was pointless. She's the only girl who's ever really held my heart in her hands, even if she had no idea.

After going back to our little hideaway and turning all the battery lights off, it's safe enough for me to walk through the house without looking like a sex-starved maniac.

"Hey, man. Where have you been?" Levi asks when I poke my head into his bedroom and find him playing on his Xbox.

"Chatting to my parents," I lie. Guilt assaults me instantly. They're only next door, yet I've only spoken to them a couple of times since I moved in here. I did go with Leah to the store the other day so I could do their shopping. That at least felt like I was supporting them somehow.

"They doing okay?"

"Yeah, or so they say." Thankfully that's not a lie. Both Mom and Dad assured me that they were fine and not yet going stir crazy locked up inside their home like prisoners.

"Two-player?" he asks, nodding at the ball game he's playing.

"Sure."

He sets the game up and we begin to play. As always, he takes the lead, but after all these years, I can read his game plan like the back of my hand. We've played together, both virtually and on the real court, since we were old enough to bounce a ball. I know how his mind works.

"I fucking miss the court."

"Not as much as sex," he mutters, stepping up to take a shot.

"That too," I agree, but I can't help let a little hope bubble up inside that I might not be missing that for too much longer. If Alyssa's keenness to return the favor earlier is anything to go by, then I should be getting some kind of action very soon.

. . .

"Motherfucker. How'd you do that?" Levi complains when I win yet another game.

"Mind games. I know how you operate, Perkins."

"Fuck off, Locke. Get the fuck out of my room."

"I'm going, I'm going." I hold my hands up in surrender and back toward the door. I pull a sulky face, but in reality, I'm more than happy to be sent to my room. It gets me closer to her, even if she is asleep on the other side of our shared bathroom.

Stripping down to my boxers, I pull the covers back and slide in.

I lie in silence, desperately trying to hear if she's awake and moving around in the next room, but all I can hear is my own breathing.

As I will sleep to claim me, I replay our time out in the woods. I picture what her body looked like beneath me. How hard her nipples pebbled when I touched her. How sweet she was on my tongue.

Fuck, I've only had one taste and I'm already addicted.

I've no idea how long I lay there with my cock once again rock-hard and the vision of her in my head, but eventually a click fills the silence and a slither of light brightens my room.

Propping myself up on my elbow, I have to do a double-take at the vision before me.

Alyssa stands with the light of her room behind her. It glows around her, making her look like a fucking angel. She's wearing a white slip which is so see-through that it might as well not be there.

"Lys. Fuck."

"I was lonely." She bites down on her bottom lip as if she's unsure of herself and it makes my cock throb. I need to feel her around me so fucking bad.

She takes a step into my room. Her hips sway, her tits bounce, and my mouth waters.

"So I thought maybe… you could keep me company?"

I sit up, the covers pooling at my waist ensuring her eyes drop to my chest. I've known for years what she thought of my body. I've always made sure to be topless as much as possible just so I could see what I did to her. I craved to know she was still interested, but equally terrified that one day she wouldn't give me a second glance.

She smiles shyly when she comes to a stop beside my bed. My eyes drop to her bare feet and slowly make their way up her shapely legs, over the curve of her hips, her slim waist, and her full tits complete with rosy-pink nipples. Her smooth neck is on full display, her hair piled messily on top of her head.

She looks utterly breathtaking.

"Come here," I murmur, holding my hand out for her.

She doesn't move immediately, and I start to wonder if she's regretting coming in here. But then her hands move to the bottom of the full skirt of sheer fabric and she pulls it up and off her incredible body, and it's then she takes my hand and climbs onto my lap.

Her legs wrap around my waist, my cock lining up perfectly with her heat.

"Hey," she says, her arms sliding over my shoulders and her fingers diving into my hair.

"Hey yourself. This is a nice surprise."

"Nice? Having lunch with your granny is nice, Locke," she sasses.

"No, it's nothing like that. It's fucking unbelievable." I brush my lips against hers, but pull back when she tries to deepen the kiss.

"Yeah?" I hate that she's questioning herself right now.

I run my hands from her ass and up her bare back, delighting in the feeling of her muscles bunching as I move.

"Yeah. Now, tell me what you want."

"Y- you."

"What of me? My lips?" I ask, brushing them across her collarbone.

"Yes."

"My hands?" I slip them around to her front and take the weight of her breasts in my palms.

"Yes," she breathes.

"My cock?" I ask cheekily in her ear, thrusting up against her pussy.

"Yes. Everything, Emerson. Give me everything."

She squeals as I flip her onto her back. I take the opportunity to plunge my tongue into her mouth and encourage hers to join in as my hands trail around her body.

I pinch her nipples and palm her breasts, making her mewl and her back to arch off the bed, before my fingers trail down her stomach in search of my final prize. I part her and find her slick and ready for me.

"Alyssa," I groan in her ear, slipping two fingers inside her and beginning to warm her up for what's to come. "Are you sure you want this to be me?"

"So sure. I've never wanted it to be anyone else," she says honestly, followed by a gasp as my fingertips find her G-spot.

"That good?"

"Mmm," she moans as I continue working her. "So good."

I press my thumb to her clit as I continue to tease her most sensitive spot, desperate to feel her squeezing my fingers again as I push her over the edge.

"Oh god, Emerson," she moans loudly. Too loudly for the fact we're in her parents' house with both them and her brother right down the hall.

I seal my lips over hers, swallowing down her pleas for more and her cries of pleasure when she eventually falls.

"Still sure?" I ask once she's come back down. I'm desperate for more, but I'm conscious of pushing her. I don't want her to think that it's all I want this early on in what I hope is our budding relationship.

She sits up and boldly pushes her hand past the waistband of my boxers and wraps her delicate fingers around my length. It twitches violently at her touch and a groan rumbles up my throat.

"Fuck, Lys."

An accomplished smile turns up one side of her mouth.

With her hand still firmly holding me, I push up and shove the fabric down over my hips to fully free myself. Her eyes drop to my newly exposed skin. She stares for a few long seconds, and if it weren't for the look of awe on her face, then I might be worried.

"I guess I was wrong, eh?"

"With what?"

"My guess that you have a tiny cock."

"My ego is fully warranted, baby."

"Ugh, please." She rolls her eyes and laughs. "So, are you going to show me what you do with it?"

"Too fucking right." Climbing from the bed, and regretfully losing her touch, I dig in my suitcase for a condom and lose my last remaining item of clothing.

When I turn back around, Alyssa is lying back on my pillow. Her dark hair is fanned over the light floral sheets, her chest heaving, and her core still slick with her earlier release.

My cock twitches with the anticipation of being inside her, but the intensity in her eyes forces me to stay where I am so she can get her fill.

"See something you like?"

"Get back over here."

She opens her legs to allow me to settle between them and I make quick work of opening the small silver packet and rolling the rubber down my length.

"You can tell me to stop at any time."

"I won't, but thanks."

I kiss up her body, my fingers back inside her, making sure she's as ready as possible for when I slide into her.

Eventually, I make it up to her lips. I kiss her deeply and I pull my fingers from her body and tease her pussy with the tip of my cock. She tenses to begin with but soon starts to relax.

Finding her entrance, I slowly push the tip inside. Her legs stiffen until I find her clit and start to circle it with my fingertip, helping her to relax and allow me to push farther inside.

"I'm so sorry," I whisper against her lips, knowing that what's going to come next is going to hurt.

"Just do it. I'm ready."

I hope like fuck that she's right, but I fear she might be lying.

Thrusting my hips forward, I grit my teeth as her tight, hot heat surrounds me. Fuck, I need to move so fucking bad, but I force myself to remain still until I know she's okay.

Her whimpers sound like screams in my ears and I hate that I've caused her any pain.

I kiss her tenderly while continuing to stroke her clit in the hope it'll spark some pleasure that will help to drown out the pain.

"It's okay. I'm okay," she whispers against my lips.

I flex my hips to see if she's telling the truth and the sensation blows my fucking mind. She's so fucking tight.

"You feel so good, Lys."

A small smile appears on her lips. "Show me."

I do as I'm told and slowly pull out before pushing back in again. "Shit. This might not last very long."

"We've got all the time in the world to do it again," she says, stealing my words from earlier this evening.

"Too fucking right."

It's only a few slow thrusts later that I know my previous words were correct. My release begins to tingle at the base of my spine long before I'm ready for it to.

"Emerson," Alyssa moans as I fold over her and take her lips on mine, wanting us connected in every way when I fall over the edge.

My growl of pleasure rumbles up my throat as my cock twitches and I release everything I have inside of her.

"Oh god," she mutters, my own orgasm bringing her closer to her own.

Next time I take her, I'll make her come with my cock. But tonight, while she's sore from her first time, I settle for making her scream with my tongue again. And that's exactly what I do the second I pull the condom off.

When we eventually fall asleep, it's with her wrapped in my arms and tucked tightly into my body. Exactly where she belongs.

8

ALYSSA

Everything that's happened from the moment I opened his bedroom door and walked into his room has been nothing short of incredible.

We both agreed the next morning to keep what was developing between us a secret for now. We're both aware that Mom knows something is going on, but it was important to us to be able to embark on our relationship without the opinions of others that we're forced to spend every day with right now.

It's far from the ideal way to begin a relationship, but equally, the sneaking around and hoping not to get caught is pretty hot.

As the days go on, the riskier we get. The little touches and the glances between us become more obvious. Mom sees most, but as far as we know, Dad and Levi are still clueless.

During the day we continue like normal. I spend most of my time in my room doing my schoolwork or talking to the girls, and he's either shooting hoops with Levi or getting worked hard in the garden by my dad. I've discovered that if I sneak into his room which overlooks the back yard, I'm able to continue working while watching him get hot and sweaty with a shovel.

Life is pretty perfect despite the disaster that is the outside world right now.

The longer we're stuck in the house, the more I crave going outside of these four walls more and more. I can't wait to be able to go and do something as simple as enjoy a meal like a normal couple, or even just a long walk on the beach followed by a milkshake at Ace's. I want to party at Ethan's and take Emerson with me to introduce him to my friends properly. They all know him. Everyone at Rosewood knows him and my brother. Together they took the basketball team to the state finals last year. Their reputation precedes them. But I want them to know him as my boyfriend, not just a legend on the court.

"Mmm... I can't wait until bedtime," he murmurs in my ear while I'm getting the dishes out ready for dinner. Mom's just taken the food out to the table, allowing us a few seconds of privacy before she returns for the glasses that are sitting on the side.

"Me too."

Everything about the evening is the normal we've become used to. After we eat, Emerson heads outside to talk to his parents. They've moved from chatting on the phone to shouting to each other across our two driveways. I know it's a part of the day he always looks forward to, knowing and seeing with his own eyes that they're both fine.

We all watch the day's updates with dread filling our stomachs. We have no idea how long this is going to last, but having Emerson, that unknown bothers me less every day. As long as I have him beside me, I'm sure we'll make it through this bizarre time almost unscathed.

After excusing myself to my bedroom not long after my parents leave us to it, I strip out of my clothes and head for the shower. It's been a hot and sticky day and I'm almost as desperate to freshen up as I am excited for Emerson to find me in here.

It's only ten minutes later when his bedroom door shuts and a shadow appears in the doorway to the bathroom.

"I could get used to this," he says, his eyes running over my naked and wet body.

"What are you waiting for?"

"Absolutely fucking nothing."

In the blink of an eye, he's out of his clothes and rolling a condom down his length. He lifts me so my back presses against the wall and pins me there with his hips as his hands glide over my already wet hair.

"I've been waiting all day for this."

I don't get a chance to respond because his lips find mine.

We're still kissing, desperate to reconnect after a day of family and work, when he lines his cock up with my entrance and lowers me down onto it.

We moan in pleasure, but both are swallowed by the other and the sound of the running water. Every time we're together I worry we'll be loud enough to arouse suspicion, but so far so good. I know each time we connect we're one time closer to being caught. This can only go on so long when we're stuck in a house with three other people.

"Your bed or mine?" Emerson asks as he passes me a towel to dry off once he's given me two satisfying releases in almost as many minutes.

The sound of Levi coming to bed is clear to hear now the shower is turned off and we're no longer distracted by each other.

"Mine. I always wake up wondering where I am when I stay with you."

"Ugh, that means I need to pack," he jokes, hanging his own towel back up on the hook and walking butt-naked into my bedroom. I shamelessly stare at his ass as he moves.

"I can feel you looking."

"Good," I call back, pulling my toothbrush from the tumbler and loading it up with toothpaste.

Realizing I forgot to bring up a bottle of water, I swipe Emerson's jersey from the floor, pull it over my head and join him in my room.

It's huge on me. It hangs down almost to my knees and shows off way more side boob than I would usually be happy with, but I know how much he enjoys seeing me wrapped in his name and number.

"As sexy as that is, I'd prefer you naked."

"I'm just going to grab a drink."

"Like that?"

"It's fine. Everyone's in bed."

"Okay. Be quick."

I slip from the room and quickly make my way downstairs. I don't turn any lights on; I don't need to. I've lived here all my life. I can navigate in the dark without a second thought.

I'm just pulling a bottle from the fridge when the light above me illuminates the room.

"What the fuck are you wearing?" Levi booms.

I spin, the shock of the blinding light along with his voice stops me thinking of the consequences.

"Fucking hell, Alyssa." He covers his eyes and I quickly cover up the excess boob I'm showing.

"Why the fuck are you...? Oh no. Oh fucking no. Tell me you're not. Tell me he's not—"

Before I have a chance to say anything, he's moving.

"Levi, come back," I cry, rushing after him. Both our footsteps pound up the stairs. I can only hope we're loud enough to alert Emerson about what's coming his way.

Levi crashes through my bedroom door seconds before me. I'm too slow. By the time I run into the room, he's dragging Emerson naked from my bed. His shoulder connects with the wall as Levi throws him into it.

"What the fuck are you doing?" he screams, pulling his arm back and planting his fist into Emerson's face.

"Levi, stop. Please, stop."

I fly at him, trying to stop him from throwing another punch but he's too strong for me. So instead of trying to stop him, I stand between the two of them, hoping that my brother still has enough sanity left that he's not about to knock me out.

"Lys, what on earth is... oh fuck," Dad barks, running into the room in Mom's pink fluffy robe. He wraps his arms around Levi's waist and successfully manages to pull him back.

I turn to Emerson, whose face is already swelling, a trickle of blood running from his cut lip.

"Here," Mom's soft voice rings out in my ear as my own robe is dropped over my shoulder.

I quickly use it to cover Emerson up before turning on my brother.

"What the hell, Levi?"

"What?" he seethes. "Don't act all innocent. He was in your fucking bed. Naked."

"Yeah, I'm aware."

He tries jumping from Dad's hold but is unsuccessful. Instead, he stands there with his chest heaving and his teeth bared in anger.

"I'll fucking kill you for touching her," he snaps over my shoulder at his best friend before turning and removing himself from Dad's arms and leaving my room.

Dad looks between the three of us before focusing on Mom. "You knew, didn't you?"

She shrugs. "I was just allowing them to explore whatever is between them in peace."

"How well did that work out for you?"

"All right. There's no need for that. You need to go and calm your son down. I'll take care of things here."

"I'm fine," Emerson mumbles from his slumped position on my bedroom floor.

Dad disappears, doing as he's told.

"Lys, go and get the first aid kit from the bathroom."

I rush from the room as she bends down to check Emerson's injuries. "I hope it was worth it," she says to him quietly.

"Every second."

With a smile on my face, I make my way down the hall to get what she needs. The sound of my brother's shouting comes from somewhere downstairs, but I ignore it. He's overreacting.

Mom and I clean up Emerson's face before she leaves us to it. She pauses when she's at the door and looks back at both of us still on the floor. "Just give him time. Don't rub it in his face. I would tell you that maybe Emerson should go back to his own room, but I know it'll fall on deaf ears. So... just be discreet, yeah?"

"I thought we were," I say as she disappears, closing the door behind her.

"Come on, let's go to bed."

I help pull Emerson from the floor and after pulling off his jersey, I climb into bed beside him and curl into his side.

"I'm sorry," I whisper, kissing the underside of his jaw.

"It's not your fault, baby. I knew it was coming sooner or later."

"Did you mean what you said to my mom?"

He's silent for a few seconds as he thinks back. "You heard that, eh?"

I nod.

"Yes, I totally meant it. He can dish out as much pain as he likes, It won't make me regret this." His arms wrap tighter around me and his lips press against the top of my head.

I lay there for the longest time, running the events of the night over and over in my head. It was my fault. If I'd just put my robe on to go downstairs, Levi never would have thought anything of it.

He came back up to bed a few moments ago. Every muscle in my body tensed as his footsteps paused outside my door for a few seconds too long. The last thing any of us need right now is for him to walk in and find us together.

Once I'm confident that Emerson's asleep, I slip from his arms, pull on my robe, and quietly step from the room.

I make my way down to Levi's bedroom and knock.

"Yes," he barks, and I push it open and step inside.

I stay by the door with my fingers wrapped around the handle, just in case I need to leave fast.

"I'm sorry."

"Are you?" He's sitting on the other side of the bed with his back to me and his head hanging between his shoulders.

"Of course."

"Sorry you ever touched him or sorry you got caught?"

"Neither," I say honestly. "I'm sorry I didn't tell you."

"Lys," he breathes, pushing to his feet and turning to me. It takes a moment, but eventually his eyes lift to mine. "I'm sorry too. I freaked out."

"A little."

"It's just… you're my little sister and he's…"

"Your best friend."

"I was going to say a dog, but yeah, that too."

Silence descends between us.

"Is… is it serious?"

"As serious as I think it can be right now."

"Oh god." He looks up to the ceiling. "You're in love with him, aren't you?"

"Yeah, I think I am."

"Fucking hell, Lys. Of all the guys."

"I know. It's always been him though, Levi."

"Well then, I guess that's how it's meant to be. Please just refrain from making me watch."

"We'll do our best."

"Now get out of here and go and look after your… boyfriend." The way he says that word makes me laugh.

Walking up to him, I press a kiss to his cheek. "Thanks, bro."

"You're really, really not welcome."

I'm laughing as I leave his room, but I come to an abrupt halt when I find Emerson leaning against the wall outside Levi's room with a wide smile on his face.

"What?" I ask hesitantly.

"Say it again." My brows furrow. "I want you looking at me when you say it this time."

"Wha—oh." I step up to him and run my palms up his chest until I link my fingers behind his neck. He's so tall that I end up on my tiptoes with the entire length of my body pressed against his. I stare into his blue eyes and swallow down the emotion threatening to clog my throat. "I love you, Emerson Locke."

"I love you too, baby." His arms come around me and I sigh in contentment; that is before the sound of my brother's voice hits us.

"Really? Right outside my door? Fuck off."

We both bark out a laugh as we apologize and make our way back to my bedroom to quietly spend the night proving exactly how we feel.

EPILOGUE

Alyssa

Six months later...

"I can't believe you're not taking me to college," I say to my parents as we stand on the driveway. Emerson's car is idling behind us, loaded with all my stuff ready to make the journey to Maddison Kings University.

"Someone can be very persuasive," Mom says, looking up and smiling at Emerson, who's waiting for me to say my goodbyes. It's crazy, the university isn't all that far away and we've already planned to come back the weekend after next for Dad's birthday. It's not like I'm moving to the other side of the country.

"I love you both."

"We love you too." Two sets of arms wrap around me and tears burn my eyes.

"I need to go."

Mom sniffles, proving that I'm not the only one trying not to fall apart right now.

"Call us when you get there."

"I will."

I climb into Emerson's passenger side without looking back.

"Okay let's go."

"It's okay to cry, you know."

"I know. I just feel ridiculous getting all emotional about this."

"It's normal. You're leaving the only place you've ever known to embark on a new life."

"Not helping."

"Sorry," he mutters, amusement filling his voice as he backs away from the house we've both spent so much time in over the past few months.

As soon as our lockdown was lifted after the scary numbers from the virus started to decline, we spent what was left of the summer enjoying time for just the two of us. We spent hours walking on the beach, chatting about what college life might hold for us. I'd managed to submit everything that needed doing and my application to go to Maddison to study art was accepted. Everything was about to change, but it all seemed so much easier knowing that he was going to be there.

I wasn't the only one heading to Maddison. I had plenty of friends going to the same university, so I knew I had support.

Emerson chats about what to expect for my first few weeks as a college student. He talks about the parties, the drinking, and briefly touches on classes.

"Emerson, aren't dorms that way?" I ask when he sails past what I thought was the turn to my new home.

"Yep. But we're not going down there."

"Why not?"

"I've got a surprise for you."

Ten minutes later and we're pulling into a small car lot behind what looks like an apartment building.

"What's this place?"

"Just wait. Come on."

He jumps out of the car and my curiosity ensures I follow him.

Pulling keys from his pocket, he opens up the front door and then pulls me toward a set of stairs and up to the top floor.

"Here," he says, coming to a stop in front of a door. "Close your eyes."

"What?"

"Ugh, fine." His large hand wraps around my face, efficiently cutting off my sight.

"Emerson, what the hell is this?"

The sound of the door opening fills my ears before he pushes me forward.

"Welcome home, baby." He pulls his hand from my face and after blinking a couple of times, a fully furnished living room comes into view.

"What the hell?"

"Surprise."

"Wha…"

I spin on the spot, taking everything in. But it's not until I spot a couple of photographs of the two of us on a shelf that things start to register.

"This is our house?"

"It sure is, baby."

"What about dorms?"

He shrugs.

"What about my parents?"

"In on it."

A laugh falls from my lips. "So… this is where I'm living? With you? Just the two of us?"

"If you'll have me."

"Oh my god, this is incredible, Emerson. Thank you." I launch myself at him and crash my lips to his, and right there in the center of our new living room, we embark on our future together as a couple. I can see a few more days of lockdown together in our future.

ABOUT THE AUTHOR

Tracy Lorraine is a *USA Today* and *Wall Street Journal* bestselling new adult and contemporary romance author. Tracy has recently turned thirty and lives in a cute Cotswold village in England with her husband, baby girl and lovable but slightly crazy dog. Having always been a bookaholic with her head stuck in her Kindle, Tracy decided to try her hand at a story idea she dreamt up and hasn't looked back since.

Be the first to find out about new releases and offers. Sign up to my newsletter here.

If you want to know what I'm up to and see teasers and snippets of what I'm working on, then you need to be in my Facebook group. Join Tracy's Angels here.

Keep up to date with Tracy's books at
www.tracylorraine.com

ALSO BY TRACY LORRAINE

Falling Series

Falling for Ryan: Part One #1

Falling for Ryan: Part Two #2

Falling for Jax #3

Falling for Daniel (A Falling Series Novella)

Falling for Ruben #4

Falling for Fin #5

Falling for Lucas #6

Falling for Caleb #7

Falling for Declan #8

Falling For Liam #9

Forbidden Series

Falling for the Forbidden #1

Losing the Forbidden #2

Fighting for the Forbidden #3

Craving Redemption #4

Demanding Redemption #5

Avoiding Temptation #6

Chasing Temptation #7

Rebel Ink Series

Hate You #1

Trick You #2

Defy You #3

Play You #4

Inked (A Rebel Ink/Driven Crossover)

Rosewood High Series

Thorn #1

Paine #2

Savage #3

Fierce #4

Hunter #5

Faze (#6 Prequel)

Fury #6

Legend #7

Maddison Kings University Series

TMYM: Prequel

TRYS #1

TDYW #2

TBYS #3

TVYC #4

TDYD #5

TDYR #6

TRYD #7

Knight's Ridge Empire Series

Wicked Summer Knight: Prequel (Stella & Seb)

Wicked Knight #1 (Stella & Seb)

Wicked Princess #2 (Stella & Seb)

Wicked Empire #3 (Stella & Seb)

Deviant Knight #4 (Emmie & Theo)

Deviant Princess #5 (Emmie & Theo

Deviant Reign #6 (Emmie & Theo)

One Reckless Knight (Jodie & Toby)

Reckless Knight #7 (Jodie & Toby)

Reckless Princess #8 (Jodie & Toby)

Reckless Dynasty #9 (Jodie & Toby)

Dark Halloween Knight (Calli & Batman)

Dark Knight #10 (Calli & Batman)

Dark Princess #11 (Calli & Batman)

Dark Legacy #12 (Calli & Batman)

Corrupt Valentine Knight (Nico & Siren)

Ruined Series

Ruined Plans #1

Ruined by Lies #2

Ruined Promises #3

Never Forget Series

Never Forget Him #1

Never Forget Us #2

Everywhere & Nowhere #3

Chasing Series

Chasing Logan

The Cocktail Girls

His Manhattan

Her Kensington

www.ingramcontent.com/pod-product-compliance
Lightning Source LLC
Chambersburg PA
CBHW020344310726
48979CB00015B/2505/J

* 9 7 8 1 9 1 4 9 5 0 9 1 9 *